FRENCHMAN'S GOLD

By Lliam West

D0544113

Tamarisk

First published in the UK in 2005
by TAMARISK

Trewynn, Lodge Hill, Liskeard, Cornwall, PL14 4EL

ISBN 0-9541911-1-0

Printed by Swiftprint, Treverbyn Rd, St Austell.

Epworth Mechanics' Institute Library
Tuesday 10a.m – 12 Noon
Thursday 1.30p.m – 4p.m
Friday 7.30p.m – 9.30p.m

qua 9 - 6. 17.

1   Please return books as soon as you have finished with
them so that others may read them

3

With a number of characters reappearing, individual traits and interpersonal tensions ready developed, *Frenchman's Gold* is probably best (if not necessarily) read as a sequel to *Pandora Inn*.

Some considered my first story 'complex'. I resist this view, and offer 'compound' as the more apt term, the intrigue having been woven from a variety of threads (historical, political, military, literary etc) and peopled by a cast of characters determined largely by the loose ends dangled to each.

I found particular pleasure in developing the literary strand, and admit (proudly) that *Pandora Inn* owes much to Shute's *Lonely Road*. To acknowledge this debt, Nevil(1899-60) featured as one of the new twists which embelish what was essentially a re-working of his own sturdy format. Other readers suggested that the link between N.S. and Norway might have been made more explicit, by means of a preface perhaps. I take their point. For this yarn one is provided.

PREFACE

(i) On the writers.

As contempories, Cyril (1903-74) and Evelyn (1903-66) have very similar aspirations. Cyril attends Eton, from where he progresses to Oxford. Evelyn arrives at the university from less prestigeous Lancing, and while neither can ever be a part of it, each develops a life-long fascination with the British aristocracy.

With regular contributions to journals such as the *New Statesman* and *Life and Letters* Cyril makes his mark as a perceptive literary critic. He goes on to prove himself an essayist of the first order with his *Enemies of Promise* (1938), a part treatise, part memoir in which he cogently warns his fellow writers of the pitfalls that can await the merely gifted. An extended novel must surely be next, and it has to be a masterpiece ..... but no. For all their fine words his characters fail to come alive. His stories disappoint, and a faltering career serves merely to underline his own argument....... that even the plumpest bud cannot guarantee a blossom. Cyril's great 20th century novel is never brought to fruition, but there is some superb journalism, notably with *'Horizon'*, the literary review that he helped found and edit during the 1940s.

The high-born rebel seems to hold particular fascination for Connolly, and come the early '50s he is quickly on to the Burgess and Maclean defections. With *The Missing Diplomats* he pioneers the kind of intelligence game dissection that would be later developed and refined by such as Philip Knightley and Nigel West. Since Cyril's death it has emerged that at the time he had been reliably informed of Philby and Blunt's complicity in the treason, and that he was likely to have been constrained from telling far more than he actually did.

By the late '60s, Philby's treachery is public knowledge, and, working now as a literary columnist for *The Sunday Times,* Connolly develops a fascination for the unsolved case of Lord Erroll, the charismatic Peer murdered in Kenya in 1941. With the young James Fox enrolled as an assistant, enquiries were followed and detailed notes made. Out of these came *'Christmas at Karen'* which appeared in the *Sunday Times Magazine* in December 1969, an article that introduced this strange and potent brew of colonial scandal and intrigue to a new generation.

Connolly died in 1974. With the notes of his mentor to hand, Fox continued the project and, in 1982, produced the book *White Mischief.....* a work which for many, myself included, begs as many questions as it purports to answer.

So can it be possible, I ask, that in his last years Cyril might again have managed to uncover a good deal more than he dared publish? Could it be, even, that he had stumbled upon a link between Philby and Erroll?

Evelyn might well have been able to furnish an answer...... had he not died in 1966, having well before then established himself as one of the truly great 20th century novelists. Whilst still in his twenties he'd penned *Decline and Fall* and *Vile Bodies* -two sparkling satires, and then his *Remote People* travelogue (replete with a section on Erroll's Kenya), plus the outrageously farcial *Black Mischief*. Similarly veined from his thirties came *A Handful of Dust* and *Scoop,* but between them (as if to placate the clerical furore provoked by *Mischief*) a reverent account of the life of *Edmund Campion*, an early Jesuit martyr.

Basil (the star of *Mischief*) returns for the phoney war satire *Put Out More Flags*, but then come the unhappy heroes of *Brideshead* and *Sword of Honour*, Charles and Guy, both staggering from the ruins of a failed marriage, wanting still to believe in love and in the obtainability of spiritual grace, but each finding little of either in a bleak, modern, war ravaged world.

(ii)   On the musicians and the poet.

Ben (1913-76) and Peter are musicians. By 1941, though still young, they are on the brink of considerable fame. Ben is a composer. Peter (another of the Lancing alumni) sings. They develop a close, loving relationship, each striving happily to complement the artistic flair, and the spiritual and physical needs sensitively perceived in the other.

Peter, raised a Quaker, is, by dint of his faith, a pacifist. Ben is convinced, no less firmly, that in a talented hand the composer's pen and the conductor's baton can prove mightier than bayonet and bullet. Encouraged by Peter he has developed, quite justifiably, an increased confidence in his own gifts.

The couple live together in the U.SA., near New York, having left their native England shortly after the outbreak of war. The move inevitably attracted critical comment, but the musicians' burden is shared, between themselves of course, and also amongst others who have taken similarly precious talents into exile.

One such is Wystan (1907-74), a poet, who has so often fed the musicians with words. Wystan is mocked by Evelyn who casts him as 'Parsnip' in 'Put Out More Flags', but this Parsnip has a tough skin. He can take all this, and more.

Like Ben and Peter, Wystan is also homosexual. For a good six years (mainly in England) he and Ben have worked closely and fruitfully, but not without tension. The poet sees in the musician a remarkable young talent, a talent of awesqme but, to him, frustratingly restrained potential. Love enjoyed as they liked is worthy of celebration he feels, and he is ready to profess this with near religious zeal.

Ben though remains true to a more reserved nature and, while the poet might be disposed to the urgent missive, so the composer prefers to refine a less forthright message. To develop and express this in his own subtle way, he needs time and he needs space.... and in these respects many detected in Ben a wariness of Wystan, particularly from 1942, a year that marks a parting of ways.

Some choose to attribute this divergence to the sharp onset of Wystan's lustful, unabashed infatuation with Chester, the handsome and promiscuous young Jewish-American who would eventually yield to ardent pursuit and settle with Wystan in devoted lifelong partnership. The poet's passion re enforced a love of America at a time when, so it is believed, the musicians were growing increasingly homesick for England. Ben's sparkling *Hymn to St Cecilia* (1942), a tender (and intriguingly interrupted) setting of Wystan's earlier written *Song* gives to the collaborative phase of their lives a final, fittingly graceful flourish.

Peter and Ben return to England. Wystan, besotted with Chester, sees a future in the States...... and there, alongside the characteristic defiance, he seems to nurture towards the musicians a degree of resentment. Letters to the composer convey criticisms, these being frostily received of course...... the recipient being so sensitive a soul. The former rapport largely evaporates and such further attempts to work together come to very little.

By 1947 there is a rift, and with both moving on to craft fresh work, separately conceived and separately published, parallel careers develop. Conventional communication largely ceases, but some listeners will detect an ongoing exchange, if not an argument then certainly a protracted debate, discernible they say, within and between the lines of many a later composition.

> *Falstaff the fool confronts forever*
> *The prig Prince Hal.**

But not quite for *'forever'*.........as, mellowed by age and physical decline, attitudes are softened, guards are lowered, and old affections are at least partly revived.

For students of the rift, this late patching offers insight. The extent of the tear is better understood, and perhaps, also, the underlying seismic strains.

* From *'Under Which Lyre'* W.H. Auden (1946)

(iii) On politics.

a) Lest there be any misunderstanding, I must state now that I hold no brief for the false creed of Holocaust denial..... on the contrary. If the enormity of the evil that was perpetrated under Hitler is not to be repeated then we must be sure that the episode in all its grimness is fully explored and the lessons drawn therefrom never forgotten. It is to this end that I suggest we might usefully question the notion of this obscenity being the sole responsibility of the one crazed individual doggedly pursuing a warped ideology in a hideous race against time.

To attribute the horror of it all wholly to one man's evil madness is to imply that all who stood against him were as righteous as they were sane. This is, I feel, insults all those who suffered...... a point often now made by the last of the death camp survivors as they not so quietly fade away. 'Think again,' I hear them say. 'It was not quite so simple.'

So I do, and with this tale I'm asking you to think with me.

As a start, rather than a phrase such as *mad and evil*, consider *maddened to evil* as an alternative........and then ask what by?

Can it be said, for instance, that Hitler might have been a victim of his own amoral arrogance in the diplomatic sphere, and that by a want of competence and caution he allowed himself to be manoeuvred towards what *for him* was an un-anticipated logistical nightmare?

b) Whatever...... life does go on and new challenges will always arise. One such is the thorny issue of modern day Palestine. During the first three post Holocaust decades it was widely felt that the remnant of the race decimated by the Nazis was now owed sanctuary. It followed that if this debt might be realised in the shape of land that their God promised to ancient forbears then perhaps the time had arrived for the Jewish people to be allowed take up an overdue entitlement.

More recently, though, it has had to be pointed out that the modern state of Israel would appear to exclude too many of its Arab occupants from the benefits of a land that they have long regarded as their home. As better brains than mine struggle to sort this one out I offer an observation that the Zionist movement of Herzl and Weizmann predated Hitler's sequence of *'Final Solutions'* by at least two generations, and that during that time, and since, it carried a spectrum of views as to how its fundamental goal, a sovereign Jewish state, might best be achieved.

It is in the nature of any political body that a pragmatic mainstream will be flanked by fanatical minorities... their solutions radical, their methods ruthless. Following the murder of Lord Moyne (Nov. 1944) even leaders so fervent as Golda Meir and Ben Gurion were ready to warn their extremists that the choice now for the future had to be between a Zionist democracy or 'Jewish Nazism'.

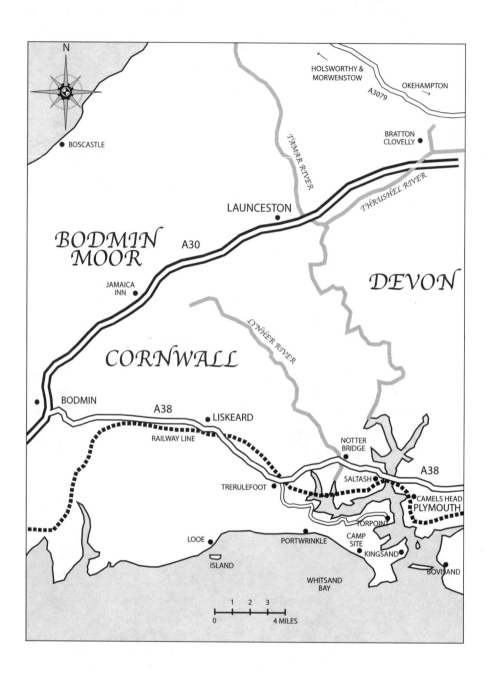

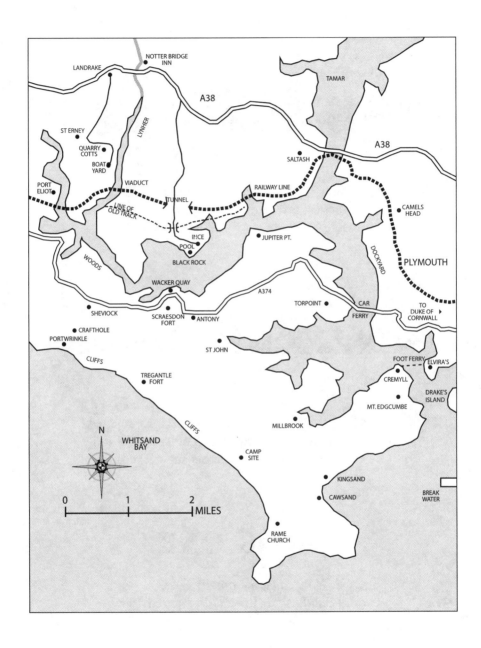

Surcouf

1929: Length 360ft: Displacing 4,300 tons: 118 crew:
Diesel powered: Surface range of 10,000 nautical miles.
Capable of 18 knots (8 ½ knots submerged)

Narval

1920s: Length 256ft: Displacing 1,440 tons: 54 crew:
Diesel powered: Surface range of 5,600 nautical miles.
Capable of 15 knots (9 knots submerged)

BOOK ONE

How came the boy by gold?
Billy Budd; Act 3 Britten/ Forster/Crozier

(i) a new century; (and a new initiative.)

1903

Memorandum

From Colonial Secretary
To Prime Minister
       Foreign Secretary

TOP SECRET

With regard to my recent negotiations with Herr Theodore Herzl concerning the settlement of as many as a million Jews (mainly Russian) on British sovereign territory, I am encouraged to hear of the positive response to our initial joint suggestions when put yesterday to the Sixth Zionist Conference, currently being held in Basle.

It was proposed to the 569 delegates present that a working group might be formed to further consider our ideas.

They voted thus;

For the proposal 295; Against 175; Abstained; 99.

We can be encouraged by this 21 vote absolute majority. It keeps alive the concept of a Greater Zion, and with it the desired prospect of our Empire gaining benefit from a timely infusion of talent, energy, and wealth. At the same time we, and Herzl, need to be wary of those in his movement who reject this concept. This is an extremist minority, not given to compromise. They are ruthless in their ambition. For their Israel they must have Palestine, the whole of Palestine, and nothing but. They suspect us of attempting to sow division, and, for that, see us as an insidious enemy.

The majority will follow Herzl, their revered leader, but having worked hard and long he now weakens in health. Should he soon die then we can anticipate an eager struggle for succession and it may be that our initiative could well shrivel under a far harsher climate of opinion.

This is not to say, however, that the passage of time will render our ideas obsolete. The Ottoman rule weakens and the Progroms of Russia and Poland intensify. For us, meanwhile, Arab oil will become a vital resource, and the Suez Canal a vulnerable artery. Political pressure on this region can only increase, and it would be remiss of us to deny to future generations of diplomats what yet might prove a useful safety valve.

My view is that even should the Jews resolve, for the moment, to bury the concept of a Greater Zion with Herzl, we would do well to keep the seeds we have planted under sheltered cultivation.

Accordingly I suggest that we might quietly impress on our respective departments the importance of keeping all related channels of communication, formal and informal, open for as long as possible.

Joseph Chamberlain

*

(ii) the 1930s

> *Far off like floating seeds the ships*
> *Diverge on urgent voluntary errands;*
> *And the full view*
> *Indeed may enter*
> *And move in memory as now these clouds do......*

From *'Look, Stranger!'*
W.H. Auden   1935

Adapted by Britten for *Seascape; Opus 11* (1937)

SEPTEMBER 1933
Evelyn

On the *SS Krajica Marija*, returning to Venice following a cruise of the Greek Islands.

"Diana Guinness, and then Diana Cooper...... forgive me Evelyn, but to fall for both after all the upset and the pain of your wife's desertion smacks as much of recklessness as it does of misfortune."

Katherine Asquith could be as frank in her advice as she could be sympathetic. "The one is too young, the other too old...... and if each can sparkle in her own way, both are unutterably spoilt and vain." She reached to softly lift Waugh's diconsolately tucked chin, lighting his impish eyes as, for the moment, only she seemed able. "You're a sensitive man, Evelyn, too sensitive to be courting pain. There is a sweetness in you still, but Helen, Trim, and I, we fear it can be too easily soured..... irreversibly soured."

"And I'm grateful Katherine, to you, and to your son and daughter. That Trim, he's such a fine lad, so studious, so devout, so respectful. He has it all ahead of him.....but to listen to Magdalen Fraser yesterday evening, at dinner, was to be assured that he is all but betrothed to her little sister Veronica....."

"..... who looks to be shaping into a true beauty."

"But what is she as yet..... no more than fourteen? I can't imagine that any firm attachment would have your blessing."

"Not until the poor girl grows out of that rather childish adulation of the eldest brother."

"The young Laird........."

".....who is coming to epitomise the want of modesty that runs through the whole family. Beauty she may be, but Trim does tire so of his ever being less than favourably compared to the dashing Simon. We can go to this place or to that......"

"...... only to find that the kilted cavalier has already been there."

"Precisely. Trim might be clever to have secured his place at Oxford....."

"...... but Simon has done all that already."

"And likewise, when Trim acts nobly, and is of lordly bearing ."

".....Simon will have acted more nobly, and he would have been more lordly. But she is young, Katherine. Dainty Veronica is young."

"Of course," conceded the eminent war widow, daughter-in-law to the late Herbert Asquith, 1st Earl of Oxford, and mother to the 2nd, Julian 'Trim' Asquith, "and if there is scope for improvement then we can hope there to be time."

"But have no worries about Trim, Katherine," Waugh assured her. "He will shine at Oxford, and prove himself worthy of the Earldom. If our acquaintence ends with this cruise then it will always be my privilege to have known him, and yourself, and Helen. Believe me, without the three of you this break would not have been nearly so enjoyable."

"And we can say the same of you, Evelyn, and it's not just your considerable talent to amuse. We've also been warmed by the sincerity of your faith....."

"..... which I know will further sustain me, as I return to pick over the rubble of my marriage. I only wish that others amongst our fellow Communicants could be as warm and open hearted towards me as yourself."

"You speak again of the lovely Magdalen?"

"Ugly as hell and as dull as mud."

"And her mother, the Lady Laura, so well known for her charm, her prettiness and her chic.....?"

".....who gets into such odd postures at Mass that no one can look anywhere else," dimpled Waugh, mischievously. "Even dear Father D'Arcy struggles to avert his eyes!"

"Take care there, Evelyn," whispered Katherine. "A proud family, that........ with Laura, don't forget, a daughter of the deeply mourned Baron Ribblesdale, whose dotage was largely spent at that hotel of Rosa Lewis's, in Jermyn Street, the establishment you mock so mercilessly in *Vile Bodies*."

"*The Shepheard's*," smirked Waugh.

"So yes, beware....... to make fun of Rosa and her Cavendish clientele is also to make fun of the Clan, and they can be very......"

"...... clannish?" offered the wordsmith.

"Exactly," confirmed Katherine. "Your time at Oxford and that of young Simon's would have overlapped. Did he make any sort of mark?"

"As a total prig..... as conceited as any that ever rode out of the Highlands. Why do they have to think that their Catholicism is so much superior to ours?"

"My friend, Ronald Knox, he thinks it something to do with the 11th Lord, the Jacobite die-hard who lost his head on Tower Hill after the '45. Nothing will so distinguish a Catholic, Evelyn, as a history of blood sacrifice."

"Magdalen and her mother, they've taken such delight in needling me over that review that appeared in *The Tablet*......"

"......excoriating your *Black Mischief*?"

"To the extent of even accusing me of blasphemy."

"Which is going way, way too far. You love Jesus, Evelyn, I know.

Those who can't, or won't see the joke, they make themselves look foolish..... and this of course is further measure of your own God given talent. See how your wonderfully despicable Basil leaps from the page. He can rile even the esteemed editor of *The Tablet*, our weekly house-paper. But don't think the whole of the Church shares that outrage. Monsignor Knox, I know, is on our side. *'Hurrah for Basil!'* he says. *'Let him live on as a Robin Badfellow, to further plague the fusty...... Cardinal, Clansman, or whatever.'* "

1945; Laura stands proudly behind her eldest son with Magdalen (l) and Veronica (r)

*

in an ideal world
1937

The *Daily Mail* reprints a letter Hitler had sent to its owner, Lord Rothermere. It reads:

All hope for the future is dead, so far as the human eye can see, unless it comes from England and Germany.

I am no new advocate of an Anglo - German understanding. In Germany I have made between four and five thousand speeches to small, large, and mammoth audiences, yet there is no single speech of mine, nor any line that I have written, in which I have expressed anything contrary to this concept or against an Anglo - German understanding.

Such an agreement between England and Germany would represent the weight of influence for peace and common sense of 120,000,000 of the most valuable people in the world. The historically unique colonial aptitude and the naval power of Britain would be combined with one of the first military nations of the world. If this understanding could be still further enlarged by the adhesion of the American nation, it would be absolutely impossible to see who in the world could disturb a combination for peace which would never, of set purpose or intent, neglect the interest of the white people.

APRIL 1937
one time friends
Ashley Gardens, London.

"Joss....... I hope you don't mind me calling like this, unannounced."

"Tom...... you catch me unprepared." Leaning nervously from his doorway, Josslyn Hay, Earl of Erroll, threw a wary glance along the street. Mosley used to be fun. Now he was an embarrassment. He was trouble.

"I've not been followed, Joss, and I know you're alone in there." The unexpected caller was almost pleading. Hay gave way with a reluctant, far from cordial nod, in that same movement stepping back against the weighty, inwardly opened door.

"I suppose you'd better come in..... now you're here."

"Forgive me, but I'm not intending to take up too much of your ....."

"Ten minutes, Tom, that's all you get..... ten more than if I'd been given any forewarning." The outside door thudded shut as the inner was held for the visitor to pass into a spacious reception area.

"You had my letter did you Tom, back in January, explaining why I thought it prudent that our former friendship be severed?"

"I did, Joss, but we'd been such great friends over the years..... I couldn't just leave it at that. We in the British Union had such high hopes of you. You cut such a fine figure in your Black Shirt. You were considered pivotal in the hoped for development of a Colonial dimension. My friends in Rome and Berlin were no less convinced of your potential, and they, like me, were looking forward to hearing the latest from Kenya. The last time you were across......"

"...... three years ago, Tom...."

"......three years maybe," conceded Mosley, "but things did look to be progressing so well. Can't we still work something out?"

"It was all in the letter Tom. I've nothing to add. Yes, we had our good times, you and I...... I remember Venice, with Olga, fourteen, fifteen years ago, and back here, at the *Savoy*, and the *Kit-Kat*."

"Meaning this is in the past now, together with those more serious matters we discussed just....."

".....*all* of three years ago," corrected Hay. "As I wrote, Tom, I am being drawn into politics, but for me, now, it has to be representative politics. Others, apart from you and your fascist friends, they too have seen in me a talent, and they have chosen me through legitimate democratic process to speak for them, to protect their interests, to voice their concerns. And I have to say now that were word of this visit to seep back to them then many would consider their trust betrayed. My career could be over, almost before it had begun."

"Very touching Joss, this new found respect for the ballot box, but that settler community of yours they'll be of pioneering stock...... hardly the most liberal minded of folk, in terms of *politics*, that is, if not personal *morality*. You wrote of my way and your way suddenly being in sharp divergence..... on what particular issue, tell me?"

"Get this straight Tom. My people, like me, will concede that Hitler has done much for Germany, as Mussolini has done for Italy. The strong line against communism is much admired, but what is questioned, and very strongly questioned, is the Fuhrer's racial policies. From a tropical standpoint this notion of Aryan supremacy is nonsense, dangerous nonsense. For each white settler in Kenya there are thousands upon thousands of black tribesmen. Currently they'll make very little trouble for us..... and why? Because as well as being in awe of our machines and our medicines they have also learned to respect the justness of our laws and the inclusiveness of our religion. But this respect doesn't come cheap. It never has and never will. We, the settlers, earn it by paying due respect to the land."

"Meaning....?"

"......doing nothing to jeopardise the sustenance it offers to the less civilised. To continue to hold sway in Africa the white man must take care to exert wise stewardship. In his approach to what he terms his 'Jewish Problem', Hitler would appear to be developing a very different philosophy."

"Fine words, Josslyn Hay, proud words, words most worthy of the grand position you'll be taking in the Coronation procession...... just two weeks away now. Less worthy is our shared past."

"Word of which would be no less damaging to your own cause, *old friend*," countered Erroll, instantly negating the implied threat. Tom Mosley, himself no less of a bounder, had to acknowledge the riposte. A nod, a ruefully lifted palm and the oppressive whiff of blackmail was dispelled. The host pressed his advantage, pointedly reiterating his new found enthusiasm for formal procedure. "In June I make my maiden speech in the Lords. We'll stay for the summer then sail for home in October. In a year's time we have the election for the Colony's Legislative Council. Voting is in April….."

"…. and you'll campaign through the winter."

"I will, and from my new base…. the bungalow Molly and I have moved to in Nairobi."

"Close to the Muthaiga, though, for sure. You can't have totally changed your spots."

"As chance would have it, yes", confirmed Joss, regretting his casual mention of Molly, his stricken second wife. He'd offered Mosley another target, he sensed….. and the thrust duly came.

"Ideal from the sounds of it, for you and your political career, and for Molly. The Wanjohi Valley, Navaisha, as beautiful as these places are, they'd have been far too remote. She'll be conveniently placed, now, to keep a watchful eye on you. That said, the word going around is that this time she hasn't been looking quite so well. She will be returning with you to Kenya, I trust?"

"Of course." A curt reply from Erroll, who could safely assume that rumour of his Countess's growing dependence on alcohol and opiates would have reached London, along with further gossip of his own perennial womanising. But he knew too that Tom Mosley was the last person to dare to suggest any causal link. For in this, here was a man who, if anything, was even worse.

Hadn't Mosley watched his own wife, Cimmie the supportive, die broken in health and spirit whilst he'd enjoyed an adulterous liaison with the enchanting Diana? And now, apparently, for all his mistress's beauty and devotion, and her reckless courage in abandoning Bryan Guinness, heir to millions, this strutting Don Juan was now struggling to stay faithful to even her! "But my dear Tom," scoffed Erroll, "it surprises me that you might think that anyone should want to listen to any advice you could proffer on the topic of marital fidelity."

Mosley knew better than to press. He eased back, using widened enquiry to cover retreat.

"And Idinia, Joss, your former wife, and an old friend of mine from way back….. does she still live out in the sticks? No lasting acrimony I trust? For you had a daughter I remember, and she must now be……"

"Dinan......? Coming up to ten. She thinks the world of me, Tom, and deserved or otherwise it's a view that her mother has always encouraged...... so yes, I have to be grateful. Idinia has taken another husband, and she lives at 'Clouds' still, where, as you say, she harbours 'no lasting acrimony'. "

"Which is as well, Joss, because this daughter who, until you produce a son, will be your heir of course, she keeps you sort of related to her, let me see.....," and the pause that followed was calculated to lend moment to what was in fact becoming an increasingly tenuous family connection, ".... to her mother's former brother in law. The uncle who, whilst we lived it up, was carving himself such an impressive career in the Foreign Office...... and who is now an accomplished spy-master, I'm told. It's said he could go right to the top."

"Good at his job," agreed Hay. "And yes, he won't be needing me to tell him you've called. I know that, but I'm certainly going to make sure he hears that you've received short shrift. Your time's up Tom, I'm afraid."

Mosley paused in his move to the door. Half turning he loosed his parthen shot. "You dress in your finery, Joss. Go to the Abbey, and afterwards speak for Empire in the Upper House. Yes, we hear you are highly thought of at the Colonial Office....... but do have a care. Assume not that the high priests of the Foreign Office must always take the same view."

*

crown imperial
MAY 12th 1937

.......and certainly more than just another day at the office for Colonel Stewart Menzies, a functionary of exceptional achievement, a confident man, well connected of course, and, within his highly specialised department, one strongly touted to eventually succeed the chief..... Admiral Sir Hugh Sinclair, head of MI6. Normally he would be indistinguishable from Civil Servants of the more ordinary sort, but on this special day he could look the part.

Having been colourfully spruced in a ceremonial tunic

21

appropriate to what had become a nominal Life Guards' rank, and having aired this on the brisk short walk from Foreign Office to Abbey he was now installed in his high gallery position. Lodged between an official camera crew and a busy group of lighting technicians he could settle to enjoy from on high what had to be the best seat in the theatre.

Rather this than the throne, he thought slipping an *Edmundesque* chuckle, for hadn't it been maliciously whispered that he was himself a bastard son of Edward VII? He'd attended the last Coronation, after the old goat had died, to watch his mother, Lady Holford, attend as Lady in Waiting to Mary, Queen then, and now widow of George V.

Naturally, Mary, in all her Highness, was to be here today........and she was entering now, to the strains of a specially commissioned anthem, *Crown Imperial*, to witness the enthronement of her second son, formerly the Duke of York until elevated by the brother's abdication to King George VI.

Crown Imperial........ mmm, not bad as these things went........ but the composer, William Walton? No, *he* wasn't going to be up to the job. A quicker and more clever talent was required. But, for the moment, back to the new King, with the acceptable new Queen, Elizabeth of Glamis, these handsomely paired figreheads who were so much more appropriately wooden than the ousted David.

With the strong and lasting marriage and, already, two very presentable daughters a smooth succession was as good as assured. The people would grow to love the Yorks. And the King across the water?....that playboy Majesty was fast fading. Already, to a fickle public, their Duke of Windsor was an oddity; but perhaps all the more useful for that, decided the intelligence officer. So many connections the man had still, and so much more usable they had become, now that those fettering strands of protocol could be quietly pared away.

For the Palace was now in the safe strong hands of this new Elizabeth, thought Sir Stewart, who was now moved to muse on the First of that name, Elizabeth Tudor.... and on *her* manipulator in chief, Sir Francis Walsingham, a true inspiration, *the* past master in the craft of intrigue. The challenge of his age had been posed by the Church of Rome. It had been faced and met, and now had arrived times no less interesting, no less dangerous. Today it was a generation of godless tyrants that were abroad, marching beneath the banners of National and International Socialism....... rival banners, fortunately.

Indeed, Heaven forbid that these totalitarian creeds might unite in common cause. This could spell England's doom. The imperative was to keep them crouching and clawing at each other...... as, at this very moment, they were pitted in the Ebro valley. Agony for the Catalans, yes, but survival for the United Kingdom...... and, to be honest, more than survival. Wars like this could be a fillip for business. '*Fillip of Spain*', he thought smirkingly. He would have to remember that one.... *a bon mot* for the cronies at the Club, Whites of course.

But jesting apart, there was real dividend in the conflict for his own department, an intelligence windfall. Mussolini, Hitler, Stalin, were, by their Iberian adventures, inadvertently disclosing the talents and tensions within their respective High Commands. Menzies could feel confident that he and 'C' had the full measure of their counterparts in Rome, in Berlin, and in Moscow.

And there was more besides, for novel political currents were being stirred here in London, and also in Washington and Paris, the three foremost of the ostensibly neutral democracies. Where ten years ago it had been only the isolated eccentric who'd muttered against the parliamentary model, now it was becoming the fashion. Fed by the fearful, huddles were becoming cliques, and cliques, factions.

See Darlan down there..... Admiral Jean Francois Darlan, supposedly representing his nation, the delegate of an elected French Government. He'd been received in London earlier in the year, then an emissary of his socialist Prime Minister, tasked to rally support for the Spanish Republic. In fact he'd done the opposite, cynically betraying his leader, betraying his people. Yes, Menzies had it on excellent authority that Darlan had used the opportunity to secretly, perversely canvas support for Franco.

This gem had come to him by way of clever young Guy at the BBC. He had an old College friend out there, St John's boy.... Harold his name.... a journalist whose reports, filed back for *The Times*, had usefully won the confidence of the Nationalist camp. With this freshly to mind Menzies had seen to it that the day's arrangements be adjusted so as to have the Admiral demoted in diplomatic station to below the representatives of Siam and Ecuador. Humiliation was intended, and it was being felt, he could see..... but sting as it might now, this was unlikely to deter. Darlan would be back, in all his slipperiness, in all his readiness to be bought.

But well done Harold, thought Menzies, and well done to himself also, for cultivating a full legion of such agents. Through Europe and across the Empire, wherever the country and whatever the movements, therein he had people in place, infiltrated so as to shadow and sometimes even influence events. So far so good, he could say.... but there could be no let up. Complacency was the mark of a fool.

There was the USA to consider, for instance, where the home security services were improving steadily, at following and reading, and even turning his own networks. It was good to know that he at least had Hans there in place, currently dormant, but ready for such time as his unique talent might be re used, the talent that had been developed so effectively, prior to his move from old world to new.

This accomplished seeker and sender of secrets had even drawn information from the top level counsels of Dr Klaus Haushofer, the eminent German professor of geopolitics whose broad theorising was coming to carry so much appeal for the Nazi High Command, and for Deputy Fuhrer Hess in particular. But then, Hans's star client, Kurt Weill no less, had had to leave Germany, and Menzies had decreed it that the composer should be followed...... first to Paris and then to New York.

One moved with one's cover, this was the rationale. Had he stayed, then Hans might have been left too exposed to be of much further use. Yes, it was better that he should go. Inasmuch as the man's professional standing was being maintained then so too was a disguise, and what had worked well in the old world should, hopefully, continue to do so in the new.

This decision made, though, there then remained the matter of a second aspect of the association, a deeper function, related but not dependent, which on separate consideration had had to be jettisoned in mid Atlantic. For if it was a truism in these matters that cover can thicken and thereby improve with time, a cypher definitely did not. The latter was either fresh or it was stale.

So thank you Kurt, concluded Menzies. Your contribution in that role now belongs to history. And Hans..... burrow while you can, but keep alert for the rising talent in the wings, the bright young talent that waits for its time and its chance. For that chance might be ours too, to nurture a second and perhaps even better flowering of your uniquely excellent, uncompromised best. Yes...... you, Mr Hans W. Heinsheimer, remain one for the future, just like Guy, just like Harold.

For today, though, there was this spectacular present to celebrate, and serried beneath him were the high born of Britain, like chess pieces, but awaiting deployment in a far greater game ..... some to be developed and protected, others perhaps to be sacrificed.

At the top, The Royal Family, by blood and upbringing, had to be pro German, naturally, because they had to be fearful of Red Russia..... for it was still not twenty years since the slaughter of their Romanov kin. And around them massed the bulk of the aristocracy, sheep-like in their fretful flock, anxious that inherited position, inherited wealth, inherited Empire should all enjoy continued protection, a protection that was no longer to be taken as granted.

Just look at that brace of Marquesses, of Londonderry and of Lothian, as true and as blue as you like, each very much of the Tory right, each trusting their fellow Peer, Lord Halifax, to speak for them in Cabinet. Halifax, the '*Holy Fox*', who commanded high position in Menzies' parent ministry, the Foreign Office. He who made no apology for actively courting the Bavarian Corporal.... a demeaning strategy, in Menzies view, demeaning and ultimately doomed, but for one whose business it was to build an armoury of pretence, a strand of policy not without worth. Nothing was to be dismissed too hastily.

And the same rationale lay behind Menzies' approval of a political rehabilitation for Sir Samuel Hoare, the former Foreign Secretary who'd been seen to be far too soft with Mussolini over Abyssinia, and, for this, forced to resign. That could have been the end for him, but now he was back at the Cabinet table, the Quaker, the man of peace. And this was the point. For if Menzies task was to protect the nation and, to do this, to identify and empower a fist of iron, then he should be also keeping to hand the velvet glove. And as such, Hoare's credentials would be impeccable. Deception, as ever, was the game, and approriately placed this man might more than persuade..... he might even convince. A principled Quaker amongst all the polluted pragmatism of modern politics..... this was a rare asset, one not to be tossed away.

Scanning across to the Dukes, Menzies now spied young Clydesdale. He was known to be doing the same as Halifax, though through supposedly more discrete, unofficial channels..... the Lisbon route, by way of the Hess nurtured connections. All around the high born of Britain were making their choice. Fascist thuggery was becoming acceptable, it seemed. To many it even appeared desirable. Someone had to confront the Georgian peasant, they argued, and as rough hewn as he presently seemed, Hitler might yet be shaped for the task.

If widespread, though, such approval was not unanimous. Even the aristocracy will have its mavericks, the most prominent hailing from families of long ago dissipated wealth, men of impeccable breeding and often impeccable education, but, after the lean years of the slump, left now with little in the way of material asset to lose to a rampant proletariat. Here was one now, protocol ordaining that he should be foremost in the procession gathering behind those of Royal birth.

Enter the 22nd Earl of Erroll, The Lord High Constable of Scotland, with his flowing robe and gold tipped baton, to cut a most impressive figure indeed. Handsome, tall, blond, and, at 36, in the prime of life, this had to be a man of considerable substance...... surely. But no, the traditional Coronation role had failed to prevent the Scottish estate from falling on hard times at the turn of the century, so hard that no lands remained north of the border and the castle, Slains, had had to be sold as a ruin. Menzies remembered this man as no more than a boy, leaving Eton to join the father, the 21st Earl, a post armistice Charge d' Affaires to Berlin.

Returning to London, the lad had then, like Menzies himself following the Great War, secured a start at the Foreign Office, but then he'd thrown this up, preferring life as a Jazz Age playboy..... and that was when the man had met Idinia Sackville, daughter of Earl De La Warr, the voracious Idinia, a vamp with whom Sir Stuart was all too well aquainted. For Idinia, remarkably, was sister to Avice, the lady he'd made his own first wife.

Sisters! And yet Avice and Idinia, like he and Joss, were as chalk and cheese. Idinia was a riot. To Mr and Mrs Menzies, so watchful and reserved and fastidious, she had been a constant embarrassment, so notoriously eager and open was her sexual appetite.

A full nine years older than he, she'd lured the future Earl into a hasty marriage and then as a pair they'd embarked on a spree of adulterous promiscuity such as had rarely been heard of since Regency times. They became acquainted with Kiki Preston and her ways, as later did the Duke of Kent..... also here today of course. And then the de Janzes joined the circus, Alice to become no less notorious than Kiki on account of a preference for shooting lead (rather than cocaine).

Soon though, as if weary of scandalising Europe, these four were decamping to Kenya, Alice abandoning her infant girls to care instead for wildcat foundlings. That would have been in '24 or '25, and as their behaviour grew ever more louche so their Aberdare enclave, by the Wanjohi River, earned its infamously lasting epithet..... *Happy Valley.*

Menzies thought back, to1928, a significant year for Erroll when, with the sudden and unexpected death of his father, the prodigal succeeded to the Earldom. His suggestion that a current lover, Mary ('Molly') Ramsay Hill, the wife of a neighbouring farmer, should accompany him back to Europe for the funeral triggered divorce proceedings to end two marriages. The cuckolded husband was outraged, but not so the shameless, careless, Idinia. There would be other men for her, but not before a family connection between Erroll and Menzies had been sealed in the person Joss's one child, a daughter, Dinan, then aged two. For if such a sister in law as Idinia was easy to disown, not so such a niece as Dinan.

So vulnerable, so innocent...... this delicate flower couldn't be simply abandoned to all that was so feckless and corrupt. Between Sir Stewart and Dinan, then uncle and niece, a deep fondness would remain, surviving even his own divorce from Avice in 1931, and his remarriage the following year.

The Earl, meanwhile, had remarried to make the former Mrs Ramsay Hill his new Countess. They returned to Kenya and farming, to mixed fortunes in difficult times. Indeed, there was accomplishment in mere survival..... but little in the way of any wealth. Nevertheless, by the mid 1930s Erroll was making his mark as a community leader, even as his wife slid into an equally marked decline. Disappointed in her hope of curing her husband's womanising, of providing him with a male heir, she sought solace in alcohol and opiates. The excesses told, her conduct giving Joss further excuse to indulge that same old weakness for other men's wives.

When last in London, in '34, the Earl had shown a strong interest in Blackshirt fascism. Mosley was being touted widely, and not unsuccessfully, as the man to revitalise the Empire. Sailing south again Joss had publicly recommended the ethos to his adoptive Colony. More recently, though, there were indications of an apostasy. He'd been heard denouncing Italian and German fascism as grave threats to the territory's fragile viability. He *seemed* sincere, but who was to be sure?

Menzies was reading Mosley's mail, and this made him better

placed than most....... but here was a man who knew better than to leap to premature conclusion. Menzies job was to be unrelentingly vigilant.

And this now had to mean stricter surveillance in Kenya, preferably before Joss Hay's return. The network of watchers laid discretely from Cairo down to the Cape needed to be tightened, particularly in the Nairobi area. Tomorrow he would be calling on an old acquaintance currently staying at the Savoy.

Percy Filmer was managing director of the Shell Company of East Africa. He and his wife Phyllis lived in 'Shell House', the company's main residence in Nairobi standing, as it did, so conveniently close to the rakish Muthaiga Club over which the Earl of Erroll had come to hold near baronial sway. The Filmers had previously represented Shell in South Africa, and Phyllis had long been useful to Menzies....... she being of Colonial background, with parents who'd served in the diplomatic corps.

As with the Errolls, Percy and Phyllis Filmer had travelled many, many miles to bathe in the prestige of this same occasion, but, as mere representatives of a mere corporation there could be no part for them in the ceremony. Like Menzies himself, they would do no more than look on.... unlike the Bonny Earl.

Just see how resplendent he stood. To behold the man now was to have to concede, whatever the side and whichever the doctrine, that here, very definitely, was a potential leader. With that build, and those looks, and with the sharpest of sharp memories, this was a man to inspire and unite and command the native..... no less a talent than that which had secured Aqaba twenty years ago. Then the thrust had been across the Arabian sands, with tribesmen on horse and camel. Now, led by fast, mechanised armour, a northward drive from Kenya to Eritrea could again secure the Red Sea, plus the Somali territories to boot. From the Horn of Africa in the north to as far as Madagascar in the south Joss Erroll was becoming a man to be reckoned with. He had the charisma, the connections, and he had the verve. The Foreign Office was alive to this, Menzies knew, and likewise were their opposing strategists in Berlin and in Rome.

Indeed, it had been reported to him that Mosley had called on Erroll at Ashley Gardens, no doubt looking to renew an old friendship. Birds of a feather they'd been during the rakish '20s, and if the old companionship was indeed being revived then the joint mischief could be of a far more dangerous kind. Mosley was being feted and flattered in

Rome. Mussolini's army would soon be placed to push south from Abyssinia, towards Kenya..

Others here were entertaining similar anxieties, Menzies knew, and they would be devising very different responses ...... men of straw, men of iron. Where was Churchill?

There.... yes, he could see him now, quite a way down, with the commoners, well beyond the transept, and, for the moment, politically, well beyond the pale. But he would be kept well briefed, nonetheless, thanks in no small measure to himself.

And naturally the same scene-stealing Earl was also drawing Winston's eye, and sufficiently for the watchful parliamentarian to be reminded that Erroll would shortly be making a maiden speech to his fellow Lords. The whisper was that he would be speaking for Kenya and the Kenyans, which would certainly mean words on the neighbouring territories. He, Winston, would follow these closely...... and, even more closely, any Foreign office response, official or unofficial. For Halifax, cheapjack-in-chief at the appeasement bazaar, he too would be monitoring Erroll's worth.

But for now, Halifax, towards the centre in one of the closer side-on ranks, was obscured. Churchill had a clearer view of the far group of Peers, facing as if in opposition. See the Lord Oxford, young 'Trim' Asquith, son of his old Liberal boss. Trim, a Balliol starlet maybe, but hardly a politician..... more of an administrator, in the mould of Lord Moyne there, the well travelled Walter Guinness. Vera, Walter's friend, she couldn't be with him, of course, being married still to Delves-Broughton..... but standing close by was the coltish young Chief of the Clan Fraser, soon to be her son in law. He'd been to Oxford too, but he was no scholar, not like his younger brother, or indeed like Trim...... but should warriors be required then this man surely had it in him to shine, Churchill was sure of that, as sure as he was that the smoke of combat would soon once again descend. For a 'Shimi' was nothing if not a man of action, born and raised to lead, to do or to die. The young stag needed a war, thought Churchill, as he did himself..... for only then would the country be in need of the man. When the call came, he sensed they might both prosper........ provided it wasn't too late.

The grinding Ceremonial was lifting, now, to one of its highlights, the Annointing. The pulsing orchestra asking, pleading, begging, and the voices answering so fully, so richly, as one ......

Zadok the priest and Nathan the prophet anointed Solomon king; and all the people rejoiced and said......

'God Save the King', mouthed Menzies, scalp a-tingle. The impact wasn't to be denied, even by one who'd heard and seen all this before. Handel, the German...... and he might have been writing for a German born, German speaking Monarch some two hundred years back, but this was good all the same, God it was good! Good enough to inspire Beethoven, who would in turn inspire Brahms and Wagner and Mahler and Strauss..... geniuses all, Germans all.

When, thought Menzies, would England find its own musical prince.... a successor, at last, to Purcell, with works the equal of Dido, and Arthur?

Maybe soon, for hadn't Hans spoken only recently of one whose musical wit might yet speak for the difficult days to come .... much in the manner that those of Weill's had ten years before, then from Weimar Germany.

And what, pondered Menzies, might this new voice say? And what might it perhaps even be made to say?

*

young 'Wricklemen'
1938
Cornwall

....and for more than a year, now, the newly crowned Monarch's writ has been running smoothly to the utmost corners of his awkwardly inherited realm, even to the meanest cottages therein, supposedly carrying the protection of the King's law to his each and every loyal subject. In one such dwelling, a crumbling two bedroomed hovel in the tiny village of Crafthole, quietly tucked into its corner of South East Cornwall, live the Wakeham family..... three fast growing brothers and their widowed mother.

In one bedroom, nineteen year old Ben Wakeham shares a far from sturdy double bed with his younger brother Vincent. Vincent is fifteen. The youngest of the three, Norman, is still only seven. He sleeps in the other bedroom, where his mother and he have a single bed apiece.

As did generations of Wakehams before them, these siblings maintain a sturdy open boat from which they fish, out of Portwrinkle. They are *wricklemen*, their traditional grounds stretching out to the Eddystone, grounds over which they can cast either seine net or line, depending on season or shoal. It affords them a living, plus a little to spare....... and this must be saved if Ben is to afford the second boat which might harvest sufficient to enable him to move into accommodation of his own.

The goal lends focus to Ben's life. He is industrious, reliable, and organised, and he expects the same of Vincent. More space will be of mutual benefit, he argues, and the younger brother has to agree.... albeit sometimes reluctantly, for Vincent is at an age when, naturally, he is wanting time to think and act for himself.

Both Ben and Vincent are fiercely, almost competitively, protective of their mother. Norman naturally idolises swarthy, broad shouldered Ben, and, of course, the freckled and fringed youngest is adored and indulged by all. In circumstances far from ideal the family functions well enough. They survive, and currently no one feels too put upon..... not even the quiet and sometimes forgotten Vincent.

Instructive is the Friday ritual of the cigarettes. Ben's weekly packet of twenty, a symbol of seniority, was purchased in the morning from the village store by his mother, together with her necessary groceries and household requisites.

These other items are now shelved in their appropriate cupboards, but not so the packet of '*John Players*'. They wait on the dining room mantle shelf where their presence is immediately checked for by Norman when he returns from the village school at neighbouring Antony. Then he must wait too, for Ben, who today arrives with Vincent at six.

They want their tea. Ben will have his cigarette later, but he must open the packet now. He must open it now because Norman is anxiously waiting for the picture card within. The current series is *Modern Naval Craft*, a theme of particular interest to the boys of Antony School where many a father or older brother will be a RN rating attached to one of the ships, or a Devonport 'yardie' employed in their maintenance and sometimes even construction. The *Warspite* for instance, she'd been Devonport built, as had the *Exeter*, and these were particularly sought after amongst Norman's classmates.

But anything British, that was the main thing, and this was far from guaranteed when only it was only fifteen of the full fifty two that flew the White Ensign. The rest were of lesser interest...... French, German, Italian, Japanese, American, Russian. In the swap market foreign ships counted for far less. Ben knows this, and he isn't above teasing the little one as he slowly levers open the packet.

"Have you managed to get a *Repulse* yet?"

"Not yet, Ben. Joseph Varcoe has a spare. I've offered him a Japanese and an Italian submarine....."

"...... because he's keen on subs."

"Yes, but he's holding out for one of the British ones. If this isn't the *Warspite* let it be the *Severn*, or the *Sunfish*."

Out came the card, but screened by Ben's palm. Ben studied it. Norman squirmed.

"Well we do have a submarine," taunted Vincent, looking over the older brother's shoulder. "That's the good news." Dismay grew in Norman's eyes, obliging Ben to end the suspense as mercifully as possible. "Because this one is French, the *Surcouf*..... number twenty two in the series." It was passed across. The child took it, his gratitude genuine, but far from enthusiastic. "Got that one?"

"No, but enough people have..... including Joseph."

"Show me," said Vincent, and Norman passed him the card. Of the three boys, Vincent the most capable reader, was always the most interested in the reverse side paragraph. "Largest submarine in the world...... does eighteen knots across the surface...... carries a crew of a hundred and fifty. That's got to be big. None of ours carries more than sixty."

"There's been arguments about this at school," said Norman, recovered now from his disappointment. "People who have the card try to make something of its size. Some say it even carries a sea plane, and that must make it really special..... but others, whose fathers crew submarines, they say that it's far too clumsy a thing to make a proper fighting machine."

"An aircraft carrying submarine?" Ben was likewise sceptical. "Neither fish nor fowl."

"But we won't know until she's called to action," argued Vincent.

"What I see is a one off. She might be the ideal tool for a job as yet un-dreamt of. War can be like that. Just as a transport she might land and take off quite a good sized raiding party. By night she can be quick, by day invisible…. plus, with that size and power, she would surely have a good range."

"So you're talking maritime performance, Vincent," said Ben, "rather than firepower."

"Basic sea going performance and, added to that, imagination. Should conflict come we can perhaps best judge the boat then, and also its crew and their command."

*

a formative influence (and informtive)

Harold 'Kim' Philby's name had gone around 'the firm' before he was recruited, and it had turned out that Colonel Valentine Vivien, deputy to Menzies in the service, had served in India with St John Philby and therefore felt able to vouch for 'Kim' (St John's son).

In July 1939 he (St John) stood for parliament in a by election at Hythe, a safe Conservative seat representing the British People's Party, an anti war group which had strong overtones of fascism and anti-Semitism. Although he attracted support from Left and Right he won only 576 votes and lost his deposit.

On the outbreak of war he tried to get into military intelligence as an Arabist attached to King Ibn Saud, but someone else got the job. He then launched himself into a scheme to raise money for Ibn Saud from the Zionists; in return for £20 million, the Jews would be allowed to take over most of Western Palestine. There is some confusion over how much Ibn Saud knew of this scheme, because he later angrily described it as an attempt to bribe him, but the principle was certainly considered feasible by the Zionists. While waiting for this, and other projects to mature, St John was peripherally involved with the publication of 'Stop the War' pamphlets put out by the British Council for a Christian Settlement in Europe……

'Philby: The life and views of the KGB Masterspy'.
p 80 P. Knightley. **Reprinted by permission of Random House Ltd.**

once a Catholic
SEPTEMBER 1939
Northern Ireland

And two young men who, as neighbours in the same Londonderry street, had learned together through the same classes at school, and taken up similar work since, and shared the same girls, stand now in earnest conversation on the southern bank of Lough Foyle. They have been friends for as long as each could remember, and in their bones will always remain so, even if now they are at a parting of ways.

"So you're decided, Seamus. You're going to enlist in the British Army."

"I am, Declan. For they've said they can support and encourage the studies I wish to embark on."

"Towards the taking of the Holy Orders. You're determined still to enter the Priesthood."

"More than ever, Declan," confirmed Seamus Mulligan.

"Yes, I can imagine quite a demand for active young Catholic Padres...... supply being rather limited."

"Obviously I don't win your approval, Declan."

"No more than I'm likely to be winning yours, with my taking up with the IRA."

"At least Declan, after I've wished you luck I can pray that Our Father in Heaven will be merciful in his judgment."

"I'm afraid it was the fate of my earthly father that most concerns me. I was barely four years old when Churchill's Black and Tans came....... dragging him from the house, to be kicked to death in the street, in front of my dear mother, who was left to struggle on alone. You wait, they'll soon be having that man back in the war Cabinet.....and he'll be in his element. He might even wangle himself the top job. Believe me, for all his fine words, he'll not have forgotten how to fight dirty."

"If that's what it takes to check the outright evil that is Nazism then so be it," answered Mulligan.

"So better the devil we know, eh?"

"This time, yes, most definitely...... for I'll tell you this, Declan

McDaid. If it's true that the IRA movement seeks to make common cause with Nazism then it invites a hell on earth. Hitler is developing for himself a private SS army besides which the Black and Tans will be remembered as a troop of Boy Scouts."

"That's as maybe," answered McDaid, reaching for a final handshake. "Like you I've made my choice, and now, in our different directions, we must take our chances."

*

Vera and Jock at their daughter's wedding. 1938

The bride and groom.

part of a letter
OCTOBER 1939

A little more than a month after war had been declared, and amongst the letters *The Times* publishes a letter from the 36 year old Marquess of Clydesdale. He has been an MP since 1930. He is also an accomplished aviator.

It contains this;

.........if Hitler is right when he claims that the whole of the German nation is with him in his cruelties and treacheries, both within Germany and without, then this war must be fought to the bitter end. It may well last for many years, but the people of the British Empire will not falter in their determination to see it through.

But I believe that the moment the menace of aggression and bad faith has been removed, war against Germany becomes wrong and meaningless......

......That day may be far off, but when it comes then hostilities could and should cease, and all efforts be concentrated on righting the wrongs in Europe by free negotiations between the disputing parties, all parties binding themselves to submit their disputes to an impartial equity tribunal in case they cannot reach agreement.

Yours truly,
Clydesdale

A year later, in 1940, the Marquess's father, the Duke of Hamilton will die. As he must to take the title, Clydesdale will then relinquish his Commons seat. He will join the RAF, and by 1941 attain the rank of commanding officer at RAF Turnhouse (now Edinburgh Airport).

*

Alan and Patsy

(ii)the 1940s

God has his ways which are not ours......
...... O tide that waits for no man,
　　　　　　　　SPARE OUR COAST!!

'Look the Storm Cone.'
　　　　from Peter Grimes, Act 1　Britten/ Pears/ Slater

The young Member
May 1940. Henlow Grange, Bedfordshire.

　　　　"From the Foreign Office you say, Alan? ...... not the usual envelope."
　　　　"This, my love, is a note from Halifax, your own Uncle Edward, personally written by hand."
　　　　"Still the Foreign Secretary......"
　　　　"......and likely to remain so for a good few months yet. Neville falling on his sword will have strengthened his position."
　　　　"Sounds perverse!" Patricia Lennox Boyd poured a second cup of coffee for her husband. The silver pot she then placed back on its tablemat,

with, carefully re-propped against it, a second as yet unopened envelope.

"Because the Party, we Conservatives, still have the overwhelming numbers in the House," explained the Member for Mid Bedfordshire, first elected in 1931 "Churchill knows that, and he knows that while 'National' in name, this compelling arithmetic has to be reflected in the hue of his Coalition. He's too wily to attempt to over-stock from his own clique, for the moment anyway. He needs to allow we of the Tory establishment to have our say at the top table, and Halifax is our leader, our spokesman. His disadvantage of course is......"

"......that he sits in the Lords."

"And hence this, my love. Read for yourself." Alan Lennox Boyd MP passed the one letter over the breakfast table. The wife took it, knowing that her husband was following the Party line, which held that as yet Churchill was still on probation...... even if Chamberlain, clearly a sick man, was obviously finished. "He conveys Neville's gratitude for the close support I've given him over the past two and a half years, and he urges that I accept any Government post that Winston might think to offer, notwithstanding the dismay that he knows we all feel at our leader's resignation following the division on Norway."

"The really depressing thing being that this was Churchill's half baked adventure." The Member's wife could be scathingly to the point. "But he wouldn't be offering you a job anyway. You were far too pro German in the Munich debate..... mind you, we did side with him against the Government's plans for India."

Boyd sipped at his coffee, allowing himself half a smile. "Whatever else we might think of Winston, he's not one to bear a grudge. I have, actually, been approached. Bracken sought me out yesterday." The wife scowled. Bracken.....to her, this man was an utter knave. "I was asked if I would consider working alongside Moyne at Agriculture."

"Uncle Walter! My father's favourite brother." And this made him her favourite Uncle, preferred vastly to Halifax, who'd come in on her mother's side by marriage. She was brightening again now. Clearly this would have been a commendable proposition....... had it not come from Mr Brendan Bracken.

"Moyne always seems to have got on well with Winston....."

"They go back a long way. Walter was, for a while, father in law to Diana, one of the Redesdale girls. The husband that was, Bryan, is my cousin....... Diana, meanwhile, is a niece to Clementine and therefore to

Winston too. I suppose in the broad stretch of thiings that makes us all related."

"Except that the marriage didn't last. Diana left Bryan....."

"......after she fell for Tom Mosley, now her second husband....... the pair currently being detained in Brixton at His Majesty's pleasure. One must assume the Diana -Winston link to be now somewhat strained. This said, a mutual and lasting regard was established between Churchill and Walter. A very capable administrator is Lord Moyne, a wise and worldly talent that Winston will have noted ......as I'm sure he'll also noted your own abilities. You're young, and you're fit...... definitely one for the future. I trust you are following Halifax's advice and accepting?" She put the letter on to the table, and as he was about to reach for and open the second, her husband hesitated. It was a moment for making himself clear.

"I can't, Patsy, and I wouldn't want to......as I told Bracken. It's got beyond Party politics. Whatever our differences on this issue or that, our fundamental pledge now has to be to protect democracy. If we need to fight to defend our whole system of Government then all of us of military service age are honour bound to enlist under the King ......"

"..... and take the command of the King's First Minister, whatever our views on him as a stratagist."

"It's as simple as that, Patsy my love, and as difficult." Hands reached. Fingers met.

"Alan, you make me so proud. Your son, when he grows, will hear of this from me......"

"Just look on it as a good long term career move," smiled the husband. "Bracken was impressed. He said Winston would be more than impressed. Championed thus, democracy was bound to win through, and in any peacetime administration he might then be required to form I could be assured of an honoured role."

"So all you have to do is survive. What irks me is the quality of those who'll move ahead in your absence. Bracken, he's little more than a bodyguard. Boothby I rate a charlatan, Eden a peacock, and Macmillan?...... 'The Prince', I call him, he can be that Machiavellian."

The M.P. shrugged away his wife's qualms.

"Forget the greasy pole my love. I'm doing what I want to. I've been set challenging, exciting tasks, tasks of critical importance....."

'Convince me,' required Patricia's sternly lifted brow.

"........just take this French Navy liaison work. We're suddenly having to consider what might be needed should Hitler punch straight through to Paris."

"You mean if France fell, its armies defeated?"

"Could happen, and what then do we do about her warships? Either we persuade their Commanders to bring them here or we attempt to destroy them. We can't let them fall into German hands."

"So what are the prospects? Are they persuadable, the French flag officers?"

"This is what my group has been set to find out. Fifty we've approached, covertly of course."

"And?"

"We might get one to declare for us."

"That's all?"

"That's all, one, and he's been brought off the retired list."

"And this is?"

"Vice Admiral Emile Muselier..... something of a non conformist, as you might expect. A ladies man I'm told, the dash of Drake, the charm of Raleigh, all stirred with a Gallic charisma. Like me, he's lost a brother to the Hun, and the whole Hitler thing he finds repugnant. In the very likely event of his coming across he'll be shunted off to somewhere quiet while his potential's sized, quite possibly the Bryce-Allen's.....the place has been requisitioned by the Admiralty for just such a purpose."

"Ince, you mean. In Cornwall, the Castle where I spent that weekend when you had Reserve exercises in South Devon?"

"Just across the Tamar," confirmed the husband. "Ideal I'd say. Remote, and yet handy for Devonport lest the Admiralty should want to deploy such talent as they deem usable."

"I loved Ince Castle..... just the kind of place I could retire to," teased Guinness rich Patricia. "Something you might bear in mind lest the owner should ever wish to sell."

"And when do you think you'll hear of me wanting to retire?" countered the husband. There would come a time, he hoped, when they could again think long term, but it certainly wasn't now. Another subject was required. "Bring me up to date on Moyne. He seems happy enough in the company of this 'Vera' of his. Is she still married to that Baronet....."

".....to Jock Broughton? No, I think divorce proceedings have been finalised. There was talk of him moving out to his coffee plantation in Kenya, and even of Walter and Vera regularising what some deem now to be a scandalously close friendship. A good five years it's been going ..... I don't see them making it official though."

"Did you ever meet this 'Jock'."

"Never, and I've no wish to either. 'Unlovable', people say. He's cowardly, and he's crooked, neglectful of former wife and children...."

"...... one of whom got married in the same season as we........... the other big London society wedding of that year. Their daughter, Rosamund, who married the young Catholic Laird. Did Jock turn up for that?"

"He did, as it happened. The bride's parents graced the grand occasion with a rare show of togetherness. Not that this would have cut much ice with the groom's people. I was surprised that anyone was ever going to be good enough for the man."

"Well this war will test the true mettle in all of us," said the MP, now opening the second letter. The two pages were closely read. The wife watched, allowing him to absorb. He would share, she knew. And he did.

"It's from Burney,"

"Bernie?" The wife knew none.

"Sending me a couple of verses, as promised."

"So this is a Bernice, or......?" The enquiry became tentative. Her husband was given to intense male friendship. She knew better than to intrude.

"Not a Bernice, Patsy, nor a Bernard."

"But definitely male?"

"Almost," teased Alan.

"Meaning?"

"That he's a sensitive soul," smiled Boyd, with enough openness to allay his wife's worst fears.

"Go on," she urged, sensing her husband's drift.

"Burney is the surname. Roger Burney, soon to be a fellow Royal Navy Reservist.... joining us when he comes down from Cambridge at the end of this term."

"A bright lad then.... and he studies what?"

"All things French..... language, literature, history, politics."

"Just what you need then."

"This was what I said to him."

"Where?"

"At Portsmouth. He was visiting the base, part of a preliminary assessment. Cleared by this, he'll then be ready for basic training, the prospect of which provokes apprehension.:...."

".... because he might be too queer a fish?"

"Partly, but more so because he's long agonised over whether he can live with himself.... either as part of the war effort or not. His closest friends are pacifists, you see, and he will have listened closely to their argument."

"But the plight, now, of his beloved France has at last braced him to enlist for the fight. So had he been part of that lefty clique up at Cambridge?"

"No, this was more to do with religion, and art. He'd got himself tangled with two young musicians, one a Quaker, the other already something of a name as a composer..... and no less a committed pacifist. That pair have taken their considerable talents abroad, to America".

"Leaving this Roger here, alone, to wrestle with his conscience....."

".... which was eased significantly on the sinking of the *Athenia* last Autumn. Remember?"

"I do, the liner, out in the Atlantic during the very first week of the war. Civilians died, including women and children....."

".... and much was made of German bestiality, of course. In the name of civilisation, the perpetrators of so indiscriminate an attack needed to be wiped from the face of the earth. Not to fight was to condone, shouted the warmongers."

"And the pacifists, Alan, what could they preach in reply?"

"Restraint...... and that might have been the more appropriate response, for, between you and I, the facts point to this incident having been unwished for in Berlin. Hitler's intent, at that time, would have been to secure Poland with a brief, limited war...."

"....and after that to pause to take stock before mustering for the next campaign."

"Precisely..... for to assist a highly active diplomatic corps, busy in Portugal and Sweden, in Rome and Washington, there had initially been a genuinely restrained deployment of U Boats. The Commanders were ordered to attack only opposing naval craft and supply ships. Passenger liners were to be left unhindered, according to the Submarine Protocol of '36, an international agreement."

"So what happened with the *Athenia*?" Patrica asked.

"Hitler was let down by an inexperienced and impetuous Commander. At the end of a restrained Naval arm this Fritz was far too twitchy a finger to have on the torpedo trigger. The *Athenia*, an unarmed liner was misidentified as one of our cruisers…..."

"……and she was attacked and sunk."

"Much to Berlin's despair, for there were Americans on board, some of whom were lost. It was looking too much like a repeat of the *Lusitania* sinking in '15. They feared the same outrage, the same disastrous diplomatic consequences. But in London, meanwhile, the warmongers are rubbing their hands with glee."

"Churchill and his chums, you mean."

"Quite…… Winston, newly re-instated at the Admiralty, can hardly believe his luck."

"A propaganda gift."

"*It was calculated*, he shouts…... *an atrocity, a war crime*, and this is where Roger Burney parts company with his friends. He doesn't know the full facts, and probably never will……but no matter. Like me, he decides to stand and fight with Churchill."

"While the others are sill inclined to give Hitler the benefit of the doubt."

"They must, because that's what pacifists do. The incident is a test of their creed. If it was a genuine mistake then Berlin must be allowed to express genuine remorse, and show repentance even….. and drawing this requires patience and forgiveness. Offer this, they would claim, and a better, more manageable Hitler can emerge. For us, though," shrugged Boyd, "this is nonsense. We have a nation to mobilise, we must demonise, and vilify….."

"…….and brutalise with escalated retaliation……"

"….. to ensure that the fearsome demonic brute raised in the public imagination then becomes reality. This is what the musicians warned. To them, for all its horror, the loss of the *Athenia* offered a moment to call for peace; and a fleeting moment at that, for once buried beneath the bluster of outrage then it was lost forever. Redemption, rehabilitation……. such concepts would be swept aside by bellicose rant."

"And likewise those politicians for whom these were core belifs, Sam Hoare for instance, also a Quaker….. and a strong voice in Neville's team. Winston won't want him"

"Mmmm...... I wouldn't be so sure," the husband was pensive. "Our new Premier can talk tough, publicly, but privately he'll be listening to advice on boxing clever, on keeping all options open. Don't write off Sam..... nor underestimate Churchill and the task that he has ahead. If he, Halifax and Hoare are as two very different kinds of cheese and a lump of chalk, don't think that they can't together be made into a potent blend. Appearances can be deceptive....... and if to us, then much more so to others. For my part, though, as it is with Roger's, I must fight. We can only hope that our efforts under Winston's leadership will be vindicated....... that by a show of force we can win for ourselves a better world."

"But one left with too many damaged people, that's what the pacifist might argue....... so does he just lie down and die, and hope that this can bring about some future heaven on earth?"

"The pacifist preaches that we demonise an adversary at our own risk. We encourage further atrocities and set ourselves the task of exceeding those excesses. And should we emerge victorious, how then do we judge ourselves? How can we say to our children that two wrongs never made a right?"

"We don't attempt to," replied Patricia. "We tell them instead that we fought a just war, in a fair and honourable way."

"*A just war*," repeated Boyd, wistfully. "So glibly do we trump the pacifist's argument, when he can hardly conceive of such a notion. That term, the just war, it has to be challenged and tested, he argues....... whatever the provocation."

"So they all run off to America?"

"I can't answer that, Patsy. This is why I stand and fight........ unless there might be something more to their conduct."

"Meaning what, Alan?"

"We don't know because we're not meant to, not me, not you, not even Roger Burney. It's as I say of Sam....... there's many a way of serving the war effort, even for those who won't carry a gun."

"But after much soul searching your Mr Burney is picking up his musket..... and you've helped confirm him in this decision?"

"All I've done is listen, and that seems to have helped..... for he sends me this rhyme."

"Show me." The top page was passed across, and Patricia Lennox Boyd read.

" 'Out on the lawn I lie in bed,
Vega conspicuous overhead
In the windless night of June;
Forests of green have done complete
The day's activity; my feet
Point to the rising moon.'

Yes, I smell that grass. And there's more.

'Now North and South and East and West,
Those I love lie down to rest;
The moon looks on them all;
The healers and the brilliant talkers,
The eccentrics and the silent walkers,
The dumpy and the tall.'

Ah, moonlight.....

'To gravity attentive, she
Can notice nothing here; though we
Whom hunger cannot move,
From gardens where we feel secure,
Look up, and with a sigh endure
The tyrannies of love'

...... how restful. Is there any more?"

"Not here."

"And the purpose of this..... is it to ornament our lives or inform?"

"Hopefully just the former."

"Hopefully....?"

"......because of what was said to me by Burney whilst we were in Portsmouth."

"Go on."

"As he goes to war he takes with him a promise, a fond promise left by those friends who have flown. Should he not survive then they say that these words shall be set to music. The piece will then stand memorial to him and and the carefree years of their youth."

44

Patricia Lennox Boyd glanced again at the verse.

"Forgive me," she murmured. "You say that and suddenly it's so much more poignant."

"We must pray he comes through," shrugged her husband . "They do sing, these words, but we must pray that they stay...... well just words, devoid of any adorning melody."

*

1940

peace..... almost

On 18-19 June Hitler met Mussolini in Munich. Ciano (Italy's Foreign Minister) recorded the event in his diary:

The Duce and the Fuhrer are locked in conference. Von Ribbentrop (Ciano's German counterpart) exceptionally moderate and calm, and in favour of peace. He says at once that we must offer lenient armistice terms to France, especially concerning the fleet; this is to avoid the French fleet joining with the English fleet. From von Ribbentrop's words I also feel that the mood has changed also as regards England. If London wants war it will be a total war, complete and pitiless. But Hitler makes many reservations on the desirability of demolishing the British Empire, which he considers, even today, to be an important factor in the world equilibrium. I ask von Ribbentrop a clear cut question: Do you prefer the continuance of war, or peace? He does not hesitate a moment, 'Peace'. He also alludes to vague contacts between London and Berlin by means of Sweden......

......The conference then continued with Hitler, Mussolini, and the military authorities. In principle the terms of the armistice with France are fixed, Mussolini showing himself to be quite intransigent on the matter of the fleet..

Hitler on the other hand, wants to avoid an uprising of the French Navy in favour of the British. From all that he says it is clear that he wants to act quickly to end hostilities. Hitler is now the gambler who has made a big scoop and would like to get up from the table risking nothing more. Today he speaks with a reserve and a perspicacity which, after such a

victory, are really astonishing. I cannot be accused of excessive
tenderness towards him, but today I truly admire him.'

Nazism 1919-1945: A Documentary Reader pp169-70
Ed J. Noakes & G. Pridham

*

Cyril
London (later in that same month)

"I trust, Mr Connolly, that you spent a restful night after that run-in with the law yesterday over at Oxford?"

"Not so bad thank you, all things considered….. and in particular the bruises sustained at the hands of an ever so gentle local Constabulary." Cyril Connolly was close to placing the man, but frustratingly at a loss for the name. Perhaps, with a clue or two…… "You look and you sound like someone equipped to proffer an explanation. What are you? Where are you from? I see you have my bag. Do I gather that it's being returned, or is this more of the same, further harassment…..or perhaps you even have a warrant?"

The caller, tall and urbane, and understated of attire save in the precision of the cut, smoothly took command of the hallway. The street door he clumped shut. He was firmly in.

"No warrant required Mr Connolly. I wield special wartime powers, and with what I have here, believe me, I could have you detained indefinitely." A wad of typed sheets was waved before the owner's eyes.

"They were posted to me, from Liverpool….."

"…. by a Merchant seaman. We know his name, *and* that of his ship, the number of his convoy *and* its date and place of departure. We know too of certain friendships that he made whilst in the States. We have plenty on how this came to you, Mr Connolly, our concern here is why."

"Sir," Connolly was defiant, "I publish *and* edit a literary review. This is literature. I've received early drafts of the author's work before, for comment, *and* I've no doubt that I shall again."

"How convenient, Mr Connolly, how very convenient." The

repetition carried open threat. "Tell me. In all of this, *who* precisely is *Paul Bunyan?*"

"Who? I don't quite get your drif…. unless…. yes….of course. You suspect or perhaps you even know of something encoded, and furthermore you presume in me an ability to decipher….."

"I'm anticipating you being able to name an individual, Mr Connolly, and also a time, and also a place.

'It is a spring morning without benefit of young persons', it says here. Dawning beneath a

'sky that has never registered weeping or rebellion'." Connolly said nothing. His interrogator read on.

"*'It is a forest of innocent beasts.*
There are none who blush at the memory of an ancient folly,
None who hide beneath dyed fabrics a malicious heart.
America, but not yet.'

Meaning some kind of New World, a sanctuary from modern day intolerance, awaiting its soon to arrive populace?"

"You tell me."

"I will, Mr Connolly, for it continues,
'Wanted: Distributors of public order,
men without foresight or fear.
Wanted: Those who have thought themselves a body large enough
to devour their dreams.
Wanted: The lost, those indestructibles whom defeat cannot
change…….' ."

Connolly remained silent.

" *'Those who have thought themselves a body large enough to devour their dreams'* ?" Repeated the caller, "*'Whom defeat cannot change……'* ?" The man's tone was becoming progressively insistent. "A *'body'*, it says. Does this mean a full race of people…..? And is it that here they are being offered a haven…..? A fresh start…… where, do you think?"

"I don't think," responded Connolly, flatly," at least not in such political terms. For me *Bunyan* isn't a person, not in this adaptation. See him as a spirit, or as an inspiration.."

"Explain."

"The author of the piece I know well. He's a poet, one who deals as subtly with metaphor and allegory as you might with secrets and lies.

47

One who long saw this war coming, as an inevitable outcome of a low, dishonest decade. And now, with those who spoiled for their fight having their scrap, just as day follows night then some kind of peace must eventually ensue. A new order must evolve, defined by its response to the challenges of a radically changed world. Old attitudes must be questioned, and modified, amongst victors and vanquished alike. This *Bunyan*, he voices those challenges, the challenges of a new and profoundly altered landscape, with all its fresh scope and opportunity."

"A better world?"

"Hopefully, but not necessarily".

"You fear the enemy will yet prevail."

"He might, temporarily, but that's not really the point. When peace comes *Paul Bunyan* will be there, pointing to the war winning technology and challenging the collective *everyman* to see all that murderous ingenuity put to a more constructive use. To believe that the common sort can respond and will meet this challenge is to be confident that this master race nonsense will shortly be consigned to history."

"So for you, the *body* in the piece will be those of the masses who can survive the outcome."

"The ordinary bloke, with his ordinary Betty......the fellow on the street," confirmed Connolly, "in their millions. The choices will be theirs, but they need to be informed, holds the poet......"

"...... of possibilities and of consequences"

"If you like, yes, and with his responsibilities starkly laid out, *everyman* can then be persuaded of his strength to meet them," offered Connolly. "Thus does an artist exercise his sense of mission. The best entertainment will often present a timely argument.... cogent and illuminating."

"As revealed in glorious technicolour at the Emerald City," scoffed the interrogator.

"If you like," repeated Connolly, finding his stride. "Look within, teaches the Wizard, find those hidden strengths and rise then to the challenge of freedom...... away with crippling superstition! Look at yourself my friend, and have a care. Today you boast special powers, and you act in their name. Tomorrow you might find them stripped, and, if we meet, what then?"

"You fail to convince, Mr Connolly, and still less do you intimidate. I smell an intellectual smokescreen. *Slim*, the cook, and *Tiny*, who he takes for a wife...... tell me that you know them as real people, and likewise *Johnny Inkslinger*. Then there are the others, the sundry creatures of the wild, and the various camp followers. The artist embellishes the legend for a purpose, I say. This is an intrigue."

"You're not convincing me," said Connolly, shaking his head. But was this bluff, wondered the other.

"You're a journalist," he said. "You might recall this......" A carefully folded page of a newspaper was produced from a side pocket. "I'll read just a few sentences .... Part of a letter written to *The Times* only last Autumn, soon after we declared war;

We do not grudge Germany Lebensraum, provided Lebensraum is not made the grave of other nations. We should be ready to search for and find a colonial settlement...... just to all people concerned.

We shall, I trust, live to see the day when such a healing peace is negotiated between honourable men and the bitter memories of twenty-five years of unhappy tension between Germany and the Western democracies are wiped away in their responsible co-operation for building a better Europe."

"That's from Clydesdale's," recalled Cyril, "without the balancing condemnation of Hitler's cruelties and treacheries."

"Well remembered, Mr Connolly, and I will say plainly now that you are suspected of being in possession of a coded communication reporting current progress in the search for the very kind of 'just' colonial settlement that was clearly and irresponsibly advocated in the letter to the paper."

"Surely you jest," blurted Connolly.

"This sort of equivocation might have been considered acceptable before the Norway debate, but now, Mr Connolly, we have in Mr Churchill's coalition a Government that vows to fight to the end. In the new climate, Clydesdale's published sentiments are close to being treasonable, and possibly too this intriguing little piece received by yourself."

"In which case, it's all yours. If you can divine hidden messages then please keep them to yourself. I'm a gentle reviewer of poetry. I want nothing of it, wishing only to continue in my harmless trade."

"And we will be watching you, Mr Connolly, to make sure you

do. These special powers of mine are very, very special. You know the score. As clever as you might think yourself, we can make your life, or even your death, far from comfortable."

"It must have been in a society magazine," taunted Connolly, bravely. "That I've seen your face, I mean." The caller turned to the door, as if in retreat. "Some time ago now, one of a couple, on the announcement of an engagement perhaps….. were you ever married into the de la Warr family?"

"Good day, Mr Connolly. I trust that I have made myself clear."

"And good day to you," returned the resident, opening and holding the door. "And be assured sir, that I do not know the score. Perhaps your threats might be better directed at someone who does!"

The caller was out onto the step and briskly down to the pavement, his prefectoral clout weightened by a solid black saloon drifting to a kerbside halt under the precise command of its army uniformed driver. Only seconds, and the passenger was aboard, and the vehicle was smoothly away…… but not before the driver had drawn from Connolly a whispersd 'well, well' of surprise, for behind the wheel was a man that he *could* positively identify.

No regular soldier this one, but, rather, as foppish a gentleman ranker as ever hung his Sam Browne on a Cavendish hat stand. Guards Club (of course), cavalry schooled, who better epitomised the absurdity of peacetime parading. He would fight, though, this was a racing certainty. One only had to see him with the hunt, relishing ceremony then dashing to be in at the kill. So why not the same in battle….. so long as a concern for the next wave of attack could outweigh that for the widely admired wave of his hair.

Evelyn would hear of this, decided Connolly. Evelyn, friend and fellow writer, who he knew to be working on the next satire, set, this time, during the early months of the war. Auden was lined up for a mocking, apparently, and now, with this link, here could be someone else to pull in.

*

Emile

A Free Frenchman
JULY 1940

Finally, early in July, there came a major 'recruiting break' for De Gaulle. Admiral Emile Muselier, a Corsican character out of an Alexander Dumas novel, arrived in Britain from Gibraltar from the 11th Cruiser Squadron, which he was commanding in the Atlantic. Muselier, with a pirate's visage of sharp swarthy features, a swashbuckling fighting personality and temper and proclaimed passion for women, was most things that General de Gaulle was not. For some reason he had run afoul of Admiral Darlan......he arrived in Britain not out of any enthusiasm for de Gaulle (in fact he had not even heard of de Gaulle) but out of distaste for Darlan and a determination to fight the Germans.

All Muselier wanted to do was fight......de Gaulle, for his part, badly needed a senior serving officer at his side, so Vice Admiral Muselier almost instantly became commander of all Free French naval forces. But it was a somewhat stormy relationship between two very disparate and strong characters......

*

51

Menzies

needs must
OCTOBER 1940.

"So the Battle of Britain has been won, Sir Stewart?"

"Fighter Command has gained us time, Prime Minister….. "

"…..and the agony, you think, will be merely prolonged," grunted Churchill, relighting his cigar to further thicken the War Room atmosphere. "Sometimes I do wonder about your commitment to this struggle."

"Have you forgotten June, Prime Minister, and Dunkirk? Hitler eased up, deceived into doing so by my misinformants. We saved your army."

"By dangling peace terms," scowled the Premier.

"We dangle nothing, Sir…… not without your permission. The peace terms one hears of so far….. which one can listen to, and then choose either to accept or reject….. they have been dangled by Hitler. They spring from his overriding ambitions, ambitions that do *not* include either an occupation of this country, or the dismantlement of our Empire. He would far rather we came to a truce, with our armed forces largely still intact……"

"……so that eventually they might fight alongside his in a grand crusade against communism. Yes Sir Stewart, I've heard all this quite often enough. We are tempted to think that the monster we would feed can be made tame, that it could be controlled, as one might a hunting dog, so as only to root out Moscow inspired Bolshevism. I say we delude ourselves. The more it devours then the greater its hunger. Gorged on the Reds, it must then turn to devour the decent doctrine of democracy….. as it has been painstakingly nurtured here, in Westminster, in our Dominions, and also in Washington. I see this, even if those in Berlin do not. As

52

individuals, Hitler included, they might *think* they can trust themselves, possibly in all sincerity, but this does nothing to lessen the danger inherent in their system. It is axiomatic......any dictator, cruel or kind, can never guarantee an enlightened succession."

"Point taken, Prime Minister. You can be assured that I would never assert otherwise. I merely remind you that when Hitler was less than ruthless at Dunkirk, it was a choice made out of an excess of ambition rather than any lack."

"..... allowing our troops to queue for the boats, bloodied but unbowed."

"And as a country we emerge from disaster with morale unbroken, indeed, if anything, stiffened. The same morale that has buoyed us through the air battle, Prime Minister. I contribute to all this, and yet you still doubt my commitment?"

"So what next Sir Stewart?" conceded Churchill, grudgingly. "What lesson will Hitler have taken from Dunkirk and the Battle of Britain? Are we to expect more focussed aims pursued with greater ruthlessness?"

"Not necessarily, for the Fuhrer is ruled by emotion. This is a man who struggles to admit any mistake. There is disappointment at our reluctance to see sense, producing anger, and frustration, all tending towards a greater *show* of ruthlessness. He will punish us more indiscriminately with bomber and U boat, but beneath this he will still cling to the hope that we can, and will change....."

"That somehow sense can be beaten into us," scoffed Churchill.

"Yes, and if we can help him to perceive in us just a twitch of movement towards his stated view that his Germany and our Britain can co operate to defeat the common foe that is Bolshevism, and afterwards enjoy a peaceful co existence, then we might *still* raise in him the the golden prospect of our imminent total conversion. For we, so he thinks, are bound to eventually see what he believes to be reason, and the more we listen then, for him, tantalisingly, the closer that elusive truce seems...... "

"......and herein persists the weakness that you think we might yet again exploit."

"A weakness long pondered, Prime Minister, to the extent that as dire as our predicament might now be, I have not neglected to equip ourselves with a range of contingencies."

"Continue, Sir Stewart. His weakness again.....?"

".....is that the closer that truce *appears* to come, then the better prepared he'll want to be to launch a surprise strike against his current ally. Last year the Poles were invaded whilst still reeling from Moscow-Berlin Pact, Molotov and Ribbentrop signing up less than a month before. The crucial point is that Hitler was ready to march."

"And when the time comes to sign with us, he'll want to be just as ready to break through the equally confused Russian lines," mulled Churchill. "So timing will be everything. While having been warned repeatedly against waging war on two fronts, Hitler finds himself anticipating a truce with London by making military dispositions appropriate to sweeping towards Moscow."

"Exactly Sir, and our task must be to encourage Hitler to wind into those dispositions an irreversible momentum, before the enticing *mirage* of truce evaporates."

"And he can be so decived, you think?"

"I do, because the man seems determined to deceive himself. We've heard it from him so often.......'So generous is the peace offered to the Englanders that they must surely soon tire of their ruinous war. The Poland they fight for is no more. Why, then, delay the inevitable.....?' "

".....as our cities are reduced to rubble," morosed the Prime Minister, temporarily dispirited by Menzies familiarity with his opponent's rhetoric, "and national morale withers for a want of food and oil. And our weaker bretheren who whisper for peace on Hitler's terms, they'll find more listeners......."

".......citing the Vichy arrangement," agreed Menzies. "Stressing Petain's *'pragmatism'*, and the Fuhrer's *'magnanimity'*, which has retained for the defeated French a more than fair measure of autonomy."

"So far, maybe,"muttered Churchill.

"We might keep our Empire....?" tested Menzies.

"And we forfeit our honour!" growled the resurgent Premier, sucking defiantly at that cigar. Even as the resultant fug thickened beneath the low command bunker ceiling, the air somehow seemed clearer. "The French can do as they want. Here we fight to the end. What mean you by this *mirage* of truce."

"It's a narrow option now, with the French collapse having been so sudden, but in some ways it could have been made more viable. Hitler neutralised the French army, and he paralysed their fleet. Only remnants came across to us...... this serving to amplify the man's conceit, a conceit that might expose him to the easily underestimated resouces that remain to us, material, diplomatic, natural."

"Natural resources?" queried Churchill. "You mean our being an island."

"Partly..... but also the Russian winter for instance, which can be ours to exploit. If Hitler wants Moscow in one campaign then he has to be on his way before the end of May .... and with the French out of the game then as soon as next May begins to look feasible."

"Provided that by then we can *look* as if we are about to accept terms. This is your mirage. How is this achieved?"

"I've been working on it, Prime Minister. Your role must be to continue with the verbal bombast. Provided I can convince them that this increasingly isolates you, both at Westminster and abroad, then it goes down well in Berlin......not least because from their point of view it reassures Stalin....."

"......who's not to suspect suspect what's afoot," said Churchill, warily. "But what mean you by speaking of my isolation at home and abroad?"

"Come the spring, from Berlin, you will have to look to be on the verge of resignation, following a stretch of months during which your position will have been seen to become increasingly untenable. This will be part of the illusion."

"And one that Dr Goebbels has always been keen to feed. So who, then, am I expected to be resigning in favour of?"

"In favour of my 'Peace' Party."

"*Your* Peace Party? Led by who? Have you a definite candidate?"

"I do, and I can come to that in a moment. First, the concept of a 'Peace Party' has for the past year been a somewhat nebulous entity."

"Riven by disagreement," scoffed Churchill.

"And if you hadn't guessed, this is largely because I have kept it so. Many people in this country want peace, perhaps a majority, but I ensure there is wide argument as to the terms they might press on Germany. At the tougher end we have those who would insist on a restoration of the exiled Polish Government. Others might demand that Hitler be gentler on his Jews. Some of the meeker might suggest that he should merely return the Channel Islands, whilst the pacifists simply refuse to bear arms."

"But we, who want war, want one thing." Pugnacity glowed from Churchill's eyes. "The defeat of Hitlerism, and on that single purpose stands my National Coalition. Therein lies its credibility, and with it my authority. It cannot be supplanted by hotchpotch, not in time of war."

"And this is why, with your approval, I am ready to turn this around by assembling a set of peace proposals, seemingly solid and coherent, around which our flakey pragmatists might settle their differences."

"Not in Parliament, you won't," said Churchill, "nor in the military, or through the press and radio. Our special power controls are far too tight, and have to remain so."

"That's good, for this in its way also encourages Berlin. For them, these controls indicate a genuine fear on your part, and that must reflect a genuine precariousness."

"So where, Sir Stewart, is your peace manifesto to be posted?"

"Abroad, Prime Minister. My mirage will first appear in the shape of an international initiative."

"From a kind of League of Nations, you mean."

"Yes….. not a bad way of putting it, Prime Minister. From a kind of League reformed specifically to address this problem of British obstinacy……. something that has gone on far too long. The talk of truce back in June was essentially a bi-partite affair…. a brief one-to-one flirt between us and Berlin. We've moved on. That can't work again. In reserve though I've kept dry this package that might be jointly proposed by a range of prominent figures from a range of concerned countries, all of whom will say that they have little to gain and much to fear from the prolongation of conflict. Some must be deceived into speaking in earnest, others can know that the prime movers in this are working for me, against Hitler."

"But public opinion here……?"

"……needn't matter so much. There's plenty else for the newspapers to write about, and no hustings of course. But Hitler, meanwhile, has his listeners out in Stockholm, in Lisbon, Geneva and Madrid…….. in Dublin also, and in Washington, don't forget. Let me have it whispered to them precisely what he wants to hear, that there is a wide foreign consensus, a reformed League, as you put it, which I like to call my *Nordic Front*, gathering momentum for a jointly formulated settlement, and that this momentum must inevitably gather in and unite

56

our home grown peace factions, hitherto so fragmented.... "

"......leaving me increasingly isolated and vulnerable, they'll think" said Churchill, pensively, "but to what? Who from the Commons would ever be likely to push for what amounts to a new fascist-friendly League of Nations..... this *Nordic Front*?"

"Berlin will hear of a positive response emerging in a firmed up extra-parliamentary opposition......led by distinguished persons assumed by them to command significant influence outside the Commons."

"And with this, a significant power...... a very wrong assumption Sir Stewart."

"I deal in wrong assumptions, Prime Minister. It is my trade. Believe me, nothing is so misunderstood and under-rated by European fascists than is the sovereignty of the Commons."

"And you can assemble these worthy personages?"

"I have Peers, many of them former Ministers. I have Dukes, some of them Royal. Landowners, press barons, industrialists, military men..... do I need to go on? As a group, from abroad, they can look an all-talented administration in waiting...... a non elected oligarchy maybe, but how much more preferable to the liquor lubricated nepotism that you would appear to purvey. My diplomatic corps stands ready. Allow me to give the word and the mirage of an imminent truce, my sham *Nordic Accord*, this can be conjured."

"And your leader in waiting is......?"

"......your recent appointment to our embassy in Madrid, Prime Minister. Nine months ago, during what some are now beginning to term the phoney war, I broached this notion of the *Nordic Front* with Neville and Edward. We were agreed that if driven to it then Sam, the principled man of peace, would make a natural King across the water..... and particularly so if the task of assembling a last ditch National Government could be left to you. This was why, back in May, Halifax was insistent that you and not he should succeed Chamberlain."

"Renouncing his own very strong claim....."

"...... because, in terms of negotiating a *phoney peace*, he could see that yourself and Sir Samuel might, each to the other, offer a truly effective foil."

"Very noble, I'm sure," said Churchill, chewing ruminatively on his stub.

"And, furthermore, Halifax is himself ready to take the pivotal role as Ambassador to Washington. I earnestly recommend that he should be given the job."

"Replacing Lothian....."

".....who recently has been looking quite unwell."

"And you truly think, Sir Stewart, that Hitler can be deceived by words and promises, by *phoney intrigues*?"

"Once sufficiently emboldened he can, Prime Minister, and to do this we must give ground." Menzies reached for the globe, on the desk to Churchill's left. "Let me show you."

A finger found the Black sea, and then the Ukraine. "Hitler needs oil. This is where it waits. Though he'll hope to take it in one, he might need two campaigns to secure it, and a lot of thirsty tanks. How does he fuel these?" The finger moved westward, no more than thirty minutes worth in time. "From here. He has friends in Rumania.... but they look vulnerable from across the Danube, to the south, in Yugoslavia and Albania, where his diplomacy has been significantly less successful......"

"......and where the Greeks have stopped Mussolini's nonsense."

"So Hitler will feel better, Prime Minister, if he can first take Belgrade and Athens. This shores up Rumania....."

"......and gives him a springboard from which to launch at the Ukraine."

"So what he needs is the pretext to sweep into Yugoslavia.....and I can give him that. Allow me to stir things in the capital....."

".....to draw Hitler in......"

"..... and he succeeds all the way down to the Mediterranean, leaving him better primed to go for Russia and even more convinced that you must be on the way out....... for us, my *Nordic Accord* being the one realistic option remaining."

"So that's it. 'Giving ground' means Yugoslavia, Albania, Greece."

"And I'm afraid there's more," said Menzies, tentatively.

"Go on," urged Churchill. Menzies took a deep breath.

"While you go on with the bombast, my role in this must be to make it seem to them that I'm undermining you."

"Which means?"

"Putting on a protracted performance, carefully paced over a number of months, hinting, promising, and then as good as guaranteeing the desired finale." Churchill frowned. Menzies continued, looking squarely into his master's eyes. "Frankly, you must allow me to take you to the very brink of capitulation. At Dunkirk we were playing for days, and words were enough. As I've said, we can't pull that again. The circumstances now are different, less fluid. To win months, and hopefully years, we need to toss them something more solid."

"But you've already buggered the Balkans, Sir Stewart!"

"Not yet...... and this is the point. We have to time things right, which means no coup in Belgrade until almost the end of March, and this leaves me with the task of keeping the *Nordic Front* at a gentle boil through a difficult winter.......an awkward interim during which to hasten Berlin in their secret preparations for a strike at Russia, I must actively demonstrate to them an earnest desire for this widely approved truce, the chimerical *Accord*, which is the *Nordic Front's* raison d'etre."

"Actively demonstrate?" repeated Churchill. "You mean with concessions that can subtly anticipate terms of that eventual *Nordic Accord* ......without giving the game away to Moscow. By sacrificing a few things of our own, you mean, as well as other people's land."

"Let's call them *tokens of good faith*, Prime Minister."

"So how solid?"

"Back in May, Prime Minister, alongside the blood, the toil, the tears and sweat you also offered our people hope. Now it's just me that can keep that hope alive, me with my sham *Nordic Accord*. Hitler has to buy it, and he will, if I can sell myself."

"Convince him of your *bona fides*, eh? And to do that, Sir Stewart you need......"

"I need land, and gold, and I need lives."

"Do you talk specific parcels, specific names...... has Berlin sent you a shopping list?"

"As good as....... and with items thereon to be provided within specific times."

"Such as what?"

"To start with, this imminent expedition being planned against Vichy held Dakar..... using the Free French, I understand."

"Later this month," confirmed Churchill.

"I am expected to ensure that it fails, Prime Minister. I ask that you sanction what amounts to sabotage. Twenty million pounds worth of French gold sits in a Dakar bank vault. Berlin knows this. They want it to remain Vichy gold. I need to show them that I am ready to allow this.......and see here." Menzies fingers were again on the globe, striding the northern Atlantic. "This small island, which is actually part of France, also hosts a similar deposit."

"We have it blockaded," said Churchill.

"We do, but they want it out and back to the French mainland........ so the test for me is to break our own blockade."

"But we can't just stand back and let them ship the stuff out. If our Navy is there, it can only be there in earnest."

"As will the force that we muster for Dakar, Prime Minister...... and similarly it must be thwarted by our stealth. Now it happens that the Free French have, in their armoury, a vessel that might have been designed for the task"

"And your phoney *bona fides* can be enhanced by getting this thing back into Vichy hands."

"Exactly, Prime Minister, and enhancement is the key concept throughout........ for I am also required to address another of Hitler's political ambitions, that's apart from securing the Ukrainian oil and eradicating the Soviet system. I speak now of as vast a project in geo-political engineering as has been seen since the herding of the North American Indian into purposely designated reservations. For this he must have land beyond Europe, and viable land at that."

"And this would be expected to be transferred under the terms of the *Nordic Accord*."

"It would, yes......but in a *state of readiness*, Prime Minister. This is the point. The land would need to be viable, and it would need to be un-encumbered."

"Prepared, you mean. Whereas a scorched earth policy might be an expression of ill-will......"

"......that would signal the very opposite, good faith."

"But we don't have gold to spare on fancy irrigation schemes and the like," protested Churchill.

"And this is understood in Berlin, Prime Minister. In fact this illustrates the whole point of the *Nordic Front*. It's an international initiative that I'm devising. It doesn't need to be just our land, it doesn't need to be just our money. The Vichy people, for example, have land to spare in North Africa, land that might greatly benefit from American dollars. If, by my oiling of the diplomatic wheels, this combination can be quietly pledged towards the deal that will ultimately define the *Nordic Accord*, then in Germany I can be perceived as a serious proponent of the same."

"So that's someone else's gold, Sir Stewart, and mainly someone else's land........ I think you also mentioned lives."

"Yes...... and with that one, Prime Minister, they're expecting a few of our own."

"Less of a strain on the Treasury I suppose," remarked Churchill, eyes twinkling momentarily from the still grim visage. "Specific lives, is it, they look for......? Not mine I hope!"

"Nothing quite so extreme, Sir," reassured Menzies, "but returning to those distant parcels of land, ours included, and the enhancement thereof, it is envisioned that this will involve more than just a reclamation from nature. Some of these areas, already the subject of discussions between the Diplomatic Corps involved, support established settlements."

"Native populations."

"In a manner of speaking, yes," agreed Menzies, now tilting the globe for a better view of Aftrica. "So what we're talking here is the elimination of the odd tribal leader who might be perceived in Germany as posing a potential threat to such plans as they might have to increase the local population. Having been awed by what their own Fuhrer has achieved then they're understandably wary of charismatic leadership, remembering perhaps the impact of Lawrence during the Great War. When the Celt or the Anglo Saxon goes native, Prime Minister, you have yourself a formidable adversary."

Churchill took the globe, scrutinising first the Red Sea, with Aqaba, of course, and then letting his eyes drop southward across the Horn of Africa and down towards Madagascar......as he did so, allowing Menzies to reach for his pocket and draw therefrom a palm sized photograph. The spymaster looked at it, and, turning it, then slid it beneath his master's eyes.

"One of our tribal chiefs," grunted the Prime Minister. "Occasionally seen in full ceremonial dress."

Menzies finger went to the globe. "And it is across this land, the White Highlands, that he holds sway. And too much sway for Berlin, where it is feared that he and his sort might obstruct, and even block the joint enterprise that the *Nordic Front* looks to move forward. As an indication of my good faith, Berlin wants to see him dead."

"And you have plans?"

"In place, Prime Minister, along with the personnel..... all ready."

A second photograph was produced and dropped clinically onto the first, as if it were an ace to take a knave. "GUSTAVE, we will know him as..... his own choice. He and his trained operatives await my command. I await yours."

Churchill examined the new picture. "GUSTAVE as a code name..... eh? Interesting, for what you have is a rival chief. Youngish......"

"......but certainly ruthless."

"Ruthless enough to ensure that none of those operatives outlive their usefulness?"

"If need be, Sir. GUSTAVE is a killer. When the time comes he will want to lead from the front...."

"......to bag more than his share of Nazis."

"Yes, Prime Minister, or die in the attempt."

"An outcome no less desirable, perhaps."

"Whatever, until then he will be the very man to oversee a thorough and proper execution of this task."

"Thank you GUSTAVE. And do we also, Sir Stewart, have a code name for the operation?"

"Not yet Prime Minister."

Churchill glanced again at the globe. "Then might I suggest 'HIGHLAND CLEARANCE'."

"Not inapt, Prime Minister."

"And the plans are thoroughly laid?"

"We would like your decision now, time being very much of the essence. We can no longer merely aim to survive in this conflict, on this we agree. It is either victory or defeat. Hitler looks stronger than ever, but there is that weakness...... his conceit. My strategy of enhancement, HIGHLAND CLEARANCE as you name it, aims to feed this conceit........ so that it might become an even greater weakness."

"Our hope being that he might be lured into fatal error," said Churchill, eyes moving with his artist hand to the Carpathians and the Urals, and the vast plain that lay between, the putative crucible of destiny, where tyrant pitted against tyrant might yet allow hard pressed liberty to cut free.

"Land, loot, and lives, Sir, we must stake all three. Are you bold enough to agree?"

Churchill glared back over his spectacles. "I am, Sir Stewart, provided you understand this. The powers I wield, so total and absolute as they might be, are, for the duration, sanctioned to me by the Commons, our elected chamber. Through them I am ultimately answerable to the people. In protecting my position, I protect their's. I am trusted, in the name of democracy, to insist that you be answerable to me. You are asking that I should agree to be seemingly taken to the very verge of failure and humiliation, knowing throughout that you are a master of the double game..... and all in the name of a mirage that you hope to project. I can allow, of course, that the occasional mistake might warrant adjustment, but I must warn you now that I will have a man on you, constantly, and he will have a gun. Should I, for an instant, detect this that you conjure to be something more solid than mere illusion, that you are indeed earnestly seeking my replacement by an unelected cabal, then your conniving brain can prepare itself for a bullet. Am I understood?"

"You are, Prime Minister."

"Good..... so you can have no objection to coming here regularly to report on progress."

"None at all, Prime Minister......once a week?"

"No, not once a week........ once a day.

*

Ince, Cornwall
(still October 1940)

Antony, Sheviock, Polbathic..... less so now, since the completion of the bridge in '61 at Saltash, but for road users of generations previous these humble place names became familiar to those crossing regularly from Plymouth to drive down into Cornwall. In those days, to take the A38 trunk route was to be ferried across to Torpoint and then have to wind westward around the quiet wood lined tentacles of the tidal Lynher.... Wacker Lake, Sconner Lake, Polbathic Lake.

Antony, Sheviock, Polbathic.... few looked beyond the signboards, remembered as these were for the order in which they could be briskly passed rather than as actual villages sheltering real communities and, with all the desperate uncertainty of the second winter of war this was what most of the residents preferred. For the understocked shops could remain their shops, and likewise their quiet pubs and their quaint churches.

In this view, Vincent Wakeham, even at an enterprising 18, is no exception. He now lives alone in Sheviock, his being one of a quiet row of tiny cottages set safely to the south of the main highway. He has moved down from nearby in ridge-top Crafthole to rent the dwelling occupied until recently by his older brother, Ben, who, as a 21 year old infantry conscript, had been shipped out to Egypt just three months before.

And Vince is steadily rising to the challenge of living alone, even though this full responsibility for a house as well as the boats had been unsought and, in truth, unwelcome. The arrangement had brought a sense of his being pushed away, to the rim of a hitherto tight family circle. Occupancy of the cottage helped Ben, and it helped the younger brother too. For Norman, back at Crafthole, could at the age of ten for the first time enjoy a room of his own and the full, doting attention of his mother.

And it was natural that this pair should, together, reserve so much pride and affection for the eldest, who was fighting dutifully for King and Country with the same first born earnestness that, even before his call-up, so easily assumed a quasi-patriarchal domestic sway. Too easily, in Vincent's view, but there would be no complaints, certainly not while the soldier was on station, defending the main lifeline of Empire.

Letters home, from the desert front, were addressed to Crafthole where the mother would read, re-read and reply as young Norman gleefully sorted the enclosed cigarette cards which Ben would beg and barter from comrades in arms. What filtered to Vincent were the reminders, constantly urging the maintenance of the cottages and the boats.... tasks usually in hand, often already seen to. Rarely were they forgotten.

For Vincent had been left with two boats to maintain, both open and masted, but each also with a more than auxiliary box housed, water cooled single cylinder petrol motor. One, for sea fishing, was kept tied at Portwrinkle. The second, in recent times very much the preference of the eldest brother, was closer. It was on the Lynher, kept anchored and tied beneath the water's edge trees of Sheviock Woods, and it was on this one that the shared suit of sails was stowed, and, depending on conditions, most often hoisted.

On the lurch from phoney to total war the estuary craft had

become the more frequently used, the more vital to the family's increasingly precarious livelihood. Fish were still plentiful, likewise customers, but difficulties had arisen with maintaining access to the latter. Formerly he'd landed his catch at Plymouth's Barbican Quay where his regulars would often wait, anticipating his approach, be it from sea or estuary. But with the imposition of the restrictions in the Hamoaze, and on the Sound, and also in the town, together with shortages of petrol, all had had to adjust.

Vince no longer ventured into Plymouth Sound. He still went to sea, but only within an arc drawn between Rame Head and Looe Island. The sea catch he landed at Portwrinkle to be barrowed over to Sheviock, and then down through the old 'George's Lane' to the waiting river boat. In this it could be taken eastwards, sometimes under sail, across to where his customers gathered close to the bank of the 'Camels Head' inlet. Skirting the northern edge of the Royal Naval Dockyard Vince would guide his river boat into the narrowed entrance to this tidal creek, beneath the Great Western girder bridge and then almost up to the brick arches of the near parallel LSWR.

Threading those arches, so as to bridge the neck of the Camels Head, ran the approach road into Plymouth from the Saltash Ferry, the smaller and less busy of the two Tamar vehicle shuttles. And, beside this road, so close to the creek as to appear, at full tide, almost to be slipping beneath its waters, stood a Public House, *The Camel's Head* of course. The pub's tight courtyard ended at a short stone quay, and this, for the duration, was serving the Cornishman and his fish buying clientele as a makeshift trading floor.

It was during the early afternoon return from a worthwhile morning by *The Camel's Head* that Vincent, not immoderately oiled, caught a first passing glimpse of a figure who, before too much later, would come to command a vivid and enduring place in his memory.

Back across the Tamar and through the Antony passage, Wakeham's boat had been beating manfully against the Lynher ebb when, from behind, he heard the gaining growl of a small aircraft. Closer it came, and louder, but without acceleration. He knew the sound, it was of a seaplane manoeuvring for take off. Could it be waiting, he wondered, for him to leave a clear stretch of water?

He looked back to check, and this was a strange one. A small single engined twin seated monoplane skimmed up behind him, balanced on the mid-most of three floats. On its straight taxi the two wing floats were lifted clear of the water, dipping only as the pilot swerved in a broad tilting turn which brought the machine around, ahead, and across a slightly perplexed fisherman.

For it was swinging in towards Ince, and as it slowed a launch was coming out to greet it. Both seats had been occupied, but now the leading was being vacated. This was a passenger, clearly, and prior to its taking flight, this unusual plane with its oddly inverted tail fin must have been requisitioned by him in Devonport as a personal ferry. Having stepped down into the launch he was able to don what appeared to be an officer's cap, and standing at the stern in a dark and immaculately fitted great coat he now cut a commanding figure. Clearly, this figure was here to assert authority.

He had to be a good fifty, but with the years there was also a grace and a balance. He remained standing in the now moving and turning launch, head up, watching, as the plane roared, sped, and this time soared Devonwards. The eyes then levelled to Wakeham's closing craft, meeting and returning the helmsman's scrutiny. With military jacket buttons a-glint, the short intense faced officer could have been a sea weathered Napoleon. If the sharper features and fuller scalp declared the man more obviously of the Mediterranean, then his bearing, less imperious, more sensual, declared him every little bit as determined.

It was spreading locally that the Castle was being used to billet high ranking French Naval officers, and Vincent quickly and correctly assessed this to be one such. What would be his status though? There were conflicting rumours. Most said that the guests would stay for no longer than they wanted, but others whispered that they were effectively interned, that, for these, repatriation to a Vichy command was not an option. Either way, Ince made the ideal pen.

Persuasive to the less dramatic majority was the retention of so many from amongst the pre war household staff, the two gardeners, the cook, her kitchen hand, and a housemaid. Each of these last three had a main building servant's room, and it was from her own small high-up window that the housemaid looked out on the river scene..... taking in boat, plane, and launch.

Jenny Cross knew Vincent Wakeham, and she was even better acquainted with his boat. Ben had often brought it across, and she'd encouraged him to the extent of his proposing marriage to her before his posting to the Middle East. Although Vincent, young Norman, and their mother were aware of a budding romance, to have sprung this provoked astonishment amongst all….. indeed there was surprise on Jenny's own part when the request was put on the occasion of she and Ben meeting for a last time prior to his departure. This after they'd been no more than five weeks into the courtship……. and what was that? Barely a month, when she'd heard tell of his walking out with other girls for far, far longer.

So Jenny Cross was entitled to feel uncertain, and, accordingly, sensibly, she'd remained undecided. She wanted time, and she'd said as much but maybe not firmly enough in the circumstances…. for Ben was taking too much encouragement from her warm and natural reluctance to overly disappoint an eager young soldier who, hours from boarding his troopship, was maybe just weeks from death.

For him, thus, it was only a matter of time, a question of simply surviving until the next leave. This was clear from his letters, and no less so from those that arrived at Crafthole than from those read by Jenny at Ince.

Ben would wait, and as he waited he could rely on his faithful brother Vince to watch. Vince, who had the cottage and who had the boat and who was, so often now, passing so close to the Castle. And today, here he was again, obliging once more.

The eyes that had been following the launch lifted to the Castle, to focus on the window he knew to be hers. Yes, she was there. And he raised an arm, which duly earned the wave in return….. but, this time, only the briefest, for Jenny was intrigued by this new uniformed arrival, an officer, not surprisingly, but the first she'd ever known to arrive by sea plane. What rank would that make him, she wondered?

For in truth, to Jenny, each novel Gallic face brought added excitement to an insular, largely Ince bound existence. Unfamiliar was the tongue, but far less so the eyes. Therefrom beamed admiration and, naturally, she was flattered.

And as Ben wooed on with his letters so Jenny found it harder to pen the appropriate response. This assumption, that he would return, war hardened, unassailable, a new generation patriarch with wife, and with children in waiting…… she was finding it all less and less a part of her dreams. She looked across to Tregantle and followed eastward the narrow heights of the Rame Peninsula. Six months before, that might have been enough…… but now she sensed there to be a wider, fuller field to play. It could be glimpsed in that corner of Plymouth revealed between Trematon and Antony, and also in the scores of window framed faces being rolled into and out of Cornwall along the GWR tracks, flanking as they did the Castle grounds to the north.

One day she would ride those lines herself, she hoped….. but with whom she knew not.

*

Night fishing
December 1940

………. and a full early evening moon had offered Vincent an opportunity to venture out from Portwrinkle on to a calm bay. He had brought Norman. The youngster had fished by night before, both with Ben and Vincent. He was unfazed by winter chill, and could be quick and competent with both line and gutting blade. He was there to earn his fare, and a good deal more should they have the fortune to encounter a thick shoal. They might scoop profitably, be back at harbour by eight, and then over and down to Sheviock with their prepared-for-morning bounty within the following hour.

Twenty minutes out now, and they were drifting at casting depth. Another five and the line was almost cast with Norman feeding and feeling for the hoped flutter. Then came the lurch, and the entangled youngster was feet first over the side in less time than it took him to cry 'CONGER!'

But no fish could have caused this, Vincent well knew. Stumbling forward he watched in helpless horror as his brother planed away from the boat. A coil had tightened around the youngster's left ankle and, whatever creature could snatch so, surely had power to dive, sharply taking the boy to the depths. But this he was being spared, and the shoreward tow was slowing. Vincent threw an oar out towards where Norman, no longer flailing, was reaching and wriggling in his endeavour to extricate himself from a now slightly slackened tangle. Vincent leaped into the water himself. The cold took his breath, and a moment was needed for him to re-find his bearings. Just a second, maybe two, and as they passed he realised the cause this mayhem.

Hard black metal was emerging from the water, gradually revealing itself to be as large a submarine conning tower as Vincent had ever seen. Its forward mounted gun turret appeared next, rising slowly from an abating turbulence, and strung Ahab-like from an imposing pair of gun barrels, fading into the darkness, was a last glimpse of the limply hanging Norman. This, unmistakably now, was the mighty *Surcouf*, the giant submarine which had been languishing in Devonport for the best part of six months since the fall of France.

It was said that then it had taken an armed RN boarding party to bring her under the Free Flag and, as if to echo the distant thunder of Mers el Kebir, a gunfight had ensued at the expense of lives on both sides. And now the monster had fished Norman, as if wanting to redress its playground belittlement...... and was the child to be just another of these tragic casualties? If he was alive then for a moment he was safe, thought Vincent, unlike himself, immersed as he was in the strength sapping cold of the sea. A powerful lamp came on making the portside sea a pool of light and all else, previously favoured by moonlight, now pitch black. The profile of the coast was gone, and likewise the prow of this vessel, its forward armament, and the sibling laced thereon.

The beam swung, for a moment meeting an empty fishing boat and then passing on and around but missing Vincent. Recovering the oar he kicked for his wallowing craft, dragged himself back over its stern, and laid low. If the light settled then the darkened side of the hull might be chanced. If he could manoeuvre forward then perhaps he might cut Norman free. But hatches were opening, and he could hear voices, French voices. This was an exercise, he thought. The Free French would be practising clandestine landings with a view perhaps to delivering or collecting agents off occupied territory.

The monster was now stilled, and Vincent needed it to stay so. Were it disturbed then a dive or even a turn might have a lethal result. Stealth was necessary, and also luck.

But the latter had expired. Another boat, like he, had chosen to make its move on the same blind side. It was a second submarine, emerging more sharply and steeply just yards to his right. The lamp swung again. There was no sense of alarm. This was an arranged rendezvous, with a species of more standard a size, one designed to surface and dive more quickly. Vincent kept back and he kept low, waiting, in darkness.

He listened. There would be more hatches, more voices, he was sure, and up they came….. French again. Now the second-up sub had its own searchlight, and from a deck hatch a small collapsible fabric raft was being hauled and assembled. Some kind of transfer seemed imminent, and why should this, in all the chaos and uncertainty of war, seem in any way improbable? Collateral consequences for the brothers might be dire, but that was how it could be for anyone whose mischance it was to be in the wrong place at the wrong time.

In the course of the cruel lottery of wartime, Vincent would have no doubt come to reflect on the other fishing craft that had struck stray mines, or had been accidentally rammed, and eventually ascribed all associated loss, including his own, to fate. But, as he listened and he watched, this encounter came to take what, even in times such as these, had to be a truly bizarre turn….. one that set a riddle, itself the baffling core of a wider puzzle, his response to which would come to shape the rest of a radically disrupted life.

Two vague silhouettes emerged onto the deck of smaller boat. One was tall and broad, loud, and of brisk movement. The other was shorter, and more slight, tending to watch and prompt with whisper as the other called up and across to the *Surcouf*. The languge wasn't entirely unfamiliar, Vincent having tangled often enough with French fishermen…… if he listened then he should at least get the drift.

The initial exchange of courtesies revealed the smaller of the craft to be the *Narval*, where the understanding was that they were talking to one Captain Ortoli….. seemingly with a view to persuading him to bring the *Surcouf* back to France, away from British and Free French control to sail instead under the Vichy flag, a course already determined aboard the *Narval*.

Vincent was hearing an appeal for a double defection. De Gaulle's name was heard, and also Churchill's, in terms and tone that were far from complimentary. Ortoli was flattered, of course, and promised Darlan's gratitude, reward from Petain, and even the admiration of the State Department in Washington where the top people, he was assured, were anxious for Britain accept the kind of generous armistice granted to France…… and in this there was a specific role for the brave crew of the *Surcouf*, a special mission that might seal already well advanced negotiations, a truly historic *coup*, it was claimed.

Ortoli, high on his tower, was listening, and this was taken as encouragement….. for the spokesman was offering now to come across to explain further his proposition. He had a collapsible dinghy to hand, which was quickly inflated from a cylinder of compressed air. It was launched, and expertly paddled from the lesser hull to the greater, bringing him closer to Vincent, while the accomplice stayed back, watching guardedly from the shadows.

On the *Surcouf*, just the one man was climbing down from the tower. One man to listen, with the one voice to then reply for all. For which side would it declare?

Up clambered the boarder, smartly saluting….. and then, as if startled, suddenly edged back. For Vincent the meaning was clear.

"You, you're not Ortoli."

"Captain Ortoli is at the helm. He waits for my order. Say what you must to me, Admiral Emile Muselier….. and show what you have come to show." Awed, the boarder complied, a hand going to the deepest of his coat pockets to draw two items therefrom, both being offered to the Admiral for inspection. First to be passed was a block. It might have been a loaf, were it not for that glint, a metallic glint. Moon-silvered gold was it? Maybe an ingot? And to accompany it there came a map, once folded, but being opened now and similarly scrutinised. "And this," weighed the Admiral, "has been brought back from here?"

"It has, Sir, from where more waits…… for a bigger boat and the boldest of men."

"Or the weakest," countered Muselier, gruffly. "You are under arrest. The *Narval*, she can flee…… but for you, with these things, it's back in to an English port. What else you might want to say you can save for de Gaulle."

Muselier now went to his own pocket……. was it to reach for a gun? The other wasn't waiting to find out. He leapt at the Admiral, tearing at the chart. The bar dropped to the deck with a clang as on they grappled. And then the boarder broke half free, sufficiently to kick at the ingot, sending it sliding along the deck and over the edge, into the sea, its glimmer fading into the depths as down it went, for a moment passing almost within Vincent's reach.

The Admiral was older, he was weakening. And now his assailant was fully free, and suddenly alert to the response of the *Narval*. The klaxon, and the clanging of hatches….. it was preparing to dive, hastily.

The command had been made, so he had to dive himself, and swim for his life. Wriggling from his coat he plunged. Into the screw-churned foam he struck. Could the hapless, spurned emissary make it back to his own metal?

He was shouting now, and the beam swung down. Would there be a lifeline?

Nothing of the sort........ instead, from below the light, from the accomplice who'd seemed so benign, there came a single sharp crack, a pistol shot, just the one, and that was enough. The swimming ceased. Dead was he? If not now, then surely soon. The light went out, and with a final thud the topmost hatch came down just seconds before the *Narval* slipped beneath a vexed and blooded sea.

The *Surcouf*, meanwhile, was turning away, seeking cover of darkness rather than depth, and this might at least give Norman a chance. He'd been taken by the right boat, that which was staying in home waters while the other, the *Narval*, was surely now having to defect.

Come daylight, then perhaps Norman would be found at the dockyard. That was his brother's hope, provided he could get himself in, and warm and dry. But he wasn't alone, not yet at least. Losing much blood, but little of his will to live, the one certain casualty of the engagement was struggling pitifully towards him, the man betrayed by his own pro-Vichy command. He couldn't be abandoned, even if he was beyond help, and Vincent manoeuvred his craft accordingly, to haul the close to lifeless body from the sea.

A shallow breath, rapid and rattling, indicated a chest wound.... blood leaking from his mouth, dripping from his drenched shirt, gathering ominously in the boat where he lay. He coughed, he groaned. He was going, this Vincent knew.... but not before a last few dying words. He bent to listen."

" Gol......," he heard. "Gold astern......," and nothing more, nothing he could take as a clue to the meaning of this strange encounter, or as a guide to how his brother might be safely reclaimed.

*

1941

Phyllis
a.k.a. Nancy

Abraham,
My servant Abraham
Take Isaac thy son by name,
That thou lovest the best of all,
And in sacrifice offer him to me
Upon that hill there besides thee.
Abraham
I will that so it be
For all that may befall.

Diana and Joss

Text of traditional Chester miracle play
Adapted for 2 voices and piano by Benjamin Britten

5th April

BBC Radio News   *"...... and still in Africa, but moving south now*
away from the war front in Eritrea, there is a report this evening of an
interesting development in the case of the murdered Earl of Erroll whose
body was found in the front of a vehicle that he was thought to have been
driving alone during the very early hours of 23rd of January. The vehicle,
a hired Buick, had left a deserted stretch of road and it was at first thought
that he might have been an unlucky victim of careless driving. On closer
examination he was found to have taken a single fatal shot to the head. A
month ago, following a series of searches, interviews, and forensic tests
the Kenyan Police arrested and charged Sir John Henry Broughton, a
more minor British aristocrat. Prior to the shooting, Sir John's wife of no
more than six months standing was reported to have spent much time in
the company of the Earl.
The Earl was a leading member of the notorious Happy Valley
settler community, a group renowned for its disregard for the normal
conventions of marriage. Sir John, a man of mature years, would have
known this, of course, and there is some surprise that an obviously proud
man should have thought of taking so young and attractive a bride into
such questionable surroundings.
Mr Lazarus Kaplan, solicitor for the accused, announced
initially that Mr Israel Maisels QC had been approached to conduct the

trial defence and that there was every indication that the prominent and successful South African barrister would accept the brief. We hear now that Maisels is unavailable for the task. Instead it will be entrusted to Mr Henry Morris QC, a leading expert in firearm forensics.

*

the devil drives
July1941 London

"Well, Sir Stewart, your HIGHLAND CLEARANCE would appear to have gone sufficiently to plan."

"It has gone well enough so far, Prime Minister," agreed Menzies, warily, "but the game is far from over. We must pray that the Russian winter is not delayed, and that Stalin will resist until it closes in." Yes.....and there were also the loose ends, reflected the Intelligence chief, privately, for not all had been disclosed to the Premier, in risky contravention of strict instruction.

"Well let's hope that fortune can continue to favour the brave," puffed Churchilll, forcing a brisk pace under the St James Park sunshine. "Things certainly look better now than they did last December. That submarine business came close to scuppering the whole project, and this before we'd hardly got the thing going."

"It was close," agreed Menzies, "de Gaulle, though, he's not at all disposed to trust his senior admiral. Never was, never will be. As it happened, he didn't over mind us wanting to keep Muselier in Brixton Gaol.....just for those few days at least. As you say, Sir, it could have been worse."

"So maybe we should be thankful..... though I would rather I hadn't had to get The Palace involved in furnishing so lavish an apology, however warranted it might have been. To have the Foreign Office grovelling, and, by implication, myself, that's bad enough.... but to also include the Monarch!"

"Well Anthony, who took the Admiral up for the insisted upon private audience, and afterwards spoke with His Majesty, he reports that King George is happy to have obliged, and also that the Admiral continues to express full satisfaction. We can consider the matter settled." Menzies wanted to be off this subject, but was wary of making this too obvious.

"And consequently, you, Sir Stewart, have been able to proceed....."

".......towards our much improved present position, Prime Minister."

"Making those few words of apology a small price to pay. This is Eden's view, Sir Stewart, and I suppose I must agree."

Except that, unknown to Churchill and Eden, Muselier had sought and gained considerably more than that. Despite the brief incarceration the Admiral had shown himself to be in a psoition of some strength. He'd demanded assurances, the best assurances, such as could be obtained only through Menzies' uniquely private access to The Throne. And while Churchill and Eden knew of, and endorsed, the Royal apology, they hadn't been told the rest...... that Muselier had also come away with the King's personally and privately given word.

But if this 'submarine business' remained an awkward topic for the Intelligence Chief, through his not having been entirely open with his master, in defiance of strict instruction, there was at least the diversion, now, of a more recently and even more spectacularly arrived loose end.

"But our cells needn't remain empty for too long, Prime Minister," continued Menzies. "We have a new possible inmate on our hands..... the intrepid flier."

"Yes, Rudolf Hess himself, dropping in on us with the full blessing of the Fuhrer. It would appear that in this respect, Sir Stewart, your ploy could have worked a little too well. I fear that in both Moscow and Washington there might now be too many who doubt the sincerity of my resolve..... however firmly expressed."

"Maybe, Sir, but the big prize is secure, Hitler's total commitment to *Barbarossa*. He won't turn back. He can't. And you are placed now to properly *demonstrate* that resolve."

"So you will tell Halifax that Sir Samuel can be stood down, and that whatever plans were being made to use my war rooms as a meeting house for the Society of Friends can be consigned to secret history."

"Thankfully yes, for no longer do we have Hitler and Stalin allied against us. The Fuhrer is hell bent on taking Moscow and we're placed to give the Reds as much or as little help as we choose."

"They'll have as much as we can spare," muttered Churchill. "It's not a great deal, I know, but it's essential now that Stalin holds out....."

".... for as long as it takes for the Americans to actively take our side. And that might be some time yet. Many in Washington genuinely supported *Barbarossa*, it being part of our ploy that such approval should have been voiced and heard. A sham so monumental and so effective isn't to be dismantled overnight."

"Indeed, Sir Stewart, for it's important that your trickery should remain a secret. Though we on this island might escape, I fear too many others stand to suffer from its consequences. The best we can do with Hess, now, is what? Do we kill him?"

"No, for that would tend to confirm Stalin's suspicion that something's being hidden......."

"....... and if he starts looking all the harder we would be fools to underestimate his ability to discover exactly what," agreed Churchill. "Particularly now we're joined in an alliance."

"Hitler, who we know condoned his deputy's carefully calculated flight, now chooses to label Hess mad," said Menzies, "and, for the moment, our best course must be to play along with that. I say we keep dear Rudolf alive, and perhaps *make* him a little mad. Then, to restore our anti-Nazi credentials, at home as well as abroad, I suggest we petition Roosevelt strongly for an extension of American Lend-Lease to Russia. Getting that one through Congress will take all the shove a President can muster."

"And, if he succeeds, you're hoping this will make Hitler cross enough to declare war on the US? I think not, Sir Stewart."

"But there is the Japanese factor, Prime Minister. Roosevelt is looking to starve them of oil. Strong voices in Tokyo argue that their war machine must be put to decisive use before it is effectively disabled. I see a real chance of their making a first strike against the US Navy....."

"...... something we shouldn't be too concerned to deter, you mean," said Churchill. "And if a grab for oil means a grab for the Philipines, you'll perhaps want it whispered in Tokyo that our resolve to hold and use Singapore is likely to be no more impressive than that displayed on Crete. The Japs then attack where..... Pearl Harbour?"

"And America is at war."

"With Japan, Sir Stewart, not Hitler."

"Yes, but the Fuhrer's anger with Washington grows by the month, remember. Putting Hess aside, by then Hitler will be furious enough to want to throw his weight behind Japan, that I promise you."

"And how soon for all this, Sir Stewart?"

"Maybe by Christmas, Prime Minister.... a proper World War with us on the side of the big battalions, Russia's *and* America's."

"Provided, as I said, that Stalin can rally and resist this Autumn, ideally with American support." A pensive pause followed. Menzies waited, allowing Churchill to reflect..... and then resume. "This is a narrow line we tread, so much being outside our control. Will Washington endorse our Hobson's choice....... the hammer and sickle over the swastika? Yes, and we have Hitler painting himself into a corner. No, and he might prove unstoppable. Is it so, Sir Stewart, that you can read Roosevelt's administration..... and influence it even? Or do you merely hope? The President himself, he shares my revulsion for Hitler, but he's so frail physically. At times he looks too much on his own."

"As with yourself, Prime Minister. But, believe me, we have weathered the worst. Since re-election, FDR has been truer to those anti fascist instincts. And we have key people in key roles. I have good information..... fed from a number of sources, through a number of channels. A loathing of Nazism hardens within the President's innermost circle. What's now more problematic is the persisting antipathy in that quarter to our friend de Gaulle. Washington retains faith in Petain. Money talks in America, and they'll persist in the hope that Vichy can be bought away from Berlin, much in the way that Madrid has been."

"A strand of State Department policy that for a while you will have been happy to encourage, Sir Stewart," nodded Churchill.

"Yes, meaning that a thorough acceptance of the Free French concept might yet take some time to establish...... even when, as hoped, Germany and the US find themselves at war."

"But henceforward, from us, it has to be unequivocal support for de Gaulle," insisted Churchill.

"And he's not to hear a whisper of HIGHLAND CLEARANCE. For him, as it must be for the people of both this country, Germany, and the world at large, Rudolf Hess is a madman who flew on a crazy whim. Hitler and you will be joint parties to the same *big lie*, and we must hope to emerge as its sole custodian."

"And where anyone sees through that lie, Sir Stewart, and on the basis of that insight seeks to make political capital, then we must be utterly ruthless, lest this time that you win for us should prove merely a temporary respite." Churchill stopped walking. Birds sang from a bough above. "Do I make myself clear?"

"Perfectly Sir," answered Menzies, who'd halted with dog-like obedience.

"Good, for just as you had a name to show me, back in the winter of our severest discontent, today in this summer month of hope, I must reciprocate with this." Churchill went to his jacket pocket. It was no more than a scrap of paper that he produced. The name, though, was clearly printed. Menzies read;

" AVRAHAM STERN YAIR "

"The man is no less sane than Hess," explained Churchill, "and, similarly, no less brave. But again the world must be fed a lie. It must be told that he is mad, and so dangerously mad that he must be hunted down and killed as if he were a rabid dog."

"A Jew," said Menzies, "and one of those active in Palestine, a Zionist."

"Who from what I've been told by Moyne, might well have guessed our game...... out of which he is fearing cataclysmic consequences, possible repercussions that he says demand radical action now."

"Action that it is essential we head off," acknowledged Menzies.

"Permanently," said Churchill gruffly.

"And you mention Moyne. Am I to suppose that you've shared our secret with him?"

"Most certainly not, Sir Stewart......but my friend Walter is an extremely intelligent man."

"So he'll know when to leave well alone."

"He will, Sir Stewart, but that won't stop him entertaining his suspicions. He and his friend Vera can be imagined to be closely following the trial of her former husband, poor old Jock. I trust that all that can be neatly tidied up. The assassin, for instance.....?"

"......was despatched on a no hope mission into Yugoslavia. Betrayed into the hands of Communist partisans, who'd been told of their new arrival having fascist sympathies..... so feet wouldn't have touched the ground, I'm afraid. Loyal, proficient....."

".....but having served the specific purpose, now dispensible.

Good. And Jock, himself…..?"

"…..will be rightly acquitted, but only so as so avoid any last speech from the scaffold. Instead, he will go into sharp decline and be dead within a year. It will look like self neglect." Menzies ruefully pocketed his crumpled warrant. "And all this in the name of the survival of British democracy," he added. "But at least we look in better shape we did six months ago, this you must concede."

Churchill glowered. He could take Menzies' chiding….. but complacency? in a subordinate?…… Intolerable!

"I don't like to concede, Sir Stewart," he snapped. "It's not in my nature. I'm not happy to have conceded Crete, for instance. I agreed to your agitating in Belgrade because you said it was just Yugoslavia and Greece that would fall. So that Hitler could feel secure in the south before striking east….. and I went with that, fine. But I don't recall any mention of Crete being on the shopping list. The Balkans, and Greece, yes, justifiable sacrifices…… but there is another side. If we're to convince the Americans that we've any kind of fight left in us then they have to see that where we choose to stand our ground we do precisely that. With Crete, now, Hitler can better sustain an army in Africa. He might go for Egypt, for Suez, and close off our oil."

"He can try. He will try….. but we ought to be equal to that, Prime Minister. His main pack is unleashed on the Ukraine. If we can't defend Egypt then perhaps we don't deserve to survive."

Churchill walked on. Was he to take this? He was, for the challenge wasn't to be ducked. This was the next test of his leadership, of his flair for selecting and deploying his generals, of his readiness to listen to and act on advice of his Chiefs of Staff. Menzies was right. Failure to defend Egypt would be his own personal failure.

"Thank you for reminding me of my responsibilities, Sir Stewart, but I'm not quite finished on yours. With the African business we can see off Broughton, and then, beyond that, rely well enough on the good old journalist-resistant aristocratic discretion. I'm less confident, though, when it comes to that submarine." Menzies winced inwardly, saying nothing. "That infernal machine….. such a curio in itself, and so, in his own unique way, is that dammed Admiral." Menzies knew this too well. He needed another subject, but Churchill, now into his stride, continued. "What about that lad who was apprehended in Scotland….. had in his pocket a return train ticket to Plymouth. Was there anything in his story of having lost a younger brother whilst out night-fishing, off Cornwall?"

"Vincent Wakeham.... currently interned on the island of Mull, wired in with Italian POWs and Irish Republicans."

"Do you have more on his movements prior to his turning up on Holy Loch?"

"Discrete enquiries were made, and an identity confirmed. He was a fisherman. He lived alone, across from Devonport Dockyard..... on the Cornwall side. No one down there was aware of his having travelled to Scotland....."

"And no one was made aware, I trust."

"Nothing was let on," confirmed Menzies. "Family, meaning his widowed mother, and neighbours had neither seen nor heard anything of him since an after dark fishing expedition, off Rame, on that same night......"

"......the night the submarines rendezvoused."

"A calm night for the time of year. The boat had come in, and it was secured, but of Wakeham there was no sign."

"And no sign either of the missing younger brother...."

".... who'd been just ten, and had lived with his mother. It was thought at first that he might have been staying the night at Vincent's. That wasn't unusual after going out at night."

"So did he ever turn up, this youngster? Was he found?"

"Decomposing remains were found washed up on Looe Island in mid February. Shoes and a belt were identified. What was left of the body was buried in a Churchyard on Rame Head, under a stone that reads 'Norman Wakeham, died December 1940, aged just ten.'"

"Any other brothers?"

"Just one..... older than Vincent, the middle, by three years. He's serving out in Egypt. He was flown back for the funeral."

"Which Vincent did not attend, I trust."

"He wasn't told."

They reached a park bench. Churchill indicated that he preferred now to sit. "Good. But you have questioned him, of course?" he asked.

"He's never said much, but we have managed to piece together some of his movements before boarding a train out of Plymouth's North Road Station the following morning. He must have gone to his home, to his cottage in a village called Sheviock. He then crossed to the Lynher to Ince in another boat of his, one kept for river fishing. He was taking a risk.

All locals know Ince Castle to be an off limits military base. We use it as a reception centre, for screening out any French Canadian Naval Officers who might be too well disposed towards Vichy. A patrol noticed the boat, and a watch was kept. In the early hours he returned to it and was challenged...."

".....and he was let go?"

"Because he gave his name, and said that he'd only been making a nocturnal visit to one of the live in housemaids, a close friend who was able to confirm that this was so, and that she'd encouraged such visits, this being by no means the first. She was promptly dismissed, and she went within the day..... in hindsight a little too hastily perhaps."

"Definitely, for if she was giving an impression that this had been some kind of romantic tryst then she was as good as lying. Vincent Wakeham would have been in shock. He'd just lost a brother, for God's sake."

"And in the hope of finding that brother he was about to cross to Devonport, thinking maybe that the boy was on the *Surcouf*, and that the submarine could have returned there before starting out again for..... wherever."

"So was it at Devonport that he found out that Scotland was the destination?" asked Churchill

"No one at the base has admitted to letting this slip. Not many were supposed to know."

"So there's a chance he might have overheard this at the rendezvous. Has this been confirmed since his capture? And what else might he have heard."

"He speaks only of an offshore squabble between quarrelsome Frenchmen. And he doesn't understand French.....so he says."

"So he says," muttered Churchill.

"And while he's spoken of hearing gunfire, he's said nothing of a body. Think of the size of the *Surcouf*. If he was head down on the one side of the hull while the action was to the other, then he would never have had the full picture."

"And what of the girl who got him off the hook at Ince, do we know where she went?"

"Into Plymouth somewhere......"

"...... and that could be anywhere," said the Premier. "As you said, they've been blitzed to pieces this spring."

"She could probably be found...."

"....if alive..."

"....but would have nothing to lose from staying with the same story," said Menzies

"So back to the fateful night and Vincent's departure from Ince, with a severe warning we can assume."

"Yes, but then a few hours later, at daybreak, he has to be spoken to again! He's got as far as the Dockyard gate, and he's asking if the *Surcouf* has yet sailed for Scotland. No one will confirm the destination, but he is told that the boat has left and is not expected back."

"And he doesn't hang about."

"Because he knows his inquisitiveness will have been noted. He can't stay around, so he's promptly off to the station and onto a train north, in true Hannay style. But pitifully, he is too hasty. As the train eases itself out of Plymouth North Road, so the Surcouf is creeping in past the Hoe, returning to harbour, the planned voyage to Scotland having been aborted....."

".....because of?"

"Mechanical problems, and the inability of a relatively inexperienced crew to cope..... the usual thing with that particular vessel."

"Leaving Vincent in plucky pursuit of a wild goose."

"Indeed, and the next morning he is found snooping around Holy Loch. He is where he has no right to be, just as he was thirty six hours before at Ince. He is arrested, and the double transgression warrants the invoking of our special wartime powers. After close interrogation we ship him across to Mull, and there, to this day, he remains."

"And the Surcouf..... ?"

"...... eventually did get to Scotland before the New Year, after spending most of the rest of December in Devonport under strict guard."

"There must have been concern, though, amongst the boys' home community? There was a mother, you say, and an older brother."

"No one down there has said anything about submarines. Two brothers had gone night fishing. The eldest returned, and after being briefly apprehended and identified in the grounds of Ince, in the early hours, he'd then fled the district. As to where, there's been speculation, naturally, and this we've sought to widen with embellishment, mixed with a few rumours of our own invention. Particularly useful were the developments at Ince. That girl who was ready to sacrifice job, home, and reputation to get the lad off the hook….. apparently she'd been as good as betrothed to his brother!" Menzies smirked. Churchill wasn't amused.

"We field hardened professionals and seek to resolve great issues," he said, "but it's the ordinary lives that are left in ruins. Those fisher folk have suffered enough. We have a brave lad here. Keep him under guard, also keep him safe."

"How long."

"A couple of years and the world will have changed, hopefully for the better."

"So if GUSTAVE asks?"

"Tell him that plucky young Wakeham is to be spared….at the express command of the Prime Minister, emphasise. In all else he is to keep up the good work."

*

Winterreise
December 1943. Cornwall

……and having journeyed long, Vincent Wakeham is at last back in Sheviock. The connections had been far from straight forward and weary, he is, from his day and a half's worth of travelling, almost continuous, totally arduous. Train tickets had been arranged, from Scotland to Euston, and then from Paddington to St Germans. His camp, a home for three years, remains a camp, but for prisoners of war now rather than internees…… as good an indication as any of the firmly turned tide of war.

He would be on parole, Vincent was told, and though there would be assistance towards rehabilitation he could also expect to be closely watched. And he could expect an altered Cornwall too, he understood that, for this war had wrought changes in everything and everyone. He knew that he would need to at least attempt to explain his absence, where he had been, and why. He'd written, but with no response he suspected total censorship. If nothing had arrived then who was to know where he was?

So now he was ready with his tale, and a remarkable one it was too, for anyone who might care to listen…..but no one was even beginning to want to, neither in Crafthole, nor Sheviock, where the two cottages now housed strangers. And not in Antony, Millbrook, Cawsand, Kingsand, or even at Portwrinkle where, amongst the boats tied and the few working offshore, he could catch no sight of his own.

He was being shunned throughout, and, with word of his re-appearance moving faster than he could trudge, he was finding the reception frostier by the mile. Doors were closing in his face. Shopkeepers and publicans were shunning his money, shunning his presence, seeing instead to the customer behind, or to the shelf that needed filling, or to the chair and table that waited to be tidied.

Back to Sheviock, and a desperate knock at the Rectory elicits a few grudgingly scowled words from an embarrassed incumbent, again a newcomer, and again, it seems, one forewarned. He would find his mother across at Rame, with the other son, his brother…. and with that he was hearing as much as could be said. And so along the cliff road he goes, climbing wearily onto the high slate headland where stands the tiny 13th century Church of St Germanus, and little else. And here in the shadow of its salt soused spire he finds stark confirmation of what had been implied, in the form of two matching slate headstones. His mother, Ruth Wakeham, and his younger brother, Norman, lie buried, side by side.

'*Died December 1940 aged 10*', reads the slightly more weathered inscription, with '*Much loved*' beneath. '*Died October 1941 aged 48*', reads the other with, below, '*Broken hearted*'.

Vincent turns away, in dismay. When he'd set off in search of Norman he'd been so sure the boy was safe, so sure they could be home together within days. Instead he'd vanished himself, obviously compounding the pain he'd sought to curb.

'*Much loved*', the words of a mother restrained in her grief. '*Broken hearted*', those chiselled on behalf of an eldest son nursing further loss, and, doubtless, a deeply felt anger. And where would he, Ben, be now? Perhaps he'd returned to the battlefield and was himself dead, lost in action and buried beneath desert sand, for wouldn't this best explain the re-tenanted cottages, and the missing boat?

For Vincent, no family remained, no home, and no livelihood…. just these matching stones, and, all around, an almost palpable hostility. There seemed no future for him here, not in this corner of Cornwall, not in the whole county, or in the whole country even. He had his skills though. He could fillet a fish as well as any, and these things were being consumed in London where perhaps it was time to seek out a few gathered contacts.

*

Evelyn

Evelyn revisited
Still 1943

And amongst all the accumulated anguish of four years of war, should we find sympathy for one such as Captain Evelyn Waugh? A man, this, who would appear to want to make his military career one long unrelieved personal disaster. He has the contacts to net himself a commision but, alas, with him, the mere donning of an officer's uniform would appear to be prejudicial to good order. He loves England, but not its men. In return, they have little love for him, and by the fifth Winter of the war he has been manouevred into the suitably inconsequential backwater of Tito controlled Yugoslavia.

With or without British help the communist partisans are going to prevail, and Evelyn is summoned there, with Randolph Churchill (no less a misfit) to help give some celebrity gloss to Brigadier Fitzroy Maclean's somewhat thinly applied backing for Stalin's placeman...... a support pragmatically switched away from Tito's rival patriot, the royalist Mikhailavic.

The task of Evelyn, Randolph, and the recently arrived Freddie Bikenhead is to marshal such goodwill as remains for Britain in this area so that it might be channelled to the advantage of the new champion. When the summons came, Waugh had scented adventure, excitement, and perhaps honour at last…… but now, after a few months, the whole thing was beginning to stink.

Communism, for him, had always been hateful creed, and this lot? As well as being ungrateful they were just so cruel to his beloved Catholic Church. But at least he had time to himself here in Topusko, time in which he could make final proof corrections to his new novel, his faith affirming *Brideshead*…… if only he could keep a clear head, something not so easily done when in the company of Randolph Churchill and Freddie who only want to drink and talk to wild excess, outbidding each other in the indiscretion of those exchanged anecdotes about their respective fathers, the once maverick now maestro, Winston, and his late friend, the mercurial 'F.E.'.

Would he manage to get away from them today, he wondered, with his wits still intact? God, it was barely lunchtime and they were opening yet another bottle of that *rakia*, the local liquor, as foul tasting as it was potent.

"Do have another, Evelyn," blustered Randolph, topping all three glasses, "and tell Uncle Freddie, here, how it was that the good war that you so hoped to enjoy turned so bad."

"Yes, Evelyn…….tell me do. Off to a bad start, wasn't it? It's said that the Commando training up in Scotland left you….."

"Left me playing catch up," confirmed Waugh, sullenly. "And then the harder I tried the worse it became. Fellow officers were making it a sport to undermine my authority."

"Like who, Evelyn?" asked Randolph. "You make a serious charge."

"It was whispers and tricks and jokes," muttered Waugh. "They didn't declare themselves openly……. cowards, like that, they were."

"Tricks such as what?" The second Lord Birkenhead sipped at his glass.

"Such as the hoax letter they gulled me with when I was given the task of censoring outgoing letters from number 8 Commando, at the time embarked on two troopships off the Isle of Arran. Supposedly being sent to a '*Herr Schmidt*,' care of one '*Vogel von Bumelzueg*', said to be living on a '*Barkhausen Strasse*' in Zurich, it purported itself to be one of a series being despatched by a certain '*Bombardier Hildebrand Hardcastle*'.

Freddie Birkenhead spluttered ill concealed mirth into his glass, almost spilling what remained therein.

"And you took this seriously?" asked Randolph, showing more control.

"I ordered that the boats be sealed, and searched by Red Caps......and then it emerged that the whole thing had been got up as a practical joke, and I was the idiot."

"And the only name you had was this *Hildebrand Hardcastle* who signed the letter," said Birkenhead, now more composed.

"No..... because he also named an accomplice. *'Gustave sends greetings'*, he wrote.

"And you've no idea who *Gustave* might have been," said Randolph, his tone implying faint surprise.

"Should I?"

"It would probably be safer for you not to," Birkenhead broke in. "It could be simple coincidence anyway, so......."

"So it sounds to me like the pair of you might know something that I don't," muttered Waugh, thinking to himself that he might now stay a little longer at this table than planned...... where at least two more bottles stood waiting to be opened, along with the two tongues that he might soon significantly loosen. "Let me pour you another, Freddie."

*

Yalta

Keelhaul
May 1945

Harold Macmillan was British Minister-Resident in the Mediterranean theatre. He was in direct and continual touch with the Prime Minister, with the principal duty of reporting the political situation. On 13 May he flew into Klagenfurt to confer with General Keighly and appraise the situation there. It was he who urged on Keighly the speedy transfer of the Cossacks......

Privately, General von Pannwitz continued to make further efforts to save his Corps from destruction. ...... Von Pannwitz expiated eloquently on the fighting qualities of the Cossacks, banging his fist excitedly on the table. He implored the British to take the Corps into their service, or to pass them on to the Americans. ......At the centre of all these operations was the Brigadier General Staff, Toby Low. Low explained at length that no promises of any sort could be made, and the Cossacks must just sit tight in their valley until a decision was arrived at.

......By 25 May arrangements were completed...... A vast fleet of three-ton trucks was assembled, each one containing a driver, co driver and two guards armed with loaded rifles. The route chosen was barred to all other traffic and guarded at frequent intervals by troops. Five artillery regiments were detailed to provide the men and equipment. An ingenious deception plan was worked out and applied with perfect efficiency. The Cossacks were informed the night before that they were being transferred to new camps in Italy: news that was bound to cheer them, since it meant that they were being moved away from the proximity of the Soviet zone. Thus they were persuaded to enter the lorries without difficulty.

For ten miles or so the trucks rumbled southwards, the Cossacks becoming ever more light at heart at the thought that they were putting an increasing distance between themselves and their enemies. But suddenly the head of the convoy swung round and began to drive furiously for the north. At forty to fifty m.p.h. the trucks flew past barely glimpsed groups of heavily armed British soldiers. Panic broke out, and a rain of watches, rings, cameras -even gold teeth- and other valuables poured onto the road. Despite the precautions, one or two Cossacks were reported to have flung themselves to their deaths. And when the column finally drew up at Judenburg, there were numerous cases of Cossacks springing from the lorries, somersaulting as they did so in attempts to break their necks on falling. All this was reported back to headquarters......

In his memoirs Harold Macmillan refers briefly to the question of the Cossacks......

'Among the surrendering Germans there were about 40,000 Cossacks and White Russians, with their wives and children. These were naturally claimed by the Russian commander and we had no alternative but to surrender them. Nor indeed had we any means of dealing with them *had we refused to do so.'*

    Does the reference to 'White Russians' mean, as it seems it must , that Macmillan was well aware of the presence of the old emigres amongst the Cossacks?

    ......The remarks in his memoirs are tantalisingly brief......

Nikolai Tolstoy *'Victims of Yalta'* pp 231-4/ 276-7

Reproduced by permission of Hodder & Strughton Ltd

*

(iii) the 1950s

The shame'll never pass.
Ay he's lost for ever on the endless sea.

Billy Budd Act 1

Schooldays
1951   PRINCE ROCK PRIMARY

"Mrs Cross...."

"Miss Cross, headmaster."

"Miss Cross, yes, well thank you for coming in."

"Is my Anton in trouble?"

"No...... at least none of his own making, Miss Cross." The head's hand patted down on the sheet of paper before him. He held the mother's eyes though, rather than looking down, conveying an impression of having digested the information thereon and already reached a firm conclusion as to an appropriate course of action. "The report I have here from his class teacher confirms the ability he's shown throughout his school life, and that's almost five years now. He's an intelligent, capable lad. If he continues to maintain expected progress he should have a bright future..... and this is why I've asked you in. In less than a year he will be sitting his eleven plus."

"You think he can pass, and go on to the Grammar?" The mother had brightened.

"He's one of our stronger candidates, certainly, but, as you know, competition is stiff. There's many a hopeful that won't make it. There's many a dark horse that will."

"I understand."

"Good, and what I want you to understand from me today is that sometimes, where there is a borderline case, I can be asked for an opinion and, occasionally, in this context, two candidates from this school can be vying for just one place."

"A difficult decision….."

"…… which sometimes can only be made with reference to the child's social adjustment and home background."

Jenny Cross coloured, partly in embarrassment, mainly in anger. But for the child's sake she would bite her tongue as she'd done so often before….. though never in these particular circumstances. How dare this man sit in judgment, she thought. Anton had always been her priority. For shelter, food, clothing, the boy had always had first call on anything she'd earned….. and how she'd earned it was her own business. Yes, there were times, at weekends, when she'd had to put the child with similarly challenged friends so as to work the bars and the kerbs of Union Street, but if needed she'd been there for him, nursing and mending, cooking and feeding.

The headmaster sensed the hostility, and as a married man blushed a little himself, privately recalling how one evening during the previous summer term he'd naughtily (and successfully) propositioned a too vulnerable trainee teacher, here in this very office, indeed on this very desk. Jenny Cross saw unease, and took advantage.

"Speak plainly headmaster."

"We both want the best for Anton, Miss Cross, and I would like to be able to say that he integrates well socially. Sadly, in this, we both know there to have been problems and I fear that at the root of these is this insistence that his father was a high ranking officer in the French Navy. He tries to put himself above the other children. They don't like it, and they gang together to try to put him down. Part of this response is the speculation that circulates as to a less elevated paternity, and I have to say that the whole thing is inconsistent with the kind of ethos being nurtured within our new style state Grammars. To put it bluntly, for me to pass this kind of thing up would likely reflect badly upon both myself and this school."

"And that would never do..... would it headmaster?" Mild words, scathingly delivered. "Now do you have anything constructive?"

"For a start, Miss Cross, perhaps your boy could get used to being called Anthony, or Tony even, and discouraged from trying to put himself above his peers by reference to this grand rank of his supposed father. He's well able enough to establish a respected identity of his own without all that. Believe me, he would be less held back, at Grammar School, Secondary Modern School, or wherever you might will. This is constructive, Miss Cross, trust me."

The mother stood. She would take the man's advice, but she dammed if she was going to thank him for it.

"I'll put it to Anton...... Anthony or Tony, he can choose, and we'll go from there." She stepped to the door." I'll wish you good day." And she was out almost before the man could rise.

*

pre-election jitters
1959 Chequers

"Dick, thank you for getting here so promptly. I'm sorry I couldn't be more explicit on the phone."

"You'll have had good reason Prime Minister, I'm sure." Dick White, 'C' to his underlings in MI6, took the proffered cigarette and selected the guest chair within easiest reach of an ash tray. He used his own lighter, and then settled, waiting for Macmillan's explanation. The P.M. was on his feet still, pacing, betraying an unusual anxiety.

"Some things can only be discussed face to face, in total privacy...."

".... and with total honesty, sir." Macmillan could be slippery, White well knew.

"Of course Dick, which is why this is being said to you, and only you, even though this should strictly be a matter for MI5."

"My old department...."

"....which I now find to be far less efficient since your transfer.

But no matter, what's lost to the Home Office is gain for the Foreign Office. I'm happy to take the positive view."

"It's nice to know I have your confidence Prime Minister. You have a task for me....?"

"Tomorrow morning, Dick..... Patricia Lennox Boyd is coming across for...."

"..... for a private chat, Prime Minister?"

"You know this already?" Alarm quivered from a usually urbane voice.

"Just a guess, sir...... and not the hardest I'm ever likely to have to make." Macmillan had sounded as nervy as Eden. The response was as genuine as it was soothing.

"Of course Dick, sorry. It's about this pickle that her husband finds himself in."

"Your Colonial Secretary..... this is the Kenya thing, concerning over robust treatment of Mau Mau detainees."

"There's pressure on him to resign, you might have read. We have a big debate coming up on the issue.....and this on top of the problems to the south, in Nyassaland."

"And this pressure.....it's from your own benches too, as well as from opposite?"

"This is so. I'm planning an Autumn election, and a new man now in the Colonial Office would shore things up a bit in what looks to be my one area of vulnerability."

"So you're letting word seep through the ranks that Alan Lennox-Boyd is not to be considered indispensable."

"As we do, quietly."

"Unfortunate then for Alan," smirked White. "As politicians go he's a sound man.......but I'm sure he can be relied upon to do the honourable thing."

"Perhaps so, but we also have this loyal wife to consider..... this Patricia, who seeks to discretely make what might well be powerful representations on her husbands behalf. At her insistence it's to be just between the pair of us. Out in the garden I've said...... in the summer house if wet. But what I want is a recording of what is said. I don't want to be taking her out of microphone range." Macmillan beckoned White to the window. "Use what you like. There's trees, benches, ornaments......"

"Shouldn't be a problem, Sir. In fact I know just the man. Let me use the phone and I can contact him now."

"Name?"

"Peter Bright, the best in the business......with MI5 still, but he'll come across and do this for me as a one off."

"So long as absolute discretion is assured."

"Naturally Prime Minister," confirmed a slightly puzzled 'C'. For what could the woman have to say that might be so sensitive?

By the next evening an answer was beginning to shape.

"Thank you Dick for your help today." Macmillan was less rattled now. This was clearly something that could be fixed. "There's been much to do. I was most impressed by the workmanship of your Mr Bright."

"He played it all back for you, did he?"

"He did..... and then, sadly, I had to ask him to erase every second."

"He won't mind. For him, it's all in a day's work." The Premier wasn't sharing, thought White, but no matter. He would make a point of catching up with the technician during the week. There would have been some kind of note made, he was sure.

"I have to say that I found Mrs Lennox Boyd quite persuasive," volunteered the Prime Minister. "So much so that I've already been in touch with Party Chairman, Lord Hailsham. He and his deputy, the Honourable Member for Blackpool, will already be putting it around that Lennox Boyd is now to be supported through the critical Hola debate. He will keep the Colonial desk right up to the election. He will stand again for Mid Beds, and very probably win. He will stay for a while on the back benches before being made up to the Lords as a Viscount in the New Year's Honours, thus enabling him to take a more active role in the Guinness family business."

"So he's now to be allowed to step down in his own time...."

".....with an unblemished record. Enoch has been instructed to produce something truly special for the debate. It should all come as quite a surprise for Alan......"

"...... because he will have been unaware of his wife's intervention."

"He's to know nothing, she said. And likewise Hailsham and Low, particularly Low..... I say that."

"So instructions are being given, but not reasons."

"Exactly. What was said this morning no one else need know."

*

(iv) the 1960s

1962

The month is May, and in the new Coventry Cathedral there is heard sung;

'......an angel called him out of heaven,
Saying, Lay not thy hand upon the lad,
Neither do anything to him. Behold,
A ram caught in a thicket by its horns;
Offer the Ram of Pride instead of him.
But the old man would not so, but slew his son,-
And half the seed of Europe, one by one.'

Rudolf Hess

from 'Parable of the Old Man and the Young'
by Wilfred Owen
set to music by Benjamin Britten (*War Requiem*)

And in that same week, in Israel, after having been tried and found guilty of complicity in Nazi war crimes, Adolf Eichmann is hanged.

1967

......sees the publication in England of Ivan Maisky's *'Memoirs of a Soviet Ambassador'* (Hutchinson). Maisky had been Stalin's main man at the Russian Embassy in London during the war years.
We read (p147):

......who is Hess? A camouflaged emissary from Hitler, or a solitary psychopath. Or is he the representative of some grouping within the Nazi top leadership, disturbed at the prospect that the war may drag out too long?

......Churchill in his *war memoirs* (Vol III p49) expresses the opinion that Hess came *'of his own free will'*, and that he was *'a medical, not a criminal case, and should be so regarded'*.

Schellenberg, the Gestapo's chief of counter espionage, asserts in his reminiscences (*'The Labyrinth'* p187), that Hitler gave Hess no instructions, and did not even know of his plans.

Ivone Kirkpatrick, (Britain's pre war Ambassador to Berlin, a close associate of Menzies, and one of the first to interview Hess after his arrival) offers roughly the same opinion (*The Inner Circle*).

However, A.M.Nekrich, the Soviet historian (*International Affairs- Russian edition No.9*) writes;

'At the Nuremburg trial there was a curious episode to which sufficient attention has not been paid. On 31 August 1946 Hess stated at a session of the tribunal that he wished to state on oath what happened to him during his stay in Britain.

"In the Spring of1941......" Hess began. But at this point he was interrupted by the British President of the Tribunal, Lord Lawrence. Perhaps history has not yet said its last word about the Hess mission. '

Whereupon Maisky, in his memoir, concludes;

However that may be, one thing is beyond doubt: all that was basic and essential about Hess's flight was known to the Soviet Embassy already at the time, in the spring of 1941.

And between these events;
In October1963, Harold Macmillan resigns as Prime Minister, afterwards to become Lord Stockton.
In January **1965**, Sir Winston Churchill dies, aged 90.
In April **1966**, Evelyn Waugh dies, aged 62.

Afterwards;
In May **1968**, Sir Stewart Menzies dies, aged 78.

*

Peter as Grimes

Peter as 'Starry' Vere

(v) the 1970s

'William Budd, I accuse you of bringing French gold on board to bribe them from their duties.'
Billy Budd Act3

A little history
1970
BBC Radio 4   One o clock Worldwide

Robert Murphy

"*Our programme today is of course dominated by the news from France. For those of you who might not yet have heard, the death has been announced of the former President, General Charles de Gaulle. The tributes have been as many as they have been fulsome, and to add his own we are privileged to have with us the Earl of Stockton who, as the Right Honourable Harold Macmillan, was our Prime Minister during those years in which France's great statesmasn achieved such eminence as a European and, indeed, world leader. Lord Stockton, thank you for joining us this lunchtime.*"

"*The privilege is mine, Mr Knight.*"

"*Now you and the General go back a very long way, Lord Stockton, both serving with distinction in The Great War of course.*"

"*Yes, and then of course I entered politics, offering my own 1930s treatise on progressive Conservatism, while he remained with the military, likewise giving his own forward looking views on tank warfare. He then forced his way to prominence early in the next World War. While many, indeed most, in his country acquiesced in the Vichy armistice he came to London and boldly raised the flag of the Free French movement.*"

"*And in this one act of leadership he took upon himself the mantle of 'Man of Destiny.'*"

"*He did, and he certainly grew into the part. So much so that he came to symbolise the new France, liberated, uncompromised, restored in integrity. We might have had Churchill to epitomise our British doggedness, but the regeneration of France required something even bigger and in de Gaulle French people certainly had a man for the part...... THE man for the part.*"

"*So on to post war Europe, and the early 1960s when his period*" *as President ran together with yours as Prime Minister. He famously rebuffed your application to join the Common Market. How hard, Lord Stockton, was this not to take as a personal slight?"*

"A man of your undoubted professionalism, Mr Knight, can surely be expected to have read 'The Blast of War', the second of my memoir volumes, published all of three years ago now."

"Parts of it, Lord Stockton."

"Then you should be able to tell your listeners that I devote more than a quarter of its seven hundred plus pages to the many months during which the General and I worked closely to ensure that the Free French movement became an integral part of the war winning coalition. Let no one doubt that he and I built a close and lasting friendship."

"Making the famous 'NON!' of 1963 all the more disappointing, I should have thought."

"I can be confident that it reflected no personal antipathy. What you must remember is that in the three years before our application my priority had to be a repair of Britain's 'special relationship' with the United States, this following the Suez crisis......"

"......the adventure in which France, along with Israel, had been a partner of ours. You don't think perhaps that your own sudden change of heart in that affair might have given the late President de Gaulle every reason to be wary?"

"If by that you mean that he was wary of the United States then to that extent I will agree, and again refer you to my wartime memoirs. De Gaulle arrived in London in the summer of 1940. Alone, we embraced his anti fascist cause, and that's more than the overwhelming number of his own military colleagues did. Most followed Marshal Weygand, the Commander in Chief, in choosing Vichy, taking their men, and the best of the equipment with them. In their opinion de Gaulle was a renegade, a traitor......"

"......who was, in his absence, sentenced to death."

"Indeed."

"And the Americans......?"

"...... were at that time neutral, I remind you, and they were to remain so for another eighteen months. And during that time it became a tenet of US State Department policy, not to antagonise Vichy. In fact Cordell Hull, the Secretary of State, at times seemed disposed to court Vichy, almost as if to espouse the French armistice as a model that we in

London would do well to copy! Central to this policy was the extremely cosy relationship cultivated between their own Admiral Leahy and Vichy's Admiral Darlan."

"A relationship that de Gaulle seemed to deliberately target when he captured the islands of St Pierre and Miquelon...... not so far, of course, from the US coast."

"They are Mr Knight, and it's pleasing to hear that your geography is as good your grasp of history...... if not better!"

"But things did change after Pearl Harbour."

"Only very gradually. Whilst we here sensed de Gaulle's potential, Washington clung to their view that he was an irrelevance...... this reflecting the diplomatic and trading ties that they'd developed with defeated France. In June of 1941 there had been the Murphy-Weygand accord, and, as late as November 1942, the now infamous Darlan-Clark agreement. These were not aberrations. They were the products of a protracted and sustained diplomatic courtship between Washington and Vichy. In this context de Gaulle's uncompromising stance...... to him, anyone who served under Vichy disgraced the name of France......was a problem. We know it was resolved eventually, but the process was painful and the scars lifelong."

"And you had a role in nursing the General through, evetually easing him into Washington's calculations?"

"I was sensitive to the Washington standpoint. They wanted to preserve allied lives, and we all knew that to attempt to land our troops in North West Africa against hostile Vichy forces could result in disaster. A better strategy, they thought, would be to attempt to buy Darlan away from Germany......"

".......getting him and his fellow chiefs of staff to change sides, you mean."

"Yes, with the offer of comparable high office in the ever strengthening anti fascist alliance. Far from being left to be persecuted by de Gaulle's Free Frenchmen they would instead enjoy US sponsored position or wealth, indeed sometimes both."

"And the Darlan-Clark agreement did indeed bring him across......"

".......together with thousands of troops and sailors, to serve now under Eisenhower rather than Petain. But de Gaulle was horrified of course......"

"......at the prospect of being placed under the man who'd been happy to put he and his followers under sentence of death."

"Indeed, Mr Knight, and Parliament here, and the press, they were no less less outraged. Churchill was given an extremely rough ride in the House...... "

"......because the deal seemed so much at odds with his usual rhetoric."

"I suppose so, but for all that criticism Winston stuck firmly to the American line."

"Had he been tipped off, do you think, about Darlan's imminent assassination? There is still doubt as to whether the perpetrator was indeed a lone fanatic...... I mean having him put to death within two days would appear suspiciously hasty."

"This will always remains a matter of speculation. As regards that particular incident, I'm in no position to confirm or deny anything."

"But you do mention in your memoirs that his death proved both timely and convenient."

"Maybe, but this still did not open the way for de Gaulle. Mindful of the immunities promised to Darlan's subordinates before his perhaps not unfortunate death, and rightly not trusting de Gaulle to honour them, Washington preferred instead to give the more the far more compromising figure of General Henri Giraud full command over liberated French possessions and personnel."

"Was this, do you think, because the Americans hoped soon to similarly turn Italian waverers and were concerned, in this context, to guard their own credibility?"

"Partly, of course, and then there was de Gaulle's near messianic single-mindedness which could never sit easily amongst the more pragmatic counsels attendant on Roosevelt and Hull."

"But that verve obviously appealed to the fighting man."

"It did, and not only to his Fighting French. The British Tommy, his Russian counterpart, and even the American GI, all felt instinctively that only de Gaulle could release France's true potential. A full six months of 1943 were wasted as the Giraud and de Gaulle factions vied for supremacy within the French Committee for National Liberation, this to be the voice of free France in the Grand Alliance. De Gaulle's supporters would harry and undermine Giraud's turncoats, 'reformed' Vichyites such as Peyrouton and Boisson, and, prompted by an offended Washington

Giraud was not above retaliating. De Gaulle was overlooked in favour of deputies of his who were known to have voiced misgivings about his autocratic leadership...... Muselier was one of these, the original Free French Admiral. I remember him being elevated, briefly, to chief law and order Minister for Algeria."

"But then came the landings in Sicily, and with the fall of Mussolini the Washington line began to soften."

"Yes, and by the end of that August de Gaulle at last achieved the primacy that most here had felt to be inevitable a good twelve months before. For the General that was twelve months of nothing less than civil war. He was adamant. The topmost councils had to be purged of anyone who'd been remotely connected with Vichy. Those not for him were against him, he maintained, and when he finally prevailed they were to be neither forgotten nor forgiven......and this included a good many in the US administration."

"And you were for him, Lord Stockton?"

"I was, Mr Knight, in the 1940s, but that didn't help me a great deal in 1960......"

"...... when the perception in France was that you owed your position as Prime Minister to an over subservience to President Eisenhower, who as a top Commander back in '42 was very much an advocate of the Darlan-Clark agreement."

"But then, as now, we could still argue the deal to have been tactically opportune. The push eastwards from Morocco into Algeria and Tunisia might otherwise have cost thousands of British and American lives. I would rather less have that on my conscience, and so, I'm sure, would Ike."

"Thank you Lord Stockton. In a few last words tell us how you think we should remember Charles de Gaulle."

"As a political giant, as an inspirational leader rather than a listener."

"...... and this was what his country needed, perhaps?"

"Certainly, yes......... but I am reminded of Lyndon B. Johnson's reaction when, as French President, de Gaulle demanded that America remove its soldiers from French soil. At Johnson's instruction, his Secretary of State, Dean Rusk, inquired whether the demand applied also to those buried in military cemeteries in France......"

"Thank you Lord Stockton...... I think we can perhaps leave it there."

*

Cyril and son, Malthew

a dead poet
October 1973 Kirchstetten, Austria

"Chester, I'm so sorry. I know how close you and Wystan were. The news came through as I was setting off. I hope you don't mind my calling."

"Of course not Cyril. You come, after all, at Wystan's invitation. That letter you sent brought back something of the old sparkle. He was truly looking forward to discussing *Bunyan*."

"He could have put it in a letter."

"He didn't want to. He wanted nothing on paper. In fact he destroyed what you'd written. Finding it was from you, he looked again at the envelope.... checking for any sign sign of it having been opened and resealed."

"Suspecting interception? Was he paranoid?"

"Not generally, Cyril, but being well aware of your long time interest in certain security matters he'll have assumed that anything from you to him would attract attention."

Cyril Connolly paused gravely for thought …. and then.

"Nothing suspicious about his death though?"

"He wasn't in good shape….. the fags and the booze and the other drugs, some prescribed, some not. If there's a mystery it's that he didn't die sooner. He went in his sleep, at midnight…..

"….with no pain."

"An autopsy will probably confirm heart failure, though when found he was lying on his left side. To me that was unique. In all our years together he would invariably sleep on his right. You'll be staying for the funeral I trust."

"I will, Chester, but let's for the moment allow ourselves to get angry. Just say he was killed, eliminated so as to prevent him responding to my enquiry. And say too that he's looking down now, from above, and he wants to spite those responsible. What would he want you to give me? There must be something written down, or perhaps a few words you could say..... before too many get here, my journalist colleagues and their like, they'll want to rifle through his papers."

Kallman hesitated. Connolly knew better than to press..... the bereft partner looked shaken, worn out, even though barely over fifty. The visitor was rewarded for his patience.

"I can give you a start, Cyril. Thereafter you'll need take it step by careful step, remembering that you're on your own. I'm not long for this world myself." Kallman reached into a jacket pocket. "I'd already taken this from his desk, thinking the same as you." An unsealed envelope was passed. Within was a plain unaddressed postcard. Connolly drew it out, and turning it he read....

MCLV HIIR=Eleanor

Uncle Crouchback knows

That was all...... nothing above, nothing beneath, nothing overleaf.

"First thoughts?" Prompted Chester.

"First line, first group, that's a date, or just a year rather...... 1155, in the Roman manner. And, following that, what I suppose must be an appropriate Royal monogram. Henry 2 Rex..... King Henry the Second, who took an Eleanor as his Queen, Eleanor of Aquitaine. Quite a formidable pair, from their union flowed a full three hundred year dynasty of Monarchs, at least four more Henrys, three Richards, plus four or five Edwards to boot..... the Plantagenets, of whom the last was Richard III, the uncle who murdered his nephews, said to have been deformed, crouch-backed maybe."

Kallman came to his Connolly's shoulder. "That's good," he said. "That's the first stage, to follow the disguise...... which most people would be content to do, learning nothing in the process. He would have wanted you to do better, though. In fact, with a prompt or two, he would have had you seeing behind the disguise, while warning that it was there for a reason...... as a kind of screen beyond which only those who are guided might pass."

"So can you prompt me, Chester?"

"This is about *Bunyan*, Cyril. Get back to the enquiry you hoped to make of Wystan, concerning some kind of rough treatment meted out to you by British Security, in 1940 I believe you said. It was about.....?"

".....about people. I was suspected of knowing who the characters used by Wystan and Ben Britten in that opera of theirs might have represented."

"And you didn't know."

"I didn't," confirmed Connolly.

"Well neither, at the time, did Wystan...... in fact not until early '42 when the job had been as good as done," explained Chester Kallman.

"Because he was merely providing the words, and while these could have been a vehicle for coded information the actual encryption thereof was done through the associated musical notation and instrumentation, a score that was subjected to near continuous revision. I guessed this at the time......"

"...... when you were left none the wiser than Wystan. But Wystan being Wystan, meaning *so* possessive, then, where Britten was concerned, he hated the thought of his collaborator being in any way under someone else's control. You might remember the resentment he nurtured against Peter, that was bad enough..... and of course there were similar problems with my friends later."

"So Wystan was determined to get to the bottom of this."

"And he did," confirmed Kallman, "identifying, first of all, a gentleman called Hans Heinsheimer, an employee of Britten's American publisher."

"This job merely being a cover. He was assembling the information and using Ben to feed it back to England, probably to Sir Stewart Menzies...... at that time, unknown to the likes of me, the Chief of British Intelligence. It was he who called on me after I'd received a sample of the libretto directly from Wystan. And Wystan must have got the gist of what was being communicated, this being preserved in this riddle of his. He's playing the code game himself."

"To protect me, Cyril," said Kallman. "I can keep it. I can pass it on. No one though need assume that I know what it means."

"I understand, Chester," smiled Connolly. "But perhaps you might at least give me a start?"

"I will, Cyril, but before that, another little secret ...... something I'll share with you provided you promise it's to go no further while Britten is alive."

"You have my word, Chester."

"A question then..... If asked to identify Wystan and Ben's last collaboration, most people would say what?"

"*Hymn to St Ceilia.*"

"The arrangement for which was written where?"

"On a ship in mid Atlantic, so the story goes, when Britten was sailing back to live again in the UK. That would have been '42."

"And it is said that the first sections of the piece had to be re-written from memory....... did you hear why?"

"Something to do US customs officials confiscating the start that had been made whilst still in America. There's never been any secret about that."

"Now that's an interesting choice of words," observed Kallman. "Take it from me, now, that this move of those so called customs officials against Ben's property was prompted by information received from Wystan."

"So I'm to understand that once wised up to how *Bunyan* might have been employed, Wystan was so strongly opposed to Ben using his *Song to St Cecilia* that he actually went to the American authorities......."

"........ who moved swiftly to invoke special wartime regulations, mirroring what happened to you almost two years before. So when you say '*there's never been any secret about that*', perhaps you are missing something."

"But what, Chester?"

"I don't know, and I don't want to know, not now, not like you...... so I just say look hard and long at Wystan's riddle. Remember his art, and how he used words to paint face upon face, and how those masks would often reveal the deeper truths about those beneath. England in 1155? Henry and Eleanor? I think not, Cyril."

"So would it be about America in 1941?"

"Eleanor.....?"

"Of course, who was married to Franklin."

"And wasn't there a married couple in *Bunyan*?

"*Slim* and *Tiny*......"

"......who could well be the ones to lead you into the riddle. Follow them, Cyril, and leave me here with my grief."

*

Young Nolwen, and Alice

Nolwen
The following year (1974)
Near Eastbourne.

"Mrs Rice...... Mrs de Janze-Rice, thank you for coming so promptly. I fear I'm not long for this world. I wish I could stand to receive you......but."

"I'm honoured, Mr Connolly, that you should be receiving me at all."

"Do call me Cyril," gasped the stricken journalist, beckoning the visitor into the chair alongside his.

"And I'm Nolwen," insisted the elegant, late middle aged widow, tenderly pressing his frail, shakily proffered hand. "Thank you for the invitation. Though a surprise, I had to come. Is this about my......?"

"......about your mother, yes, because of all the letters that came back to the *Sunday Times* in response to our *Christmas at Karen* piece....."

".....five years ago now, and a rare hornets' nest you did stir!"

"Five years," sighed Connolly, "and I summon you today to hear that nothing that's come back to me in all that time on the Erroll matter

105

has touched me so as those words of yours. I wish, now, that I'd contacted you sooner...... but better late than never. I was truly moved by your loyalty to your mother, the mother by whom you'd been virtually abandoned, who you could have barely known."

"It matters, Cyril, because I am heartily sick of my mother being cast as a promiscuous, drug crazed, gun toting psychotic. What happened in Paris back in the '20s was a complete aberration. She was loving, a creature of beauty and grace. My sister and I, even from so far, we felt that love...... as did the animals she tamed, as did Josslyn Hay. She would have no more killed him than killed me."

"Yes, Nolwen..... you're right on that, I'm sure."

"She had a gun, and in the end she used it on herself, but that was Africa. People there *did* have guns, and when the cancer spread then to shoot herself made, for her, African sense. Stricken pets she would despatch with no qualms at all, and this differed little."

"She wasn't going to linger."

"She wanted herself clean away, Cyril."

"She could be eccentric, your mother, she could be passionate, but I agree...... she was never a murderer."

"But at this distance, Cyril, years and miles away from a world that has gone now forever, my mother's contribution to the Happy Valley scene will be taken by any Sunday Newspaper man as an absolute gift."

"Even by one working for so prestigeous a title as the *Sunday Times*," acknowledged the host, eyelids sheepishly lowered. "You made this point in your letter, Nolwen, and I will accept now that I allowed those unconvential ways of Alice to distort my analysis of the case. If you feel owed an apology then, Nolwen, you have one."

"Accepted, Cyril, but for you to have brought me here...... this is about more than contrition."

"Quite, for that I might have offered in a letter of my own."

"You have more?"

"Not on your mother......"

".....but on the case. Concerning the actual assassination..... sufficient to put Alice de Janze more positively in the clear?"

"Certainly, and, in a sense, too certainly."

"Too certainly?"

"Because what I have, Nolwen, points to a truth that could be dynamite."

"An explosive tale."

"So much so as to warrant extreme care in handling."

"So you have no wish to go out with a bang?"

"I've been tempted, Nolwen, but there's my darling Deirdre, who'll soon find herself a far from wealthy widow, with Matthew, my sweet infant child. I must be mindful of their security, their life chances."

"So you feel there's a threat..... that you're being watched?"

"I do, and it's only over this last year that I've begun to understand why."

"But you've sensed something for far longer."

"For more than thirty years, Nolwen......since 1940."

"Taking us back to when my mother was still alive, and also Erroll. When they were in Africa....."

".....and you still in France, and I was in London, producing *Horizon* and making the occasional visit to Oxford." Connolly reached to a shallow side table drawer, sliding it open to produce a once folded sheet of writing paper. "But before going back to those times I must show you this, hand it to you, in fact....."

".......and explain, perhaps," added Nolwen de Janze-Rice, baffled by the brief, strange message.

MCLV   **HIIR = Eleanor**
(step backwards)   **(IST)**

Uncle Crouchback knows
(vaguest variation)

"That outside the brackets was given me last year, by Chester Kallman.....heard of him?"

"Remind me, Cyril."

"Long time companion of Wystan Auden, the poet....."

"......who died."

"He did, and just before I could get to him.....which is why it gladdens me so that you've reached here in time. Chester was passing on what had been left for me by Wystan, a riddle."

"And in the brackets?"

"You see there my additions. They are from me, to you."

"Hardly explicit, Cyril!"

107

"Mnemonics, they are Nolwen, as discrete as they will hopefully be effective..... provided you listen closely to this that I intend now to explain, which hopefully you can retain and perhaps, in safer times, re-tell."

"So it's a dangerous story, Cyril, and this is all you're giving in writing."

"Because it's all that you should need, provided you listen, and watch, and move with stealth and patience. There's an old guard, like me, slowly dying off. Some avenues of enquiry will be rendered less perilous by the passsage of years. Fresher talent might emerge, better fitted to the opportunities and challenges thus presented."

"But dynamite remains.......dynamite."

"So speak softly, Nolwen. You will be carrying a big stick. Tell me...... what think you of the music of Benjamin Britten?"

A strange question, thought the visitor, but surely no digression, not when so earnestly posed.

"For orchestra, very good," she replied.

"And for voice?"

"Even better."

"So of his operas, which would be your *must* see?"

"*Grimes*, I think..... the first.

"Most would say that, I fancy," nodded the ailing host, "overlooking the fact that there was an earlier work, composed in America at the start of the war...... Wystan providing the words. 'Incoherent' was the general view, few performances, constant revisions. Wholly forgettable..... and Ben would have appeared to agree, for years the project has been shelved."

"So I can be forgiven."

"But since Auden's death, last year, this neglected runt of a piece has started to stir. Parts are being revived for a recital programme at this year's Aldeburgh Festival. I would have liked to have gone.....so perhaps you might."

"And this has a bearing on what you show me here," said Nolwen, glancing down, "and to the myth that's been built around my mother?"

"Very much so," said Connolly. "This story, which I can begin and you might help to finish, must, for me, start with *Paul Bunyan*."

Times change
Another year on (1975)
Ince Castle, Cornwall

"Alan, have you seen this is today's paper?"

"In what section, Patsy?"

"Foreign news.... the piece about the big military funeral in Israel."

"I've not. Show me." Lord Boyd was at his desk. His wife placed the paper, appropriate page outermost, within his reach. Sliding it a little closer, he read.

JERUSALEM: *Thousands of mourners, including Prime Minister Yitzhak Rabin, today filed past the coffins of Eliahu Hakim and Eliahu Bet-Zouri prior to their internment in the sacred burial ground set aside for the founders of Israel. The pair were hanged in 1945 by the British Wartime Administration in Egypt on being found guilty of the previous November's murder in Cairo of Lord Moyne, then our Government's Minister Resident for the Middle East Area. The corpses were recently reclaimed from the Egyptian Government as part of an exchange for twenty Arabs jailed in Israel as enemy spies.*

The assassins, now feted as martyrs, had been members of the then notorious 'Stern Gang' whose vicious terrorism at that time attracted the revulsion of moderate Jewish opinion. They even drew condemnation from the radical 'Jewish Agency' who at that time were even prepared to commit their Haganah (secret army) to help the British Colonial Police root out those who planned and perpetrated a succession of similar atrocities.

"Thirty years on, Patsy, and your uncle must be spinning in his grave."

"Likewise Winston, Alan..... so much has changed in the ten years since his death. I'll never forget his Commons eulogy to Uncle Walter. In terms of raw fanaticism he could see little to distinguish the Stern Gang from the hated Nazis...."

".......and didn't he say as much, in no uncertain terms?"

"He did, but too many saw it as no more than the usual Commons bluster. "

"Spiced with genuine grief, Patsy...."

"....and perhaps a measure of guilt. I know this from what Uncle Walter told me shortly before he died."

"I'm not sure that I want to hear this, my love. Moyne was a good man. He was family, I know, but for better or for worse the world has moved on. We are no longer the nation we were. It seems beyond us even to sort out the mess that is Rhodesia..... don't ask me to get worked up about the squabble between Arab and Jew." Lord Boyd pushed the paper back towards his wife.

She picked it up, hesitantly. Perhaps Alan was right. The secret, her secret, was becoming less of a burden now.... it was only rarely now, when stopped by articles like this, that she again felt its weight. She was impelled, though, to say her piece.

"Listen Alan," she implored. "This sort of thing has to worry me. It ought to worry you. The world isn't getting any safer, and there are people out there with long, long memories. I'd be less concerned if only you stuck to that decision to retire from active politics."

"I am in the Lords, my love, and, as I've said before, if we can't make ourselves useful then we strengthen the case of the abolitionists. I might be struggling against the tide, but I have to believe that when the time comes I can leave the place stronger than how I found it. This is part of my brief from the Party."

"You owe the Party nothing," countered Lady Boyd. Her husband of almost forty years was unapologetic

"Deserved or no, they can count on my loyalty......"

"......and they see a soft touch. They take advantage, always searching you out for those odd jobs...... Foreign Affairs tasks because of your old colonial contacts in Africa..... Home Affairs tasks because of your work with the Prison Reform League. You're being drawn into it again, Alan. This woman who's taking over from Ted, I can see her winning the next election. She'll want to put fresh faces on her front bench and, for balance, take a few old hands on as backroom boys. Old Thorneycroft's going to be turning to you, I know. I see you getting ever busier and frankly, you and I, we don't need the danger."

Lord Boyd leant back in his chair. He reached for his wife's hand. "If it's worrying you this much then I'm listening..... but not to those same veiled warnings that I've heard before." He looked across again to the discarded newspaper. "Tell me now Patsy…. What's this really all about?"

The wife turned away. She had been tempted, but now, at the crunch, she couldn't say. She wouldn't dare say. This was the bind. To know so much, and to be able to say so little to one she loved so, so deeply. For the situation was changed now, so changed as to have been quite unimaginable to the assassinated uncle.

*

(vi) 1983-6

My subject is war, and the pity of war.
Owen

A grievous loss
1983 London
A restaurant on The Fulham Road.

"And how did he put it?" guffawed Boyd. " '*Quite black inside and full off beaks and shot and inexplicable vertabrae……*' "

"….. and we all knew this had to be the Cavendish," sniggered Bryan Guinness, the second Lord Moyne, and cousin of course to his companion's wife. "Yes, and nothing could ever better typify Evelyn's style then, that early genius for lampoon. With broad brush he would paint us a grotesque, and then finely ink-in the tellingly authentic detail….."

"…..those parts that tended to stick in the throat."

"And in this case, quite literally," snorted Moyne.

"And were his victim to take umbrage then naturally the barb would sink all the deeper. Because Rosa Lewis couldn't laugh at herself she was all the more identifiable as *Lottie Crump* …… and how did we get on to *Lottie* and her *Shepheard's Hotel* anyway?"

"Because the other day Patsy and I were down in Kent, at Saltwood, for a 'do' hosted by Alan and Jane Clark."

"Something of a rogue, that man….. definitely a whiff of the Mosley about him."

"Quite," acknowledged Boyd, politely wishing to avoid the

subject of Diana, even though it was now half a century since the break-up, "but what's relevant to Evelyn Waugh, and to your family, was the presence there of Clark's stepmother, the Lady Nolwen."

"Ahaa...... Nolwen de Janze. An interesting marriage that, so late in life for Lord Clark....."

"......and so soon after the death of Lady Jane, but I suppose she brightened Lord Kenneth's final years."

"Little love lost between her and the sons though. That Alan, he loathes the woman," tattled Guinness, at the same time sensing there to be a further, deeper reason for the mention of her name. His tone lowered. "Might," he began, more seriously, "might this perhaps be something to do with her mother, the infamous Alice? Are we talking *Happy Valley* and the *Muthaiga*, Joss Hay, 'Jock' Delves Broughton and all that?'"

"We are, Bryan. Murder and old ermine, and it seems that sweet Nolwen has a thing about her late mother so often being cast as a chief suspect. With each new account of the murder, increased emphasis is given to the poor woman's instability."

"Not unnaturally, I suppose."

"Unless this is being done deliberately, so as to further bury the truth..... this is what Nolwen feels, and apparently, before he died, she was quietly encouraged in this view by Cyril Connolly......"

"..... who himself researched the case. I remember his piece in the *Sunday Times*. That would have been.... what, a dozen or so years ago now?"

"At least," agreed Boyd. "But for a good while she's kept what he chose not to include under her hat. Cyril's widow was left with debts, and also a young child. To spare them potential embarrassment things needed to be allowed to settle."

"So what Connolly put in the paper was only part of his story....."

".....the better part of valour being discretion, but with the passage of time Nolwen has been emboldened. Carefully, she's been pulling a few of his loose ends together."

"And this is where the incorrigible Evelyn Waugh crops up, I take it, no doubt because of those valuable connections he cultivated. Bracken was a friend..... helped him into a good rank in the army it's said. Then, later, he was teamed with Randolph Churchill and Freddie Birkenhead, for special operations in the Balkans."

"Evelyn did, it's true, make many a valuable friend..... but he also made many an implaccable foe."

"As we've said."

"Except that I speak, now, not of the dotty Lotties, but of men of rank and position."

"The ruling classes of Abyssinia were far from amused by *Black Mischief*. I do remember that."

"And look too at some of his other stories, and how they might have similarly offended a few amongst the ruling classes in this country of ours. Dangerous, some of them, secretive and ruthless....."

".......definitely not the sort one would want to upset, eh Alan?"

"Particularly if active still, to this day."

"Exactly, Bryan, so we take care."

"By?"

"Well I made sure that I was seen to be receptive to Alan Clark's opinion of his stepmother. He loathes the woman....."

"..... but of course she comes with the inheritance."

"And he's stuck with her," confirmed Boyd. "But he wastes no opportunity to whisper it around that Nolwen is no less loopy than was her mother, who, according to Alan, was absolutely barking. Listen further, and the disparagement is extended to Connolly, who was quite a close neighbour down there on the south coast, and also, going back again to the '30s, quite a close friend of Alan's father....."

"Lord Clark, the late Sir Kenneth."

"So it is with some authority, Bryan, that Cyril's style of history, speculative but nonetheless informed, is roundly rubbished as crackpot musing."

"To which Connolly has been prone, of course. Don't I remember an obsession with the true identity of Jesus, and then the true identity of Shakespeare. Complete tosh, all of it Alan, so why should any theory he had on Lord Erroll be any different?"

"A good question, Bryan, which brings me to this that I have here with me, which today I've brought back from Berlin."

"Berlin..... we go from Africa to Berlin, and still with Connolly?"

"Because amongst all the fools' gold, the Christ and Shakespeare stuff, Cyril did bring up some true nuggets.... and one of these was the piece he did more than thirty years ago on the Cambridge spies, *The Missing Diplomats*."

"Burgess, Maclean....."

"...... and make no mistake, he knew about Blunt......"

"...... a fellow associate of Sir Kenneth......"

"...... and he'd good reason to strongly suspect Philby."

"Who was more than just a diplomat....."

"......having burrowed to the very heart of Menzies' MI6, where he was well placed to monitor the British response to Hitler's peace overtures prior to his *Barbarossa* campaign."

"And there were peace overtures?" queried Gunness.

"The Hess mission," answered Boyd. "It's a matter of fact."

"And this was significant?"

"Far more so than could be admitted at the time, Bryan, and also since."

"So what I hear, Alan, is the suggestion that Hess was as good as invited across...."

".... this being merely the visible element of a wider deceit, Bryan, with which Hitler was lured into opening that eastern front, a deceit achieved on the strength of far more than diplomatic double speak. Cyril Connolly's suspicion was that there was a Colonial dimension to all this......"

"..... with certain territories in East Africa being placed on the negotiating table, Tanganyika for instance, the former German posession. Hadn't the appeasers been keen on that one, back at the time of Munich?"

"They had, Bryan, so perhaps, by '41, with our cities being pummelled by the Luftwaffe, that same deal was being resurrected..... with a few other Crown territories being thrown in for good measure. And it was early in '41 that Erroll was shot, a man with much to say on behalf of Kenyan Settler and native."

"So he had to be silenced," said Guinness. "And you're suggesting that Cyril Connolly might have worked this out."

"And this happens, Bryan, when your father was Colonial Secretary."

"Poor old Dad," sighed the heir, "in an age of political dynasties I was always going to be something of a disappointment to him.... me a mere author. He had high hopes for you, though. Rarely was he so happy as when confiding these in young Patricia, his favourite niece."

"So I begin to gather, Bryan, and because you are family, and a fellow Peer, concerned like your father was, and I am, for the future of our Upper Chamber, I feel that you ought to allow me to confide in you with this that I was given in Berlin."

"And this is why you brought me here." As he spoke the second Lord Moyne glanced down at the brief case propped closely against his companion's chair.

"It wasn't what I went for, Bryan. I don't go looking for trouble"

"......but you've been persuaded to bring it back, and you're finding it a hot potato."

"As hot as anything I've known."

"So first tell me exactly where you went, and why."

"It started off as a job I was asked to do by Margaret. She's a little nervous of the Human Rights Court in Strasbourg."

"Our methods in Ulster have attracted their close scrutiny, this I know."

"Well, I think she put it with me because of the prison reform work I've done."

"And you are a qualified lawyer, Alan. Too many forget that. So where were you sent to in Berlin."

"Spandau....."

"*Spandau*," whistled Moyne, "because no one, however evil, is to be denied humane treatment, even....."

"Even prisoner number seven," confirmed Boyd.

"So you can report, I trust, that this country fulfils its obligations?"

"I can, Bryan. Hess is being well looked after......"

"....but?" Moyne's prompt elicited only silence. He persevered. "There has to be a 'but', Alan."

"I was targeted......"

"....by?"

"A group declaring themselves to be keen to hasten the end of the Soviet Empire."

"You were targeted by the good guys, then."

"Just a small group, in Berlin, a discrete cadre drawn from both sides of the wall whose long term wish is to see Germany re-unified...... as a democratic nation, they say, peaceable and prosperous."

"A heartening prospect."

"Yes, but they're worried Bryan. Looking ahead a little, they feel progress might be jeopardised by one of the most renowned of our fellow Peers."

"One of Our Lordships? Which?"

"Stockton."

"Macmillan......Harold, your old boss."

"The same, who these people fear might get drawn into a tangle with young Nikolai Tolstoy. You might have read his books."

"I have read of his books, Alan...... '*Victims of Yalta*' and then '*Stalin's Secret War*'. I know he has a real go at Macmillan, for supposedly ordering the hand back to Stalin of the thousands of Russians liberated from German captivity by the British advance, mainly through southern Europe."

"Some having to be forced, at gunpoint, to return to death or slavery," said Boyd grimly. "I've been told that a third book is on the way, this putting Macmillan's role under an even closer scrutiny."

"But why should this be laid at Harold's door, Alan? Back then he was well junior to Eden, who in turn would have run this in front of his own boss, the top man, who was Winston."

"Churchill died in '65, Eden in '77. Neither can reply, nor bring any action for libel."

"And this is what Tolstoy wants?" Bryan Guinness was puzzled.

"I think he does," replied Boyd, "no matter what it might cost him. For what young Nikolai really craves is his day in court, and all the attendant publicity this must inevitably create. He can say what he likes about the dead, and have his efforts dismissed as no less loopy than those of Connolly on Jesus and Shakespeare. What Tolstoy needs is a live target....."

".....however inaccurate his fire. And this cadre in Berlin you speak of, they find this an alarming prospect?"

"They do, Bryan, because Tolstoy's ultimate target must be the Foreign Office, and information held therein. Macmillan can be regarded as a gatekeeper, a figure of true stature who, in his efforts to defend his reputation, might well crack open the whole edifice......"

"...... which could well suffer a significant seepage, this is the rationale. So tell me, Alan. What kind of stuff do these people in Berlin fear might be spilt?"

"This kind of stuff," answered Boyd, reaching towards the floor to pat the briefcase leaning against his chair. "I'm to personally deliver it to the Lord Chancellor..... tomorrow now, because I was too late today."

"Pivotal position that," nodded Moyne. "On the Woolsack, in the

Cabinet, heading the Judiciary......"

".….. making him the ideal man to avert a what could build to a constitutional crisis with the gravest of international consequences. What I have here is potentially a time bomb. Those people in Berlin see it as such, and I do too."

"And there is agreement that Hailsham might be best placed to defuse it."

"And also best equipped," added Boyd. "He has the contacts, the inside knowledge, and the means of exerting subtle control, of finding those forms of words which will say just enough and yet not too much. I'm anticipating that Harold might soon be pointing to some vaguely worded and too easily misunderstood Foreign Office or Defence Department directive, attributable to some anonymously staffed *ad hoc* committee, long disbanded of course. As a Government admission, it wouldn't need to be detailed or profound.….."

"...... but it would be enough to give Macmillan a much needed smokescreen. There'll be doubts, and he'll benefit."

"And the grave charges of 'complicity in war crimes' can be blunted by emolient whispers of 'tragic misunderstandings'."

"So what is it you have in there, that you feel might persuade them to go to such trouble...... are you about to tell me?"

"Not here, Bryan. I'll show you later, at the flat. At the moment I'm looking across the road at that shop window, the one displaying antiques. It's giving a reflection of a side street thirty or so yards along, on this side. There's a car there, waiting. If it's occupied then I might be under surveillance. If you just sit with this a moment then I can cross and check. I'll pretend to be interested in antiques. If you can be ready with your coat and the briefcase I'll flag down a taxi."

"You be careful Alan."

So tall and so lordly, Boyd rose from the table, covering the bill with a more than adequate £50 note. A waiter fetched both coats, and Bryan Guinness watched his cousin's husband slip out on to the pavement. He was looking along to the side street as he came to the kerb, and then across to the shop.

He was waiting for a break in the traffic, and now he was striding out, because he'd seen one he thought. But it didn't exist, and in an instant neither did he. He'd been struck, and thrown, and he was dead. And Moyne had seen it happen, in all its sudden and brutal finality. Quickly, instinctively, he was out onto the road, and part of a throng all hoping to comfort..... but finding only the broken corpse. Patsy, he thought, he must phone Patsy now..... from inside the restaurant, where that brief case should still be.

Within minutes the news had reached Sir Clive Faulds, and he was swiftly and discretely away from his Chief Secretary's desk so as without delay to be in the absolute privacy of his Hampstead home.... there to be ready by the specially installed phone, its line more secure than any in the whole of Whitehall, Downing Street included. The call would come, he knew, probably within an hour of his return.....and this was it now. The unique ringing tone summoned. He reached, and taking a deep breath, scooped the receiver to his ear. Through came the voice, as stern and as steady as ever, despite the events of the afternoon.

"We need to meet. Very soon."

"Where are you?"

"In London still, and not so far away. I can be at *The Spaniards* in fifteen minutes..... usual bar, near as possible to the usual corner."

"I'm on my way, Sir."

The brisk walk took Faulds past a darkened Kenwood. The name 'Iveagh' drew from him a brief glance, but then it was on without breaking step. Irony wasn't to detain either him or his flow of thought..... so heavily now did this meeting loom. He would need to be at his sharpest, at his considerable best, for this had to concern HIGHLAND CLEARANCE, which he knew to be strictly GUSTAVE's domain.

Things had gone awry, and now the chief would be wanting the situation rectified. But he, Faulds, didn't need to be too apologetic. He might have done better, this was true, but that he hadn't was not entirely his own fault. Though happy enough to use his skills and his team, GUSTAVE had been reluctant to confide in him the full import HIGHLAND CLEARANCE. For too long now he'd been kept in ignorance, and left to gain no more than a shadowy conception of the project...... one informed largely by speculation and contradictory rumour. If he was to be engaged now in the task of putting things to rights then he would need to be told far more. On this, as he sucked at the March night air, he was almost ready to insist.

GUSTAVE was waiting, as promised, in the customary corner,

and rising now, stiffly, to greet him. He looked older, of course, for at that age two years can alter a man greatly. The chiefly bearing remained though, clearly undimmed. The table had been suitably furnished...... the two empty glasses, the full half bottle of scotch and, naturally, the small porcelain jug of water.

They settled, Faulds accepting the proffered whisky and charging each glass to a careful, respectful depth.

"He's dead?" GUSTAVE began.

"He is."

"These things happen, Sir Clive." Neutral words, but warningly intoned. Faulds shuddered. "That briefcase was recovered I hope. I trust it didn't escape your surveillance people."

"I'm afraid, Sir, that....."

"Damn...... and if there were other teams in the field and they've got it then we're in trouble. Though we might not know exactly what Boyd was bringing back from Spandau it has to be assumed to be highly dangerous."

"Some kind of testimony this would be, from Hess...... an affidavit perhaps?"

"That kind of document," nodded GUSTAVE, "and our best hope now is that it has been destroyed. Believe me, the wrong words placed in the wrong hands could precipitate calamity."

"Moyne rushed out to see what could be done for Boyd. The briefcase had been left by the table. We were slow to realise this......."

".......but others weren't."

"It might have been filched by a common criminal," offered Faulds in desperation. "We could put the police on alert."

"A bag snatcher lurking in a select restaurant? Think, Sir Clive...... and besides there are as many 'wrong hands' in the Police Service as anywhere else. Why risk putting them on alert too. For the moment we're best to sit tight and wait. If it has survived then there's some consolation in Hess's want of credibility. His words won't properly persuade until substantiated, and this might be partly why Boyd was singled for the errand."

"Because he was thought to have had independent access to something of substance, that might make the difference, something sufficient to make Hess believable," ventured the other.

"Perhaps," hedged GUSTAVE. "It's very possible, but I can't be sure...... and now he's dead."

"So what about this testimony from Hess? What would he have been saying? You must have some idea there."

"Yes, Sir Clive, I can make a good guess, but it's not one that I can make aloud, not at this point."

"Because it's me that's listening?"

"No...... because there's this chance of it having been destroyed. If it has gone, like Boyd, then it's best to allow the whole thing to die. I wouldn't wish to trouble you."

"Sir, whether we find this to be gone or not gone, if I'm to be any help now then I need to be troubled."

"Perhaps you do, Sir Clive, perhaps you do." GUSTAVE was weakening, Faulds sensed. He knew better than to press.

"Well there's no perhaps about Boyd being dead. He is ... incontrovertibly so."

"Quite, Sir Clive, but the key to his involvement might have been a family connection, and this still exists."

"Explain, please."

"When made Colonial Secretary back in the '50s Alan was dealt the poorest of hands...... last ditch stands in Malaysia, in Cyprus, in Kenya, the latter culminating in the Hola debate. He was lined up to take the full rap....."

"....'59, the prison beatings, I remember."

"But his wife, Patricia, she wins him a last minute reprieve. She goes to Macmillan for a quiet word and proceeds to alarm him with an unsuspected and closely kept knowledge of HIGHLAND CLEARANCE."

"A trump card......"

".....which she must still hold, Sir Clive."

"So why this uncertainty about her late husband?"

"Because that knowledge was so closely kept. We can't even presume that it was shared with him, Sir Clive, even if those who collared Boyd in Berlin were obviously hoping so."

The logic was sound. Faulds was impressed.

"So *her* knowledge of HIGHLAND CLEARANCE came from where?" he asked.

"Macmillan understood that it had been handed down by Walter Guinness, the 1st Lord Moyne, before he died...... he being her uncle."

"Shot, in Cairo, '44," punctuated Faulds, "Bryan's father of course. "

"But the son would have had no need of it, so instead it went to the niece, as I kind of insurance policy for her husband's political career….."

"……which she utilised in '59….."

"……without his knowledge, then, she said."

"But we don't know if he was made aware subsequently."

"But whatever," shrugged GUSTAVE, "this can't matter now, for Alan Lennox-Boyd is out of the game. Patricia remains though, and with the disappearance of that document we must be all the more concerned for her security, and ours. The Hess business is a can of worms, always was, and what festers at the bottom of it must be kept firmly out of the public domain. To his credit, this was what Boyd was hoping to achieve, by getting what he had to the Lord Chancellor."

"Where better to keep something covered than under the woolsack?"

"This was what he'd been persuaded, and we were ready to nod this along, for Hailsham would have been ready to share the exact contents with us. Transport, though, will always involve risks…… so we had to be watchful, Sir Clive, and now, worryingly, it looks like we weren't watchful enough. Instead of being lidded securely down our can of worms has been mislaid, very possibly into the still very capable claws of the bear. He could soon be on the prowl, I fear. I hope I can count on an improved vigilance." This was Faulds' cue.

"Perhaps, Sir, if it could be more fully explained to me just what HIGHLAND CLEARANCE was about……?"

"……then maybe you would be better equipped for the task, eh?" GUSTAVE pondered, looking into his tumbler. It was a fair point, for no one was getting any younger and the burden would have to be shared soon. Faulds, here, was as well qualified as any….so yes. Why not now? The whisky was swilled, and sipped, and the glass then lowered. "HIGHLAND CLEARANCE, Sir Clive, was the brainchild of Sir Stewart Menzies, conceived as a contingency in the late '30s when he was a departmental head under Admiral Hugh Sinclair…."

"…. who died in harness at the beginning of the war, Menzies then taking the job of running MI6 for a dozen more than eventful years."

"Eventful, Sir Clive, and pivotal; years during which this country was brought to the brink of destruction...."

".....and yet survived. Hitler having been vanquished....."

".....while Stalin was empowered. It all seems so inevitable now, in hindsight, but believe me Sir Clive, it was the closest of contests. Without HIGHLAND CLEARANCE we wouldn't have edged it as we did."

"So it was a plan that worked, Sir, a contingency for which the time came."

"Let's say it worked well enough. Had it worked better then maybe we wouldn't be meeting like this, Sir Clive, more than forty years on, having to address loose end after loose end......"

"......such as the today widowed Viscountess....."

"..... and also Lord Stockton, the same Sir Harold with whom she sparred so effectively back in '59. In fact it is through Stockton and his present day predicament that the consequences of HIGHLAND CEARANCE threaten to upset the current balance of world affairs. For forty and more years Mac has enjoyed a generally good press....."

"..... making him one of our best loved senior public figures," said Faulds, "as would befit someone who bears one of the most powerful names in publishing."

"Yes," agreed GUSTAVE, taking the point without fully endorsing the couching cynicism, "but over the past five years or so things have radically changed, due largely to the persistence of one man."

"You speak of young Nikolai Tolstoy, and his crusade on behalf of the repatriated Russians...... the Cossacks, the POWs freed from the Nazi camps, and as many of the statelesss *Whites* that Stalin could scoop back from the west."

"All of whom Stalin perceived as a threat, and was keen to enslave or kill. And Tolstoy has chosen to identify Macmillan as Uncle Joe's main accomplice, even though at the time, relative to Churchill and Eden, he was a junior minister."

"But *he* is still alive," said Faulds, "and capable therefore of issuing a libel writ, the ticket that Tolstoy seems to crave...... bankrupt him though it might. And this, as you've said, is where Boyd, with that errand, was hoping to pull the plug."

"But he failed, Sir Clive."

"With the loss of that briefcase merely adding to the problem. Where can we go from here?"

"Macmillan isn't going to live for ever, Sir Clive."

"So are you considering hastening Stockton's death?"

"Not yet, Sir Clive, for while we have Macmillan at the hub, we still have matters reasonably under control. Aldington waits in the wings, remember, one who might prove far less manageable. But more on Harold and Toby in a moment, for in the regrettably untidy scheme of things those two were relative latecomers."

"Things already having gone too *aft a-gley*." Faulds was warming to the Scotch.

"Yes, for while not being too fatally flawed, HIGHLAND CLEARANCE was compromised almost from the off."

"As Menzies might have been, for wasn't Kim Philby one of his proteges?"

"Indeed he was, Sir Clive. Philby, Burgess, Maclean.....with hindsight we see them being firmly planted, the seeds of nemesis. How they did prosper in the warmth of Sir Stewart's achievement. And while on this reprehensible bunch perhaps it might be the moment to mention our friend Lord Rothschild."

"Victor Rothschild..... also a traitor? There have been whispers, I know but....."

"......*you*, Sir Clive, can be assured that they are totally without foundation. Yes, he was a close friend to Burgess and Maclean during the war, but he was as true as they were false."

"So why raise his name now?"

"Because he retains a formidably forensic mind, and with this, through his long standing Cambridge connections, a ready access to the furthest frontiers of natural science."

"And this warrants an alert?"

"Because of the assistance he has recently seen fit to give to Mr Chapman Pincher....."

"......the journalist? The man's a joke, surely. According to him every other one of us is a mole. He takes the whole thing too far."

"True," agreed GUSTAVE. "On his own he wouldn't normally have me losing any sleep, but with his access to the popular press he tends to draw to himself the disaffected, and one such has been Mr Peter Bright, the former MI5 listener, now retired and fallen on hard times since trying his hand at farming in Tasmania......"

"......and who, in an effort to stave off insolvency has written a memoir, the publication of which would contravene the Official Secrets Act. If this has been produced under Pincher's guidance we can expect to be liberally spiced with largely imagined KGB subversion."

"And generally, Sir Clive, that kind of thing has become harmless old hat."

"But in this case?"

"More by chance than design old Pincher has introduced Mr Bright to Lord Rothschild and the pair now seem to be enjoying a free standing association....."

".....and it's of this that you are wary."

"Because in the course of his career as a listener Bright did, I know, hear an occasional snippet pertaining to HIGHLAND CLEARANCE, but to him these would have meant nothing..... limited mind, limited resources."

"But should they be brought into the den of the forensic wizard....."

"........ an alchemy might be triggered to produce a whole that might worryingly exceed the sum of the hitherto disparate parts."

"But if Victor Rothschild is, in your opinion, so loyal, why can't just a quiet word suffice?"

"If Hailsham can be trusted then why not he?" considered GUSTAVE. "Chancey, Sir Clive, on two counts. A 'stay clear' at this point, even if heeded by Victor, would only work to sharpen and focus the curiosity of the others."

"..... and?"

"We don't know that such a heeding can be guaranteed. Think of the name ' *Rothschild*'. This is a family that has done much to enrich this Nation. In the last war and since Victor Rothschild has served with valour and with industry, but even the most fervent of loyalties can be strained, even to splitting point."

"So, might you at last be able to explain?"

"Yes, now I can, Sir Clive. So I'll go back forty five years, to the very beginning."

*

the gardener
INCE CASTLE

Under a sombre morning sky the stunned household begins to grieve. The drive is almost busy with cars, gently, respectfully driven, the familiar vehicles of shocked neighbours and friends, making their brief calls. Occasionally a relative will arrive to stay longer, for the funeral. Patricia Lennox Boyd carries her heartbreak with dignity, accepting and offering comfort with thoughtful grace.

It is natural that she should be seeking out those amongst her staff who were known to have been particularly close to the late Viscount, and one such, Declan McDaid, looks sorrowfully up from his hoeing as he hears the unmistakable footsteps.

The Viscountess will call him Declan. To the Viscount he had been simply 'Dec', since long before he'd sold-on his diligently developed milk delivery round some ten years back now.

Ince had been part of that round when the Boyd's had taken up residence, the previous occupants having enjoyed a good dozen years of the man's cheery and reliable Trematon based service. But back in the 50s Saltash had had its own creamery. St Stephens was a village, and Burraton almost a rural crossroads. Then came the bridge, and the bridge brought the developers, and Saltash spread. Fields to the south of the new A38 were soon in-filled and, as the estates grew and grew, Mc Daid found himself facing cross-border competition...... aggressive and well equipped.

Come the late '70s and the choice was simple. It was time to either invest or to deservedly cash in on one of what was a succession of increasingly attractive buy-out bids. He'd never married, there was no family to consider, and indeed he was ready to move into a less rigid lifestyle..... so he took the money, while he had the time and the health still enjoy it.

He was able to add to this by selling the Trematon house, most of the capital being put into a pair of adjoined cottages in quiet St Erney, the next parish to the west, just across the Lynher River. He lived in one, and the other was let...... initially to a sitting tenant...... the rental income supplementing the returns on a few paper investments plus what fluctuating amount might be made from the kind of casual work that had today brought him to Ince. At this time of year he might garden here for up to twenty hours a week. In the shorter days of winter, though, he would be more often found scraping off or painting on at the Old Quarry Boatyard, a leisure craft concern tucked along his side of the water just a little way upriver of the railway viaduct.

At an active 60 the large frame of younger days remained, though more stooped and angular, and where once he filled his clothes now they flapped loosely. Hair was greying (with beard to match), teeth were yellowing, and a voice was losing its earlier steadiness….. but not its accent. Other Gael emblems had long slipped. Gone was any hunger for the Roman Eucharist, and likewise any thirst for stout, or any yearning for the music and the dance of the ceilidh. Yes, he would often whistle whilst working, and sometimes even break into song, but usually to the tunes of Hank Williams and Slim Whitman. Rarely would it be a John Mc Cormack. Those, like so much else, had been smothered under the soft Cornish cloud, but not that strangely un-withered accent which seemed almost to want to flourish in its contented isolation.

And now he is aware of the widow's approach. The weeds in the barrow can wait, his bonfire will slowly smoke. He must be attentive. It appeared that the bundle of old papers she carried might be for him…… for him to burn, for they were lowered into the barrow, on top of the weeds, but as yet with no instruction.

"He was a good man Ma'am," said the gardener. "One that I was proud to know."

"And your friendship meant much to him, Dec. He was never happier than when tending to this garden with yourself. I think, at times, he would confide more in yourself than he would me."

"Because his instinct was to protect rather than burden….. and me, I've always had broad shoulders. If he wanted a listener, I was here. Those things for the fire…..?" Patricia Lennox Boyd hesitated. But it was time they were burned, for there'd been nothing yet to suggest her husband's death to have been anything but an accident, unless…….

"Had he said anything to you about that trip to Berlin?" she asked.

"He regarded it as routine, a finding out about facts. He was more concerned about this bindweed and how much further it could spread before he got back."

"So there were no doubts that he would get back."

"None that he expressed to me, Ma'am."

"So yes, Dec, this lot we can burn." And with that the papers were lifted and poked into the smoking pile.

"A few minutes and they'll properly ignite, Ma'am," McDaid assured her, and then he looked across through the trees to the drive where a familiar vehicle moved towards the Castle. "Looks like your son. Shall I go across and call him over?"

"No. If you can stay here and see to this I'd rather take him inside." And with that the gardener was left to prod his fire into true flame….. but these papers needed to be rearranged first, for as they'd been dropped they merely dampened the flow of air through what was already a far too green a pile. They wouldn't go up, they would just gently smoke, so Declan McDaid crouched. And he crouched close enough to read, just a few of the words, some of them names, and this name, yes, it was one that he'd heard before, a long, long way from here, and a long time ago, but even so, one that he was never likely to forget. Perhaps it was unconnected, but then again perhaps not, and if not then how intriguing this was, that such a name might reappear in circumstances so tragic as these. Maybe he needn't be in such a hurry to complete this task. No one was watching. He had deep pockets, with room too inside his shirt……
and what was saved from the flames would be presumed destroyed.

*

the veteran
JUNE 1984. PLYMOUTH SOUND (local radio).

PRESENTER: '……and today and all this week we are commemorating the Normandy landings of forty years ago, the crucial first days of the assault on Nazi occupied Europe that would eventually culminate in the final surrender of Germany almost a year later. With me as guests I have a veteran of the campaign and with him a distinguished military historian. The latter, already familiar to most of us, is The Honourable Alan Clark, currently Employment Minister…… a man we have often heard speaking on this station, though usually of course in his capacity as Member of Parliament for Plymouth Sutton. Good morning Minister.
CLARK: '*Good morning. Thankyou for inviting me.'*
PRESENTER: We are indeed honoured Mr Clark, and no less so to have alongside you Mr Stanley 'Peg' Willis. He now lives peacefully near

Landrake, but forty years ago he was a sergeant in the 6th Airborne Division, the British contingent that spearheaded the assault.'
WILLIS: 'Good morning.'
PRESENTER: 'Well, in a moment Peg, -- if I can use the name most know you by--, we will listen to your D Day story, but first I have to ask the Minister to briefly outline the concept and the evolution of the airborne assault. Mr Clark...'
CLARK: 'For thirty years now we've been able to bus troops around the battlefield by helicopter. They can be put down, picked up, and put down again. Before that it was the parachute and the glider. Once down the men had to fight where they stood, and with no more than the equipment that could carry from their planes. They had the gun, and the grenade, and precious little else. Where the target was well defended they relied upon surprise, accuracy, speed, and absolute ruthlessness.'
PRESENTER: 'No prisoners.'
CLARK: 'No prisoners. The idea was to take and protect strategic objectives that lay ahead of the more heavily equipped ground forces, until relieved by the same. The text book example was the German capture of the Belgian frontier forts in 1940. The following year the German paras were again deployed to capture Crete.'
PRESENTER: 'Successfully?'
CLARK: 'Just about......but the losses were heavy, too heavy, leading Hitler to lose confidence in the technique. My book on Crete will......'
PRESENTER: '......but no loss of confidence on our side. Bearing in mind that we're here to talk about 1944.'
CLARK: 'Not until September 1944, Arnhem......'
PRESENTER: '......which proved a bridge too far.'
CLARK: 'Exactly, but by which time Peg and his comrades had shown their worth in Normandy, particularly in the crucial action that secured the Orne crossings, the two left flank bridges spanning the side by side canal and river.'
PRESENTER: 'And their significance......?'
CLARK: '......was that they offered access to the high ground to the east of SWORD, itself the easternmost of the invasion beaches. Had the Germans been allowed to gather their artillery there then they might have pinned our boys on the beaches. This is what the Turks had been allowed to do on Gallipoli, the sacrifice of the ANZAC divisions earning nothing. Then, a bit more dash and initiative in breaking inland from the relatively

128

lightly defended beaches would have won the day. ......

PRESENTER: 'So this was what was asked of the Commando brigades landing on SWORD beach.'

CLARK: 'Exactly. With their tanks, they needed to win the race to the lightly armed parachute boys. The bridges had to be taken intact and held so as to facilitate just that. Were they not, then the disaster that came three months later at Arnhem might well have happened in Normandy, with even more calamitous results.'

PRESENTER: 'And Peg, short for Pegasus I believe, you were there......Peg.'

WILLIS: 'That's right, and a close run thing it was too. I was in the Ox and Bucks, D Company, under Major Howard, one of the group detailed to take the canal bridge, to this day named Pegasus Bridge. Being the more vulnerable to counter attack, this was the most crucial of the two. We went in with gliders, and I was in the second one down. The pilot was accurate enough, save for the fact that we skidded over quite a deep pond and one of the men jumped into the darkness only to drown. For the landing part, he was the one loss.'

PRESENTER: 'But plenty were to fall over the next few days.'

WILLIS: 'Sadly, yes. The bridges were not well defended, and we'd trained hard......you know up at Exeter where the main road goes over canal then river? We'd spent nights and nights there, storming the crossings and storming them again.'

PRESENTER: 'And you did the business on the Orne.'

WILLIS: 'With a will, but what we couldn't be prepared for was the ordeal of the counter attack. We were like the circled wagon train fending off onslaught after onslaught, desperately waiting for the cavalry. That was the Commando Brigade, and it was about more than linking and seeing them across. Once over we had to follow their tanks into the drop zone and, joining with the rest of the paras, help effect the highland clearance.'

PRESENTER: 'Highland clearance, I see you use those two words on the sketch map you've brought.'

CLARK: 'Show me......Was this a code name you were given, or perhaps heard? I see there's a 'Gustave' here too, next to the arrow marking the Commando thrust down to the crossings an over into this higher ground to the east. I've read several accounts of the operation but never before encountered these.'

WILLIS: 'On D Day plus four a German bullet shattered my right knee. The field surgeon saved my leg, but it never worked again as it should and that was the end of my war. Anyway, during my second night in the forward casualty station a Commando officer was stretchered in to be treated alongside me. Morning came and I was moved out...... probably to make room for more of the worse injured. But he'd taken a back full shrapnel. He was screened off, not expected to last I suppose, so I never got to see him...... but I did hear him. Most of the time he was under sedation, occasionally though he would surface and start moaning about 'Highland Clearance', and about 'Gustave' having to 'See this job through, at all costs'. Then he was wanting a priest, I suppose he must have been Catholic.'

CLARK: 'And was there a Priest?'

WILLIS: 'There was. A Padre had dropped with the landing Brigade. By then the officer was sinking again under sedation. I'm not sure how much of a confession was heard, but certainly the last rites were administered.'

PRESENTER: 'So this 'highland clearance', that he had to see through......'

WILLIS: '......I took to have been the kind of pep talk he might have delivered to his Company, a ' G Company' perhaps, G for Gustave, before the ramp dropped and they charged from landing craft to beach, and then on and up. The man was reliving all this in his delirium, driving his men forward, killing their way inland. No mercy was given or shown on that first day. We'd listened to similar in the glider.'

CLARK: 'And did he survive?'

WILLIS: 'I can't be sure. I saw no face, I heard no name. it was just a voice behind a screen.'

CLARK: 'And was there anyone else there who might have heard?'

WILLIS: 'I would have been the only one close enough.'

CLARK: 'If I may I'd like to take a copy of this, Peg. Perhaps we can run one off here, before we leave.'

PRESENTER: 'Sounds though there could be a project for you in this, Mr Clark, for when thy throw you out of politics and you have to once more make an honest living. We've had 'Crete', we've had 'Barbarossa', next up you might give us 'Pegasus Bridge', or 'Highland Clearance' perhaps . And what about this name 'Peg'?

WILLIS: 'Pegasus after the flying horse on the famous beret. Mine

hangs behind the bar at Bullers Arms, my local. My nick name, 'Peg', was coined by the regulars there.'
PRESENTER: *Yes, in Landrake, just off the main road, ten minutes beyond Tamar Bridge, and this leads us nicely on to the traffic news......after which we can return again to these heroic exploits of forty years ago. Stay with us to hear about his ordeal by sniper and the fearsome 'moaning minnie'......*

*

on the trail
1986
OAKSEY, Malmesbury, Wiltshitre

"Lady Clark..... welcome to 'Green End'. That's quite some journey, all the way across from Kent for just the one day. You could have stayed the night, or perhaps two."

"That, Mrs Huxley, I would have had to explain to my stepson. As it is he'll assume this to have been no more than a day trip into London."

"Do call me Elspeth, Lady Clark, and please accept my condolences. A great man, Lord Clark....... I particularly enjoyed his television series."

"Thank you Elspeth., and you must call me Nolwen. I wasn't married to Sir Kenneth for long....."

".....I know, my dear, I do know, but no one doubts that you brightened those last difficult years."

"How kind, Elspeth, and how kind, too, that you should have agreed to my calling like this. I'm thrilled to be in the company of someone who knew my parents so well, the celebrated Elspeth Huxley no less, she of *The Flame Trees*, and *White Man's Country*, doyenne of the colonial chroniclers....."

"......who took so much of her inspiration from your wonderful father, Frederic Janze, author of *The Vertical Land*, a peerless work." Elspeth led her visitor into the Cotswold stone farmhouse. Soon they were settled at the kitchen table.

"So your stepson is not to hear of this visit," probed the host.

131

"For the same reason that I prefer to speak with you like this, face to face, rather than on the phone or by letter. His father, Sir Kenneth, he was a sweetie to me ...."

".....a gentleman, I remember, whereas young Alan?"

"Less of one, Elspeth, and this is to put it mildly. If this shocks you, then believe me, it's nothing to what he will say to people about me."

"But do I sense a wariness with the contempt?"

"You do, because I know him to be too well in with the Government spooks, those tasked to listen in on telephone calls and intercept mail."

Elspeth leaned back in her chair, eyes narrowing slightly as they searched into those of her guest.

"I think I see where this conversation might be leading," she said. "Something to do with your mother?"

"Yes, it's that book that came out a couple of years ago."

"*White Mischief*, you mean. Written by a Mr James Fox..... the latest raking over of the Erroll business. Fox actually worked with the late Cyril Connolly on the *Sunday Times*. He helped with that colour supplement piece put together back in the late '60s. My impression was that Cyril might have found out a lot more than he dared publish. Ironic really, for the old boy had long striven for the one big story that might have at last secured the kind of recognition so many had predicted."

"And have you also read *White Mischief*?" Nolwen asked.

"I have, because Mr Fox came here seeking my help..... as I've no doubt he came to Saltwood seeking yours."

"And your impressions, Elspeth?"

Elspeth Huxley hesitated. This woman had come a long way, and she herself was getting old, approaching 90 now, so this could be a last chance.

"I was disappointed..... where you've probably been angry, and quite understandably too. There's talk now of *White Mischief* being made into a film, and of Alice de Janze being a plum role for the likes of Sarah Miles. Sarah Miles....!

"Which means we know what's coming, don't we?"

"Doe eyed, dotty promiscuity," sneered the host. "It sells Sunday papers, it sells books, it puts the bums into the cinema stalls, and....." Elspeth checked herself again.

"....and," prompted Nolwen.

"And it can serve as a useful smokescreen."

"To hide what, in your opinion?"

"The truth, Nolwen, which I can't profess to fully know......"

"...... while being fairly sure that Mr Fox doesn't come come near."

"I don't think he even tries to come near, Nolwen. He gets some good leads from me, and what does he do? He ignores them!"

"Concluding that it had been *crime passionnel*, that Jock Broughton was the culprit," added Lady Clark, "and that the jury were wrong to acquit. You don't agree, obviously, and you suspect Fox might have been warned off.....or bought off, with a fat film rights fee, paid in advance. So *White Mischief*, the book and film, it's just more and more smokescreen."

"Unless one focusses on the glaring omissions."

"Glaring, that is, to one such as yourself, Elspeth, one who was out there in '41, living through these events. Be specific."

"There's a man and there's a woman, two people, two names. Both I mentioned to Mr James Fox. The man is studiously ignored."

"And the woman....?"

"......appears only briefly, Nolwen, under a what I would deem a conspicuously strange alias."

"Quite," agreed the visitor, "any alias from an author purporting to present 'the last word' must be a contradiction."

"I speak of his '*Mrs Wirewater*', the married woman with whom Erroll was involved when Jock and his wife arrived in Kenya, the mistress supplanted by Diana Broughton."

"She gets sidelined by Fox," continued Nolwen, "by virtue of a trip she has to make down to South Africa, taking her son to his boarding school. The serious action, the whirlwind fresh romance and the shooting, this all takes place in her absence. You would know her real name, Elspeth?"

"Phyllis Filmer. Her husband was with Shell Oil, based at Shell House Nairobi, Nolwen, this also being an out station of the British Secret Service. Erroll was being closely watched."

"By British agents?"

"By German too of course, and by American...... and there would have been others, which brings me to the second character."

"The man....."

".....who, for me Nolwen, gains particular significance from being so totally absent."

"So again, Elspeth, you have the name....?"

"Israel Maisels..... Mr Israel Aaron Maisels, a distinguished barrister, based in South Africa. Now what would you make of a name like that?"

"It's about as Jewish as you can get."

"And this is the point, Nolwen. On the advice of one Lazarus Kaplan, the Broughtons' solicitor in Nairobi, Maisels was the initial choice to represent Jock at trial. He was approached, and he agreed, but was then obliged to stand aside......"

"......allowing Henry Morris KC to take the case, and win the acquittal."

"Something of *a tour de force* according to Fox," continued Elspeth Huxley. "And by not mentioning Maisels, the author avoids discussion of how the first choice came to relinquish the brief. I've heard that he was pressured to do so by the South African Government, with Smuts, at that time, being closely involved with the High Command in London."

"And this pressure might have been something to do with Maisels and Kaplan being Jews."

"And in particular the place of the barrister in the international Jewish network........ which then concerned itself, of course, with political as well as business and cultural links. I think it significant that Maisels had contacts in all corners of the Zionist movement."

"*All* corners?" Lady Clark was puzzled.

"Famously splinter prone, the movement was never so riven as during the early years of the war, escape for the Jews from Nazi persecution being thwarted by the British White Paper restrictions placed on immigration into Palestine."

"So they were in a jam."

"With some preferring to seek a way out through constructive negotiation," explained Elspeth, "while others wanted to fight. There was a spectrum of opinion, and Maisels had access to every shade."

"So Maisels was forced off the Broughton trial, you think, because his standing in the international Jewish community wasn't going to lie comfortably with all that lay behind Erroll's death."

"I know nothing for certain, Nolwen.....but I have heard

speculation take this direction."

"And are you going to repeat this now?"

"I will, Lady Clark, but first a warning."

*

the pamphleteer

On the same day, in a busy London bookshop.

"*And* the next, please."

"My turn, yes….. there's three books that I ordered last week. I was told that they should be here by today, for collection."

"So your name, sir, was…..?"

"Watts, a Mr Nigel Watts." The spectacled female assistant scanned her latest print-out, giving the customer more than amoment to admire the jet black shoulder length hair, and the smooth skin tapering beneath a subtly filled blouse of white silk.

"Yes," she eventually said. "I have you here now, on my list, and the three books….. all written by Nikolai Tolstoy; *Victims of Yalta, Stalin's Secret War,* and *The Minister and the Massacres.*" She looked up. "I can fetch them now from the stock room." The assistant was briskly and attractively away. She had good legs, and knew as much. He might come back when there was less of a queue. And now she was returning, but with only two books, and a yellow post-it sticker that she was having to scrutinise. Something was awry. It was a chance for him to use the name on her company issue brooch….. an unusual name.

"Three books, you said, Lillia. Is there a problem?"

"I'm afraid, Mr Watts, that *The Minister and the Massacres* is no longer in stock. We only have the two earlier works….."

"…..because you've sold out of the most recent, I suppose. If I re-order, then when you have some more….."

"…..except that it seems that we are unlikely to be having any more. We didn't sell out of *The Minister and the Massacres.* Half went, quickly enough, and then the rest we had to send back to the publisher."

"A product recall."

"In effect…. though not due to any quality issue. We understand

135

it to have been on the advice of their lawyers."

"The publisher's?"

"As I said, their lawyers..... not ours. I think there might be a libel issue. The decision could be part of a settlement. They'll have taken them off library shelves also. You are still happy to take these other two? Less the deposit they come to fiteen pounds." Watts passed his credit card.

"I would have been happier taking the three, Lillia," he muttered, "and that's an unusual name, an interesting name. It wouldn't happen to be......"

"It is, it's Russian. Lillia Ostrovsky. If you're not already familiar with that surname, then before you've finished the first of these books you will be."

"So you've read them?"

"Only bits..... those pointed out to me, relating how narrowly my grandfather escaped being delivered back into the hands of Stalin at the end of the war."

"In accordance with arrangements made between we British and the Soviets at Yalta, you mean. You can claim a personal connection with this same chapter of history that so exercises Nikolai Tolstoy."

"And which so obviously fascinates yourself, Mr Watts," added the young woman enticingly.

"So of this most recent of the three books, you did manage to sell some."

"Just a few."

"And they'll be rarities. Tell me, Lllia, did any of those customers leave a name, as I did mine?"

"I couldn't say, Mr Watts."

"Not today, no, but perhaps you might be able to find out..... maybe if I came back in a few days? We could do lunch perhaps?"

Ben

Roger

Wyston

BOOK TWO (1987)

Evil is unspectacular and always human,
And shares our bed and eats at our own table,
And we are introduced to goodness every day,
Even in drawing rooms among a crowd of faults;
He has a name like Billy and is almost perfect,
But wears a stammer like a decoration:
And every time they meet the same thing has to happen;
It is Evil that is helpless like a lover
And has to pick a quarrel and succeeds
And both are openly destroyed before our eyes.

W.H. Auden 1940; from '*Another Time*'

(i) Whitehall
London; April

"And our last item today concerns the Prime Minister's holiday arrangements. You will recall my raising this with you briefly during our last meeting, Captain Daniels, and now I can say that subject, of course, to our final advice on the security aspect, she and her husband hope, within the next month or so, to accept a long standing invitation from the Viscountess Boyd of Merton to stay at Ince Castle."

As he spoke, the most eminent Sir Clive Faulds produced from his file an aerial photograph of the chosen retreat. Captain Colin Daniels, a security specialist of no mean standing took it with all the respect due to the man who stood now as the most unassailable of the current Cabinet Secretaries. Faulds had long been an executive heavyweight, reflected Daniels, but through this second term for Margaret he'd unquestionably joined the super division.

No one else so so regularly chaired the meetings of the Joint Intelligence Committee. Through him, operations concerned with intelligence gathering and covert action, whether at home (MI5) or abroad (MI6) could just about be said to be democratically accountable. Each agency had its special powers, of course, and beyond, to supplement these, a carefully nutured range of irregular devices and personnel to cover any glaring gap in effectiveness. Though ever available to report his overview to a busy political mistress, Sir Clive was entrusted with a wide but judiciously used discretion. Of some things she would be keen to know, of others, just as keen not to.

Captain Colin Daniels studied the picture. Previously of the army, now with MI5, his remit was VIP protection. He had a proven field record and could be trusted to plan and execute close personal security with military rigour, this making him the ideal subordinate for Faulds, he so much more the career administrator.

Sir Clive had risen through the Foreign Office. It was said that the key to his climb to Mandarin status lay in a readiness to embrace the mood of the Trend Report. During the mid 1970s there had been suggestions, strongly voiced, that UK intelligence services continued to suffer the effects of lasting Soviet penetration. To quell these, Prime Minister Harold Wilson had persuaded Burke Trend out of retirement to review all available evidence.

So had Roger Hollis, Director General during the Macmillan years, been under Soviet control, and likewise his Deputy, Graham Mitchell? Probably no, possibly yes, concluded Trend, but these men were safely dead now, and joined in their long night by most of their close associates. With this in mind the point could be firmly made that it was an improved future that mattered and that over-zealous and over-prolonged mole hunting was likely to be no less detrimental to the effectiveness of MI5 and MI6 than any supposed subversion...... a point long appreciated in Moscow.

Daniels had embraced this rationale and in the previous decade as a junior MI5 officer he'd been careful to stay clear of that stubborn faction within the organisation whose introspective obsessions with Philby and 'Sonia' had cultivated the *Wilderness of Mirrors*. If once they had been the 'Young Turks'; now they were just old men scraping by on eroded pensions, some finding this harder than others. Yes, Stalin's Englishmen had, in their day, wrought grave damage.... but this had been contained, and with the running repairs looking to have held, the game was moving on.

Career-wise, Colin Daniels' 'look forward' stance had been vindicated. So was that it? Was he indeed 'made'...... with continued clean-nosed upward progress assured?

Not quite.

For this was no more than a qualified, up to a point vindication, that point being marked by a final disturbing irony. The brave new world that beckoned was suddenly requiring of him a re assessment of the man who, throughout all before, had been his guiding mentor....... he that, since childhood, he'd known as Uncle Vic.

Though not a true uncle to Colin Daniels, Lord Rothschild had been far more caring and useful to him than most who were. He'd been close to his father in a firm friendship that had stretched back to their Harrow Schooldays. They'd shared many a holiday since, but then Michael Daniels had died of a sudden heart attack, just prior to his son's passing out from Sandhurst, and from that cruel moment there had always been time for young Colin in Uncle Victor's busy prestigious life. The obvious aptitude for army intelligence work was encouraged and, likewise, the phased task by task transfer to MI5.

The Rothschilds, of course, had made theirs one of the great names in British banking. No dynasty could ever better exemplify the benefits of an assimilated Jewry. The family had enriched its adoptive country morally and culturally as well as financially, and in Victor it had offered the service of one of its ablest and bravest sons. Decorated for his wartime valour, his life as a public figure reached its apogee with a top advisory role to the Heath Cabinet in the early 1970s. For Colin Daniels here was valuable, discretely laid patronage, and also a source of wise and measured counsel.

Edward Heath had consulted Rothschild on security matters, and, from listening to Victor, and others, it had been made clear to Colin that even the likes of Sir Clive Faulds would have struggled to have attained their current rank had it not been for his Uncle's forward thinking recommendations. And this, sadly, was what had rendered the more recent developments so unpalatable.

Yes, Victor Rothschild could have been more circumspect perhaps, but that was hardly the point. The assistance he'd given to Peter Bright with his '*Molehunter*' memoirs said everything about this generous nature. Had he refused to help then the surprise would surely have been greater. So help he offered, and by doing so Rothschild himself had blundered into that same *wilderness of mirrors* that he'd guided so many away from and around ...... and this being for *their* safety, for *their* sanity, and not, *most certainly not*, to conceal anything dubious in his own past.

But no wilderness can be without its wolves, and it was to the pack that Uncle Victor had been so ungratefully abandoned........ and worse than that if you believed, as he did, that word of he and his wife's close wartime social contact with the Cambridge spies had been leaked from MI5 at Sir Clive's instigation.

Yes, the Director and their Chiefs were angry with Bright at his seeking to publish those sensitive revelations, and yes, it was understandable that they should seek to deter others from giving the kind of assistance that Rothschild had lent.... but to stoop to dredging all that up from so far back, this was despicable, not least in that there were so few left now who could present the true facts in their proper context. Instead, predictably, the scandalmongers had done their worst. Sensation is what wins circulation, and money, and fame...... and, having been skewered, Uncle Victor was then duly roasted.

The hypocrisy....... this was what Colin found so hard to

swallow. All right, Victor may indeed have been the one who recruited Blunt into the intelligence service.... and, OK, he and his mother had sublet that London apartment to Guy Burgess, but this had been during the war when, for all their eccentric ways, these people were regarded as being way, way above suspicion by all...... to the extent of course of being entrusted with the very highest secrets of State.

It should have been remembered, rather, that Victor had often been abroad at that time, risking his life for King and country, defusing unexploded bombs, dismantling lethal booby traps. And again, the time and the effort he'd more recently put into his Government 'think tank' work had been given unstintingly. Yet now, today, all this had come to count for nothing, just because he'd seen fit to help a fellow patriot in his attempt to enhance an insultingly meagre civil service pension.

Victor Rothschild had been as good as abandoned. Abandoned beneath a cloud of whipped up suspicion, abandoned when he was old, when his faculties were fading, when he was less able to rally and respond and refute. And why? *Pour l' encourager les autres*? No, this was careerism, a minnow minded exhibition of top level cleverness.

Duplicity had to have its part in the great game of diplomatic bluff, but that wasn't to say there could be no place for common decency. Maybe it was inadvisable, what he'd done, but that said Uncle Victor could and should have been spared this. And that he'd not, had meant no one could feel secure...... and this was what could be so corrosive to morale.

It was high time Faulds' own initiatives were subjected to scrutiny, thought Daniels quietly. As often as Sir Clive had been heard to laud team spirit, by his own repertoire of tricks that same ethos could only be undermined. The man was due a come uppance...... so said Uncle Victor, and, privately, Colin Daniels was certainly disposed to agree.

And this is what had led him into the occasional company of another disaffected eminence, another upper-housed malcontent who likewise considered himelf in receipt of very poor reward for his years of competent, loyal service to King, Queen, and Country. A former soldier, this, and later a Conservative politician of no mean accomplishment. And he'd risen on merit, had Lord Aldington, as he was now, to feature in the Heath administration almost as prominently as had Rothschild, again as a trusted advisor and close confidant. For a too often beleaguered Party Leader and one time Premier, famously unmarried, this pair had been true bricks.

But now, with the prayers of the faithful finding answer in the form of the 'Blessed Margaret', Sir Edward was very much out of fashion and these disaffected friends cruelly out on their own. Whilst enduring very different slurs, it was all too apparent to Daniels that each had been cast in the same unhappy role, each was a scapegoat...... a fate that could just as easily be his were he to be less than watchful of his own back.

Thinking of Sir Edward Heath reminded Daniels that Ince had been considered as a Prime Ministerial retreat a dozen or more years before. He'd heard this from his Uncle Victor, who could clearly remember Sir Clive's predecessor firmly vetoing the motion. It was interesting that Faulds, in all else so conservative, so very careful, should now feel able to adopt the idea with such enthusiasm.

Equally uncharacteristic was this odd reluctance to pass down responsibility for the finer details of this operation. Daniels was accustomed to hearing of the 'where', of the 'when', and of the 'for how long', the 'for whom' and the 'with whom', and then being left to recruit and make such dispositions of personnel as he, himself, saw fit.

If it had been somewhere unfamiliar then preliminary enquiries and visits would be undertaken at his own discretion. This time, however, Faulds appeared strangely unready to pass the reins. For the moment this photograph was being shown rather than given. It was something to chew over here rather than be taken away and digested.

"Looking down like this, Colin, we see the beauty of the place..... I mean for our purposes. Though not an island, it has what's virtually a full box-like perimeter...."

"..... with the water on three sides, and the main rail line along the fourth," observed Daniels.

"And you see that the sole vehicular access is by this lane which crosses the narrow spur saddling the short rail tunnel."

"Which can be barely a third of a mile from portal to portal." Daniels' finger traced along the distance as he spoke.

"For this operation I have decided on a strict division of labour," declared Sir Clive. "I will assemble and personally supervise a team to guard the length of the road down to the Castle itself. With your team you will watch the length of the river shore and the boundaries to railway property...."

"......including the tunnel itself?"

"Leave the actual track and the tunnel to me," said Faulds.

Daniels would have preferred things otherwise, with either he or his senior taking total operational control, but for the moment he could voice no practical objection. His tacit agreement was accepted, and the subordinate left to suppress a niggling sense of vulnerability. The arrangement was such that he could find himself carrying the can for errors of another..... and, dirty for dirty, this meant that he ought now to move into place a potential scapegoat of his own, just in case, for an effective lieutenant never took the full rap. He was there to share it, and see it dispersed amongst his *own* subordinates.

'Be wary of Faulds,' Uncle Victor had often warned. 'Assume an undeclared personal agenda. Play along, but be alert.' If there was one in this then, as yet, even to a man who made vigilance his profession, it remained obscure. But he could speak with his mentor, who also knew something of the place, and he could prepare, lest indeed it was an arena in which the over-mighty Sir Clive might be tempted to over-stretch.

Such was the context of Daniels' own team selection. Craft was required. The right kind of talents, placed and primed and suitably provoked, they might be the key to inflicting that measure of embarrassment felt to be Faulds' due.

"What about to the south, across the water?" continued Daniels, quietly wondering if geography might offer cover, natural and convenient, beneath which to shield and incubate his germ of subterfuge. "Will we have firm control on the facing bank of the estuary?"

From a brief sift through a miscellany of stacked desk documents and Faulds produced a standard 'Land Ranger' OS map. Just the one quarter of its full extent sufficed to illustrate his reply.

"You see the Tamar flowing from north to south....."

"......to enter the Sound with its breakwater, with this being the English Channel beyond."

"Well discounting the Plym, over here, which enters the Sound separately from the east of the City, the Lynher is the lower of the two main tidal tributaries."

"The other being the Tavy, joining here, from the Devon side," pointed Daniels, "above the Saltash bridges."

"But, below the railway, just there, Ince sits on the northern shore of the Lynher. It looks across what can be full tide water or low tide mud to Antony....."

"..... the village here, on the A road that makes towards the car ferry at Torpoint."

"Yes, and as you see, Antony sits on an isthmus. Even by helicopter, from there to Mount Edgcumbe and Rame, along here, at the end of the peninsula, is a good four miles..... but with the way it carves into South East Cornwall, Whitsand Bay brings the open sea to within two comfortably walked miles."

"Not so comfortable if you're climbing from the shore. Those cliffs look daunting."

"Indeed so, and this means that to command the isthmus at Antony is to be well placed to defend the Dockyard from any assault or bombardment launched from the Cornish side. One hundred years ago Plymouth and its Dockyard were considered so important as to be worthy of a ring of stout fortifications and the two westernmost of these were constructed, less than a mile apart, just here.... the twin forts of Tregantle and Scraesdon."

Daniels' finger went again to the map.

"This is Tregantle, the highest, overlooking the coast.... still in use, it seems."

"With Scraesdon, disused apart from an occasional war game exercise, a little lower, just a bit to the north, right next to Antony village. In fact the main road has to veer around the structure. So overgrown is it that not many motorists appreciate this. The route naturally seeks the line of the riverfront and eyes are drawn towards the water. The twist past Wacker Quay is always remembered while Scraesdon, high but tree screened, goes relatively un-noticed. When the forts were built a short military railway was installed to bring supplies up from thte quay. The line has been long dismantled, but the old engine shed remains."

"Down by the water, here." Daniels was tapping the map. "Looks to be a quiet little picnic spot, one for the birdwatchers."

"Ideal, but more so in winter..... for in recent summers it has become a regular haunt for travelling folk." Faulds' tone conveyed more than a hint of distaste.

"Of the New Age variety, you mean?"

"All sorts..... benefit scrounging drifters, itinerant market traders, the more traditional sort of Gypsy, every species there is. They slip in and slip out with their caravans and their trucks. You won't find it empty."

"So Scraesdon overlooks them, and the Lynher estuary...."

144

"..... including its far shore..."

"..... on which stands Ince Castle."

"And it might be useful to you to know that both forts are still Ministry of Defence owned. With Scraesdon, disuse has brought disrepair. Tregantle however is in frequent use."

"It holds soldiers?"

"Soldiers with weapons, and live ammunition. It looks out over the sea, and set into the cliff-side are firing ranges. The fort itself gives accommodation...... draughty by all accounts. To warm them up they have bayonet drill."

"Charging at dummies, and all that?"

"Drop in at the local, *The Finnygook*, and you might hear rumour of sheep being trucked over from Liskeard Market. Whatever, just bear in mind a possible resource. You've liaised with the MOD before."

"Do they have anything else? What about here, where the chain ferry comes across from Devonport?"

"The Navy are big on the Torpoint spur." Sir Clive, an RN conscript spoke with authority. "This spread here is HMS Raleigh, an important shore based basic training establishment.... and they have the use of Jupiter Quay, an all tide jetty, accessed through the grounds of Antony House. That could be useful for patrolling Ince from the East. But be careful. Too large a team, too much liaison, and too many people know. Word gets around, and security is compromised before we even start. For the moment I'm asking for a small team, one placed essentially to protect. You're not to be diverted from that task, not by anything happening across the water, or on the water, on the railway, or on the road. In any such event, pull back. Think about establishing a tenable perimeter around the Castle itself."

"So I leave any pursuit to yourself," checked Daniels.

"I'll have personnel appropriately equipped," confirmed Faulds, "and briefed."

The exchange was moving onto controversial ground, sensed Daniels. Shoot-to-kill, licensed at top level, a regime off-limits to all but the invited, himself *not*, as yet, included.

"We can be relied upon to be looking the other way." Daniels spoke calmly, without looking up. Yes, he mulled, he would certainly guard the principal as instructed ..... but he might also needed to guard his own position, and this required a closer scrutiny of his superior's as yet opaque motives. The game was on.

*

(ii) girl and boy

Brown eyed Sally Shaw, 17, with the pale skin and the shoulder length chestnut hair, long in the leg and lithe of movement, is an only child. She lives with her parents in the tucked away bijou village of St John, found between Torpoint and Millbrook. Having graduated from the small village Primary in Antony she has now, for six years, crossed the water to the Devonport High School for Girls, the most reputable of the City of Plymouth's state Grammars.

She loves words, and languages, and sport. Her ambition is to be a journalist, like her father, but rather than entering his field, which is local radio, she hopes her break will be into Newspapers, at national level. Her parents and her teachers are supportive. She has flair, she works hard, and few doubt a big time potential which is already being developed by the regular weekend and holiday work experience secured for her at Harmsworth House, the George St H.Q. of the City's provincial Daily.

Each Wednesday, after school, she will stay in Plymouth to assist with the assembling of the Thursday edition of *The Western Morning News* .... and those six hours, divided equally and successively between the features, the news, and the sports desks, go so, so, quickly, particularly that last period when, during the season, the late midweek football action has to scramble for space before the falling deadline.

For herself, though, swimming is the main sport. She represents her school, with regular success, and this helps to an all round self confidence which falters a shade in just the one aspect of her life...... that concerning boys, young men with similar interests and aspirations, of about the same age, perhaps a little older. There will be plenty, she knows, when she moves on to College, but for this she is feeling a little unprepared.

There were none at school, of course, and very few in the village. Her time would come and she would cope. She knew that, but a little more practice now...... this would be nice. So where was she to find opportunity for such?

Maybe at Bovisand, she was thinking to herself. For with each session there, young Chas was looking more and more to be of the right mettle. Chas Cross, who hated being called Charles, because that too easily brought to mind a grey ruin of a church on a traffic roundabout, a police station, and an ugly concrete carpark. He found her attractive, she was sure of that, but there was his natural inhibition...... understandable, maybe, but frustrating all the same. For while he might be an admirer Chas, no more than a year older, was also her instructor.

His father, Tony Cross, operated the diving centre where Sally was now mid way through her twenty week Saturday morning SCUBA course. As young as he was, Chas was qualified, capable and trusted. Routines had to be closely observed. Concentration was essential. Safety depended on authority, and to flirt would be to compromise both. Sally realised this, admiring his sense of responsibility, but hoping none the less, for the lingering glance and the smile, and an invitation to make and privately share a little spare time.

But to passively hope and dream had never been her way. She could actively impress, and, if not immediately with Chas then certainly with his father Tony, she would. He was running a business, and positive mention across the local media had to be desirable. A girl with contacts, at the *Morning News* and, through her father, with *Plymouth Sound Radio*, was to be courted.

There was a story in this man, Sally Shaw could sense this. And it was one he was ready to have told, and have her tell.... and so it was that at half term, while Chas was at his day job as a dockyard apprentice, she had taken a tape recorder across to Fort Bovisand and encouraged Shaw senior to tell as much as he wished.

She learned that the master diver's widely respected expertise, together with most of his investment into the Bovisand venture, had been hard earned beneath the North Sea rigs, over many years his bread and butter. But this wasn't to say that he'd never indulged a gambler's streak. More than once he'd hired himself to a decidedly chancy deep sea salvage operation, and more than once emerged from a profit share arrangement with a firmly negotiated slice of precisely nothing.

But, for Tony Cross, that was life when lived at the limits. 'No venture no gain,' he would say, the appetite for risk insatiate.

This reckless vein had been a factor in the failure of his marriage to Chas's mother, but in fairness he had been as keen as she to have the boy focus his energies into the valuable apprenticeship he'd secured at the

Dockyard. Now though, as if through some perverse gene activated by discouragement, many of the father's traits and talents were emerging in the son.

Any time spare, and too much that was not, was spent in neoprene, and now, it seemed the latest initiative was one jointly conceived, a scheme that to begin with would need to be kite-flown across the community. If it was to be financed then it had to be sold, and this required first a sounding, and here was where Tony Cross hoped Sally might help..... with the column inches.

And that hope had been realised. Within a week the transcript had been submitted and discussed, and within two it became a finished article.

SIR FRANCIS: A HOMECOMING?

The remains of Sir Francis Drake, committed to the deep off Panama almost 500 years ago, could now be found and retrieved claims Bovisand based diver Tony Cross.

"The position was carefully logged," he says, "and the depth and local currents have long been charted. We know too that Drake was honoured with a leaden coffin the detection of which should now be within the scope of advanced sonar and remote camera technology."

Plymouth born Cross has had long experience of working at the extreme frontiers of the divers realm, having been deeply involved in the installation and maintenance of offshore oil and gas equipment in our North Sea fields. He looks forward to working in warmer tropical waters.

"Ideally I would like to get a film company on board, for we have here the makings of a splendid documentary...... the suspense of the search, the exotic location, a wonderful story from the past, replete with cast of colourful historical figures. It could go all across the world, creating global interest in Plymouth and also, of course, in any local firms who might feel persuaded to assist with sponsorship. This said, I realise that as a community we first need to debate the issue of where, if at all, in Plymouth, or in Tavistock, or elsewhere, Sir Francis might finally be laid to rest."

Tony and Chas were delighted, as was Sally of course, for as well as being a story that might run it wasn't yet so important as to require being put into more experienced, more professional hands. The delight, though, was to be short lived.

Perhaps Sally had been too pleased, for certainly she was too hasty in putting it to her father that he might use the story for an item in his radio programme, the weekly hour long phone-in slot scheduled for the following day. He could invite spontaneous on-air comment, she suggested, but neglected to clear this, both at the paper and at Bovisand. And suddenly the whole project was jeopardy...... before it was really begun.

"......and furthermore, Mr Shaw, I don't mind saying it to the rest of your listeners that this one is of the view that Mr Tony Cross is no more than a disgrace to all we who are proud to call ourselves Plymothians."

"Strong words there, Mrs Eileen James of St Judes......and do call me Graham, Mrs James ...... Would you care to give us your reasons?"

"Correct me if I'm wrong, Mr Shaw, but I've heard it said that Tony Cross was a member the team that dived down to wreck of HMS Edinburgh......"

"......sunk by the Germans during the last war, somewhere to the north of Norway. I have heard of the wreck, and the salvage attempt, but I know nothing of Cross's involvement".

"She was torpedoed whilst fetching a payment being made by Russia to Britain of gold bullion, then valued at £20 million."

"And most of this was successfully recovered, and split three ways I believe, between the two governments and the salvage team......."

"Led by a character named Jessop, and he had expenses to meet, after which he was into clear profit which, by the laws of our land was subject to tax."

"So your point is, Mrs James......?"

"...... firstly, that the amount left behind in the wreck, on the stated grounds that it was inaccessible, was in fact very accessible. Indeed it was made so by Jessop's men so as to enable a Russian team to perform a later salvage, the worth of which could then be quietly halved. The tax man doesn't hear about this, of course, so we of the British public are twice cheated."

"And there's another point......?"

"That ship, Mr Shaw, is a war grave. There have been reports that the divers conducted pranks with human remains, the bones of British *sailors, some of them possibly Devonport based. Go up to the Hoe, to the Naval Memorial. Read the names listed at its foot, thousands of them, all lost at sea. By their conduct Jessop and his men have insulted every single sailor there, together with their forefathers, those who served under Nelson, and yes, those who served under Drake. And now Mr Cross wants us to sponsor the ultimate desecration."*

"So you say no, Mrs James."

"I say it's time the man was run out of town. Fort Bovisand is Ministry of Defence property. He should be evicted, and he should be brought before the Inland Revenue and audited down to the last halfpenny."

"Thank you Mrs Eileen James. Certainly a strong reaction there. Is there anyone brave enough to differ, I wonder. The phone lines are still open. Keep calling, and we'll have more on this after the lunchtime News and Weather."

Sally blamed herself. She was appalled. How could she face them now? How could she continue with that course?"

*

(iii) Kate, James, and Enid

Kate Rogers, formerly of the casualty department at the Truro City Hospital, and before that with the Queen Alexandra Nursing Corps, is embarked on a second career move. She remains a nurse, but is retraining now to work in Psychiatric medicine. For more than a year she has been attached to St Lawrence Hospital, in Bodmin, the vast spreading institution that rolls down and away from the forbiddingly walled old County Asylum, some of the wards of which are still put to use. 'Sinister use', say the ignorant and fearful, but such rumour will ever seep from walls so thick and tall.

Content to live alone now, Kate rents a small grey two bedroom terrace cottage in Ruthernbridge, a sheltered streamside hamlet no more than two and a half miles to the west of the hospital. She keeps a twenty year old Morris Minor car, mainly to take her to work, but often she will leave herself time to enjoy the pleasant walk, knowing that colleagues driving the same lanes can be relied upon for assistance should they find her delayed by unexpectedly inclement weather.

Sometimes she will sing as she walks, rehearsing choral pieces, for she has joined the Bodmin Choral Society and needs to practise when she can. For across a dozen years of disuse the once reliably firm schoolgirl alto has, as if to sympathise with her figure, thickened to a matronly contralto with a slightly disquieting upper range wobble. But no matter, for she has been told that such voices as hers are scarce in these parts and, after passing a suspiciously perfunctory audition she has been warmly encouraged by the committee's view that with regular and careful exercise her younger form might yet be regained.

The Society would frequently join with the Mid Cornwall Orchestra and, on major projects, sometimes stretch to hiring in professional soloists, the amateurs feeling more comfortable in the preparation and performance of a solid accompaniment. But the paid principals' rehearsal time was limited, of course, and so it was that Kate had found herself filling some of the solo parts as a kind of rehearsal understudy during the preparations for this year's production of Britten's *Spring Symphony*.

The work was new to her, and the parts by no means easy…. but how well she had risen to this challenge. Her musical soul seemed to have responded to the composer's choice of lyric. She'd surprised and impressed with what by any measure was a remarkable contribution, one fulsomely appreciated by chorus and orchestra alike…..some even confessing to having been inspired.

And here was one now, in his car, slowing to squeeze past as she turned with a smile and a wave. He might have stopped if she hadn't been now almost within sight of the hospital, for James Busbridge knew well that this was where she was headed, even though not strictly a colleague.

Once he had been a patient. Years before her time, that was, and on discharge he'd chosen to keep up a contact through membership of 'The Friends of St. Lawrence', a charitable association with a long and worthy history of raising much needed funds for equipment and also offering lay support to patients' relatives. He too is a member of the Choral Society, and it had been largely through his efforts that they had secured the use of the hospital's Foster Hall as an ideal rehearsal venue. It was comfortably large enough and, during the winter, far warmer than Bodmin Church where the concert had eventually been staged early in May.

James Busbridge was a baritone, and if the voice was weakening as he approached 60, the benefit drawn long ago from a good Cathedral School musical education was his for life. In the choir he was very much a leader, but not so in the 'Friends'. Amongst this group he was content to leave committee matters to those who could better defend their integrity, being that his original introduction to St Lawrence was by order, in the form of a sentence handed down by a Crown Court Judge.

Like Kate, Busbridge lives alone. His cottage is in Tremorebridge, no more than a mile upstream from Ruthernbridge and, if anything, even more secluded. Well off the beaten track, one would say, and in the car age certainly so, but not since forever. For the valley between Tremore and Ruthernbridge carries the ancient 'Saints Way', a route by which voyaging early pilgrims could traverse the county port to port, between Padstow and Fowey, rather than risk a hazardous circumnavigation of Penwith, the Lizard, and the Dodman.

And now this signposted modern version has been brushed up. Linking footpath and byway it can offer the hiker a rewarding alternative to groping along a fog bound coast..... but few will think to pause at Tremore. For diversion they might instead climb to the elegant Church of Withiel village, or drop to Grogley where the gentle Camel swerves sharply northward to the Atlantic as if summoned by the rumble of Doombar surf. James Busbridge and his few neighbours can meanwhile be left to their treasured tranquillity.

Lean, balding, and easing now from sprightly middle to active old age, the fellow keeps up a neat, if slightly frayed-cuff appearance. Seldom is he seen out without jacket and tie. His home never lacks for maintenance, nor his hedges and lawns for a trim. Those neighbours would agree him to be polite.... but affable? No. He is too brisk about his business, and, in such homely surroundings as these, far too guarded.

Outwardly, such fastidiousness suggests an unremarkable respectability, but this can be misleading. Take a little more time, look and listen a little more closely, and a less conventional cut will emerge. Ask for instance after an employment history, so often the accurate tell-tale, and find, by piecing fragment to fragment, that here is a character who is considerably more than just fairly unusual.

A meritorious National Service was followed by skilled work in the Naval design office of Vickers Armstrong, a job to take him across the world and also bestow a specialist's insight into the arcane intricacies of international arms procurement, an insight which he can admit to have drawn the interest of MI6.

So does this mean that on coming to live in Cornwall he was able to name his price in the local market for labour? Evidently not, for it seems that the best that he could initially find was a job in the despatch section of a local bacon packing firm, Couch's, a large and growing concern, in which for a good man there had to be scope to rise.... and did James Busbridge? No..... far from it. Something possessed him to start filching from the orders. He was found out, dismissed and prosecuted.

Reports were submitted and imprisonment was avoided, but not so the criminal record. He was in a hole. For a man of his age it was deep, and the sides steep. But all is never fully lost. For there was time now to read, and soon a lively interest in intelligence matters was taking him from library, to bigger library, and on to archive. The reading became note taking, and then writing.... letters at first, dashed off to the local press, usually touching on Naval incidents, the earliest of several being the loss of the M1 submarine back in 1925, and the latest, the disappearance of 'Buster' Crabb in 1956.

The letters were well received. Space would always be found for they could be guaranteed to raise reader response. He tried then the national broad sheets, and from the wider public came similar approval. Soon he was giving interviews, writing commissioned articles, and the next thing had to be a book.... *'Secrets of the Seas'*.

'Popular' rather than 'learned', he seemed to thrive on the contentious premise, the shedding of new light on old intelligence mysteries. There was the loss of the *Glorious*, and ordeal of convoy *PQ17*. His way of mixing drama with controversy rarely failed.

Penetrative research, that was his trade mark. Rarely would he descend to the spurious. He seemed to have a nose for the right file, even amongst records claimed by others to have been deliberately shuffled or weeded. And if the file begged an interview then no distance or expense seemed too great to secure the relevant testimony.

Indeed, to Defence Ministry and Foreign Office officials he was beginning to be an irritant, so adept was he at pointing out inconsistencies between the records of this department and that. It had even been considered that maybe he was being used by a person, or even people, on the inside as a means of circumventing secrecy law constraints. Such suggestions amused James Busbridge, indeed he found them quite pleasing. They lent an extra credence to his work, plus, of course, extra entertainment to the reading public.

For denial can be counterproductive, of course. Far better it was to add to the intrigue, and lend extra spice to the paranoia..... and this he'd done recently by admitting that he was distantly related to Peter Bright, the retired and embittered MI5 dirty tricks specialist whose written in exile memoir, *Molehunter*, was causing such consternation amongst Government's legal advisers. Were they really cousins, and did they maintain frequent contact? These kind of questions were encouraged only to be evaded. It suited Busbridge, and his sources, that he shouldn't be taken too seriously. The image preferred and projected was that of the inspired amateur.

Not that he was ever likely to be taken too seriously by the inhabitants of the parish of Withiel, for even prominent celebrity can struggle to cut ice in Cornwall.... and this man is a long, long way from achieving or even from wanting that. Between his sporadic forays into the big wide world James Busbridge likes to keep his head well down. But this isn't to say that the he has no interest in what for a dozen years now has been his adoptive locality. He likes the sea, and shows a particular taste for the havens along Cornwall's wilder north coast. Trebarwith is a regular haunt, as is Port Isaac, and just as often, further down, St Agnes and Porteath.

But it is in Bodmin that he is most likely to be recognised, in his nearest large town where, naturally, he is well known amongst regulars at the Public Library. And then there is this interest he maintains in St Lawrence. In his brush with the law, almost ten years ago now, Busbridge was deemed unwell rather than dishonest and accordingly referred to the hospital for an apparently successful course of psychiatric counselling. The sessions ended, and the new investigative persona blossomed, but not, it seems, without holding to a sense of security drawn from the very fabric of the institution, its staff, and latterly its 'Friends'.

Did this betray a hunger to belong? No, and neither did he crave understanding..... he just liked to feel accepted, and to be useful.

And useful he certainly was, not least in his apparent concern for those patients who were in to stay, the incurable. Their degeneration might be remorseless, but for as long as he could be recognised, and even after, he brought comfort...... to the afflicted and also to family members and friends who could still bear to visit. James Busbridge showed interest in them, and in their memories of happier times.

This was more than mere morbid fascination. In fact, if challenged, he would be quite open. He liked to circulate this thesis that some amongst these patients might be victims, that they were suffering from either having worked at or having lived too close to the now disused Nancekuke chemical warfare research facility sited on the old wartime airfield laid some twenty five miles distant, between Porthtowan and Portreath, a short way from Scorrier. What he was learning from gentle exchange with patients, and families, and friends, he was noting; and while there had been no pattern as yet, he remained hopeful that in time one might emerge to in some way complement observations made on a range of basic samples collected from the north coast shore....... water from its cold rock pools and dank, dripping caves and, with this, its feeding weeds and molluscs, and even shrimps and small crabs.

Fastidiously he would compare like with like, looking he said for blemishes, and for impaired reflexes..... but, as yet, without luck. And naturally this had become somethiing of a joke amongst the hospital staff. For here was Don Qixote with a scatter-gun, preposterous but well meaning, absurdly harmless, and, lovably useful.

Kate Rogers knew this, but left it to others to scoff-off or patronise these dilettante ways. She held the man in firm respect, not least for his musicianship. The words 'odd', or 'eccentric' were too dismissive. She preferred 'curious', a description all the more apt for its ambiguity. For if, in some ways, to be curious is to be alive then James Busbridge is indeed a curious man.

And we can stay for the moment with Kate, as she walks the lane to work, and pick up a fragment of the duet that she is currently working on with the curious man, this at the suggestion of one of the female elders of the Society. Always a spinster and a far better pianist now than singer, Enid is attempting to coax the pair to a performance of Britten's fifteen minute Canticle *Abraham and Isaac*.

Were they to put this together between them then for her this would be the realisation of a long cherished dream. *Billy Budd*, she feels, is the composer's masterpiece, the work that stands as the lasting monument to his genius, and with this Canticle, written soon after its completion, she finds a distillation of that most profound and puzzling moment in the grand piece when Captain Vere must tell his loyal young crewman that he is to hang from the yardarm. Like Britten she has read Herman Melville's original story in which the writer portrays his Vere as one who '*may in the end have caught Billy to his heart, even as Abraham may have caught young Isaac on the brink of resolutely offering him up in obedience to the exacting behest*'.

For that last interview which Vere must conduct, the composer can find no words...... just music, in the succession of chords that end Act Three. They must, surely, in all their measured intensity, reveal something about about the composer himself, but what? Many had speculated, but it was a puzzle still unanswered. For when in his own life had Ben been felt compelled to sacrifice the innocence of another? Was it, as some maintained, about a struggle within to suppress pederastic lust? No, Enid wasn't accepting this, and the sweetly resolved Canticle was her argument that it could never be anything so sordid. For Ben had his Peter, and while together they might enjoy their fantasies, these could remain their private affair, and as such an absolute right ...... like it was *her* right to enjoy *her* own. Fantasies they could harmlessly, discretely, and decently stay.

Those chords, to her they spoke of a far more permanent and weightier concern than any that might stem from fleeting carnal lust, and if expressed enigmatically rather than explicitly, then so be it. For since when did great art have to be fully and precisely understood? With the best and most lasting it will often be enough to merely enjoy. And enjoy this Canticle, she now would.

James would manage Abraham reasonably comfortably. She had long felt that, but the right partner had been elusive...... until now. For here was Kate with the potential. If she really worked at it, and they didn't fall out between the three of them, she promised to make a more than passable Isaac. And so far, so good, all is harmony. Busbridge is confident enough, Kate is still game, and beneath her pinned silvery bun, cotton frocked Enid stokes this, her pet project, with growing enthusiasm.

She says that back in the '60s she sang under Britten himself, this when the War Requiem was premiered at the rebuilt Coventry Cathedral and she was in one of the choirs. She can recall a profoundly moving occasion, and laud particularly the contribution of Heather Harper, '*the great*' Heather Harper she would say, who'd been summoned in to 'rescue' the event when Galina, the planned and rehearsed soloist, had been at the last moment barred from travelling to England by the Russian

Government.

But *her* Heather had held the whole thing together, Enid maintains, with a performance which, while if not perfect, was as heroic in its own way as *her* Kath's had been of Isaac back in the early '50s.

Kate was left to wonder on that possessive..... sensing in it a sapphic intensity, an unmet desire long sublimated to music.

'*Farewell, farewell, forever and forever......*' trills the nurse, Enid's frail fingered piano chords chiming brightly in her mind's ear as on she strides.

A shade over an hour later, and James Busbridge can be found in Bodmin's ring road car park, sitting at the wheel of his trusted two door Viva. He has taken and almost used an hour's worth of ticket, sufficient to call at his favoured Fore St baker, at the fruit shop, and at the newsagent's between. He has the *Telegraph* delivered every day, but not The *Western Morning News*, unless engaged in one of his periodic letters' page exchanges. At the moment he is not, so just one copy a week can keep him abreast of the regional news agenda and today's will be it.

By chance, though, on his return to the car he'd spotted a two day old edition crumpled into the bin near the ticket machine. Now, before addressing the fresh news he uses his remaining minutes to smooth and scan the staled.

Soon most of it will be re-binned, but less the half of one page that this scavenger decides to tear off, fold, and tuck between the pages of his fresh paper. Such are the ways of curious men.

Busbridge then feels into his pocket, and he has change enough for a further half-hour's parking. Another ticket is bought and displayed, and the car re-locked. Back he climbs to the Fore St, this time to use the Public Library. He finds and searches through the Cornwall and West Devon telephone directory, and is soon emerging with the number. He crosses to the newsagents seeking extra change, successfully, and then continues down towards Mount Folly Square where stand the public telephones.

As he waits his turn he re-reads what he was lucky not too have missed. His call is answered, and he is fortunate. Mr Cross is there, and he can come to the phone for the 'quick word' requested.

"Mr Cross?... hello, Mr Cross. We've not met. I could give you my name, but I would rather not. I phone from Bodmin though, from a call box, and I have before me the pieces that have appeared in the *Morning News* this week."

"......and?"

"We need to talk."

"...... and you're ready with sponsorship support. Either that or you think the whole idea in extremely poor taste, a desecration."

"Neither, Mr Cross. You speak with a historian. Earlier this year I went to the main French Naval archive, the Vincennes archive. You know it, don't you?"

"Research is part of the diver's business."

"Granted, Mr Cross, but by chance, I happened to call up the very same file that you had inspected the previous day. It hadn't been re-consigned to the vault, and when the assistant produced it so remarkably quickly he carelessly volunteered the name of the English person who'd made this preceding enquiry."

"So you were given my name......"

"...... to go with the object of your research, which I want neither of us to mention now. I obviously have an interest in the same thing. You have reasons for masking that interest, and so do I. Maybe a face to face chat could be of mutual benefit?"

"Early next week would suit me. Say where, say when......"

*

(iv) Eamon Carroll
London

Eamon Carroll rents a three-roomed basement flat in Queens Park. Most who ride through London in his traditional style black cab would put him at forty. In fact he is a worn and slightly paunchy thirty five. His vehicle, no less shabby, has had three previous owners, and, as durable as these taxis will often prove, this one is becoming expensive to maintain. For running costs must be measured in time as well as money and it's becoming too often now that half a day needs to be given to under the bonnet work.

He has no garage. The cab has to endure all weathers and the tools and the spare parts are beginning to clutter Eamon's already cramped living space. It was whispered to him a while back that 'the movement' might help finance the purchase of a newer model, but hopes raised were starting now to fade. There were still the half dozen pub collection boxes, the monies from which he gathered and forwarded...... but his contribution in terms of active work had lessened considerably during the past two years. While remaining on their list of people movers he had slipped way, way down, and no longer did they come for those old fare-timing clocks, a speciality of his to the extent that he still had a bedroom drawer full of the things. A lethal business, working with explosives, a nasty business, but war is war, and so far as he knew such components as he'd supplied had been faultless. They would knock again, he was convinced.

It had just become dark when the rap came. Eamon Carroll waited, and there it was once more, in the coded rhythm, distinct on the door panel. He moved cautiously to the door. Bending, he pushed at the letter flap.

"Password?"

"*Shannon*," replied an outside voice. The latch was turned, the bolt drawn, the door pushed..... and suddenly Carroll was on the floor. He was pinned. Four men were through, at least three of them heavyweights, but all with the one concern. They were here to take man rather than property. Gag, blindfold, cuffs, applied simultaneously by at least six hands, concerted and strong, rendered the assailed powerless. He was hauled to his feet and as good as dragged from his home, up the steps, and across the pavement to the waiting van.

He was bundled into the back, two following him to bind his legs as the doors thudded shut. The driver was in and the engine started. The van lurched away. To struggle was senseless. The best Connors could do was to attempt to use his intimate knowledge of the street patterns to divine a direction. Locally, he could be confident. He could sense speed, and corners, and gradient. He knew all the twists of the unavoidable one way systems, and he even had a feel for the rhythms of the traffic lights.

They were moving towards Paddington, he was sure. No more than ten minutes from his flat, he knew the railway terminus well. He was a regular on the rank. He anticipated the girder-bridge to the west of the platforms. The ironwork offered a sound of its own. This would be confirmation, confirmation that they were headed towards the river. And there....? Connors shuddered at the thought.

They were making the approach, the small traffic system, and the gently curving rise onto the bridge deck.... except suddenly this was no longer happening. Instead of vaulting the tracks they had edged into the filter lane, that which fed the parcels platforms beneath the northernmost of Brunel's arched canopies.

This could only mean a train journey. Metal riding mysteriously, distantly, on hard metal rather than soft rubber on familiar London street. So where was he bound now? He knew not.... but at least it wasn't to be that murky river.

*

(v) St Erney

Cornwall, meanwhile, still enyoyed twilight. Declan McDaid was finishing an evening's tidying in and around the quaint, slate walled, squat towered church that sank so snuggly into its simple sloping graveyard. The damp clippings lay in his wheel barrow, weighted and brightened by the tools he'd brought to use ..... the orange power strimmer with its yellow extension lead and the pair of red handled garden shears. He wouldn't need the strimmer tomorrow at Ince, but VIPs were coming, apparently, so the shears he would, when sharpened, and this job he could do back at the cottage. He'd used a brush also, and a rake, but these had been paid for from Parish funds and will, for their consecrated status, rest at the back of the rather damp and dingey bell tower next to the long handled feather duster with which he'd just taken to the worst of the cobwebs spun within.

Declan McDaid stows them together, into the corner, carefully, so as not to clutter the space needed by the ringers when they come on their once a fortnight practice evening. He turns then to leave, on the way pausing to straighten the small notice that hangs close to the plaque which names 'The Fallen' of two World Wars. Above the notice hangs Peg's maroon beret, rescued by McDaid from the *Buller's* last autumn when the

160

brewery changed its management.

The notice would often need adjustment. In the dim light it was near impossible to read without being lifted down and angled towards one of the windows. It was gratifying to think that people were taking the trouble to look, thought Declan as he again read through the words, his own words.

Worn by Stanley 'Pegasus' Willis, lately of this Parish, who as a soldier with the 6th Airborne Division was one of the first to land in Normandy on the 6th June1944.

On the 5th September, following 91 days of continuous fighting, his unit, D Company, was withdrawn from front line combat. All told, by death, wounding, and capture the unit had been reduced to a complement of 40, from an original D Day strength of 181.

For many months after his disappearance, almost three years ago, McDaid had hoped that his former neighbour, tenant, and friend might return, just as suddenly...... but it wasn't going to happen now, deep down he knew. It had to be accepted, that Peg had rejoined those comrades who had never grown old.

So he turns wearily away, and out into the near darkness, closing and locking the door. He pockets the key, and he savours the peace of the yard...... as the brave veteran would have himself so often done, for, before Declan's assumption of the duty, this tidying of the church had been one of Peg's jobs.

Albert Willis had been McDaid's first, and only, proper tenant. Previously he'd occupied a cottage on the Menabilly estate near Fowey, then the home of Tommy 'Boy' Browning, former General of his Regiment, the Paras, fighting under whom he'd sustained the leg wound shortly after the D Day landings. While never again enjoying full mobility he could still drive well enough, and he was able to prove himself also a reliable and efficient gardener and handyman. But then Tommy had died, and with the celebrated widow moving from the main house, Peg Willis looked to be at a loose end, but not for long. Something similar was found, courtesy of the Earl of St Germans. Work awaited him on the Eliot Estate, and accommodation was found at St Erney...... rented, fully furnished, from Declan McDaid.

As part of the pay off from Kilmarth Peg had been given the last of Browning's boats, a sturdy little cabin cruiser which had long been kept moored on Polkerris beach, within the lee of the sturdy harbour wall, and this craft he brought with him. In fact it was how he plus a meagre collection of belongings had arrived, following a full calm day's coastal cruise from the Gribben to Rame, into the Sound then, and the Hamoaze, and the Lynher. He negotiated a tie up at the Quarry Boatyard, and the vessel became his means of commuting….. down river through the Lynher viaduct before cutting back J-wise across the Tiddy confluence to St Germans Quay. While varying with tide times his hours would always be fully worked, and it was said that regular users of the Cornwall-Plymouth trains would look out for his boat and sometimes draw an acknowledging wave. But then, without warning, he was suddenly gone….. no Peg, and no explanation.

The rent had been paid in advance, together with a deposit, so McDaid had no grounds for feeling cheated. Then there were the few belongings that remained, a a few ornaments and clothes, and a selection of serviceable tools. All were left save for clothes that he would have stood in, the double barrelled twelve bore shotgun which was in fact kept kept on loan from the Eliot estate, and that map of the Orne crossings, the one he'd traced at the local Saltash library to proudly take to his radio interview.

He'd had it framed, and it had hung on the cottage wall. McDaid was intrigued that it should have been one of the few things to disappear with his tenant…… intrigued, but, on reflection, not totally surprised. And in so much as this particular item had not vanished totally without trace then perhaps it might prove a clue as to its owner's whereabouts, and for a while, at least, could even offer some hope of a return……but not such hope as to share too widely. But then days became weeks. The police were alerted, and there was a search of sorts, and enquiries made, but all to no avail, as weeks became months, and months, years.

The boat was taken from the water, but at McDaid's insistence, and expense, it was stored rather than sold. It was suggested to him that he might himself use it to reach Ince, as an alternative to the drive up to Notter and down, but no, he would stay with his ready established short cut. For all his capability and industry in the boatyard, he showed no desire to prove himself on water.

The empty cottage became an inexpensive holiday let, enjoyed particularly by the anglers who came for the sea trout and the late running

Lynher salmon, and soon it was generating more than Peg had ever been likely to pay. But if and when he came back, it could still be his. This was the man's home.

Mid morning, the next day...... and having been early into the grounds of Ince Castle, Declan McDaid is well on with those sharpened shears. Lady Boyd breaks into his snapping rhythm, she speaks and he ceases. She is pleased with the amount done, and tomorrow, she says, he needn't come..... nor for the rest of the week, including the weekend, and this leaves him correctly guessing that the VIP guests are to be Mr and Mrs Dennis Thatcher, Prime Minister plus the husband, and that the pair can be expected within twenty-four hours.

There had been a previous stay, six, perhaps seven years ago, this when the Viscount, still very much alive and active, was helping a young Government tidy the few remaining African loose ends, including having to 'observe' the organisation of the first 'free' election in Zimbabwe. While willingly taking the task, the former Colonial Secretary was, in truth, finding it distasteful, for clearly this was going to be about resolving ancient tribal enmities rather choosing any aspired for future. Turning a blind eye to corrupt practice could do little to allay the stench...... this was what had been whispered to McDaid in the privacy of the walled garden, Declan being as attentive as ever.

For Boyd was a man who'd sat with the highest councils in the land. Nothing he offered was to be ignored, for who was to say when anyone might be taken, whatever their rank, and forever silenced, be this by accident or design. And then, sadly, soon afterwards, it had been the Viscount himself who'd been taken, and after that, no more than a year or so later, Peg Willis too had vanished. The accident, and then the total mystery, unconnected probably, but possibly not, for in each instance a name had been dropped, the same name, casually, incidentally, perhaps co-incidentally even..... but then again, perhaps not.

In the years since, McDaid had become even more a part of the household, commanding a near automatic security clearance, reaffirmed by simple reference to the Viscountess....... who in the alternative might indicate, as this time she did, plainly and politely, that he was to stay clear. He would do as directed, he had no choice....... save in what might be his preferred route for walking back to St Erney, a decision made less than straightforward by what, through the day, had grown to an irritating infestation of security personnel.

They were swarming, compounding the oppression of the day, with their binoculars, their radios, and their guns. Declan despaired. Ince he was happy to leave to the hostess and her guests, but why should he allow those spooks the pleasure of counting him out?

He would baffle them, he decided, by using the track..... joining it in the tunnel, and following it westward along the cutting to the Lynher viaduct. He checked his watch. It was almost four. While the railway people had never complained, it was always best to avoid the trains. If the 6:15 down was on time he could use the comfortable forty five minute window that followed.

A far off rumble of thunder prompted a glance at the sky. Clouds were building beyond Plymouth. Above and to the west the cloud remained thin. For the best part of an hour he could scratch with the hoe, then, on returning it to the shed, at the same time pick up and prime the spirit lamp he would take into the adit.

This 'adit' was, more precisely, a cave. To venture in was to soon realise that it long pre-dated the railways. From before Napoleonic times there had been rumour of a smugglers' route into Saltash. From Portwrinkle, or even as far as Cawsand, contraband would come by cart or pack animal down to Sheviock Woods, from there to be ferried across the Lynher to Ince where caves afforded storage and, by emerging onto a copse hidden farm track, what amounted to a back alley into Saltash...... useful in those years when even for the owners of the Castle it was a struggle to make the land pay.

Then the railway arrived, accompanied by more affluent and ordered times. The original broad guaged line was cut to almost within a stone's throw of the Castle, but then abandoned in 1907 with the northward re-routing of most of the Saltash-St Germans stretch. New stone viaducts were built to span Forder Creek and the Lynher, and a linking tunnel driven through the spur between.

It was in the boring and the bricking of this that the adit was unearthed. Land-wards it was sealed, but river-wards it was followed and a brambled-over mouth was found low in the nearer bank of the soon to be abandoned old broad guage cutting, midway between the Castle and the neighbouring Wivelscombe Farm. It again proved useful. The tunnel engineers had cut beneath a spring. It could provide storm drainage, as it still did, for while now, in summer, the adit could be walked, in winter it was more often paddled.

On reaching its top end, Declan would there need to bend from stoop to crouch, and turn so as to backwards emerge next to the down track some 80 metres in from the tunnel's eastern portal. He would extinguish his lamp, for being straight and short the tunnel was dim and shadowy rather than truly dark. The gardener could be through in less than ten minutes. It was a further thousand metres to the viaduct, plus the hundred for the crossing to take him almost to the boatyard and his cottage beyond.

But first he had to cross the old disused track, using the one narrow stone bridge that carried the one narrow approach lane to Ince. Once over he could double back to the cutting wherein lay the concealed entrance to his bolt hole.

Reaching the bridge he was surprised at the absence of any guard...... but he suspected this a temporary lapse for there was a van parked further along the lane, on the landward side of the cutting, facing him, with the rear doors open and around them a huddle of perhaps half a dozen functionally uniformed 'heavies'. Declan didn't linger. That wasn't a hamper of sandwiches being broken out, it was a case of rifles. His movement was being noted. He'd drawn eyes, and recognition...... so no immediate alarm, but tension was gathering. Little was being left to chance.

He was by the stone stile now. Climb this and he would be through the hedge and on the path that followed the dismantled line. He was nimbly over, and relieved to be leaving the armed team behind as they were being set, it seemed, to fan over the crown of the tunnelled ridge.

He was into the bushes now, out of their sights, beyond their stern scrutiny. The familiar solidity of that old stone stile had been reassuring......he wasn't to know, though, that it had just been used for the very last time.

He scrambled down into the cutting. Reaching the adit he paused to pump and light the spirit lamp. Then, easing back an ash bough and ducking low, he slipped into the darkness. Now he could straighten and stride forward...... just thirty metres, then, from behind, a loud thud, as if from the slamming of a distant heavy door. Unheard of this was, and enough to halt McDaid, but he didn't turn, for there was no door, he knew that. It had to be that thunder, he thought, and pressed on.

If punctual he would be hearing that train soon, and should it pass at speed he would be feeling its gust. But maybe it was a little late, he thought, holding the lamp up to check his watch again before climbing on. He was close to the tunnel now….. and there it was, the sound, not of the wheels on the track, yet, but of the loco horn being sounded by the driver…… again, something unusual.

The train was approaching, but slowly. So slowly that Declan was out of the adit before the diesel had even reached the tunnel. His lamp now snuffed, he kept well back against the wall. He wouldn't want it to be seen from the cab.

The locomotive was in now. Faintly, beyond the western portal a green light glowed. The gardener anticipated acceleration…..but here was none. The engine and six assorted parcels wagons rolled slowly past, at little more than walking pace now, brakes grinding on rims.

The rearmost van squealed by, and Declan once again had the light from the portal to his right. He glanced that way, and there were men out there. Three he counted, crossing stealthily from his side of the line to the other. Uniforms again, and guns….. this was part of that armed team. Could the train have attracted their suspicion? Maybe, but they'd moved from sight now, and the wheels were still rolling. Should he follow it? No, for the moment he could wait. Anything might happen, he thought…… and caution paid.

For on that last van a door was opening, and something was being lowered to the side of the track, barely thirty metres from where he stood. It was dropped rather than thrown, and it landed much as would a large sack or mailbag. McDaid glanced again towards the portal. No one was coming in for it, not from this end. He could move for a closer look, and as he did his eyes made better sense of the thing…… as did his nose. For the bundle was moving, and also it stank, of human ordure. This was a person, a man, now dragging himself to his feet, dirtied and disorientated. The figure stumbled clear of the track, to the wall, and like McDaid watched the train…. for now, steadily, it was gathering speed. A swirl of diesel fumes settled over the exposed rails, subduing their glimmer until yet more light was offered as the stock cleared the western portal.

And in that light, in that portal, a distant figure strode out to stand between the tracks. One figure, raising one gun, to fire just two shots in quick succession. Declan heard the ricochets chasing towards them, he and this other who'd been dropped from the train, who wouldn't, as yet, know of his own nearness nor of the presence of those others in the armed team who had to be covering the eastern portal.

A set up, realised McDaid. Those shots from the west were to drive this victim back, into an eastern portal ambush, into the sights of at least three well-trained rifles.

"Jesus...." Just the one groaned profanity, that was all the gardener needed to hear. This was an Irishman, and just for this, in these circumstances, one surely packaged for summary execution. He was moving, coming closer. Those scare bullets had done their work. Declan had to think quickly. As confused as this stumbling unfortunate was, he would in seconds realise the predicament, and realise also that he wasn't alone. And anything might then happen, particularly as more bullets started to fly.

McDaid wanted to be back into his bolt hole. A distraction was needed, perhaps another shot from the west. And as he peered along, there was........ not a bullet, but something no less effective. It was a diesel on the up-line, running light, now briskly into the tunnel and rattling towards them on the far track.

Unscheduled traffic will sometimes catch maintenance teams unawares, and never so often as within half a mile of passing an opposite bound train. Accordingly, as well as with a sharp blast on the horn, the driver greeted darkness with the switch-on of a front headlamp. And with that, Declan was seen...... not by anyone outside the tunnel, not by the driver even, but by the paunchy figure who was by now less than ten metres away.

McDaid decided. The diesel would surely distract the ambush team. Virtue fused with necessity. He stepped out.....

"You're with me," he said, gripping the man by his arm. "Into here......I can save your life. Quickly."

"Jesus, Son of God.....," groaned Eamon Carroll, and despite the bruises from his bumping, and the sores from where the bindings had cut, quick enough he was. Into the adit they ducked, and with the lamp re-lit Declan led his new acquaintance down and out of the trap. The rescuer emerged first, keeping low, and scrambling to the rim of the cutting to check. There seemed to be commotion away to the right, back towards the bridge and the stile, where a thinned pall of dust and smoke hung above where path met lane. People were gathering and here, from the left, was one more person hurrying to join the group, the footsteps and panted breath approaching and passing along the path.

No uniform, this one, and no gun….. that was good. He was security, yes, but unforewarned, sensed Declan, and probably unaware of the thwarted stroke attempted in the tunnel. He'd come from the shore perhaps, and peering that way McDaid found confirmation from a small inflatable which had been pulled up onto what a set of shallow footsteps indicated to be a shale firmed stretch of tidal mud.

He slid back down to the adit. A face emerged.

"I smell explosive," it brogued. McDaid could only smell the man.

"You're one chance is the water, less than a hundred yards……
that way," Declan pointed. "There's an inflatable on the mud. Tug on the cord and the outboard should start. If not, then there should be oars."

"You don't think I'd be too exposed?" The man was out now, giving Declan opportunity to size figure, and face, and clothes. They weren't unlike, this fellow and the guy who'd passed on the path, presumably after leaving the dinghy. The age had to be about the same, and the tousled hair and the generally unkempt clothes. The paunchiness, perhaps needn't matter. There was a chance. It was slim, but it had to be grasped.

"Get out on the water. The more exposed the safer. No one's going to shoot you in broad daylight. Lurk in cuttings, loiter in tunnels, and you give them their excuse. Head down river. The big city is Plymouth. Blend in with the throng. You need money? Take these two tenners." Declan reached for his pocket, but the hand was stayed.

"Keep it," said the other, who'd already drawn a wallet from his back pocket. "It seems I was packed off with all I could need."

"Including identification….. all they would need, I suspect."

*

(vi) 'STANLEY' writes
early in the next week

Harold a.k.a. 'Kim' or STANLEY

……and GUSTAVE, at home, welcomes his weary visitor with the customary scotch, the authentic highland blend, gratefully received.

"And thank you, Sir Clive, for travelling so far to brief me personally."

"I merely report as instructed, sir, and only to disappoint, I fear."

"So nothing was found." The host's mouth tightened with frustration. "But you were thorough?"

"We took the place apart, as per your strict instruction, and yes, there were the odd, long hidden away fire-arms, even a Colt .32."

"With the six grooved left hand rifling.....just what we don't want."

"I'm sorry for that, but we did do our considerable best."

"Of course, of course, you did well. It's just that I know precisely what was used, a .32 Smith&Wesson, with the five grooves, twisted so as to impart clockwise spin on the bullet. And it's because others could know this too, Sir Clive, that the damned thing is so dangerous."

GUSTAVE prowled moodily back to the tray, decanter in hand. Faulds sought bravely to console.

"Well if it really is at Ince, Sir, then be assured that it's very well concealed. And remember, it's been four years now since the late Viscount was killed. In that time, there might well have been a full clear-out."

"Maybe, Sir Clive, but there's almost a lifetime's work at stake here. Hence the measure of my frustration. I find no fault with yourself."

"But why the sudden flap now?" asked Faulds, further emboldened. "If this is linked to the written testimony that Boyd was bringing back from Berlin, from Hess, the affidavit that went missing on the night of the fatal accident...... might we not have moved a lot sooner?"

"As I said at the time," Sir Clive, "There was a chance then that it had been lost forever, just as there was a chance that you might, last week, have found that particular gun. Either would have done........"

"...... to put the whole HIGHLAND CLEARANCE thing back into bed."

"Quite, but in neither instance have we been so lucky, so to go with the history of this that you had back when Boyd died, it's best now you now be brought up to date on more recent developments."

"So this from Hess, might have disappeared forever...... but it hasn't, has it? It's turned up....... At the Kremlin perhaps?"

"That, Sir Clive, wouldn't be so bad." GUSTAVE went to his bookcase, to a particular shelf from which he drew a particular one of a series of tall matching volumes. Opening it he drew therefrom a letter, the writing filling both sides of some three sheets. "For two months I've sat on this. Success at Ince might have rendered it irrelevant...... but this wasn't to be. I can accept, though, that you did your best. You deserve to know the worst." The letter was passed. "You will see that I am addressed by the code name given me by my masters. He signs himself, likewise, with the name given him by his."

Faulds read:

April 1987

To   'GUSTAVE'

From   'STANLEY'

Subject   'HIGHLAND CLEARANCE'

Dear erstwhile colleague

Greetings from the heart of Moscow, even from the Kremlin itself! I compose this letter in the sole presence of General Secretary Gorbachev, currently the leader of this, my adoptive country. He adds his own best regards and wishes it to be known that he is in full agreement with all I write, indeed it comes to you at his personal behest.

You will know of General Secretary Gorbachev's view that some aspects of Soviet society require adjustment, hence his twin reformist initiatives, Glasnost and Perstroika. In these he has my wholehearted support. Accordingly I am strongly persuaded that the sterner approach of Stalin, while no less valid and supportable in its day, now belongs to history, and that the time has come to dispense with the more authoritarian aspects of his legacy.

Alas, though, there are many here, and more again in our satellite territories, who, from their hitherto entrenched positions of considerable power, cannot share the leader's progressive view. If only in the interests of simple self-preservation they can be expected to attempt to block, and even reverse attempted reforms. A good number hold high rank in the military, and should General Secretary Gorbachev falter then with all the hardware and personnel at their disposal they might well be tempted to effect a seizure of power...... indded, it might be said that a good excuse

170

is all they need.

This brings me to a document that has come to be known, here in the Kremlin, as 'The Hess Affidavit'...... a little piece of mischief procured from Spandau by a member of your House of Lords back in '83. This written statement touches upon operation HIGHLAND CLEARANCE, the project conceived by the man who was your chief, and mine, when we fought together in the struggle to defeat Nazism, what is termed here our 'Great Patriotic War'.

The Peer in question was the late Viscount Boyd of Merton. The nature of the document, added to the fact that the man was a trained barrister, suggested intended use as a part of some kind of formal or informal legal submission, but before any deposition could be made the Viscount was killed in a street accident, and his bag, containing the affidavit, was mislaid, lost, or stolen during the fuss that immediately ensued.

"So when STANLEY writes here of you and he working together during the war, he means under Menzies....."

"......when we were both entrusted with knowledge of HIGHLAND CLEARANCE," added GUSTAVE, "but with him it was a trust misplaced. What wasn't realised then, of course, was that he was already working for Stalin, that his first loyalty was to the Reds. It has long been said that Stalin suspected that Hess had been lured to Scotland..... as if this was part of the paranoia that came to characterise the last years of his tyranny."

"But this wasn't suspicion, paranoid or otherwise."

"Because STANLEY had put him in the know..... read on".

For as long as nothing further was heard, it could be guardedly assumed, on your side and ours, that on being considered valueless by some petty thief the crucial content might have been destroyed. We could only watch and wait.

Recent developments, however, have convinced us that we are not yet at the end of this story. Belatedly, but reliably none the less, we are informed that within a week of Boyd's death the document was securely in the hands of STASI, the East German security agency.

Perhaps they had a watcher too...... as we did...... but one that moved a little more quickly. Perhaps, more innocently, because the affidavit was written in German with frequent reference to 'Berlin', some well meaning Londoner took it upon him or her self to mistakenly 'return' this item to the East German Embassy, a place run, as you well know, by the STASI.

Realising its historical significance, and at least something of what it might come to be worth to them politically, the hardline East German ruling elite seems to have decided to keep this thing beneath its collective cap......up until now, that is, when, with this new loosening of mood in Moscow, they begin to feel perturbed. It is their turn to be in the bunker, and if the tide is to be stemmed then every asset has to be used, including 'The Hess Affidavit'.

"Interesting," commented Faulds, coming to the end of the first side. "Boyd feared, back in '83, that a testimony given by Hess might prove awkward....."

"......and needed to be scotched," added GUSTAVE, swilling his glass. "But he wouldn't have been anticipating this kind of awkwardness. Boyd's concern was strictly for the future of the House of Lords, his fear being that all this might emerge in a libel action brought by Macmillan against Nikolai Tolstoy, an action that could have ultimately been referred to the Lord Justices of Appeal......"

"...... who, in turn, might have found themselves stymied by the Foreign Office."

"But, as it has proved, on that score Boyd needn't have worried. You'll remember last year, Sir Clive, when Stockton's action over *'The Minister and the Massacres'* ended as a total walk over. To Tolstoy's frustration, his publishers had no stomach for the fight. Relieved to still be in business, they settled cheaply, agreeing to take the books back off the the shelves for hasty pulping."

"And that was enough to satisfy Macmillan. Old and tired, but handsomely vindicated, he was to die at the turn of the year with reputation higher than ever. So even should it be found, whither then for the missing 'Hess affidavit'? Dead minister, dead letter."

"Far from it," scowled GUSTAVE, gesturing Faulds to turn the page.

Faulds complied. He read on.

I am informed that the testimony of the last top Nazi tells of how he was persuaded to embark on that seemingly bizarre solo flight of May 1941, just prior to Barbarossa. He explains that he (with the rest of the German high command) were mistakenly convinced that after landing in Scotland he might conclude at least a truce between Britain and Germany, with a strong possibility of this being developed into an anti Bolshevik alliance, a 'Nordic Accord' that might have even included the USA, with Washington being ready to mediate a redistribution of Third World colonial territories enabling the 'Jewish Problem' identified by Hitler to be solved in a far more enlightened manner than he ultimately chose (or was driven to, some might say).

In captivity, Hess was soon to realise that in fact there had been no 'Nordic Accord' on the table and that he, with Hitler, had been the victims of a deception, the deception that we know as HIGHLAND CLEARANCE. At leisure, he has also been able to reflect on the later consequences of my having passed details of this typically Churchillian ploy to Stalin.

For good reason, HIGHLAND CLEARANCE had been a top secret initiative, and, from the British standpoint, in the interests of the post war settlement it was, and is, felt important that it should remain so. Thanks to me, however, the Kremlin knew, and Stalin was able to exact a price for staying silent...... the magnitude of which came to be spelt out to the British delegations sent to the summit talks held at Yalta and Potsdam as the Reich crumbled under the Russian tank offensives.

You and I know that this price was met, at particular cost to those millions of unfortunates who young Nikolai Tolstoy terms 'The Victims of Yalta', the Russians and other Soviets who Stalin wanted to punish for fighting with the Germans, or for surrendering to the Germans, or for merely having fled to the west during the years prior to Barbarossa. Bluntly, wherever such citizens found themselves under British control, expecting and often pleading for British protection, Stalin was placed to demand that they instead be repatriated without appeal, to face either the firing squad's merciful bullet, or years of Gulag privation.

The enormity of these recriminations of Stalin has, for many years, tended to deter his successors from making any more of Britain's unhappy complicity, and also any further exploitation of our knowledge here of HIGHLAND CLEARANCE, the despearate throw which left Hitler diplomatically out-manouevred in '41, only to give Uncle Joe the whip hand in '45, at Yalta and Potsdam.

But times have changed, and desperate men now consider desperate measures. If they can blacken the west, they feel, then maybe Gorbachev, the westerniser, can be trumped.

So can the Hess affidavit blacken the west?

"Good question," muttered Faulds. "Can the Hess affidavit still blacken the west?" GUSTAVE nodded him on. He moved to the next page.

Not on its own, for Hess himself is too easily discredited. His words need to be substantiated by something more solid......and because they briefly found their way into the hands of Alan Lennox Boyd there has developed, rightly or wrongly, a suspicion that one such item might indeed have lain within his reach, after possibly having been passed down to him by his wife's uncle, Walter Guinness, the first Lord Moyne, who'd held the position of Colonial Secretary in 1941.

We have known all along that the Hess' peace initiative was far from unbidden, and that it wasn't with just words that he was persuaded to fly. He swallowed the hook only after having been thrown a rich ground bait, a spread of events designed to make it appear that despite Churchill's rhetoric, Britain was in fact more sincere with what were carefully made truce moves......subtly framed, discretely voiced, but no less enticing for all that.

Connected with this was the murder, in Kenya, in the January of '41, of Josslyn Hay, Lord Erroll. You might recall that later in the year, shortly after Barbarossa, Jock Delves-Broughton was tried and acquitted of the shooting, the case having been brought on an assumption that here was a crime of passion, the recently married accused having been motivated by jealousy and hurt pride, on seeing his bride fall so quickly and completely for Erroll's seductive charms.

"Yes, Delves-Broughton," remarked Faulds. "I've read about this quite recently, in the papers. A film is being made......"

"......of a book titled *White Mischief*," continued GUSTAVE, "written by one James Fox, who as a young journalist back in the '60s had assisted with the late Cyril Connolly 's investigation into the matter. Fox is good on the fire-arm forensics, the mishandling of which allowed the accused to walk free. STANLEY's snalysis of the evidence, which you'll see there, follows Fox's very closely….."

"……to the same conclusion?" asked Faulds.

"No, here they differ. You'll see."

Broughton might have hanged, had not the case been mishandled by the prosecution who attemped to CONCLUSIVELY link the bullet prised from the victim's head to a .32 Colt handgun of which Broughton was the registered owner.

The defence easily proved that the fatal bullet could never have come from such a weapon, and claimed therefore that the bullet must have been fired by some one else……even after similar bullets had inexplicably been found on a private practice range used by Broughton.

Those who afterwards considered Broughton to have been guilty, and therefore wrongly acquitted, suggest that the prosecution might have done better to use the similarity of the murder and practice bullets to instead argue PERSUASIVELY that Broughton could well have held an unregistered handgun IN ADDITION to the Colt, almost certainly a .32 Smith&Wesson, and that it was with this that he'd shot his rival in love.

But such a gun could not be produced for the jury. It was established, though, from the bullet and its entry wound, that it certainly had a five grooved clockwise rifling (as against a Colt's six, set anticlockwise), that it had certainly been loaded with the older and less common black powder charged style of cartridge, and that probably it was of that (non Colt) design in which the revolving cylinder will fall out sideways for reloading.

It has been held (most recently by Mr James Fox) that Broughton was guilty and that he was lucky. The prosecuting counsel was incompetent, they argue. We, though, are placed to disagree. We know that at that time .32 Smith&Wessons were issued to British Secret Service operatives, and that one such might have been used for the deed, the suspicion for which will always stay with Broughton thanks to the cleverly contrived inconclusiveness of Court proceedings in Nairobi. Further to this, it should have been of little surprise to us when, within a year of the trial, we hear that Delves Broughton has also died in debatable circumstances.

So with Jock dead too, is this the end of the story?

No…..for if we accept what James Fox writes in his book (White Mischief) then we must be strongly inclined to disbelieve Rudolf Hess. But what if that murder weapon HAS survived, and it CAN can be found, and it can then be shown to have been USED ELSEWHERE in other special operations that we might know to be associated with HIGHLAND CLEARANCE, operations far, far distant from Jock Delves Broughton and Kenya? If this can be forensically established then the Hess account starts to look the more likely. Particularly if, as I've heard it said, Erroll was in fact shot by a trained assassin, flown in from and back to Cairo, where the weapon was then left when the agent was sent to certain death on a purposely compromised mission into Greece. Deliberately betrayed into the vengeful hands of a group of communist partisans, the now superfluous operative is thought to have met with summary execution......cruel reward indeed for the special services rendered.

But the gun itself is not so easily disposed of. It stays in Cairo, until a year later when, with Rommel close to putting our brave boys to rout, the whole place is in panic. The thing cannot be allowed to fall into Nazi hands, and who better to ensure this than the man chosen for the position of Minister Resident, Lord Moyne, who seems to have performed the task well...... too well, perhaps, for when he himself is assassinated in '44, by the Zionists, the whereabouts of Lord Erroll's bane, almost certainly a Smith&Wesson .32, is left as a continuing mystery.

"The .32 Smith & Wesson," nodded Faulds. "This is what you hoped I might turn up down at Ince....."

"......and thereby de-fuse a potential political time bomb...... but you still have a couple of sides to go."

The view here is that the weapon might well have stayed within the Guinness family, as an heirloom of considerable political weight......but of little use to Bryan, the son who seems to have had no ambitions in that field. But there is a niece, with a husband who picked up the torch and carried it forward into the brave new post war world...... Sir Alan Lennox Boyd, no less, the same who just prior to a sudden and untimely death, had been singled out to receive the Hess affidavit.

The STASI has long thought this too much of a co incidence. For them it suggests that the gun exists and that it probably lies somewhere within the fabric of Ince Castle, Boyd's old home, where the Viscountess still resides.

Faulds shook his head.

They are intent on finding it. A search team has been assembled, which currently might be engaged in making preliminary observations, with a view to moving in when ready, perhaps under the guise of a property maintenance firm, offering to inspect for rot, say, or to point brickwork, or to paint windows. I've seen photos of the place. Something of that sort will always be waiting to be done.

"I think he's right about the upkeep challenge down there," remarked Faulds as an aside.

And be aware too, that whilst in the area, these searchers can be expected to sniffing back to another HIGHLAND CLEARANCE related episode, one closely predating the slaying of Erroll. It concerns the early wartime movements of another weapon...... one far larger but, sadly, just as lost. We must expect them to have been briefed on the mysterious career of the French submarine, the Surcouf.

Docked in Devonport when France fell, the vessel had to be forcibly seized by the Royal Navy before a subsequent assignment to the Free French. Stalin infiltrated some good men into de Gaulle's early makeshift Command, and though not specifically mentioned in the affidavit, there is, in their reports, strong indications that the Surcouf could also have figured as another component in the deception practised on Hess.

The point of this letter is to put you on alert. The STASI has the Hess affidavit, and that's a start, but for them, rather more is needed......further and better particulars, ideally corroborated by hard evidence, ideally that gun used in Africa, and with this, if possible, any reliable first hand account that might bring the Surcouf more firmly into play .

Be aware, GUSTAVE, the search has begun, a search that could end with their identifying yourself, as well as your closely guarded secrets. But that would come later. Their first goal will be to find something that can publicly withstand legal scrutiny, and in respect of their gaining access to open court with such material you will hardly need reminding of the threat posed by the recent antics of Nikolai Tolstoy.

"Tolstoy....... this keeps coming back to Tolstoy," said Faulds, "of whom you've said that Boyd might have been needlessly wary."

"Four years ago, yes," qualified GUSTAVE, "but times do change. Keep reading.

Money would appear to be no object for this young tyro, for libel as outrageously as he may, there will always be friends to back an appeal, even to the highest court in the land. Lose as they must, they'll pay that much merely to say their piece in such an elevated forum.

Boyd was carrying that affidavit in anticipation of this eventuality. Having read 'The Victims of Yalta' it was reasonable for him to fear that a continued and sustained assault against the reputation of Harold Macmillan might bring the whole edifice which is the House of Lords into total disrepute. To avert this he hoped that the affidavit might soften the Foreign Office, and that this most inscrutable of departments might yield a limited admission, delicately measured so as to take the heat off dear old Mac, the individual in Tolstoy's sights.

But Lord B dies, and the affidavit is lost. And then, with 'The Minister and The Massacres', Tolstoy in fact contrives to overplay his hand. He forges a far too cumbersome a sword, too heavy, too blunt, and against one as well armoured as Macmillan, too easily deflected. Out of a natural fear for his own commercial life, the publisher sensibly drops it. Then, within a matter of months Macmillan is dead. If he is to make the Courts then Tolstoy must have another target, and there is one. He can erect Lord Aldington, who'd actually rated no more than the briefest of mentions in the first book. So Tolstoy sharpens up his pencil, and his invective, to this time fashion a far stealthier weapon...... which is his pointed revision of a pamphlet originally penned by a Mr Nigel Watts, a man carrying his own separate grudge against the former Brigadier.

Faulds paused, frowning quizzically from the page.

"This 'Mr Nigel Watts'..... remind me."

"Character assasination...... this is Nikolai Tolstoy's strategy, and in this context the publishers of '*The Minister and the Massacres*' found themselves in the business of executing a clumsily conceived contract killing."

"With the weapon provided, that book, being far too unwieldy..... as STANLEY says. It was never going to hurt Macmillan. It was too imprecise."

"And as the writs started to fly, the firm were quickly wanting out."

"And then Macmillan dies. Tolstoy's chase is over, the grim reaper has taken his fox."

"But by dropping his sights," continued GUSTAVE, "he might yet get the contest he craves......"

"..... if he can sufficiently rile Aldington," added Faulds, "character assasination again."

"Yes, but he's learning. Who is going to print for him a book on Toby Low? Who is going to even buy and read the thing?"

"No one..... so a different kind of weapon needs to be devised."

"Yes, and see," continued GUSTAVE, "here is one ready made almost, courtesy of an aggrieved policy holder with Sun Alliance, an insurance company for whom Aldington held a directorship. Mr Nigel Watts, a humble policy holder, has refused what he feels to be a good claim. He is cross. Some one must pay, he feels......"

"......, and why not Aldington?"

"Yes, a man with an interesting history, whose 'good war', it seems, might have involved him in a dark secret. This is what was suggested in Tolstoy's accounts of KEELHAUL, so why not distill those mentions of the Jobsworth Brigadier, scattered widely across three books, into a concise pamphlet, something easy to print, and to pass around rather than sell? And you have to hand it to the man, Sir Clive, he does hit on the neatest of ways to sharply question an only vaguely suspect integrity."

"So originally this was an idea of Watts, to focus on Aldington?"

"It was," confirmed GUSTAVE, "and he was well on his way to the finished article before Tolstoy even became aware him....."

"..... and the potential of his project."

"Indeed, Sir Clive, for whereas Stockton had seen that last book coming and almost contemptuously managed to deflect the intended blow, this eventual pamphlet, honed now by Tolstoy's late revisions, has indeed caught Aldington off balance."

"So no easily dodged sword for Aldington......"

"........instead he encounters a stealthily thrust stilletto."

"And whereas Harold's lawyers merely had to tease up and exploit the natural reticence of a wary publisher and nervous booksellers, poor

Toby is left to counter the uncompromising attentions of a zealout, one sufficiently spite-crazed to be handing around his own pamphlets!"

"Indeed, Sir Clive, and we can expect him to go to Court to defend his name. It follows that we will hear Toby appeal for the kind of establishment help that I suppose he deserves....."

"..... but which we know can never be fully given. Tolstoy, though, he'll not complain, for in the publicity stakes he's merrily sucking on a fresh tank of oxygen. While Watts......?"

"...... he just likes to see the mud being thrown. Some will stick, it always does, and to that extent he can satisfy his craving for revenge." A flicker of disgust crossed GUSTAVE's lordly countenance. "Watts' motives look to be as ignoble as Tolstoy's are noble......"

"...... it's a potent blend that they make, though." Sir Clive tapped at the page just read. "And it would appear that your Kremlin correspondent can accept that the surface agendas hide nothing else."

"So far, perhaps, but he and I have been similarly taught, by training and experience. At this level one takes nothing at face value. See what he says next."

Faulds returned to the letter.

And in this newer combination Tolstoy does look to be conducting a more effective ploy. The Foreign Office haven't moved and Aldington, caught in the open, is angered. He ducks, he dives, and resolves to have his day in court, and this, I say, should be bringing for us no less concern than that felt by Boyd back in '83. Indeed it should be all the greater now, for with the changed mood on this side of the Iron Curtain, there might be far more at stake than just the future of the House of Lords.

In the event, Macmillan v Tolstoy came to very little. A year on and it is history, and no more than a footnote at that. But what looms before us now is Aldington v Watts+Tolsltoy, a spat which at this critical time might undo 35 years of painful post Stalin progress. We must remain ever watchful.

Of Tolstoy, we know plenty. He boldly fronts his campaigns and it is likewise with this chippy Mr Nigel Watts with his naked spite. What we see there is what we get. We can be reasonably sure that as individuals, neither harbours any hidden demons. But this said, do we know enough of how they were harnessed into a collaborative pair?

Our information is that Watts' trawl through Tolstoy's books for details of Low's war record brought him to the attention of a vaguely constituted agency claiming to be active on behalf of the White Russian émigré community, and that it was with the encouragement of these people, and through their offices, that he managed to secure the author's endorsement of the project, and ultimately that actual assistance with the finally produced and circulated pamphlet.

And who exactly are these people, these facilitators? We don't know......and until we do we have to be wary. And why.......? Because what we do know is that White Russia, in its time, was no less absolutist than have been the Stalinist Reds who inherited their Tsardom.

The Whites are slippery......as proved by their survival. Now, though, they wish to do more than that. They have old scores to settle. Do not believe that from sheltering in the west they have become westernised. Assume not that they are ready to embrace Glasnost, Perstroika, or even Strategic Arms Limitation. What they hunger for is their former power, and, if it might be reclaimed thereby, it is to the disaffected amongst our Warsaw Pact military elites that they might go......to those who might justifiably feel themselves a newly endangered species as our General Secretary here looks to slash our once sacrosanct arms expenditure. It comes back to the immense wealth the Whites still command. As the Reds run out of Roubles, here might be a source of fresh sponsorship.

Strange bedfellows......? No more so than Molotov and Ribbentrop in '39. So much is in the melting pot. Discount nothing, particularly if the West and its ways can be discredited. And this, in our view, is why nothing of HIGHLAND CLEARANCE must ever be allowed to be substantiated in a public forum, and why the reformers here look to establish common cause with yourselves.

Accordingly, for the moment we feel there is little to be gained from cluttering your Parish with agents of our own. Your strategy, clear, and sensible, and occasionally ruthless, has been to keep your secret to as few people as possible. You command an admirably tight ship, and our view is that we do best by merely alerting you to what is in the wind. The task of searching is left to you and those of your capable and trusted assistants you might care to deploy.

It has been many years, GUSTAVE, since you and I have worked together. When I left there was bitterness, I know, and this was understandable. But I regret nothing. Given that time again then I would probably do just the same. But times change of course, and I hope this letter can go some way towards bridging the rift with a view to restoring a once effective working relationship.

Yours truly

STANLEY

"So" grunted Faulds, "my Cornish caper is now explained. You're obviously ready to believe this man, after all his treachery."

"Can we afford not to?" countered GUSTAVE. "I don't think we can...... though it grieves me to say as much, we must take something of the joy that is in heaven over the one sinner that can at least partly repent."

"And what a sinner, eh? Kim Philby..... re-inventing himself as the Protector in Chief to Mikhail Gorbachev. My apologies for not coming up with that gun, but be well assured, that place was fine-tooth combed. If the gun is there, then it's too well hidden......"

".... for you....."

".... and for anyone else," Faulds insisted. "We went into every room, every corner."

"So perhaps if we let them come and search as you did, Sir Clive, in vain, then they'll waste their own valuable time..... but they must be identified and watched."

"But you see no reason to disturb, to frighten off."

"I don't, Sir Clive, at least not yet, but there is this other thing down there, the submarine. You've had access to the file on that for quite some time now......"

".... and I was going to tell you, Sir, that I've had it out again, only last week."

"So I've been informed." nodded GUSTAVE. Faulds shuddered.

"The *Surcouf*, sir, was a curio. It still is, and, as such, will always attract the curious......."

".......and to over-react is sometimes to further whet their curiosity. I take that, Sir Clive, but do I nonetheless detect from you a niggling concern?"

"You do, over a home grown development which hopefully we've nipped in the bud....... for it could only have complicated this other probing from the east."

"How very prescient, Sir Clive. Do enlighten me."

"Amongst the curious one naturally has to expect the occasional professional salvor. This is their trade, after all, and it's a competitive business. They must move with stealth, sometimes adopting disguise, and all this we can usually indulge, quite happily."

"Except .....?" GUSTAVE almost demanded.

"....... when we suspect a disguised interest is being shown in the *Surcouf* by a Mr Tony Cross."

"Tony Cross, eh? That was well spotted, Sir Clive. And I agree, we certainly don't indulge that one. But when you say 'We've nipped it in the bud', that's you and who else?"

"I speak of our quick thinking friend at the DTI. This cropped up in Plymouth. He was there, as he often is, on the spot, on the ball...... "

"...... to once again do the business. That's good," said GUSTAVE. "Well do, once again, convey my gratitude. I would say he's earned a glimpse of this letter. I've a copy here for you to take back."

"And I can show it to him?

"To him only."

*

In London, meanwhile.....
(vii) a head rolls

"Suspension......?"

"With immediate effect," answered Colin Daniels, "in response to disquiet at the very top level."

"At Number Ten ..... because putting a fine tooth comb through that place cost she and her husband three days of their precious holiday?"

"Having to forego his planned afternoon's golf at St Mellion put Dennis into the grimmest of moods. The Prime Minister is demanding a full report, and it will be recorded therein that the person almost certainly responsible for the attack was allowed to escape, your dinghy being the means. A full internal enquiry has been promised. While it proceeds you will be paid, of course, but you keep well away from this department. Our work continues without you."

"I was just following orders Colin, your orders. In the event of any incident I was told to fall back from the shore so as to help more closely defend the Castle perimeter. I hear an explosion, I react accordingly. Was I meant to have been carrying that dinghy on my back?"

"I too had orders to follow, don't forget. You will be interviewed by the enquiry panel, so will I. Should we feel that something needs saying, then that will be the time."

"So I just sit back, and allow myself to be stitched up?"

"Not necessarily. View this as 'garden leave'. That alias you've used before down there, 'Alan Grigson', it gave effective cover, and there's more mileage to be made out of that yet, I would say. Giving some time to the cultivation of that persona might well pay."

"So you don't mind me snooping into that corner of Cornwall?"

"Not at all. But you'll be on your own, remember, no back up team this time. I'm trusting you to tread very carefully."

"A boat?"

"No," scoffed Daniels, "you can't look after the things. But what you can take, if you want, is that old VW Camper. It's not been used since the Roseland job."

"Grigson the freelance has already done something on the Lynher, remember."

"He has, yes, so perhaps he might have a follow-up project.......
a book or a tape on Scraesdon Fort for instance. Get into natural history. The place has become a sanctuary for threatened species, plants and insects. I'll get it nodded through with the MOD. Garden leave, very good."

*

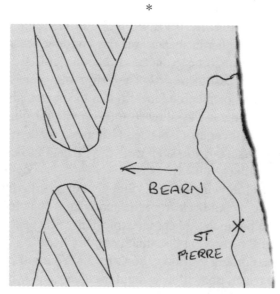

A copy from the Vincennes archive

184

(iix) while in Cornwall
The next day

Kernow Mill sits next to the Trerulefoot traffic roundabout, the junction where the 'new' bridge road and the 'old' ferry road meet. It's a modern shop, a purpose built out of town clothing store offering old fashioned quality rather than the recent and racy. For the car owner in South East Cornwall, and even Plymouth, it's a place easily found and reached. Parking is plentiful and free, and before leaving few will resist a clean and airy tea-room.

This was the meeting place suggested by James Busbridge, and Tony Cross was pleased to comply.... showing himself one willing to come half way.

Busbridge was there first, as he said he would be, waiting in his Viva, and, as promised, there was plenty of space for Tony to roll in alongside with his venerable, salt scarred Volvo estate. He was led to the tea shop where, again, there was ample room. Though knowing the place well enough, Cross was content to let Busbridge assume the role of host, and stand the first tray of coffees...... for the best divers rush at nothing. Surface pleasantries are important. Plan to dive, they say, and dive to plan.

"Now, Mr Busbridge...."

"Do call me James,"

"And I'm Tony....... James, you tell me that we share an interest in the same subject."

"This not being the bones of Sir Francis Drake, Tony. Good idea though, this trying to launch your quest under the cloak of an old sea dog......"

"...... but one that looks to have backfired." A rueful tut registered the diver's dismay.

"Yes, but this might yet be to your advantage. If I've managed to suss your game then it's to be imagined that others far better equipped than I will have done likewise..... and this is why I'm pleased not to be talking through the phone."

"So my game, Mr Busbridge, is what?

"Big game, Tony. A lot, lot bigger than just the coffin of one man, however famous. The big fish that you seek took to the bottom how many?.... One hundred and....?"

"One hundred and twenty nine French sailors," Cross was coming clean, "plus the three of the Royal Navy's liaison team, Leading Signalman Warner, Leading Telegraphist Gough......"

"...... and Sub Lieutenant Roger Burney," completed Busbridge, as if to confirm an equal diligence of research. "They all went down with the *Surcouf*, which might, very possibly, very conveniently, lie close to where Sir Francis was committed all those centuries ago."

Tony Cross nodded resignedly. "So what exactly might be to my advantage, Mr Busbridge?" he asked, returning to the formal mode of address.

"I think you might have enemies, Mr Cross," matched Busbridge. "And I think they might have used the press and the radio in an attempt to blow you out of the water. The same tactics were used against Jessop, your old boss. Negative publicity about desecration on the *Edinburgh* became a constant thorn, I remember....."

"..... and then the Inland Revenue was deployed," agreed Cross. "Damn near ruined the man. So I ask again. What might be to my advantage?"

"The fact that these enemies might have opened up on you so soon. When a sniper fires he gives away his position. He also leaves spent ammunition. Look closely and we might also glean clues as to identity, which in turn could offer clues as to what it is that needs to be so closely protected......"

"......and why."

"Which is more my territory than yours, Tony, but two heads have to be better than one. I say there's a story in this, a lucrative story. Everything I've read on the *Surcouf*, everything I've been told, suggests to me that the thing was a brimming can of worms..... far more so than the *Edinburgh*. That, in the end, is a tale of just one consignment, one last voyage. With the *Surcouf* we have more than eighteen months of end to end intrigue...... rumour and cover up all the way, beginning with the never fully explained on board gunfight by which she was brought under the command of our Admiralty........"

"....... and ending with her never fully explained loss."

"You will have taken your own copies of this, no doubt," continued Busbridge, reaching into a plastic Co-op carrier to produce a photo copied chart....... which, by its one uneven margin, in fact declared itself no more than a torn away part of one.

Tony Cross recognised it immediately. "Mine's in the car," he smiled. "Obtained, of course, from the Vincennes Naval archive over in France. There's one in the *Surcouf* file, another in Muselier's, and a third in that headed 'St Pierre and Miquelon'. All the same, all copies......"

"....... and with no sign anywhere of an original from which those copies were taken," added Busbridge, "or any indication where the missing half might be located. For all that's on what we have, it could be showing us anywhere."

"Anywhere where there's a 'St Pierre', on the coast presumably....... which would be this line here," Cross traced with his finger accordingly. "But from this, who's to say which side of it is land and which sea. I suppose this might give us a degree of orientation." His finger went to a small, centrally placed, arrow head marked **BEARN**, level with and to the left of the **ST PIERRE**. "Then if that way is north, we can perhaps turn these shaded bits to the top......."

"........ and read them as what, though?" asked Busbridge. "High ground........ or they could be shallow water, or anything you like. I suppose we have to be somewhere in the vicinity of St Pierre and Miquelon, for this was where the *Surcouf* and Muselier covered themselves in glory."

"Much to the fury of the State Department in Washington, the Americans still being reluctant to join all out hostilities against Vichy France....... even just after Pearl Harbor. Yes," the diver agreed, "those two islands off Newfoundland have to be favourite." He then swivelled the map on the table, scrutinising it for a last time before sliding it back to the owner. "But I still think we keep an open mind. Something firmer to go on, we need. Where can we find it?"

"Maybe in this response you've had to that newspaper piece," suggested Busbridge. "It stirred a few things up, and more, possibly, than just the sensitivities of a few little old ladies. See how it got me here......"

"...... and if you were alert, why not others too."

"As I said, Tony. So look on that as a dividend. We need to know our enemy and, in that respect even bad publicity can help. Your problems seemed to have started when this was picked up by the radio people. If you had contacts at the station then maybe you now feel disappointed in them?"

"Naturally I was annoyed, and so was my son who was best placed for getting it all checked with me beforehand....... but that said, I suppose people were only trying to help."

"And maybe they have, even if not as anticipated….. so where relationships might, because of this, have become strained or fractured, I would recommend rapid repair. A rebuilt bridge will often offer the best way forward."

*

That evening, some 20 miles to the west.

Kate Rogers fumbled for her key. Beyond the door her phone was ringing. The late night shopping had to be dropped gently, and her handbag opened quickly. It was well past nine. She was curious as to who this might be at such an hour.

At last she was through, and the phone, still ringing, finally within reach. The door remained ajar, the bags on the step. Now the receiver was to her ear.

"Hello?"

"Kate?"

"Speaking."

"Alan here."

"Alan …..?" Kate's heart quickened. She knew, but she wanted to hear it from him.

"Alan Grigson."

"Grigson…… Alan Grigson. It's vaguely familiar," she fibbed. "Talk on and it'll come to me."

"You're cross Kate?"

"And that should surprise you? I let you enjoy me, use me. You then disappear…… and for nearly a year I hear nothing, until suddenly, out of the blue, when it's almost ten at night, you're on the phone, expecting all to be as it was I don't doubt. I thought you'd ceased to exist!"

And he had in a sense, but she was meaning this in a very different way.

"Look, Kate, it'll take too long to explain now. I need your help….. "

"Naturally."

"I'm in trouble at work. At the moment I'm suspended."

"Mixing business with pleasure, was it?"

"Look, you've made your point. You're a big girl now. I'm bothering you because I'm in a corner, on my own."

"So you expect me to do what, Alan?"

"I want to get in touch with Jeremy."

"And you come to me! He and I might still have been together were it not for you."

"Now that is pathetic, Kate. I don't recollect you needing much encouragement….."

"Because I fooled myself into thinking that your interest me might be of a more lasting nature." Kate half hoped that Alan might defend himself, but he didn't, because he couldn't. And realising this from his abashed silence she could only soften. "He lives in Bath now. I've forwarded letters, but we've not spoken since….."

"Since he almost got himself and me killed."

"…… since we hurt him, Alan."

"OK, but let's hope he's over that. For all his faults he's a man of considerable talent, a talent I could use. Give me his address."

"15c Belvoir Crescent, Bath. If he's moved on again you'll have to ask there." There was a pause, presumably while this was being written down.

"Thanks Kate. Now what about you? Busy at the Accident and Emergency still?"

"Nice of you to eventually enquire," replied Kate, cuttingly. "Actually I've transferred to a hospital in Bodmin….. and also moved to a village nearby."

"I'm pleased then that you kept the same phone number."

"The change I made from military nursing to A and E was psychiatrist prescribed," continued Kate, "you know that……"

"…. and it worked….."

"….. but only so far, only until my cosy routines and relationships became disturbed by a Mister 'here today, gone tomorrow' Grigson. I discuss this with the same Doctor, and it's suggested that it might be time for a further career change. This I try, and again it would appear to be working…. so far."

"I refuse to believe you're so delicate, Kate Rogers," scoffed Alan, and he was as correct as he was confident. This 'Doctor', a psychiatrist, was in fact more of a personal friend, Rosemary, her name, and she'd

189

listened and advised as such, rather than in any clinical capacity. But Kate wasn't saying this now, not while she was wanting every defence in place.

Rosemary had likewise had enough of the military culture, and similarly taken a civilian position........ in her case to be based at Moorhaven, a psychiatric hospital in Devon, on the southern edge of Dartmoor, close to the village of South Brent. The equivalent in Cornwall was St Lawrence, and it was here that on Rosemary's suggestion Kate had sought and was finding her new challenge, aspiring now to heal the psychological wound rather than the physical.

"So where is it you work?"

"St Lawrence, Bodmin..... a psychiatric hospital of the old sort, massive. I'm no longer so accessible I'm afraid, but perhaps that's not such a bad thing."

*

(ix) a find

Sally fretfully paced her room, too anxious to sleep, and too embarrassed venture much beyond its door. If she was serious about her diving then by now she should have contacted Bovisand to confirm the weekend's session. But it was all so awkward, so depressing. She'd upset Chas, she was sure, and, more than anyone, she'd let down his father, Tony. And she was disinclined, too, to share all this with her own parents. The guilt was hers. It was to be borne alone.

She heard the phone downstairs. On another evening she might have hastened to get to it first, but not today...... in fact she near dreaded it being for her. But it was, and her mother was calling up.

"Chas Cross," she called up, leaving the receiver and tactfully moving back to the lounge before the daughter was even half down.

"Chas," the girl acknowledged, rather limply.

"Sally, we're sorting out Saturday, and we hadn't heard."

"The phone-in, Chas. That was my fault..... your father, he must have been livid."

"It did come as a shock, this is true, but dad was quickly over it, remarkably quickly. He says that this element of controversy that you've injected......"

"......inadvertently...."

"..... has prompted other direct contacts, some by no means

190

negative."

"That's a relief." Sally couldn't muster the nerve to pry.

"And dad himself, he said that we need to keep customers like you, good pupils who will achieve and hopefully recommend. So if the weather's nice….."

"……. as it promises to be….."

"……. he's allowing me to take you around to Whitsand Bay. Can you make both morning and afternoon, bringing sandwiches, enough for me too? I can get the kit sorted, then come across and into Kingsand to collect you on the way. Should the weather play up unexpectedly then things can be changed with a quick phone call."

"Sounds good, shall we say, what…… ten?"

"Ten at Kingsand," confirmed Sally, much cheered.

And Saturday did dawn fine. Sally was through Millbrook and over the crest to Kingsand in good time….. likewise Chas, after a smooth crossing of the Sound. The air was warm, and the sea blue, clear, and so still that it barely lapped at the pebble and studded shore. The sturdy sea going inflatable could be gently idled in to knee depth, enabling the girl to be smartly up and onto the bow. Her rucksack, replete with towel and packed lunch was stowed with the kit, and then, trimmed and balanced, they were away.

First, Chas had to negotiate the inshore moorings. He would need to concentrate, so she could save the chat…… and admire. He was good at the helm, with his neat, evenly tanned legs, the thick, flowing, sun bleached hair, and bright brown eyes. To have this specimen to herself, for so much of the day, yes, all to herself……. she'd thought it could get no worse, but now, hey, could it ever get any better?

They were through the buoys and the boats, clearing the breakwater and rounding Penlee Point. It looked plain sailing, and she felt so secure. It wouldn't be a new start, though, until the past was tidied. It had to be addressed, as delay could only foster pretence.

"And that debate provoked by the radio broadcast," she began, "it hasn't totally scuppered things?"

"It wasn't anticipated, but if there's a snag looming then it's best to know of it sooner rather than later. At the start of the week my father was not a happy man, most definitely not…… by Thursday, though, he's totally changed. And this after driving over to Cornwall to speak with some guy coming up from further down, a Naval historian with a good knowledge of the seas off Panama. Exactly what they'd discussed he was keeping to himself."

Sally sensed exasperation, and perhaps hurt too.

"He's learned to be wary of you saying something to me, and me passing it on....... understandable."

"Well you needn't be beating yourself up, Sal. He was keen that I should contact you. What's done is done, he said, so whatever went off between him and this bloke has to have been positive."

"But the kindness is coming from you, Chas," smiled the pupil. "I bet you bring all the girls out here."

"Only those who I know will cope." The girl giggled, and then Chas was chuckling too. "Do what I say and you'll be OK. I think I can trust you to follow instructions."

"And trust me too to keep your secrets," teased the girl. "No one to hear us out here."

Chas hesitated, then reached for her hand. He was being serious. "I think I might take you up on that," he said. "You know my parents have split...."

"I do."

"Well there are things I'm not sure I could say to either."

"That's not so unusual, Chas, even when parents are together still."

"But I'm talking things that I sometimes want very much to share, but can't. I did have a gran, and we were close, but she died back in the winter."

"Having reached a good age?"

"Not really...... mid sixties, that's all. It was cancer."

"Leaving your grandfather?"

"There never was one, not officially. She'd been a single parent......having had my father when really young, a teenager still, in the days when this was less accepted."

"So your father was....."

".... he was born out of wedlock, to poor Jenny Cross, a girl barely older than yourself. Dad was her only child, just as I am his."

"You must have been very precious to her."

"I think you're right, and part of this was what I see now, looking back, as a kind of need in her, a need to offload her story, the story of herself and my father, and also his father."

"The father that he never knew."

"Of whom gran seems to have spoken more easily to her one grandson than she did to her one son. The guy was never far from her thoughts. You could see this towards the end…… she never forgot."

"So your father, Tony Cross, has he ever spoken to you of this."

"No, because as I've hinted, he was never properly told, not like I've been. In fact, you could say that I was groomed, almost, to be the sole recipient of what she was determined and perhaps almost desperate to say, this that I can't forever keep to myself. It was different, though, between her and dad….. and she did tell me why."

"So the explanation….."

"…..was that such fragments of the tale as were passed, were passed clumsily, to say the very least."

"He was too young, you mean."

"And they threatened to become a crippling burden."

"And this was realised…… so he was spared any fuller detail."

"Quite. Life for the little lad would have been uncertain enough as it was. Further complication had to be avoided, Sally, and maybe this is why we have the big-hearted survivor you see today, confident, buoyant and brave."

"So it had been too much too soon for young Tony….."

"……. who had actually been christened Anton. The preference for Anthony, afterwards shortened to Tony, was but one adjustment amongst many, all made with a view to damage linitation."

"But still there remained something in all this that Jenny Cross was anxious to preserve, something she had to pass on before she died, to the new generation."

"Which is our generation, Sal. And her wanting to do this, and her achieving it, this was the core of the special intimacy she and I enjoyed."

"Because it was to stay between you and her. You weren't to take it to your father."

"She made me promise, Sal. The Tony Cross that you know she likened to a timepiece…… steady enough and reliable, but in truth, not so solid as it might appear. His was a personality delicately assembled, she said. And while I could be given a better understanding of its construction, I was never to attempt to open it up and meddle."

"So to the extent that the son has been disburdened, now it's yourself, her grandson….."

"……who has been left to carry what his father has been spared. But gran was right, it's a far lighter load for one a generation removed, for one older and better prepared. I can be equal to it, I'm sure."

"But if there's no sharing of this with your own Pa, then who can you confide in?"

"That's up to me, Sally. I've been trusted to choose wisely….. to be careful with the placing my own trust. And it's more than a matter of who gets told and how much they'll hear. The when and the where have also to be considered. The time and the place must feel right."

"As well as the person," soothed the girl, softly, unassumingly, irresistibly.

"So don't think I bring all my pupils out here," smiled Chas. "Why are you out here today? I did say."

"Capable…?"

"….and?"

"Trustworthy?"

"Exactly," chuckled Chas. They were closing on Rame Head now, losing the angle they had on the church spire of St Germanus, while winning a clear sight of the tiny point lodged chapel of St Michael. "So ready yourself. Sally Shaw, you are about to be put in the picture……. and, hopefuly, recruited to the challenge that it presents."

"You speak as if I were in any position to walk away," chided the girl, looking out to a hazy Eddystone.

"No pressure, Sal……..the choice, in the end, will be with you. Hear me out, now, and accept that I bring you here merely to illustrate my narrative."

"To set the scene?"

"Yes, and to show you as best I can where the challenge lies."

"OK, I'm listening. Where are you going to start."

"With me. According to my grandmother, Sal, you are now being helmed by the grandson of a French Admiral." Chas hesitated momentarily, wary of derision, but needlessly so. He continued, encouraged. "They met early in the last war, he being one of the very few of that rank who abandoned the French Vichy Government to join Charles de Gaulle's Free French movement, maybe the only one"

"And your father was never told this?"

"He was, but at an age when the most natural thing in the world is to boast such a revelation to every corner of the school playground. Imagine it, one of the poorest kids in the class coming up with something like that..... amongst all the ruin and hardship that Plymouth was at that time, the late '40s."

"No one believed him."

"Whether they did or didn't, wasn't the point. What mattered was that no one was going to forgive such crowing. He was teased and he was bullied. And a counter rumour grew that in fact he'd been sired by a Cornish fisherman who'd been found one night in the House where she'd held a house maid's position. Summarily dismissed she'd then found herself abandoned, for the fisherman had vanished, it was said, leaving her to whore herself a living along Union Street."

"And she repeated this to you?"

"So that I might understand my father's pain, and his need for it all to be kept buried. At the same time she was wanting the truth to live on. The rumours were not totally without foundation, she said, but the fact remained that her child had been fathered by this distinguished Frenchman."

"So what became of him?"

"He fought under de Gaulle...."

".... to help liberate his country."

"Yes, and after that he dabbled in French national politics. He died back in '65. He was a good bit older than my mother, you see."

"Big send off I should think."

"Not so big as one might expect... that is if one didn't know that both military and political careers were decidedly patchy. From the little I've read it seems there were problems between him and de Gaulle. They both hated Hitlerism, true, but beyond that, in temperament and taste, they were poles apart."

"Sounds like he might have been a bit raffish."

"Quite, and bearing in mind that Gaullism became a political movement in France....."

"....which lasts even to this day...."

".... well we can imagine that those who dared express misgivings about their nation's saviour left themselves exposed to strong adverse comment."

"OK, but I don't see why, over in flattened Plymouth, a poor abandoned single mother should care too much about the reputation of the man so largely responsible for her predicament"

"To every mother her own child is special. This one was no exception. Jenny Cross wanted her child, christened Anton, to grow up to be brave and honourable"

"And this," reasoned Sally, "was why she'd been moved to tell the little lad that his father was a very distinguished person."

"But she wouldn't have, at least not then, had she known of the hurt that came….."

"….. but that said, Chas, I'm sure that all who've worked with him consider your father a responsible and resourceful man. Any mother would be proud of him, and any father. What was his name, the Admiral? You said you'd read of him."

"Emile Muselier, he was called, and yes, he is said to have had a roguish streak. Gran knew that."

"Only too well."

"But this wasn't going to stop her taking vigourous exception to one particular charge laid against him."

"Which was….?"

"That during the war he was tempted to waver in his opposition to fascism by an offer of gold from the Vichy people, those in France who'd accepted defeat by Germany."

"So he would never have been bought, she says ……. and she actually knows this?"

"Because she was told as much by someone who happened to be right there when the offer was made," said Chas.

"Right where, for heaven's sake?"

"Here, Gran told me that it happened out here, in Whitsand Bay. And it was seen by a local fisherman she knew….."

"The fisherman?"

"I think it must have been. The fisherman, out here at night, with a younger brother, doing his job, witnessed a surface rendezvous between two French submarines…… the first of these pulling that brother from the open boat, sadly never to be seen again. He did see the gold though, and heard the inducement. He heard Muselier refuse it and attempt to arrest the agent, and then, as he sought to escape, he saw the tempter shot in the water by one of his Vichy colleagues. The submarines crash-dived, leaving the fisherman to hook the dying agent into his boat."

"With that gold?"

"No….. because he saw this drop in the struggle and slip from the submarine to sink to the bottom of the bay. What he did save though was part of a map which had been torn in the struggle."

"So the fisherman knew Jenny Cross, and knew too of her involvement with Muselier, a guy who he'd been able to recognise presumably after some previous sighting."

"Must have, because before that night was out, the poor lad had called on Jenny…..he being in a state of utter desperation."

"Having lost his younger brother, of course."

"The first submarine to surface had been Muselier's. It had fouled the boy's line, dragged him from the boat, and lifted him into the night air on its forward armament. The fisherman knew, though, that this vessel had come out of Devonport, and of a chance that it might return there…..where the boy might be safely delivered up."

"Did this happen?"

"No. He was to learn that Muselier and his submarine was bound elsewhere, to Scotland in fact, and he set off in pursuit."

"Plucky!"

"Until one imagines his reluctance to face his mother."

"He had an explanation, though,"countered the girl. "It had been mischance."

"He had an explanation, yes, but could it be safely given? He'd seen a man shot, seemingly by a colleague, possibly for knowing a deal too much. He chose to act rather than talk."

"So he went alone, telling no one save your grandmother….."

"…..who he hoped might squeeze the Admiral for information. That's why the he left the part map…..hoping that it might earn her some sort of consideration. The lad would have warned her, though, that it was a scrap that had already cost one life."

"And then he was on his way."

"Thereby putting himself firmly in the frame when the paternity issue arose." Chas managed a wry smile. "Hardly his night, was it?"

"So where did she entertain these men, your gran? One of the big Houses I suppose. You spoke of her being in service……where? Mount Edgcumbe? Antony? Sconner?"

"She had a position at Ince Castle, having been kept on there after the place had been requisitioned as a kind of clearing house for high ranking French Canadians. Muselier was seen as someone who might help weed out any that were over sympathetic to Vichy."

"So would she be remembered by any over there now?"
The grandson shook his head.

"She spoke of having gone back there once in the 70s, with a few gentle enquiries. She learned that the present owners had arrived in the early '60s, bringing with them their own staff. None of the old guard remained."

"This would have been the Lennox Boyds. Lady Boyd, now widowed, lives there still….. the Lord, a former Minister, and therefore Viscount, having been killed in a London street accident, some three years ago. The Viscountess, as we should properly call her, she is one of the Guinness family, the big Dublin brewers. In recent years the Prime Minister and her husband have been entertained at Ince, in fact it's only a few days ago that they were down to see the old lady again. The papers weren't making much of it for security reasons. My father heard a whisper though, through the journalists' grapevine…. "

"…….but he'll get no whisper of this I trust."

"My lips are sealed, Chas, and I mean that. What really intrigues is how this tale is meant to affect you. You weren't told all this just so you could sit on it."

"Right, Sal, and I'm not intending to."

"So you're contemplating action. Something that could involve me, but definitely not your father….. lest painful memories be revived."

"As I've said, I think you're ready to go diving in Whitsand Bay."

"Diving for gold, that's what you're saying. Real gold, real French gold……. and you think it could be out there, an ingot lying amongst the rocks, just waiting for us? Isn't the area crawling with divers?"

"But you have to know what you're looking for. They don't, we do. Treasure from the sea is always a gamble. To win it….."

"…..you have to be in it."

"Just look at my Dad. He's ready to trawl the western Caribbean for a lead coffin… that"s further away, deeper, and all for an item that's been down there a lot, lot longer. I have to give it a go. I owe this to the pair of them, Jenny and Emile."

"And also to that fisherman, wherever he might be…… in this world or the next. I'm with you on this, Chas. Go for it, I say. Clearly, you're not going to be satisfied unless you do. Are we equipped to sound for metal?"

"Whitsand Bay is like a scrap yard, Sal. We use our eyes."

"This fisherman, did he leave any clues as to position?"

"Between Portwrinkle and Eddystone, that's all."

"So that part chart doesn't help."

"Not in the least. I can say that because I have it at home."

"So I can assume that the Admiral never came back."

"It seems so.....and she was never to see that fisherman again either."

"And the lost youngster?"

"Some months later, in the *Morning News*, there was a brief piece on the remains of a child found on the rocky shore of Looe Island. Cause of death was obscure, decay being so advanced, but this fitted the time lapse since the fateful night venture out of Portwrinkle..... and there were a few durable scraps of clothing to suggest that this indeed was what was left of the lost brother."

"And your Gran was convinced?"

"It was at the height of the blitz. Tragedies were coming too thickly and too quickly to be hung up on just one." Chas circled the inflatable, then cut the motor.

"And what did she make of that part chart? Come to that, what do you make of it?"

"The best thing is to let you see it. I keep it in my bedroom." Sally turned away, not wishing Chas to notice her rising blush. But if he did, he wasn't making anything of it. "It's there in the same old envelope given me by my Gran, between the pages of an old school atlas. I'm not to take it out on the water. She insisted that I guard it closely....."

"..... as she'd done previously."

"As she was reminded to do after almost losing it forever."

"To some one at Ince?"

"Not at Ince." Chas slid the anchor over the side, feeding it slowly with measured chain. "No one knew of it there, she said, but she did seek an opinion after she'd moved into Plymouth. She went to a small shop over in Bretonside, Dalton's, in Bilbury Steet, a navigation chart specialist, hoping that as an expert this guy might recognise what she assumed to be a stretch of the French coast."

"This assumption being based on what?"

"The only discernible letters.... denoting a 'Mt. P'."

"A tenuous assumption."

"And the chap in the shop made exactly the same point, adding that as well as the coasts of France, north, west, and south, there were also those of her colonies to consider! Not surprisingly he wanted to keep the thing for a day or three. If he was to fix this Mt. P he would need time. And Gran did initially agree to leave it with him, but then, when almost home, thought better of this and went back to collect it, allowing Mr Philip Dalton no more than a hastily traced copy....."

".....but your gran, she left with the original."

"She did."

"So was he able to find where this place was."

"We'll never know, for neither he nor his shop survived another night. Even the family went. They lived above."

"A bombing raid?"

"There was a cellar beneath, and that's where he went on raid nights, preferring not seek shelter outside the City. They were as safe there as anywhere really, but they were unlucky. If the bomb had your name on it there was no escape. This one was a stray. On that night, according to Gran, scores came down to the west of Derry's Cross, perhaps a dozen on the Hoe, but just the one on Bretonside."

"And that was the one."

"Which also, fatefully, carried a delayed action fuse. There was no detonation until it had penetrated every floor. Then it took out cellar, foundations, proprietor, wife, child, the lot..... leaving nothing, just a rubble rimmed crater."

"So it was as well that she'd changed her mind and retrieved that chart." Sally looked across to Portwrinkle. "What about the fisherman, do we know if he ever sought her out?"

"He didn't. She was left to assume that he'd built a life elswhere....."

"..... as she'd had to."

"And this would have been for the best, she thought, for it was obvious from the whispers following her and the baby, that any homecoming to Sheviock or Portwrinkle would be met with hostility."

"Even from close family?"

"All the more so, since after the grief stricken mother pined to her death there remained just one brother, an eldest brother who'd been away soldiering. Had he not been, then it's likely that Jenny Cross's child would have been rumoured to be his..... for she and he had been betrothed you see."

"And the poor man's plans were thrown into total disarray. Is he.....?"

"He died in the '50s. He stayed with the military. He was shot in an ambush out in Cyprus, and that's where he was buried."

"So they've passed on, and all that's left now is this lump of gold, waiting there for us to pluck it from the depths. You don't think it cursed in any way? ....Rheingold," she trilled, "Rheingold."

"This is no fairy story, Sal."

"OK, say we bring it up. What do we do then, tell me? You don't walk into the local Post Office and say 'cash this please'."

"I think we take it all to France, the ingot and the map. That's where they came from."

"And your grandmother would have wanted this?"

"Because she wanted Muselier's name cleared of that lingering whisper that he'd listend to fascist bribes. My father's parentage needn't be an issue. The story comes from a fisherman. It was passed to gran, and from her to me. We find them the gold, they have it analysed, and this substantiates the story........ should put us in line for a reward. After that we might negotiate something with a newspaper You're the budding journalist. How's your French, Sally?

*

(x) M4
The same day: BBC Radio 4

"Lord Aldington, thank you for coming in today to speak to us on One o' Clock Worldwide."

"Thank you, Mr Knight, for the kind invitation. Having been made out by some to be a monster, I'm grateful for any opportunity to show myself as I truly am...... one who has always tried to give good service to this Nation of ours."

"As an MP, yes, and as a close advisor to the Heath

administration, and of course now as a member of the House of Lords."

"And before all that, Mr Knight, as a loyal soldier during the last war......loyal, dutiful, and humane."

"Which you are keen to stress, Lord Aldington, in refutation of this recent pamphlet authored and circulated by a Mr Nigel Watts, with Nikolai Tolstoy who......"

"......and in particular it is the second of this pair who needs to be taught a lesson, Mr Knight. Forgive my interruption, but I want your listeners to know exactly where the mischief comes from."

"And to do this you intend to commence libel proceedings......but against both."

"I have already instructed my lawyers. Together we are gathering the evidence from the relevant Ministry archives."

"But I understand that some of your friends have misgivings about such a course. They make the point that last year Tolstoy made a big enough fool of himself over his attack on Stockton, whose lawyers forced 'The Minister and the Massacres' into the pulping bins."

"Except that without his lies being tested in Court it was merely his publisher's lack of nerve that was exposed. That's what he argues......"

"......and you want this stopped."

"He's made a fool of himself, you say. Well I will make that a bankrupt fool. He writes that I am personally responsible for......and I quote......'a combination of duplicity and brutality without parallel in British history since the Massacre of Glencoe.' I am 'a major war criminal,' he adds, 'whose activities merit comparison with those of the worst butchers of Nazi Germany or Soviet Russia.' Now tell me, Mr Knight. Why should I allow that kind of invective to go unchallenged?"

"Some have suggested, friends again included, that confrontation gives Tolstoy what he seeks, his day in court, with all the attendant publicity. He's out to promote a fishing expedition into other areas of British policy towards Russia during the last war, they say, and these might prove dangerous waters. If it can be established that your role was minor and innocent, this will do nothing counter a widening realistion that Stalin was appeased......and then of course the extent of that appeasement begs the question why. Sometimes, in the National interest, a measure of reputation has to be sacrificed."

"So long as it isn't yours Mr Knight, or theirs. So long as it is mine. I see this also as a test of friendship. The 'friends' you speak of

sound to be of the fair weather variety. There's a better sort, I remind you, of whom I still have plenty."

Alan Grigson reached for the tuner. It was an ageing van and this radio looked and behaved as would an original. Any more drift in the reception and he would lose the thread of the programme, just as it was starting to fascinate. He was Bath bound on the M4 and, dropping from the Berkshire Downs, beginning now to get used to how the VW handled at speed.

He was much improved in spirit. It was good to be on the road, and heading again for the south and west. The camper had benefitted from a lick of paint since last he saw it….. blue now, with a red roof in shades not dissimilar to those that graced the boat, his *Speedwell*. She was no more, so why not let this van take the name? Yes…..the *Speedwell* she would be.

He checked his watch. He would make Bath by mid afternoon, and in a place so compact he should be able to locate the address fairly promptly. Suspension made him no less a professional.

But would Kate have warned Jeremy that he was on his way, he wondered? Probably not, for she would be wary of getting re-involved, he felt….. and who could blame her for that?

That operation down on the Fal had been closed out quite neatly though. His superiors had certainly been impressed, even if this seemed to count for very little now. He glanced ruefully across to the passenger side door. The armour had done its job then, he thought. He hoped it might again.

*

(xi) Whitsand Bay

From the shore the Bovisand inflatable looks to be hemmed amongst a far too crowded cluster of such craft. It seems that the divers beneath must be having to jostle for space. In fact, they have ample, even in an area so popular. A day as good as this can draw as many as a dozen groups, but as yet it's not half that. This is ideal……. space for all, and yet the added safety of no more than sufficient number. A look out would always be on the surface, watching and ready should any wayward helmsman threaten their ground.

At this moment, though, neither Chas nor Sally need stand watch. Their station is empty. It is anchored, firmly, and they are beneath. Chas swims free, but only after equipping the girl with a light tether that slides on the anchor line. She can reach the bottom whilst being confident that neither she nor craft will stray.

But no longer is Sally the novice. Here is one well taught, with an instructor to whom the seabed below is no less familiar than any patch of his native Plymouth. Sometimes, when lying in his room, Chas could imagine himself down here under darkness, with the wartime submarines inching in above him at periscope depth. Black and long against the moonlit surface, they then rise to break into the night, each trailing its silvered wake. They close, but apart lies the small smudge that is Wrickleman's bark, and then comes the glint of the down spiralling ingot. He watches it to the bottom and sees it nestle amongst the rock and the weed, where it waits for him now.

Such a cosy dream this once had been, with all the warmth of a shared secret, a special secret. But when Jenny Cross had died so, for the grandson, had its lustre. Instead, being his alone, it chilled......until today. To once more share this hope of treasure was to re-ignite that imagined glow. This was their second dive. He glanced at his watch. They'd been down for almost thirty minutes, and that was enough for now. There was time and there was air to do another later. He swooped to tug playfully at his companion's tether. She turned, opening herself to his gentle touch.

Chas tapped at his watch, and pointing upwards he kicked for the surface. Sally signalled compliance but chose to sink the last eight or so feet to the seabed, preferring to launch upward with a crouch and a spring. But the under flipper firmness she sought wasn't quite there. The right foot had loosened something. It was giving way and, though buoyant, instinctively her arms were out for balance, and she was kicking again at what she'd dislodged. It was rolling away, she felt, but in a lumpy man moulded kind of way. She could look down now and reach. If this was a block of metal, then why not a block of precious metal.....*the* block of precious metal, maybe.

Chas broke an otherwise barely rippled surface, perhaps twenty metres from the inflatable. He anticipated Sally's appearance between, and soon, but he was having to wait. Where was she..... on the other side of the craft? He sculled for an angle to look around, no sign though. He peered down, and here she was, almost to the surface now, but under leg propulsion only, for there was something she was clinging to, with both hands.

The anchor? No, for the line was as taut as before. Whatever, his help would be needed as she emerged, lest this prize be dropped back. He dived again so as to come up beside her, which he did, at the same time using the line to drag the inflatable to within easy reach. He was placed then to take the thing and hold it while she hauled herself into the craft and from there, with his support, land this this intriguing catch onto the tough laminate deck.

She helped him aboard then, and off came the tanks and the masks and the flippers. They could talk now, and properly move.

"That thing's heavy," gasped Sally. Chas weighed it from hand to hand, then reached for the oily rag kept beneath the outboard. He polished at the block, conjuring a glow that seemed almost to want to feed off the sun.

"Beginner's luck?" asked Sally, afraid to use the 'G' word.

"It might be that you've hit the jackpot," said Chas, now wrapping the ingot with the cloth. A thought flashed through the girl's mind. This was hers to swaddle so, not his....... a second's worth of indignation, before realising how instantly she'd fallen prey to the long fabled instinct for sole possession. Partnerships forged in the quest for wealth can quickly unravel on its dicovery...... the old story. It couldn't happen with them, over this, surely? But already, for Sally, here was a warning that it might. "We take it in for a closer look," continued the boy. "You see Portwrinkle, there's a quiet stretch of sand along from there, to the west."

The strip of sand was visible, raised above a ragged fringe of ebb-exposed rock through which, from the prow where she sat, Sally could see no navigable way. Chas, standing at the tiller, knew better. Carefully, nimbly, he found water enough to nudge a way into to the shell strewn shore. The tide was filling. Coming out again would be easier, but first the boy wanted their craft higher on the beach. And quite a haul it was, offering a measure of the boy's uncertainty as to their next step. Jackpots are dreamt of rather than expected, and still less is such a prize planned for. They could take time though, to confirm and to consider and to discuss..... provided secrecy could be assured. And could it?

They thought so, for there was trust between them they decided, and they would move and speak with care...... but already it might not be that they'd been sufficiently watchful. That flash of reflected sun high on Rame Head, it had gone unheeded. For them it might have been a mirror on a car or bike, or a tilted bottle.

In fact it had been thrown by a raised lens glass.

*

(xii) Bath

Jeremy Barnes rose from his kitchen table. For all of the full five hours he'd given to the marking of these 'A' level coursework projects the stack that he was now shoving away to the far end seemed neither lower nor lighter. A lonely and wearisome task this, but it would help finance a cheap fortnight in Greece, and also help nurture a few local contacts. Yes, he'd wanted to come to the area, but he still felt less than at home.

He would have a mug of coffee, and with it a little of the light relief that he'd left open next to the kettle..... *Put Out More Flags*, his paperback of the moment.

English Lit. was very much a minor option at his college. Understaffed, under re-sourced, it was hardly a department at all, but they were commendably keen in there, he thought, and for the coming autumn he'd allowed himself to be enlisted to teach a term long module on the novels of Evelyn Waugh. And what this meant, of course, was that during the summer he would need to re acquaint himself with the man's canon.

He'd read *Brideshead* first, as so many did, when it was put on the telly six or so winters back. Then *Decline and Fall* and *Vile Bodies* within the year, but interest swiftly dwindled on a failure to finish even the first part of the *Sword of Honour* trilogy..... so it had been quite some time. But just before his Easter break a perceptive female colleague had dangled *Black Mischief* in front of him. He'd taken the intended bait and he was now re-hooked, firmly so, on the excruciating barb that was Basil Seal.

For Charles Ryder and Guy Crouchback with their agonised loves and their profound spiritual quests had been altogether too serious, too burdened perhaps with their creator's own angsts..... but Basil, he was the child of a formidable wit, of a certain *apercu* that deftly pointed up so much of the political and social humbug of the time. Jeremy recognised Basil as no less a creation than Becky Sharp or Barry Lyndon had been nearly a hundred years before. Waugh, with those two tight little tales, *Mischief* and *Flags*, was surely the Thackeray of his age.

The colleague, Penny, with her charming and obviously devoted female partner, had even taken him on an excursion or three to sample a few of the local and not quite so local places that had figured strongly in the author's life. On one such they had driven him as far north as Madresfield Court, a moated manor house nestling in the lee of the Malvern hills, home of the Lygon sisters where, in the early '30s, much of *Black Mischief* had been penned. On their way back they'd taken in Piers Court, the grand house close to Dursely purchased by the author for his second wife Laura on their marriage in '38, and where they'd lived with their young children until the mid '50s.

Another distant outing had been westward to Chagford, in Devon, to the Easton Court Hotel, another of Waugh's 1930s working retreats, the return this time taking in his last home at Combe Florey, and nearby Pixton where Laura had enjoyed her girlhood. The favourite for Jeremy though had been the short spin over to Midsomer Norton, returning via Mells, a tour that since he'd more than once repeated on his own. As a child Waugh would holiday to Midsomer, staying with his aunts; and then later, at the time of the collapse of his first marriage, he was to be made welcome at Mells by Katherine Asquith and her children, all under the gentle matriarchal watchfulness of the Lady Horner.

The devoutly catholic Katharine, daughter in law to Herbert Asquith, was probably foremost of the generation of single mothers widowed by the Great War..... a status that resonated with Jeremy whose own father's father had been taken in the same cataclysm.

He was back in his chair now, with mug and book, averaging perhaps three sips to the chortle, and slipping back to the early months of the war...... when there were footsteps, outside on his staircase.

Not unusual, this, for there were flats above. Why should he stir? They would probably climb on, but not this time.

The firm rap jerked him from his page. Resentful of its authority he moved first to the sink to swill and rinse the mug. It could wait. The same rap was repeated, if anything more firmly. Was this the law? He pulled open the door.

"Jeremy...."

"Alan Grigson. To what night I owe this pleasure….. or should I say 'to whom'?"

"It's just me, Jeremy, and I need your help. Can we talk…..inside?" Jeremy stepped back. Alan eased past.

"You come here, expecting my help! Bit of a nerve, wouldn't you say? Mr smooth talker Grigson…… this will have to be good."

"Might be, Jeremy. Listen, I'm here because *you* were good, Jeremy, in the sense that you got to the heart of the *Kampala* thing on your own. I was fronting a team. Thought I had every angle covered….. and yet you came at it from the past and in the end left me standing. OK, you got yourself upset over the woman and allowed spite got the better of diligence, but that takes nothing from my assessment of your talent."

"Sit down Alan. I was about to make myself another coffee, so….?"

"Yes please, milk and just half a sugar."

"Where then is the action?"

"Cornwall again. The other end, up towards the Tamar this time."

"But it was Kate who gave you this address wasn't it?"

"Over the phone."

"Keeping well was she?"

"Changed jobs, but much the same apart from that. I hadn't spoken to her for some time….. as I tried to explain to her, it's in the nature of my work not to…...."

"…..not to give too much weight to people's feelings. But I'm sure she'll have made hers known, all the same."

"She did," confirmed Alan, sheepishly, "but the pair of you, you made adult choices. Why should I be made to feel totally responsible. If I look after my own self then so can you. I don't see that I have that much to apologise for. In fact, considering how close I came to being blown up, I think you and I, Jeremy, are just about even."

"So you need my help, you say, and it's the Tamar you're doing this time. Have they given you another love boat?"

"No boat."

"So where's your accommodation?"

"Outside actually. I'm using the old camper van. It was in action on the Roseland. So busy were you with chasing through fifty years of history, I doubt if you noticed."

"And the rest of your team?"

"No boat, no team either. This time I'm truly on my own. I've been suspended.... told to regard myself as being on 'garden leave', pending the findings of a departmental enquiry."

"So when you say you 'need help', this means you're in trouble."

"They want me stitched up Jeremy, I can feel it."

"Isn't that how the covert departments operate? Every so often someone has to be thrown to the wolves. You've just happened to pull the short straw."

"And I'm not accepting it. This is why I'm here. If we get to the bottom of this thing my career can be back on track."

"So what's in it for me?"

"You would be doing what you love. The media down there made quite a lot of Old Jack. It was an opportunity you opened, then missed out on. No promises, but this might be your second chance."

"Let's hear it then. What's this jam you've got yourself into?"

"You've heard of Ince Castle?"

"No."

"Alan Lennox Boyd?"

"Yes, a Tory politician, made up to a Lord..... Lord Boyd I suppose. Dead now I think."

"Killed in a London street accident four years ago,"confirmed Grigson, "sadly, quite a way from his home and family. He had a place in Cornwall, just, near Saltash...."

"....... this Ince Castle."

"To where he'd retired, and there he was known to entertain a wide selection of top Tories, including Margaret and Dennis Thatcher. They so much enjoyed the place that they were delighted to return there this summer at the invitation of the widow, the Viscountess."

"So your task....?"

".... had been to help implement the security arrangements, and with the place being all but surrounded by water these should have been straightforward."

"But there was an incident."

"The detonation of an explosive device, Jeremy, but fortunately before the arrival of the star guests....."

"..... who nevertheless got to hear of it."

"They did, and they also learned that the prime suspect for this outrage was allowed to slip away, from right under our disjointed noses.

He made his get away in an inflatable dinghy, the very craft in which I'd earlier been patrolling the shore. Maybe I shouldn't have left it where I did when the bomb went off ......"

"..... but you did, presenting yourself as the sacrificial lamb. Heads had to roll. Your neck was nicely stretched across the line. Oh dear, Mr Grigson..... and you think there's more to this do you?"

"There always is Jeremy. Isn't this what experience tells us?"

"So where do you look?"

"I'm going down there. I would like you to join me. I'll scout the area as it stands, you could look into its past...... as only you can. I hear the brain ticking already. Come on, Jeremy...... Alan Lennox Boyd, there must be an episode you can recall. He was a Cabinet Minister.... "

"Under Macmillan, yes, Colonial Secretary before Macleod, which means before the '59 election and the subsequent 'Wind of Change' tour of Africa. Hola, that's the episode. Alan Lennox Boyd will be remembered for surviving the Hola scandal. That was at the tail end of the Mau Mau thing, in Kenya. Pity he's dead, but never mind, could be a good one all the same. Macmillan was peaking, and we catch him at his most Machiavellian. Boyd was odds-on to be forced out, a scapegoat....like you.... but in that instance to ease Harold's re-election..... not that he need have been worrying, in the event he coasted it. It didn't happen like that, though. Boyd must have had something up his sleeve."

"Some kind of insurance provision?"

"In effect..... but exactly what, no one's sure."

"So maybe he hung on to it, taking whatever it was with him into eventual retirement. You could sleuth it out, Jeremy, I'm sure. It's your forte, this kind of thing."

"Certainly a challenge, Alan."

"And I think you could have a way in, via a quiet little chat with your old friend Sir Edward. Still squeezable, I reckon.... Don't you? I know you tried to cut some kind of deal with him. Are you with me?"

Jeremy Barnes stood. He walked to the window, and considered. Grigson waited. Finally;

"Where will I find you?" asked the lecturer.

"I see on the map that there's a campsite above Whitsand Bay, atop that ridge that goes on to make the Cornwall side of Plymouth Sound. Go through Plymouth, find the car ferry over to Torpoint. Cross, drive out to Antony, the first village, then keep bearing left until you find the sea.

There'll be room for you in the camper van."

"I'll be down by the weekend, but first it's a cheap day return into London. As you say, Sir Edward might be just the man. He'll certainly remember the Hola debate."

"But you don't mention me, OK."

"Don't worry, I'll be giving nothing away," said Jeremy, escorting Alan to the door. Hand on handle, he spoke again. "A final point….. for all of our combined talents, yours and mine, our success down on the Fal was achieved primarily through the boy, young Steve. That guileless usability of his was the key. He became an in-tray for unguarded confidences, proffered by both good guy and bad, and it was from that accumulation that the solution was sieved….. through his innocence, an innocence that was, as a result, largely lost. Be on the lookout for anything similar."

*

(xiii) London (Hampstead)
Two evenings later.

"An interesting letter," said the Minister, passing it back, "very interesting."

"And you can understand, now, why I asked you here, to my house, and the privacy of this study, so that you might share this?"

"Of course I do Sir Clive, for this is hardly to be mixed with Parliamentary or Departmental business. Thank you for calling me in. But of course my association with GUSTAVE stretches back far longer than yours, back to when I was primarily a historian, the capacity in which I was initially engaged. I trust that he's keeping well?"

"Remarkably so, given his age….."

"…..and those war wounds, of course," added the politician. "So I find it comforting to have the confidence of the man I must assume is being groomed as a successor."

"And thank you Minister, for it comforts me to know that should the time come then you might favour me with the same loyal assistance." Faulds rose, signalling an interview almost done.

"As I look forward to my political career continuing to prosper,

Sir Clive."

"But there's life in the old dog yet, Minister," said Faulds, snapping his guest, the Honourable Alan Clark MP, back to the present. "He asks me to convey his gratitude for your recent efforts down in Plymouth...... with this, I gather, not being the first time you've displayed a talent for thinking on your feet."

"Two things, Sir Clive, GUSTAVE will guard to his grave. Remember this for when the mantle passes, for the same will be expected of you."

"So we must guard HIGHLAND CLEARANCE......and also?

"You guard your identity."

"Yes, of course, most important....... but before you leave, Minister, there's a footnote in one of the files he's passed to me concerning your stepmother. Is she still.....?"

"She is .... she's totally barking, which isn't so surprising, Sir Clive. Runs in her family, of course. When any one asks me about her mother and Africa I just send them straight around.... and they're delighted, of course to be speaking with a real live de Janze. But Nolwen was never there, of course, any more than you or I were. So what can they ever learn from her?"

"It mentions here that there's little love lost between the pair of you."

"I can certainly confirm, Sir Clive, that no amendment need be made to that entry."

"I think then, Minister, I can safely leave you to the weighty responsibilities at the Department of Trade."

"My car waits at the door."

"So I will bid you good night, Minister. I'll be in touch."

*

While in Belgravia.

"Mr Barnes. I thought I'd seen the last of you ..... and paid good money for that privilege. If it's more that you've come f......"

"It's not money I want Sir Edward."

"But you do want something. You're not here, in London, knocking at my door just to enquire after my health..... which could be better, I might add, were it not for this kind of interruption to my afternoon rest:"

"I'm involved in a research project, Sir Edward."

"So you want help......"

"...... which I feel you might be uniquely qualified to give."

The retired Conservative Member for Plymouth North stepped back to usher the lecturer through. It remained as one of his life's dwindling pleasures that people would now and then remark on having seen his name as a footnoted source in this publication or that, usually a political or historical monthly, occasionally a book.

"When we last spoke you were considering a move away from Cornwall. I trust you found....."

"I lecture in Bath now, Sir, and that's where I live. Since moving I've not been back to Cornwall once."

"I don't get down so often myself."

"But your son, and the family.... they're keeping well?"

"They are, Mr Barnes, thank you. But you're not here to talk about Carwinion. I'd be obliged if you could get to the point."

"Alan Lennox Boyd, Sir Edward. Died four years ago, knocked over in a London street. .... main memories of the man, as they come to mind."

"Long Parliamentary career, he was an unusually young entrant. Originally won his seat back in '31, like Ida, but his was a shire constituency, safe as houses. Bedfordshire I think. He married well, into the Guinness empire, and that really is well, financially and politically. That Patsy, she had a truly awesome pedigree. Moyne was a brother to her father, the Earl of Iveagh, and I think it was her mother's sister who married Lord Halifax."

"Awesome indeed," concurred Jeremy.

"But he fought and survived an active war, did Alan, we can credit him there. Then, resuming in Parliament, his political career peaked in the late '50s. He was given the Colonial Office....."

".... at a very difficult time."

"Indeed, there was the Mau Mau thing in Kenya, the communists in Malaya, and the Turks against the Greeks in Cyprus, another thankless police action. He stepped down in '59, shortly after the October election.

He'd comfortably retained his Bedfordshire seat, but then in the spring of the next year he was relinquishing it, having been made up to a Viscount. Many of us expected him to resign his desk sooner, before the '59 election was called. For a while the word from the top was that this might be for the best, particularly in the weeks before the Hola debate."

"The Kenyan prison camp scandal."

"It was feared that if anything might lose us that election it was Africa, and that if Boyd went early enough then perhaps a line might be drawn beneath what was an admittedly shameful episode...."

"..... and perhaps the sting drawn from that particular issue."

"At the last minute, though, the whispers changed. This man had to stay, even if it was just for a few months, and he did, toughing it out against the opposition before stepping down in his own good time with honour and reputation intact. Strange business really, but politics is like that. A week, Mr Barnes, can be a long time...."

"....especially with an election approaching. The prospect of losing a stout contribution to the campaign fund might just about have swung things, eh?"

"*Stout contribution*, from the Guinness fortune, very good..... but I'm not sure that electioneering was all so much about money back then. There could have been other factors in play."

"The family's political sway, rather than financial...... is this what you mean?"

Trembath hesitated, weighing his words.

"Let's say a posthumous sway, exerted by one particular member. When Lennox Boyd married Patricia Guinness, I think in '38, he was himself already a Junior Minister under Chamberlain, and Patricia, as I've said, was a niece to Lord Moyne, he an extremely influential Tory Grandee. Many saw in the union a potential Chamberlain style political dynasty. Well travelled, well read, extremely well connected, smooth tongued Moyne was an accomplished administrator. We can guess that Alan and Patricia gained many an insight from her Uncle Walter. He was very close to Churchill, but by no means a sycophant. In fact one particular difference led to his death."

"I think I've read something about this, perhaps ten, twelve years ago. It was in the papers........ to do with a state funeral in Jerusalem."

"Yes, for the exhumed remains of the two men who'd been hanged for Moyne's murder. By '44 he was Churchill's Minister Resident in Cairo.

He was targetted by the Zionist terror group, the Stern Gang, and gunned down in the street, together with his chauffeur."

"So why should they have picked on him......?"

"...... after we plucky British had fought so stoically against the genocidal Nazis? That's the history we know and love, and you've taught often enough, no doubt." Did Jeremy hear scepticism? Trembath continued. "We have to go back to '41, when Moyne was installed as Colonial Secretary, and this would have been prior to *Barbarossa* when Britain stood alone. We governed Palestine then......"

"...... under a League of Nations Mandate, as we did Tanganyika....."

".....and as did the French in Syria, meaning the Vichy French, of course, in '41. And since the previous year's armistice this amounted to a worrying pro-German presence to the north east of Suez, an additional threat to the narrow strand by which we clung to Empire and drew on our Arabian oil assets. Palestine, predominately Arab populated, had to be held as a buffer....."

"..... and the natives had to be kept sweet," prompted Jeremy.

"It was essential. In the '30s there had been a serious Arab Revolt against increased Jewish settlement....."

"..... needing to be bought off by the famous 'White Paper', enacted just before the war to severely restrict the admission of Jews."

"And our basic Foreign Office line was to uphold this new strict quota regime, for fear of again alienating Arab opinion, at a time whem we could ill afford to."

"And Churchill," continued Jeremy, "who had been known to speak up for Zionism....."

"......when he came to power, at the head of a National Government, he had to heed his Foreign Office advice, disappointing many a Jewish friend, of course, friends he valued, particularly those in the American diaspora."

"So it was natural, Sir Edward, that the sterner utterances and decisions confirming this pro Arab policy should have been passed down to figures such as Moyne to voice."

"Exactly, Mr Barnes."

"But after reacting strongly against the White Paper, the Palestinian settled Jews did, by and large, rally to the British side when Hitler went into Poland."

"Most of them did, it's true. While still anti-quota the Irgun signed that truce and put many of their members under British Command. This was how Moshe Dayan famously lost an eye, fighting with the Palmach to secure the Levant border. Moyne had been given the decidedly tricky task of securing this truce. This would have been through late 1940 and early '41. He was allowed scope to offer concessions and, fatefully, to give assurances......"

"...... such as lifting the quota restrictions for Jewish immigration into Palestine?"

"There were all sorts of ideas..... even talk of buying a wedge of Sinai from Ibn Saud, and providing refugee havens in other Colonial territories. For those Zionists already in Palestine there was seeming approval for the formation of an independently led all-Jewish armed division which might take the fight beyond Damascus, to the alarm of the Arabs, of course......"

"....... who sensed that once formed and deployed with success, such a body might prove impossible to dislodge and disband, impossible to deny."

"Exactly, Mr Barnes, but Moyne, straining to ride two horses, was making it look as if the British were amenable...... and on the somewhat dubious strength of his vague assurances the truce you mentioned, with the Irgun, was bought."

"But such promises, if that's what they were, couldn't be delivered."

"Not in the face of Arab disquiet," confirmed Trembath. "Oil won the day, yet again, with Moyne becoming the focus of redoubled Jewish resentment. Trickery was suspected, probably unfairly...... at least so far as he had been personally involved. My guess is that he'd been negotiating in good faith and had himself felt let down. While sovereign in the Colonial Office, for the Foreign Office he was no more than a pawn."

"So it was embarrassment for Moyne."

"Embarrassment and heightened danger, Mr Barnes. Extreme disappointment breeds extreme anger......."

".....and extremist reaction. The Irgun splintered, a breakaway group rejecting the truce."

"Yes, the Lehi, for whom British vacillation was tantamount to a sham diplomacy, of the kind that which would only exacerbate the plight of European Jewry. The Irgun hope was that for the millions facing persecution in Europe, the truce might open Palestine as a stepping stone to safety. The promised land would be a vehicle of escape...... freely accessed, self-policed and defended by their own militia."

"While for the Lehi, this lifeboat was nothing but a cardboard mock-up, a deceit......"

"......and a trap for those who might place any reliance thereon. Few foresaw the Holocaust during those early years of the war, Mr Barnes, but in the Lehi there was a strain of opinion that almost certainly did. Some were even ready to argue that impending disaster might best be averted by the negotiation of an alliance with Hitler. An approach was made by the infamous Avraham Stern, offering to raise a force to help drive the British out of the middle east, the pay off being Nazi sponsored Zionism...... a racially pure Jewish state, run on fascist lines."

Jeremy offered a wry smile. "Strange how things turn out," he added.

The irony hit home. "Indeed," responded Trembath. "Maybe that Stern was not, in fact, the lunatic he was made out to be. But nevertheless he had to be hunted down and shot, I think in '42, and it was as part of the continued insurrection of his disciples, the Stern Gang, that Moyne was also shot in '44. He was down in Cairo then as Resident Minister, having left the Colonial job early in '42."

"So he relinquished the post of Colonial Secretary just as Hitler's extermination programme was beginning....."

".....as the Panzer divisions pressed eastward on their make or break bid to take Russia."

"A bid that foundered at Stalingrad."

"Stalin's star thereafter being on the ascendant, Mr Barnes."

"And you say that Moyne's posthumous sway over the events of '59 has to be somehow rooted in this pivotal sequence."

"And also in the Colonial Office, perhaps, for that would appear be a common factor. Macmillan did the job after Moyne......bear that in mind too."

"So something Moyne knew, or had, was handed down to his niece...... as an insurance policy, is that what you are saying?"

"Already I've said enough, Mr Barnes."

"So where do I go from here?"

"In Cornwall.......? If you were headed again for the Roseland then Lord Shawcross has a home in St Mawes. He'll use it often at this time of year. He keeps a yacht on the Percuil, the *Talisker*. Hugh will occasionally crew for him. As a main Prosecutor at the Nuremburg Trials he would have looked closely at '41, Hess having stood in the dock. He's a very discrete man, though, is Sir Hartley.......what you want is someone far less child immune. Someone who likes to talk, as my son Hugh did for the boy, Steve wasn't it?

"It was."

"And that worked well for you." Sir Edward was pensive. "Now if you were to similarly find yourself a pretty young lass, then you might find a way of sounding out the MP for one of the neighbouring constituencies to Plymouth North."

"Owen?"

"No, I speak of Mr Alan Clark, the honourable member for Plymouth Sutton......"

"...... currently main man at the DTI, a fair bit younger than yourself, and a lot younger than Hartly Shawcross. And he would be an authority on '41?"

"The renowned historian, who wrote so fulsomely on the *Fall of Crete*, and on *Barbarossa*? I would say he knew quite a bit, and also there's an intriguing family connection. Five, perhaps six years ago a book that came out on the Erroll murder, the Lord who was shot in Kenya, also in '41. Did you read it?"

"I didn't."

"Do so. I think it's being made into a film.....which might be complete by now and awaiting release, so there'll be copies in the shops still. The name you'll read of, and hear of too, when the film comes out is de Janze, Alice de Janze, a close and devoted friend to Erroll. One of her daughters became Clark's stepmother, his father, Kenneth, of *Civilisation* fame, marrying again late in life. Lord Clark has died since, but the Lady Nolwen Clark survives him, living in more modest accomodation within the grounds of Saltwood Castle........ Quince Cottage I think they call it."

"So could you be suggesting a link between the Erroll murder, and the killing of Stern, and the consequent assination of Moyne?"

"I'm suggesting nothing, Mr Barnes....... merely recalling your question for me when we first met. You called at Carwinion, and it was ......?" Jeremy thought back. He remembered.

"Who killed Harry Oakes?"

"And you were in...... under my guard, with all that further agenda concerning Old Jack Butters, young Cairns, Mosley, Monckton, Shute. The Erroll and Oakes cases have similar ingredients; the famous victim, the disapproved of love affair, the trial that went wrong, the wartime subtext. Do your homework, find and prime a female ingenue for our Alan's delectation, and you could well be in."

"I'll see what I can turn up, Sir Edward, but whilst in Kenya, give me your take on the Mau Mau thing of the '50s, and the Hola scandal."

"Fleet St went silly on the Mau Mau. Spontaneous, they said, totally unforeseeable. 'Mass hysteria!' we were to believe. While we had hula hoops and Davy Crockett hats the Kikuyu had a matching craze for this weird ritualistic violence, part of an irrational perverted religion, orchestrated by oath administering witch doctors."

"This was what we were meant to believe."

" The popular press loved it, but Boyd was an intelligent man, an experienced lawyer, and whatever was being spun to Joe Public, his understanding of the thing had would have been far more measured, more informed. He would have appreciated a continuum stretching way back to the start of the century, perhaps even before, an ongoing anxiety about land.... similar in theme to the troubles of the middle east. But an emergency had to be declared......"

"......and it was policed with excessive zeal."

"Out and out Black and Tannery....... you would have thought lesson had been learned........ but no, and this is where Boyd can be criticised, for turning a blind eye."

"And Hola was the climax of such criticism, Sir Edward, with the cover up scandal effectively ending Boyd's Ministerial career."

"Not so disastrously as it might have. As I've mentioned, he came out of the debate well, when only a week before it was being predicted that it would be the total undoing of the man's reputation. The knives had been out for him..... and I mean on our side, behind his back. He was to be the scapegoat, the offered up sacrifice for which the gods of the ballot box would perhaps look kindly on our coming election campaign."

"So he was to carry the can."

"He would have to resign...... the bush telegraph dictating that there could be no other option. But suddenly, on the eve of the debate it was all change, with the *Volte Face* coming from the very top, from Macmillan."

"Now there's a surprise," smirked the Suez soaked lecturer.

"Lennox Boyd was to be backed," continued Trembath, not wanting to dwell on the earlier, deeper trauma of a lost Eden. "For, suddenly, it was now wished that he should stay. And he stood again for re-election, and won again, and gracefully relinquished ministerial office on the formation of an entirely new administration."

"Then, as you said, the following year he went up to the Lords with head held high."

"This is almost thirty years ago," sighed Trembath. "And yet I can remember the Hola debate so clearly, almost as if it were yesterday. Prisoners beaten to death, and a stupid attempt at a cover up. They were said to have died of something like dysentery, and there they were, clubbed to a pulp. Barbara Castle was good, always a class act that one, but then Gaitskell allowed Enoch to steal the show, memorably so.... because a former Minister won't normally be critical of another Department."

"..... and Boyd slipped off the hook," pressed the lecturer, "because Moyne had held that same job back in '41, and he'd perhaps known something, and passed it down, that posthumous sway. The Erroll thing..... remote people, distant lands, distant times, are there any survivors to hand?"

"Diana, Lady Delamere, formerly Diana Delves Broughton, wife of the accused, mistress of the victim, she just about survives. She's here, in and out of a London clinic, in the final stages of a terminal illness...... but stay well clear. There's a posse of journalists plus, no doubt, the usual insinuation of secret service agents masquerading as the same. They sit around in vicinity pubs, vulture like, waiting to swoop on any death bed revelation. Join them and you're a marked man. I wouldn't put it beyond that Grigson fellow to be amongst them."

I don't think so, thought Jeremy. Insofar as he could be certain of anything about Grigson he understood differently. But this had to be kept to himself.

*

(xiv) Bodmin

Kate Rogers has finished her day's work. She is in good time and good fettle for the arranged rehearsal with James and Enid. As usual they will use the hospital hall, but she prefers that they should meet in the small cafeteria run by the 'Friends'.

Early, she is first to arrive. The two to come will probably be late, but not because James is at all un-punctual. He will have called for Enid, expecting her to be ready and, as usual, there will be one last thing she *must* do. This will irritate the man, but Kate is un-bothered. There is nowhere else she needs be, and no one else she needs, or even wants, to be with…. certainly not in Bodmin.

For as much as she enjoys the challenge of a very different branch of healing, with the fringe benefits of the singing, and even this quiet table and relaxing tea, she cannot yet warm to the town into which St Lawrence cuts such a deep wedge.

She sees slate, and granite, and more slate…. the hospital to the west balanced by the old Regimental Barrack to the east, and scant comfort between. From the northern edge of town glowers the ivy draped ruin that was once the County Gaol, re enforcing the hard hearted mood set at the centre by the thick pillared Mount Folly Court House.

Its days as a County Assize are now numbered. Soon the proceedings will move to stylish new accommodation being prepared in Truro and, as if conscious of this impending desertion, the old building stands grey and steadfast in an almost monumental sulk, determined to perpetuate the feel of far meaner times.

Something of this gloom might be lightened, thought Kate, were it not for the town having to endure such a disproportionately heavy share of the County's rain. Wadebridge on the Camel will be dry, likewise Lostwithiel on the Fowey, each within six miles….. at Bodmin, though, on the edge of its twin peaked Moor, the old stone Beacon can needle even the calmest southern breeze to an oppressive sweat.

And this is partly why Kate will prefer to chug across to Wadebridge for her shopping, or to use bank or post office. For as well as enjoying its extra sun, Wadebridge, like Truro heads an estuary. It draws in the tide and with it some of the scents and the sounds of the sea….. simple things, but missed since moving away from the Cathedral City.

So, singing apart, when Kate says she is comfortable in her new life she means when at home alone, or at work in the hospital, with her colleagues, her patients, and those who come from across the county to visit. And this makes sufficient, for just in itself this institution amounts to a good sized and surprisingly varied community, even if many of the Victorian ward blocks now stand abandoned and neglected.

Across ten years a 'Care in the Community' push had seen a three quarters full establishment contract to one now approaching three quarters empty, but, as yet, with no demolition programme to match. Sceptics hold that the flaking shells are being held in reserve lest some sharp policy review or drastic pharmaceutical failure necessitates that the halfway-housed thousands should return. Kate, though, was no sceptic. Such views were an anathema to her fresh sense of mission. Anything with more than two floors, Victorian or not, she would happily have flattened...... but not quite yet, not before she'd built for herself a picture of how the old wings might have functioned when the 'bin' processed its unhappy customers by the score. And this was how she had been drawn to the long stay ward, St Mabyn Ward, where she had first noticed, then spoken with, then lightly befriended James Busbridge.

She was short term inquisitive. He was long term curious. And, to the extent that each was looking to find out more, there was overlap, and a consequent rapport, a rapport then made less transient by the music, for it was sure to have otherwise dwindled on confirmation for the nurse that the stricken of St Mabyn were far, far beyond any hope of repair. For, where she could, Kate Rogers wanted to heal, and it was more to the severely shocked mind that she felt she might make a difference, rather than to the irredeemably decayed.

But she was getting to know some of these unfortunates by name, and she would mention them to James so as to encourage him in his concern for their condition, so worthy were his attentions, and seemingly so thankless. For she was aware, of course, that Busbridge too had been a patient, and that this role he had styled for himself as a 'Friend' was bracing the ladder by which he was himself climbing to sounder health.

This was progress to be consolidated, she thought. It had to be helpful to him to be feeling useful and listened to. And hence it was that one day, when he came back with a new name, she responded maybe a little too readily..... forgetting that a curious man might also be a crafty man, one who could be seeking to profit from being patronised, one who might even have been carefully working and waiting for just such a moment with such a nurse.

'Gordon' was the name, and whether first name or surname Busbridge couldn't be sure.... not yet. For no other name had ever been said or written in his presence, though he'd listened long and watched closely. Gordon was not a St Mabyn patient, any more than Busbridge was himself, but he seemed to come there every day, more often and for longer than any doctor or nurse.

Gordon was the bringer of food. He would trolley it up from the central kitchen, serve it on to plates, help spoon it into mouths, then clear and cart away what remained. And throughout those meal times, which could extend across more than two hours, Gordon would say nothing.

No one could be more reliable. Ordered, he could understand and obey. Shown how, he could copy. What he would never do, though, was speak.

Apparently he had his own small room, upstairs in the kitchen block. There he could sleep and keep a small functional wardrobe of clothes. He enjoyed shelter, warmth, food, laundry. He was settled, he was comfortable, he was occupied, and for being so constant he earned that kind of affection that might be happily enjoyed by a reliable beast of burden.

Busbridge had told Kate that he understood Gordon to have been a war casualty, knowing that battle trauma came firmly within her interest and experience. He'd heard that the man had been brought back to England almost twenty five years ago after having been released from three traumatic years in a North Korean prisoner of war camp. He'd carried no identification, it was said, apart from the number given to him by his captors. In fact there was no proof that he was a British soldier, and no proof even that he'd ever spoken a single English word.

For what he understood, he might have picked up at Moorhaven, the equivalent psychiatric establishment serving South Devon, but which was now shrunken even more severely than St Lawrence. It was in the kitchens at Moorhaven that Gordon had first shown his aptitude for catering, and it was from the unhappy result of a well intentioned attempt to develop this talent that he'd come to be eventually moved from South Brent down to Bodmin.

This was as much as Busbridge had so far gleaned. Vague details, but enough to prime an under-experienced Kate who, true to her fresh enthusiasm for this calling and her concern for this dapper baritone, with his kindnesses and his enticing fund of military knowledge and experience, maybe allowed herself to overlook the insidious manner in which gossip can sometimes undermine a strict line on patient confidentiality. She was the professional, enjoying access to clinical files, and what was he? A curious man….. no more, no less.

But what she'd got today was good, too good to keep to herself. It had come down from Moorhaven courtesy of her friend Rosemary. And with James entering with Enid now, and the accompanist excusing herself to the toilet for a moment, Kate was quick to share a little of her excitement.

"I've got more on Gordon, James, from Moorhaven. Will you have time after?"

"Once I've lifted Enid home, yes, of course. How long, and where?"

"Six now, seven by the time we've finished, that still leaves us more than two hours of daylight. I want you to come back and pick me up, I'll be at the main entrance."

"And then?"

"Well the old tonsils should be ready by then for a good cool drink…. so where better than *Jamaica Inn*?"

*

(xv) London (St James Place)
Lord Rothschild's flat.

"If anything the pressure is increasing, on both of us."

"On Peter Bright *and* yourself." Daniels, alone with his regular host, re-saucered a thrice sipped cup. While welcome, his tea was, as yet, a little too hot.

"And we struggle, still, to understand as to why," continued Lord Rothschild.

"But we know it's to do with Peter's book, '*Molehunter*', and the fact that but for your encouragement, Uncle Victor, he would never have put pen to paper. He contravened the Official Secrets regulations. You were an accessory."

"But it can't be that simple," countered the Peer. "There's nothing particularly new in the book, and nothing particularly new about a retired agent going to print."

"Bags of precedent, and no great mischief....... and yet still that panic for a court injunction, and then the negative press briefings that you've had to endure."

"Bullying...... this is what it amounts to."

"Maybe there's a higher up feeling threatened," suggested Daniels.

"But unnecessarily, surely...... at least from where I stand."

"And is that how Bright sees it too?"

"Almost," Rothschild hesitated. The words were being carefully chosen. "But rather than being about what he has written....."

".....so far...."

".....he wonders whether what might be feared is a sequel, a second effort containing further revelations."

"So it's about wanting to strangle Bright's writing career at birth."

"Prompting him to think back through a varied career in intelligence, sifting for tasks and incidents that might now command a greater significance than hitherto realised."

"Not easy," said Daniels," being now so far from events, both in years and miles."

"But it seems that we have helped to jog a still formidable memory."

"We.....?"

"Because of something *you* told me a month or so ago, about Sir Clive Faulds. You might remember your saying about his keenness to oversee security arrangements for a holiday visit by the Thatchers to Ince Castle in Cornwall, on the invitation of Patricia, widow to the late Viscount Boyd. I mention this to Peter, and within the week he's back to me, recalling two tasks previously considered in isloation."

"And he now finds a link?"

"Not yet...... let's say he's been alerted to that possibility. He's certainly interested to know how those security arrangements were implemented."

"So tell me first of those two tasks," said Daniels, "we'll have it then in sequence."

"It was carried out at Chequers, back in '59, at the request of Macmillan......"

".....the then Prime Minister."

"And it features Patricia Lennox Boyd, before she was a Viscountess, and before she and her husband moved down to Cornwall. They were living near Bedford, where her husband, Alan, was a safe seat MP. He was also Colonial Secretary. An election was due that autumn, and during the spring and summer Alan Lennox Boyd was looking a liability. Problems in Africa....... he could easily have lost his job, and it was certainly looking that way until the wife called on Sir Harold at the PM's country retreat. Peter had been brought in to record their conversation. It seems she had the benefit of some useful knowledge passed down to her by Lord Moyne before he died during the last year of the war."

"Powerful knowledge......?"

"..... hinted at, rather than explicitly professed. She mentioned certain code words, thereby indicating a familiarity with an obscure wartime operation, clearly top secret."

".....and that was sufficient to deter the Prime Minister from issuing the old 'black spot'."

"The husband was reprieved. He was eventually able to step down on his own terms, with honour and reputation intact."

"Interesting," acknowledged Daniels, reaching again for his tea, "and the second task.....?"

".....was commissioned far more recently, on his moving to Tasmania."

"On his retirement.....?"

".....which initially was not as acrimonious as it subsequently became. As you know, the intelligence operative will only rarely go into full retirement. A controller will always have his number, and always there will be the odd little watching brief, assignments done on a casual basis."

"Even in far away Tasmania."

"Paticularly in far away Tasmania, a place ever attractive to those from this hemisphere looking to cultivate anonymity..... not that Vincent Wakeham was looking to escape any great notoriety."

"So it's a 'Vincent Wakeham' who's the principal in this instance."

"He *was* the principal, Colin. He died back in '85."

"Natural causes?"

"To the best of Peter's quite considerable knowledge, yes. Though not that old, the fellow had been in ailing health for some time. Smoked heavily, heart gave up. "

"And the possible link, would that have been with Macmillan?.....
with the Boyds?......Africa?"

"For a start, with Ince Castle," said Rothschild. "This much Bright
had been told when briefed. It was said that this Wakeham was a
Cornishman who'd been interned during the war after being twice
apprehended within the wire at off-limits military instillations, all within
48 hours. The first transgression had been Ince, close to where he lived
and worked as an inshore fisherman. The second had been in Scotland, at
Holy Loch......"

"The submarine base."

"Correct. He'd been out in his boat at night with a younger
brother, and the boy had been pulled into the sea after they'd hooked a
surfacing submarine. He'd hoped, vainly as it turned out, that the lad had
been taken into the vessel."

"So find the submarine, find the boy. Discovering that it was
headed for Scotland, off he went, by train......"

"......not returning until almost three years later, and that's when he
finds that a body identified to be the missing brother had been recovered
from the Cornish rocks. The lad had been buried in a cliff top graveyard
where, within a year, the grieving mother had joined him. There was an
older brother away in the army, but Vincent doesn't hang about to take the
opprobrium. He heads for London, and from London he sails to Australia,
and then Tasmania. All this much Vincent will, over the years, divulge.... "

"......but very little more," concluded Daniels.

"Precisely, and here lay Peter Bright's task. He was to listen
closely and report back should he hear anything that could suggest that
Wakeham was beginning to talk of this submarine episode in any greater
detail."

"But this didn't happen."

"No," continued Rothschild, "and it seems that our Vincent was an
easy man to lose interest in...... a view that Peter was ready to encourage,
particularly as the subject became ever more reclusive in his decline."

"Bright having other things to concern him," added Daniels.

"Quite....... his farming enterprise began to falter and, as it did
so, there came this resentment at the paucity of his pension. *Molehunter*
could be the answer, he decided."

"And if this was to be assembled then there were far better stories
to be concentrating on than that of Vincent Wakeham."

"Yes, and if, in airing these, he would be holding the intelligence service up for public scrutiny, and even ridicule, then clearly there could be no further role for him as their supernumerary eye....."

"..... for all trust would now be gone."

"So it was, perhaps, now for the best that Vincent Wakeham should be firmly forgotten," continued Rothschild, "in the interests of effecting a clean severance from the intelligence establishment."

"But he couldn't have been too firmly forgotten, not for you to be raising his name now."

"This is the irony, for it was in the act of handing the story down, like an outworn suit of clothes to a poor relation......."

"....... that there emerged, from a neglected pocket, something that was felt might be valuable."

"Exactly, Colin, for on one of his visits back to this country, in pursuance of the book project, he passed the Wakeham tale on to a cousin of his who lives in Cornwall....."

"......inviting him to make of it what he can."

"Yes," said Rothschild. "and you might have heard of James Busbridge. He writes too...... for the papers mainly, usually Naval stuff. He's not afraid to speculate, wildly at times. Some consider him a crank, and he'll often be ready to play up to this image."

"Hamlet style, perhaps, preferring to be taken less seriously than he ought......"

"..... while certainly being in earnest about his work, work that has included an ongoing investigation of a wartime submarine called the *Surcouf*, regarded in its formative months as the centrepiece of the Free French Navy. Busbridge notes that in his memoir, de Gaulle writes puzzlingly of a crisis in his high command over the '40-'41 New Year. The General tells of a senior French admiral getting himself out of jail, quite literally, after having been falsely accused of a arranging an attempted defection of this *Surcouf* to Vichy control. When Bright passes Wakeham's tale to his cousin he promptly hears back that this is one vessel that is known for certain to have been at Devonport during the autumn and early winter prior to this crisis and, that after leaving, it next appeared in Scotland, at Holy Loch. So maybe....."

"......it could have been the *Surcouf* that took Wakeham's brother."

"And before Bright set off again for Tasmania it was also

228

established that the Admiral concerned, an Admiral Muselier, had also been in the Plymouth area, spending time both on that submarine and at Ince, the big house having been used for receiving and screening French Canadians of officer potential."

"Was all this put to Wakeham when Bright got back?" asked Daniels

"Peter was a couple of days too late. The man had died."

"So might there have been anything about the *Surcouf* with his belongings, at his house still?"

"Nothing …. so at this point, for Peter Bright the matter was as good as closed. For Busbridge had been to the cliff top churchyard and found the graves, and also learned from talking amongst the locals that the eldest brother had given his life too, whilst soldiering on into '50s, out in Cyprus."

"So they're all gone, the three brothers, leaving no trace."

"Almost no trace," corrected Rothschild. "As might befit an eminent Cambridge scientist, one who has worked closely with those engaged in the further development of innovative forensic technique, I'd suggested to Peter that on getting back he might discretely obtain from Wakeham something in the way of a tissue sample."

"Not knowing that he was at death's door…..the idea being to draw a DNA profile, this to be preserved on file," reasoned Daniels. "But as you've said, Uncle Victor, the subject was by then no more, so nothing could come of your suggestion."

"That's what I'd assumed, Colin, but then, recently, Bright hears me tell of your work taking you to Ince and he is reminded that after being informed at his local hospital of Wakeham's death, he was asked if he might take away with him the few personal effects left in the bedside locker."

"And this Bright did."

"And the bag given him by the hospital was taken home to his garage where it went into a box, to be stowed on a rarely reached shelf."

"Where it stays undisturbed for the best part of two years."

"But he has it down now, for he recalls there having been a hairbrush amongst those effects, and on an inspection of this he finds and recovers and sends a quite presentable little lock of hair."

"And using this, you have manged to draw a DNA profile….. for what it's ever going to be worth, with brothers and single parent all long dead. Mind, I suppose a paternity issue could still crop up….. "

"…..but that now has to be extremely unlikely," conceded Rothschild. "This, though, has not deterred James Busbridge in his endeavours. In fact he's been spurred."

"In what direction? Where could he be hoping to go with this?"

"As I've said, this character is nothing if not speculative. Back when Busbridge had first been told of the brothers Wakeham……"

"…..two years ago…."

"…. he had quietly entertained the possibility that the youngest brother, named Norman……"

"……whose gravestone he'd seen, along with the mother's….."

"……might not, in fact, lie dead beneath that turf. What is known is that the remains eventually found and buried were little more than crab-cleansed bones, identification hanging on no more than a few shreds of clothing….. a tough canvas shoe, the leather belt. This was during the height of Plymouth blitz. Young bones were plentiful."

"But if the clothing was real, then we're talking deliberate deception…… delberate and cruel."

"In the interests of secrecy, according to Busbridge."

"So conspiracy," said Daniels. "But this has to be fanciful….. for what could be the big secret?"

"The same that left Vincent to languish in an internment camp for most of the war….. and by which the French Admiral levered himself from his incarceration in the Brixton Gaol, to the extent of even being invited to the Palace to receive a Royal apology. Make no mistake, Muselier had gotten hold of something truly heavy. And he might, claims Busbridge, have also been able to insist that the boy be accorded a special Royal protection. Being suddenly dragged from his boat, into the winter sea, that must have been an ordeal……."

"……. physical and mental."

"Meaning hospitalisation," said Rothschild. "This is how Busbridge is thinking."

"Secure hospitalisation…… yes, I get the drift, perhaps *permanent* secure hospitalisation."

"For even where well treated, we know that the effects of deep mental trauma……"

"…..can long outlast the effects of hypothermia," reasoned Daniels. "And of course, rather than well treated, in this instance a loss of memory could have been welcomed."

"So for Busbridge now it's hunt the amnesiac."

"No easy challenge."

"But at least, Colin, we now have this sample, and the profile therefrom. For Busbridge it's a template....."

".....to take into the haystack," added Daniels, sceptically.

"But every little helps," chided his Uncle Victor. "This is why I'm eager to hear of events at Ince. What was Faulds up to?"

"I suspect he could be searching for his own needle."

"With any success?"

"He went in with his own specialist team, supposedly in response to the premature detonation of an IRA bomb. They had detectors of every kind...... sound, X ray, dogs, the lot."

"Looking for more explosive."

"So we were meant to believe....."

"....but?"

"From what I heard, unofficially, it was thought that there were guns in there."

"And guns were found?" Rothschild asked.

"They found a number," said Daniels.

"But they would, Colin, in a place like that. I can imagine they turned up some rare old relics, some having lain undisturbed for generations, even centuries. Would you say that Faulds was pleased with his haul?"

"As regards number, is this what you ask?"

"Partly I suppose, but more in terms of any specific type of weapon that was turned up?"

"Bullet rifle, shotgun, that sort of distinction....."

"...... or a handgun," angled Rothschild, "of a sort that might have been issued during the last war?"

Daniels shook his head. "There were a couple of pistols, yes, but neither appeared to warrant any great rejoicing."

"So rather than with anything actually found, you would say Faulds' contentment was derived from having at least given the place a thorough going over?"

"Yes, Uncle, I think I would."

"In which case I trust you have made your own arrangements for keeping a discrete eye on things down there." Rising as he spoke, the Peer took the drained cup. The audience was done. Daniels stood. Rothschild had said earlier that he would be going to the club to dine with Toby Low. He would need time to collect his thoughts.

"Be assured, Uncle Victor, I have made dispositions." An appreciative palm dropped on Daniels' shoulder, guiding him doorwards. Four, five steps and then farewell, but space yet for a few more words. "Aldington...... he came on the radio a few days ago. Did......?"

"Yes, I did listen Colin. The man's under presure, just as we are......Peter and me."

"Meaning you suspect a link?"

"I do, and more than ever, now, after listening to you."

"So is it Faulds?"

"He's in on it, as he's in on most things......but he won't be the one behind it all. It's too big, and goes back too far. It has cost too many lives. No less than you and I, Colin, he's having to tread very carefully."

*

(xvi) Bodmin Moor

The rehearsal was over, and for James in his car, with Kate beside him, it was but three miles now to Jamaica Inn. The session with Enid had gone well, their director was happily delivered back to her home, and two well exercised voices could be gently eased down. For here, where the A30 climbed the western edge of the moor, the chill granite landscape spoke bluntly for itself.....words barely necessary.

The nurse, she was content to take it in, acre by rugged acre, leaving her companion at the wheel to quietly indulge his natural optimism. For the excursion held promise. Might this at last be the nugget so painstakingly sifted for? Or was he again following the glint of the fool's gold, so plentiful around these parts.

He'd handled Kate patiently, though, and she'd been so responsive. He sensed reward. She had something on this Gordon, she'd said, something that she was keen to share..... so he needn't press. When they were in the bar she could spill at her own pace.

Temple lay to their right, whispering a Christian message of

232

Celtic times, as taught by the pre industial ancients...... just as Trewint, only a few miles ahead, would voice that which had been revived during the age of the steam pumped mines. Before them now, though, stood *Jamaica Inn*, a shrine to the long dark interim, skulking here in all its recalcitrance and looking the last place on earth to inspire one to prayer.

Save for the unrepentant wrecker who leers down from a weathered signboard, all is grey..... the cobbled yard, the slate hung granite walls, the windows, the tarred roof and, even in summer, the wood smoke that smoulders from the potless slab of a chimney. Here is solid, unrelieved shadow, a structure that will carry more glow under low cloud mist than it might ever raise beneath a bright evening sun.

With the car parked, they were briskly to a quiet table in the wide lounge......where there was at least some comfort to be drawn from the privacy enhancing gloom. The lager was cool. It was welcome, and, settled now, Kate could begin.

"You remember my saying about Rosemary...."

"....your friend, who works up at Moorhaven. You wondered if she might have something on Gordon."

"And she has. She phoned me last night. The first thing, Jim, is that Gordon has only been Gordon since arriving at St Lawrence...."

So who is this? Thought Busbridge, knowing better than to actually ask..... for Kate had more to say.

".......and something else that's been invented is the story about his having returned from Korea. The file that Rosemary glanced into mentions this renaming, and the rewritten history. In fact it mentions all this being prescribed after he'd come to work here, in this very pub, as a kitchen hand."

"Work? Here.....from South Devon!"

"The place is run by an Exeter based chain, and they were persuaded that they might find live in work for the likes of our Gordon."

"The steady trusty sort....."

"....which is what Moorhaven had him down as, after years of sterling service in their kitchens. But sadly, in the event, he turned out to be anything but. It was going well enough for a month or two, and then, totally out of the blue he was throwing this violent tantrum..... one made all the more alarming and inexplicable by the absence of any verbal clue."

"So a dumb rage."

"Totally out of character, Jim, and totally unacceptable to the employer."

"Do we talk, then, of people having been hurt? Customers? Staff?"

"Most of the damage was sustained by the fittings here. There was some blood, but that was all his own. A heavy glass ashtray was thrown against one of these pictures, probably one of these framed collections of old cigarette cards. One or two hang here still, I see. Then his hand went into it, and his fingers of course were cut. He had to be restrained, and a doctor was summoned, the police, and ambulance. He was sedated and brought to St Lawrence...."

".... where the storm was allowed to subside."

"And with Moorhaven being phased down it was considered best that he should stay...."

"....with a new identity," Busbridge reminded her.

"Yes, for St Lawrence he became Gordon, placid Gordon. Friend to our subterranean community of bats, his true friends with whom he likes to regularly commune. If he can't, for any reason, then apparently signs of anxiety will emerge."

"In him or the bats," joked Busbridge.

"Both," smiled Kate.

"So he's known to Rosemary as....?"

"....one Trevor Dalton, who was orphaned during the Plymouth Blitz, when ten. An only child, he was pulled from the rubble of his home and thought to be suffering from nothing worse than concussion."

"But then it became apparent that this muteness was not temporary, and the poor lad was compelled to grow up in Moorhaven. Was there any treatment tried?"

"All sorts of things were suggested, you know how things came in and out of fashion. All were ruled out though."

"Mercifully, in some instances, I suppose one could say....... no shock treatment, and nothing experimental."

"Quite." Kate was pleased. The man was reading her.

"So the military aspect that we hoped to use isn't there......something of a shame, me being not so far off his age, and having done National Service, and yourself with your own experience of the military....... but maybe if I can mug up on the Plymouth blitz. The city took a pasting through the difficult winter of '40-'41, the raids coming to climax in the spring that followed. With the Luftwaffe working out of

France, Plymouth was within easy reach. Should this be when our Gordon was taken into Moorhaven it could be worth having it confirmed. We might construct a calender of notable events immediately prior to his world being bombed to pieces."

"Not a bad idea," agreed Kate, "and what about the cigarrete cards he took exception to? Those across there on the pillar are warships. He might have lost his father before the bomb fell that took his mother. Maybe he was on a Devonport based ship, or perhaps it was a brother. I'll ask the barman if he can take it down for us."

She did, and the employee obliged, to the extent even of dusting away some of the cobwebs on the back. He brought it over.

" *Modern Naval Craft*'," read Kate.

"Of all nations, I think," added Busbridge "As presented by *John Player*."

"But not so modern now. Cigarette cards went out with the Ark, in fact there's an *Ark Royal* here."

"The first carrier of that name," observed Busbridge.
"The one built in the '30s and lost out in the Med during the war."

"And it looks to be the only carrier pictured in this frame,"said Kate, still checking down each of the three columns of nine cards. "But no..... at the bottom here we have two more."

"Just the one more, actually," corrected James. "Whoever mounted these made a mistake. They put in two of one card. The French carrier, the *Bearn*, is repeated..... and seeing how the ships are grouped by nation, with battleships to fore in each instance, followed by a carrier, and then by a submarine or two, this duplicate sits right where one might expect to see the very acme of France's pre-war undersea technology. I talk of the *Surcouf*; a giant of a submarine that left us a giant of a mystery. I'm hoping to do a book on her soon."

"Sounds like you've done some research already."

"I have, and there's an intriguing connection with what we've been doing with Enid."

"Enid?" With her quizical glance at the cards, and then at James, Kate was clearly wanting to know more.

"Does the name 'Roger Burney' mean anything?"

"Not particularly," answered the Nurse. Should it?"

"It would to Enid, I know that, because she was there.... as she never tires of telling."

"Where, Jim?"

"At the premier of *The War Requiem*, at Coventry, the other phoenix city. She would have a score, probably several, and will have noted the names of the personal friends to whom Britten dedicated the piece. Men lost in combat, some killed, some crazed, and amongst the former...."

"......that name."

"Roger Burney, who was serving on the *Surcouf* as a Royal Navy liaison officer when the vessel was lost with all hands in '42."

"Where?"

"Just this side of Panama. It was at night. She was on the surface, heading for the canal. It's thought there was a collision with an American freighter, a failure of communication."

"So accounts are vague. You know I had a boyfriend a while back, he would have loved this. To me it sounds a cock-up. For him, though, it would be conspiracy."

"And his name?"

"Jeremy...... he and I had a place together in Truro. Good to me, he was, when I think back, but then someone else came into our lives. Suddenly he seemed rather unexciting."

"Hurt?"

"And angry......."

"..... and it seems to me that you harbour a measure of guilt, and perhaps regret..... this new lad having disappointed maybe?"

"Something like that, James, but I didn't bring you here to talk about Alan, or Jeremy, or even Benjamin's friend Roger. This is meant to be about Gordon. Or shall we call him Trevor?"

"Let's stick with Gordon," chuckled James. "You never know, it might change again!" Kate thought this a joke. Busbridge quietly hoped otherwise. "As we're holding this now," he continued, " I'm going for a long shot."

"You have a hunch?"

"I do, Kate. A hunch that we might be looking here at a hasty repair. That this has been re-framed after having been damaged."

"Perhaps we could ask that helpful barman," suggested the nurse. "He looks as much a fixture as any of this stuff on the walls."

Busbridge nodded. Kate rose again to carry both picture and enquiry to the bar, James staying at the table, from where the ensuing conversation was encouragingly long…. long enough, and deep enough to be broken and resumed a number of times as other customers came and ordered. In one such pause Kate slid back to James, offering to refill his glass. She was able to bring him up to the moment on a fruitful exchange.

The barman *did* remember Trevor, and with some affection. He also recalled the incident…… as baffling, he said, as it was alarming. He was pleased to hear that his former colleague had found a settled niche in Bodmin.

As to the picture, Kate had been told that in all the intervening years, they were first to notice the duplication. The lost card had indeed shown a submarine, he remembered that, but neither name nor nationality. A number of cards had been beyond repair, but a replacement for that particular one hadn't been located, and the duplicate *Bearn* had sufficed. But the damaged originals were still in the pub, in an envelope which should be still attached to an inventory of the hangings. It was together with the repair receipt, appropriately filed in the office, but this was closed at the moment. If they wanted to see it, and perhaps had the time and interest to seek out the elusive replacement, then they were welcome to come back in a few days.

"How damaged? Ask him that," urged James, softly. And off she went, to return again after a short while.

"It was tightly crumpled," she reported. "In fact it had to be levered from a clenched and bleeding fist."

"So screwed up……. and in need of straightening."

"Like all of us," said Kate, "and remains creased because of that, and bloodstained."

"But not torn. It is intact."

"Sounds like it," the nurse confirmed, tentatively. "So did the *Surcouf* have to be captured, at the expense of British casualties?"

"And would this explain all that stored up anger? Well, there was an incident in Devonport, where the boat happened to be tied when France fell, and there were a couple of RN lives lost, but this was just a boarding party seizing control at night. There was no action on the high sea….. and this, in truth, was the story of the *Surcouf*. For all its size and apparent firepower, and its place here, framed amongst these most prestigous and powerful of vessels, it was, as a weapon, worse than useless. Think in terms of lives being lost on it, rather than to it."

"But let's not jump ahead," said Kate. "For all that you might be able to tell me about the *Surcouf*, and those who served on her, we can't, as yet, be sure that this is the submarine that made up the cigarette collection."

"True," answered Busbridge, encouraging her caution.

Had she known anything of his protracted quest, so devious and discrete, then she might have realised that she'd just helped the man to his most promising lead yet, and maybe sensed in him his concealed surge of excitement. For her, for now, it was just a maybe…..the *Surcouf*, bent and bloodied, just might surface from that filing cabinet. For James Busbridge, so remarkably well informed at times, and at others merely curious, this was now a near certainty."

*

(xvii) itch

Two days on, and for a successive night Sally hadn't slept well. The find, *her* find, was eating at her customary composure. She'd thought she might hear from Chas the next day….. but nothing, so why? What was he keeping to himself, what plans? Question after unanswered question, the itch becoming a nibble, and the nibble then a gnaw….. the gnaw of mistrust.

Something was getting to her, this her parents could see, but how could they divine it to be sea-bed treasure? The boy was involved, they knew that….. and plainly it was a simple matter of being patient. For wasn't it said that youngsters were wiser these days, that relationships came with a health warning? And what was three days, after all, at any stage of any courtship? In what was not even the broad scheme of things it was nothing, even at that age.

But gold, hastily buried gold, hastily buried and left, this can cast a very different spell. Perhaps it would have been better had it been he who'd pulled it from the deep, but the fact was incontrovertibly otherwise. It had been her. So where was he? What was he doing? Who had he been talking with?

They'd buried it together, in a cave beneath the cliff close to where they'd beached, with a pact that nothing of this was to be mentioned to anyone, at least until they could meet again. But Chas had not said when…… only that he would be in touch, and so far…… nothing.

Save for a last few tepid gulps of coffee Sally's father had finished his breakfast. He was up and now circling the table with the day's post. The bills he could leave for later, but not the hand written envelope, the content of which was already almost fully read. This, he thought, might be the kind of distraction required.

"Something for you here, Sal." He placed the two page letter next to her juice.

"For me?"

"Addressed to me, and written to me, but mentioning you also. Remember a guy called Alan Grigson?…..had a boat."

"The *Speedwell*," recalled the daughter.

"That's it. Down here a couple of years ago, doing pieces on the estuaries. Camera, tape, notebook….".

"….and we helped him, gave him bits and pieces on Millbrook, Cremyll, Mount Edgcumbe."

"He's coming back, this time for a closer look at the Lynher," said the father. "He mentions Scraesdon and Ince."

Sally was already onto the last side. The two names had registered, particularly the second, for hadn't Ince been mentioned by Chas in his tale? According to his grandmother, his father, Tony Cross, might have been conceived there, consequent to her seduction by some mysteriously maligned French Admiral. And, in so far as this man's reputation might be salvaged with the gold that she had herself plucked off the sea floor, it was a tale that now included herself. She had to be interested. This could be a chance to search out more, and without giving anything away, not even here, now, at the table. She scanned back through the letter, looking for the something else that she might comment upon. And yes…..

"Says he no longer has the boat. Using a camper van this time…… booking into the holiday site up at Whitsand."

"Nowhere else, is there?" harumphed her father, being firmly of the view that but for a want of choice of site this corner of Cornwall might make much more out of summer tourism. Sally looked to her mother. She could respond to this, and she did.

"Not unless he prefers roughing it down at Wacker."

"Room down there, do you know?" scoffed the husband.

"Why do you say?" asked his wife.

"Scraesdon, Ince..... where better?"

"And he seems to think that I might help show him over the old fort," joined Sally, looking, for the moment anyway, to leave Ince at the very margin of the conversation.

"Good opportunity," said her father. "He'll not have forgotten your enthusiasm for the flora thereabouts, within the walls, and down in the deep surrounding ditch. Let him use you, Sal, and at the same time you use him. This is how journalism works. Jobwise it's how you make your way. If that's your chosen direction, then believe me, you're never too young to be cultivating contacts."

"Have him around then," said Sally feigning indifference. "We might hit it off, we might not. I'll decide accordingly."

"There's others I can put this with."

"No Dad..... at least not yet." And the father knew immediately that he wouldn't need to....... as did the mother, who, seeking to jog the conversation along, returned to briefly mentioned Wacker.

"You do know that old Megan is back...... another pair of minders with her. She might be of interest to Mr Grigson. This has to be her third year now."

"The old herbalist again," said Graham Shaw.

"Looking fitter than she's ever done. Seventy if she's a day, I'd say, and the perfect advert for those potions that she hawks around."

"And it's the same caravan," confirmed Sally, "but a different van to haul it."

"Which is no surprise, given the weight of the thing," added her father. "Built to last, that trailer....almost a fairground job."

"And it needs to be," said his wife. "It's a home, it's a factory, it's a warehouse. The van can take some of the stock, but there's also the knock-together stall, plus the tent they take around the shows. Last year it was the Indian couple with their silks and beads, and before that the oriental pair with those hand crafted chess and backgammon sets. Chinese were they, or Korean? True, the stuff will sell down through a season......."

"......but with each new summer she's juggling with a different kind of clutter," said Sally.

"And this year's fellow travellers...?" enquired her father.

"Look like Africans," replied the wife. "Asked in the Post Office the other day, one said he was Nyassan."

240

"And their special offer.....?"

"Carved ornaments," said Sally,"out of tough native wood, and also that light stone, easily shaped, easily glazed...."

".......and too easily broken," added Graham Shaw, "but fear not, for another twenty container loads wait on a Mombassa quay. And these vendors, they'll look the part I'm sure, but do they genuinely speak the part...... or are they third generation Brixton? Nyassaland went out of existence twenty five years ago!"

"But why should that matter?" protested Sally. "If it sells, and obviously it does, then either way they're giving people what they want. That's enterprise. I suppose you would rather have them selling drugs, just to confirm your prejudices."

"Well said Sally," chuckled the mother. The girl was at last sounding more herself. "Well said."

*

(xviii) strange meetimg *(I knew you in this dark)*

Though clearly signed the campsite above Whitsand Bay is easily missed. Unusually for Cornwall it is both high and sheltered, tucked as it is behind the seaward rampart of yet another disused coastal fortification. While close to the cliffs there is no sea view, a drawback well compensated by a fascinating northern prospect that stretches across Millbrook 'lake', and the Hamoaze, to Devonport and the heart of Plymouth, and then on to Dartmoor beyond..... a vista that can be enjoyed from levelled and well drained ground. Look to the northeast and the city feels near. Turn, climb the few yards to crest the battery and, in an instant, urban Devon is far, far behind. Instead, listen to the hiss of the sea stretching away below along as remote and rugged a shore as might be found anywhere Cornwall.

The contrast is never so marked than at night time, when the moon is veiled by a warm low-cloud south westerly. Plymouth offers then a calmly glowing grate of anthracite, whilst to the south the dark and fretful waters of the bay quiver beneath the swinging beam of the Eddystone.

So it is on this blustery summer night, and Eamon Carroll is understandably drawn to the sea..... there to once more pray for the shaft that might illuminate a path from his predicament.

He should have been dead. Instead he was saved and enabled to flee. And fled he had..... inexpertly by boat to Plymouth, and then, expertly, by night, in carefully a stolen cars, back to the capital. The second of the two he'd abandoned on the edge of Scrubs Common, choosing to walk the last few miles to Queens Park, and this, after almost five hours of driving, had allowed him time to consider.

His abductors had been with the security forces, of this he was convinced. They'd known he was with the movement, and known too that he was a mere minnow. They'd wanted to kill him, by shooting, at a specific location.... and probably at a specific time, possibly as a part of some kind of diversionary strategy. And if that time was now expired then so, perhaps, was that particular danger.

But the movement would be watchful now. Their once useful lackey would be regarded as a wayward risk. Rather than merely neglected, as before, he could expect to be totally cut adrift, or even hunted down.

A fresh start he could make, here perhaps..... or perhaps not, for as safe a place this might make for a rural semi-retirement, it wasn't the life he knew and loved and missed. He had to get back, but not yet, not without an explanation. This was why he'd travelled, for it was never going to come to him at his Queens Park flat, nor would it appear at a an airport or London station cab rank. Sitting and waiting could only bring more problems. He needed to move, and move smartly while any loose ends remained un tidied. Converting the taxi to cash and drawing on his savings he'd purchased himself an early model Cavalier saloon plus a several times owned Sprite caravan.

Hitch fitted, hooked up, and he was away, M4, M5, A38, and across the bridge and into Cornwall.... where Trerulefoot was far enough. Railway and water and Plymouth were to be kept together, in sight, and this, his map had told him, meant cutting back along the ferry road towards Torpoint. Four miles, and there on a loop of old road was a hefty caravan tucked close to the edge of a tidal creek, but these were obviously travelling folk. He'd paused, as if using the lay by, and, looking to the furthest shore, he'd identified the scene of his ordeal, but then moved on. Wary of appearing conspicuous he sought a touring site, for safety in number, and he'd found Whitsand, and this, as the season developed, was proving ideal. For a growing throng also offered Eamon scope for earning himself a little cash.

Plymouth had the shops, the theatre, the cinemas, skating and bowling...... tempting damp day options made all the more attractive by a quick and cheap taxi service down to the ferries. Cremyll or Torpoint, Eamon was ready to take to either, and even pick up later at a specified reasonable time.

The site owner was amenable. Eamon, he was personable, and the car, reliable. The arrangement was proving a success. The savings he'd drawn on could now be preserved.

All well enough, but a night like this would remind Eamon that a season was just that, and no more. What he continued to draw on was valuable time. This had to be more than a refuge. He knew this, he was trying..... but making little progress.

He reached to his shirt pocket for a cigarette, then felt for his lighter, without success, for it was in the car, he now remembered.

"Borrow this...." A quiet voice, male, from behind at first but now moving unthreateningly to his side. "Mind if I join you?"

"Do," said Eamon, taking and using the proffered lighter. Now both were smoking.

"Well..... nice evening."

"Er.... yes," And that was as much as Eamon could muster in reply. For he knew this face. It had been part of that ordeal, a knot in the mesh through which he'd slipped. Were the rest of them here, now, around him the darkness, or was this man on his own? If he'd wanted to kill again then a good chance had been passed up. It was dark. They were close to the edge of the cliff. A weighty rock would have done it, or, equally, an expertly delivered karate blow..... why mess with guns or knives?

"You run the taxi.... yeah?"

"That's me. You staying on the site?"

"I am."

"Alone?"

"Alone."

"Like me, but on holiday."

"Not really. I'm a journalist, freelance. My current project brings me here. Fascinating area."

This was a lie, Carroll knew. Why should this man bothering to invent? Perhaps recognition wasn't mutual.... and this was puzzling, for surely he would have seen photographs as part of the planning. There could have been a mistake. Maybe someone else should have been abducted and bundled off that train, unless knowledge of the shooting was restricted to those with guns.... an inner security force, a squad within a squad.

This kind of thing wasn't unknown, thought Carroll. That boat he'd borrowed....... if this fellow had left it then he could have been using it to genuinely patrol the shore, and been no part of what had been arranged for the tunnel. And this meant that this strange meeting here, tonight, might in fact be coincidental, and, possibly, an opportunity.

"Extremely fascinating," echoed Eamon. "These forts for example..... the whole area must have been bristling with guns. You writing about them?"

"It's radio stuff I do. Put down on tape, edited, then broadcast."

"So how do you move around?"

"In my camper van. I'm in and out of the site."

"Have I seen you out in a boat before?" asked Carroll speculatively.

"Might have done, before I lost it." Grigson was assuming this meant the *Speedwell*, two years before. He was happy to confirm that he'd pottered these parts, implying accidental loss in a storm or collision.

"And are you in trouble for that? It was found, I presume." An incisive probe, and suddenly Grigson was unsure. There was another boat, one that he'd lost more recently, more unusually. Was he being expected to answer for that one? To this man, here? Surely not, although there was that accent..... and one could never be certain.

"What do you mean?"

"That it wasn't yours to lose? That it was taken perhaps? And that you could stil be trying to work out how it could have happened?" Eamon was gambling, inviting the man to come clean. If he did, then they might have much in common, and scope perhaps for working together. Which way would it go?

"Are you a Republican," Alan spoke softly. Eamon drew on his cigarette.

"I can confess to having collected funds for the movement......"

"....but not to laying explosives, locally to here, a couple of months ago?"

"And if so, would you expect to find me still sitting around?

244

Believe me, I would be far, far away by now."

"But you've recognised me. You know about the boat. You must have been there."

"Yes, yes, and yes,"smiled Eamon, "but someone else was behind the explosion. And I can't say who......because the movement assumes it to have been me, acting alone, without their approval."

"A grave matter, I understand. Guard those kneecaps. Can you explain being at the scene?"

"Near the scene, Mr....."

"....Grigson, Alan Grigson, but just call me Alan."

"And I'm Eamon. I didn't hear the bomb, but I did see and smell smoke, just before seeing you and then being directed to your boat."

"And you had just landed there, as if by Tardis?"

"Think back, think hard, and you might remember a train entering the tunnel from the east, just before the explosion. The train was slowing....?" And Alan was nodding. Yes, he could remember.

"It was vans rather than carriages.... and you were in one of those?"

"About to be thrown out, thrown to the wolves. You think the Provisionals a bunch of lawless thugs? They're not the only ones. You weren't carrying a gun, I saw that. You wouldn't have been expecting that explosion, why else would you have been running to the scene, leaving your boat. But some people were carrying guns. They were expecting the explosion....."

"..... and were expecting you...."

"....in that tunnel, with orders to shoot to kill. I was meant to be shot. My body was meant to take the blame for that bomb."

"But instead you got away...."

".....and a scapegoat has to be found for that." The Eddystone glowed briefly from a vaguely defined horizon. Grigson was with him. Carroll asked; "Can I take it that you too are at odds with your own high command?"

"It's as you say. I'm the scapegoat."

"Cast out, like me, into a limbo existence, an escape from which requires answers."

"Like who it was that really set off that explosion, and why," agreed Grigson, at the same time wondering how this person could have got out of that tunnel alive..... but there would be another time to ask this.

"I say, Alan, that two heads must be better than one."

"So shake hands now, Eamon, and forward together eh? I've a friend coming to join me soon, and between us I think we might have the makings of a merry little band."

*

(xix) Scraesdon
The next day.

"Had I known, then I might have equipped myself with a smarter pair of trousers," mock-moaned Alan Grigson. "This is my worst pair of jeans, selected with a view to scrambling through thorn and bramble."

Sally smiled sympathetically, but beyond that it was just the curt 'left here' as, dropping into Antony off the Tregantle ridge, they needed to turn sharply into the quiet lane that led up to the near abandoned fort. It was a fine, almost windless evening, and the girl's father had been delighted to bring her as far as Tregantle, where Alan had waited with the *Speedwell*, parked on the wide space opposite the turn off for Freathy.

Graham Shaw, an occasional golfer, kept a half set of clubs ready bagged for just such evenings as these. Sally had heard them clatter into the boot. He would be taking on the back nine over at Portwrinkle, and it was natural that he should suggest that his daughter be brought down to the clubhouse once they'd scouted Scraesdon. He would buy them both a drink, he'd said when driving off, but had overlooked Alan's far from appropriate garb.......hence the latter's understandable reticence, now, to take up the invitation, however well meant. Alan's style was to blend. Local rules were to be observed, and to arrive at the nineteenth in Levis went against every instinct.

The girl apologised for her father, with polite expression of regret. Inwardly, though, she was far from disappointed, for she knew that beneath those clubs in the boot had lain the hobby weight metal detector which was always brought on the frequent Sunday spin to either to coast or moor. So later, she thought, if the light was still good and her father still playing, she might make a solo excursion with this, beyond Portwrinkle harbour, over the rocks, and along beneath the cliffs, to the cave where the gold lay buried. If she could only hear the buzz that would indicate it still to be there, that would do…. and to this degree of reassurance she had to be entitled, for again, this was her find.

But that possibility was for later. Now they were at Scraesdon, mere minutes from Tregantle, and what a contrast it made from the boldly flagged coastal fort. Tregantle, on its sparsely treed clifftop ridge, is visible for miles, but not so Scraesdon, the neglected twin, crouching on its less elevated river spur, under the shabby disguise of a near century's worth of scrub wood. Only from the air, or from actually within, can one get the full measure of those still formidable walls.

The camper is parked discretely in the lane, and Sally leads the way….. across the corroded, long seized drawbridge to the heavy door, firmly bolted under the heaviest of padlocks. But Alan has a key, and they can ease beneath the crumbling arch into a world apart. For Scraesdon is a walled Eden, a stubborn redoubt against farm chemicals. Surrounded but never overrun, it provides sanctuary to a wealth of flora and fauna which, outside, on local fields and hedgerows, dwindle to extinction under a protracted chemical purge.

They can thrive here, explains Sally, alongside the common daisy, under the protection of the bright foxglove and the vivid buttercup, behind the bramble, between fern and thorn, and Alan is certainly impressed….. but also slightly puzzled. For the girl's enthusiasm for the rare blooms and butterflies seems less than it might be, given her close knowledge. This was a distracted enthusiasm, he felt, of a mind pre occupied. He should be wary, he decided, lest she might likewise detect an ulterior purpose in him.

For as unique as this site might be, Alan was primarily concerned to assess his guide as a possible recruit. Jeremy was right. As deftly as he'd handled the secrets of Carwinion it was through the youngster that they'd been unlocked…. and another such key would be priceless.

But Sally, here, was no Steve. The boy had been a Parsifal, an Alice, blundering into a Wonderland of intrigue to draw the poison therefrom through that malleable innocence of his, a quality not nearly so apparent in this girl. And why should it be, on this, her home ground, where she had her own way to make, exams to pass, friends to keep, space to find? Mutual benefit would be the game here, finding overlap. Jeremy was a knowledgeable lecturer, and if this girl was a conscientious student then there had to be some scope. First, though, he would need to engineer an introduction.

"You don't seem too much interested in botany," said Sally, breaking Alan's reverie.

"Well I was just thinking maybe the same about you," countered Alan, starting to sound bunged, nasally, and needing to sniff before the question that was to follow. "Do you think I might be better off with that pair over there?" Two figures, both male, both black, each shouldering a canvas mailman type bag had appeared in the northernmost corner of the parade. They would have probably climbed through the woods from the river before picking their way along the ditch to a scale-able section of wall.

"Hay fever," said Sally. "You get the pollen in here, like pea soup. And those guys might well have the answer. They're up from Wacker Quay, picking Hawthorn leaves, or flower, or stripping bark, something like that. This will be for Megan, their companion, the old herbalist. She'll be down below...."

"In the basement, mixin' up the medicine!" As nasally as this attempt to sound hip was intoned, Alan was woefully off mark....... by a generation at least.

"We can call down there. She's bound to have something. I don't like to hear a man suffering."

"Good idea..... first, though, Id like to get up onto that far end wall. It has to give a good view across the Lynher."

"We'll need a gap in the trees," said Sally. "Follow me." There were paths across the overgrown parade, but at this time of year the grasses closed high to the waist. Sally waded on, Alan spluttering behind. Reaching the wall they climbed onto an emplacement, where Alan could at last gulp at the breeze as a goldfish might for its floating food. A distant glimpse of Dartmoor confirmed that he was through the worst, before the trees briefly parted to reveal the full blue width of the Lynher River, with weathered red-brick Ince glowing resplendently amongst the more stately trees of the far bank.

There it was, just as Alan had expected, and just as Sally had been picturing it, more and more, in her increasingly troubled mind. And suddenly Alan was hopeful...... for see, she was scrutinising the place more intently than anything else she'd looked upon in the full hour just past. But words, the right words, these he found elusive. He needed to say something though, before the chance was lost...... an open question maybe.

"And what do you know of that place, Sally?"

"Ince? There's been a Castle there for centuries, in various styles and states of repair. Compared with that, this masonry beneath us is young."

"Ever taken a closer look?"

"Only last year. About once a month through the summer the old lady throws the gardens open for charity. I think it was the Heart Foundation when we went across."

"The old lady....?" Grigson knew very well, but Sally was talking freely now, and this was to be encouraged.

".....being the Viscountess Boyd. Widowed when the Viscount went under a car in a London street..... three years ago now, I'd say. Two years ago you were last down here, wasn't it? Weren't you filled in then?"

"Then it was more this side," explained Alan, " Mount Edgcumbe, Antony House, Torpoint rather than Saltash. When did the Boyds move in?"

"Early '60s, after he was finished with politics. They've rescued the place. Spending money on the buildings, spending time on the gardens, they've made up for years of neglect."

"It looks to be the kind of place that might have featured in the Civil War. There was a plenty of action around these parts...... that much I did learn when last here." Alan was testing.

"And in the last war it was used as a billet for French Canadians," continued the girl, showing an encouraging preference for more recent conflict.

"Rather isolated down there, but as a group, in 1940, they had to be watched..... assessed. You find that era interesting.....?" Alan was angling.

"Very, in twelve months I'll be sitting History at 'A' level, with a view to possibly going on with it to university."

"Then you would get on well with a friend of mine. He's keen on the subject. He lectures up in Bath. I'm expecting him down. He'll be staying with me for a few weeks over at Whitsand. I'd like to introduce you."

"Sounds good," agreed Sally attempting to convey earnestness rather than excitement, and just about succeeding.

"The early post war years, Jeremy likes. He actually knows Sir Edward Trembath...."

"…..who was returned for Plymouth North how many times…..six, seven?"

"I lose count," smirked Alan, hiding ignorance. "And this place, Sally, what a piece of archaeology! Jeremy will be no less fascinated. It's owned by the MOD, I know that. I applied through them for the key. Do they use it at all?"

"Training….. they send units over from Tregantle. You get them clambering through the ditches and over the walls, often carrying the tools of their trade. The weapons, the radio, food and first aid things, but not live ammunition….. they save that for the coastal ranges, and for over there." She pointed towards Dartmoor. Under a clear November westerly it could stand crisp, mainly pale but patched in vivid bracken brown. Now, though, it was a basking chameleon, low and grey under a simmering July haze. "We can follow this wall along, back to the camper. That gives us a good view of the old lift incline. You'll know about the railway that ran from Wacker across to Tregantle."

"Quite a climb….."

"…..requiring the track to be laid in two separate sections, one at river level, the other from Fort to Fort. Joining them was an inclined plane, up which the uncoupled trucks had to be steam winched one at a time. There must have been some kind of stationary engine."

"Sounds like a lot of huffing and puffing…."

"….. because, when it came to the defence of the Realm, no expense or effort was to be spared. This was the way it was all brought……. ammunition for the guns, victuals for the men, plus fuel, of course, for heat and light."

As quiet as this place was now, with just the occasional car wending the road below, the sights and the sounds of a hundred years before sparked Alan's imagination…... the hiss of steam, the clang of couplings, the smell of burning coal and warm oil, and the grumble and squeal of burdened rail. And all this for just the westernmost two of a full ring of forts which, in its totality, had to stand as an astonishing feat of construction. Was the purpose fulfilled though? Had a potential invader truly been deterred by all this, or did they stand now on a monument to paranoia, a grandiose folly?

The *Speedwell* was rattled back into life, eased down to Antony, then it was westward along to Wacker. Megan might recognise him, Alan explained. He'd tried her hawthorn jelly two years ago.

"Haemorrhoids," he whispered, as if such a confidence could confer privilege..... and then more normally, apologetically almost, "but I've had no trouble since."

"Good," responded Sally, trusting that laconic indifference might spare her further detail. It was as well that they were now just seconds from Wacker.

"Yes, I can see that you're suffering with this. How often will it affect you this badly Mr.....? I'm sorry, I do remember you, and the boat of course, but I've forgotten the name."

"Alan Grigson, and don't apologise. You had a stand at that Fayre over in the Eliot estate. Of dozens of customers I was but one. You had no reason to ask my name, I had no reason to give it. I sailed by a few times, and waved, but never pulled against the quay. This is my first time of calling here."

"Well you must call again," insisted the weathered nomad. "And if you're living in that van then, as you can see, we have room alongside."

"And the lady's question, Alan, was how often does it affect you this badly."

"Very rarely," replied Alan, meeting the girl's feigned exasperation with feigned contrition. Was she feeling a little left out, he wondered. If so then he could take encouragement. Resentment was an improvement on indifference..... anything was. And if she was now better engaged, it could be that this had been precipitated by Ince, and perhaps even by that mention of Jeremy. "And never once as bad as this," he added.

"Do you have a handkerchief?" enquired Megan.

"I don't."

"You can use one of mine." The caravan rocked slightly as she stood to reach one from an eye level shelf. "It's clean." She then stooped to slide out the mid-most of a five-high chest of shallow drawers. One small bottle was confidently selected from a tightly packed range which to the two watchers appeared confusingly similar. "Keep it folded, thus, and occasionally moisten with a few drops, so." She unscrewed the narrow top to demonstrate, spreading a strangely re-assuring waft of tincture. "Then hold beneath the nose and breath there thorough as best you can."

The wad was passed to the patient, and the bottle to Sally who treated herself to a cautious sniff. It wasn't hawthorn. Her mother had some of that at home…. to help her through the 'off weeks' she said

"And the magic ingredient for this one grows up above us in the fort?" the girl asked.

"Magic doesn't come in to it my dear," the headscarfed practitioner gently chided, her bright brown eyes more than matching the glint of the bottle. "Two of the active ingredients will, on a good year, be found here, yes, but what matters just as much, if not more, is the preparation, the blending, the storing ….. trade secrets of course, nothing more mysterious, or sinister."

Grigson nodded approval, for already the itching and the running had eased. Here was a clever woman indeed, but what about that voice? The command of English was easy, but the accent was so well travelled as to defy location. Roma, he decided, allowing himself the fullest scope for error. Jeremy's proven ear was the more expert, he thought, so let him listen and say.

"And this year you've taken a pair of Africans as business partners," said Sally. "We saw them up in the fort. From the west are they, or from the east, or the south?" Jeremy, dosing on his vapours, approved. He might have put the same question.

"Next time, if they're here, you can ask them," replied Megan cordially. "You know you're always welcome, together or singly."

"I'm sure we'll be back," confirmed Alan, readying himself to leave. "If only to top up on this stuff. What do I owe you?"

"Nothing," insisted Megan. "Consider it a free sample."

*

(xx) *Jamaica Inn*

As Alan and Sally leave Wacker for Portwrinkle, James Busbridge and Kate Rogers arrive once again at *Jamaica Inn*. The same drinks are purchased, and these are taken to the same table. They are recognised by the same helpful bar assistant, and he has been as good as his word. Soon they have before them the damaged card which makes up the full set. It is crinkled. It has a tear, and it is marked. The stain might have been wine, or gravy, or sauce, but they have been told that it is blood, and this they have no reason to disbelieve. Pictured is the *Surcouf*, as hoped, and this curious man is scenting a lead.

But he can't dispense with Kate, in fact he needs her all the more..... so his tactic, for the moment, is to allude to his possible usefulness to her.

"Do you think it possible that Gordon might talk again? You've spoken of an interest in trauma linked psychiatric conditions so, as a possible case, would our friend be deemed treatable...... or beyond remedy? He was a child, it was almost fifty years ago. Too deep seated, do you think, too long term?"

"This can depend...... on the severity of the emotional shock."

"And how much might be known of its circumstances?"

"Indeed," agreed Kate, "especially where an attempt is being made to restore an erased memory....."

"...... a form of treatment not without controversy."

"Any new treatment will encounter controversy," countered Kate. "To challenge tradition is to challenge vested interest." This is radical-speak. Busbridge is encouraged.

"A historian might say the same thing," he chuckles. "Hear this. Yesterday I went into Plymouth, to the library, where one can find a record of '40/'41 blitz casualties."

"Deaths you mean....."

"....plus addresses of deceased."

"And you found Trevor's parents....."

".......I found a Philip and Christine Dalton."

"And others, I would have thought, Dalton not being an unusual surname."

"But these had a son, Trevor, living with them."

"So survivors were listed?"

"No." Busbridge has the *Surcouf* in his fingers, he turns the card and flicks pensively at a limp corner. "This Trevor Dalton, aged 10, died with his parents. The three were pulled from the rubble of their Bretonside home and buried together, I learned, in a mass grave in Efford Cemetery." Kate sips at her lager, and considers.

"So we conclude what?" she asks.

"Nothing, at least not yet. Possibly there are two Trevor Daltons."

"Not too much of a co incidence, I suppose?"

"But enough to alert us to a second possibility. We know of one change of name...."

"..... to Gordon."

"So perhaps the purpose of this was to mask a previous one."

"To Trevor..... from?" The natural enquiry from Kate, and now James hesitates. Instead he looks down at that card again. The nurse reads his eyes. "This is something else to do with that submarine," she says. "To do with an action she was in...... the seizure in Devonport perhaps?"

"Certainly related to this. For when this happened, the majority of the crew, like most in France, were content to accept Hitler's far from onerous armistice terms. Many were allowed home, and these had to be replaced, of course. A core of Free French zealots could be kept on to control and train these draftees, but the quality and the loyalty of their material was variable, to say the least."

"French seamen of the not particularly able sort."

"And not particularly trustworthy either," continued James. "Few being fully convinced that Churchill and de Gaulle together could come close to matching the combination of Hitler and Darlan. A view confirmed by fiascos such as that at Dakar. Winston's bellicosity was empty bluff, it was thought. He would soon have to resign to allow more fascist friendly successors to accept a similar Vichy style settlement."

"So if this *Surcouf*, which barely works as a weapon, starts then to become a focus of intrigue, why isn't it towed off somewhere to be scuttled?"

"Good question Kate....... I suppose it was an emblem for de Gaulle, that's got to be part of it"

"But not all?"

"This is what I'm hoping you can help us to ascertain."

"Me?"

"You and Gordon."

"Who we know to have been a Trevor, and you think might have been someone else before that. Who else?"

"You will have heard of Peter Bright, of *Molehunter* fame."

"The spook, ex MI5, now living in Tasmania," confirmed Kate. "He's at odds with the Government, his former employer. They tried to stop him publishing that book. He says he needs to, the pension they gave him being so paltry."

"He's a cousin of mine. We're in touch, and he can't understand the Government. What should they fear from him? he wonders. There wasn't a lot that was new in *Molehunter*."

"But there's the precedent, and the principle."

"Others had written memoirs before, some a lot more revelatory. This was about him, he concluded, and something he might know, something really hot, which they didn't want appearing in any sequel. The irony is that he hadn't so much as even considered what this might be."

"But now he was alerted...."

".....and he thought back to when he first retired to Tasmania, and to an apparently insignificant task he'd then been happy to fulfil just to keep his hand in, really. For it had been realised that Cousin Peter was going to be living close to Vincent Wakeham, a private man who had lived quietly in Tasmania since emigrating from England shortly after the war. He was no trouble, this man, but it was wished that he should be kept under a casual but permanent surveillance. He'd outlived the one previous watcher and as Peter was arriving in the right place at the right time......."

"He would make an ideal replacement."

"Exactly...... and, as it happened, Peter was to discover that this wasn't to be a long term task, for Vincent Wakeham, he soon learned, was mortally ill. He had an ailing heart. Within eighteen months of Peter himself taking on the task the poor fellow was dead."

"So the duty had been discharged......"

"It had, but not before he'd spoken with the best of the few friends that Vincent had made over his years as a naturalised Tasmanian."

"And your cousin, as a trained listener, he would have pulled together what they had gleaned of his background."

"From which a report was produced. This was sent back for his controller....."

".......and then largely forgotten about."

"Yes, because what he'd pieced together appeared unimportant. And then Peter himself began to feel largely forgotten about. Resentment grew. *Molehunter* was written....."

".....which provoked a seeming over reaction in London."

"Which in turn had Peter returning to his Vincent Wakeham notebook. Something in this might be more significant than originally thought, he concluded, and the summary sent to London is re composed for my scrutiny."

"And you learn what?"

"That Vincent Wakeham was originally from Cornwall, and that during the war he was interned on an island off Scotland...... this because he was deemed a security risk after having been apprehended close to the Holy Loch submarine base in Scotland."

"A long way from Cornwall."

"He was searching for a younger brother who'd been lost while night fishing out of Portwrinkle. A surfacing submarine had snagged the line, and the boy, named Norman, had been dragged from their boat."

"And this has to be the *Surcouf.*"

"From which members of the crew are seen to emerge, and hopefully they untangle Norman and take him below. Vincent gets to Devonport the next morning only to be told that the sub has set sail for Scotland."

"And that's where he heads...."

".... by train, yes, and that's where he gets arrested."

"The internment camp is well stocked with Irish Republicans, apparently, and the lad picks himself up a passable Irish accent. After the best part of three years he is released, and he can head home to Cornwall. Here, though, he is shunned. His brother's body had been washed ashore. Vincent finds the grave at the local cliff top church, and also that of his mother who'd been lain alongside Norman on her death shortly afterwards. Vincent bids them farewell and travels first to London, where he lives out he rest of the war....."

"...... and then, with peace," said Kate, "he decides on Tasmania, and a fresh start."

"And being a fresh start he offers new found friends only a vague narrative concerning an up-bringing in Cornwall, the wartime tragedy, and the internment."

"So in reality, those who'd instigated the surveillance had nothing to fear."

"Not from Vincent, or even from cousin Peter, then, but in choosing to antagonise him they fashion a rod for their own backs. The story he has of Vincent is sketchy, but he can be sure that the vessel involved was the *Surcouf.* Its move, for crew training purposes, from Devonport to Scotland at the end of December 1940 is a matter of open record. No other submarine, British or French, was similarly transferred. There can be no confusion on this...."

"…..but…."

"….secrecy still surrounds the actual base to base voyage."

"And secrecy breeds speculation."

"Speculation and rumour, Kate, and enter at this point another French submarine, nominally Free French, more conventionally sized….."

"…… named?"

"Named the *Narval*. The crew is smaller and, unlike in the *Surcouf*, the men are trained and capable. But there is, it seems, the same crisis of loyalty. The boat has just left Portsmouth on its last operational patrol. It has strict orders to sail to Gibraltar, there to await further directions."

"But something went wrong. You said it was a last patrol."

"The *Narval* did reach Gibraltar, Kate. It left replenished, and then it disappeared. Somewhere in the Mediterranean, it's thought, but quite how has never been made clear."

"And speculation has followed," said Kate.

"Some saying that she was chased and sunk by our Navy following an attemped defection to a Vichy port. Others suggest sabotage."

"Just because she was lost without trace? Perhaps there was an accident, or encounter with an enemy mine."

"Maybe," acknowledged Busbridge, "but looking at the movements of both the *Narval* and the *Surcouf*, some have suggested that the two boats might have rendezvoused between Portsmouth and Gibraltar, and perhaps discussed a joint defection."

"And this might have been off Cornwall."

"Indeed, where upon some theorists, Kate, will introduce a truly intriguing character……."

"…..this being….."

"…..the most senior of the Free French naval officers, one Vice Admiral Emile Muselier, who would have been on the *Surcouf*, it's claimed."

"Claimed?"

"Because again the known facts are vague. What has been established for certain is that while the *Surcouf* is making for Scotland, this Muselier is arrested by the British secret service and thrown into Brixton Gaol. Amongst other pro-Vichy machinations he is accused of plotting to sell the *Surcouf* back to Darlan. Some will go as far as to say that de Gaulle wasn't totally displeased to have a leadership rival brought so low, but whatever, in the event Muselier was able to plead his innocence so strongly that apologies had to be proffered by all, by Churchill, by his intelligence people, and even by His Majesty the King!"

"So from bread and water in the dungeons it was suddenly the best sherry in the Palace vault," wowed Kate. "Sounds like he had something truly persuasive up his sleeve."

"Enough to confound de Gaulle's studied indifference, certainly….."

"…… and possibly enough to pin the guilt where it belonged, embarrassingly so, perhaps."

"But no one can say now what it is he had," explained Busbridge.

"Because the agreement would have included a confidentiality clause. It was a done deal, ratified by the Crown, no one else to know, no comebacks."

"But what if there were witnesses?" posed Busbridge.

"To a submarine rendezvous? All on the *Narval* were lost with the boat, you said, likewise when the *Surcouf* went down barely more than a year later."

"I don't mean on the *Narval*. Nor do I mean on the *Surcouf*. I'm thinking more of casual bystanders, unlucky fishermen for example."

"But they're both dead. One dying on the night in question, the other expiring in Tasmania forty years later."

"Maybe, but what if there was a misidentification, or even a deception in hand when the boy's body was washed up and buried? This is the possibility that Peter entertains….."

"…… and one that he's obviously asked you, James, to explore."

"Something looks to have put Vice Admiral Muselier into quite a strong bargaining position," reasoned James. "Also he has fished himself a boy, a lad who might have seen and heard far too much."

"Too much to be allowed home, and he's too young to be interned, and maybe he's traumatised….. to the extent that he is unable to speak."

"You get the drift, Kate. Muselier insists that the boy be cared for. This is agreed. Where better then for the youngster to be entertained at His Majesty's pleasure than……"

"……. at a secure hospital, at Moorhaven, or latterly at St Lawrence."

"And if such a boy was rendered speechless by the shock of such an ordeal then it is going to suit some that he be not prescribed any remedial treatment. Tell me, Kate, would you have access to Gordon's case records?"

"I might do, I don't know," blurted the nurse, realising now where this might be leading her….. deeper into trouble. In fact already she was compromised, and so by extension was Rosemary, her friend. A confidence, both professional and personal had been betrayed, and this because it had seemed to her that Gordon was no more than a sad case of neglect, a case that might even fall within her scope to mend.

Now, far from his having been allowed to sink down into an institutional sump, she was hearing that Gordon's predicament might have been positively determined, on decisions reached amongst extremely powerful people. And though it might be that they'd now passed on, this wasn't to say that fully empowered trustees were not still active…….. so what was she to do?

Cut and run? No, for this would be provocative, and she would be squandering such control of the situation that remained to her. What she'd so far given to Busbridge was his, to be used how he liked. She needed to keep her nerve, to show an interest still while, if necessary, finding discrete ways to obstruct and delay…… until what? Until some kind of assistance might be found, or until some other stronger leads might appear to render redundant those foolishly opened by herself. Ideally it would be a mixture of the two. It would certainly help if she could share all this….. but with whom? And as for the case records?

"I don't see why not," she said, having found sufficient composure.

"So could you be able to locate a birth certificate? It might be an original, salvaged from the rubble of the Dalton's home….."

"Or a replacement, available on application, even after an individual has been registered dead….. the Jackal trick. But that wouldn't be signed by either of the parents, of course. I'll have to move very stealthily with this. You're not to rush me. What will you be doing with that card?"

"Seeking a replacement for the pub, and also sending this up to a contact Peter has in Cambridge."

"At the university?"

"Involved on the science side, where I'm told there's a group developing advanced forensic techniques. Their realm is molecular biology."

"DNA analysis, and you think they could use what's on there?"

"Not necessarily to a criminal standard of proof, but there could be positive indications, and they might ask for instance for a larger and more up to date sample." The statement was loaded, the last part being phrased to hang as a request.

And Kate was appalled, but this was hardly the place to make this known, or to even sound merely lukewarm.

"I'll be interested to know what they make of it," she said, as if awed by nothing more than the pace of scientific progress. "And what about the churchyard that holds the graves, of the washed ashore remains and also the boys' mother. Have you located that yet?"

"I have, and I've been there, and it's a place I think we could now visit together. Ever been to Rame Head?"

*

(xxi) Portwrinkle

Set down in the clubhouse carpark, Sally pauses to reflect as the Speedwell grinds back up the hill to Crafthole. She'd agreed to meet Alan again, and with him that friend of his, the lecturer, but only if she could herself bring Chas. He shared her interest in Ince, she'd said, and on some aspects he would be more knowledgeable. And Grigson had been happy to agree, likewise considering four a less daunting number.

They'd seen Graham Shaw on the way down, still three holes from home, calculated Sally, and behind a somewhat sluggish looking foursome. Time, she had, to turn to the west, to beyond the harbour where the cliff foot shadow seeped across dark weed draped rocks, slowly gaining on the ebbing tide. She could use that gloom, as she could also use the lasting glow of the sinking sun, thrown inward off the still bright pool that was Whitsand Bay. She had the best part of an hour, she reckoned, and soon, metal detector shouldered, she was scrunching herself a fresh path across the shaley storm line shingle.

The cave had been aptly chosen. Beachcombers and dog walkers rarely ventured so far, and from both sides the entrance was screened by a paralleled pair of naturally up-angled slate outcrops. The faulted cleft between tapered towards the cliff as a deepening naturally walled gully, a narrow avenue of sheltered wave-ridged sand, beaded to each edge by string of glassy shrimp-grazed pools.

To notice the cave one had to be in line with this gully. To enter the cave one had to take that avenue, as Sally now did. There it was, gaping ahead, and it looked dark, far darker than it did on that afternoon when the sun had still been high. Then, within the cave, they'd had a good half light. Now, for her, not yet to the entrance, it was barely a quarter, with the damp feeling damper, and the cold more cold.

But the detector was on, and it was working. She swept and it sought..... and there was the signal. And this was all that she'd really come for, that comforting buzz. But now, with that ingot calling, this was never going to be enough. She had to see this thing again, she had to hold it..... and why not? For this, she again told herself, was her find. What harm was there in digging and looking. She certainly wouldn't be taking it away.

So down she was on her knees, scooping back the coarse, dry, grey sand. Going deeper, having to lean, now, and reach for the something that would be hard to the touch.... which this was, at last. If she could just dust around the edges, and down a little, then there should be a corner to lift. But this time there seemed to be no corners, though she had an edge now and it was starting to lift. So she pulled, and up it came..... to bring a realisation that whatever else she had hold of, this was not gold, or even metal. It was bone, old bone. It could be a shoulder blade, of a sheep maybe? They would sometimes be over adventurous on the pastures above, and some had been known to slip, and be killed by fall, or lie injured to drown.

The blade would do as a trowel, she decided, and wielding it as such she crouched to widen her excavation. She had something again, and she was working around it. She could get her fingers beneath now, and again it wasn't metal, but there were sockets and it was coming as she tugged...... so light it was to lift, and then, suddenly, she was having to drop it in alarm. For glinting in the shadows were teeth. This was a skull, a human skull, unmistakably so, alarmingly so. She wanted to get out, well out. Had she not tripped on the detector it might have been left, but she snatched it up, and now she was running. Distance was the imperative. She had to be clear of the gully, a soft cloying tongue that might yet roll her back into that dragon's mouth, to face again that fiendish detritus.

It was panic, and, as she glanced back, blind panic. For while dashing on, without watching ahead, there was nothing to warn her of the two strong enveloping arms. Nothing short of the contact, of the being held, and lifted from her feet….. and by whom ? By her father? By Chas? What could she say, and what might they say?

Nothing….. for this was neither. Released, she had to turn, turn and meet two faces, warm eyed, warm land faces….. part puzzled, part amused. She placed them at once, as the pair seen at Scraesdon. These were Megan's trusted African minders, and how much more reassuring were these smiles, with their rows of living teeth. They still had those bags, and one now lay on the sand having slipped in the collision. Amongst the spill of blossom and leaf lay a scattering of shells, and these people's presence here was explained. Having collected for the herbalist this was for themselves. Gathered for their accessory lines they would be fashioned later into buttons, brooches, bracelets.

Embarrassment supplanted fear. She would help re-gather this spillage. She owed them no less. Clutching still at the detector, she stooped to lend such assistance as she could, and this was appreciated, particularly by he into whom she'd run. He held the bag open with one hand, so that with the one free hand each they were gathering with two. But his colleague had stepped away, and he was peering cliff-wards along the gully, naturally curious as to what might have triggered such fright.

Sally glanced nervously. The guy would be thinking that another person was involved. A live person, of course, and why not he whom they'd seen her with earlier, up at the fort? The companion had turned assailant, this would be the suspicion.

"It's just me," she said, coyly, explaining nothing. "No one else."

But she wasn't believed, that was plain. And now she had to be on her way, pleasantly, as if her strange conduct was in some way normal. She bade the puzzled pair an apologetic farewell and strode eastward. How could she just hang about? She had too many questions of her own.

She hadn't found what she'd sought….. so was it, or was it not still there? It probably was, for something other than bone had activated the detector. But how could they have missed her grim discovery before? Was Chas aware of those remains being there? Surely this wasn't a deliberately contrived scare…. unless the whole thing was a hoax. But she couldn't believe that, not after having found the gold herself. If he'd brought it to the surface then maybe…… if it were not so elaborate, and in such bad taste.

No, she decided, this was real, and so was the predicament. Those Africans would enter that cave, she knew. They might have a torch now. If not, they would be down there in the morning..... and then? The prospects were dire, but what could she do?

*

(xxii) a phone call
The next day 8.30am. At the camp site.

"Jeremy.... Alan here."

"Alan.... speaking from a call box are you? I can ring back"

"How soon can you get down?"

"As soon as you like. I'm near enough prepared. Give me forty minutes to wash, dress and pack, and from Bath it's what...... three hours at the most? Suggest a meet up."

"The *Notterbridge*, know it? A pub set back off the main road.... about five minutes out of Saltash, where you cross the next river after the Tamar."

"I'll find it. A clear road and I should be there before one. Met any interesting people?"

"Two or three, and one I'll be bringing with me."

"Good, and I've been given an intriguing lead.... "

Alan was heartened. Jeremy Barnes, the academic, was enthusiastically on task, and sounding keen to pool his dividend.

*

(xxiii) damage limitation
Wacker 8.45am

Sally taps nervously at the caravan door, hoping she isn't too early, and hoping even more that she hasn't left this too late. It opens. She takes a deep breath and looks up. Megan, as prim and as perceptive as ever, beckons her in, almost as if expected.

"Coffee, young lady?"

"Please." The girl glances around, to check they were alone......but immediately sees the ingot, on the floor, beneath the table at which she is about to sit.

"No school today? I see you're in uniform."

"Later perhaps."

"So as far as your parents are concerned you're on your way..... but instead you've come here."

Sally had had to, having not slept a wink.

"The ferry bus comes out to Antony before doubling back. I walked from *The Ring o' Bells*."

"On a matter of some urgency it would appear. Is this yours?" The old herbalist shoves at the block with stretched out foot. It doesn't move.

"I found it."

"And where did you find it?"

"On the sea bed, out in the bay, when diving."

"So you wouldn't have been alone."

"Just one other, my instructor, but I was the one who found it," she repeats.

"But he chose the place for hiding it..... and a very good place too, except for this problem we have of the sitting tenant. My colleagues have gone back down to piece him together. This gold, I take it, is a secret between you and....."

"...... Chas. Yes, or at least it was."

"And have you contacted him since yesterday evening?"

"Not yet..... I wanted to check here first."

"Did he know you were going down there?" Sally shakes her head. "So what do I do? Give it you back and ignore the skeletal remains?" The girl has no answer. The steaming kettle whistles derisively. "You find treasure, then you find a body. I think, at law, one is obliged to report both."

"Let me....."

"..... and Chas, who is yet to be told of the bones?"

"But he will be."

"Will he really?" The woman frowns sceptically. "I think you need my help, the pair of you. There's three things here that need sorting..... your relationship, this lump of metal, and that pile of bones. How soon can you get your friend here?"

"Possibly by this evening. He lives in Plymouth."

"I want it to be just him, you, and me. And you say nothing about yesterday until he gets here. I won't be going anywhere or saying anything, and neither will Makesi or Juma, my companions."

*

(xxiv) Notter
1pm

Jeremy was comfortably on time. Alan and Eamon, standing with the parked taxi, hadn't long arrived. The lecturer brought his green Astra gently in beside them, leaving himself room to climb out and stretch arms, legs and neck, and suck in the balming Cornish air.

"Barely across the border," he said approvingly, "but it's Cornwall, all the same. Great to be back!"

"And good to see you again," said Alan. "Meet Eamon, and Eamon's taxi. Just how they come to be plying their trade in this corner of Cornwall is a story best left to him."

"And one best begun inside," added Carroll. And thus, huddled around a corner table in the lounge at the un-busy *Notterbridge* Inn, Jeremy Barnes heard mainly from Eamon how his and Alan's paths from had crossed. The latter had brought in a standard OS map, and to any casual observer the three, with their pasty apiece, would have been discussing the possibilities for a pleasant walk in the country..... taking in an old church or two, a mix of railway architecture and industrial archaeology, plus one or more of the big houses, at Port Eliot, Ince, or Trematon.

But not every observer need be casual. Unknown to either, Alan and Eamon have been recognised. Their arrival together was noted by one of the public bar occasionals, and his surprise at seeing each is only exceeded by an astonishment that they should be together. He has to know more. He slips out to check the car park. With their motors still warm, it should be possible to work out which of the cars they might have arrived in. That would be a start.

The three inside, meanwhile, are on to a second round of drinks..... half pints of course, to be safe, and after having had the best part of Eamon's story it was the natural moment for Alan to prompt a contribution from Jeremy.

"You and I, Eamon, we take the lie of the land. Jeremy here, he brings historical insight. On the politics of recent times he's the best I know. I'll be disappointed if he hasn't already got an angle on the Viscountess Boyd and her late husband."

"Well I have made a start," began the lecturer. "I've been up to London to call on Sir Edward Trembath.... another Tory politician, Eamon, MP for a Plymouth seat. Retired in '79. Back in the '50s he was a colleague of Alan Lennox Boyd, then MP for a Bedfordshire constituency. Boyd went up to the Lords in 1960. He'd been a Minister, for the Colonies, hence the title of Viscount. Shortly afterwards they moved down here to Ince." And for his own benefit Jeremy half opened his map to check exactly where the Castle lay in relation to the pub. "The Viscountess still lives here," he continued, his finger finding the residence. "She having been widowed four years ago......traffic accident in London."

"And Trembath was ready to talk about Lord Boyd?" asked Alan, too well aware of the lecturer's propensity for digression.

"He was pleased to. Assumed I'd turned up to discuss money....."

".....for some reason," smiled Alan, "and would have been well relieved that your questions concerned someone else's political career, relieved and grateful. So could he help?"

"He could, and yes, I think he did. He suggested we might initially focus on Kenya, and an illustrious predecessor at the Colonial Office."

"Named," prompted Eamon.

"Lord Moyne...... Patricia Lennox Boyd's Uncle Walter. He was at the Colonial Desk for just over a year, his span covering 1941.... a crucial phase in the last war."

"For you British, a year of military disaster," said Eamon.

"And one of diplomatic disaster for Berlin," added Jeremy, "epitomised, some say, by the baffling antics of Rudolf Hess."

"Who flew to Scotland....," mused the cabbie, ".... a long way from Kenya, so why focus there?"

"Because Trembath associates Boyd primarily with the Mau Mau emergency, in the 50s."

"A police state," commented Eamon, "like Ireland in the'20s".

"Quite," agreed Jeremy. "A cruel suppression, one of the worst episodes being the Hola Prison Camp scandal..... chain gangs, prisoners being beaten to death, cover-up lies, the lot. An enquiry was commissioned, and put to the Commons. On the eve of debate Boyd's position looked to be untenable. He would have to resign, it seemed, accepting enduring blame and disgrace..... but then, on the day, to Trembath's lasting amazement, the Minister was let off the hook. He was allowed to see things out. He could stand down later on his own terms."

"So he had an insurance policy," deduced Alan. "and it sounds like a last gasp revelation."

"This is what Trembath was implying..... and perhaps actually cashed in by someone other than the insured."

"So who?"

"The whispered word was that perhaps his wife had been quietly holding something, something left to her by her Uncle Walter, Lord Moyne."

"When?" asked Alan.

"Before he died, or soon after in a letter posthumously received."

"So his death was in....."

".....1944," offered Eamon, knowledgably, and Jeremy was reminded how much, in terms of organisation and method, the modern IRA had learned from Irgun practice. "He was shot in Cairo, where by then he'd been made Minister Resident. Assassinated by Zionist gunmen....."

".... who were ready to alienate our British Government just when we'd established a war winning position," said Alan, looking to Jeremy for explanation. It seemed so perverse.

"Quite how he should have found himself in the firing line remains a matter of conjecture," said the lecturer. "The one certain thing is the current status of the assassins. Caught and hanged immediately after the murder, their remains are now venerated. Recently reclaimed from their Egyptian lime, the bones are now interred in the promised land, amongst the graves of the martyrs."

"So no regrets there," observed Eamon.

"But what link might there be between Moyne and Kenya," wondered Alan. "Some wartime thing would it be? You must have asked that of Trembath."

"I did, and on this he told me he'd made it his business not to be curious. Yes, it was whispered that the Hola debate was skewed, and perhaps by Moyne, posthumously, through his niece…… but as to the nature of the actual lever that might have lifted the blame from Boyd, this was understood to be strictly secret."

"I can believe that," said Alan, "Trembath being there to keep his head down, we know that….."

"…..and for his son's sake he'll be wanting to keep well clear of the parapet now."

"But if he were you, Jeremy, determined to dig on, where would he go with his trowel?"

"He pointed to something that was common knowledge then. Before and during the war Moyne had a very close lady friend. She travelled the world with him in his spanking great yacht. Vera Broughton, her name was, and while they never married she was seen very much as part of the Guinness family."

"Whilst staying a Broughton." Using a name could some times help Grigson to retain it.

"Being her married name, kept after divorce from a more minor aristocrat, one Sir John Henry Delves Broughton….. known to most as 'Jock' Broughton. Ring any bells?"

"Should it?" Alan blankly answered, clearly speaking for Eamon too.

"What about 'Lord Erroll'?…… Eamon?…..Another assassinated Peer?….. Kenya?" Eamon was at a loss, but for Alan it was coming.

"Happy Valley," he said. "There's been a book, *White Mischief*, and they're making a film, I think. Lord Erroll was a womaniser. He was shot. A jealous husband was put on trial."

"And this was 'Jock' Broughton," explained Jeremy "He was acquitted, and the crime remains unsolved….. although some say this was only down to the mishandling of good evidence. Broughton's defence was full of gaps….."

"....but no less so than the prosecution's case," said Eamon, caustically. He'd seen enough protestant gunmen walk free to presume conspiracy rather than cock-up. "So have you read *White Mischief*, Jeremy?"

"Not yet..... though I did buy a copy whilst in London, and with it a copy of *Black Mischief*....."

"......from which the title is obviously derived," said Eamon.

"And that I have actually read before," chuckled Jeremy.

"Me too," sniggered Alan. "Evelyn Waugh at his sharpest..... warning against premature de-colonisation."

"Premature de-colonisation!" repeated Eamon, reacting, in truth, to being out of the joke. "Only those schooled in imperialism could conceive such a notion. What next..... premature justice?"

"Relax Eamon," said Jeremy. "Waugh lampoons native, settler, and administrator alike. The books are in the car. I can show you a few choice passages. It's a hoot, you just see. I'll be back right away." The lecturer rose and slipped out.

"You'll get used to him, Eamon," charmed Alan. "Very knowledgeable man, sometimes wants to be too much in control..... but we can all be like that at times."

"A very British trait," observed Eamon, smiling now.

And here was Jeremy, back already with those books..... but looking strangely concerned, wary almost. Something had happened, outside. Damage to his car maybe?

The books, still in their bag, landed on the table. Jeremy remained on his feet, eyeing the small side window, just an empty table away, with its slightly opened upper sash. It looked out onto the river, and the narrow strip of bank along their wall..... and yes, the man needn't have been inventing this. He could have stood there outside, unseen, back against the wall, listening to every word they'd said.

"Something wrong Jeremy?" asked Alan.

"I was approached in the car park. This bloke, he looked to be just one of the regulars, elderly but sprightly enough, and he was Irish sounding. Said he'd recognised the two of you at once, as soon as you came in. He thought it strange that you should be together, so he went out and edged around the side here to pick up what he could of our conversation. He'd heard '*too much*,' he said, but '*again*' we were '*lucky*'. He can '*help*' he reckons. He got me to write his address on my bag, here."

Eamon swivelled the wrapped books, and read… first;
"*Quarry Cottage, St Erney*" and then the words beneath,
"*on boatyard road,*
halfway down, on right."
Jeremy sat at last. Alan re-opened the map.

"Just here, he lives. Little more than a mile, but there's no road along the valley. To take up the invitation we climb to Landrake and turn down the spur to St Erney, which is a church and little else. Then the lane drops to the boatyard, passing a large old quarry."

"Halfway down, as he said," added Jeremy. "Do we go?"

"Sounds like we would be silly not to," replied Alan, hoping to sound less foolish than he felt. "but we'll give him half an hour to prepare for our arrival."

"Eamon…..your opinion?" The Irishman was studying the map, pensively.

"We go," he said, "because there's only one person hereabouts who could recognise the pair of us *and* be surprised to find us together. I've met him, and we've spoken; but Alan, as yet, he will only have seen. It has to be the guy who got me out of that tunnel, the one who saved my life. I'm going, definitely. You two can please yourselves."

"We all go then," said Alan, "and remembering that already he's been listening to us….."

"…..we go there to listen to him," said Jeremy.

*

(xxiv) the truant

Sally had taken the ferry, but not the route to school. The day's remaining lessons could be missed, she'd decided, for having phoned the Diving Centre she'd found that Chas was at college rather than in the Yard. This was his release day, and he might be obtainable between lectures. Instead of taking the Milehouse/Outland Road bus she'd climbed seawards, across Devonport Park to Kings Road, where the brightly built FE establishment had risen from the long levelled Southern Railway terminus.

She knew his block, and placed herself to intercept when he emerged for a lunchtime break. It was an uncomfortable wait, but she had to keep her nerve. Delay would only bring further difficulty. Here he was, now...... surprised, and naturally so.

"Sal..... shouldn't you be at school?"

"If I didn't need to speak with you."

"Now?"

"It's urgent. It's about that gold and......"

·".....and?" Chas took her hand.

"And, there's a body, dead. I panicked, and I wasn't so careful as I wanted to be."

"You've been down there?"

"Because it was disturbing me. I needed to know it hadn't been moved."

"But I was trusting you, so....."

"..... why couldn't I do the same? I don't know."

"It was there?"

"It was, and I'd only intended to check. It was going to stay, but I uncovered these bones, human bones I think, and I ran from the cave ..... straight into a couple of African guys who were working along the shore, gathering shells. I had to leave them down there, wondering what had scared me so. They would have followed my footprints into the cave, uncovered the rest of this skeleton and also the gold. I'm so sorry Chas. This is the second time I've let you down..... and that was your dream, finding that gold."

"So you know that they found it, and that it was moved?"

"And I know to where. Those Africans are working and staying with Megan, the old herbalist who comes each year to Wacker Quay. They do ornaments and jewellery, some embellished with shells. I called this morning at Megan's caravan, and yes, the gold was there."

"And she was keeping it?"

"There was no taking it back to the cave, she said. She wants to see the pair of us together, as soon as possible."

"In which case I'll come now. We'll go down to the ferry queue..... see if we can't scrounge a lift. Some one's sure to know you. They can ride us out to Antony. If not then we walk."

*

271

(xxv) Quarry Cottage

They went in the two cars, Eamon and Alan together in the taxi, Jeremy following. Quarry Cottage was easily found, and McDaid was there, waiting to greet them.

Eamon led the other two forward, taking the man's proffered hand and shaking it with warmth, and vigour, and hearfelt gratitude. This was definitely he who'd pulled him from danger, who'd led him to freedom. Introductions followed, and further handshakes before the guests were taken in and settled.

"So where to start!" began the host. "Apologies I suppose; to you, Alan, for encouraging Eamon to escape in your boat; and to you, Jeremy, for the ambush just now in the pub car park; and to all three, I suppose, for the eavesdrop."

"Which I trust you found interesting," said Alan.

"Very interesting….. and more than just a little worrying."

"But you say you can be of help."

"I can, I think, but only if you first heed this warning. You were far too conspicuous down there at the pub. I couldn't believe it. Bullets you've had, and explosives…… if that lot can't alert you to danger then tell me what will. You were lucky just now, lucky it was just me. Others might have been listening, others less disposed to assist. Never assume that they are not, that's my advice, particularly when gathering in a place so public, and so local."

"Wise advice," agreed Eamon. "Now venture an explanation. I'm hauled from my London flat, bound, loaded into a train, and thrown out into a tunnel, to land at your feet, hundreds of miles down the line. For a start, is it a normal thing with you….. to be walking around in railway tunnels?"

"Not unusual. I do casual gardening work over at Ince. Sometimes I'll walk, using the viaduct and tunnel as a short cut."

"So what did you make of Eamon's appearance?" asked Jeremy.

"It was to do with the explosion. Someone had to carry the blame, someone who wouldn't talk."

"Someone who was dead," added Eamon, "but in this they were thwarted. I escaped."

"Meaning further blame," continued Alan, "this time for me. So we must ask who or what is this '*they*', the party that was thwarted? If that explosion was an attempt against the Prime Minister then they were miles

272

out with their timing. and yet there was Eamon right on cue. As a terrorist bungle it was choreographed to the second!"

"To me that makes it a fake," said Declan McDaid, "staged by the security people." All looked at Alan.

"By me?"

"By an element within your people, Alan. If a terrorist movement can sprout factions, then why not a security force." McDaid turned again to Eamon. "And if it's any consolation to you, my friend, it might be that as well as yourself, and British Rail, this faction that I envisage could also have been using the Prime Minister."

"To what purpose though?" asked Jeremy.

"The purpose that was achieved," answered Declan, "Ince Castle was immediately evacuated. Every room in the place was subjected to a thorough search, even the most private."

"And was anything significant found?" asked Eamon

"I don't know, but I do know what wasn't found."

"You do know what wasn't found," repeated Jeremy, smilingly in a mock brogue.

"Because it might be that something of what they were searching for is here," countered McDaid," in my possession. I speak of letters, letters that pertain to what you were talking of in the pub...... but if you're not interested."

"We are," insisted Alan.

"Then you can try this for a start." The first of four hand penned pages was passed. Alan read.

Cairo
August 1944

My Dear Patricia,

I have instructed that this letter be given to you in the event of my death, a constant possibility, even as we appear to be slowly winning a safer future for the world. I must hope, of course, that this will not be for many years, I fear though that you might be having to read this while the Country is still at war, with Alan still serving as a Naval Officer.

Alan is a fine and honourable man, an asset to our family and the Nation. We should all be proud of him. I hope he can return to politics after the war and resume a sparkling Parliamentary career. He deserves to rise to one of the topmost offices of state. He is able, energetic, and loyal.

The concern of this letter is to ensure that you are equipped to help him make the best of these qualities in a field where advantage, and advancement, will too often accrue to the less principled.

The old Tory Party of Stanley Baldwin and Neville Chamberlain is no more. A strong Labour recovery can be anticipated, and to counter its excesses a new Conservatism must evolve. The likes of Anthony Eden, Oliver Stanley, and our Alan will naturally be prominent, but each must be wary of a new crop of Machiavellian upstarts; men like Macmillan, my successor at the Colonial desk, whose ambition is only exceeded by his want of scruple. Already I note his toadying up to the Titans of the future, Stalin's henchmen and Roosevelt cronies.

My old friend Winston is exhausted by the war. He will be lionised for his leadership, and rightly so. Beatification, though, would be inappropriate.

The awkward truth is that difficult times necessitated difficult decisions, the consequences of which will vex our world for many a generation. A full knowledge of such decisions is closely guarded by a powerful and select few of (certainly to me) obscure identity, some of whom will be charged with ensuring that the details remain their exclusive preserve. In this context, depending on how it is handled, a partial knowledge might become either a very useful or a very dangerous thing.

While pleased to say that I am not one of the select few burdened with a FULL knowledge of these matters, I can tell you that a few clues as to their secrets have fallen my way...... more (hopefully) than they can suspect, and perhaps enough from which to draw something of the full hidden picture.

While only a little, with time it might go a very long way. Even where its meaning can only be guessed at, the mere use of a nomenclature might impress.

(i) On GUSTAVE, HIGHLAND CLEARANCE, and the unexplained death of Lord Erroll.

You will know that my close companion, Vera Broughton, was formerly married to 'Jock' Delves Broughton, the Baronet who was tried for the murder of Lord Erroll in Kenya, in 1941. You will also know that at the time I was Colonial Secretary, subsequently moving to Cairo as Deputy Minister of State, and latterly Minister Resident. Although acquitted, many will still say that Broughton was guilty, usually pointing to the incompetence of the prosecuting team.

My informed opinion is that jury came to the correct decision. I mention the above to persuade you that I was, and still am, well placed to hold this view. Furthermore, I can add that since the trial I have obtained possible 'exhibits' that the jury was prevented from seeing, evidence which could only have further confirmed them in their decision. The fact that this evidence was suppressed serves to underline the extent to which, firstly, the murder was planned and, secondly, the trial was manipulated.

The murder was planned and executed by a British Secret Service unit, overseen by an officer known by the code name GUSTAVE. The 'hit' was part of a wider operation entrusted to him, code named HIGHLAND CLEARANCE.

Jock Broughton was a member of part of GUSTAVE's team. Possibly his new wife, Diana, was too. Also a member of the team was Phyllis Filmer, the married woman with whom Erroll was conducting an affair prior to the Broughtons' arrival in Kenya. Neither of these women shot Erroll. Each had a sound alibi. The killer was a trained Secret Service assassin who was able to lure Erroll to the scene of his murder mainly with the assistance of the 'slighted' former mistress.

Mrs Filmer lived at SHELL HOUSE Nairobi. Her son, though, was at school in South Africa, and it was while taking him there to start his new year's term that Erroll became enamoured with the newly arrived Diana. Hearing of this, Phyllis wired Erroll to tell him that she was returning to SHELL HOUSE with a view to addressing their futures, either together or not. She would phone him, she said, on her arrival, with a view to arranging an immediate meeting for sorting this matter as it should be.

The wire was sent, and a telephone call made. A hasty meeting was arranged, at an appropriately remote location, but instead of finding Phyllis Filmer there, Erroll was instead surprised and killed by his assassin.

The wider purpose of HIGHLAND CLEARANCE is unknown to me, as is the identity of GUSTAVE. I am equally at a loss to explain why his operation should require the elimination of Erroll.

I do know, however, that the assassin flew into Kenya from Cairo and returned there immediately, bringing the murder weapon and also what I shall term the SHELL HOUSE TELEGRAM. This having been removed from a pocket of the deceased victim. Subsequently, the operative was eliminated by way of a purposely betrayed parachute drop into Yugoslavia. With this indication of GUSTAVE's ruthlessness in mind, perhaps the ony surprise is that he didn't conspire for Broughton to be found guilty and hanged! In the event, having returned to England, developed a habit for opiate, and then overdosed, Jock died within eighteen months of the acquittal.

By this time, following the summer 'flap' of '42, I had seen fit to firmly secure the items left in Cairo. Now, both the SHELL HOUSE TELEGRAM and the gun lie together. They will be found in the SHELL HOUSE. Seek the African Tiger.

(ii)   On the summary execution of Avraham Stern.

Avraham Stern Yair was shot dead in Palestine in '42, many months after the assassination of Erroll, and many thousands of miles away. One was a Peer of the Realm, the other a Polish born Zionist rengade impelled to fight on against the mandated British rule in Palestine, in defiance of the majority of a kin who were, at that time, ready to bury differences with Westminster and join the wider struggle against anti Semite fascism. In terms of past and current situation the pair could hardly be more different......and yet I have it on excellent authority that the same GUSTAVE, who accounted for Erroll, also oversaw the hunting down and killing of Stern a little over a year later.

Again, with this second target, one cannot over emphasise the sheer ruthlessness with which the victim was despatched. In the hunt that was mounted, which lasted for well over six months, the normal police procedures (for which I carried a measure of responsibility) were suspended. We were specifically instructed that this man was NOT to be arrested and brought to trial, even were he to surrender himself in this expectation. Accordingly, were information to be provided as to his whereabouts then this had to be passed to a special armed unit which had licence to shoot on sight......to kill.

Clearly Avraham Stern was feared, and probably because he was perceived as a threat to whatever the hoped for outcome might have been to OPERATION HIGHLAND CLEARANCE. I do know that he championed a strain of Zionism which, following his conquest of Poland and France, regarded agreement with Hitler as the best means of securing a Jewish homeland, and with this the safety of the millions of Jews who had fallen under Nazi 'protection'. His proposition was that a Jewish army might fight alongside German troops so as to oust we British from Palestine and Egypt, and ultimately all places to the south and to the east.

When the history of these times is written we will, I am sure, be told that this was a madman, and maybe this will be for the best. I fear, though, that he might have known something that I, as yet, do not, and reached his opinion of this country and its rulers through a process of clear sighted logic. I wonder, also, if a fear of his being in contact with Stern led to Broughton's solicitor's first choice of barrister, Mr Israel Aaron Maisels, being prevented from taking the case.

Though the man himself was eliminated, Stern's disciples live on. Inspired by his 'martyrdom', they are busy. I have been told that having been taught well, by GUSTAVE, they might be planning to take up the art of assassination themselves......with me perhaps being singled as a target.

In the event of such a fate, it might happen that I shall never be any the wiser than this as to why Erroll and Stern were shot. With this letter I nevertheless bequeath to you the little that I already know. It could be that more will emerge in the future so as to enhance its value.

In the meantime, take the nomenclature and use wisely.

Remember;
GUSTAVE
HIGHLAND CLEARANCE
SHELL HOUSE
PHYLLIS FILMER
AVRAHAM STERN
ISRAEL AARON MAISELS

As regards the whereabouts of the missing gun (a SMITH & WESSON) and telegram my current itinerary precludes better information.
If I'm spared, and I can return to England. You shall then have something more concrete.

Ever yours, your loving uncle.

From Alan to Eamon, then to Jeremy, each page was passed and read. Jeremy, last to finish felt obliged then to speak.

"But he wasn't spared, was he. The Stern Gang got him, probably not long after he wrote this."

"And the '*something more concrete*' promised on his return is unlikely to have materialised," added Alan.

"At least he can acknowledge a shoot-to- kill policy, " growled Eamon, with all the resentment of one who'd been on the receiving end of the same.

"But an *African Tiger*," frowned Jeremy. "I wonder what that might be when it's at home."

"Seems like you might need to travel to Nairobi to find out," said Alan. "That's if the old Shell House is still standing. Probably is. A company like that wouldn't have stinted..... built to last I should imagine."

"We could find out," said Jeremy. "Perhaps Mr McDaid has already?"

Their host shook his head. "I wouldn't really know who to ask. Moyne does advise discretion, bear in mind."

"I think it has to be something ornamental," suggested Alan, "either in the House or in the grounds....... a statue, or a picture, perhaps even a shrub or tree of some sort. So how came you by this letter, Declan........how, where, and when?" Blunt words from Alan, but politely delivered, and McDaid readily told of his years as milkman to Ince, and latterly as a gardener, then companion to the late Viscount.

"She brought it into the garden just after he died. I'd just started a bonfire. She wanted it burnt. She put it on the fire, but it hadn't quite caught before she was called away."

"So what was it that made you think that it could be worth saving," persisted Alan..... and McDaid hesitated, appealing to the others with an evasive shrug.

"Curiosity, I suppose. The man was a friend. He would confide in me often, but never completely..... because you wouldn't expect that from one who'd done, and was still doing, important Government work."

Jeremy was nodding sympathetically. He wouldn't have wanted it to burn, of course not, but the historian's instinct to preserve wasn't to be automatically ascribed to a milkman turned gardener. There was more to this, Alan was sure, but for the moment it could wait. He wanted to be invited back, and it was the moment to allow Jeremy a turn with the questions. He could perhaps bring a fresh angle......

But it wasn't the lecturer who spoke. Eamon was in this too, and fully engaged.

"So this name 'GUSTAVE'...... in all your long and close acquaintance with the Boyds was it ever mentioned by either?"

"No, there was never anything from them."

"Meaning?" prompted Eamon.

"That there has been something from someone," suggested Jeremy, looking to their host for confirmation.

"Strangely, and perhaps disturbingly, yes."

"Someone at the Castle?" pressed Eamon.

"Closer, much closer. Someone next door. I own both these cottages. He was my tenant......"

".....until?"

"Until his sudden unexplained disappearance, three years ago now."

"And that's after the Viscount's death," said Jeremy.

"Correct," confirmed Declan. " And compared to me, Peg, as we called him, was a stranger to Ince. He worked for the Earl of St Germans, around at Port Eliot."

"Peg?" queried Alan.

"After Pegasus, the winged horse on his beret. Peg Willis, a para during the war, helped with the taking of Pegasus Bridge, an airborne swoop essential to the success of the D Day landings, and it was in this context that he suddenly came up with a mention of both GUSTAVE and HIGHLAND CLEARANCE. It was bizarre. There was I, not daring to breathe a word about these things, even to my closest friends, and then suddenly my neighbour was broadcasting those very names across the whole of Plymouth and beyond."

"Broadcasting?" Jeremy said.

"He was on the radio. It was forty years on from the landings, and he was talking about the bridge, and the link up with the Commando thrust from the easternmost beach. After four days or so of fighting he was wounded and became one of many who had to be patched in a field hospital. Another soldier was brought in, one far more gravely injured, and it's touch and go for the poor bloke. He's drugged and delirious, but occasionally lucid..... and, when so, an OPERATION HIGHLAND CLEARANCE is mentioned repeatedly, and a GUSTAVE is spoken of, one who must see this thing through at all costs. They'd been fighting to clear and hold the higher ground beyond the Orne River so it was natural for Peg to assume these to be code names for specific aspects of this push."

"But the interviewer, Declan, he wasn't going to know any different...... surely?"

"I can agree there, Jeremy, but there was a definite reaction on the part of a second interviewee; a man introduced then as an authority on military history, but better known now as a leading politician."

"And this was.....?" asked Jeremy.

"Alan Clark, MP for Plymouth Sutton."

"Of course," said Jeremy, again thinking back to the call made on Edward Trembath. "though I would associate him more with the Eastern Front, and Crete perhaps."

"1941," said Declan, "the pivotal year."

"So what kind of reaction?" probed Alan.

"You must have heard the man on the radio, normally so suave, so self-sure and in control."

"A supercilious git," opined Jeremy.

"Well, for a moment, he seemed anything but. Instead of the smoothly phrased intervention, immaculately timed, I was hearing something unchracteristically desperate. The man was rattled. If the interview was a car, and the presenter the driver, Clark was like a back seat passenger attempting to grasp the wheel. He'd suddenly seen danger ahead......"

"...... and it had to be avoided," added Eamon. "So you want to link Clark with HIGHLAND CLEARANCE and the old soldier's unexplained disappearance."

"He can certainly be linked with the HIGHLAND CLEARANCE spoken of in that letter," said Jeremy. His step-mother features in that *White Mischief* book, in fact I think there's even a picture of her, as a child, next to her mother."

"The mother being.. ... ?" said Alan.

"Alice de Janze, another colourful denizen of Kenya's notorious Happy Valley. Totally loopy by all accounts...... there's another portrait of her, a portrait from after she'd abandoned the girls, this time with a pet lion cub in her lap. I'll get the book, it's in the car." the lecturer slipped out, giving McDaid an opportunity to fill in a little more about Willis.

"Here......Alice de Janze," resumed Jeremy, re-entering with the book already opened, "looking a lot happier to be nursing a baby lion than her own daughter!" The others leant in, and there they were, her and the cub, both gazing across to the facing print, the gruesome close up Erroll's fatal head wound. Could a femme ever look more fatale? All must have thought it, but it was Declan who said......

"Could we be looking at the '*African tiger*'? What do you think, Jeremy?"

"She was certainly no stranger to guns. In France, in the '20s, she'd wounded a lover and herself, and then in Africa, later in '41, she was eventually to kill herself with one, after being told she had cancer."

"Drama after drama," remarked Eamon. "Perhaps the gun that Moyne wrote of came down to her daughter...…"

".......so as to equip Mr Clark with a similar insurance policy," added Declan.

"And maybe explain why such a poser can command such profile," muttered Jeremy, with all the natural envy of a rival historian.

"A possibility," Alan reminded them, "one of many, and among them the proposition that Peg Willis could have met with an un-natural end."

"As did Lord Boyd," continued Jeremy, "and Lord Moyne, and, before him, Lord Erroll."

"And we can throw in this Stern-Yair character," said Eamon, "and but for yourself, Declan, I could have been the latest on the list..... the fourth to have been deliberately shot. Remind me how Boyd went."

"Street accident in London," answered McDaid. "Knocked down."

"But that sort of thing can also be contrived," said Connors. "Another execution?" no one answered. "Anything else fall out of the bonfire Declan?"

"A newspaper cutting...... quite recent, telling of the bones of Moyne's hanged assassins being returned from Egypt to Israel; plus a personal letter, sent to Boyd by a friend of his, who also served in the Navy. It was written in the first year of the war, spring 1940, before the fall of France, and Dunkirk. The main thing in it is a poem."

"And the sender of this letter, is this a famous person?" asked Alan. "One still alive......"

".....who might know the identity of the sinister GUSTAVE,"

continued McDaid, shaking his head, "and be sufficiently aware of any link with Alan Clark MP, which could perhaps shed light on the where abouts of my neighbour and tennant, the valiant 'Peg' Willis? I wish it were so simple."

"Never is," joined Jeremy, "but you do have a name....?"

"Roger Burney...... who, so far as I can ascertain, achieved nothing by the way of any renown."

"And it was just the one piece of correspondence," checked Jeremy. "There's been nothing received since the war."

"Not that I've seen," confirmed Declan.

"So he might have been lost in action," Alan deduced. "These things can be checked."

"And on thiat point at least, there might be a clue for us in the actual letter." McDaid was on his feet. "It's upstairs. I can fetch it down."

*

(xxvi) wise counsel
Wacker Quay

"You asked too much of her, young man. You can't dangle this kind of bauble in front of a young woman and expect her not to be hypnotised. My boys, Makesi and Juma, they could tell you that!"

Chas broke into a smile, and Sally, so embarrassed, could at last take some comfort. Megan did indeed have a healing touch.

It was soon agreed......she and her lads would see to the skeleton, while the gold ingot could stay a matter for its finders. Both metal and bone would have to be reported to a coroner, she said, but the sensible thing was to keep the issues separate..... for that's surely what they were. The gold had been found on the sea bed, out in the bay, while the body had lain buried in that cave. The temporary juxtaposition had been chance.

She'd cleaned and inspected the treasure, but found no indication of origin or ownership. It was, in her view, likely to be deemed crown property, and that for finding it and turning it in, the youngsters could be in line for as much as half its value in compensation, perhaps more.

"This is by far the safest course," the woman advised. "Also the easiest, and, in the end, probably the most profitable. The longer it hangs about, the more it disturbs. Gold is like that. It poisons friendships, strains trust." The girl nodded meekly. She couldn't feel any smaller. "But it might be asked if you just happened upon the item......or whether you were acting upon information."

That last phrase was left to hang. Was this a statement, a warning..... or was it a question? Sally glanced across to Chas.

"Complete chance," he said, having checked with the girl on their way here that she'd earlier divulged nothing of what Chas had confided off Rame.

"That's fine," said Megan, "because we should all be concerned to keep within the law. The public are quick to complain about travellers, and the police can be swift to act. One has to be wary of giving them any excuse. Our story will be that my boys happened across that skeleton whilst beach-combing, for shells to polish and for driftwood to carve. There will be nothing to suggest that anyone with a metal detector had been down there. As I said, travelling folk are distrusted, and likewise the metal detector fraternity. Police, landowners, the revenue people...... none will be too impressed by a combination."

"Point taken," acknowledged Chas. "So you're trusting us to trust the coroner."

"Coroners...... the skeleton we can report to the one who covers East Cornwall. Plymouth is a different district...."

"....meaning different office, different man."

"So you go there, yes, but first you might deposit your treasure with a bank and ask that it be assayed. Then you'll have your own professional report, a copy of which can be delivered up to the coroner with the gold......... and I would appreciate a copy also, if that's OK."

"So you'll know that your advice has been followed?" said Sally.

"If you like," returned Megan, now standing..... and that was enough. Any flicker of defiance had been snuffed. In the same moment she'd slid the ingot from the table and placed it into Chas's lap. "Take it away. I'd prefer not to see it again...... but I'm here for you both should you need."

*

(xxvii) Jeremy hits his stride

> " ' .... *though we*
> *Whom hunger cannot move,*
> *From gardens where we feel secure,*
> *Look up, and with a sigh endure*
> *The tyrannies of love.*' "

The first two verses Jeremy had read silently......the last part he was moved to voice softly, repeating that last line;

"*The tyrannies of love.* It's rather good. It would make a fine book title, don't you think?"

"For a marriage guidance manual?" quipped Alan.

"We have a cynic, it seems," remarked Eamon.

"Definitely," confirmed Jeremy. "A man of many guises..... but no soul."

"So this was sent to Alan Lennox Boyd by a fellow reservist," continued Grigson, undeterred. "A guy named Burney, and Patricia has tucked his letter away with this second that later came to her, from the Uncle Walter. And while used to protect her husband, it might be that the content of Moyne's missive stayed private to her."

"And is there a link between those documents?" wondered Alan.

"The Viscountess is the one to answer that," suggested Connors.

"But she now thinks them bonfired," McDaid reminded him. "A belief I would prefer to see maintained. We were considering this Roger Burney, and the clue as to whether he might have survived the war. Had he been lost then those verses were supposed to have been set to music. He writes here of his musical friends in America who'd promised as much."

All looked to Jeremy, the academic. He scanned the poem again. "I can't claim to be an expert on this, but to me it has the ring of *Parsnip*."

"*Parsnip*?" repeated Eamon, clearly not expecting a further riddle.

"This is me getting too much into Evelyn Waugh. At the pub I spoke of *Black Mischief*, written in the early '30s. Ten years after this we are treated to the return of the incorrigible Basil in *Put Out More Flags*. This time our rakish adventurer is back in England, working at the Ministry of Information during the phoney war."

"And this *Parsnip*, Jeremy?" enquired Alan.

"….. is a poet in the story, one who decamps to America at the start of the war, thereby attracting popular wrath, and Waugh's sharply penned derision. The real life model for *Parsnip* has to be Wystan Hugh Auden, who likewise went to America. And with Auden went Christopher Isherwood, a fellow poet, and also Ben Britten, who might be termed a tone poet, plus Peter Pears…..."

"…….who were musicians," added Alan, quietly.

"But any of those three could fit the bill for *Pimpernel*," continued Jeremy. As more of a composite parody, this *Pimpernel* far better represents Waugh's satirical style than does *Parsnip*….. his concern usually being to pin down a certain *type* rather than needle any one specific individual. But that said, there are conspicuous exceptions… and perhaps many an inconspicuous."

"And this could be reflected in the names," said Alan, "*Parsnip* being so prosaic, so solid and so pointed…… while *Pimpernel*, that's altogether more elusive, more disguised."

"But those lines in that letter, Jeremy," said McDaid. "It is Auden that you hear."

"It is."

"And did he continue to collaborate with those musicians whilst in America?" asked Alan. This, he thought to himself, was Jeremy at his most useful.

"With Benjamin Britten and Peter Pears?…..for a while. The association goes way back into the '30s, to the *Night Mail* and all that, but whilst in America something happened….. something to snap the relationship. Both went on to do greater works, but the joint output was as good as finished."

"And the cause of the fracture?" persisted Alan. Jeremy shrugged.

"It's fashionable to talk of sexual tension…."

"…..but you sense something deeper?"

"Maybe. Ben and Peter were gentle people, they liked to work things out quietly, privately. Wystan was different, he preferred to flaunt his homosexuality, particularly after taking up with young Chester. He liked to think himself a cheerleader for the cause….."

"…….whereas Ben and Peter?"

"They didn't do marching tunes."

"So go deeper, Jeremy," prompted Alan. "This is why I've brought you along."

The lecturer reached again to Moyne's pages. He tapped the topmost.

"We find it here in this letter, so why not look at Auden's own concern for the oppressed Jew? A concern as real and perhaps as intense as that carnal lust for young Chester Kallman. It can be traced back for years in his poems, a recurring theme, and this was more than just clever words. It was an active concern, pushing him as far as to take a Jewish wife; making a marriage of convenience, just to get the woman out of Germany."

"So do you suggest that a lack of a matching concern from those musician friends led to the rift?" probed Alan.

"Stern-Yair's rationale might have crossed the Atlantic," reasoned Jeremy, "and if it could polarise opinion in the Diaspora....."

".......then why not also amongst the English exiles? Do you suggest, then, that Auden might have been responsive to the Stern Yair logic...... but was left to despair at his friends' indifference."

"Something of that order," agreed Jeremy.

"What a rich seam of speculation," remarked Alan. "And all loosened by those stories of Evelyn Waugh. Any other nuggets glinting therefrom?"

"Maybe," said Jeremy, "it's about Cyril Connolly, the guy whose investigations feature so strongly in *White Mischief*, this recent book about Erroll......"

".......coming out soon as a film," added Alan. "Tell us, Jeremy, about Cyril Connolly.... do"

"My strongest memory of him is from back in the early '70s when he was with *The Times*. There was this TV documentary about the wartime Ministry of Information, and as well as writers such as Priestly and Orwell he was keen to reminisce too about Waugh....... mentioning that he himself had been affectionately lampooned in one of Waugh's wartime novels. He was cast as one *Everard Spruce*, and his literary review, '*Horizon*', that had become '*Survival*'. The parallels were obvious and amusing, recalled Connolly, but in one respect not entirely accurate. He was at pains to say that the animosity to *Parsnip* and friends, attributed in the story to *Spruce*, was in fact far more Waugh's own than his. He, Connolly, had respected the exiles' viewpoints and their decisions, and had always been ready to make space for their work in his publication."

"But he wasn't forthcoming on the fall-out between Auden and Britten," said McDaid.

"Because Jeremy wasn't there to ask the right questions!" stated Alan.

"And within three or four years Connolly was dead," continued the lecturer.

"And this would have been all of ten years ago," said Eamon. "Who might tell us now? Burney, if he is still alive….. and if someone's ready to familiarise himself with the Britten-Pears songbook, we could find this out. Who's ready to go to a library, or to a record shop?"

"I can do that," volunteered Jeremy, remembering something about Kate…… but holding it to himself.

"And there's Alan Clark," suggested McDaid. "It seems he could be eyes and ears for someone….."

"…… a dangerous someone," joined Eamon. "If Peg tripped an alarm and then disappeared then watch out the rest of us."

"So now could be the moment to deploy a scout," said Alan, as if prepared.

"And you have one to hand?" asked Jeremy.

"Waiting to meet you……tomorrow perhaps? Just say."

*

(xxiix) The Minister

Gen. Sec: Minister; PM.

5 Days later; and the following article appears in the *Plymouth Evening Herald*

WARTIME REMAINS

The human remains recovered earlier this week from a cliff foot cave a short distance to the west of Portwrinkle are thought to be those a male serviceman whose body came ashore during the early part of the last war. The complete and largely undamaged skeleton suggests a death by drowning rather than from any explosive or small arms trauma. A lack of clothing remains suggests interment and decomposition to have been a protracted process engineered by the steady relentless movements of sea and sand. No identity 'dog' tag has been found, and no insignia that might indicate service branch or rank.

And two days after that;

"Friends?" whispered Sally. "Alan and Jeremy? They're close in a kind of complementary fashion, but I wouldn't say they were friends."

"Two-way respect, certainly," agreed Chas.

"But full trust?.... I don't think so."

Five days had passed since the pair of them had been introduced to Jeremy, a period that had accommodated two further meetings, the first with Alan the second without. The purpose had been to prepare them for this, the sixth day, the day of a hastily arranged audience with no less a personage than the Honourable Alan Clark MP, chief Minister at the Department of Trade and Industry.

How well it had fallen into place. Forty-eight hours notice had been enough. The Member for Plymouth Sutton could give them an informal fifteen minutes before the first of the morning's regular surgery appointments.

Chas, this week on the evening shift, had met Sally, now broken up from school, off the Torpoint ferry. The twenty minute bus ride had given them opportunity to re-rehearse their roles and, if anything, the boy was the more excited.... a measure of his personal fascination with Ince, something not mentioned yet to either Alan or Jeremy. And now, as they sat and waited for the secretary to re emerge from the consulting room, hopefully to usher them before the Minister, they'd nervously fallen to a whispered discussion of that pair who'd put them up to this charade.

"As regards respect, I can agree Chas, but can't you also sense a rivalry there? They can work together, and can even live together in the confines of a camper van, apparently, but somehow it doesn't feel like they're buddies.... or ever can be."

"Something from the past, is that what you suspect?"

"Where else," replied Sally, and that moment the door opened and hearts leapt. They were being beckoned through.

Two chairs waited and Alan Clark MP was standing over them,

having risen from his to come around a very organised desk. Chas was his constituent, the potential vote, but he was left to float rather as the suavely smiling Minister concentrated a practised charm on the girl.

"Sally," he said, adjusting the position of one of the chairs ever so slightly, "you can sit here."

And she did of course, while he hovered lasciviously, as if on the scent of prey. Here was a wolf, she knew immediately. She'd known teachers to do the same…. harmless of course, but disturbing nonetheless. She didn't look up, preferring to have the desk between them before she gave her eyes, and by this modesty at least some attention was deflected to Chas.

"And you, young man, you take that seat and show me what it is you've brought. Something to do with a College course I believe?"

"At the Further Education Institute over in Devonport ….. where amongst other things we've both been studying aspects of film and television production, largely technical."

"Shooting, sound recording, lighting……that sort of thing? Not really my area of….."

"Of course not Mr Clark," said Chas. "But what we've been following over the past term is a project on the history of British film making since the war, and an aspect Sally and I have been given to explore during the holiday is the change in the way that the British presence in Africa has been portrayed."

Jenny was nervous. Chas was doing well she thought, but the kind of response that this might elicit was anyone's guess.

"Still hardly my field, but I've promised you fifteen minutes so what have you done up to now?"

"Watched a series of films, three to be precise, the earliest from the early '50s, set against the Mau Mau emergency, then '*Zulu*' and '*Khartoum*' from the '60s, and soon, when it's out we'll finish off with *White Mischief*."

"I certainly remember *Zulu* and *Khartoum*."

"It's the next element that we thought you could be of particular help," joined Sally, gathering in confidence and even venturing a flutter of eyelash.

"Go on," encouraged Clark, leeringly.

Sally reached for the book that Chas held and placed it on the desk.

"Back in September it was anticipated that by now a film of this story, *'White Mischief'* would have been through the cinemas, and we could have been able to come fully up to date."

"Had it all gone to schedule, we would have seen it by now," said Chas, "but as usual there seems to have been delays......."

"....... and you think it possible that I've sat through a preview, don't you?"

They didn't actually. Jeremy hadn't presumed, let alone suggested, any such thing, and now they were having to respond to the unexpected. There was brief moment of embarrassed silence, each waiting for the other to reply. Nothing was coming and, suddenly, for both, fifteen minutes seemed a long, long time. The Minister shot a mischievous smile to the secretary. Were they about to be shown the door? Or, worse, having seen the fabrication for what it was, was he about to un-pick? Sally held her breath.

"Well I haven't," continued Clark. "Despite....or because of, perhaps, my stepmother's tiresome strictures I have remained immune to her fascination with the *BongoBongo Lands*, and the brutal histories thereof."

"So you can't help.....?" In reaching for the book Sally pinned the Minister with a disconsolate pout, a last flirtatious throw.

"Actually, young lady, I can," he smiled, "because you happen to be in luck, you two. Today I can pass you on. A case of fortune favouring the brave, I think. Dearest Nolwen is here, in Plymouth, now. You can have it straight from the old nag's mouth. She'll be delighted, I'm sure, to give you a lot longer than fifteen minutes. Indeed, this could make her day. I brought her down yesterday, from Saltwood in the Rolls. I booked another room for her over at *The Duke of Cornwall*, for last night and this. Tomorrow she sails on the ferry across to Brittany.... she has family over there still. They'll meet her at Roscoff. If you care to wait outside I'll phone the hotel now."

They rose and the secretary escorted them out to the now lightly populated waiting area. A last backward glimpse of the Minister for Trade caught him dialling on their behalf. Barely a minute elapsed and the secretary was out again, with a brief note of introduction to Lady Clark, signed by the stepson, and an instruction to present this to the hotel's reception desk at 10.15am.

They had to move. With the clock fast climbing to ten, the

distance, Mutley to almost Millbay, offered a stiff challenge even for young legs. They needed to make haste, for the impression was that Lady Clark might be keen to meet them.

It had to be either the Drake Circus subway or the North Cross, and it was the second they chose, cutting down through North Road East and under, before using the uncluttered sweep of Western Approach to skirt the bustle that was the grid laid post-war retail centre. They skipped barriers and dodged traffic to negotiate Union Street, and then it was the quick rise between *The Continental* and *The Pavillions*.

They'd made it, just. In they went, and with Chas flourishing the note, up next to the reception desk.

"Yes, you are expected," confirmed the receptionist, calmly. "Lady Clark is already in the lounge. I'm instructed to take you through."

They followed and were led to a low table around which three light arm chairs had been purposely arranged. Exquisitely dressed, immaculately groomed, Lady Clark stayed in hers and bade the youngsters sit. Close to seventy, thought Sally, noting the Gallic grace which she'd always imagined would distinguish the French aristocracy from its earthier English counterpart.

"Lady Clark, it's good of you to see us at such short notice," began Sally. "Sally and Chas...... he's the Plymothian. I'm from Cornwall, just across the river."

"The pleasure is mine. My stepson only had to say the magic words. If I can help, then I will." The French accent served to emphasise an easy command of English, and the eyes, blue and compliant, yet searching and knowing, told of an enchantress who perhaps wasn't to be so easily deceived as the stepson .

"The magic words?" queried Chas.

"*White Mischief*," replied Lady Clark. "Book, or film of the book...... I've a close interest in both, as I have in the actual events which each purports to represent."

"Purports ....?" Chas wasn't letting this pass. "Scepticism is this?"

"It is," confirmed Lady Clark, "and this is what irritates Alan so. Then he turns on me, but that makes him all the easier to read. I can see he feels threatened."

"Threatened by what, Lady Clark?" asked Chas.

"My background."

"Your background?"

"Which creates a tension between the two things he holds most dear, his reputation as a historian and his political career."

"Which combine well, I would say," remarked Chas.

"Yes, to produce that smooth, buttery smugness," continued the man's stepmother, "but allow too much of me into that mix and it soon curdles. All looks to be nicely in balance, as you say, until some rancid relic of the past dares disturb the politics of now."

"Forcing a choice between academic integrity or political expedience?"

"Quite, and for dear Alan the prospect of having to merely consider such a choice poses a threat…. and this is why he bullies. He will even tell people that I killed his father, that I'm as wicked a stepmother as ever tricked her way into a wealthy widower's affections."

"A bit off," commented Chas.

"The pain is his. He won't upset me. His father, Sir Kenneth, warned…… such an egotist the boy can be, but this isn't what you are here to learn."

"Our task is to compare *White Mischief* with *Zulu*, another film on Africa made 20 years ago," explained Sally. "What do they say about the British audience?"

"*Zulu* was made when the British, and the French also, were being driven out of Africa. The white man's decency and bravery is unquestioned. He can walk away with his head held high, we are told. All he yields to is arithmetic."

"And *White Mischief*?" prompted Chas.

"Will show us a ruling class who are unworthy of the 'white man's burden', as Kipling had it. If ever the audience felt guilty about a continent being abandoned to corrupt, anarchic chaos, it can rest assured that the white stewardship was far from spotless. It won't do justice to the book."

"You know this?" queried Sally.

"Because there is no place in it for Cyril Connolly, or for the author Mr Fox, who was and still is the Watson to Cyril's Holmes. Did you ever see that film made of the Watergate cover up in America, with Redford and Hoffman….."

"….. as Woodward and Bernstein," said Chas, proudly. "Quite good."

"*White Mischief* could have been just as good, better even, but instead it will be just cheap voyeurism, and as such just one more bucket of whitewash. Mr Fox ought to feel as disappointed as I….."

"….. although consolation will be found in the cheque for the film rights," reminded Sally.

"Maybe," said Lady Clark, "but have either of you read the book?" Two heads shook. "Do either of you even have the book?"

Chas patted a jacket pocket. "It's been lent to us by Mr Barnes, our lecturer….."

"……at?"

And suddenly they were having to lie, and the façade that had stood so firmly before the MP started to crack.

"Chas here goes to the local F.E. college…..," Sally stuttered.

"But no matter," said Lady Clark, seeing the girl's embarrassment. "Perhaps he would like to meet me. I'm only in France for four days, and then I'll be back here for another two nights. With this number he can reach me here in my suite. I'll write it in his book." She drew a pen elegantly from her handbag. Chas produced the paperback, passing it to to the lady.

"Tell him to call me," she said, putting her number down on the inside of the cover. "And tell him too that I'm interested to see what he can make of this." They watched her write on, and, when the book came back, and centred beneath the figures were a puzzling mix of letters and names;

MCLV   **HIIR=Eleanor**
(step back)   **(IST)**

Uncle Crouchback knows

"It was given to me by Cyril Connolly, tell him. Plus a little more, but first we'll see what he can do with this."

Chas looked to Sally, who leant closer so see.

"Roman numerals?" she ventured. "Have we to step back to a year….. 1155? So over to the right might be Henry the Second, who married Eleanor and began the Plantagenet Dynasty. And this was ended by Richard the Third, down here, the deformed uncle who reputedly mudered his two nephews, before going down at Bosworth."

"The crouchback," minced Chas. "*Now is the winter of our discontent......* "

"Thank you Chas," said Sally, meaning *please* shut up.

"A nicely developed interpretation," said Lady Clark, to Chas's momentary delight...... until he realised that she was speaking of Sally's stab at the riddle, rather than his slighted dramatic flair. "One to put to your Mr Barnes, but I would be disappointed were he not to pick up on a couple of errors."

"Significant or slight?" asked Chas. Lady Clark smiled, and thought, and then answered;

"Depends, I suppose, on how he rates himself as a historian." The statement was authoritive, to the extent of being the defining moment of the interview. There was little more for either of the youngsters to add. A rather nervy serve had been clouted back with penetrating depth. Could Jeremy find the response to sustain the rally?

Sally and Chas couldn't say, for they didn't really know the man...... but Kate Rogers did, and had she been there, courtside, following this exchange, watching and listening, then her answer would have been an unequivocal 'yes'.

*

(xxix) Rame

But that wasn't possible........not quite, even if, at this moment, she wasn't so far distant. She was nearing, and soon the youngsters and she would meet. For now, she was looking down on *The Duke of Cornwall*, together with most of the rest of Plymouth, through the front passenger side window of James Busbridge's Viva.

High to the west, they were now skirting Tregantle Fort, taking the sweeping cresting turn from which a briefly offered panorma of the city below will capture the attention of any passenger in any car, and that of too many a driver also. But this time Busbridge wasn't to be distracted, neither by Devon's famous naval port to the east nor, as they turned down onto the cliff top road to thread the Freathy cabins, by a breathtaking extent of Cornwall's southern coast. The road was too narrow and too winding, and the man at the wheel in too much of a hurry.

They'd left Ruthern in what seemed like good time, only to meet more than the customary delay at Dobwalls….. and now it would be tight. There ahead was the stone spire, prominent and deceptively close in the clear air.

"Ten minutes," said the driver, glancing at his watch. "We might just about make it." Swinging at the wheel, working through the gears, every inch of the road had to be used, and every ounce of torque. Kate gripped at her seat belt in queasy silence, tongue drying to a leather gag. This was worse than the South Atlantic. She turned for a moment, glancing rearwards for the stability of a distant horizon, for the Dodman and the Lizard. And there they stretched, pencilled with ominous clarity beneath a thickening wedge of grey frontal cloud….. heavy weather!

She was clinging on, white knuckled, and how indicative this was of her position. What had once seemed comfortably in hand was moving inexorably from her control. But there was no jumping clear at this stage. The man could yet be reigned back, this she had to believe. A fast burn on limited fuel must soon create a taming hunger for more. She just had to hold her nerve.

The hearse gaped at the lytch. The door of the church hung open, and the organ groaned faintly from within. The ceremony was under way. They could let this follow its brief course, they decided, and move around to the burial ground and wait there, respectfully, to observe its conclusion.

A veteran undertaker's assistant stood white haired, drawn faced by the grave, carefully arranging the straps in readiness. Looking up to acknowledge Kate and James' approach the slate eyes were in that instant drawn past them, suddenly enough for each in the pair to glance behind to a second group of latecomers. Three, they made….. an elderly headscarfed woman, grey haired, weathered of complexion, but moving easily enough without any assistance from either of two young and colourfully robed black companions.

This had to be unusual….. despite the stoney unsurprised demeanour of the assistant, for whom it could be believed that nothing was new. A frail, smartly sleeved arm was extended, to indicate where the full five might wait.

"Still nameless?" enquired Busbridge, quietly.

"And always likely to be," anwered the undertaker's man. "Not the first of such in this yard and, I'm sure, not the last."

Kate enquiringly scanned the spread of gravestones. "Wakeham," she said. "Young lad, drowned back in 1940, not much more than ten."

"Over there, with his mother who died soon after... not far from the father, who died when the boy was an infant."

"An only child, or were there siblings...... alive still perhaps?"

"Two older brothers, both of whom died abroad. The eldest, a career soldier, he fell in Cyprus......what, thirty years ago now?"

"About that," Busbridge concurred. "And the other?"

"He went to Australia after the war. Never came back. Estranged from the eldest, little was heard of him until there was word of his death...... two, three years ago I suppose."

Busbridge nodded appreciativly. For the moment he'd heard enough. The last to come were closing to within earshot. The assistant greeted them, presenting the Africans to Kate and James as 'the gentlemen who found the deceased', and Megan as 'their fellow traveller', whereupon the attention of all went to the near door of the Church. The Vicar had appeared, climbing from the door to the slightly raised level of the burial ground, and behind him, lightly hoisted by four assistants, a precariously borne coffin. A police officer and a coastguard followed, and next, with beret, tie and medals, a representative of the British Legion.

Just two more and the procession was complete; one, notepad to hand, was clearly here for a local newspaper, and the other? Kate knew immediately. It was Grigson...... fixing on her face now, and, for a second, being taken no less aback than she. And no wonder, for he would surely have recognised James Busbridge too, and what was to be made of he and her combined as a joint presence?

Alan would be guessing, she thought, as the straps were looped through the handles, guessing, and not even coming near...... for how was he to read her growing wariness of Busbridge, this recent and rather oddly adopted acquaintance? He couldn't of course, any more than she, from her side of the grave, was placed to read in him an equivalent concern for his own career.

What she did know, though, was that Jeremy wouldn't be too far away, and that the pair were no doubt sizing for themselves a well ripened mystery, one dripping with the juice of history..... and that it would have been in connection with this that Alan had showed, if only just to see who else would attend...... so what, indeed, could he be making of this?

Whatever, there might be opportunity here, she thought. If she wanted his help then now was the moment to signal for assistance.

Do so then, instinct told her. The professional she remembered would certainly be useful, he had to be. He would carry those team resources still, that access to high level councils, and proven capability with the low level loose cannon. Who better to quell the fervour she'd over-stirred in Busbridge?

The logic was as soothing as it was sound, and by a slight shrug and a slow tilt of the head, her plea - join me, Mr Grigson - was subtly conveyed. The reply, instantly nodded and smiled, seemed positive, and flatteringly so, but only because she was believing what she wanted to believe, that Alan was still everything he had been. The clinician in her might, perhaps, have urged caution.

For logic can be fallible. Like brickwork, even the finest can totter, and never so often as when erected on a wishful premise. For the man Kate had before her was not the Alan of old. No longer was he an establishment approved, establishment equipped outrider, briefed to watch and protect. Out on his ear now, he was having to take a turn as the cause driven maverick, a re-casting that the nurse was neither aware of, nor requiring......her concern at this moment being to dampen Busbridge's burning curiosity. Instead, unknowingly, she risked bringing more fuel to the fire.

The committal was read, and with the bones finally at rest the small gathering began to disperse. The vicar, shaking this hand and that on his way, went with his book, back to the vestry, leaving most of the rest to follow the undertaker back to the lytch and through to their waiting vehicles beyond. But not Alan, who'd been approached by the reporter, who held him in quiet conversation, and not James, who was moving towards where it had been earlier indicated to them that the Wakehams lay.

Unsure as to whether she might wait for Grigson, Kate hesitated, conspicuously, and this prompted him to break off from the reporter to join her. Both then followed Busbridge.

"Kate..... this is a surise. Mr Busbridge one might have expected, but not with yourself as a companion."

"A long story, Alan, and you might as well hear most of it from James himself. How am I to introduce you..... journalist? spook?"

"As an old friend, then leave the rest to me. I'll not ask you to

297

lie….. for your man there, I know, is nobody's fool."

"Did you catch up with Jeremy?"

"I did."

"And how did you find him?"

"With your help."

"Don't be funny, Alan," pouted the nurse. "You know what I mean."

"I found him on good form, as I need him to be. I've persuaded him to join me. We're at the campsite just along the cliffs."

"So you're finding him useful."

"He's got a good brain, just like your friend here. You know how I like to spot for talent….."

"…… and how you like to recruit," added Kate, having the last word in this initial exchange. They'd closed on Busbridge, who'd found the stones. Small, weathered, tilted slightly from a former alignment, but garlanded touchingly, naturally, by a spreading wreath of ivy….. the mother and her son.

"Mr Busbridge," said Alan, warmly, extending his hand. "The prolific and highly respected man of letters."

"Good morning….. you seem to know Kate here, but I don't believe I've yet had the pleasure."

"Alan Grigson," responded Kate. "An old friend, from my casualty days down at Truro."

"And you're in that same field?" Grigson was being invited to invent, and Kate knew well enough what to expect. He would be some kind of free lance again, magazine work, radio work, the usual stuff. She glanced away. She'd heard it all before…….but this time? No.

For what was there to be gained from mendacity or obfuscation, Alan reasoned, with Kate already knowing so much? She and Busbrigdge might appear an odd pairing, but they were together. That was how they'd arrived, and it would be how they would leave. He could be frank he decided….. and suddenly Kate was on the wrong foot.

Astonishingly, alarmingly she was hearing Alan tell things as they'd actually been. That he'd been working for the Government, down on the Fal, with a surveillance team into which Kate and her boyfriend of the time had been co-opted. The pair had done well, he added blithely. The operation had been a success.

"Good," responded Busbridge, as perplexed as he was flattered.

Rarely would so gentle a probe yield such rich reward. "I must thank you for your openness in this. One does weary of the guessing games that your people will so often favour….."

"This is good to know," agreed Grigson. "For no longer are they my people. Bluntly, Mr Busbridge, I've been thrown out."

Kate was suddenly having to adjust a flawed strategy.

"So you're no longer………"

"……the same man?" smiled Alan, sensing something of her quandary with Busbridge, and that rather than being re-asserted, this might be control further lost. "I'm on my own, and I'm resentful," he explained, more seriously "I will sort it though. I know I can, but this time it comes down to me only, and such resources that I can personally muster. This is why I've pulled Jeremy in. I must trust him, as I must also trust you, Kate. And so that you might trust me, it's better that you should hear of my difficulties in person, rather than through him."

"True."

"Yes, and suddenly we have, sprung upon us, an ideal opportunity. I come here today, and, quite fortuitously, you arrive also, bringing with you the added bonus of Mr James Busbridge, the widely respected Mr James Busbridge….. as perceptive a commentator as any on intelligence matters, always so well informed, and with that renowned appetite for the awkward truth. Just the sort of man I need!"

"We can listen," said Busbridge, modestly. "And perhaps there can be advantage for us too. We're not here for the sight-seeing, any more than you. We have a project of our own. We come to investigate possible connections, as you probably do. If there's overlap, then this indeed might offer scope for joint progress."

And for mutual admiration too, feared Kate, with the corollary of mutual encouragement, threatening a doubled disregard for her job prospects. Her hopes for Alan had been totally misplaced, and now Jeremy loomed with his own brand of sleuthing. Doubled jeopardy stood to be re-doubled….. but still she had to hang-on in. With the situation slipping further from her hands it was even more essential to maintain some kind of overview. There was no running from this. Developments would have to be tracked.

"So these graves….., " said Alan.

"We were just curious," answered Kate.

"About a mother and her young son, Norman, both of whom died during the war?"

"And also the boy's two older brothers, both of them dead...... so we are told."

"One lying in Cyprus, the other in Australia," added Busbridge.

"Quite a scattering," remarked Grigson.

"Which we think might owe something to the circumstances in which young Norman here was lost."

"But this wouldn't be to do with today's internment of those bones," probed Alan.

"Maybe," shrugged Busbridge, "maybe not. We'd planned to come sometime....."

"..... then we read of this funeral," continued Kate, "so why not today, we thought."

"We wondered who might turn up," confessed Busbridge.

"And look who you've found," chuckled Alan. "Is it right, Jim, that you have a cousin who went to Tasmania..... our Mr Bright, the redoubtable *Molehunter*."

"It is right, and actually I was told of Vincent Wakeham's death by the very same. What I heard just now was merely confirmation."

"So your cousin was watching this Vincent....."

"...... because when he first went out there, to Tasmania, he was asked to, by British intelligence, as a kind of part-time retirement number. Gentle observation, that's all, modest tabs......"

"So why would they have been taking this bother, we ask," said Kate, to see if Busbridge could be so open as he had been at *Jamaica Inn*.

"The question that exercised cousin Peter, but at the time only briefly..... with his having then considered the task trivial. More recently, though, since having to endure all this *Molehunter* fuss, he's been looking again at such matters."

"Being less inclined, now, to dismiss them as innocuous." Kate was hoping to prompt Alan. It worked.

"And this leads him to what?" he asked.

"An intriguing hypothesis," replied Busbridge

"Which holds......"

"......that Vincent's brother, young Norman Wakeham might not in fact be dead."

"Even though we stand here at the boy's grave?"

"Which could, conceivably, hold the remains of another

youngster, one of many killed around the same time, during the Plymouth blitz."

"So you're suggesting a deliberate switch, Mr Busbridge," said Grigson. "For what good reason?"

Busbridge straightened, scanning the greying sea to the east. Prawle Point glimmered still in the last of the sunlight.

"Did you ever hear of a vessel named the *Surcouf*?" he asked.

"A submarine, French...... for her day, huge," said Alan.

"And hugely controversial, because she happened to be in Devonport when France fell.... and as our Navy shelled a thousand and more French sailors to death at Oran so the *Surcouf* had to be boarded and taken at gunpoint. Then, naturally, she went to the Free French, only to figure prominently in a mysterious crisis within their high command, as Christmas 1940 became New year '41. Parts of this episode are well documented, but only so as to beg more questions."

"So de Gaulle would have been involved," smiled Grigson.

"Also his highest ranking Naval officer...... Vice Admiral Emile Muselier, who found himself being marched off to prison, our Secret Service having supposedly foiled an attempt by him to sell the *Surcouf* back to Vichy."

"So it was into the cells for poor Emile....."

"...... until the accusations were shown to be groundless, and so effective was the refutation that he was able to exact an apology from no less a figure than our Monarch, King George VI."

"So what he said would have to have been big," remarked Kate.

"And had the *Surcouf* been allowed out of Devonport?" asked Alan.

"Orders had been given for just one voyage, from Devonport up to Holy Loch."

"Off the Clyde, in Scotland......."

"The instructions were received before the end of November, but the crew was inexperienced and the machinery notoriously unreliable. She was to eventually make it after Christmas," explained Busbridge, "after a number of false starts during the weeks before."

"And this," said Kate, "is where Vincent Wakeham comes into the story."

"Vincent and Norman Wakeham," corrected Busbridge, patting the latter's gravestone. "The date here, could well mark one of those abortive departures...... on the same evening that these brothers were preparing to fish in their open boat, out of Portwrinkle." He pointed to the cliffs to the west. "Just down there, beyond Tregantle, and neither came home, even though the boat had been brought back to the harbour. The body of a boy came into shore some weeks later....."

"..... to be buried here," said Kate.

"But Vincent was nowhere to be found. There would have been rumours, no doubt, and we know, here, that the mother died within a year, but it's only much later that anything equally certain emerges, and this from the other side of the world. Favoured friends in his local Tasmanian community learn from him of an urgent dash from Plymouth to Scotland, in search of a brother who has been dragged from their fishing boat by a surfacing submarine...... for it had been to Scotland that he'd been told this submarine was headed."

"But with the countermand, his information is wrong," said Kate. "He gets to Scotland, while the submarine doesn't."

"And the failed quest ends with Vincent being interned for the best part of three years on bleakest Mull, in conditions of strict security. On release, he returns to Cornwall, only to suffer ostracism. A move to London follows, and then, with peace, emigration."

"Sketchy," remarked Alan.

"Naturally,"countered Kate. "Australia, then, was where people would go to start a new life. It wouldn't have been the done thing there to pry into the old."

"And prying certainly wouldn't have been Peter's brief," continued Busbridge. "It would have been about keeping a distance, cultivating mutual friends and business contacts, listening mainly, and just slipping in the occasional casual enquiry..... a task in a way made simpler as the subject became mortally ill."

Alan nodded. Secrets can often expire with life.

"And when it comes to getting to know what there is to find out, Peter Bright is good," continued Busbridge. "Always was."

"So as to the finer detail of what happened down there in the bay," Grigson pointed, "and after, in Scotland, with the arrest and the internment....... we can assume that nothing of this ever emerged."

"And never will," added Busbridge, "at least not in Tasmania. And now, on reflection, Peter concludes that such seepage as was feared in this regard might have been what he'd been engaged to monitor. As it was, in their sketchiness, those details were just about tolerable. Had there been anything more to report then some kind of gagging measure might have been triggered.... conceivably lethal."

"And that ought to signal caution," said Kate, wanting to impress with her gravity...... but from the two men there was little to indicate that she had.

"So your cousin shares this with you, James, and who else?" asked Alan.

"To my certain knowledge, only with his early mentor in this *Molehunter* business..... Victor Rothschild."

"Lord Rothschild, the brain."

"The very same, and it was at his instigation that Peter managed to gather what has been explained to me as a genetic fingerprint.... this from no more than a lock of the man's hair, taken from a left behind hairbrush, one of a few seemingly worthless bits and pieces that had to be cleared from the deceased's hospital locker. Courtesy of a spare shoe box, and an empty space on a garage shelf, this thing was preserved......."

".... to possibly make all the difference," enthused Grigson, "as the chance survival of a neglected remnant sometimes can."

Kate, sensing where this might be leading, was less sanguine.

"Sounds like it might have gone for DNA analysis," she said. "Where?"

"I can only guess," shrugged Busbridge. "Peter and Victor maintain a distance these days..... and I don't hear so much."

"And that guess," persisted Alan.

"......is that having been brought over a year or so back, by Peter, it was taken then, by Victor, up to Cambridge where he has access to the newest in forensic science."

"Sounds as if your cousin also wants to keep you and his Lordship apart," said Alan.

"And that suits me. I know my place."

"So were it possible now for us to reach into this grave and extract one of the poor lad's molars, could it not be sent to the same place to confirm fraternity?"

"I have been furnshed with a box number address," said Busbridge.

"In the hope, obviously, that you can indeed turn something up." Alan glanced down, taking the length of the grave, sizing the task. "But you can't just stroll into a graveyard and start digging...... and what could a switched corpse have to say anyway?"

"That, irrespective of whether this might be conspiracy, the real Norman might still be alive and kicking......"

"...... but not talking, Mr Busbridge," reasoned Alan. "For if he was still with us, wouldn't you have thought he'd have had something to say about this, in all these years?"

"Call me Jim, Alan...... and consider for a moment the kind of fear that a lad of that age would have felt."

Grigson glanced at Kate, and back to Busbridge, then to Kate again. She coloured slightly. He was working it out, she could tell.

"You've found someone," he said. "You're talking trauma, severe and long term, debilitating...... a case for psychiatric care, your new field of work, Kate. And you, Mr Busbridge, you'll have got your sample, without having to dig for it. And you will have sent it off......"

"...... but nothing is back yet. It can take weeks, and it could be that that which has been sent is insufficient."

"More hair?" asked Alan.

"An old bloodstain," said Busbridge, "perhaps too old."

"Which was not procured by myself," added Kate, pointedly. "It seems that a mightily disturbed boy has grown into a mightily disturbed man. Normally placid, he reacted with uncharacteristic violence against a cigarette card sized picture of the *Surcouf*. Blood was spilt, on the card itself....."

"...... and this is what I've sent off," confirmed Busbridge.

"Just to see, before you attempt to talk with the man."

"He doesn't do talking, Alan," said Kate. "The poor fellow is a total mute, and has been for as long as anyone can remember. Like you said just now.....'but not talking' "

"Induced, are you saying, by the trauma?"

"Could well be," answered Busbridge," by an experience which might in itself be the key to a programme for rehabilitation."

"For him," agreed Alan, "and, for you, maybe the key to a less than tidy war time cover-up. This business of the Vice Admiral attempting to sell the *Surcouf*...... anything in that, do you think?"

"Something we do know," replied Busbridge, "is that at the time Vincent and Norman could have encountered the *Surcouf*, there was a second Free French submarine on the high seas."

"Name?" asked Alan.

"The *Narval*, which earlier in December had left another British port on what would come to be a final mission. Final and fatal, for before Christmas she was to be lost with all hands in the Mediterranean, off the coast of north Africa….in somewhat intriguing circumstances. Details of any action are sparse, but it has been said that the sub was running for a Vichy port after defecting from the allied side."

"Ah haa!" Alan was liking this.

"It is possible that both the *Surcouf* and the *Narval* surfaced off here, to rendezvous with a view to a joint defection. If so, then the brothers Wakeham might have witnessed a very interesting debate…. and if we are to believe that young Norman was actually taken aboard the *Surcouf* then implications for him become grave. The boat might be hobbling back to Devonport….."

"…..rather than Scotland," said Kate, "or anywhere else…."

"….. but on no account will this lad be allowed home."

"Poor Norman," muttered Alan. "A nightmare."

"Severe trauma," said Kate.

"But this remains speculation," Busbridge reminded them.

"Of course," conceded Alan, "but, all the same, I'd like you to meet my associate."

"Mr Jeremy Barnes," intoned Kate, as if his was an intervention pre-ordained.

"And if you've an hour or so," breezed Grigson, "then there's an opportunity now. He'll be waiting down at Mount Edgcumbe….. and if I could beg a lift then all the better."

"Mount Edgcumbe for lunch, then," said Busbridge…. and Jeremy for afters, thought Kate, yielding without question to the vicissitudes of fate.

But maybe she was over-worrying, for there was in fact little risk of any 'scene', and Alan, in this short time he'd been with Jeremy, had come to realise as much. Of course, thanks to him, the nurse and the lecturer hadn't parted on the best of terms, but the latter was mature enough to realise that their former relationship had for too long relied on what had been merely a temporary need. The cosseting he'd offered had worked. Her appetite for excitement had been healthily re-found and indulged. The manner of the break had wounded his pride, but he was over this now, and enjoying fresh challenges of his own.

Already he was at Cremyll, lingering at the gate to the avenued drive that led bold and straight up to the main House. Alan would be coming alone, he still thought, but before him he was expecting Chas and Sally who'd said they would cross from Stonehouse on the foot-passenger ferry. This was going to be interesting, hearing what Alan Clark had had to say for himself.

There was a ferry crossing now, he could see. He turned, to look back towards the walled orangery, with its tea room and sheltered italianate garden. They could go in there and wait for Alan, maybe finding time to flick through some of those photographs in his copy of *White Mischief*.

Since reading Moyne's testimony the book had become even more intriguing, and in some ways newly puzzling..... for the author, perceived previously as a hard hitting investigative journalist, fearless and thorough, was, when more closely re-read under this very different light provided by Declan McDaid, perhaps pulling a few of those punches.

Why, for instance, wasn't Fox making more of Erroll's relationship with Phyllis Filmer, Joss's current and quite firmly established lady-friend when Jock and Diana Broughton arrived in Kenya? Leaving aside the significance placed by Moyne on the Shell House telegram, the woman was still worth as much space in this book as the likes of Alice de Janze and Kiki Preston, surely. But no, the author couldn't bring himself to so much as mention her by name. Instead he invents a weird pseudonym, this *'Nancy Wirewater'*. No one else in the book is favoured with such a cloak, so why then was she? And such a strange name too...... like a cheap wig it was more a flag than a disguise. So perhaps it was indeed just that, a flagged up clue to something that an intimidated author feared to explicitly state.

And then there was the solicitor to the accused, one Lazarus Kaplan. When, in '69, Cyril Connolly, with the young Fox as an assistant, first researched the case for a *Sunday Times* article, this Kaplan fellow had been eager to help...... until, strangely, the enthusiasm suddenly evaporated and the man was wanting nothing to do with the project. Then, within the year, he was dead. Was this again indicative of duress, or perhaps something even more sinister? Whatever, Fox wasn't following it through. So who was to say he hadn't been got at too?

Alan Clark, so famously incautious of tongue, maybe he will have had something to say on this, thought Jeremy, and, as if on cue, Sally and Chas appeared before him. What had they drawn, anything?

The pair certainly looked pleased with themselves. This was encouraging.

"Well," began Jeremy, "did we get our Minister to try on his historian's hat?"

"We didn't," answered the girl. "In fact we were in and out in minutes." The lecturer's face dropped. "But don't despair. He sent us across to *The Duke of Cornwall*......"

"......where his step mother has been staying," continued Chas. "She was the one to answer our enquiries, he told us...."

"..... and I think you'll agree that he was right," smiled Sally, proudly.

"His step mother....?" Jeremy shouldn't have needed prompting, but Sally wasn't waiting.

"Nolwen, " she said.

"Of course, Nolwen Clark, widow of Kenneth, and a daughter of Alice de Janze." Jeremy took the book back from Chas. "See here, we have a picture of her, as a child." He flicked to a block of thirty or so monochrome plates, and there she was, in the fourth, three years old perhaps, standing by her mother who was seated with the youngest of the two sisters on her knee. Alice with Nolwen and Paola, stated the caption, shortly before the mother left the girls in France to take up permanent residence in Happy Valley.

The youngsters scrutinized this print, of more than sixty years before.

"She's certainly interested in you, Jeremy," said Chas. "I'm not sure that she wasn't seeing through what you were trying to do....... but that's not to say she had any objection."

"There's no love lost between her and her stepson," continued Sally.

"Open warfare," added Chas

"And she likes to recruit people to her side," added the girl.

"No problem there," said Jeremy. "Our man at the DTI is either liked or loathed, and, frankly, won't give a damn which."

"While she thinks the tales of her mother's notoriety are over done," continued Sally. "She'd hoped for better from Mr Fox, in his book, and, from the bits she's seen and been told of, she's appalled by the portrayal in the film. Things might have been set straight, but no......"

".....and instead they're now set to go from bad to worse," added Chas.

"So is there something she knows?" wondered Jeremy.

"Very likely," replied Sally, "but whether she might choose to share this with you is going to depend on your response to a riddle."

"Devised by her?"

"Posed by her, certainly, as it was previously posed to her by a Mr Cyril Connolly....."

".....who's been dead now for a good dozen years," Jeremy told them, thumbing quickly to the last of the book's photographs. Here was Cyril, shortly before his death in 1974, said the caption..... and with him in the picture stood his young son, slightly older than Nolwen had been almost fifty years before, but carrying the same uncertain expression. "And I suppose we can't even assume it to have been devised by him."

"Now look inside the front cover," said Chas.

Jeremy did.

"We've had a go," said Sally as he studied the mysterious group of letters and words.

"And it was a good go, she told us," added the boy, "but I think she's hoping that you might do better."

Jeremy had it before him. What could he make of it all?

MCLV	HIIR=Eleanor
(step back)	(IST)

Uncle Crouchback knows

The lecturer perused the matrix for the best part of a minute, to then break the respectful silence himself.

"And you say you had a go at interpreting this?"

"History we thought," said Chas. "Step back to 1155, to Henry II, and his wife Eleanor....."

".....of Aquitaine," acknowledged Jeremy, though obviously far from convinced. "But Uncle Crouchback ..... what are we to make of that?"

"Richard III," offered Sally, less confidently now than in the

The Duke of Cornwall. "Henry was the first of the Plantagenets, and Crouchback, murderer of his nephew Princes, he was the last."

"Yeah.....good try, very good," acknowledged Jeremy. "You were having to think on your feet...... and you did. But he was a clever man, old Connolly."

"Clever enough to be more precise?" asked Chas.

"Quite," confirmed Jeremy. "I see what I think Nolwen wants me to see."

"Which is?" asked Sally.

"A mock-medieval veil, but not hanging quite as it should, through having been made faulty by design."

"How though, and why?" said Sally. "If there is a more obscure message to be read then it can only emerge from a precise identification of those mistakes...... and this is what Nolwen wants, Jeremy, for why else the prompting. Do you see anything?"

"Well, for a start, there's sonething wrong with the date. Henry and Eleanor did marry, but that was in 1152, I know because this is how I used to remember it...... Henry two was her husband number two, and they wed in fifty two, before they were crowned."

"So maybe '55 was when they were crowned," offered Chas.

"The Coronation was in '54," corrected Jeremy.

"So question mark over the date," said Sally. "Anything else, obvious to a professional's first glance?"

"This Uncle Crouchback." queried the lecturer, "that's a very tenuous Richard III....."

"..... because Shakespeare was inaccurate with his history," said Chas. "The hunchbacked psychopath being an invention, you would say..... a mix of poetic licence and Tudor propaganda."

"I don't think 'hunchback' even comes into the plays. Margaret of Anjou, Queen of curses, she rails against a '*pois'nous bunch-back'd toad*,' I do remember that..... but hunchback? I don't think so, and Crouchback?..... No, never."

"You're that sure?" checked Sally.

"Because for me Uncle Crouchback belongs to this century, in fact he flits briefly through that book, *White Mischief*. Kenya was a stop over on his *Remote People* tour."

"So you still mean Royalty, Jeremy," said Chas, hoping to be still at least a little right.

"No, sorry Chas, Royalty this is not."

"Tell us then who Uncle Crouchback is," said Sally, taking the book from Chas and passing it back to Jeremy.

"Guy Crouchback is a fictional soldier, created by Evelyn Waugh. He earned the epithet 'Uncle' when he joined up at the start of the last war, as in real life did the novelist."

"And Connolly knew Waugh?"

"Very well.....too well to underestimate, as many did. Like the fool in Lear, Waugh was adept at cultivating powerful connections, forming penetrative insights, voicing profound opinions. *Remote People* was an early travelogue project. It took him to the far corners of Empire and beyond. Whilst in Kenya Waugh stayed with Raymond de Trafford, an absolute rake who seemed to bring out the worst in Nolwen's mother. It was he who broke up the marriage in the '20s, and she actually shot the fellow at a Paris railway station, in full public view......but he survived, and when they met later in Kenya the pair married, but only for a matter of months."

"Melodrama!" remarked Chas. "I'll borrow that book when you've finished."

"Eventually he was himself jailed for manslaughter. For Nolwen and her sister it had to be the stepfather from hell. Kiki Preston was another who Waugh met in Kenya, and she too came to a mysteriously sticky end...... after teaching George, the King's youngest surviving son, how to mainline in morphine and cocaine. Back in the '30's Evelyn drew heavily on these misfit types to colour his characters....."

"..... and then, after the war, he drew on himself for this Uncle Crouchback," Chas added.

"The failed first marriage, the earnest Catholicism, the loathing of any form of socialism, and the revulsion towards the wartime alliance struck with Russia, all this was Waugh's own," said Jeremy, "but at the same time the character never quite becomes the author's alter ego. While Waugh's personal wartime experiences are chronicled, and many of the vivid personalities he encountered are wheeled through the chapters, Guy's reactions to these events and these people are distinct from his creator's. His Crouchback is more honourable, more trusting, more loyal. He can suffer a fool gladly, and be chivalrous to even the most undeserving of women. Waugh, himself, was altogether more spiteful and bigotted. To his credit, he could at least admit this."

"So his adventures of Guy Crouchback can be read almost as an apologia," Chas suggested.

"Indeed, as throughout the *Sword of Honour* trilogy this 'uncle' creation nobly endures a procession of characters who approximate to the sort who got right up Evelyn Waugh's real life nose. And while this might not be the actual key to Lady Clark's riddle….. "

"……you could demonstrate to her that you've at least located a hidden door," said Sally. "And if she's sufficiently impressed then perhaps you'll be fed a little more in the way of clues. She gives you her phone number there. That's for her suite in the hotel. She'll be returning on Tuesday's daytime crossing, to stay another couple of nights."

And Jeremy relished the prospect of that return, for unknown to the youngsters he was, thanks to McDaid, well primed to give as much as he might be getting from this woman. Given the chance, he could hit the old girl with '*Phyllis Filmer*', and follow this with '*Shell House*', things not mentioned, certainly in print, by either Connolly or Fox…… and see then how well she liked her reaction coming under *his* scrutiny.

"So I'm to contact her?"

"Her, and her only," said Sally. "She was adamant. From now on this game has to be strictly between us and Nolwen. The Honourable step son is to know nothing. He's out of the loop, she insists, and there he must stay…… and here's your buddy now, with a couple of friends picked up along the way. We might need more than one table."

Jeremy stood and turned to move, but didn't. For he was looking at Kate, and rendered stock still. But she was still walking, still coming, with nothing more than a look of faint embarrassment. Forewarning, she'd had….. obviously.

The youngsters exchanged glances. They couldn't know the story, but they could well enough sense a previous something….. a debt, a hurt, some kind of wrong, or wound even, healed but still tender. They watched….. until Alan, lagging a little with Busbridge, stepped forward to seize control, and this too was interesting.

"Kate and Jim," he announced proudly to all, brimming bonhomie. "Meet Chas, and Sally….. and Jeremy here who's actually known Kate for far longer than I."

"But who I've not seen or spoken to for quite some time….," returned Jeremy, composure recovered, the voice calm, steady, but slightly puzzled.

"Perhaps, later, we might catch up on things," suggested Kate tentatively, and with a gentle humility that Jeremy couldn't have expected.

"Yes, later," agreed Jeremy..... almost forgivingly, noted Chas.

"Good, so that can wait," continued Alan. "For while we are honoured by his company, I should also be making a fuss over Mr Busbridge here, Kate's companion." Busbridge was beaming. "For anyone choosing to delve into the events of '40 and '41, this man has to be as good as a library. If getting behind the official version is the game then we have ourselves here a past master."

Kate glanced downwards. She was proof. Officialdom included hospital staff, from the highest to the humblest. She'd been trusted with a position therein and now felt compromised. And just listen to Alan..... so impervious he was to her discomfort. She lifted her eyes briefly towards Jeremy, and met his.... when conventionally they might have been sizing James. How well did her former man remember her.......could he guess her distress, merely from body language, from eye movement? If so, would *he* be interested in particulars?

He would notice surely, how much Alan was taken with James, and see how a tie-in there could offer promise to both....... but not how this might pose further difficulty for herself. This would need explaining, that it was becoming a matter of sides. And then, could she really expect him to take hers?

Jeremy moved now to lead all into the orangery. The youngsters followed him as a pair, then herself, with Alan and James together behind, still locked in conversation. Yes, Grigson seemed more interested in her companion than in the youngsters, who were closer to Jeremy ...... and therefore, as a couple, those youngsters were probably his team, being groomed by him to assist with his particular angle of enquiry. And if she knew the lecturer, then as such, for him, they would be closely held asset, one not readily relinquished to the direction of another. And good for Jeremy, thought Kate, for it was becoming clearer by the minute that, in his overriding concern for himself, Alan was slipping inexorably towards a natural alignment with Busbridge.

So her response now had to be to gently show a little interest in Chas and Sally. Jeremy should feel this to be a gesture of support, and perhaps look to reciprocate.

The tearoom was well filled, and this was helpful. Two small tables were available to them, close enough but not adjacent. They would have to split.

Kate kept the youngsters together, to sit with them, and complete one group of three. Alan, Jeremy and James were thus left to make another, and make another converstaion too, for as the men srtuggled to determine who was going to the self-serve to fetch what for whom she was stealthily and chattily away, impressing and re-assuring the teenaged two with her knowledge of Jeremy. He seemed a 'clever sort of man', said Sally, and Kate agreed, 'even if sometimes he might be a little too clever for his own good'. They weren't to be daunted by him, that was her theme, and it did loosen from them a little of their morning's errand. They mentioned Alan Clark, and the stepmother of his who was so concerned for her own long dead mother's reputation, and they spoke too of the riddle that she'd set for Jeremy. The lecturer was well up for such a challenge, Kate heard….. and, far from surprised, she well imagined he was.

They were sipping at their drinks now, and Kate looked across to the other table. With Busbridge there to give guidance Alan was re-telling, as best he could, what he'd heard earlier up at Rame. Jeremy was attentive. He needed to be, and, for the while, what he had himself gleaned through those youngsters was having to wait. Good, thought Kate. This suited her fine.

"So who else was at the burial?" Chas asked her.

"Not many," replied the nurse. "The police were represented, and the coastgurds, a reporter, and then there were the people who found the remains."

"The two young Africans….," said Sally, falsely.

"….. and with them a woman," added Kate, deceived, "a good bit older, she…..European."

"We know them," said Chas. "In fact we were hoping to call on them later."

"Travellers," explained Sally. "Currently staying around at Wacker."

"Wacker….. where's Wacker?"

"If you're headed back down into Cornwall….?"

"Soon," said Kate glancing at her watch. "My shift starts at two."

"Then you'll pass close by. If you could fit us in we can show you," said Sally. "It's an old creekside quay, not far off the main ferry road. The woman, Megan, she's becoming something of a perennial…….does a neat line line in herbal remedies, mostly hawthorn based. Blossom, leaf, berry, she'll use it all, singly and in any combination. Mum goes for a syrup, as a natural diuretic. I know you're a nurse and all that, but I could arrange a consultation if....."

"I'll bear that in mind, Sally," smiled Kate. "I suppose her lads help with the stall running and the housekeeping."

"And they carve driftwood, and make jewellery from shells," said Chas. "This was how they happened across those bones.... beachcombing."

"And just bones?" smiled Kate, with gentle scepticism "Can you really believe there was nothing else there..... no tags or buttons or coins, that might indicate service branch, rank, or nationality?"

A second's pause, and then the split response;

"Why shouldn't we?" from Sally, and, from Chas,

"If we weren't there....." Voiced simultaneously it hinted contradiction and concern.

"I'm a military nurse," explained Kate "I served on the *Kampala*, the hospital ship in the South Atlantic. We treated friend and foe, often indistinguishable save for what was holding their clothes together. They might have been shredded, they might have been burnt, but always, somewhere, they would be buttoned."

"And your friend, Mr Busbridge, he's thinking the same?" angled Sally.

"But the coroner must have checked this," said Chas. "That's his job, surely."

"Should be his job," said Kate. "But James thinks they can be leant on."

"By?"

"By the powerful, Chas, seeking to avoid the awkward question."

"Well I wasn't there," repeated the boy.

"And.....?" Kate's eyes had turned to Sally's, drawing colour to neck, then cheeks.

"And ...and I believe Chas," she insisted, wanting to convey firmness, but merely sounding flustered.

"Time's up anyway." Kate looked at her watch again. "Ninety minutes I've got. One of us here is having to hold down a proper job. Before I break up that happy threesome over there I want to leave you with my phone number. I'm not sure that Jeremy knows this one. If you could perhaps make sure that he does...."

Chas, slightly relieved, and marvelling at Jeremy's magnetism for phone numbers, was pleased to oblige with a pen. Next to his chair sat his college rucksack. He rummaged deeply to draw one out, along with the large envelope given to him at the the bank the day before. He could write on this, he thought, but care was needed for it was unsealed and as it came up the contents were slipping clear of the cover, contents which for the moment were for no one's eyes but his and Sally's.

The girl reached, to hold them from sliding to the ground...... copies of the coroners office receipt and the assay report from the bank. It was as well that each had been sharply folded against any casual disclosure of its business. She straightened them, Chas writing as Kate, now standing, dictated the number. But it was Sally's hands that kept the nurse's attention, for shuffled amongst those copies there was also an old foolscap sized manila envelope. That which Chas had been left by his grandmother..... she having taken it at the chart shop, from the owner when, back in early '41, she'd suddenly decided against leaving him with her oddly acquired part map.

With its archaic wax seal, broken and dulled, and frank-smudged stamp (George VI) it looked worn and delicate. An elegantly black inked address had paled to a barely readable grey, but readable nonetheless, and while Kate couldn't know anything of this item's history or its contents, how interesting it was for her that it should be that name, and that address.

How very interesting, and also very noteworthy..... for, hitherto, to her, it had been a name closely held in a confidential medical file, a name she'd foolishly fed to James's beguiling lay curiosity. Opprobrium had seemed inescapable, but now in this unexpected turn of events, there might be opportunity for her to mitigate something of its weight. The name from the 1940s that had tripped far too loosely off her tongue..... it was seeking another route out into the '80s and, from her standpoint, surely such an escape had to be encouraged.

But carefully though, for clearly these youngsters were wanting here to keep this thing to themselves, and maybe with good reason. For the moment she would say nothing...... save, perhaps, for just a quiet word later with James, the curious man, who could be trusted to widen such a trickle as this into a channel, a course that might lessen the strain placed on her career.

*

(xxx) a mentor

Later, at Wacker Quay.

"It's good that you've come over, especially in this weather."

"We did get a lift Megan," said Sally.

"And I'll make sure you have a ride back," said the herbalist. "Makesi and Juma, will be back soon with the van. They went across to Downderry.... shouldn't be too long, not in this rain."

The caravan rocked slightly, pressed by a strong gust. The patter of rain sounded more like hail, and a loosely braced side window thudded back into its frame.

"We were told that you all went to the funeral," said Chas.

"By Alan..... we saw him, and he was with another man and a woman, quite an age difference."

"She being of previous acquaintance," Sally explained, "up from Bodmin, and on their way back now. They were our lift."

"So you met them....."

"..... at Mount Edgcumbe, where we'd arranged to meet Jeremy, a friend who's working with Alan...."

".....while he was up at the church."

"That's right," continued the girl. "But like we've just done to here, Alan cadged a lift down to Cremyll in Busbridge's car. That's the older guy's name....... James Busbridge, who Alan seems to know by reputation. The pair certainly seemed to hit it off, in fact all three do."

"You mean the woman too....."

"Actually I was thinking of the three males; Alan, Jeremy, and Busbridge. All of them, they have this thing about 1941."

"But you've said nothing to any about finding that gold."

"Nothing," confirmed Chas.

"And those who attended the funeral, did they have any thoughts on the ceremony or the unknown deceased?"

"From Busbridge and Kate, who's a nurse, there was some surprise at the reported absence of any service tags, or buttons and buckles," answered Sally "There ought to have been something, they felt."

"So was this doubt directed towards my lads? It was dark for them in that cave, and getting darker. You know that Sally."

She did. Nodding, she had to agree, but it hadn't been so dark as to prevent their lifting that gold.

"Directed, I think, more towards the coroner," said Chas. "That James Busbridge has little faith in coroners."

"Too widely empowered," added Sally.

"Well we've no cause to share such concern, not in East Cornwall District," said the herbalist. "Any complaints about how the gold was received by Plymouth District?"

"None at all," answered Chas.

"And you have the receipt?"

"I do, with a copy for yourself, together with a copy of the assay done by my bank." The envelope unintentionally aired at Mount Edgcumbe was again produced and tipped, the contents sliding onto a still damp lap. What had been promised was passed, briefly inspected, and gratefully accepted..

"Yes……nothing here to suggest this can't be claimed wholly by the Crown. Has to be to your benefit, of course, with no third party to dilute your interest."

"No mark of origin detected, you mean," said Chas. "I would have thought that unusual."

"But we have the bank's assay….. and something else there?" The woman's eyes had settled on the old envelope. "Also to do with your find…… must I presume?" The words carried authority, compelling authority.

"I put this in today to show Sally, because the gold was her find….."

"…..and whilst coming across on the ferry I did snatch a look," added the girl. "But that hasn't made Chas or me any the wiser."

"So may I?" asked Megan.

"And why not?" agreed Chas, easing a painfully fragile document from its tissue thin envelope. The herbalist came to the table where it now lay, wishing not to over handle it.

"A chart, or map of some sort," she murmered, leaning forward to peruse, "or part of one at least. We have the three straight edges and one torn….."

"…..and it's been in and out of the water, so I have been told."

"By…..?"

"My grandmother, before she died."

"When she said about the gold bar."

"Correct."

317

"But there was never any mention of a fatality that might account for the bones?"

"Not for *those* bones, but there was a lost child, the remains of which were recovered and......" Chas paused, wondering how much he should tell, before deciding; "Look.... I'll give you the story. As you know about the gold, then you might as well have the rest."

And so it passed. This tale, privately gathered by Chas at his gran's deathbed, then told by him to Sally out on Whitsand Bay, was now recounted before this wise woman of Wacker, the trusted holistic oracle.

She heard of the of the two young wricklemen and the two submarines, both French...... like the Admiral who'd come to Ince, and met a young and vulnerable Jenny Cross, the girl who was to be told of that gold and also given the piece of map, then left to survive as best she could, with a baby son, on the shattered streets of Plymouth town. But survive they did, the child to eventually become his, Chas's, own father, the master diver of Fort Bovisand.

Megan listened closely, to every word, and by dearth of interruption allowed the story to be told in less than twenty quick minutes. Only with the facts, such as they were, delivered did she begin to probe gently at possibilities.

"So your Gran, Chas, while knowing of an argument and a tussle out there on the *Surcouf*, was not made aware of any adult fatality."

"Of that I'm sure," Chas re-affirmed. "Had she, then I think I would have been told."

"But this isn't to say that the fisherman had himself been entirely frank with her. It could be that he saw more than he let on. In wartime, to pass information is to pass risk. To protect you sometimes have to withold." Megan looked down on the envelope that lay next to the map, then softly stroked at the address with the side of a thumb. "As young Jenny Cross might have been starkly reminded when these poor souls were blown to high heaven. There's much to indicate that we might have here what's been an extremely dangerous scrap of paper, dangerous and perhaps powerful."

"If only Vincent Wakeham were here to help explain why," added Chas. "But we are told that he too has now died, in faraway Tasmania, where he went to put all this behind him."

"But this said," cautioned Megan, "I think you could be taking far more care with this part chart than you are. Like the metal, it should be in a safe or strong room, under lock and key. Have copies made. Carry them when asking opinions. You don't want to be wandering around with the real thing, it's far too precious."

"Good advice," agreed Sally.

"Thank you, young lady," Megan turned, pulled at a small drawer and produced a neat pair of scissors. "But while we have it here, why don't we snip off just a little piece of margin….. off the corner, at the top here where the tear begins. I could keep it with those other things you've brought."

"Why?" asked Sally.

"Because, as you've explained it to me, Sally, a trust has been betrayed." The admonishment registered. The girl coloured, and Megan relented. "But worry not, for gold can do that, even between the very best of friends. And trust can be rebuilt. It soon will be, I'm sure, to something stronger than before……and this is what I seek to nurture. You've followed my advice, and that treasure is now being safely looked after."

"In Plymouth," confirmed Chas.

"As these documents attest," continued Megan, "and while I have copies, plus this snip, you will each have an independent access to me, here at Wacker…… where I'll be equipped to verify, firstly, each one's stake in the jointly raised bullion, and secondly, the authenticity of that part chart."

"But that's only up until the end of October," said Sally. "It's then that you usually move on."

"By when you'll be knowing each other better, trusting each other better……and, if not, then maybe you'll have found someone else to take my place, to put themselves to similar trouble."

Chas looked to Sally. She shrugged, he snipped, and in an instant Megan was at the table with an unused glass ointment jar, the small moth wing of a wedge to be slid therein and fastened.

"We could have enquiries made about getting this dated," she suggested casually.

"For a positive fix," agreed Chas, "date of origin, place of origin….."

"……without disclosing this, the main part," said Sally, "which depicts what? Ideas anyone?"

"Not a lot to go on," said Chas, "but if we're talking submarines and admirals then this unbroken but unevenly curved line must be a stretch of coast."

"So which side would be land," asked Sally, "and which sea? We only have those three letters...... 'MT P' ."

"Four, if you count the cross beneath," offered Chas. "Unless 'x' marks the spot......"

"......of a mountain perhaps," suggested the girl, "if we're talking land on this side. A mountain near the coast, presumably visible from the sea. Not many of them in France itself."

"But plenty in French Polynesia," said Chas. "Hundreds, I wouldn't wonder. Did you ever see *South Pacific*? Poor old gran, she loved that film. 'This nearly was mine'.......that was her song. ' .... *Only to fly as night flies to day*.....' ," he sang.

"I'm not sure that I have," frowned Sally, "or, indeed, that I want to!"

"So if we can't identify a place," said Megan, "what about a purpose? You will have speculated Chas, I know, so what's your best hunch?"

"That more gold waited for Muselier and the *Surcouf* at whatever place this might be..... that the missing part must be far more informative. Pity we don't have it. Maybe it'll turn up. What I do know, though, is that almost a full year after this incident in Whitsand Bay, the *Surcouf* was involved in the one serious action of a far from distinguished Free French career. This was with the capture of the Vichy held islands of St Pierre and Miquelon, in the mouth of the St Lawrence....."

"......between Newfoundland and Cape Breton," remembered Sally.

"It was a de Gaulle initiative, taken independently of any British Command, and probably against the express wish of the U.S. But it did go down well with those fighting the Battle of the Atlantic. It was known that radio beacons on the islands were signalling to U boats, briefing them on convoy movements. Some have said that Washington's habitual wariness of de Gaulle can be traced back to this one small doorstep coup."

"And was your grandfather there?" asked Megan.

"He was. He led the force, the *Surcouf* being his flagship."

"So could this also have been about Vichy gold," Sally wondered. "If the plans had been laid as much as year before then the idea might have been to pay Muselier to sabotage or betray them in some way......possible?"

"Not impossible," said Chas. "But whatever was attempted, he

320

wasn't taking the bribe. Perhaps that James Busbridge might have something on the episode. He's a bit of a naval historian I understand."

"Good idea," said Megan, "and perhaps you might also consider broaching some of this with your father."

"Against his mother's wishes?"

"Can we say that, though?" countered the herbalist. "The tale was entrusted to yourself so that you might pass it on to your issue, to be passed down, if necessary to their children's children. The chances were that this would be necessary, that generations would have to search before any discovery was made, and we would have to say that it was in this realistic expectation that your father was passed over..... for he might have been reluctant to instigate this chain, not wishing to visit his own childhood torments on you or any children you might have."

"But with Sally having helped me to this breakthrough, then perhaps none of this need apply," agreed Chas, but uncertainly. Greater openness between father and son might be healthier, yes, but there remained sensitivities over which he had no wish to trespass.

"If you want, I could help in this," soothed Megan, acknowledging those misgivings. "A mediating voice will sometimes help."

"As it has done so far," agreed Sally, earning a smile from Chas.

"So perhaps you might bring him here," Megan suggested, "along with a copy of this map."

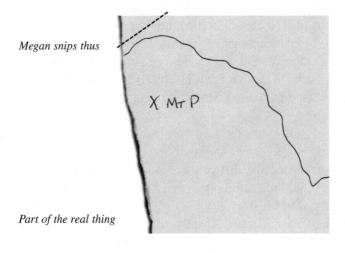

Megan snips thus

X Mt P

Part of the real thing

*

321

(xxxi) an audience

Wednesday, mid afternoon.

"See over to the left Kate. Now, across the water...... you get just a glimpse of Ince, amongst the trees." Jeremy, driving, had his eyes ahead. Kate looked, and there it stood, momentarily, before the woodlands of Antony House intervened and they were turning away from the lake-smooth Lynher, so calm, so shallow, to drop to the choppier Hamoaze with its yards of wharf and bustle.

Jeremy had used both numbers. A meeting with Lady Clark had been arranged, as suggested, and he'd also phoned Kate, inviting her to join him. She would be pleased to, she said. Yes, together they would go to *The Duke of Cornwall* and meet a daughter of the famed Alice de Janze...... and now they were on their way, having met at Kernow Mill, the nurse having come thus far in her Morris, which would wait there for her later return.

They were early, and could use the ferry. The waiting and the floating time might, Jeremy hoped, ease away some of their edginess, a nervousness admitted by neither but felt by both. Initially, from Trerulefoot to Polbathic, the conversation had been stilted and one sided, with Kate hearing first what she already knew, and indeed, in her small way, had helped arrange.... that the lecturer was back in Cornwall at Alan's behest.

She learned then of Eamon Carroll and the far from fully explained events at this place called Ince, amounting to a security lapse for which Grigson had been held primarily to blame. Suspension had followed, as she was aware, and this was offering time for perhaps getting to the root of the matter. The role for himself, Jeremy understood, was to delve a strongly sensed historical dimension, and his start in this respect had been encouraging.

She should know that the Lady of Ince Castle, the Viscountess Boyd, was the widow of a former Colonial Secretary, Alan Lennox Boyd, who'd held the post during the difficult late '50s. She was also a niece to Lord Moyne, who'd held the same office in 1941...... as pivotal a year as any in 20th century world history.

The advice from Edward Trembath, explained Jeremy, was to approach Alan Clark MP, he who'd forged a formidable reputation on a close dissection of the main events of that same year. So with the help of the youngsters he'd ventured an enquiry, and indeed found reward. The Minister was busy...... of couse he was, but they were in luck. The MP's hated stepmother was in town, the Lady Nolwen Clark, and she would be willing to talk, for she was only too eager to voice her thoughts on a soon to be brought out film, a picture inspired by a book titled *White Mischief*, which purported to solve the wartime murder in Kenya of Lord Erroll. Set mainly in '41, it featured a far from flattering portrayal of her mother, the troubled Alice de Janze, whose besieged reputation Nolwen felt bound to defend.

Just this one slender strand he'd had at first, but now, intriguingly, it promised to twine with a second that had emanated independently from Ince...... a line with which Nolwen would surely be impressed. He was going to surprise her today, and please her, he hoped, sufficiently to perhaps draw further disclosure.

The ferry waited, having comfortably swallowed whole what queue there might have been. The gantry light shone green, beckoning them through to the slip and across the the lowered ramp without delay. Now Jeremy could cut the motor. He turned and smiled.

"Not quite the old King Harry," he quipped, "but plenty here to get my teeth into."

"Sounds like it," said the nurse. "and all without involving yourself in the tangle over that blessed submarine."

"You mean your friend's pet, the *Surcouf*. Do I sense tepid enthusiasm? I took it that you and he were together on that one, that as a helpmate you were equally enthralled."

"To begin with, yes......"

"......but no longer?"

"It's my fault, Jeremy. James, you see, was once an out patient at St Lawrence. That was before I started there....."

".... and he seems well enough mended."

"He is, but not so well as to want to completely sever all connection with the hospital....... at least, that's how it first seemed. He helps with 'the Friends', a support group, and, as worthy and useful as this might be, I saw no harm in also cultivating a shared outside interest."

"To help wean him away from the institution, you mean. But since when, Kate, were you ever interested in the history of submarine warfare?"

"Since never. The shared interest was in singing, something I took up again on moving to the new area. We're both members of Bodmin's choral society. I'm rusty, of course, but James is good. He went to a choir school and was properly taught."

"So in an after-care sense, he might be said to have been your pet."

"A few months ago, yes. I would have had to agree, not suspecting then what I've since come to realise....... that Mr James Busbridge has been quietly manoeuvring so as to further an agenda of his own. I see now how he was, in fact, subtly grooming me. He knew precisely what he was looking for....."

"...... and he'd worked you out as just that kind of talent."

"And useful I have been to him, Jeremy, by breaching patient confidentiality, a basic principle. I needn't have, I shouldn't have....."

"......but that's done, it's in the past," consoled the lecturer. "Distance yourself. Disengage."

"Sounds simple...... except that professional misconduct can't be so easily shrugged. What I've done is traceable. It can't be wished away."

"So now, for you Kate, it must be damage limitation ..... tricky task."

"Tricky, Jeremy, and solitary..... but then, in the churchyard, I see Alan. I try to signal to him my unease with James........"

"......but in vain."

"So it felt, and I thought it was me...... but I realise now that he'll be thinking about his *own* career."

"And naturally, in this context, he picks up on the tale of 'that blessed submarine'. It's a good one, though, as tales go...... that you must admit."

Kate admitted nothing. The ferry slowed. The dropping ramp grated onto Devon. The gates swung.

"You'd better start up the engine," she reminded him, seeing that their line would be first off. Jeremy did, to take them promptly off, and on their way, threading Devonport, dropping to Stonehouse, and then leaving Union Street before the old Palace Theatre to cut along the edge of Millbay. *The Duke of Cornwall* loomed ahead. They found a parking space behind, on West Hoe Road.

Jeremy liked it. The afternoon was progressing smoothly. Clearly, and perhaps thankfully, they could never again be the couple of old, but there was a warmth still. The way Grigson had come to him, seeking help, that had patched a tattered pride...... but pride, he'd learned, went before a fall. Kate was bringing something more, something sweeter, rarer, as yet only faintly sensed. It spoke of a distant prize, one to be earned rather than awarded. He'd drawn the hallowed scent of redemption.

For there had to be more than just the one way into the forest of intrigue that was 1941. Busbridge, with Grigson seemingly in his thrall, he was following the *Surcouf*, and a trail of victims, damaged and mostly dead. Would this really lead them to perpetrators and underlying motives? Jeremy wasn't so sure, and this emphasised the importance of the coming interview. If, now, he could impress the Lady Nolwen, daughter of Alice de Janze, then perhaps he might emerge better clued as to where he might beat a wholly more rewarding path.

The receptionist was expecting them. A quiet corner of the lounge had been arranged, to which they were shown, and in what seemed seconds Lady Clark was down from her suite. Silver haired, but neat and erect still, she exuded refinement and warmth. Both rose to shake hands.

"Mr Barnes, and....."

"Jeremy and Kate, Lady Clark. How do you do."

"Kate , Jeremy...... do call me Nolwen. How good of you both to come."

"And how good of you to give us this time.... and to have been so helpful to the youngsters."

"But what an interesting enquiry they brought," smiled Nolwen Clark, bidding them sit again before settling into the spare chair.

"And such an interesting riddle they came away with," countered Jeremy. The book was produced and the cover turned, the **MCLV** now ringed in pencil, and likewise the **Uncle Crouchback knows**. "It was quite a good attempt by them."

"As I did say, at the time."

"Adding that there could be aspects of their construction that I might be moved to query." Jeremy showed the page. "And, well, you can see there what I've circled."

"But not your reasons for doing so."

"Well if I may......"

"Do go on. Do."

"Firstly, if this was about the Plantagenet dynasty then I would have expected a scholar of Mr Connolly's standing to be more exact with his date."

"Good...... and down here," pointed Nolwen. "Crouchback....?"

"......for me, has nothing at all to do with Henry and Eleanor's illustrious line."

"But it will have something to do with something....... or with someone."

"Someone like Evelyn Waugh, the writer," stated Jeremy, watching closely for a reaction. A gentle nod urged him continue. "Connolly and Waugh could be said to have been of the same feather.....and the latter, he does crop up in '30s Kenya, when your mother of course was very much part of that scene. I've read that on his *Remote People* tour he actually stayed a while with Raymond de Trafford."

"Very good Jeremy," acknowledged Nolwen, glancing across to Kate and noting puzzlement. "He might not have told you, my dear, but this Raymond de Trafford briefly became my stepfather. Married and separated in the same year..... I would have been about nine, and living in France."

"So you never really knew him," said Kate.

"Only by reputation," said Nolwen.

"And that's been quite considerable," added Jeremy. "In this book we have him as the '*epitome of the remittance man*'...... always some scam on the go."

"Quite," agreed Lady Clark. "It was racket after racket. With one it was catching and selling gorillas to a Berlin zoo. Think of it."

"I'd rather not", shuddered Kate.

"And you needn't," said Jeremy, "for Crouchback, I would say, is about Waugh and the range of far more influential people he encountered, particularly during the war years. People such as Brendan Bracken, Churchill's crony in chief, with whom he was on first name terms. And then he drank and gambled with young Randolph, the pair ending up in Croatia together, in '44, along with Freddy Birkenhead. Make no mistake, as the court gossip went around our Evelyn would have heard it all...... and this, I think, is the message that Cyril Connolly was seeking to convey to you, Nolwen, and you alone."

"So why this riddling?" asked Kate.

"Because Cyril thought better of responding openly to Nolwen's very natural concern for her mother's reputation. The official line on the *White Mischief* case, the murder of Lord Erroll, holds that it was a crime of passion."

"But the accused was acquitted," said Nolwen, "and no one else charged."

"So the theorists sharpen their pencils," continued Jeremy, "and it's time then to stoke up a good smokescreen....."

".......the smuttier the better," said Nolwen, "and here's the ready made part for my mother. Whenever the story re-emerges there she is, getting dottier with every re-telling. For the scandal rags she'll sell copy, in the film she'll steal scenes."

"But Connolly knew a different story?" asked Kate.

"He had strong suspicions," said Jeremy, thinking back to Moyne's letter as he put the book on the arm of Kate's chair.

"But wasn't going public," said the nurse, picking it up.

"I think he was onto a top level conspiracy," continued the lecturer, "orchestrated by powerful and dangerous people."

"And rather than risking the grim consequences of their displeasure he chose discretion." Kate looked at the page. "But not total discretion."

"Would you agree with that, Nolwen?" asked Jeremy.

"I would," replied Lady Clark.

"Good, because now I'm going a little further. I'm moving on, into this actual book, *White Mischief* .... written after Connolly's death by his assistant, Mr James Fox. Now I suspect, Nolwen, that just as you received clues from Cyril, so too did Fox....... and he, like his mentor has declined to examine them openly."

"Similarly intimidated, you mean," said Kate.

"Yes, but look closely and maybe he is passing them on."

"An example?" said Nolwen.

"See this photograph of Connolly." The plate was found and shown. "Of the thousands available, why choose that..... taken in '74, just before his death, sitting in portrait next to his young son? This is no coward, says Fox. It's a man who fears more for his young lad's future than his own."

"Perhaps," conceded Nolwen, receptive certainly, but wanting more.

"And why, in an account that's generally so strong, should we get these moments of utter feebleness?"

"Such as?"

"When he considers the possibility of political assassination. It's dismissed in barely a paragraph...... on the word of Diana Mosley would you believe! Are we really expected to swallow that?"

"Good point again," conceded Nolwen. Jeremy was into his stride. Clearly he had more.

"Then we get this strange volte face from Lazarus Kaplan, Broughton's solicitor. Still alive in the '60s, he was initially more than willing to help Connolly with his investigation..... until suddenly losing his nerve. Something frightened him away, and he was dead within the year. There should be more on this, but Fox just leaves it."

"Inviting us to speculate," added Kate.

"This is it," said Jeremy. He glanced at Lady Clark. How would she take what he had for her now? "And the best one has to be the mysterious 'Nancy Wirewater'." He drew a deep breath. "Why this pseudonym, so oddly chosen and so strangely and uniquely used? It has to be an invitation to explore."

"And have you...... explored?" asked Nolwen, gently, but probably not believing for a moment that he had. Jeremy was ready primed though. She was about to have it straight.

"I am reliably informed, Lady Clark, that the name 'Nancy Wirewater' hides the identity of a woman called Phyllis Filmer, she being the established mistress of Lord Erroll before the arrival of the Broughtons. She lived at Shell House, Nairobi, her husband Percy at that time being the managing director of Shell East Africa. Both moved in diplomatic circles, and both made themselves available to British Intelligence. In fact some will say that Churchill's Special Operations Executive used Shell House for an East African base, and it was from here that the shooting of Erroll was planned and carried out, Phyllis having been instrumental in the plot."

"Impressive, Mr Barnes," said Nolwen, losing none of her composure. "Very impressive indeed. Can I ask who your informant might be?"

"This was in a letter, a private letter written by none other than Lord Moyne, at one time a father in law to the aforementioned Diana Mosley. By the time of the murder and the trial he was Colonial Secretary. He moved on to become Minister Resident in Cairo."

"Where he was shot by the Zionists in....."

".......in 1944," said Jeremy, "not long after he wrote this letter. It seems he was fearing for his life."

"And who was the recipient?"

"His niece, Patricia. She married Alan Lennox Boyd, who took the Colonial desk under Macmillan. When he was done with the Commons they came to live at Ince, just across the water in Cornwall. He did twenty years in the Lords, only to be knocked over by a car in a London street. More than four years ago, that was, and shortly afterwards the letter was thrown on to a bonfire. It was meant to burn....."

".......but didn't."

"And you Nolwen, and Kate too, now join the select few who know this....... so maybe I deserve to be told more about Henry and Eleanor, and this date we have, which I'm thinking might not be a date after all."

"Yes, maybe you do," conceded Lady Clark, but first I must firmly repeat what I told Chas and Sally. Nothing of this must get back to my stepson. While not a dangerous man himself, he is beholden to a few who most certainly are."

"We hear you," said Jeremy, and Nolwen was reaching towards Kate for the book, taking and turning it towards them, holding it lightly in both hands opening the cover. An index finger was then elegantly extended to mask the bracketed 'step backwards' and 'IST'.

"Connolly came by this in'73," she explained, "and only this, he said. What I'm concealing now were his own additions."

"So this hadn't entirely been of his devising," said Kate.

"Far from it..... as you see," confirmed Nolwen.

"And he was working with less than we," remarked Jeremy.

"Not really," said Nolwen, returning the book to the lecturer. "For what Cyril had been handed was a coded commentary on a hitherto unexplained scrape that he'd personally experienced early in the war, more than thirty years before."

"So it was first hand," remarked Kate, "and never forgotten."

"Never," confirmed Nolwen. "This was when he was running *Horizon*......"

"...... his famous literary review," chuckled Jeremy, "lampooned, of course, by Waugh."

"But not at the time, for newspaper and magazine space was then at a premium. Any kind of writer looking to nurture his or her public would also be looking to Cyril Connolly. He became quite an influential figure, receiving new work from all across the English speaking world, often brought by hand rather than mailed. One such contributor was Wystan Auden, the poet."

"Then living in America," said Jeremy.

"He was," continued Nolwen, "and a current project of his in 1940 was the libretto for an opera."

"A famous opera?" asked Kate.

"Not particularly," replied Lady Clark, "but the composer of the music, he was famous enough. The collaboration was with Benjamin Britten."

"*Grimes*," said Kate, "that came out towards the end of the war, and there's few more famous."

"But you're not familiar with any of his before that," said Jeremy. The nurse shook her head.

"So you've never heard of *Paul Bunyan*," said Nolwen. "Well don't for a minute think you're alone. After the first few performances in America it was shelved, the critics having been far from impressed. I think parts were given another airing just before Britten died, but for the thirty odd years between it was left to gather dust. Part of the problem with the thing was the constant chopping and changing it had to endure during the lead up to those first few full performances. Not all of this was to Auden's liking, apparently, and rather than seeing the pruned away fruits of his labour go untasted he arranged for an early draft to be brought across the Atlantic for Cyril's scrutiny. Connolly picked it up in Oxford….."

"…..where lived many a mutual friend," quipped Jeremy.

"And perhaps a few who might have been wary of the communication, for before he could return with it to London poor old Cyril was arrested and interrogated…… in a far from friendly manner. It seems that he was suspected of knowing how some hidden political meaning might be drawn from the work."

"That was encoded therein, you mean," said Jeremy. "Some kind of underhand subversive communication….."

"…….of which, at that time, there was much," continued Nolwen. "But Cyril successfully protests ignorance and innocence, both genuine, and he concludes that if there was anything in this then probably it lay with the music. It would be a combination of syllable with notation, the former relying on the latter for anything more than face value. People did say to him later that the idea wasn't new……that not long previously, in Europe, similar use had been made of the combined talents of Brecht and

Weill. Britten's settings of Auden's verse could be said to be an added rotor in a machine ready developed within the New York and London offices of the composer's publisher."

"But Connolly obviously managed to work something out before passing this to you," said Jeremy, returning to the book. "Who exactly did it come from?"

"It was given to him by Chester Kallman," replied Nolwen, "Auden's boyfriend of more than thirty years….. not always devoted, but towards the end very much so. They lived together in Austria, and Connolly went across, hoping to speak with Wystan before he died."

"On this particular matter?" asked Kate.

"So Cyril told me. For years, Auden, and Britten seemed to want to pretend that this piece of theirs had never happened. But Cyril had written, and an exchange began, and then came the invitation."

"But in the end this was too late," concluded Jeremy.

"By just a matter of hours. Chester was distraught, naturally, but he did manage to pass over Wystan's note."

"So the riddle comes initially from Wystan Hugh Auden….. and he is saying something about how his words were used," said Jeremy.

"And Chester helped Cyril on his way," said Nolwen.

"The '**H(II)R=Eleanor**' represents three individuals who stood together politically. We have a book-keeper and a married couple, and cleverly they have matching personas in the opera……"

"….. but not with their real names, of course," said Kate.

"**H(II)** represents Henry Morgenthau…..," said Nolwen

"…..Junior," joined Jeremy, getting the gist. "He headed the Treasury."

"And in the opera is one *Johnny Inkslinger*, appropriately a book keeper."

"Leaving **R=Eleanor**," said Kate, still none the wiser.

"Jeremy?" prompted Nolwen.

"Must be a married couple….. so why not Roosevelt and his wife, who was an Eleanor? Was there a couple in this opera?"

"There was. Unusually for Britten, the work features a successful courtship. *Hot Biscuit Slim* wins the hand of *Tiny*, and, together with that *Johnny Inkslinger*, they are very much the heroes of such drama as there is in what appears outwardly to be a somewhat feeble story….. the President, together with his feisty First Lady, and the Head of his Treasury Department."

"Wow," whispered Jeremy, "and is it implied that this tight knot of immense political power might have been under pressure? 1940 was an election year.... but I've always thought that one to have been a shoo-in."

"On domestic matters, yes, they made a formidable triumverate," agreed Nolwen, "but far less so when it came to foreign policy..... with an agenda having to be hidden, a see-saw ridden."

"Very Audenesque," quipped Jeremy, picking up on the couplet.

> " *'From gardens where we feel secure*
> *Look up and with a sigh endure ......' ,*"

offered Kate, meekly, as if not wanting to be left out of some kind of fun..... but drawing from Jeremy such a sudden glare that she could only feel that she'd somehow offended.

' *......the tyrannies of love,*' he mouthed to himself. How weird it was that he should be hearing that. He couldn't find, let alone say the words ..... and his amazed scrutiny could only be taken as censure. "Sorry," she blurted. "It's something I've sung, with the society, in Bodmin."

"And it's perhaps something to discuss later," intervened Nolwen Clark, "along with your homework, which is to see what you can make of Wystan's **MCLV**, for which you've already had Cyril's prompt." She was pointing now to the '**step backward**' beneath. The finger went then to the '**IST**' below the '**M(II)R= Eleanor**' "This one you now know..... *Inkslinger, Slim, Tiny.*"

"So, for that **MCLV**, there will likewise be an equivalent in the opera," checked Jeremy, "**step backward** being the clue to the clue."

"Take it away," directed Lady Clark, affirmatively re-stowing her pen. "Make something of that, and we'll then have a look at what Connolly drew from **Uncle Crouchback**. Tomorrow though," she sighed, "I must return to Saltwood."

"And we contact you how?" Jeremy almost implored.

"You'll find my address and number in '*Who's who*', but be careful when writing or speaking on the the phone. I'm more than happy to travel again, but I'd be trusting you to make such a meeting worthwhile." She rose, and so did Jeremy and Kate. "I must leave you now, but not before saying, with absolute sincerity, that I greatly look forward to meeting you both again."

They went for the bridge to cross back into Cornwall. The evening rush was building, the gathering traffic of Pennycomequick and Milehouse setting almost to a jam at Weston Mill. The lights, where once stood *The Camel's Head*, were against them. Away to their left a westbound train express clattered across the low bridge, girding itself for the short climb through St Budeaux, determindly on track for Brunel's masterful leap of faith.

Jeremy was clearly pleased, but thoughtful so far, rather than talkative. Kate knew better than to disturb. He would speak when ready and, switching off the car radio, this was now.

"Kate," he began.

"Your thoughts…..?"

"I was weighing that metaphor she used, the political see-saw to be ridden……"

"…… linked as it was with the agenda to be hidden."

"So how did she mean with that see-saw? What kind of activity is that?"

"Well you have a partner," said Kate,"you have an end each, and you take turns……giving and taking., pushing and riding, up and down."

"So it's a trade off….. endeavour for pleasure. The reciprocal exchange being negotiated through the medium of simple physics.

"Yes, if you want to make it sound complicated, I guess it is."

"So where can this notion of a hidden agenda fit in?"

"You tell me, Mr Philosopher."

"I don't think it can, because you're either on one side or the other."

"Going up, or going down," added Kate.

"Exactly…… so there's no scope for bluff, unless….."

"Unless?"

"Unless you're in the park on your own," said Jeremy, "or you're the last to arrive of three…… and then how might use choose to ride the see saw?"

"Standing over the middle," answered Kate. "holding the balance. And if you're good enough on your feet you can bring in something of a concealed agenda by keeping the others guessing a little…… as to how hard they need to push or how quickly they'll drop."

"So where as at the ends it's a game of negotiation, for a smart operator in the middle it can be a one of manipulation. And this, I suspect is what Nolwen could have been alluding to. President FDR, his wife Eleanor, and Henry Morgenthau at the Treasury made a powerful anti fascist triumvirate. Once in the war they were in with a will, pushing all the way for an unconditional surrender. Make no mistake, the victory in the west was their victory. This said, it took Pearl Harbor get them truly fired up. Before then, as the low countries and France were over-run, and then the Balkans, there were strong voices in America, and particularly in the State Department, that advocated stepping in with a negotiated peace plan. Despite forcing through Lend Lease provisions the three in the White House were not having it all their way. Running counter to the economic support being sent to this country was that being channelled, for instance, to Vichy France...... in open defiance of our Naval blockades."

"So this other group of letters, Jeremy, the **MCLV**, you think it might represent some of the proponents of that alternative programme."

"If I can get down to the library in Torpoint I'll see if I can't check out a few initials, my premise being that in 1940 and early '41 there was a delicately poised balance of power in the States, and that to a degree this was being monitored and even manipulated from this side of the Atlantic, Ben Britten having a role in that operation."

"People here though would have been backing the White House, surely."

"Well nowadays this is what popular history would have us believe," said Jeremy. "At the time, though, there were many who despaired of America joining the war, saying instead that our best hope for survival lay in fracturing the pact between Germany and Russia, the deal that saw the end of pre war Poland, and provoked our declaration of war agaist Hitler."

They were over the bridge, through Saltash, across the Lynher, and climbing now to Landrake. In less than ten minutes they would be at Trerulefoot, and Jeremy was wanting to shift the topic. Something else had emerged from the afternoon's foray to The Duke of Cornwall. He was loathe to let it pass.

"That snatch of poetry you gave us in the hotel, Kate ......can I hear it again?"

Kate obliged.

" '......*from gardens where we feel secure*
Look up and with a sigh endure ......' "

" ...... *The tyrannies of love.*', " finished Jeremy. "So where did you get that?"

"Audenesque, you said...... and that's about as much of Auden that I know. It's part of a song that Britten includes in his *Spring Symphony*. And with that work you have about as much of Britten that I know. James could tell you more."

"Were I to ask him, which I'm not." Jeremy was emphatic. "He's become far too much of a worry for you, that I can see. Let's leave him to his submarine, and Alan too.....good idea?"

"Good idea."

"Right, because I've seen those words before. They were in a letter that had been kept with that same one I spoke of in the hotel......"

".......with that written by a Lord....."

"Lord Moyne, who was strongly of the opinion that the murdered Lord Erroll had been a victim of a political assassination. And while I wasn't saying this in the hotel, I can add now that his goes on to state that this murder was part of a wider operation named HIGHLAND CLEARANCE overseen by a character codenamed GUSTAVE."

"And the link between this and that song.....?"

"For the moment, only that Moyne's letter and that written by a young Naval Officer, one Roger Burney, have for some reason, best known to the Viscountess Boyd, been kept together. What you do confirm for me, though, is that Burney was killed in action. The letter says that he knows Britten and Pears well, and should he be killed there was agreement from them that his chosen verses would be put to music."

"Fascinating," said Kate, "for I've heard James speak of Burney. He says he was lost with the *Surcouf*, that submarine again. He knew about the friendship with Britten, this from the fact that the sailor was listed amongst those to whom the *War Requiem* was dedicated." The nurse looked thoughtful. They were passing through Tideford. Jeremy needed to concentrate on the road. "That HIGHLAND CLEARANCE operation," continued Kate. "Might this have been concerned to get Russia and Germany at each others' throats? This is what actually happened, I know."

"Yes, and it did get us off the hook," agreed Jeremy. "But what do you have to link *Barbarossa* with HIGHLAND CLEARANCE?"

"That song, and the way it ends," answered Kate.

"With the '*tyrannies of love*'?" Jereny was puzzled.

"But there's more, isn't there?"

"Is there? I didn't know," said Jeremy. They were passing beneath the railway bridge now, Kernow Mill was in sight. "How does it go on?"

Kate was ready;

"And gentle do not care to know ,
Where Poland draws her eastern bow,
What violence is done;
Nor ask what doubtful act allows
Our freedom in this English house,
Our picnics in the sun."

Jeremy offered no immediate response. "What do you hear in that?" asked the nurse as they rolled in next to her car.

"It's a 'keep clear', a 'don't ask.' It's the voice of a manipulator. His hands are dirty and he's saying 'avert your eyes for a moment and just be grateful that I can steer us through this mess.' "

"So the shooting of a Peer of the Realm...... a doubtful act perhaps?"

"By anyone's standards, Kate. We could be on to something here. Britten is certainly saying more than he was asked to by Burney, and that was in.....?"

"Spring Symphony...... '49."

"And eight years earlier, when Erroll was shot, he could have been staking out the American political landscape in *Paul Bunyan.* We need to crack that first block of letters,";

"**MCLV**," obliged Kate, "with (**Step backwards**) being our clue."

"Who might help us, then?" asked Jeremy, "apart, that is, from James Busbridge?"

"Enid!" chimed Kate, climbing from the car. She was on her feet now and ready to close the door. "Of course, you can come down and meet Enid. If any one knows the score then it's her. I'll set up a meeting for the three of us. James needn't know..... and you wouldn't tell Alan, would you?"

"Not if you don't want me to, Kate. I'll phone"

He had to let her go. She needed to be on her way. But this, indeed, was progress, reflected Jeremy, leaving the carpark himself now to return eastward, back again on the Torpoint road...... and progress made with Kate, independently of Alan Grigson and James Busbridge.

But a curious man is never to be found short of a lead of his own to pursue, and had Jeremy lingered at Kernow Mill he might have recognised a car seen once before, the previous week, as its owner had set off from Mount Edgcumbe with Kate and youngsters as passengers. Almost certainly, he would have then scouted the store, with its tea shop at the back, and there at a table found James Busbridge in close conversation with one who would have been cordially introduced to him as Mr Tony Cross.....father of Chas, and diving instructor to Sally.

But today, with the lecturer happily on his way, James and Tony were able to continue undisturbed.

"So yes," stressed the latter, "while my son has held this for more than a year, I was made aware of it only yesterday evening." He tapped on the photocopied fragment that, save for the minor nick off the margin by the tear, completed a map which previously they had only half known. The uneven line of the tear, registering faintly on the copy paper brought the two images to a convincing match. "We were over at Wacker when he produced it...... and I was to learn that it had been given him by his grandmother, just before she died."

"That's your mother," checked Busbridge."And, hitherto, he'd kept it from you at her express wish."

"A last wish," acknowledged Cross, "which he respects...... until yesterday's sudden change of mind."

"How is this explained?"

"He heeds wise counsel, and, on careful consideration, is led to the conclusion that had she lived to see this matching up of a complete map then she would of probably swung away from the strictly preventative line taken against her boastful child, who been told far too much at fat too young an age, turning into an adult Walter Mitty,"

"Clearly something you are not."

"Thank you, Jim, for that opinion....but this," Cross tapped on the chart, "this now amounts to a persuasive contemporary source, a document that begins to verify a tale which previously verged on the risible."

"So the story was remembered by you, despite your mothers efforts....."

"And I've always been fine about it.....she needn't have feared as much as she did."

"So this fully vindicated 'wise counsel' was from ....?"

"Megan, she calls herself, the old herbalist camping at Wacker, and now it's all out between myself and my son then I am happy for you to have as much as the detail as she's had from him."

"So tell on, do," urged the curious man.

"I, Tony Cross, grew up as an illegitimate child, this at a time when such a status carried no little stigma. It didn't help that I carried the name Anton. It was too unusual, certainly for a primary school in downtown St Judes. Why Anton? I asked my mother..... and she informs tender young me that my father had been an Admiral in the French Navy."

"The Free French?"

"Yes."

"So it would have been *the* Admiral."

"Muselier, yes, but back then it was simply 'an Admiral.'"

"Something you were delighted to repeat at school."

"Naturally...... only to provoke doubled derision, of course. And this was felt to be reducing my chances of winning a place at Grammar School."

"So you were re-styled as an Anthony."

"I was, and this humbler version of me did pass his eleven plus and moved on to join a fresh set of fellow pupils who were never to know me as anything other than Tony Cross. If I was to fit, and progress, then plainly this was what I had to be."

"So the French Admiral story was dropped," said Busbridge.

"At school, certainly, and between my mother and myself it was, just like the *Surcouf*, never to resurface."

"But likewise again, not totally forgotten. Your natural interest in your parentage becomes a closet fascination, and one perhaps sharpened by your mother's discouragement. It wasn't just treasure hunting that took you to the French Naval archive."

"And I find now that she, rather than trying to forget all this herself, was attempting to discretely preserve it for the next generation."

"And succeeding in this, it would appear." Busbridge glanced down at the map. "But you, Tony, did you actually come to the name 'Muselier' when he was still alive?"

"I did, before I left Grammar School. And I remember then when he died......taking to his grave that old question mark over his loyalty to Charles de Gaulle. You will be acquainted with the General's war memoir, and his confused account of my father being thrown in to Brixton Prison......."

"...... following vague allegations of a traitorous approach to Vichy with a proposed deal. It was said to have involved a hand-back of the *Surcouf*."

"Not the kind of thing one likes to see written about one's father......"

"......and certainly not the kind of thing you would have wanted to raise with your abandoned mother......"

"...... any more than she might then have been inclined to raise it with me. But do bear in nind, Jim, that she and I never agreed to not talk about the war. It was an arrangement, yes mutually observed......"

"....... but individually determined, by two distinct mindsets," added Busbridge.

"And both, in the view of Megan, the old healer down at Wacker, are now totally obsolete. My mother as good as admitted this, she argues, by confiding in Chas as she lay dying. She'd accepted that if the story was to be kept alive then it had to be properly shared."

"And already the pooling bears fruit," said Busbridge. "But I don't quite see yet where this Megan woman comes from."

"Clearly she's won the confidence of young Chas."

"Yes....... but how?"

"The link is the girl, Sally, our pupil at the diving centre. He seems to be growing quite fond of her."

"Enough to confide that deathbed tale.... and this fondness is reciprocated, I trust?"

"Looks that way, sounds that way," confirmed Cross.

"So this old Megan......?"

"....... is a Wacker perennial. Sally has known her for a good three years now, and she told Chas this after it emerged that it had been the woman's companions who'd stumbled on that recently found skeleton, the one said to be dating from the early war years."

"I went to the burial, " said Busbridge, "up at Rame Church, and I think this Megan was there. There were two companions, much younger, both Africans."

"That would have been them."

"Also, I've a feeling I could have met your son Chas and his girl....... on the same day, but not at the funeral. This was down at Mount Edgcumbe. They were with a chap called Jeremy, a lecturer...... he being a friend of a of a friend of a friend. It was all by chance and....."

"........and you weren't as attentive as you're now wishing you should have been," smiled Cross.

"This is so," admitted Busbridge. "and it wasn't for lack of opportunity either. When we set off back to Bodmin your lad and his girl begged a lift as far as Wacker."

"Yes," nodded Cross,"and this would have been subsequent to my Chas having first sent the girl down there on her own...... he wanting to know more about that body, and thinking that Sally might be the best one to enquire, she having become acquainted with the woman over two or three summers." The diver was a convincing liar. "But the use of that familiarity in fact backfires. Megan is perceptive. She detects in Sally a changed manner, the manner of an edgy emissary."

"And this is where Megan suggests that Chas be brought before her, so that he might be told directly what he wants to know..... which is what?"

"About items," dissembled the father, "clues that might have been found with the bones..... metal tags, buttons, coins, that sort of thing."

"The sort of stuff not mentioned in the papers, or in radio and T.V. reports. I wondered about that too. Could she help at all?"

"She could, but having heard Chas's tale about his grandmother and me, and seen that other part to the map, she insisted on my presence too. I went across with my car in which I happened to carry a copy of the archive sourced part of the map."

"I get it..... and when you suddenly produce a matching half for your mother's part, now Chas's, then the concilliation that the old woman was attempting to propagate is ready to spontaneously flower."

"And I've got a copy of the whole for you Jim......save that is for the little snip just here that Megan took off the original, Cross pointed. Busbridge leant forward for a closer look.

"I see, yes."

"For the moment, though, I'd rather you kept it under your hat. It was agreed in that caravan that nothing said there was to be repeated to anyone else outside."

"Of course," acknowledged Busbridge, well flattered, and also lulled.......for as well as dissembling on how the two youngsters and he had been summoned to Wacker, Cross was purposefully omitting any mention of his having been told about the discovered gold; where it had been found, and then hidden, and where it now lay. All of this he now

340

knew, but for the moment wouldn't divulge.

It counted for nothing that he was fundamentally an honest man...... evasive occasionally but seldom untruthful. Again it was that gold, ever corrosive to scruple. To lie was suddenly so easy.

Such a find just *had* to be kept secret and, if there were pangs of compunction then he had a ready salve in the shape of that map. He was sharing this, and, if not of the same crown jewel material, it was by no means dross. Sop, maybe, but it could be a beguiling one nonetheless, and made all the more so by this Megan woman with her suggestion that...... but this was something that could be shared in a moment. He would see first what this curious man was making of it by himself.

"So now we have the full chart, Jim, where are we?
St Pierre and Miquelon? Can we confirm this?"

"No, not there..... I've looked at maps at home. This is somewhere else," shrugged Busbridge, "and anywhere really."

The diver was now leaning in closely. Their heads almost touched "The St Pierre is complete now, and see. What we said might be the coast, tailing towards the bottom, now continues upwards before wrapping around to come down again, over here to the right."

"Shaping either a headland or a bay," remarked Busbridge. "And the significant new label within this feature is this **Mt P** .... which signifies what, though, Tony? A landscape feature? A ship or a light, off the coast?"

"Listen to this, Jim," the diver was ready, "and then, when you get home, get those maps out again. The old woman's an expert on thorn based remedies...... right?"

"Right."

"And she's travelled Europe, and she knows what goes down well in different countries, countries including France."

"Big country, France...... a lot of coast."

"So the stuff can vary region by region, soil by soil."

"Like their wine does," added Busbridge. "some areas producing a distinct flavour."

"Exactly, and she tells us there's one particular district of France which in the thorn trade is totally unique. The bushes grow in limited number under a tropical clime on a freshly laid volcanic soil, and their fruit is known to her fellow apothecaries as the Pelee berry........ so named after the mountainside from which the roots draw their curative power."

"So 'Mount Pelee', she's suggesting, for **Mt P**," said Busbridge, "making this side land."

"And if I said St Pierre could therefore be a port, and at one time a capital city, before its destruction by the Mount Pelee eruption....... you should be able to tell me, Jim, which distant part of France this is."

"Martinique, of course. Martinique...... and over here, these shaded parts mark two stretches of coastal water off St Pierre. They might have been mined during the war, part of the our Naval blockade."

"But there is a gap," prompted Cross.

"Which could be a way through, deep enough at high tide to cover a submarine, shallow enough at low tide to preclude the laying of mines. So what about where it says **BEARN**?"

"The *Bearn* perhaps," offered Cross. "The Vichy carrier impounded by the blockade. They could move her around the coast of the island, if nowhere else. And look, in this position, aligned according to that arrow, she will appear from dead ahead to be exactly mid way between the cross for what must be the summit of Pelee and this cross for St Pierre..... probably a church tower or the like."

"Yes," said Busbridge, resparked, "and see where the sharp end of the *Bearn* points....... straight for the gap between the shaded areas. At a certain time the ship might have been thus positioned so as to provide a navigation aid....."

"..... for a submarine attempting to run through the mines into Martinique. And once behind the *Bearn* the sub has found cover. Now who would have wanted to send the *Surcouf* into Martinique, Mr Busbridge?"

"The Vichy people. Like we, when fearing the worst in '40, sent gold to Canada and South Africa, so the French sent much of theirs to Dakar and Martinique. Money talks, but as you know from the Edinburgh loss, the words are empty when the bullion can't be shifted....... hence our blockade. Vichy wanted it out, and either back to France or at least into a friendly mainland bank. Leaving aside her fighting capability, the *Surcouf* looked very much the boat for the job."

"Worth her weight in gold," quipped the diver, "quite literally. But they had to capture her first, or persuade her to defect, and we know she did neither."

"We can't be sure that she didn't defect on her final voyage, Tony. Her end, early in '42, was as unexplained as that of the *Narval* fourteen months before."

"But we do know that fourteen months before she didn't then follow the *Narval*, as this map suggests she might have been invited to. If this was what the local rendezvous was about then it sounds like my father resisted the suggestion. This is what I want to believe."

"And why not....... but this leaves us struggling to explain why he should have put in Brixton," said Busbridge, "and how he then managed to win such a grand apology for this inconvenience. As for the *Narval*, if that boat was genuinely bent on defection, why did she not then steer straightway for a Vichy port? Plenty of questions yet, you see."

So may be it's as well that you know nothing about Sally and Chas finding that gold, thought Cross, all smugness, and all unaware of the ambush that awaited. In his excitement, he'd forgotten that this meeting had been arranged, at Busbridge's behest, a whole afternoon before his own fruitful introduction to Megan at Wacker. Had he remembered this then he may have been better prepared when, with a glance at his watch, James Busbridge proceeded to raise a topic of his own.

"And before we finish on this, here's something else," he said, flicking back through a tattered notepad. Looking over a sequence of roughly compiled, part scratched-out lists....... research, shopping, earlier research, and shopping the time before. "Somewhere...... yes here." Busbridge turned the pad, pointing. "This name and address...... I thought it sensible not to mention it over the phone. It has come to my knowledge that there might be a connection with the map."

"Where did you get this? How could you have known?"

"Tell me first. Do you know of any connection, and if so, then for how long?"

"Only since......"

".....yesterday evening?"

"Since yesterday evening," confirmed Tony Cross. "So did the kids say to you......?"

"They've said nothing...... although my friend Kate who was with me when we were introduced at Mount Edgcumbe, she did notice the name, with an address, on an old envelope that Chas had with him. But it only registered with her because she had seen both before."

"Where?"

"In a medical record. I was going to alert you to this because we'd at least worked out that Chas was your son. Why he should have been carrying it was then far from clear, but now I would hazard that the part of the chart held by your mother came briefly under the expert scrutiny of that man, Philip Dalton."

"Very briefly….. so Chas was told by his gran. Hardly so much as an hour, it stayed, before she thought better of leaving it……."

"……. and returned to the shop, to be given it back in that second hand envelope."

"This is the tale that's been handed down," confirmed Chas's father. "and, apparently, that very night, the whole family were killed. There was an air raid. A bomb penetrated to the basement. Nothing was left, a direct hit…."

"……from a stray bomb," added Busbridge. "The rest of that night's damage being concentrated in the Millbay and Stonehouse areas, on the other side of the Hoe. I'm not discounting murder. In the short time he held that map, Dalton might well have placed an enquiry…..he would have had contacts over at Drake, the Dockyard naval base."

"Where someone might have pressed an alarm button," Cross added grimly, "leaving my mother to perhaps vaguely suspect……."

"…… and go to ground, Tony, just in case."

"But some forty odd years later she's thinking the coast is clear, and her grandson can have what she'd kept so close for so long."

"But is it?" posed Busbridge.

"Is what what?" Cross wanted to be sure as to Busbridge's precise meaning.

"The coast…… is it really clear, even forty odd years on? Your proposed trawl along the inshore waters of Panama, and the opposition it provoked ……someone tossed in your connection with the *Edinburgh*, who exactly? Local outrage, you can say……but all of it? You needn't get paranoid but……"

"……. it could bear looking at again," nodded Cross. "I shall."

"In the meantime," said Busbridge, proudly, "you can hear how the name Philip Dalton came to my attention, in the course of my search for a long lost Wrickleman, the youngest of the three brothers Wakeham …… and it is with the full three that I must start."

*

(xxxii) Eamon visits Quarry Cottage

And as the second cup for each was poured at Kernow Mill, so Eamon Carroll was being handed his first mug at not so far away Quarry Cottage. Unannounced, and made alone, the call on McDaid was, for all of this, not entirely unexpected. That chance encounter in Wivelscombe tunnel had brought to Declan a unique understanding of the man's predicament..... and to the fortunate Carroll, of course, a unique appreciation of his rescuer.

"To begin with," explained Eamon, "my joining with Grigson seemed as much a step forward for him as it was for me. He was so anxious to introduce me to his friend Jeremy, and we were the three of us together, of course, when you invited us here."

"But now, increasingly, there is this feeling of being put to the margin," said McDaid. Carroll nodded. "And you must feel slighted, understandably, for whatever concern that Alan might have for his job, and however specialist might be the input from his pal, it's only for you that this whole shooting match has a been just that..... as I was made only too vividly aware."

"But it's not that together they're cutting me out.......more, it's that as individuals they're being drawn away from me by their separate lines of inquiry."

"And they're expecting a simlar autonomy from you," suggested Declan, shrewdly. "Might this be why you're here?"

"Not consciously," replied Eamon, after some thought.

"So tell me how the two buddies have diverged, Eamon."

"Grigson, the watcher, he's been quite taken with those wartime bones found across at Portwrinkle. It's been on the radio....."

".....and in the local press. I did see something."

"Well he went to the burial......"

".....over at Rame...."

".... and there, by chance, he met an old friend, a nurse, and she introduced him to the companion who'd brought her along. A fellow called Jim."

"And he was just curious?"

"More than that...... he'd come in pursuance of a strong interest in a wartime submarine, a French vessel. The *Surcouf* it was called. There's another body in that graveyard, that said to be of a youngster, lost while while fishing out of Portwrinkle late in 1940, on a night when that sub could have been setting out on voyage to Scotland."

"So this fellow, he's thinking there might have been an incident..... an incident that perhaps claimed two lives?"

"Yes......but possibly no."

"Possibly no?" echoed McDaid. "You've lost me."

"Possibly," emphasised Eamon, "we have here a case of mistaken identity. Our man Jim is out to prove that the youngster who never returned from his fishing trip is, in fact, still alive."

"So who would have been laid in that grave?" asked McDaid.

"Someone of similar age and size, a blitz victim perhaps, disfigured and decomposed beyond any certain recognition....."

".....that just happened to float ashore?" Declan was sceptical.

"Unless things had been so arranged," countered Eamon, "and remembering how close I was to being the dead meat over in that tunnel......"

"...... then why should we, of all people, think to dimiss such an idea. I can see the appeal in all of this for Alan Grigson. And this man's name.....?"

"Busbridge, James Busbridge."

"And he thinks he's found someone who might be the lost boy.....?"

"In the big psychiatric hospital down at Bodmin, with an altered name, and in a kind of a permanent state of shock. He doesn't speak. He can't, and this could be from the lasting trauma of that night out on the water. It's as if his memories have been locked away in a box and the key lost, perhaps deliberately."

"But, being the psychiatrist that he is, our Dr Busbridge is prepared to attempt to pick that lock, and hopefully restore the closed down power of recall."

"You're on the right track, Declan......"

".....except...."

".... except that James Busbridge is no psychiatrist, in fact he's no doctor."

"And not even a nurse."

"Not even a fellow nurse."

"But he was with a nurse, Eamon, so...."

"....so one could say that he was working with a measure of

clinical insight. This Kate, she works at that hospital, the St Lawrence Hospital in Bodmin. She's freshly trained in this branch of medicine, and would probably admit to being a little naïve in her enthusiasm….."

"……making hers a somewhat modest measure of competence," said McDaid. "So wouldn't you say this to be a little irregular, to have a nurse encouraging a lay person to dabble in clinical matters?"

"I put this same question to that Jeremy, for he's known this Kate for even longer than Alan, apparently, and yes, he was puzzled too…… enough to quietly raise this with her."

"And…..?"

"Jeremy is informed, just as quietly, that she herself is far less happy with the situation than she was allowing herself to appear….."

"…… when in Busbridge's company," added McDaid, "Implying that she is in some way bound…… that she might even be under a degree of duress?"

"Not quite, there's nothing she's being made to do. She could choose to walk away……but having made her error she wants to be placed so as to mitigate any fallout."

"And that error?"

"Was to have underestimated this Busbridge fellow. What she's done, is to allow him to groom her to his advantage. She hadn't realised it, but right from the off this man knew exactly what he was looking for, and exactly the kind of helpmate that was required……"

"……and this was her."

"Quite……the soft touch novice, whose rash enthusism could cause her to overlook basic principle. He cultivates a social relationship and, when luck gives him his break, there she is …."

"…… in the right place at the right time," prompted McDaid.

"His milch cow….. having fed that enthusiasm, he now squeezes for profit. And though to her, at the time, the yield of just a name seemed such a small thing, such an innocuous piece of confidential information, suddenly it shapes as a link in what might prove to have been quite a momentous chain of events…..."

"……meaning publicity, with, for her, a high embarrassment potential. So what can she do, Eamon, having already sold the pass?"

"As I said, Declan, she stays with it, monitoring for any adverse repercussion, looking to nip it in the bud. And this is her position now. I suspect she might have hoped for better from Grigson, on meeting him at the burial. She'd known him before, you see."

"But hadn't realised the extent of the trouble he too has found himself in, is this what you mean?"

"I do, for rather than being open to her plight, as hoped, she instead finds him pre-occupied by his own," explained Eamon, "and perhaps Busbridge could be the one to help him solve this, he thinks."

"Such is the enchantment of that tale of his, this submarine mystery."

"It does tend to ensnare," sighed Connors, "I've felt the tug myself...... and of course Kate, she suddenly feels out numbered."

"So naturally she is turning to the other friend, this Jeremy, before it becomes three against one. Is there a chance of them finding each other useful......what do you think?"

"I'm not sure, and I don't think even Jeremy is. What I can see, though, is that there was a time when they knew each other very well indeed. A split occurred, and maybe this was something to do with Alan, maybe not. Whatever, both would now appear to be ready to leave Busbridge and Grigson to each other."

"With a view to refinding the lost togetherness? *Misery re-acquaints women with estranged bedfellows*', one of the bard's best lines."

"On that, we'll have to wait and see," smirked Eamon, warmed by this snipe at Shakespeare...... the inalienable right of any Irishman.

"So this name that the nurse has let slip..... is it now common knowledge amongst the five of you?"

"I've not heard it," shrugged Connors, "but then, I've not asked."

"Has Barnes, do you know?"

"I don't."

"So what do you know?"

"That the patient in question hasn't always been at St Lawrence. That there was a previous institution where, according to the confidential record, he went by a different name."

"The name on the youngster's gravestone?"

"Nothing so obvious, I'm afraid, for behind the first mask it appears there might be a second. The previous name is verified by a birth certificate, and this naturally lies on his file, but on examination this document reveals itself to be a replacement, issued from the National Registry early in 1941. Busbridge suspects a switched identity."

"By switched you mean a one for one, that this birth certificate might properly go with the remains that were buried at that time, over at Rame."

"That's his theory. He wants to believe that this patient truly is Norman Wakeham."

"Norman Wakeham," repeated Declan, "the boy whose name is carved on the stone...........who is now grown to a man physically, but not mentally, the young mind having suffered this long term damage. Nice theory, Eamon, but, sadly, one lacking in proof."

"At the moment, Declan, but perhaps not for long. Forensic evidence could be forthcoming. One of the older brothers was traced to Tasmania, where Busbridge has a cousin..... this is the Peter Bright you might have heard of in the news. Before the brother died Bright obtained a sample of the man's hair, and since, on one of his many visits back to this country he has placed this with a research lab, I think in Cambridge, specialising in advanced molecular biology."

"DNA science," said McDaid, hoisting his eyebrows.

"Sounds like it," continued Connors, "and now a bloodstain left by this unfortunate in St Lawrence has been sent up by Busbridge for comparison......"

"..... and possible matching. So the results fom the lab will be eagerly awaited."

"Certainly by Busbridge, and Grigson, and with some trepidation by Kate...... but Jeremy, he prefers to plough his own separate furrow, this very much in the direction pointed by that epistle of yours, bequeathed by Lord Moyne."

"Good for him, and good for the rest of you. You wouldn't want to be carrying too many of your eggs in the one basket. So how goes it then for ploughman Barnes, is he turning himself some good rich soil, or is it stiff and stoney?"

"A promising tilth, from the sound of it."

"He had this idea," remembered Declan. "He would use a kid to get beneath Alan Clark's radar....."

".....yes, and this seems to have paid off handsomely. The Minister's stepmother happened to be in town. An interview was arranged for Jeremy and Kate together, and I gather that the old duchess didn't disappoint."

"Sounds promising," said McDaid. "We're going to have to get them down here. I like the way these pairings have developed. There's balance, and there's tension..... a productive combination."

"Except that I'm left floating between."

"You are." McDaid reached to slap a firm hand on his guest's shoulder. "So I think perhaps you might help me."

"By continuing to keep you briefed on their progress?"

"More than that, Eamon. Busbridge and Grigson look set to discover more about that submarine, its business in these local waters, and the characters caught up therein. Jeremy meanwhile, with Kate's assistance, his inclination is to explore a wider historical context. As you say...... the tissue sampling as one route and Moyne's letter the other."

"And you regret revealing this?"

"Not at all, Eamon.......indeed, far from it. But for both, these journeys are into separate pasts from where it is unlikely they can return with any information on my erstwhile neighbour, and tenant, and friend, Mr 'Peg' Willis."

Easing himself from his chair McDaid moved to his solid mantle shelf clock to lift the A4 envelope dicretely propped against its back. He opened the flap to slide out an unfolded torn off sheet of greaseproof paper. The ink was clear. Here was a carefully and firmly traced map, probably taken from a book. It was passed down to Connors, still seated .

"Take a look at this."

A firmly printed heading stood out clearly.

"*The Bridgehead over the River Orne*," read Eamon, audibly. "With this river flowing in a north easterly direction before looping into the sea here at the town of Ouistreham, and next to it is cut the Caen Canal, making this Normandy, in '44, on D Day, for to the west of the estuary we have the Brigade Landing Beach."

"We do, and some three miles inland a single road seperately bridges both river and canal, joining the villages of Benouville and Ranville. While not marked as such on this map, from that day forward the canal crossing, the one nearest to the coast, became known as 'Pegasus' Bridge......"

"......because it was captured by those bastard Paras," spat Eamon, deeply versed as he was in Derry's Bloody Sunday.

"It was, and had this map been taken from an Airborne Division account of the action then the 'Pegasus' label would surely have been here."

"But it wasn't, Declan, so......?"

"So I'm thinking that it was traced from an account given by a beach landing soldier, a member of the Commando Brigade which fought it's way inland to support the lightly equipped glider and 'chute dropped troops who'd taken the crossing with their pre dawn surprise attack."

"And should this matter?" wondered Eamon.

"To the person who found and traced this map, yes, I think it did."

"You speak of this 'Peg', your tenant next door."

"Who as well as being a neighbour, also became a close friend. 'Peg' Willis was a veteran of Normandy, one of the glider borne troops who took that bridge."

"A former Para!" said Carroll, the three words combining outrage, distaste, and puzzlement. "A friend?" The contradiction had rankled since his first visit here.

"Hence Peg," repeated McDaid, offering no hint of apology. "He pencil traced this three years ago, at the library in Saltash. Transferring it to proper paper, and inking it in, he made a presentable little map which, after his radio broadcast, he had framed."

"And you don't have that."

"It disappeared when he did," McDaid confirmed. "But I did find this tucked away, which I've inked over similarly."

"Was he a member up at the library," asked Connors.

"He wasn't....... infact he considered himself 'word blind'."

"Dyslexic," spat Eamon. "A common complaint amongst the Paras..... why else would they be given written rules of engagement?"

"So very rarely would he be found in any library," continued the host, ignoring the emerald bile. "On this occasion, though, he was seeking to prepare himself for that radio interview. *Plymouth Sound* were doing a forty years on from D Day programme, and with a map he felt he might better explain his role to the presenter and his fellow guest."

"And you tuned to that broadcast?"

"I did, and Peg was good."

"So the map did help."

"Certainly..... and possibly too well."

"I don't understand," Connors looked again at the document. "Explain."

"The fellow guest for that programme was Alan Clark MP."

"Him again, the Cabinet Minister...."

"..... and also, as a military historian, a considerable authority on

351

Second World War. Naturally, Clark took a very close interest in Peg's account, the taking and holding of these Orne crossings. The action enabled the Commando brigades fighting inland from the beaches to establish themselves a perimeter on the ridge to the east of the river and canal."

"Quite a famous tale, I believe," said Connors, at last coming off the Foyle.

"And, this time, interestingly embellished, as Peg referred to the drive off the beaches to the bridges and beyond as an 'OPERATION HIGHLAND CLEARANCE', a task to be performed under the leadership of one code named 'GUSTAVE'. Peg had picked this much up from the overheard ramblings of a fellow casualty, an officer, possibly GUSTAVE himself."

"But he'd never heard of those code names before...."

"....or since."

"But you had, Declan. In '83, a year before the broadcast, and in the totally different context of Moyne's letter to his niece. You must have been quite......"

"........ astounded, Eamon, extremely so. But I say nothing, and then shortly afterwards Peg vanishes."

"Leaving you to wonder if the Minister might have been equally astonished, to the extent of being positively alarmed......"

"...... dangerously alarmed even," whispered McDaid. "For I've read plenty since on the OVERLORD landings, the capture of Caen, and the subsequent breakout, and in all of this I've never once seen any mention of HIGHLAND CLEARANCE being used as a code word for any aspect of the campaign....."

"...... and no mention either of any GUSTAVE."

"Nothing....... but that casualty, he knew something."

"And was Peg able to identify him? Do we know if he lived even..... or will his bones be amongst the thousands that lie between Caen and the coast?"

"One of the Brigade Padres was brought in, Peg had explained. A young Catholic Priest this one, for it was to administer the Latin Rites."

"So it must have been touch and go for the casualty."

"Yes, but occasionally a few of the stronger ones would survive."

"So if this one did, and we could find him....."

".....we might be finding GUSTAVE, the high executioner

mentioned by Moyne, who presided over HIGHLAND CLEARANCE, and who could, conceivably, lead us to Peg Willis."

"Or have our heads to go with the rest he's been collecting," said Carroll, grimly, and shuddering as he thought back to the dark barrelled tunnel and its lethal whining lead. "So you're saying, Declan, that a war wounded GUSTAVE might have survived, to be still alive and active now, with a concern that Ince might be a chink in the armour that he has built and maintained around HIGHLAND CLEARANCE."

"And with Peg's words on the radio, and his nearness to Ince being relayed to him by Alan Clark, he might have thought to have had him swiftly removed."

"So we tread very carefully."

"A point I emphasised when you came here last, from the pub. Guard that map closely. For all Grigson's interest in French submarines and the Wricklemen, and all his lecturer friend's fascination with Alan Clark's stepmother, it's this that might offer the best lead as to the real identity of the sinister GUSTAVE."

"So did you check at the library, where Peg went."

"I looked in all they had on Normandy……. and nothing. I thought of asking at the counter, but then decided against. Powerful people can have books removed from library shelves, and record made of those who come seeking them."

"So where am I meant to go with this?"

"It'll be your choice Declan…… but think. That was a Catholic Padre. How many of them do you think would have landed with the first wave into Normandy?"

"Not many."

"And of those that did, and came back, what sort of proportion do you think would have been carrying an Irish sounding name?"

"Most, I suppose."

"And they would have had to have been young and fit……"

"……so the one mentioned by Peg might also be alive still….."

"…..and traceable, maybe?"

"And you're thinking, Declan, that he might identify that casualty."

"Why not, Eamon? It's just a name you want, hardly a confessional secret….."

"…. but for us a start. And to begin with I enquire where….. with a military archive, then a clerical directory?"

"Unless you go straight to the agency which, I'm sure, will have done that much already." It took a second or three for Declan's meaning to register, but when it had….."Yes, you've worked with them before," he added.

"I have," said Eamon, "the Movement, and the information we want off the Priest might be worth something to them……. yes, so maybe this map could be my ticket to re-instatement. The others meanwhile, Jeremy and Alan, you wouldn't want me involving them in this little initiative."

"Because they're outsiders, Eamon, and each has plenty to be getting on with. When you're around them, then just keep listening to both……"

"…… as they piece together what they separately gather."

"Exactly," said Declan. "Take that Jeremy, and this window he has back into the '30s and 40s, the scribblings of Evelyn Waugh. We hear it at the *Notterbridge*, and later we hear it here."

"Waugh, the writer. *Brideshead* and……."

"…… and a lot more besides." insisted McDaid. "He knew the pre war settler community in Kenya well, and later he trained as a Commando. He was also a staunch Catholic…… and whilst individually these might be slender coincidences, who's to say they can't twine to something more substantial."

"And the other one, Alan Grigson……. what might there be to pick up on with him?"

"He's an intelligence man, Eamon, and so too will be an active GUSTAVE, though far more exalted in rank. As in any hierarchical body there will be the manipulators and the puppets; those who 'need to know', and those who must be sacrificed on the altar of expedience. Is it not the same with the movement? Maybe Grigson belongs with the betrayed, his career having been put on the line."

"On the line," echoed Carroll, for this man a compelling idiom. Perceptively observed, sharply made, it not only compared Alan with Jeremy it also begged Eamon to likewise ponder the comparer, his enigmatic rescuer, Declan McDaid. Like himself, here was a sole trader of Irish descent, replete with quiet loyalty and staunch independence, and yet surely this was more than just a one time milkman. Gained somehow, from somewhere, was an appreciation of a very different sort of domain……. one strictly regulated, and ruthlessly officered.

"You can take this," he said, folding and passing the map for Eamon to wallet. "I've copies enough."

"I will," said Connors, freshly fired. "And as soon as I can I'll be on my way."

THE BRIDGEHEAD OVER THE RIVER ORNE.

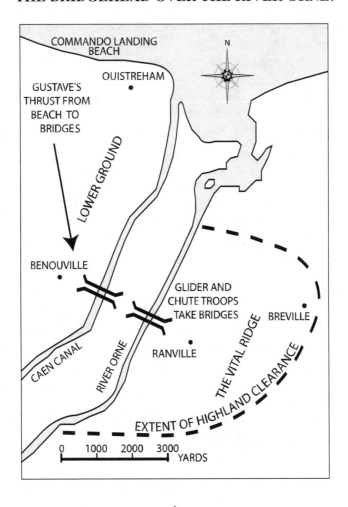

*

(xxxiii) at Lord Rothschild's
The same day.

"Progress!" announced Victor Rothschild, "definite progress, this is why I've asked you here, and why I'm delighted you've both been able to come."

"Our privilege," responded Lord Aldington, Daniels modestly confining himself to a nod.

"You've had something from Peter in Tasmania?" enquired the latter.

"Indeed I have," confirmed the host, "following a sudden spate of messages he's received from his cousin...."

".....that James Busbridge," continued Daniels, "the fellow who lives somewhere down in Cornwall."

"From the very same," confirmed Rothschild, "confirming that a promising sample has been submitted to one of my top Cambridge labs."

"For forensic testing, you mean," added Aldington. Gaunt, intense, here was a person living on his nerves. "Rigorous testing, I presume."

"DNA science," confirmed the host. "As yet in its infancy, but a positive outcome would be encouragingly persuasive ...."

"..... in establishing what, exactly, Victor?" asked the fellow Peer.

"A true identity, with the grounds and the means therein to challenge a forged one....."

"......and perhaps establish who it was that did the forging, and why," added Daniels.

"Yes, why?" Rothschild repeated. "And I can say that in this repect there have been other leads for our busy Mr Busbridge."

"And specifically?" pressed Aldington.

"Three names," answered Rothschild. "Three names, and one precious commodity...... the *Surcouf*, a submarine; Emile Muselier, the Free French Admiral, made second in command to de Gaulle; and Martinique, that piece of France out in the Caribbean, to which, on the outbreak of war, the French Government despatched as much as twenty million pounds worth of their gold reserves."

"That being your commodity," said Aldington.

"But with defeat," continued Rothschild, "the Vichy version was to find themselves doubly constrained in their access to this by separate British and American naval blockades. Getting it out was the problem, and the *Surcouf*, an exceptionally large boat, could well have been seen as the answer....."

".....if it could be persuaded to defect," said Daniels.

"But it didn't," added Aldington, testily, "and if thanks to Muselier, or no thanks, I fail to see what bearing this might have on our predicament now."

"But this might yet emerge," contended Rothschild. "Peter Bright is of the suspicion that so desperate was the position of our Nation at this time, and so hopeless the cause of Poland, dismantled as it was from west and east, that Vichy felt there to be a strong chance of their gold buying something of far greater moment than just a split in the leadership of the Free French. If they could only get at it, they felt that it could be enough to even buy themselves a revolt here in Westminster, within Churchill's Coalition......."

".....and Roosevelt's additional blockade might have been imposed to help deter such," reasoned Colin Daniels.

"And," said Rothschild, "if there was traitorous encouragement for Vichy, voiced by big names in UK Government circles, names mentioned to Muselier when petitioned out on the sea, perhaps overheard and remembered, then by staying resolutely anti fascist the Admiral can, with this knowledge, respond very strongly from a more than useful hand of cards."

"But how might this have give Stalin such a powerful lever at Yalta in '44?" Aldington was sceptical. "He demands those Cossacks and from the Foreign Office it's simply 'here you are...... just take them' "

"Worse than that," remarked Daniels. "If we are to believe Tolstoy, we provided free delivery."

"Bright puts this down to the Free French being riddled with Soviet moles," explained Rothschild. "But he can be like that, we know. Start him off and he'll have a Red under every bed there is."

"And laced with paranoia, the speculation becomes wilder," despaired Aldington.

"So what this cousin down in Cornwall hopes he has found is a witness. A child at the time, who was out fishing, with a brother, at night, close to Plymouth. Dragged into the sea, probably by the *Surcouf* as it surfaced to rendezvous with a second sub, it's thought that the lad might then have been taken ashore under Muselier's protection, to since then languish in a succession of mental wards in Devon and Cornwall. The trauma was such that he doesn't speak, but this needn't mean that the memories are permanently lost. In fact our man is hopeful that prompted by appropriate cues they might be restored, and at long last shared."

"A big ask," said Daniels.

"Which might take a while," added Aldington, wanting to be convinced that this wouldn't be time wasted.

"But there are possibilities here," argued Rothschild, and who was to disagree? Certainly not Colin Daniels, whose placemen, actually there, on the case, seemed as content as the accomplished Victor and Peter were to wait upon the curious probings of Mr James Busbridge.

*

(xxxiv) post
Two full days pass

……..before another morning, which finds James at his cottage door, annoyed by the fumblings of a postman who, having found a pen, was momentarily unsure as to exactly where on his pad this recipient's signature was needed. For the addressee, this was it, at last…… the anticipated registered letter, sent from Cambridge. The formalities patiently completed, it was now in his hand, the official confirmation, he was sure. He closed the door and opened the envelope, glancing at his watch in doing so, calculating what time it would be in Australia, where Peter would have been pacing as restlessly as he.

He had the report now in his hand. Placing it on the kitchen table he smoothed across the fold, then sat and read.

*

(xxxv) at Enid's

Kate, meanwhile, was working an early shift at the hospital, during which, as she passed an upper floor window, she caught a fleeting glimpse of Norman trolleying breakfast bowls back from St Mabyn. For her, James' news was having to wait until afternoon......and late afternoon at that, for on finishing her eight hours at two it would be straight down to the *Borough Arms* where it had been agreed that she and Jeremy might meet, prior to their arranged call on Enid.

From here, the accompianist's home, overlooking the old gaol and close to where a branch of the the old Southern Railway once probed the town, was quickly and easily reached. Jeremy drove, Kate directed the way.

And it was she who led along the path to knock at a smartly painted terraced house door. It was opened, for Kate to be warmly welcomed, ...while himself more coolly so perhaps, out of an understandable reserve, he thought, initially, until an awareness grew of the dearth of male-ness about the place. The net curtains were as a veil, part concealing so much that was of feminine hue and shape. Britten was here though, he noticed, in the framed monochrome photo that graced the piano, between his merry Peter and a stoically smiling Kath; as well as beneath, in the shape of the composer's name on an open page of music titled '*Chorale After An old French Carol*', a setting with words, it stated, by W.H. Auden.

Jeremy was encouraged. Before settling into the deep offered armchair he paused to inspect the piece, Enid having glided to the kitchen, to ensure freshly boiled water for their tea. It was one of the Auden's miniatures, an artists' litany;

> *'Inflict Thy promises with each*
> *Occasion of distress,*
> *That from our incoherence we*
> *may learn to put our trust in Thee,*
> *And brutal fact persuade us to*
> *Adventure Art and Peace.'*

If the price of inspiration was pain, then yes, thought the lecturer, with this poet the world had found a god given talent ready to pay. Enid re-appeared to set down her tray.

"Good stuff," ventured Jeremy, moving away from the piano to resume his seat.

"Words or music?" asked the host.

"Any verdict on the latter would best be left to you. Good old 'Parsnip' is all I say."

"Yes.......and good old Evelyn Waugh," smirked Enid, alive to the allusion. "Another who certainly endured his share of distress." And with this such chill as might have lingered was chuckled aside.

"But returning to Ben and Wystan," continued Jeremy, resisting, for the moment at least, an exploration of Enid's take on the author, "to the musician and the poet......Did they not fall out?"

"They did, and from all I've read and been told, I suspect that short Chorale there on the piano might offer a clue as to why. What I do know is that Wystan was utterly in awe of Ben's technical genius. It really was a rare and prodigious talent...... in my view, one to almost match that of Mozart. And because of Britten's feeling also for words, Auden knew that this man could and should do something truly special in the field of opera...... and I talk world opera, not just British."

"And there was a collaboration, I understand," ventured Kate.

"*Bunyan*," confirmed Enid, to Jeremy's delight. She was 'on message'. "For Wystan, a far from auspicious debut. The composer, though, was on his way to far greater things, the poet was sure.... save for the one reservation, and this he was bold enough to actually put to Britten. The composer's life he suggested was too protected, too cossetted."

"There'd been too few '*occasions of distress*' in his life, you mean," remarked Kate, looking across to the piano, and the piece thereon.

"Exactly, my dear," said Enid. "Ben's life until then, thought Auden, was lamentably short of '*brutal fact*', and if it was the task of an artist to help draw from his audience the pain of such, then something of this had to be first sampled."

"I think I would agree," said the psychiatric nurse.

"As I do too," said Enid, "and as I think Ben came to..... in time."

"Once he'd gotten over the impertinence of such, a suggestion," smiled Jeremy, "the immediate offence."

"Quite," said Enid, "time proved Auden to have been prescient with that little say. The words appear to have been heeded more closely than the composer could ever admit....."

".....save through the quality of his output," said Kate. "But while

360

long term constructive, career-wise, in the short term, friendship-wise, this advice was destructive."

"You have it," confirmed Enid.

"And the distress that Wystan challenged Ben to find was evident in the greatest of the subsequent operas, you would maintain," continued Jeremy.

"In *Budd*, yes, …. and also in miniatures such as *Abraham and Isaac*, as well as in the monumental *War Requiem* in which the 'old man and the son' re appear. The pain of Captain Vere is the pain of Abraham."

"And this is succesfully conveyed?" asked Kate.

"For me, definitely," answered Enid.

"So have you ever speculated how and where, in his cossetted surrounds, our Ben might have himself encountered such distress as suddenly he is able to communicate?" asked Jeremy.

"Many have," replied Enid, "but the answers remain tantalizingly obscure. Something changes him. *Peter Grimes* is fun, it's good, it's clever, and ground breaking in it's way, but it's only after that, that whatever it was truly kicks in. I've read that he toured Germany just after the war, playing to concentration camp victims. This may have affected him."

"Plenty of brutal fact there, " commented Kate.

"Whatever, the next major work is the *Spring Symphony* ……"

" ……. his hymn to resurrection," said Kate.

"And then comes *Billy Budd*," continued Enid, "which to *Grimes* is what the butterfly is to the caterpillar…… a transfiguration. I only hope that Auden appreciated it……"

"…… because it was all he could have wished," reasoned Jeremy.

"That and more," insisted Enid. "The chords at the end of act three, when the Captain has to tell the boy he nust hang…….. I find that section utterly profound. A statement that's beyond words, words that Britten doesn't so much as attempt to provide. I can only reach for those of Wystan's that you see there on the piano. They can't give the answer, I know, but they do provide comfort."

"Fascinating," said Jeremy, it was moving enough to be merely listening to the woman.

"So how were things between Wystan and Ben by '49?" asked Kate.

"Cold," replied Enid, bluntly. "They were continents apart,

literally so.......and yet...."

".....and yet, paradoxically, we have '*Out on the lawn*' bringing such tang to the Spring Symphony," said Kate, "my song."

"And Kath's," Enid gazed wistfully across to the piano top photo."It was never recorded though, and neither was her Isaac."

"And if I said to you that it was also Roger Burney's," said Jeremy, "what would you make of that?"

"Roger Burney," repeated Enid, in only half recognition. "I know I've seen it......but when and where?"

"*War Requiem*," prompted Kate. "I've heard you tell of the premier, at Coventry, of being in the choir. If you have the score still..... at the very top?"

"Yes, it comes back. One of the lost friends, amongst the group to whom the piece was dedicated." Enid turned to Jeremy. "And is there something to link him with the *Spring Symphony*...... through this song, *Out on the lawn I lie in bed*?"

"In a letter of his that I've seen, written in the very first year of the war to a fellow Naval Officer. He tells of having secured a promise from Britten and Pears. Should he die then they were to set those words to music....."

".....in remembrance of good times enjoyed together before the war," suggested Enid, thinking back to her own college days, with the gals, and the luxuriating '*in gardens where they could feel secure.*'

"Except that Roger Burney's three verses finish at '*The tyrannies of love*'......."

".....while Kate tells you of a fourth," nodded Enid.

"A last, that mentions Poland," continued Jeremy. "So where might that have come from? Could it perhaps shed light on that quarrel between musician and poet? Was the fate of Poland an issue between them."

"Both hated violence," said Enid, "but Auden did actually go to war against fascism, in Spain. Something Britten would never have done. The tyrant should be given the benefit of any doubt, so runs the argument in *Grimes*. To confront is to further alienate and antagonise."

"Scope for redemption diminishes," added Jeremy. "Danger escalates."

"So as regards Poland.... " pressed Kate.

"It could be said that Wystan was the more vociferous on behalf of the persecuted Jew," offered Enid, cautiously.

"That he *came* to be more vociferous," modified Jeremy, "I would say, that when looking back, after the Holocaust, Wystan *was tempted to cast himself* as a pre-war Cassandra."

"You mean that he wanted to say to the likes of Britten that he'd had the gift of prophecy and should have been listened to more closely," said Enid, "but you query this stance?"

"I do.....and I think Ben did, himself, in his choice of a last verse from *out on the lawn* for its *Spring Symphony* setting."

"Enjoying a picnic under an English sun," joined Kate, "that's all that mattered to Wystan then, in the early '30s. The Poles, Jewish and otherwise, they can look after themselves!"

"A pointed riposte," said Enid.

"Made, perhaps to counter a thrust from the poet of a very different order to any we've so far considered," continued Jeremy, firmly. "Thank you for your reflections on *Grimes* and *Budd*, Enid, but it's *Bunyan* that has come to exercise us the more. What do you make of that one?"

"I've only heard bits and pieces, Jeremy. There's good tunes, and there's plenty of cleverly phrased social comment..... but no argued out premise, no message."

"None that you can detect," said Jeremy, almost discourteously.

"Jeremy......!" scolded Kate.

"Nor many others, actually," responded Enid, curtly. "But if you think I can be educated......."

"What I mean, is that perhaps not even Auden saw the message....... at first, but on realising what was being made of his words then this was enough to crack what, up until then, had been a robust friendship."

"Forgive me," said Enid, confused. "I'm missing something here. You're saying what, exactly?"

"I think he might have a hypothesis coming on," warned Kate. "He's a lecturer...... further education."

"Then hypothesise, do," invited the host.

"Neither Wystan Auden or Ben Britten are apolitical. Wystan, with his many close Jewish friends and keen imagination is at last waking to early signs of what might develop into an undreamt of peril to European Jewry. Ben, as a pacifist is attracted to international peace initiatives........OK?"

"OK," nodded Enid, cautiously.

"Wystan provides Ben with words, as he had done often before. To him, that's Wystan, all they have above their face value is a certain poetic charm. Ben, though, the musical technician, he can give them a lot more than that......in fact, by giving others the necessary insight into a range of specific techniques, he can endow those same words a totally changed meaning. Set to music they can say far more than anyone else would realise, Wystan included."

"A cipher, you think," responded Enid. "Do go on."

"And remember that America was sharply divided then, between those who wanted to confront fascism, led by the President and his First Lady, and those who felt that a fascist Germany could be reformed and accommodated by the international community......."

"......as Ellen hoped *Grimes* might be accommodated by her fellow villagers," said Enid.

"And there were countries, such as Italy and Spain of course, from whom this kind of acceptance was already as good as won," continued Jeremy, "but America was still very much, and very evenly, split......a good number there being unwilling to fight for democracy in Europe."

"The *Isolationists*," said Enid.

"This a misnomer, maybe, if one remembers how ready they were to intervene at a diplomatic level....."

".....With mediations that plenty on this side of the Atlantic were ready to encourage," said Kate, "but obviously not the Churchill crew."

"Hopes were placed in the Vichy people in France," continued the lecturer, "and in their friends in Sweden, Portugal, Spain. There was encouragement for some big names in this country, around whom a Peace Party might have developed a momentum sufficient to have actually dislodged Churchill. As it happened, though, he was alert enough to head this kind of thing off. Roosevelt stood firm, Churchill took encouragement, and then, with Pearl Harbour......"

"......the rest was history," said Kate.

"But for almost eighteen months, between the fall of France and Hitler himself declaring war on the U.S. of A., all was in the balance. It was touch and go."

"And this," agreed Enid, "was when Auden and Britten were working on *Bunyan*, with the score being constantly chopped and changed."

"Yes, with proof after proof being sent across the Atlantic, ostensibly for the perusal of Ben's London publisher."

"And you think they were being read by a peace movement," said Enid. "That, in America, Ben was being fed critical information pertaining to the delicately poised balance of power in Washington, so that he might encode this in the form of musical notation."

"This is my hypothesis," confirmed Jeremy.

"And you have evidence?"

"So far, just scraps, Enid, but interesting scraps nonetheless."

"For instance?"

"Kate was told by James that Roger Burney was attached to a Free French submarine, one rumoured to have come close to defecting back to Vichy. Perhaps it was to deter this, that it spent so much time over on the far side of the Atlantic......before it was lost with all hands, Burney's included, somewhere off Panama. I'd be interested to know if the poor soul spent any of his shore leave time with his old friends, Ben and Peter."

"Well, if there's anyone capable of finding that out, it's our Mr Busbridge," said Enid, "but what can this prove?"

"Pivotal to any prospect of an early negotiated peace were the attitudes within the Washington State Department towards the French split…….. between Petain, in Vichy, and de Gaulle, in London, at the head of his Free French. Coming to terms with fascism meant repudiating de Gaulle, and this was something that plenty in America seemed ready to do, including many a big commercial interest. Imagine the conversations at the officer's mess table, in that submarine. All this would have been thoroughly and frequently aired."

"But Britten, he wouldn't have been encoding just table talk." Enid was hoping for better. This was good. Jeremy was encouraged. If he'd captured the woman's imagination then this might be the moment for Nolwen's riddle. He'd come prepared, having copied their top line progress to date onto a fresh page.

MCLV	HIIR=Eleanor	
(Step backwards)	(IST)	
?	Morgenthau	FDR= Eleanor
	Inkslinger	Slim = Tiny

"Have a look at this. I've been set to work it out." The page was passed. "The right hand side, here, has been solved..... but not by me, I hasten to add. Originally there were two question marks."

"And this, down here, explains what's above," checked Enid. "The three top Washington politicians corresponding with three of the principal characters in *Bunyan*, the book keeper and the married couple....... very good."

Kate reached across, her finger tapping on the '**IST** '.

"And this was the key," she said, "three letters, three initials...."

"...... three characters," completed Jeremy.

Having absorbed the solved side, Enid pointed to the clue above the remaining question mark. "So these four letters, to the left, over here, they might match with four more of the opera's characters."

"And we thought you would be the one to tell us which," said Kate. "If anyone was to know the full cast......"

"Well there's a '*Hel Helson*'......but he might be too much of a man apart. If you want a grouping of four, there are the four Swedish lumberjacks or, singing just one blues number, a *Quartet of the Defeated*....... but the parts are small, even together they don't come close to balancing *Inkslinger*, *Slim* and *Tiny*." Enid was shaking her head. "Besides," she added, "any link with this 'step backwards' I'm afraid eludes me."

"So what parts are there that could match those of the Commander in Chief, his wife, and the top man at the Treasury?" asked Kate. "Come on Enid," she quietly urged, "like *Inkslinger*, *Slim*, and *Tiny*, they would perform throughout."

"Well there's a group of pets, but...."

"......and for them, yes, the key would fit," interrupted Kate.
" '**Step**' spelt **backwards**. What do you think?"

"Pets, of course," said Jeremy. "Well done Kate!"

"Except that there are only three pets," cautioned Enid, "a dog, *Fido*, and two cats, *Moppet* and *Poppet*...... given to a colorataura soprano and two mezzos. They were an innovation, just for the opera, to lend it more female voices. The characters can't be found in the old Bunyan legends."

"So pick just three of those four letters, '**MCLV**'," muttered Jeremy, "but which?"

"The first three?" ventured Kate.

"Your reason....?"

"Because if the whole thing is a commentary on a power struggle then '**MCL**' is pitted *against* '**HIIR=Eleanor**'......"

"..... and the '**V**' can be the against, as in the legal shorthand, or the sports fixture. I'm with you," said Jeremy, on his feet now. "Yes, v for versus..... Kate, you're a gem! You ought to compile crosswords." He crouched by her chair, smiling, leaning into a brief hug. Their first touch, this, for so long...... and was this how it had once been? No, not quite, not yet, but lending promise of something different and better...... presaged maybe by the softest of sighs from Enid, half charmed, half disappointed.

As for Kate, though, she was now unstoppable.

"So come on, Jeremy. **M** is for; and **C** is for; and **L** is for who, who, and who? You're the political historian. You said you were going to find a library. We're after a pro Vichy clique in Roosevelt's administration."

"Did he have an Ambassador to Vichy France?" asked Enid, now recovered.

"Yes, an Admiral Leahy," beamed the lecturer.

"So that leaves just two," said Kate, "**M** and **C**?"

"**M** has to be the Robert Murphy, the powerful State Department official who negotiated the Murphy-Weygand Accord early in 1941. This set up the commercial supply links between the US and Vichy controlled French North Africa....... while we, with de Gaulle, were attempting to impose a blockade."

"Thwarting our war effort," followed Enid.

"And **C**?" pressed Kate again,"maybe another agreement?"

"General Mark Clark perhaps, whose cosy-cosy with the Vichy Admiral Darlan eventually produced the 'Darlan-Clark Agreement', signed late in '42, when the US had been at war for the best part of a year, and supposedly committed to support for the Free French. Effectively this opened the door for Darlan to change sides, with a view to lording it over the likes of de Gaulle and Muselier, the leaders who'd risked all reputation, and even life, in making their stand against fascism. After a month of this nonsense Darlan was assasinated, and most accounts now will write this up as an ill-advised lightning romance...... but, more likely it was a protracted secret courtship, conducted over many a long month, stretching back more than a year."

"Progress being covertly minuted along channels such as this," concluded Enid, obviously warming to the intrigue. She reached to the arm of Kate's chair, whereon lay the now answered riddle. "And I'll add something more to this," she said. "Ending their exile, Ben and Peter had sailed for Liverpool in the March of '42, and during the voyage the former re-wrote the first section of his setting of Auden's *Song to St Cecilia*, largely from memory...... a task made necessary by the manusript he'd completed in America being confiscated by the authorities at the dockside. Clearly it was thought suspect......"

"....... by the OSS probably," suggested Jeremy. "An early incarnation of what was to become the CIA, formed by the President to supplement and also curb the FBI. The 'Boss', J Edgar Hoover, was considered to be over powerful and too fascist-friendly."

"He had a down on Eleanor," said Enid wistfully, "as he would have had on Britten, Pears, and Auden."

"For their lifestyles, of course," said Jeremy, courteously, having sensed in the host a parallel proclivity. "That was good Enid...... thanks."

"Something else for us to tell Nolwen," added Kate, drawing for herself a bullet glare of censure from the lecturer..... which, like that name, Enid might not have missed. For Nolwen's was amongst those that Jeremy was looking not to disseminate, and now it was out, irretrievably. There might be little risk with Enid, her sweet useful self, thought Jeremy, but she was known to be acquainted with a fellow of guaranteed curiosity, whose scrutiny, for the moment, he was more than content to evade.

"Nolwen....... who waits with further riddles does she?" probed their host.

"Which are not to do with Auden and Britten," acknowledged Kate clumsily, her bid to recapture the released indiscretion merely inviting further enquiry.

"*African tiger*," pre-empted Jeremy, as neatly as he knew, remembering and grabbing at an alternative species of conundrum, the one coined by Moyne, which should also have been exercising Alan Grigson...... through whom Busbridge might have already attained a measure of conversance. "Where in this world would one find an *African tiger*?"

"And as a clue?" Enid was certainly game. Jeremy was hesitant, and Kate, totally nonplussed. "Where am I?" pressed Enid. "Tell me.......where in time, where in space? She closed her eyes"

"You're in Colonial East Africa," began Jeremy, speaking slowly, "back when Ben was in the US. And it's a busy capital city, where the massive Shell Oil Company has chosen to install its regional headquarters. Think of what style of building they might choose......"

"Oppulent," offered Enid, "prestigeous."

"And the furnishings and the hangings therein?" suggested Jeremy. "Pictures, ornaments, rugs....... you're going from room to room, upstairs and down...."

"..... and I'm looking for the *African tiger*," said Enid.

"Which might be big enough to conceal something the size of a battery torch, or a reflex camera," prompted Jeremy.

"But I don't yet see it ," she sighed.

"In the gardens perhaps," suggested Kate. "A kind of tree, or bush, or flower, of striped pigment?"

"I've never travelled," said Enid, eyelids lowered still, "but I've seen pictures of the frangipani, and the jacaranda. I've imagined the scents...... of the fuschias, and the lilies."

"Tiger lilies?" wondered Kate, unsure if such a thing had ever existed outside of never-never land.

"No, sorry," Enid woke from her reverie. "Not even dreamt of, let alone imagined."

"Well think on and it might come," said Jeremy lamely, readying himself to leave whilst this hastily lain smokescreen remained just about aloft.

And this evasiveness was more fully justified than he could know, for when leaving the *Borough Arms*, together in Jeremy's car, the pair had been seen by James Busbridge, the curious man just chancing to be second in a line of vehicles waiting to emerge onto the Wadebridge road from the linking lane that ran across to the old A30. His intention, after skirting the hospital, had been to turn left, down to the Camel, and then out to Portquin, his choice for a coastal stroll that might help him fully absorb the implications of the morning's communication from Cambridge.

A result, this, at last...... the result, a copy of which he'd promptly faxed away to his distant yet closely involved cousin, from whom a response could be expected on his return. But the cliffs of Pentire and 'The Rumps', those rocks of ages, now they could wait just a little longer. He needed to check where this pair were headed. Turning townwards instead, he'd kept them in sight, at a distance, and then, on realising their destination, had discretely parked and watched. Eventually they would emerge.

He saw them drive away, but did not follow. James stayed, waiting a little longer before presenting himself as another, this time unexpected, afternoon visitor for Enid.

*

(xxxvi) Elvira's
Two hours later.

"Dad gave me this." Sally pulls a tape cassette from her bag, then slides it delicately across the café table towards Chas. "It's for your father." The pair had met at the yard gate, as arranged, and decided to take a bus over to Stonehouse. Here, at Elvira's, they could take a beverage and bun prior to Sally making for home (from a day's holiday work at Harmsworth House) via the foot ferry to Cremyll, the bus onward into Millbrook, and then a short, fine summer evening's walk into St John. "He called in at the studio yesterday, asking about that phone-in."

"The phone-in....... on the finding and bringing back of Drake? I thought we were over all that." Chas has the tape in his fingers, and he turns it as if an inspection of both sides might reveal to him his father's motive. "I'm sure he'll be grateful," he adds, no wiser of course, as he buttons it into his shirt pocket.

"And there's this too." To take with it, the girl produces a thin sheaf of typed notes, the pages stapled at the corner and folded once. "It's a transcript, and as well as what went out on air you have the prompts of the producer, and those at the switchboard. So that listeners can speak on cue they'll usually be called back from the studio, after being asked to leave a number......"

"........and I see, the numbers have been written in the margin to the right," says Chas.

"I've not had chance yet to properly look." Clearly, for Sally, the

370

episode lingers as a source of embarrassment.

Chas lifts the topmost page. He hadn't heard the programme….. so how interesting, particularly this piece now, coming up to that troublesome call.

"Aah……yes, here she is, the good old irate woman listener, and this time it was a Mrs Eileen James, who was calling from St Judes…." He hesitates. "But is that number right? Let me just check." And Chas feels down into a pocket of his small rucksack. He finds his diary, with its list therein of phone numbers, the most recently added being ……. yes, it is, and re-checking with the transcript, he can confirm. "The number written there is the same as this," he declares. "Put into Jeremy's book by Lady Clark"

"from where you copied it before it went back to him."

"And he phoned her, we know, when she returned from France. So he must have used it….."

"….to reach her in that room in *The Duke of Cornwall*, Chas, with its own direct line."

"So would she have been there on this day also….?"

"…… mimicking an irate woman, giving a misleading address? Difficult to imagine."

"But to put it down to coincidence, Chas." Sally is shaking her head.

"Is just as difficult, I agree. I'll pass the tape and the paperwork on to Dad. On the number, though, we're best putting that to Jeremy. If there is an explanation……"

"…….then he'll be best placed to find it." Sally finds a pencil in her bag. "I'll take the number across with me."

The ferry is waiting at the hard, and likewise the compact single decked bus on the far bank. Within twenty minutes Sally will be climbing the steep rise out of Millbrook…… to be home inside the hour.

*

371

James Busbridge had likewise walked...... for him a gentle saunter along the valley from Tremorebridge, down past 'Goosemills' to Ruthernbridge. As disappoining as the morning's post had proved, Kate needed to be told....... that according to the laboratory there had been no tissue match, and therefore, from those samples, no proof of biological fraternity.

"I find that hard to believe," she responded, as genuinely surprised as she was secretly relieved. "Can we be sure as to the infallibility of this test, when so much else appears to indicate otherwise?"

"So you suspect either error or manipulation," said Busbridge, "cock-up or conspiracy."

"I suggest we dismiss neither," said Kate, shrewdly applying a gentle brake. "Nor should we forget that it may be our error. What we certainly do, if continuing, is we move with the utmost care. The name on the birth certificate, do you know yet how the youngsters came by this."

"I do, and this is something more to stoke the conspiracy take."

"Go on."

"It goes back to the Wricklemen, the French Admiral, and the submarines. There was a map, and it was torn, half of it somehow coming ashore and into the possession of a local girl who was carrying the Admiral's child, a boy who was conceived at Ince Castle, where she worked. He, now, is Tony Cross, a professional diver. The Chas we met, he that you saw with the name, is Chas Cross, his son...."

"..... and grandson, therefore, of Emile......"

"Emile Muselier," confirmed Busbridge. "And shortly after being thrown out of her job, the grandmother sought to find out something more about this part map, thinking initially to leave it with this marine chart specialist."

"Philip Dalton."

"But in the event, he was to hold it at his shop for no more than part of an afternoon. She'd returned, thinking better of leaving it overnight."

"And was that the night, when a bombing raid claimed the whole family?"

"It was, if we believe their place was hit by a stray Luftwaffe bomb. To find that birth certificate on that medical file, though, invites us to suspect otherwise."

"That this was murder, and that only the bodies of the parents went into the mass grave, young Trevor's being saved in the sea somewhere until sufficiently decomposed to be passed off as Norman Wakeham's. So where are we to go from here, Jim?"

"Remember what happened at *Jamaica Inn*, the sudden outburst of ill-will that brought Norman to St Lawrence."

"Prompted by a picture card of the *Surcouf*."

"And then, you say, that with his residency at the hospital, he has settled to a sustained demonstration of good-will, in particular towards his friends."

"Friends?" queried Kate. "His only friends are the bats which thrive in the darkness of the cut and covered service ducts."

"That's right."

"And this leads us where?" Kate was still puzzled.

"To the possible conclusion that Norman's distress on being snatched and devoured by this monster vessel was to an extent allayed by the means of his being disgorged."

"But bats?" queried Kate.

"I think he might have been flown ashore," explained Busbridge. "The *Surcouf* had its own little fold away sea plane, kept tucked in a small hangar built aft of the conning-tower. It was a long night. The submarine could have surfaced again later, and that plane might have been used to bring the boy in, by moonlight, perhaps to Ince."

"Leathery wings, having to be unfolded...... so yes, maybe."

"And the whole machine had an upside-down look to it, the tailplane with its rudder dropping from the fuselage, rather than rising. An almost unique feature this, so if I could find some pictures of the thing......?"

"Do that," agreed Kate, cautiously, trying to appear helpful while wanting to stall. "And I'll put my mind to how they might be sensitively presented to our patient. It could take time."

"I'll contact Tony Cross. I've made enquiries with him before, on deep sea salvage matters. He'll have diagrams, pictures, I'm sure. That can be one way forward...... another might open were we submit a more clinically procured tissue sample."

"I'll work on that too," promised Kate, emptily.

"And this afternoon, Kate, I dropped in on Enid," he added, the affected nonchalance almost overdone. "Quarter of an hour earlier, she told me, and I would have found you there, you and also that Jeremy. Nice young man, she thought."

"He's interested in Britten," explained Kate, nervously. *Bunyan* if possible, and certainly Nolwen, these names she was preferring to avoid. "I thought he might like to pick her brains. Did she say that Roger Burney's name cropped up?"

"She didn't. How? Tell me."

"It emerged from Ince. Lennox Boyd and he were in the Naval Reserve at the start of the war. Some of their officer training was done together. Quite a fondness developed. Family man though he was, it seems that the MP wasn't averse to a little close male companionship."

"And on this theme, Lennox Boyd hears of Roger's affections for Britten and Pears."

"He does,"confirmed Kate, "and there's a letter, I'm told, sent from Burney to Boyd, and this says that should the former be lost at sea then the musicians have promised to commemorate their friendship by setting part of a specific Auden poem to music......and this is the one that begins *'Out on the lawn......'* "

"Which you sang in the rehersals for the *Spring Symphony*."

"The very same," said Kate

"And this letter is what has emerged from Ince?" probed Busbridge. "Into whose hands?"

"There's this former friend of Boyd's, he still helps in the Castle gardens. Jeremy, and Alan too, I think, they got talking with him in one of the pubs that way." By her manner, one of mere vague concern, Kate implied this to be the extent of her knowledge...... and, as she'd hoped, this together with the mention of Alan's name prompted her visitor to rein back his curiosity. He was placed to take this up with Grigson himself at another time. "I think he might also have been the custodian of the *African tiger* riddle we left with Enid."

"Yes, she told me of that," said James, lightening somewhat. "She was still exercising her imagination with that fantasy walk of Jeremy's. Quite taken with it, she is."

"Still challenged, you mean."

"And quite happily so," smiled James. "And were it not for my having so much else to fathom, this elusive creature you've set loose might have also had me in its claws."

"So you've no time for such frippery."

"I mean I've riddles enough already...... but if I can suggest something?"

"Go on," urged Kate.

"Why not put it to the Africans?"

"Africans?"

"The Africans we saw at the funeral, with the old woman."

"Of course......the Africans, staying down there by the water, on the Torpoint road....."

".....where we dropped those youngsters....."

"....Sally and Chas," Kate reminded him.

"Sally and Chas," he repeated, "who your pal Jeremy thought to use on Alan Clark, I understand. And if they did that then they ought to be no less qualified for running this mysterious *African tiger* past a little native wisdom."

"Sounds a good idea," conceded the nurse. "Shall I put it to Jeremy?"

"You needn't. I could get the boy to phone me. I'll be speaking with his father later. I can leave a message."

*

(xxxiix) Two phone calls
(i) to Quince Cottage (Kent)

"Yes, of course, I would be delighted to meet you Mr Barnes. There's so little one can truly convey on the phone. I trust you've made some progress?"

"A dog and two cats, Lady Clark, and all quietly wishing to remain neutered...... unlike the top three."

"Very good, I can reward you with your final clue. Are you ready to travel?"

"If I can bring Kate again. That I've got this far so quickly has been down to her."

"That's no problem at all Mr Barnes. Where shall we make it?"

"How well do you know Bath?"

(ii) to St John

"Chas......?" Sally knelt next to the narrow hallway table given to the phone. "A pleasant surprise........it was only this morning you called. Nothing wrong is there?"

"Something new. I said this morning, didn't I Sally, about that phone message. The one that came through to the centre for me yesterday......"

".....from that Busbridge fellow, to whom you got back to, and he was wondering about this weird notion of an *African Tiger* ......"

"...... and he was hoping that I might find a way of drawing some sort of response on this from Juma or Makesi. What I didn't know, when we spoke this morning, was that I would have an opportunity to broach this with them this very lunch time. They were down on the Barbican, selling their wares. I'm not sure, Sally, how well I made myself understood."

"Little wonder, Chas, for '*African Tiger*'...... that can't be an easy concept to get across. And there was a mention too of the Shell Oil firm, and how they liked to dress up their overseas outposts, back in the days of Empire. Would these guys have any understanding of those times?"

"This I put to Mr Busbridge, Sally. But they'll know about the multi nationals, he said. Have have no worries there. True, our imperial writ might have expired, but this wasn't to say that the giant companies of the wider petro-currency world cannot still call the shots. In fact, with the check of Crown proccess no longer in place......"

".....they'll have an even bigger shout than before," continued Kate, "bcause the new Africa is corrupt, with so many of the new leaders on the take. The whole continent now works on back-handers, is this what he implies? His generation will always believe in their Colonialism...... something to do with the Boy Scouts and Kipling, Onward Christian Soldiers and all that."

"Maybe, but Busbridge's point was that for any average African, Shell House stands as securely as it ever did...... the firm knowing that it had to adapt and prosper, or die."

"So was there a response?"

"There has been since, Sally, for this evening, less than an hour ago, I'm getting another call from Megan."

"Megan.....from a call box?"

"From the one in Antony, ……. and she's suggesting we go over there, with a tent Sally, for this weekend."

"To set up next to her, on Wacker Quay?"

"She says that the boys might be on to something……"

"You mean with this *African Tiger*?"

"I suppose I do. She wants me to come up with the inflatable, and, if possible, she wants you, Sally, to bring that metal detector. The one you put to such effective use down at Portwrinkle. Is this feasible?"

"Shall we put this to Jeremy?"

"At this stage she's preferring that they not be told."

"So you've agreed to all this, Chas?"

"I said that you might insist on your own separate tent," he chuckled.

"A separate sleeping bag, maybe," countered Sally.

*

(xxxix) DTI (Westminster)
The next day

"Welcome Lord Rothschild and Lord Aldington," said the Minister, striding to the door of his spacious office. "It's just a short chat I wanted us to have. My invitation was necessarily curt. I'm grateful that you should have responded so promptly, grateful and flattered.

"You are a member of the Government, Mr Clark," Rothschild reminded him.

"And such an invitation, from a Cabinet Minister, is perhaps best regarded as a summons," added his fellow Peer who as the door was closed behind, glanced uneasily towards a fourth person in the room whose un-notified presence awaited remark.

"Yes, and as you see, I have with me Sir Clive Faulds," obliged Clark.

"A figure more readily associated with the Foreign Office," remarked Rothschild.

"Indeed," said the Minister, "and it might not surprise you to know that it is essentially a Foreign Office matter that we've brought you here to discuss."

"Good afternoon Your Lordships," said Faulds, "and if we can remind ourselves that Privy Council conventions must strictly apply......"

".....then perhaps we can begin," added Clark, with an officious frown, resuming his own chair, now, having ensured all were comfortably seated.

"So why not a matter for the Foreign Secretary?" enquired Aldington.

"Because it needn't be at this stage," answered Faulds.

"And because the matter crosses what is widely known to be for me a specialism," continued Clark. "I speak of a particular period of history."

"You mean like 1941," Rothschild broke in.

"Yes...... exactly Victor," admitted the Minister. "The year that a European war that we could only lose became a World War that was eventually won."

"The conjuring trick of all time," pressed Aldington, "the secret of which remains the preserve of a magic circle, which perhaps, as yet, doesn't include Geoff Howe....."

"..... nor even the blessed Margaret herself," ventured Rothschild.

"Such speculation we can neither confirm, at present, nor deny," responded Faulds. "The Founder of our order died twenty years ago, but not before commissioning Alan, here, to produce his accounts of *Barbarossa* and *The Fall of Crete*. The last Prime Ministers who I can definitely say to have been in the know were Mac and Alec, both of whom played an active political role during that vital time."

"So Harold, Ted, Jim......" reeled Aldington.

"We don't know," said Clark.

"And as for our Margaret," sneered Faulds, "after her revocation of the immunity granted to Blunt, I doubt if she can now ever be trusted."

"By whom, tell us," said Rothschild.

"By the original grand wizard's chosen successor...... formerly his enforcer in chief, selected for his ruthless efficiency and likely longevity," answered Sir Clive.

"And in neither aspect has he proved a disappointment," added Clark. "Indeed, it's that first quality that must deter us from divulging his identity, as well, of course, as his closely gurded secret."

"So why bring us here today," asked Aldington. "Is it to frighten us?"

"No," said Faulds," at least not primarily. Your growing resentments have been noted, and actually they are sympathised with. Victor....... the whole *Molehunter* business was mishandled. It was meddlesome Margaret again. And Toby, likewise you deserve better for the fine service you've given to the nation over many years."

"That young Tolstoy should have been silenced long ago," added Clark. "But too late, now, of course, and with international developments as they are, I'm afraid you're still having to be hung out to dry."

Aldington's chin dropped, in the manner of a unjustly chastised puppy. Rothschild shook his head dismissively. "It's a sour tasting sympathy, Sir Alan, that can't be sweetened with an explanation."

"Of course, and this might be what you'll have," said Alan Clark, " but from neither of us. Instead, you are here to be informed that the chief man in all of this can, in a few days time, grant you a personal audience."

Aldington straightened. "So we will learn his identity?"

"Yes and perhaps even the full story," added Faulds. "But the decision will be his. Much will depend on how you present yourselves on the day."

"So where?" asked Rothschild. "And when? Here, Minister, in your office?"

"No....... at my country home, where he has invited himself for another of his short and far from frequent stays."

"At the Castle you mean," said Aldington, "down in Kent."

"No, a little further I'm afraid. He has always preferred my farm...... being something of a cattle man himself."

"And your farm is where?" asked Rothschild.

"Not far from your accommodation." A brochure was passed. "*Jamaica Inn*, on Bodmin Moor...... very comfortable, easily found. I've provisionally booked you in for two nights...... that's three separate rooms. I can collect you after your first breakfast. That will be Sunday August 16th, the day will then be ours."

"Three rooms?" queried Rothschild. "So Sir Clive will be staying with us?"

"He won't. In the absence of your friend Mr Peter Bright, my guest would be pleased to become acquainted with his cousin. A Mr James Busbridge, I believe his name is. We understand that you can be quickly in touch. Shall I leave you to ensure that he knows of the invitation?"

*

379

(xl) a garage workshop

in a small market town between Belfast and Derry.

"........and you do understand, Carroll, that even by such small involvement as you've had you are nevertheless pledged to observe our movement's strict code of discipline."

"Something I've always understood, Mr McBeamish ......sir." Eamon, blindfolded and handtied, rocked forward, but the knots were unyielding. He found no give, bar in the joints of the hard wooden chair to which he was bound.

"So you must also understand that any breach of that pledge invites stern punishment, to the extent that this renders you as much a fugitive from us as you ever where from the British."

"I do," confirmed Carroll.

"And yet you arrive here at Belfast Airport with a return seat to Bristol booked and paid for, openly seeking to re-establish contact with us........ as if you considered yourself due a welcoming committee. Is this foolishness, I want to know, or desperation, or an unsubtle attempt at a plant?"

"It's confidence, Mr McBeamish," replied Eamon, bravely.

"In us? Are we perceived to be turning soft?"

"In the potential of the information that I bring, a potential I'm sure you can recognise...... and help to realise also."

"So long as we are not being mis-informed, Mr Carroll."

"This is no ruse, Mr McBeamish, I can assure you of that. Hell and high water, I've had to come through."

"You can spare me the detail for now. You speak of a potential .... to do what, tell me?"

"To persuade, Mr McBeamish. We try the bomb, and we try the bullet, and do those Anglos bend? They don't. In fact they stiffen."

"So instead.?"

"Why not embarrassment....... as a weapon to penetrate the very top Foreign Office departments, and reach those who up to now have shown little concern for this untidy back yard which is Ulster. They're so full, you see, of securing a pro-west resolution to the Cold War, with developing the European Union, and trying to make some sort of sense of the Middle East. And why not, when over a number of years they've built for themselves a certain standing in these affairs. Quite an influential standing, provided, of course, that it's not undermined."

"So this is what we can threaten to do, with that which you've started to put together."

"Yes, and to buy us off they might start to budge on the six Counties."

"And Eamon Connors, in that London cab of his, he's going to drive down Whitehall to deliver this threat!"

"It'll be big," replied Eamon, ignoring the sarcasm. "It'll be big and it'll be strong, but I first need to find and fit two important pieces."

"And you know where to look?"

"Here, Mr McBeamish, because the keys for finding and slotting those pieces could well lie within your archive."

"Go on Mr Carroll."

"Firstly, I look for a Priest, probably in his 60s now."

"Plenty of them."

"But this one served in the British Army, as a Catholic Padre, landing in Normandy on D Day, either with the 6th Airborne or !st Commando Brigade……. Can't be many of them."

"And the second?"

"Concerns a character named Declan McDaid…….said to have grown up in Derry, in the '30s. Father was in the movement way back, in the '20s. Declan himself might have joined for a while just before World War Two. Then, during or just after, he crossed to the mainland and stayed…….. no longer the avid Republican."

*

(xli) Bath

"Robert **Murphy**, Mark **Clark**, Admiral **Leahy**, '**v**' for versus, Henry **M**, Franklin **R** and **Eleanor**…….. it's a delicately poised power struggle, being contested amongst those considering US foreign policy options during those sixteen or so months between the French surrender to the Germans and the Japanese attack on Pearl Harbor." Jeremy had the page further filled at Enid's out on the table. He swivelled it for Nolwen Clark to inspect more closely. "The tunes given to the pets, over here, and to Johnny, Slim and Tiny, on this side, they chronicle the moves and counter moves of the major players."

"Very good," acknowleged Enid, who was clearly enjoying her day's excursion to Bath. She'd come by train, to be met by Jeremy and Kate at the station, they having driven up through the morning. Together they'd walked up river to take themselves a table at a spacious licensed tea room, close to the Pulteney Bridge. "But for whom were these communications destined?" she added. Jeremy hesitated, then;

"I can give you my thoughts on that, but first a question for yourself."

"Ask on then," invited Nolwen, graciously. "Do."

"How many times this year have you travelled to Plymouth?"

"Just the once."

"And how often will your son in law have stayed at *The Duke of Cornwall*?" Jeremy produced a pencil.

"Four times at least, maybe five or six."

"And one of his bookings, might it have included this date?" Jeremy wrote day and month in the ample space above the **MCLV**.

"It did," confirmed Nolwen. "I can remember him saying. He came down for the weekend prior to those nights he booked for me."

"And if I said that a woman phoning from that suite, on that day, had got through to a local radio broadcast, and on air had purported to be calling from elsewhere, then who......"

"......might that have been? An oldish voice?" Probably a secretary either with the Ministry, or at the constituency office."

"Thank you Lady Clark," continued Jeremy. "And answering *your* question, I would hold that no one was likely to be following the gradual shaping of *Bunyan* more closely than those, here, discretely seeking to promote an early negotiated peace. Any accord reached between Washington and Vichy offered them a paradigm."

"Unless the whole thing had been rumbled by the authorities......... and was being monitored maybe?" suggested Nolwen.

"But assume not that all within the establishment were totally loyal to the Churchill line," cautioned Kate.

"Nor forget that the totally loyal will sometimes have licence to play for advantage by feigning disloyalty, " mirrored Jeremy. "Hitler was never so gullible as when he was being told that along with the swathe upon swathe of territory, he was also winning admirers."

"Very good Mr Barnes," conceded Nolwen, "and either way, I can tell you now that Cyril Connolly was fairly sure that our security people knew something, but as to how much, and how loyal they were......."

"....... he was probably reluctant to speculate," muttered Jeremy. "Dangerous ground that...... but what we can say is that the links being forged between Washington and Vichy looked to be substantial, certainly from Berlin, and being commercial rather than martial they would have certainly had appeal for Britten, and any other principled pacifist."

"While Auden," said Nolwen, "the provider of words....."

"...... he would have been less impressed, and we know that the long friendship between musician and poet foundered at this time. An oft voiced concern for the Jew suggests, in him, an instinct for confronting rather than pandering to fascism. Even if there's evidence of indifference ten years earlier, my guess is that by '42 he would have been strongly of the view that the Quakerist stance of the musicians was dangerously supine."

"And, with all the horrors that came to pass, who would now argue?" said Kate, confidently.

"Plenty, actually," replied Jeremy, "and with his historian's hat on Nolwen's step-son is unafraid to count himself amongst them. Of course, the debate is now academic, but there remains this view that had London accepted the truce offered by Berlin in '41, prior to *Barbarossa*, then not only would our Empire have held together for longer, but also Hitler could have been guided towards a final solution for his 'Jewish Problem' that might have been very different to that which he was left to so wickedly pursue. Britain, France, Portugal, Belgium, Holland...... we all had colonial posessions, and therefore land to spare."

"To absorb deported Jews," continued Kate.

"And it can be argued,"said Jeremy, "that it was to this end that what eventually became the death camps were initially set up......... primarily to hold their inmates, prior to transit across peaceful waters to appropriately prepared land......"

".......flowing with milk and honey," added Lady Clark, implying that at best these poor souls would disembark to the kind of reservation endured at the end of the nineteenth century by the North American Indian........ the slow death camp.

"But for the fit and the resourceful there would have been a fighting chance," insisted Jeremy, "which is more than they had during the grim three years that began early in '42." His finger went to the page. "Robert Murphy, here, of the Murphy-Weygand 'accord'....... we could say he was laying on a pilot scheme. What he could achieve in the way of making French North Africa more refugee-friendly might be offered as a model for the British in East Africa, or for Belgium in their Central areas. For a while, prior to *Barbarossa*, Jews were actually being tranported out of Germany down to camps in southern France in preparation for being shipped across the Med."

Neither Kate nor Nolwen demured, leaving Jeremy momentarily amazed, not least at himself, for had this been a student of his making the same point, in class, just a month ago, he would then have been more than pleased to summarily rubbish such a reading. No, he would have said. Washington's early war pro-Vichy diplomacy was merely the typically American response to the communist element within the Free French.

But now, sharply, in his own mind an old history was being displaced by a new, and the reason wasn't so much in those *Bunyan* riddles devised by Auden, developed by Connolly, presented by Nolwen, as it was in that letter he'd read at Quarry Cottage, left by Moyne for his niece, and rescued from the fire by McDaid. So well did Murphy suit the purposes of HIGHLAND CLEARANCE, and GUSTAVE, that the man might have even been a puppet. But for the moment Jeremy could keep this to himself. He'd already produced for Nolwen. It was there on the table, all that was asked for. He needn't be squandering more.

He could reach again for the page, and take his finger down, to the space beneath the Roosevelts and their banker.

"So 'Uncle Crouchback knows', Lady Clark. That's what Auden tells us...... so how is Cyril going to help us there?"

Nolwen produced her pen, as she had at The Duke of Cornwall, and reached without hesitation to rewrite the final element, as promised;

Uncle Crouchback knows, she printed, beneath adding;
(**vaguest variation**)

This done, she returned the page into Jeremy's hands, ensuring that it was he who would be sharing this final clue with Kate.

"And this, now, is everything," checked Kate.

"All that Cyril gave me, and all that I can pass on to you."

"So you can't offer the complete solution," said the nurse.

"Because you've done well enough without this ever having been promised," Nolwen reminded her. "Put your minds to it and.....".

......and Jeremy already was.

"It's another anagram," he said. "A variation of vaguest...... pen, Lady Clark, please," and its return to her bag was forestalled. "Uncle Crouchback knew the identity of.....," and he spoke as he spelt, "G...U...S...T...A...V...E. This is another name that's come out of Ince," explained Jeremy.

"With Roger Burney's?" asked Nolwen.

"Sort of," the lecturer replied.

"Meaning.....?" prompted Kate.

"Meaning through the same person, and from the same period in the war...... and possibly from the same episode. Burney was a real name, of a man now dead. GUSTAVE, though, that's a code name for a person in high authority, one who might still live, and be wielding this authority with a practised ruthlessness."

"And Uncle Crouchback, we've established, was modelled by Waugh on himself," Kate said.

"Who managed to network himself into some truly exalted circles," said Nolwen.

"Working closely in Yugoslavia with Randolph and Freddie, sons to Churchill and F.E. Smith," cited Jeremy. "Let's say that Waugh encountered this GUSTAVE, and then caricatured the man in those same *Sword of Honour* books that figure Crouchback. Then Cyril, who suffered the same treatment, and knew how to read Waugh, he sees in this a way of preserving his own insights for posterity."

"Dangerous insights," continued Nolwen, "gained piece by piece. It starts during the war when, as editor of Horizon, he receives from America a sample of the Auden's work on *Bunyan*, incurring for him a third degree interrogation which couldn't, at the time, have made much sense. But the experience is never forgotten, and later, on delving back into the world of firstly the Cambridge spies, and then Happy Valley, he starts to more than just imagine connections."

"He contacts Wystan," continued Jeremy, "who might have told him more, but sadly the poet dies......though not before bequeathing these clues for Chester to pass on."

"And Cyril does derive an interpretation," said Kate, "but one he feels he has to cloak rather than openly announce."

"Because he will die soon enough himself, and naturally he wants the best for the widow he will leave, and their young son," said Nolwen.

"So those clues of Wystan's stay clues," added the lecturer, "but on to each he hangs a cryptic embelishment….. for the likes of us."

"So that we might be eased towards the solution that he saw, but turned away from," explained Nolwen, "not wanting to detonate what, then, was a powder keg. He hopes, though, that with time all this might be more safely handled."

"And we can hope the same." Queasily, Jeremy remembered Eamon, and Declan's concern for his tenant Peg.

"But this novel by Evelyn Waugh," breezed Kate, "that's hardly going to blow up in our faces. Do you have a copy Jeremy…..up at your flat?"

"I don't, but if you wait here I'll get one. I can be down to Waterstone's and back in less than fifteen minutes."

*

(xlii) curiouser and…..

"James Busbridge……and as I was passing, Mr McDaid, I thought……."

"No, I don't mind at all Mr Busbridge. Do come in. A surprise, yes, but I'm delighted that you should have made time to drop by."

And Declan McDaid was indeed pleased to be answering his door to this man of whom he'd read and, more recently, heard so much. This said, he couldn't be entirely surprised, not after having so prompted the enquiries of Alan, and Jeremy, and Eamon.

"Perhaps Mr Grigson has mentioned me," began Busbridge tentatively.

"Not so much Mr Grigson as an acquaintance of his and mine, a Mr Eamon Carroll, who if you've not met, I'm sure you soon will…."

"…… but for the moment he's been called away for a few days, so I understand from Alan."

"Yes…..as I do too," added Declan, less than accurately. "Back to London perhaps…… we all have housekeeping. But your business, I've been told, is to do with an oversized wartime submarine, French, and with a pair of brothers named Wakeham, the youngest of whom you might have located in the St Lawrence Hospital. It's been said that a tissue sample has been obtained for possible matching. Has this confirmed you in your suspicions?"

"It hasn't, but the fault could well lie in the sampling process rather than the premise. So much else, you see, points to this having been correct."

"Such as?" McDaid's tone conveyed sympathetic interest.

"His very condition, the irregularities in his medical record, and a treatment regime that seems geared to perpetuate rather than rectify his lasting amnesia. Then there's a range of coincidences. They begin with the total destruction of a Plymouth shop back in '41, together with its proprietor, and his family....... the child's remains possibly having been used to account for the missing Wakeham, to the extent even of being buried in Rame churchyard."

"And ending with......?"

"The circumstances of the admission into St Lawrence, after the lad had been cared-for for so long at a similar institution over in Devon."

"This would have been the violent reaction in the pub. Alan did say...... to do with a picture on the wall."

"A picture of the *Surcouf*......"

"...... which appears to have revived an old anguish, a nightmare, and yet you would appear to be ready to pitch the poor fellow back into it all. If I understand Grigson, you can tell him that his mother died, heartbroken, shortly after his disappearnce, and that his brothers fell out with each other, until they too were to die, each far from home. A bit much for a fragile temperament to sustain, I would say....... leaving aside how he might take the loss of forty odd years from his own life. Should he not be best left undisturbed in what sounds to be a reasonably comfortable niche?"

"It would need to be handled with care," conceded Busbridge.

"With extrene care, I would say. For what, in the end, is he, Norman, likely to gain from this, apart from turmoil and regret. And what could you possibly gain, besides? However well his memory might be re-sharpened, what understanding would he have had, at such a tender age, of a stand up row conducted in French?"

"Fair point," admitted Busbridge, "but by ascertaining the identity

I can then move on to the next questions. Other innocents were slaughtered. This one was spared. Why, and how?"

"But *he* wouldn't be able to say."

"No, but there night be a hidden away case record, and perhaps this could shed light on another charmed life, that of Vice Admiral Muselier who at around the same time was able to extricate himself from Brixton Gaol, to be received at the Palace for a personal apology from no less a figure than our Monarch."

"Consideration such as wouldn't have been bestowed for nothing," conceded Declan.

"Exactly, Mr McDaid. And I imagine Muselier to have picked up on something truly big. So big as to allow him to summon a protection wide enough to include secure provision for the youngest Wakeham. In my scenario I see the boy being flown off the *Surcouf*, to somewhere like Ince....... pending the outcome of negotiations, which could well have included that business at the Palace. And Ince Castle is the reason I'm here. When it comes to that place you seem the fount of all knowledge"

"And I guess from Ince, it could have been on to Moorhaven, maybe by rail, the line passing so close to each place. But going back to your 'something truly big'........ what was this? Let me hear you speculate Mr Busbridge."

"There was a stash of gold, French gold, sent to Martinique, in the West Indies, prior to the surrender to the Germans. The island, as part of France, declared itself Vichy governed. It was promptly blockaded by the British Navy, our units then being shadowed by a fleet of US ships concerned to prevent any precipitate action. I've evidence, in the form of a map, that Vichy, wanting the use of its gold, regarded the *Surcouf* as an ideal vehicle for bringing it out...... but of course it had been impounded in Plymouth, and subsequently claimed by the the Free French. I suspect that the Wakeham brothers witnessed an attempt made to buy the *Surcouf* across to Vichy, an attempt resisted by Muselier, second in command to de Gaulle, the Admiral happening to be on board."

"Interesting," acknowledged McDaid after some thought, "but even if he proved himself loyal to the Free French and the British war effort, I still don't see how this might give the Admiral so strong a lever against the British establishment."

*

(xliii) Sword of Honour

"I bought two." Jeremy was slightly breathless. "They had an offer going in Penguin Classics. One for you, Nolwen….. Kate and I will share."

"Near seven hundred pages," said Kate, fanning through the lot.

"Because originally it was three separate books," Nolwen informed her.

"And Guy Crouchback, he's the hero in these stories."

"I suppose he is, Kate," said Jeremy, "but in a most unheroic way. Well past the first flush of idealistic youth, we have him stumbling through the early years of the war much as the nation did. Fascism and socialism are equally repugnant to Waugh, and that the challenge of the first was met by a sell-out to the second causes him more shame than it does pride. Military training is a farce, an offensive operation to capture Dakar, a fiasco, and the defence of Crete, a tragedy. He quests for a sense of honour, but too often he finds himself pursuing a mirage."

"And is there a heroine to guide him to this elusive grail?" asked the nurse.

"More of an anti-heroine. We'll find her name here, it's Virginia, the former wife of Guy. Many consider her to have been far from fondly modelled upon Waugh's own first wife, by whom he was abandoned during the early years of far too hasty a marriage. Virginia might be unworthy, but this does little to alleviate Guy's sense of failure and humiliation."

"And there's a second aspect," added Nolwen, "in how this marital calamity cuts across Guy's agonised response to the teachings of the Catholic faith."

"But Virginia pays," continued Jeremy, "ultimately with her life, to a Luftwaffe bomb, and before that by being paired with the contemptible *Trimmer*, who must rival any as the least attractive character in the whole Waugh canon. If, through Virginia, the author shovels spite by the bucket-full, with *Trimmer* it is discharged by the boat-load."

"So they deserve each other," said Kate. "And this *Trimmer*, is he a fellow soldier?"

"He is, and as inept at this as he proves, when assigned to a Hazardous Operations unit, he is selected by the Ministry of Information for manufacture into a war hero….. in the interests of public morale, of course."

"So both man and honour are totally phoney," said Nolwen.

"But as such, appropriate to the waging of modern wars," said Jeremy, "and, I suppose, modern love affairs." Kate shifted slightly in her chair. Was that accusation she'd heard in Jeremy's tone..... or might this have been merely imagined, out of her own sense of guilt?

"So for a real life candidate for *Trimmer*," Nolwen continued, "where would we look?"

"Perhaps north of the border, for I think I remember him entering the action as a cod Scot, a *Major McTavish*," said Jeremy. "'*Ali' McTavish, short for Alistair, you know*," he added, adopting a cod Scot's accent...... to the reward from Nolwen of the briefest and most Ladylike of giggles.

"So, for all that, hardly a GUSTAVE," said Kate, thumbing towards the centre of her volume.

"Except, emerging from Ince with the code name GUSTAVE was an operation HIGHLAND CLEARANCE," reminded Jeremy.

"And definitely a Caledonian flavour there," said Nolwen.

"And yes......!" Kate was up on her feet, and around to behind Nolwen and the other book. "Here..... I've got it. Chapter Six, '*Happy Warriors*' . *Trimmer* is on leave. He finds a hotel in Glasgow, and in the hotel he meets Virginia, and she recognises him from before the war, when he was a hairdresser on a transatlantic liner...... who then called himself *Gustave*, she recalls."

"And, you know, though I've read a good bit of this, I'd forgotten," said Jeremy. "Well done Kate......again." He took her copy. "It must be just that once that this pseudonym crops up, because *Trimmer* he stays for the rest of the book."

"But Cyril Connolly, he wasn't going to miss it," said Nolwen. "Think hard now, Jeremy....... *Trimmer*, who else might know?"

"There's a Trim, I'm aware of."

"Who wouldn't, himself, be *Trimmer*?" wondered Kate.

"No, because this Trim and his family were held in far too deep affection by Waugh. Trim Asquith would never have been held up to such ridicule."

"That's Julian, isn't it?" Nolwen was well versed in her Debrett's. "Grandson to Herbert, son to Katherine, and current holder of the Earldom."

"And he lives quite locally." Jeremy glanced at his watch. "When's your last train?"

"I've got a good three hours."

"Ample time," Jeremy dedclared. "I say we go to the Manor House at Mells to ask Trim, as he was and is known to those close to him, who he reckons this *Trimmer* might be. For today we are graced by the company of her Ladyship here, and who better to gain us an audience with his Lordship, the 2nd Earl of Oxford and Asquith."

"Fine," agreed Nolwen, rising elegantly from the table. "We'll waste no more time."

*

(xliv) Father Mulligan

"The Catholic Church at Stonebridge Park, NW10."
And that was about as much as Eamon Connors had heard his minder say, since having been met by him at Bristol Airport. For a west London cabbie, though, little more was required. It was just along the Harrow Road, hardly a twenty minute bus ride from Queens Park. How strange, that he should have had to journey so far to be directed to place so close to home.

They were on the North Circular, and having crawled across Ealing Common, and through Hangar Lane, this was the junction. Filtering right, Eamon passed the bus depot and the 'rec'. The tower blocks were on the rise ahead, and leaving them to his right the large modern Church would be on his left, just a little way along from the freight link railway cutting.

Bordering the parish to the south, across the main Euston passenger line, was Park Royal, a vast industrial estate producing inter alia Heinz Beans, McVities' Biscuits, and Guinness beers, through busy plant that had long drawn on immigrant labour, much of it from Catholic Ireland. Some of the pubs here-abouts had given well to the movement, he knew, but not this particular Church.

It seemed, however, that they were expected. Eamon was tersely advised to use the small parking area, and as he did so the Priest appeared at the main Church door. And it was the Father Mulligan that he'd imagined, hair white and whispy with age but standing erect, still, and alert....... the military man of old. Eamon was greeted cordially by name, but not so the minder, who was left to slink guiltily away as though each sole placed on consecrated ground was purgatory.

"I do come in peace Father," said Eamon.

"So I understand, from the Province."

"Where they told me that you fought in the British Army, with distinction, particularly in Normandy."

"Many Catholic Irishmen enlisted to fight Hitler, Mr Carroll, and not all from the North. In so far as I served as their padre, I am proud to count myself as part of the contribution they made."

"So you carried a gun."

"And I was taught how to make a lot of noise with the thing. With it, on D Day, I was put in a glider."

"Two wings, a prayer, and no engine."

"Me being the middle part....... and we landed early in the afternoon of that first longest day, close to the Orne bridges that had been captured and held since dawn. From the moment I crawled from that shattered contraption I was hearing men screaming for me, brave men men who'd suffered mortal injury just in the business of landing. My gun I gave away, and I've not touched one since."

"And as well as ministering to the lads of the Air Landing Brigades, there were also the Commandos fighting inland from the beaches."

"One of whom you wish to locate."

"And I was hoping for your help. All I have is this map," it was produced, "traced from a library book, and the two code names written thereon........GUSTAVE and HIGHLAND CLEARANCE."

"Written by whom?"

"Originally by a wounded para, who remembered hearing them in the garble of a particular commando, also wounded, in a field hospital, not far from those bridges which, by the sixth day, the Germans were straining to retake. That para also remembered a Priest being in attendance."

"And that indeed was myself, Eamon."

"So what can you tell me?"

"About HIGHLAND CLEARANCE......? Precious little, my son. For what is said to me by a man preparing to die must remain a matter strictly between myself, him, and his maker. As ever, I must observe the sanctity of the confessional. It's on this principle that I've won the respect of all sides involved in the Anglo-Irish troubles."

"But if I said this was in the interests of peace?"

Father Mulligan turned. Stepping into his church he beckoned Eamon to follow.

"In the interests of peace, I've wrapped you a package. It sits on that pew over there," he said, pointing. "Just a book, it is, a memoir. I'll lend it to you."

"A copy of the book, you mean......with a map in it, which matches this."

"But without those added code words, of course. I give you no more than what the author himself wanted the world to know."

"So there's no mention of them in the text."

"Nothing of HIGHLAND CLEARANCE, nothing at all .... but you will learn that the author is still alive, and also where he'll likely be found."

"And then?"

"From my standpoint, any discussion of the topic becomes a matter for him........ and yourself."

"On my own head be it, eh?" Carroll drew a deep breath."Worry not, Father Mulligan, I know too well already how dangerous GUSTAVE can be..... but having been spared, I'm thinking maybe this was for a purpose."

"Maybe," repeated the Priest, "and if you've nothing else to ask......."

"Just one thing, and then I'm gone. I was told that you grew up in Derry, in a Catholic neighbourhood."

"I did."

"Quite a tight community."

"In those days, indeed it was."

"So did you ever know of a lad named Declan McDaid?"

"Did I ever.....?" The Priest was shaking his head, but in fond reminisence rather than denial. "Now there's a name I never expected to hear again. As boys, Eamon, we were the closest of friends, indeed we were, but then it was time to gow up, time to decide. For myself, I chose the Cross. I would fight the devil."

"And he, for himself?"

"The tricolour....... He was going to fight the British."

"So you lost touch......."

"…..without entirely losing track, for news would filter through our families, in both directions."

"Things to be kept secret, I suppose."

"Yes, but perhaps no longer, Eamon."

"I'm listening Father Mulligan"

"You are? Then see what you make of this……."

*

(xlv) Mells

……..has a time at a standstill charm. It's an oolitic fossil, almost, a Larkrise, or a Candleford, lovingly preserved in Mendip limestone. Comfortably found but easily missed, it lies a little off the main highway linking Shepton Mallet and Frome, no more than three miles short of the latter. The High Street, broad and straight, offers easy, hassle free parking, while the *Talbot Inn* and the Post Office will each trade attentively on its gentle stream of regulars, and the occasional visitor.

Behind, and near shadowing the *Talbot*, quaintly accessed along New Street, stands the serenely crafted Church of St Andrews, with its clock tower chime ringing down on those Lutyens styled churchyard headstones, commemorating the Horners and Asquiths, the Lady Bonham-Carter, and the poet, Siegfried Sassoon. Having been here often enough before, to absorb the unique ambience at leisure, Jeremy felt he should be introducing all this to the others, all this and more. But he couldn't, of course, for they were too pressed for time…… and they were here for what they could sneak away with, almost as a possee of thieves.

"We can leave the car here, outside the pub," suggested Jeremy. "The Manor House is this big place next along, set back behind the high stone wall that goes up to the driveway gates. To appreciate the true size of the House you need to be on the other side of the wall."

"So we walk along to the drive," suggested Kate.

"We don't," said Jeremy. "At the back of the pub, the Churchyard and the Manor house court yard meet, to be divided by a high stone wall through which the household had its own access to the Church by way of a wooden door. It's heavy and it's latched, but rarely bolted……. for before now I've taken a peep through. You see the back entrance of the Manor which faces across a wide gravelled courtyard to a walled garden beyond. Guests, it seems, are encouraged to use the yard for car parking. It's at the back door where one rings the bell...... so I've been told."

"So it's to the churchyard first," said Nolwen.

"Down New Street, here," confirmed Jeremy, leading them off the High Street and along to pair of black wrought iron gates, nicely painted, smoothly swung. Through, they then had to veer away to the left, towards the high wall with that strangely forbidding wooden door..... a solid symbol of ecumenical divide.

Dare they open this thing, thought Kate, and even Jeremy seemed tentative as he lifted a heavy latch with the utmost care and pushed himself a gap for no more than just a tilted through head.

"Just the one car in the yard," he said, as if this were a reason for his now moving more boldly, "a Roller, looking very much in its element."

Kate squeezed him on, allowing Nolwen, last through, to edge herself a clearer view....... and that was enough. Without warning, she shrank sharply back into the Churchyard, hurriedly regaining the cover of the wall. Alarmed, Kate drew back also, concerned and confused, wanting to hide while knowing not what from........ but grabbing at Jeremy who had to likewise fall in with them, rearwards, swinging the door shut as he did so.

"Nolwen," said Kate, "is it a ghost you've seen?"

"Yes," whispered Lady Clark. "The roller, it's Alan's.......his Silver Ghost, and he's here. And I mustn't be seen. You have to get me back to Bath, immediately."

"Of course," said Jeremy, his head fast filling with questions. But they weren't for now. Nolwen, his best source, she was the priority. "I'll back the car into New Street. Get over there and wait inside the Church. I'll come in, and you can walk out between us."

"But then leave me here," insisted Kate. "Put Nolwen on her train, then come back and meet me in the pub."

"So long as you're not over inquisitive," said Jeremy.

"Or under. I think it best if I can be as inquisitive as any normal tourist..... no more no less."

Kate saw them away, watching the car turn left onto High Street with Nolwen peering anxiously to the right across Jeremy's back, then coming to the junction herself she chose the same direction. Jeremy had left her his camera, and she thought initially to return down to the attractive village war memorial. Also, according to Jeremy, of Lutyen's design, it had to be worth a print or three.

Sixty or seventy metres along the street it was, and she hadn't covered half before the Ghost swept past. That could have been close, she thought, instinctively steadying herself to snap the car with its unaccompanied driver from the rear.

Nolwen was clear though, the nurse knew, for with four or five minutes start Jeremy would, by now, be well on his way to Bath.......and besides, the Honourable member for Plymouth Sutton would, on hitting the main road, probably be heading in a totally different direction.

*

(xlvi) a diversion

As also was Eamon Carroll, who having earlier left London on the M4 was now just to the north of Bristol, filtering through the Patchway interchange onto the southwest bound M5. He was buoyant. The traffic could be sticky here, but today it was moving and his vehicle was cruising well.

And he could reflect on a a fruitful expedition. All that had been suggested to him at Quarry cottage was achieved, that and more. Having stayed overnight in Queens Park, where he'd found all secure, he'd even found time in the morning to fix a spare TAXI sign to his car roof.

Forty, fifty minutes, and he was across the Avon, and the Yeo, around the Mendips and onto the Somerset levels, fleeing Sedgemoor, leaping the Brue and the Parrett, with its feeder, the Tone away to his left.

He would bridge this at Taunton, close to Junction 25 where he was having to pull out for a large-ish vehicle edging in from the left, and now filling his nearside mirror. The grill with the mounted wraith announced itself to be a Rolls Royce, being driven as if to assert absolute ownership of the road..... all six lanes of it. Eamon knew better than to contest, he was going to have to ease back and fall in behind, but not before a sideways glance at this ostentatious twit, who he thought he might recognise.

And, on a second glance, yes, he most certainly did. This was Alan Clark, of whom that Jeremy had made frequent mention, and also Declan had said something....... a significant something, because it had been to do with that map. It was about the radio programme, the one on which his tenant, Peg, and the MP had been interviewed together.

So where might the Minister for Trade and Industry be headed now, wondered Eamon Carroll. Perhaps this was an opportunity to find out. He could stay behind him now, without attracting suspicion. For wasn't this where he'd been so firmly put?

Easily said, yes, but not so easily done as the Rolls breezed over the Whiteball ridge, stretching away from Eamon's flagging motor with every uphill yard. But he was still in sight from the crest above the Culm Valley...... the straight descent bringing a chance to make up the lost ground, particularly now that his elegant quarry had moved in again to the slow lane, so perhaps there was no need to charge.

Definitely so, for look, he was pulling off at the Tiverton junction. This was interesting. Was he headed for North Devon, taking the Barnstaple road, or picking up petrol at the the services, or could he be calling at the station here...... Tiverton Parkway? If this, then care was needed. But that said, taxis tend to be more naturally drawn to railway stations than do Rolls Royces. All options remained open, at least until he had the mischance to attract custom!

And it was the station, with its large carpark affording continued scope for discretion. The Rolls parked and the driver waited, and leaving him the widest practical berth Eamon did likewise, taking the opportunity then to lift a Western Region timetable from his glove compartment. An express whistled through, prompting him to wonder how many services made a stop here. Very few, the timetable told him. In fact, there wasn't one in either direction for more than an hour.

So what was the explanation? Ministers of the Crown have full diaries. They won't often go in for trainspotting. Was he meeting another car here, perhaps? This was intriguing.

The answer came in fifteen minutes...... a down train slowing, slowing, gradually to a stop. And perhaps *unwontedly* it seemed, for no one had been waiting on the *bare platform*. Until a door was opened, from the inside, just the one door on that one end of just one of the first class carriages. And Eamon Carroll realised, for he'd known something like this before. But it hadn't been a first class carriage then, nor indeed such a conveniently raised platform. He was thinking back to a rough ride that took him to a dark and dangerous tunnel, and to this same irregular feature…..an unscheduled stop.

Could such manipulation of the railway network lie within the power of this Minister, wondered Connors. Or was the MP himself being manipulated by a more sinister agency? Two figures had alighted, and as they found their bearings Clark had brought his car to the station entrance, where he was climbing out to greet them. Though neither of the pair was young, one, the taller, seemed significantly older. He was of slighter build and more aristocratic bearing. Something in him was familiar, thought Carroll, and he reached to the back seat, for the book he'd been given the previous day……. that, as yet, he'd only glanced through, scanning for maps and photograhic plates.

Now he was thumbing for the last of these, taken in '44, well over forty years go now…… and yet there was a clear likeness. Allowing for the passsage of years, this could indeed be the same man. And his companion, who was shorter, stouter, and now lifting both their bags, it would appear was carrying a limp, so……

So he would continue to follow, decided Eamon, and while waiting as they loaded into the Rolls he would look again at that timetable so as to confirm, from the Bristol and Taunton stop times, a strengthening suspicion that this train would not have been a Paddington departure. This was so. Instead, it had come down from the north east, and maybe they had too, all the way, from the far north east……. but where to now? Back to the motorway, and on to Exeter and Plymouth?

If so, then why hadn't they stayed on the train, to the scheduled stop at either place. Strange, until, as the Rolls pulled away, it became clear that the Minister was about to take the Tiverton road, the A361, a route unfamiliar to Eamon, but which he understood from the signs would take them to Barnstaple, thirty miles distant, were they to stay with it. But they weren't. Ten minutes and they were approaching Tiverton itself, filtering from the dualled by-pass to find the edge of town roundabout, but not to take the town centre exit. Instead it was another A road, this one, to Crediton, along which they followed the River Exe to Bickleigh before twisting away to the west, reaching Crediton and climbing to the ridge beyond which the A377 dropped with the Taw valley towards the northern coast.

But this wasn't their direction either. The mass that was Dartmoor was drawing them in again, there was no escaping its relentless pull.

Okehampton appeared on the signs, which Eamon knew to be on the A30 trunk road. They were taking a broad short cut, avoiding Exeter. Would they strike for Bude now, or for Launceston? The preference for Okehampton over Hatherleigh suggested the latter, and they were almost to the edge of Dartmoor now, the northern slope gloriously defined uinder an early evening sun.

But then, sharply they were turning away on a B road signposted for Holsworthy. So why, ten miutes before, hadn't they taken the better road through Hatherleigh rather than a route which described the roughest two and a half sides of a square? Perhaps his dogged pursuit had been noticed. If they were testing a suspicion then it was time to let them go. Why risk all when he'd done so well already? Besides, his fuel guage was showing alarmingly low.

*

(xlvii) African Tiger?
Wacker Quay

" 'Shell House', Chas, these were the words that put us on our mettle."

"But Megan, they all seem fairly sure on that. The bit that's baffling them is this mention of an 'African Tiger'. Where the devil can one of those to be found? Tigers don't roam Africa any more than polar bears do the South Pole!" The tent had been erected next to the caravan and the inflatable firmly tied. As the sun sank towards hill hidden St Germans, Megan and the two youngsters could now enjoy a brew of tea. The supper could wait for the boys' return. They were collecting again across at the cliffs.

"The first mention, though, this did emerge from Ince," probed the herbalist.

"In a letter, apparently, that I've not seen, Megan, but Jeremy has, and Alan."

"And also Eamon, that Irish Londoner they've struck up with at their site," added Sally. "He does a taxi service."

"So where were they shown this letter, and who wrote it?"

"At a cottage close to that boatyard," replied Chas, "the one just above the viaduct, across there on the Lynher. They met the live-alone resident down at the *Notterbridge* pub. They got talking. Declan they call him."

"Another Irishman," said Megan.

"Who's lived there for donkey's years. He delivered milk, then sold up his round to do odd jobs. He helps with gardens at Ince...... got quite friendly with the Viscount. The letter was amongst things the widow was throwing out after he died."

"So it was to the Viscount, this letter?"

"It wasn't," answered Chas, "and Jeremy says we can't even be sure that he knew of its existence. It was written by a predecessor of his at the Colonial Office."

"By a Lord Moyne," joined Sally, "and it was addressed to the Viscountess, she being his niece. Forty years later the gardener saves it from a bonfire."

"And the uncle, he knew of a Shell House long before the Boyd's came to Ince," reasoned Megan.

"This has to be the HQ of the Shell Oil Corporation in Kenya," explained Chas. "Apparently, during the war, the building doubled as an out station for our Secret Intelligence Service. The story runs that a political assasination was planned and perpetrated from the place. A notoriously dissolute Earl was bumped off."

"Why was that?"

"No one's exactly sure," replied Sally. "Probably something to do with peace moves." Megan nodded. Chas continued. "The whole thing was muddied by the arrest of a fellow aristocrat, who was charged and tried for supposedly shooting the man in a fit of passionate jealousy, the Earl having seduced his wife."

"Ah," responded the herbalist, "I think I do recall some of this. He was found not guilty."

"That's right," confirmed Sally, trying to remember what she'd gleaned from a hasty flick through of *White Mischief.* "I think because the prosecution overplayed the significance of a gun that the accused owned. It was proved by the defence that this particular gun could not have been the murder weapon, and this sowed sufficient doubt to win the acquittal.

The possibility that the accused might have borrowed or stolen a different gun to do the deed might have been more thoroughly explored......"

"......but wasn't," added Megan, "making the whereabouts of this real murder weapon, and the identity of whoever concealed the thing, the keys to the solving of an ongoing mystery. The pair of you certainly seem well briefed on the case."

"Jeremy let us have his book about it all," Chas told her. "written by a guy named Fox...... but he doesn't mention that Shell House, in fact it seems he could have been dissuaded from ferreting into that aspect."

"So, much as with the trial in distant Africa, all those years ago, the possibility of a political assassination remains under explored," said Megan. "That's intriguing."

"And all the more so for us having come into Moyne's tip. OK, he sets us a riddle, but that in itelf is a privilege. The vital gun, Erroll's bane, will have been concealed in that Shell House.......perhaps in the grounds, or in the fabric of the building, or under some piece of ornamentation."

"In *that* Shell House," repeated Megan, cryptically.

"Because apparently the wife of the main executive who was in residence there could well have been implicated in the killing," said Sally. "She'd had a fling with the Earl too, but perhaps this might have been part of a watching brief, she also having been recruited to the intelligence service."

"Sounds complicated," remarked Megan, "and too much so, possibly, for if you went across to Ince now and asked the old Lady there straight, about a Shell House, she wouldn't take this as an invitation to talk about her uncle's memories of Africa....... would she? You'll have been there often enough, Sally, and done the gardens. Tell me, what would she assume you were wanting to know about?"

"About *her* Shell House, the summer house in the corner of the garden. Yes I'd overlooked that.......but, understandably, for while Moyne was killed in '44, the Boyds didn't move down to Ince until the 1960s. The building of this small garden feature wasn't started until after that, as a project to slot between those odd retirement jobs that a former Minister will often be roped in to do."

"So after he'd cleared his Colonial desk," said Megan. "Having the time now, with his no longer having to constantly dash off to the far corners of Empire."

"Something like that," agreed Chas.

"But if he wasn't travelling, where would he have found those shells?" posed Megan.

"He would have collected them over the years," suggested Chas.

"And stored them where?"

"In Bedfordshire," supposed Sally. "At his former home."

"And maybe he was given a start with this collection. Perhaps Moyne had gathered a few sackfulls in his travels."

"Yes, fairly likely I'd say," conceded Sally. "In *White Mischief* it's said that Moyne was famed for his interest in zoology."

"So he was linked to the case......directly?"

"By virtue of the very close friendship he'd formed with the accused's former wife."

"Interesting," said Megan. "And if he came by that gun in the course of his work, and realising its potential decided to hide it......"

"Then he might have concealed the thing amongst a pile of shells that he was saving for a retirement project of his own," said Chas. "And there could have been an understanding, between him and his niece, that should he not survive to enjoy such a retirement then what he'd so far gathered would be for her and her husband."

"The gun included, you're implying," added Sally. "So this African Tiger........ might it be a species of shell?"

Megan shrugged. "The boys, we can ask the boys," she said, with a snap of her fingers. "Here they come now."

*

(xliix) room at the inn

"Ah yes...... Mr Barnes," the manager of the *Talbot Inn* selected a key from his rack. "We just had the one double room, which your wife has already booked. I'll show you up." Jeremy was speechless. "And it would only be the one night, she said. If I could leave this breakfast menu with you then maybe you could advise me on your selections before turning in."

"Of course," blurted the lecturer, struggling to contain a heady blend of surprise, joy, and trepidation. If this is what it was, he'd never imagined rconciliation could be so...... well, so sudden. "But she's gone out again?"

"I think they went around to the Churchyard."

"They?"

"Well she was in here, waiting for you she said, and she got to asking about Lord Oxford, and the Manor...... the usual questions, concerning the mother and her religion, and the Horner family as well as the Asquiths. And as I was starting to fill things in for her, who should walk in but the old boy himself."

"Julian Asquith, the second Earl. He comes in."

"I wouldn't say he was a regular, exactly, but once a week, at least, he'll look in. He owns the premises, like he owns a lot of this village and plenty of the farmland around. But he's a good landlord, one who sees no sense in coming in unless it's to be sociable...... and what I did, of course, was to introduce him to your wife." They were at the top of the stairs now. "That's your room there."

Taking the key, the lecturer unlocked the door. The room was perfect, cool and dim, with a small thinly curtained window bringing from the solid oak cupboards and crisply linenned bed a gently balanced glow, and from Jeremy a deep spasm of desire. Yes.....she did it still for him......and how, and she knew it, and was wanting to.

"So how long ago was it they went out?"

"Less than an hour, more than threequarters maybe."

"I'll wait here then...... and if I could trouble you for a bottle of your best red, and a couple glasses."

*

The Manor House, Mells, with St. Andrews Church beyond. The gate in the dividing wall is to the right of the tower. It was through this that Nolwen spied her stepson's 'ghost'.

BOOK THREE

'J'ai seul la clef de cette parade sauvage.'
(I alone hold the key to this savage parade)

From '*Les Illuminations*' by Arthur Rimbaud
Set to music by Benjamin Britten (*opus 18*) 1939

(i) Wacker

Just the few sharp words in Swahili from Megan, and Juma and Makasi were launched into earnest and animated discussion. Chas and Sally watched, uncomprehending of any close meaning but taking encouragement from what looked to be a series of affirmative gestures……. the nodding of heads, and hand movements that might be indicating shape and size.

They walked away then, towards the edge of the Quay, taking Megan with them.

"We could be on to something here," whispered Chas. He turned towards Ince "Sally, do you know exactly where that Shell House is over there."

"I think I could find it," the girl replied.

"Even in the dark?"

*

(ii) *The Talbot*

"A true gentleman…….. so, so sweet. And I think he enjoyed my company, as a pleasant change after that of Alan Clark. I was left with a distinct impression that the Minister's call hadn't been the highlight of his day."

"And this was volunteered by Lord Asquith."

"Give me some credit, Jeremy. I didn't interrogate the man. I know better than that."

"Of course you do, Kate." Jeremy swivelled so as to ease his feet up onto the bed. Suitably propped he then reached for his glass of wine.

"How then did you get him on to the illustrious visitor?"

"It was with the mention of Evelyn Waugh."

"So you managed to broach the subject of Evelyn."

"I didn't have to…… he did, initially, when we were in the Churchyard. Having paid our respects to several generations of Horners, and Violet Bonham Carter…..

"….. and Sassoon of course….."

"We then found the name Ronald Knox, and this meant nothing to me, I had to admit."

"Should it have?"

"If I was seriously a Roman Catholic, then yes. "

"But you're not."

"As his Lordship came to realise….. but he said that if I wanted to know more about the man I should look out for his biography, this having been written by Waugh. Knox died back in the late '50s having lived for the last ten years of his life in the Manor, as a personal chaplain to Katherine Asquith, Julian's mother. As you've said, Waugh took his Catholicism seriously, and Knox and the then Lady of the Manor were the closest of friends. This went right back to the early '30s when Evelyn wrote *Black Mischief*, a novel that some in the Catholic establishment considered blasphemous. Knox and Katherine, both prominent in the Church, they defended him stoutly. Twenty years later, Evelyn helped nurse Knox as he slowly died of cancer. I would imagine it to be an affectionate biography."

"So did he say more about Evelyn?"

"He did. He said that few had been as good as he at lifting his mother from her periodic bouts of melancholy. She wasn't one for mocking people herself, being far, far too good a soul……"

"……thus denying herself the therapeutic benefits often drawn."

"Exactly, but with Evelyn to hand she could share in his jokes and taunt, as it were, by proxy."

"You said this?"

"And Lord Oxford was quite impressed. He asked if I'd read any of Waugh's satires, and I said *Brideshead*, adding that for all its spritual earnestness it has some really funny parts. He agreed, recalling that it had been written during the war, and at this I brought up the *Sword of Honour* books….. but warily, because I haven't read them."

"So you said……?"

"…..that I understood they reflected many of Waugh's own wartime experiences, and perhaps lampooned a good selection of his and his mother's mutual acquaintances."

"Good, good, go on Kate ….. did you mention Trimmer?"

"No, I didn't." Jeremy's face dropped.

"Because I didn't have to," chuckled Kate, squeezing kittenishly at his thigh. "For he did," she added, in triumph. "'*Only just now*', he said,

'*I had someone at the door wanting to talk about Trimmer*'. 'Trimmer?' I said artlessly. '*Who'd always drawn a smirk from my mother*' he continued '*although it's only now that I see the joke myself.*' "

"So did he say who it was aimed at?" Jeremy had scented his quarry.

"No, and yes," teased Kate. Now it was Jeremy going for her thigh. "The name he mentioned was Veronica Maclean, the widow of one Fitzroy Maclean."

"I've heard of Fitzroy Maclean," confirmed the lecturer. He was our main man in Yugoslavia, towards the end of the war."

"Well the Asquiths, and also Evelyn, they knew this Veronica when she was a girl, a teenager, and apparently she had this elder brother who eventually came to distinguish himself during the war..... but before then, by all accounts, was as conceited a prig as could be imagined, this conceit having been stoked by the way his mother and his sisters had always idolised him. To them, the sun would ever be shining from his backside, and in comparison poor young Julian Asquith, Trim to family and friends, was always considered second best."

"I get it," announced Jeremy. "To those who knew what Trim had had to suffer, it wasn't difficult to work out who Trimmer might be."

"And the joke targets both him and the sister. To Katherine Asquith and Ronald Knox, who knew Veronica's family well, all this would have been a hoot."

"While for good natured Julian himself, it would have appeared to have gone over his head.......until today, you say, and this visit from Alan Clark." Jeremy was intrigued. "But Lord Oxford didn't give you a name for this Trimmer, you say?"

"He didn't, and I wasn't going to ask for fear of seeming over inquisitive, and staunching a copious flow of information. Tomorrow we can call at a library, find a *Who's Who*, and see what we can find on Veronica and Fitzroy Maclean. That should tell us her maiden name....."

".....and also identify Trimmer, who has a number of aliases in *Sword of Honour*....."

".......including the name Gustave."

"Well done Kate, bloody well done." Jeremy pulled her close. "What a team we are."

"And there's more yet," said Kate, pressing a restraining finger against the end of his nose. "Lord Oxford told me that not so long ago this

Trimmer produced a memoir. He'd owned a copy, even, and would have lent it to me had he not just given it away this very afternoon......"

"......to Alan Clark....."

"......as much to get rid of him as anything, that's the impression I got."

"So Clark had just turned up, wanting to talk about this soldier?"

"Well like you, Jeremy, he is a historian. Research you call it. They would have looked at the book together, and perhaps also taken *Sword of Honour* off of the shelf....... for somehow Clark let Trim in on the joke."

"But I fancy it to be more than a coincidence that he's turned up here today. Perhaps he's getting the measure of Nolwen's game. If he knew she was coming to Bath, just a taxi ride away, maybe he was moving to close off a potential weakness in someone's cover. I've told you about 'Peg' Willis's disappearance......"

"......just after they'd been on the radio together."

"Clark would have had a hand in that, I'm sure. His neighbour thinks it was to do with a map that Peg brought to the studio. He'd traced it out of a book he'd found in Saltash Library."

"Sounds as if it could have been that self same memoir," said Kate.

"Once we've got the name, we ought to be able to search out our own copy."

"A specialist military book shop, you'll need."

"In Plymouth there's one," said Jeremy, "down towards the Barbican. Loads of second hand stuff, he's piled to the ceiling."

"So tomorrow," smiled Kate, "it's early to rise."

"And tonight," nuzzled Jeremy, "early to bed."

*

(iii) Sourton

Abandoning Clark's tail, Eamon stayed with the cross-county Bideford to Plymouth road. Soon he was at Sourton Cross, where it ducked beneath A30, just to the west of Okehampton. A service station offered the chance to refuel before continuing southward. Having paid he checked his where abouts by browsing one of a selection of local maps.

Yes, he would continue on this road to Tavistock, and there strike westward to cross the Tamar at Gunnislake. It would be Callington, Saltash, and then Trerulefoot for the familiar first exit to take him towards Torpoint.

On the same map he tried to make sense of Clark's choice of the A3079 for Holsworthy. How strange this was......unless his actual destination lay within the Holsworthy/Okehampton/Launceston triangle, probably somewhere near Roadford Reservoir, between the catchment of the River Thrushel, which fed the Tamar, and that of the Torridge bound River Carey. He could raise this with Jeremy. The lecturer, he knew, was in touch with the Minister's step mother. She would be the one to ask. An interesting weekend loomed.

*

(iv) Tremorebridge

And, as he pressed his sharpest trousers and ironed his least cuff-frayed white shirt, James Busbridge was thinking much the same. Tomorrow he would be making his way up to *Jamaica Inn*, to the reserved accomodation, and the illustrious company that would await. Peers of the Realm no less, not one, but two...... both of whom had been so much in the news. And on the following day they were due to be collected by a Cabinet Minister who, whatever his merits and de-merits as a politician, had to be counted a formidable military historian.

Busbridge thought back to his last two visits to the inn and what they'd produced. There would be some kind of link, he was sure, but its exact nature remained elusive. Today he'd tried to contact Kate, but without success. She was away, he'd been told ..... and possibly overnight.

(v) Wacker

That night, at forty five minutes past midnight......

Chas, Sally, Megan, Juma, and Makesi were ready to go. Half a moon might be enough, thought the girl. For the inspection of the Shell House the boys would have with then a lamp. The tricky bit was the tide. It was lowish still, but, luckily, fast filling. Their approach should be rowed, it had been decided. By the time they were over, the mud would be covered.

Juma and Makesi were positive. Cowrie shells were common along the coast of East Africa, ranging widely in size and marking, and while different tribes gave them different names they did know of a species that the european liked to call 'the tiger cowrie.'

"So how big?" Megan had asked.

"Big enough," Juma had replied, spacing his hands to indicate shoe box dimension.

"And striped, obviously," Chas had ventured, only to incur sharp correction. While tiger coloured, these shells were spotted, leopard-like. Indeed leopard cowrie might have been the more appropriate name.

Sally, for a moment, quietly entertained misgivings as to Megan's ability to cope with this foray, age mitigating against mobility...... but then, seeing how nimbly the woman embarked and how eagerly those eyes caught the glow of moonlight on water, the girl knew better than to voice such concern.

In climbed Sally with her metal detector, then Juma and Makesi with lamp and lump hammer, and finally, pushing them out and starting the outboard, Chas. They were on their way.

*

(vi) *The Talbot*

Certainty, fidelity
On the stroke of midnight pass
Like vibrations of a bell......
......but from this night
Not a whisper, not a thought,
Not a kiss nor a look be lost.
(from *Lullaby*; W.H. Auden)

........and, window filtered, the light of the same soft moon blanches the single form of two naked lovers, finding thereon not a shadow of guilt. Theirs tonight is the sleep of the freshly absolved, the fully and firmly forgiven. For both, never had love been made more deeply or warmly than it had here, beneath the chime of Mells Church.

*

(vii) Ince Castle

Having pushed downriver, against the tide, to be almost level with the big house, Chas cut the motor. The boys, with an oar each, could now pull them off the main current, back into the shallower lee of Black Rock, where a land fall might be achieved a field and a half to the west of the tight spinney that shelered both castle and gardens. The way in then would be along the first hedge, as far as the outdoor swimming pool, from where a path entered the main grounds at the very corner where the Shell House stood.

If there was a dog, then surely it would be guarding the approach from the other side where the drive came in, having crossed the tunnel and then the old bridge from the north.

Sally led, carrying the detector, then it was Megan, her boys with their tools, and Chas to the rear. No need to rush, thought the girl, keeping low. Were she to stumble she might damage the detector, the vital implement. Likewise, Megan might sprain or fracture a wrist, or, even worse, a femur. So it had to be steady here, at this first stile, so that all could be safely over.

Another stretch of hedge and they were at the pool. Sally took the torch, suggesting that all save her might wait under the cover of the changing shelter while she scouted the path for their goal. The others concurred, Chas holding the detector. Sally was confident, but her heart raced nonetheless.

"Back shortly," she whispered, thinking perhaps five, six minutes...... but actually returning in less than four. "Follow me," she rasped.

She led them through, all in that same order, until the Shell House loomed, sentry-box-sized, externally walled and roofed with Bedfordshire brick and local slate, but within, rendered wholly with as an exotic a collection of shells as might be found anywhere outside of a Natural History Museum.

The torch was passed in to Makesi. Juma crouched with him as they examind the back wall first, from the bottom up. Sally, meanwhile, activated the detector, opting for a silent mode setting then testing it on the metal strap of Chas's wristwatch as the boy peeled a few strands of ivy off the outside.

As its seconds ticked, the Africans within moved from back wall to side, muttering to each other in Swahili as they progressed. No cowrie yet..... so, outside, Sally moved around also to scan up and down with the sounder.

And then a reading....... the indicator lit up. She felt the vibration.

"Here, try here." She tapped against the wall. "Shoulder height, hand to elbow's distance from the front corner."

Juma and Makesi were quickly there with the torch.
"Could well be," said the former, reverting to English. "Right size, and certainly mottled........ deeply set though."

"So we might need to knock off some of that cement," said Megan, passing the hammer through to Makesi.

"Stand back," said the African. "If it's been sawn and restuck then pieces might fly. Protect your eyes." The hammer was swung. Two blows and that was enough. The cowrie caved, giving a glimpse of rag within and a whiff of oil.

"He wrapped it too," said Megan, taking the hammer again. "Good man...... it might even still work." Slidding his fingers carefully

412

between the jagged edges of broken shell, Makesi tugged the package out. And a gun it was, he knew by its weight and shape even before it was unwrapped. Out they came. Juma trained the torch.

"According to Fox, in his book, that's likely to be a Smith & Wesson .32," said Chas, "with a five grooved barrel which gives the bullet a clockwise spin. Anyone ready to confirm that?"

"Not in this light," said Megan, re-wrapping the pistol, but not before securing the scroll of paper rolled loosely around its barrel. "Let's get out of here. We've got what we came for. Get back to caravan and I'll do us some cocoa."

"Sound thinking," agreed Sally, attempting to mask the damage with a hasty re arrangement of the remaining ivy. "Follow me again. No need to rush, we want no accidents….. not while carrying a gun!"

*

(vii) A303
The next morning

"So you'll allow me to take you to your door," smiled Jeremy, as he eased his car onto the Ilchester by-pass, the busy A303. On an August Saturday it could be slow going to Exeter, though once on the A30 the flow ought to improve.

"I'm having to work tonight, Jeremy." Kate dusted affectionately at his knee. "And by tomorrow I'll be needing my sleep."

"So what would you like me to do?"

"I want you to rejoin Alan, and impress upon him the progress you've made."

"*We've* made, Kate. I'd be nowhere without your help. And, I suppose, if you want Alan on board then so it has to be…..."

"……because it's the pressure from Busbridge that's been getting to me, and without seeing it Alan has added to this."

"I thought you said the DNA testing was inconclusive."

"Yes, so he thinks I should oblige him with a better sample from his putative 'Norman'. Also he's gathering together some drawings of this small folding plane carried by that submarine he's so taken with."

"And he wants you to brandish them in front of the poor fellow."

"But without proving anything, that could be dangerous. Our patient might fly off the handle, just as he did when working at *Jamaica Inn*." Kate looked at her watch. "If we have time we could call in there on the way through. Just briefly...... I can show you something."

*

(ix) Wacker

Let us sleep now.........
In paradisum deducant te Angeli (War Requiem; Britten)

Crouching, Megan lifted the tent flap slightly, and there they were. Her darling Babes, sleeping so soundly.......
as they would for a good twenty four hours yet, by which time they would be truly secured, together with all that they'd so trustingly brought to her. Ideally, though, she just needed the one more witness....... just in case. For prisoner number seven could hardly be expected to be in robust health, not at the age of....... what was it..... 93?

The boys were already on task, a doubled task, in fact; the summoning of the waiting ship, with, at the same time, the making of a necessary reconnaisance. It was about noon now, she judged. They would be back with the van by eight, and the ship should be inside the breakwater for dark.

*

(x) *Jamaica Inn*

As he swung into the carpark, Jeremy thought back to his last time here..... two years before, and that return from Exeter, on a surge of anger that too easily led him so far astray.

He glanced at Kate. Her eyes met his, briefly, fondly. This was

414

indeed more than a mending.

A coach waited for them to take a space, diverting Kate's attention away from what she might otherwise have seen...... James Busbridge's car. It wasn't until they were in the bar that she spotted him. Jeremy was headed for the counter. She checked him.

"That's James over there," she whispered.

"By that framed picture....."

"......which is what I wanted to show you, but not now. He hasn't seen us......"

".....and you would rather he didn't." They turned for the exit, Jeremy checking with a last glance back. Nothing was said. Within minutes they were back on the road.

"Those two guys with him," Jeremy began, at last.

"I didn't really see," said Kate. "Was he showing them what was on the wall?"

"That same picture."

"Which is actually several. It's a collection of old cigarette cards, warships......"

"Including his favourite submarine?"

"No...... but that's the point. Too long a story or now, though."

"That's good," said Jeremy, "for I'm more intrigued by the eminent company he would appear to have gathered."

"You recognised those men?"

"Both, Kate, are prominent life Peers, each having been closely supportive of Ted Heath when he was PM. Now, for reasons other than this association with an outmoded style of Toryism, each is finding himself personally at odds with the present Government."

"So who were they?"

"The Lords Aldington and Rothschild, both of whom have been engaged in defending what they strongly feel to be unjustly sullied reputations."

"Whose reputations?"

"Their own."

"So not quite the same as Nolwen......"

"..... whose concern is for her mother's," agreed Jeremy, "but finding Busbridge in there with them suggests a link."

"That this is all to do with the same deep laid conspiracy, you mean?"

"I do, but as yet any sure connection evades me. Were we to identify GUSTAVE, things then might become clearer.

"Shame there wasn't a *Who's Who* in Launceston Library," sighed Kate. "And Bodmin's will have closed by now."

"Never mind......I suppose Busbridge hadn't mentioned it to you that he would be hob-nobbing with the Peerage?"

"He didn't.... any more than I said to him that we would be seeking out Lord Oxford."

"When I catch up with him I'll ask Alan the same, but for the moment it looks as if your friend James might be on a frolic of his own."

"Like us, you mean," giggled Kate.

*

(xi) Whitsand Bay campsite.
later

"Where've you been all night, " asked Alan.

"A place called Mells," replied Jeremy, economically. "Did you say that Eamon is back?"

"Yesterday evening, he got here. He too has been wondering where you were. He wants us to call on Declan McDaid. Eamon has been to Ulster, this at Declan's suggestion. After flying back to Bristol, he then went up to London....... checking out his digs."

"So is it over to Quarry Cottage this evening?"

"As soon as he's back from his last fare down to the ferry." Alan tugged at the camper curtain. "In fact here he is now. There's a chippy down in Millbrook. He said he would bring some up." Now he stood, procurring a small bottle of ketchup from a flap-fronted, eye level cupboard.

But there was no time for that. Having seen Jeremy's car, Eamon wanted its owner and Alan in his...... without further delay. They could eat the chips as he drove. Save for the two or three he snaffled as Alan fiddled with his keys, he would forego his share.

"I won't be saying too much yet," the driver began "for I'm not wanting to repeat things again for Declan's benefit."

"Sounds like you've got something," angled Jeremy.

"I have....... something on GUSTAVE certainly, and maybe also on that missing neighbour."

"'Peg' Willis," helpd Jeremy.

"Plus a little something extra on Mr Declan McDaid. But as it was he who put me up my two day fact finding tour....."

"..... and also saved your life," added Alan.

"Perhaps it can wait for a less hectic moment. Is there any news yet from Mr Busbridge on the forensic front?"

"There is," answered Grigson. "The hoped for match wasn't made, much to his dismay."

"No need for that," said Eamon. "There's conclusions to be drawn, whatever the result."

"But he won't be budged from his premise," said Grigson. "The sample wasn't good enough, he maintains. With Kate's help I guess he'll try for better."

The driver nodded sagely. Enough said on this topic. "So what about those youngsters?" he asked. "Any more use to you, Jeremy?".

"They're on the trail of Moyne's African Tiger," broke in Alan. They'd reached the roundabout at Trerulefoot. "Somehow Busbridge has got wind of this little conundrum, probably through Kate, with whom you, Jeremy, might have shared it."

It would have been through Enid, Jeremy knew....... but he wasn't disposed to explain. "Might have," he conceded.

"Well James thought it a good one to take down to Wacker, to the Africans there, and using the same tactic you employed, Jeremy, with Nolwen, he put this task with young Chas. Jim, apparently, knows the boy's father quite well."

"So it'll be interesting to hear what they come back with," said Eamon, as they climbed from Tideford, indicating then both urgency and a growing familiarity with the area by ducking across into Tredinnick Lane, dropping between the high hedges into Hay Lane Bottom before climbing to St Erney past Vicarage Woods.

In the back, Alan Grigson glanced down at a wide soft cover road atlas, and beneath, half cooncealed, a substantial paperback. '*March Past*', announced the title, boldly, and finely beneath, '*a memoir by*' ...... and the rest was obscured. And so it stayed, the passenger being unaware of its possible significance.

McDaid was there. He welcomed them in, and sat back as if impressed and encouraged as Eamon moved to initiate discussion.

"Declan, if I can presume to use your first name, I've not yet told Mr Barnes and Mr Grigson here of my travels, nor anything of the dividend gained therefrom. With your permission, I would like them to hear what I bring back for you."

"Go ahead," responded the host.

"Well if anyone has a solid handle on this HIGHLAND CLEARANCE mystery then it's you, Declan. In fact, you have a number. You knew Boyd. You came by Moyne's letter. You heard Peg Willis on the radio with Alan Clark." McDaid nodded. "You also saved my life and, since then, you've been sensitive, as you all have, to this limbo predicament of mine between the British security people and the Republican movement." Carroll turned to Alan and Jeremy. "To you two, I can say now, that with a view to resolving this predicament Declan suggested that I might travel to Ulster, to Bellfast, and there meet the IRA command. This I did, equipped with a map given to me by Declan, the tracing from which Peg made the very map that he took to the radio studio....."

".......and which disapperared when he did," added Declan. "The grease-proof I found amongst his those few books he owned and left."

"The proposal to them, the IRA, made in person to Martin McBeamish himself, was that if they were to help me identify our man GUSTAVE, then such insights that might as a consequence be gained into HIGHLAND CLEARANCE would be shared. They would then have a lever, I argued, that might prove more effective in their cause than any amount of bomb and bullet."

"The lever that Patsy Lennox Boyd might have used to against Macmillan prior to the Hola debate," said Jeremy, "relieving the pressure on her husband."

"Fine," said Alan, "but how were the IRA meant to help you identify GUSTAVE?"

"Through a Catholic Priest," explained Declan. "One mentioned, though not actually by name, by Peg Willis in his broadcast account of the fight to take and hold the Orne River crossings. He spoke of a Padre with the D Day Air landing Brigades, and he was Irish.....now there couldn't have been many of them, could there?"

"I suppose not," answered Grigson.

"Well this one was summoned to the field hospital that Peg spoke of, where he'd heard the names GUSTAVE and HIGHLAND CLEARANCE in the ramblings of a wounded officer, one close enough to death to warrant an administering of the last rites."

"A soldier that might well have been GUSTAVE himself," added Eamon, "and my hope was that the movement could help me trace this Padre, who, in turn, might divulge the real name."

"That was our plan," confirmed McDaid, eagerly. "Now tell us what it produced."

"Plenty," continued Carroll. "I was sent back to London, to north-west London, to a place not far from my home in Queens Park......"

"......where you were told you might find this Priest," said Jeremy.

"Which I did."

"So you have his name, at least."

"Father Seamus Mulligan." Eamon Connors announced slowly, searching into McDaid's eyes...... to find, as expected, not the slightest flicker. "And he gave me a book to borrow, a memoir written by that selfsame soldier, who survived those wounds and who is still very much alive now....... for I think I might have seen him, only yesterday. The book's in the car."

"*March Past*, it's on the back seat," said Alan "I'll get it." Darting out, he returned in seconds. "*A memoir by Lord Lovat*" he read off the front. " '*Fiercely exciting and poignantly moving*', according to the *Spectator*, so it says here."

"And in that book you will find the map used by Peg Willis in Saltash library," said Eamon, proudly.

"Less any mention of GUSTAVE or HIGHLAND CLEARANCE," said McDaid.

"Unless you look really closely," countered Eamon, "which I did before turning in last night..... at certain sections anyway."

"Chronicling D Day, or earlier?" asked Jeremy.

"Earlier," continued Eamon, "much earlier, at the prompting of yourself, actually. The parts I perused chronicle what looks to me to have been a feud, a protracted personal feud stretching way back to his time at Oxford. Though he writes as recently as the '70s, fifty years on from those University days, this man is still twisting the knife. The spite is unrelenting. In pages and pages he'll not summon so much as one simple word of forgiveness." Eamon took the book from Alan. "See where I've pencilled." He found the page, and turned and passed the book then for the lecturer. Jeremy read out the marked phrases:

" *'Evelyn Waugh was cordially disliked by every combatant officer in the brigade......*

......a greedy little man - a eunuch in appearance......

......there was a malignant element - it was worse than spite - that I had not previously encountered in a grown man.

......a misfit personality, who joined through the back door......who made no attempt to train or to learn his trade; when he emerged from protective custody it was in 'shit order' "

"I think we're starting to get the drift," quipped Alan.

"And there, across the page," pointed Eamon, "something about 'Nemesis stalking at Uncle's elbow'. Now when you've been talking about Waugh, Jeremy, the name *Uncle* has cropped up."

"It was the nickname given to Guy Crouchback, the far from heroic hero in *Sword of Honour*. Most have assumed the character to have been based on the author himself, and his own wartime experiences..... and this Lord Lovat is obviously no exception."

"And the nemesis takes the form of a practical joke," said Eamon, "a hoax that Lovat himself proudly admits to having had a hand in."

"I see, yes, we have it down here," said Jeremy. "Waugh was given the task of censoring outbound mail, and Lovat and a pal, they together compose this letter in which they make themselves out to be a couple of spies."

"Which is reproduced there, on that page," said Eamon. "Read it closely."

Jeremy did:

Herr Schmidt, c/o Vogel Von Bumelzeug,
6 Barkhausen Strasse, Zurich.

Dear Schmidt,
ime is short and I will soon be on my way to the
destination already referred to. It is some weeks since we

met and I hope that, according to plan, you have reached
this address in a neutral country. The Dutch route is
dangerous and must be discouraged. I have said enough.
On this chance I am writing. It is not possible for me to
see A, but if all goes well I hope to meet B where I am
going. He will keep you informed.
Gustave sends greetings.
(Signed) No. 89706,
BOMBARDIER HILDEBRAND HARDCASTLE
IN TRANSIT

"I see, yes," said Jeremy. "The name *Gustave* crossed Waugh's desk, and while taking it at face value at first, he was later to find out that it was a hoax impersonation......"

".....and perhaps, eventually, also identify the impersonator," suggested Eamon.

"Who he then, by way of revenge, held up to ridicule in his *Sword of Honour* novels," continued Jeremy. "And if that hit home then it can explain this prolonged slagging off Waugh gets in this memoir, written so long after Evelyn's death......."

"......and in which he might have otherwise barely warranted a footnote. He must have touched a pretty raw nerve," said Alan.

"By painting a fiction that ran so close to the truth that it drew this over-protestation," explained Jeremy. "Lovat does a Gertrude, and halfway outs his own secrets."

"So exactly how far is halfway?" asked Grigson. "What does all this mean, and where does it leave us?"

"We have a name, now, and a scenario," replied the lecturer. "Lovat was an exceptional soldier attached to an ordinary Commando regiment, so exceptional as to be selected for a special assignment."

"Pertaining to the highly secret OPERATION HIGHLAND CLEARANCE," added McDaid.

"In which, when orders were received or issued, the code name GUSTAVE was to be used. By the summer of '42, with the war winning Grand Alliance now well in place, Lovat might have considered HIGHLAND CLEARANCE a done task and grown a little careless..... to the extent of using the code name on that hoax letter, obviously assuming that Waugh could never divine his true identity. That's until ten years later when, in *Officers and Gentlemen*, the second of the *Sword of Honour* trilogy we are introduced to the absurdity that is Trimmer, alias Ali McTavish, alias also *Gustave*."

"And, by then, the true weighty significance of what HIGHLAND CLEARANCE was, and still remains to this day, had become apparent to Lovat," said McDaid. "And his least favourite author was giving him reason to regret his being so free with that code name. For anyone sufficiently clued up on HIGHLAND CLEARANCE, as we are, courtesy of Moyne in his letter and Peg on the radio, Waugh's wartime trilogy offers a key to the identity of one of the main players......by now, perhaps, the main surviving player."

"But doesn't he then compound this discomfort by including the hoax anecdote in his '70's memoir?" asked Eamon.

"Not really," answered Jeremy. "Waugh is dead by now and unable to answer back, Lovat can be as vituperative as he likes, and also feed the impression that so far as he was concerned the name *Gustave* had been devised solely for that hoax, any other connotation being falsely derived from, at worse, mere coincidence."

"A risky ploy," remarked Alan.

"It might easily have worked," said Jeremy, "but the fact of our dicussing this, here, today, obviously means it hasn't...... and we can thank others, Declan, besides the late Moyne and the missing Peg. There's this Priest that Eamon's searched out, who's lent him the book here. And then there's the independent line of enquiry opened for me by the lady Nolwen Clark, carefully preserved and handed from Wystan Auden, through the remarkable Cyril Connolly. That's what got me on to *Sword of Honour*, only yesterday in Bath. Then, on my way back, I must have come within a couple of hours of finding my own copy of *March Past*. It wasn't to be though, and I needn't have worried, for you, Eamon, are the man..... the one who's turned up trumps."

"So where did you come so close," asked Alan.

"Place called Mells, near Frome. We had Nolwen with us?"

"We........?"

"I was with Kate too," answered Jeremy, as casually as he could. "We'd hoped to call on Lord Asquith, a friend of Waugh's who still lives there in the Manor....... and we would have, had not Nolwen taken fright."

"But she's a Lady," said Alan, "and he's a Lord. What was the problem?"

"Her stepson," replied Jeremy. "The Minister….. Plymouth MP and military historian, who co-starred with with Peg on the radio, back in '84."

"And what time was this," asked Eamon.

"Mid afternoon. I didn't see him. Nolwen, though, recognised his car."

"Which was what?" pressed Eamon.

"A Rolls."

"This figures…… for by four-thirty he was on the M5, like me."

"So you saw him too." Alan was amazed, and faintly put out that so substantial a surveillance could have been effected without his involvement. "Where was he headed….. west or east?"

"He joined the westbound carriage-way at Taunton, obliging me to fall in behind him. But this enabled me to follow."

"All the way to Plymouth? Will he be at *The Duke of Cornwall* do you think?"

"Nothing so predictable, Alan,'" answered Eamon. "Where you got that book just now you'll also find a road atlas."

Grigson went. Jeremy smiled to himself, unused to seeing Alan being obliged to fetch. He was soon back. Eamon took the atlas on his lap, opening and turning it for the others to see.

"Now," he began, "If he left Mells, over here, then rather than tangling with the traffic in Glastonbury and Street, he's probably decided to strike southward from Shepton, down the Fosse Way, and then across to the Taunton junction past Langport. I think he likes the old style country road motoring.

"So you then follow him along the motorway," prompted McDaid.

"But only thus far….. to Tiverton Junction station, here. He comes off, and so do I. He is meeting people at the station, two people, one of whom I now think could be Lovat himself."

"And you can say that for sure?" Alan was doubtful.

"Obviously he must look far older than in any of the book's photos, but some things about a man's bearing will never change……. and also I checked with my train timetable."

"So he has a special train!"

"In a manner of speaking, yes Alan, he does. Firstly, no one else gets on or off. Secondly, looking in the timetable, I see that each day a service runs from Penzance, all the way up to Inverness......"

"...... and a corresponding service will run in the opposite direction," added Jeremy, "crossing in the Leeds/Sheffield area, where the crews will probably switch."

"And Lovat, he lives in Inverness, at Beaufort Castle, the ancestral home of the Clan Frasers," continued Eamon. "It's all in that book."

"Go on," urged Jeremy.

"The Inverness to Penzance service runs through Tiverton Junction, and that's what I saw Alan Clark meet."

"Interesting," conceded Alan, "but hardly cast iron."

"Perhaps, but certainly lent solidity when one finds out that the train should be passing through that station at one hundred and twenty miles per hour," countered Eamon. "Nothing was scheduled to stop there at that time......"

".......and, as you say, no one else got on or off." Jeremy bent forward to look more closely at the map. "So where to then...... back to the motorway?"

"It wasn't." Eamon's finger found junction 27, before tracing a route westwards "From here it was across to Tiverton, and then down to Crediton for a short stretch on the Exeter- Barnstaple road before striking across to meet the Okehampton to Bideford road, this one, here, just to the south of Hatherleigh."

"So was it right, there, or was it left?" Alan's interest was deepening."

"Well look at the map, and say you wanted to get to Holsworthy."

"I would turn right," answered Alan.

"And were you wanting to get to anywhere else to the south or west of Okehampton?"

"Then left down to here, on the A30, the Sourton juction where I've used the service station."

"Well Clark turned left, following the road so far, and then swung off to the right, along this minor road that goes back up to Holsworthy."

"I hope you didn't follow," said the professional. "After all that distance he could have been testing you out."

"I let him go, yes, but I still think it more likely Clark had a place in mind, a destination in this Okehampton, Launceston, Holsworthy triangle....... so where?"

"One side or other of that damn great lake," suggested Jeremy.

"What I could do, is ask Nolwen. I have her number."

"Use my phone," offered Declan. "It's through there, in the kitchen."

Jeremy slipped out. Alan flicked through *March Past*. Eamon eyed their host. He wanted to tell him that the Movement was indeed very interested in HIGHLAND CLEARANCE, and also discuss much else besides...... but perhaps now wasn't the moment.

"You know," he ventured instead, "I've a strong sense that GUSTAVE is staying somewhere in this area, and if we don't find him together then he could be seeking us out, one by one......"

"....... just as he might have done Stanley 'Peg' Willis," agreed McDaid.

"And then there's those kids," added Jeremy, re emerging from the kitchen. "It was through their chat with Clark that I initially made contact with Nolwen. He might remember this. We want to be sure Chas and Sally stay safe."

"So....... Lady Clark," Grigson closed the book, positioning himself to again scrutinise the road atlas "Did she pick up the phone? Was she helpful?"

"Her stepson has a country retreat in a village called Bratton Clovelly. Town Farm, he's had it for years."

"Got it," said Alan. "Here, just to the east of Roadford Reservoir, right where you would expect it to be. Well done Jeremy, and very well done Eamon. I think we can assume them to have been unaware of the tail. Our famed leader of the Lovat Scouts has been out-scouted."

"So what now?" asked McDaid.

"I reckon we confront them," said Eamon. "I speak as the fugitive......the one who's had an attempt against his life, and can expect another at any time. We go together and from my stand-point there would be safety in numbers. Also we go as soon as possible."

"Tomorrow?" Declan's suggestion met the approval of all......only Jeremy expressing slight reservation.

"So what about Busbridge and Kate?" he said.

"More than four and they'll think us an army," cautioned Eamon.

"And Kate's working tonight," remembered Jeremy. "Yes, she'll want to sleep tomorrow. And as for James, well we only saw him this afternoon, up at *Jamaica Inn*."

"And he saw you?" checked Alan.

"I was unprepared," replied Jeremy. "We kept out of his way, he being with friends, and very distinguished friends at that...... the Lords Rothschild and Aldington."

"At *Jamaica Inn*." Alan again bent to the atlas. "From there to Bratton Clovelly, here, wouldn't be more than thirty minutes. Chuck in Lovat, and that's a remarkable number of Peers per acre."

"More than you'll sometimes get at Westminster," quipped Eamon. "And Kate, she was equally unprepared?"

"She was," confirmed Jeremy.

"In which case I would say we're best leaving him to it," said Alan. "But when turning up at Clark's, don't be surprised if we have that lot to contend with too. It could all be to do with HIGHLAND CLEARANCE. Rothschild got himself mixed into the Government's attempt to silence Peter Bright, Busbridge's cousin over in Tasmania. He who'd been set to keep a discrete watch on that Vincent Wakeham, the Wrickleman who lost his little brother......"

"......Norman," said Eamon," who our James thinks he might have found down at Bodmin. You'll rember me telling you, Declan."

"I do," acknowleged McDaid. "But Aldington...... how would you explain that one?"

"Aldington's current well publicised concern," began Jeremy, "is to defend his honour and reputation agaist an attack mounted by a customer of his insurance firm, a Mr Nigel Watts. Watts, feeling that he has been defrauded of a contractural entitlement has chosen to take the attack to Aldington by publishing a pamphlet criticising his war record. For ammunition he uses the research done by Nikolai Tolstoy on the treatment of Russian nationals, and others, who were either liberated by, or surrendered themselves to, advancing British forces during the final years of the last war. In '41, Stalin had ordered his troops to fight to the death. Those who hadn't were therefore deemed traitors."

"And it follows that very few wanted to return or be returned to to his far from tender mercies," reasoned Alan.

"Indeed," continued Jeremy. "And rightly fearful for their lives, they pleaded with the British authorities, meaning the Foreign Office, to be allowed to stay under our protection. Similarly entreatied, the authorities in the USA, our other partner in the 'Grand Alliance', did, by and large, give that protection. Our Government did not."

"And the big question has to be 'why?'," stated Declan.

"Tolstoy would appear to suspect a top level deal forced on Churchill by Stalin, a kind of secret protocol signed at Yalta, but of course, if any relevant documents remain, no one's allowing him near them."

"And besides," said Declan. "Churchill died over twenty years ago."

"He did," said Jeremy. "So Tolstoy's tactic has been to focus his attack on the surviving Lieutenants in this sorry business, suggesting that they personally took it upon themselves to exceed orders with their thoroughness in these repatriations. For many years a prominent target was Macmillan, a junior Minister at the time."

"But he died at the turn of the year," remembered Alan.

"Not long after his legal team managed to get Tolstoy's last book pulped," added Jeremy. "But young Nikolai is far from deterred. Dispensing with the pusillanimous publisher he instead joins forces with a devil-may-care pamphleteer......"

"......to take a stab at Aldington," said Alan, "who wouldn't even have been a Minister."

"He was no more than a Brigadier," confirmed Jeremy. "Brigadier Toby Low....... and yes, forty years or so pass and now the Foreign Office appears to be quite happy to let him stand there and take the flak, a convenient Aunt Sally, unless, of course, someone divines that his predicament might have something to do with HIGHLAND CLEARANCE."

"Aha." McDaid saw where this was going....... but not, Carroll.

"In what sense?" he asked.

"How could Stalin lean so strongly on Churchill at Yalta?" posed Declan. "Perhaps he had an insight into something that Winston was desperately wishing to keep secret. Something to do with 1941, and of course the names Hess and *Barbarossa* spring to mind. Stalin often hinted at a link between the two, and of course this would have been rubbished by the authorities here....."

"..... where we've always been encouraged to believe that Hess was crazy," added Jeremy. "But maybe he wasn't, particularly if those in Berlin had been fed the impression that it was Churchill who was about to mentally implode and be ousted from power."

"And it might be that HIGHLAND CLEARANCE was to do with this," suggested Declan, "that this could be the link between Hess and *Barbarossa*, and that Stalin had been clued up on it all by the likes of

Philby, one who had access to top Foreign Office levels."

"So are you saying that the ruthless Lord Lovat might have reason to fear this little man that is James Busbridge?" Alan sounded sceptical.

"In as much as he might, at one time, have also felt threatened by Evelyn Waugh," argued Jeremy. "A pen will sometimes prove mightier than a sword."

"And would this mean that Busbridge is in danger?" asked Alan.

"Not while he's in the company of their Lordships." Jeremy looked thoughtful. "But this would make him more biddable perhaps. I reckon Lovat and Clark could be trying to soften the three of them up. I'm thinking now of the gaps there are in *White Mischief*. It might be that James Fox was bought off..... I wonder"

"Shooting at people in tunnels, though," said Eamon. "I was very nearly bumped off."

"You were," agreed Declan. "And lest we might forget, there's still 'Peg' Willis to consider."

*

(xii) Bovisand
Sunday 16th August 9am

"Hello...... Diving Centre. Tony Cross speaking, how may I help?"

"Mr Cross, good morning, this is Diane Shaw, Sally's mother."

"Good morning Mrs Shaw. This must be about the youngsters. Are they OK?"

"I should think they are, yes, it's just that I thought I might have had a phone call from Sally yesterday. Have you heard from Chas at all?"

"I haven't, but that's not so unusual..... given, of course, that he shares his time between myself and his mother. They'll be all right, I'm sure. They're pretty grown up, the pair of them."

"I suppose they are...... and the old lady in the caravan, she's been coming for years. Perhaps they've gone down to the coast in that van her boys get around in. Sally did take the metal detector, I know."

"As soon as I see them, or hear from them, then I'll let phone."

"Thank you Mr Cross, and I shall do the same."

(xiii) Town Farm, Bratton Clovelly
10:30 am

"Lord Rothschild, Lord Aldington, Mr Busbridge....... I would like now to formally welcome, and also thank you for gracing Town Farm with your presence. My other two guests will be with us presently. As I set off for *Jamaica Inn*, they did also for a morning stroll down to the Thrushel."

It was a fine warm morning, enabling Clark to settle the three into as opulent a suite of outdoor furniture as could ever have been devised. Behind them a tall stone wall gave shelter from the light westerly which rustled the tall elms away to their left, towards the neighbouring Old Rectory, whilst from their right, there wafted the comforting aroma of roast meat being sizzled gently towards its customary succulent readiness, as savoured by regulars of the mid-day Sunday carvery at the close by *Clovelly Inn*.

Ahead the garden sloped away, Thrushel-wards, to open an un-interrupted view across the valley to Dartmoor, risen now in vivid, almost touchable, summer splendour. Along its rugged horizon the naked drama of boulder and tor could only emphasise an absurdity in the lawn's tame decorum, the broad sunshade spread above the tabled coffee pot and a gathered brood of delicate china such as might have been imagined by Lewis Carroll, or even Evelyn Waugh....... a mad Minister's coffee morning replete with their Lordships as the Tweedles dee and dum. But for James Busbridge, what a thrill! With his cup brimming so, the curious man could not but anticipate a feast.

The click of a gate latch prompted Clark to turn. Was this the main course? The three rose as one.

"You've lost your companion," said the Minister.

"He saw people going into the Church," the Scot replied, the voice aged yet authoritive. "He decided to join them, perhaps thinking himself a little in the way here."

"So yes, we can get on with the day's business. Lord Lovat, you'll know the Lords Rothschild and Aldington. It remains for me to introduce Mr James Busbridge."

"Mr Busbridge," a frail hand was offered, "I have read some of your work...... with interest."

"As I have read of your valour. Sir, I'm honoured."

"And today you're privileged, the three of you, to be told by me that you speak with GUSTAVE. Moreover, when you've heard all that I will now say, you will be trusted not to abuse that privilege. While you will be aware that Alan, here, can be one of our more freely spoken politicians, in these matters I have decided now to disclose, he has, for more than twenty years, been discretion itself."

"So would this be about HIGHLAND CLEARANCE?" From Rothschild, so knowlegable in all else, this was pitiable.

"It is," replied Lovat. "And it's also about reputations, and loose ends."

"You mean the tidying of the latter at the expense of the first," chipped Aldington, resentfully.

"Partly," conceded Lovat, "and this makes it all the more important that you should better know the broader picture, in which reputaions far more illustrious than your own have been forfeit....... and that, long before any thoughts of a cover-up."

"So we're talking 1941," said Busbridge, now finding his tongue. "The year of the *Fall of Crete* and *Barbarossa*....... episodes so vividly and comprehensively examined by our host."

"Before that," said Lovat. "three, four years before that, when what I will term the *Nordic Front* was conceived as a mere contingency...... its author, Sir Stewart Menzies, still at that time being a deputy to Sinclair. And me, what was I?"

"Still waiting the call to do battle," smiled Clark.

"So the *Nordic Front* was what?" enquired Aldington.

"Essentially a sham anti communist alliance," explained Lovat, "at that time, of course, meaning anti Russian. It presumed a worst case scenario in which German Fascism had come to pose a critical threat to the survival of democracy in western Europe...... and you have to remember that even with the outbreak of war over Poland this was still regarded unlikely."

"But within a year the picture was very changed," added Clark. "Hitler's armies having exceeded even his own expectation."

"And this was the key to Menzies' success," continued Lovat, "for the *Nordic Front* was in essence a confidence trick. Fascism was the future, Hitler proclaimed…….. and to prove this, if the rest of the civilised world were to fall in behind him, he would lead a crusade against Stalin. There was just the one temporary snag."

"This country," said Rothschild. "For Hitler's generals a war on two fronts had long been unthinkable."

"But this said," joined Clark. "Looking to the east, Stalin would never be more vulnerable than during the early summer of '41. The Red Army, which had even struggled against the Finns, was there for the taking…… so perhaps if Britain, while not yet quite to the peace table, was nevertheless on the very verge of coning to terms, then it might be the moment for Hitler to consider taking a calculated risk, as he'd done before, of course, with remarkable success. Before him, perhaps, was an opportunity to save himself a lot more bother later."

"To strike while the iron was hot," nodded Busbridge.

"So what he needed and so wanted to know was that the task he'd been hammering at on his other anvil was now as good as complete," continued Clark, pounding the same overwrought metaphor. "That in the west this *Nordic Front* initiative had gathered an unstoppable momentum, and that non adherents such as Churchill and de Gaulle were, on borrowed time and money, merely digging their own political graves."

"Democracy was as good as suspended in Britain anyway," added Lovat, "so what serious objection remained to a Peace Party assuming power?"

"This a group of eminent, if largely un elected, establishment figures," explained Clark, "with a readiness to negotiate a dignified settlement which would surely include signing up to the widely desired, and seemingly inevitable *Nordic Accord*, the green light……"

"……that in the end Hitler couldn't wait for," added Busbridge, "the consequences of that impatience ultimately being disastrous. The *Front* having been a diplomatic feint, an *Accord* being a total illusion."

"Ultimately, yes, but at the time, for us, it was just about survival," said Clark, "and this was Menzies' achievement. The home grown Peace Party was his invention, a sham, as was the internationally fostered *Nordic Front* to which the Peace Party appeared to be a response. Both were part of the same lure."

"A lure that had been painstakingly cultivated from at least the time of the civil war in Spain," continued Lovat, "but as a contingency, remember," he stressed. "This is important for us here because the particular circumstances of the winter that followed the Battle of Britain required that it should be given extra dressing. The hook had to be more deeply diguised with a few extra tasty morsels.....and this was where I was brought in, as GUSTAVE."

"So to Berlin, Menzies was wanting to make it seem that he was on their side," said Aldington.

"By seeming to be undermining Churchill," added Rothschild. "But they could never have been entirely sure of course."

"So what they sought," explained GUSTAVE, "were interim tokens of good faith....... an occasional murder, or betrayal, a minor political or diplomatic coup, or perhaps something financial, that kind of thing; each indicating progress, slight but real, towards the state of affairs that they were assured would crystalise during May '41. These tokens amounted to HIGHLAND CLEARANCE, the culmination of which was the putsch in Belgrade against the the King there, this giving Hitler the opening to storm into the Balkans on the pretext of lending legitimate succour to an assailed neighbour."

"Slight," queried Aldington, "why not more than slight?"

"It was to our advantage that Berlin had to be wary of arousing suspicion in Moscow," explained Lovat. "Russia and Germany were allies remember, and it was important that Hitler should hold Stalin's trust until the very eve of *Barbarossa*. The *Nordic Front* had to, therefore, remain a shadowy concept. In fact there were people in Menzies own department feeding Stalin good information, warning him of all this, but he chose to ignore it."

"Thinking this to be dis-information," smiled Clark. "Stalin, you see, was pathologically mistrustful of Churchill. At this vital moment in the history of civilisation, Winston's history of anti-Bolshevism worked in his and our favour. Later, though, the whole thing would rebound........"

".........but more of that in a moment, "said Lovat. "Stay for a moment with the theme of reputation. In the cause of this Nation's very survival a number of true patriots allowed themselves to be recruited as associates of Menzies' fake Peace Party. Lord Halifax for instance, and the great David Lloyd George, The Duke of Hamilton, the Duke of Windsor, he too would make the right noises."

"And Sam Hoare," said Busbridge. "Was he another?"

"Slightly different, he," replied Lovat, "a special case which we might leave for a moment. Think now in terms of the valiant men who having fought the Hun with might and main during the Great War were ready, if the hour came, to cast aside their laurels so as to hopefully be condemmed in history as discredited, even disgraced fascist sympathisers. Do you not find that humbling, Lord Aldington, when all you have to cope with is a spite motivated customer turned pamphleteer?"

"Maybe but......"

"And you, Lord Rothschild, might you not consider swallowing just a little of your pride and renown, in the same cause, that of democracy?"

"If democracy was still imperilled, yes..... I suppose so."

"Good, for what is imperilled now is the fragile prospect for an expansion of democracy........ as the Russia bequeathed by Stalin at last begins to question its future."

"Which brings us to the matter of loose ends," said Clark, "which cannot be allowed to unravel."

"And this is why the Government has been advised to come down hard on Peter Bright," explained Lovat. "Not so much for what he put in *Molehunter*, as for what might appear in any sequel, should he not be checked. The prosecution was somewhat heavy handed......."

"......but not so the sniping at those who have given him assistance," said Rothschild, his mouth edging briefly to a sullen smile.

"Yes, I'm afraid so," said Lovat. "But you're big enough, Victor. We all know that."

"But I don't see how reputation can concern me," challenged Busbridge. "You invite me today because I'm a worry to you. You know me to be on to the same something that you fear my cousin could blow open. Something to do with the *Surcouf*, and a Vice Admiral Emile Muselier."

"Which was the very first of a number of these loose ends," nodded Lovat, in a faltered tone and starting to look his years. "They begin, Mr Busbridge, with this sub full of Free French sailors, and they end with your Cossacks, Toby, being ferried off to death by the shipload....... and if this weren't nightmare enough, in between there lies worse."

"But we did as a nation survive," said the Minister, reacting sharply. "We kept the flame of democracy alive. You did!"

Lovat looked up, wearily. "Thank you Alan.......seems like you might have visitors."

433

Clark turned to the gated driveway beside the farmhouse. Four men were coming through and edging now past the parked Rolls. Busbridge knew them all, but said nothing.

"Excuse me a moment," said the Minister. "This will happen now and then...... one of the drawbacks of being a public figure."

Eamon led the way. "Leave this to me," he said over his shoulder, at the same time drawing a small folded note from a pocket.

"I'm afraid this is private property, gentlemen," announced Clark, briskly.

"I need to speak with GUSTAVE," said Carroll firmly, much to the Minister's amazed consternation. The note was passed. "Show him this name please and tell him I bring the man with me. He has an interesting story...... and no great wish to take it elsewhere."

Clark returned to his guests. Eamon edged forward, knowing they would be beckoned....... and they were, as the host went to a solidly made garden shed to fetch out four more chairs. Eamon, Alan, Jeremy, Declan...... all were soon settled.

"Now christian names please," said Lovat, pointing first to the lecturer.

"Jeremy," said Jeremy, then......

"Alan," followed Grigson, and

"Eamon," joined Carroll. Lovat then glanced down at the scrap before scrutinising McDaid.

"Leaving Vincent," said GUSTAVE, to render two of those first three wide-mouthed in astonishment. "Neither of you others being old enough, of course. We meet again young man. You wouldn't remember me. I was present at more than one of the many interrogations you underwent when you came to Scotland, way back in December 1940. I can tell you now that you were fortunate not to have been shot."

"Eamon, how long have you known this?" demanded Jeremy.

"Only since Thursday."

"So why didn't you say yesterday?"

"I was saving it....... like Declan was, I suppose. Declan?" All turned

"My local community knows me as Declan McDaid," said McDaid. "I would like this to continue. Mr Busbridge, I should apologise. You and I discussed this patient that you suspect to be Norman Wakeham, and I chose not to reveal that you were speaking with the brother, Vincent."

"Don't apologise," responded James, pleased now to be able to discount the disappointing result of the forensic test. "Perhaps I should have guessed, so brotherly was your concern for his well being."

"You informed me that he was alive, and happy, and well cared for. That's good to know. I should be grateful, and I am. I'm wary though that any attempt to restore memory could inflict a re run of the trauma that led to its catastrophic loss. I insist now that such ideas be abandoned. I can tell you what happened out on the Bay. If this helps GUSTAVE too, then in return he might oblige us with an explanation as to what was going on in those submarines."

"Fair enough," agreed Lovat.

"But before I proceed on that," said Declan, as he wished to remain, I have a question each for Eamon and the Minister......Eamon first."

"Ask away."

"Who told you I was a Wakeham?"

"No one," answered Connors. "You told me to seek out the Padre mentioned by Peg Willis, he of the left flank in Normandy, who comforted the injured and dying, not only of Peg's paras but also of the beach landing Brigade that won Sword Beach and thrust inland under Lord Lovat here."

"And on the 12th of June I took a back full of shrapnel," joined GUSTAVE, "and it was my turn to receive the last rites. You have found this Priest...... one Father Seamus Mulligan?"

"I have."

"I trust you found him well?"

"Extremely well, he still works.......he has a Parish not far from where I live in London. While not divulging anything you might have said, he loaned to me a copy of your memoir, *March Past*."

"But how could this have got you on to we Wakehams?" asked Declan.

"Through my using the movement to locate Mulligan, ironically at your own suggestion. I also enquired about a Declan McDaid who'd grown up in Londonderry, which had been Mulligan's home town also. Ask him, they said."

"And you did......" said Declan.

".....to find out that the pair had grown up together, that the families were still in touch; and that while Seamus had joined the British Army, Declan had joined the IRA. He gets himself interned, and in the camp he meets and befriends Vincent Wakeham. After the war they meet in London, and with each wanting to live down a past, they switch identities, the real McDaid eventually reaching Tasmania as Vincent Wakeham."

"And the real Vincent returning to Cornwall as McDaid," concluded Busbridge. It was that simple, he thought, and yet so easily missed.

"Very resourceful, Eamon," said Lovat. "Do give my regards to Father Mulligan whe you next see him. Now next, Declan........ you had a question for the Minister."

"It's about Peg Willis. He remembered the Priest from being in the same field hospital. He spoke of this on the radio, the member for Plymouth Sutton being part of the same interview. I want to know what happened to him."

Clark looked at Lovat. "Later," said GUSTAVE. "You'll have an answer for that later. This we promise. Tell us now what happened out on the Bay, then I'll give the bigger picture."

"The *Surcouf* surfaced first," began Declan, "dragging Norman from our boat. The line had tightened around his ankles. I got to the stern of the sub, but that's a good way from those main guns which had taken our gear, and him, like a fork might spaghetti. Then up came the second sub. They were parallel, no more than 30yards apart. Lights came on, hatches opened, and you could hear and just about make out people. Initially it was tower to tower hailing. I heard the name *Narval*."

"The other boat," said Busbridge, listening keenly.

"And it was from a hatch on this that two figures emerged, dragging with them an inflatable dinghy. The taller of the two then paddled across to the *Surcouf* to engage a man he addressed as Admiral Muselier in earnest discussion. A map was produced and inspected, and then what looked like an ingot of gold. Muselier then attempted to effect an arrest. A struggle ensued. The ingot dropped into the sea and the map was torn as the boarder broke free and dived into the water, attempting to to get back to the *Narval*. Both subs wanted to be away. Alarms were sounding, the screws churning, hatches clanging. And then the other figure who'd brought up the dinghy must have had a gun. A shot was fired, just the one, and the poor swimmer had been hit. The lights went out and the subs slipped away leaving him to die, from the bullet, the cold, or drowning......maybe all three. There was no sign of Norman. I could only hope that he'd been taken into the *Surcouf*."

"As he must have been," said Alan.

"The guy who'd been shot was still alive when I dragged him into my boat. By the time I'd got him to the shore, though, he was gone. I buried him in a cave just to the west of Portwrinkle."

"The bones that were found quite recently," said Clark. "A couple of African guys who craft shells were down there picking them up. Everything went through the coroner."

"Everything?" queried GUSTAVE. "The bullet hit him where?"

"In the chest," answered Declan.

"And did you notice an exit wound?"

"No."

"So there should be a bullet...... but none's yet appeared."

"No one's reported finding a bullet," said Clark. "I'll find out how closely those bones were examined for any bullet damage. They were buried at a Church close by. We could have them up again if need be."

"And perhaps we might run a check on those Africans," suggested GUSTAVE. "When you got him into your boat, Declan, was he still alive enough to say anything?"

"There was something about the gold. This was a Frenchman, speaking with his dying breath. The English wasn't going to be the clearest........ '*gold astern*', I think I made out."

"And the torn map.......did you manage save his part of that?"

"I did, and I took it with me over to Ince Castle where I'd seen Muselier before. I knew a girl who worked there, Jenny Cross. She was engaged to Ben, my older brother."

"The place was off limits, you were apprehended, and she covered for you," said Lovat. "This you told us in Scotland, but you made no mention of the map. We do know, however, that the girl was pregnant, probably by Muselier."

"So I believe, " said Declan, "and after she left Ince it was put around that I was the father. She must have gone into Plymouth, carrying the baby through those terrible months when the city was blitzed to pieces."

"My understanding is that Jenny took the piece of map to a dealer in Bretonside," offered Busbridge, "to one Philip Dalton, seeking expert opinion on its origin."

GUSTAVE shook his head, ruefully. "Word of this reached my chief, Menzies. Moving quickly, he had the premises destroyed......"

"......complete with occupant and family....."

"......and, he hoped, that vital piece of evidence."

"It survived though," said Busbridge. "As did Jenny Cross and her unborn child. She'd gone back on the same day to retrieve it. You'll know who the son is, of course."

"Mr Tony Cross, the Bovisand based diver," confirmed Clark.

"Whose plans for a fishing trip to Panama you helped scupper," said Jeremy. "He's found this out I'm afraid, the number having leaked from the radio station. Irate Plymouth housewives won't normally call a phone-in programme from the poshest suite in *The Duke of Cornwall*."

"One of your legion of lady friends perhaps?" said Busbridge. The host squirmed visibly. GUSTAVE rode to the rescue.

"We know plenty about Tony Cross, and also about you Mr Busbridge. Fort Bovisand is MOD property. The phone line has long been monitored."

"So it will come as no surprise to you to know that both Tony and I each have a copy of the full map. We've been separately to the Vincennes archive in Paris where Muselier's half is available."

"But only as a *copy*," punctuated GUSTAVE.

"And we've located the piece Jenny Cross clung to."

"An original piece, I'll assume," said GUSTAVE. "This is where?"

"She passed it to her grandson Chas."

"Excellent.......and what have you made of the whole, Mr Busbridge?"

"We think it shows a way in to the French island of Martinique, a course which on a certain day, when the tide's right, would have evaded the blockades imposed by the British and American Navies. The alignment of the Vichy carrier *Bearn* with Mount Pelee and St Pierre might be significant. We've just heard mention of gold. There was Vichy gold on Martinique. Can we assume that the *Surcouf* was seen as the vehicle to bring it out?"

"Correct," said GUSTAVE.

"And that those on the *Narval* were attempting to persuade it to defect to Vichy."

"Correct again, but Muselier was on board .... unexpectedly."

"And, as we've heard, he wasn't having it."

"No…….. and he smelt a rat. Had he been convinced that the proposal was genuine he might not have attempted the arrest. A polite refusal would have sufficed maybe. But earlier in the year, before the surrender, he'd escorted a shipment of gold to Martinique. He'd actually seen the stuff, and was familiar with the French Treasury hall marks. What he was shown that night was from our vaults, with our markings eradicated, but still clearly something other. Menzies was behind it, you see, as he had been when so much went wrong at Dakar, a month or so previously."

"And where as that little sweetener for Berlin had worked," said Alan, "this one wasn't going to, thanks to Muselier…….."

"…… who was looking now to take his man in for questioning," continued Lovat, "and how embarassing that might have been for Menzies. The gold would have been examined, and dicovered to have been of British Treasury origin…… just as that map had been drawn on what similarly could be proven to be Admiralty paper."

"I can see why that guy wanted to get back to the *Narval*," said Eamon.

"And why he was shot," said Declan. "He was delaying the get away, and couldn't be left. He had to be silenced."

"We tried to frame Muselier as a turncoat. We even had him taken to prison. Had it not been for his scrap of paper he could have been shot……. but this, he maintained, was with a loyal fellow officer, in a sealed envelope, together with a letter explaining its probable significance."

"And this might have been de Gaulle?" ventured Busbridge.

"We don't know," replied Lovat, "and we didn't want to find out. Just the threat was enough to win Muselier a grovelling apology….."

"From the King, no less," added Busbridge. "What happened then to the *Narval*? There's a variety of stories."

"Both boats were meant to defect. That one hadn't, rendered the other a problem. After my sharp shooting operative was disembarked at Gibraltar it was felt that the crew knew too much. They were confined to their boat, which was then sent out into the Med on patrol…….. with a couple of limpet mines attached, set to go off at fifteen fathoms."

"He could be a ruthless bastard, that Menzies," muttered Rothschild. "Sounds like that operative was fortunate to survive."

"Too valuable," GUSTAVE said. "HIGHLAND CLEARANCE was ongoing, and an assignment awaited in Africa for which she was irreplaceable."

"She?!" chorussed at least four voices, Jeremy being quickest with a supplementary question.

"Because of her likeness to someone, in voice, in build, in appearance?"

"This is so," confirmed Lovat.

"Someone named Phyllis Filmer, a.k.a.*Nancy Wirewater*?"

"I can see you're on the case," said Lovat.

"The case?" enquired Aldington.

"The assasination of Lord Erroll, in Kenya, little more than a month after after the disappearance of the *Narval*," said Lovat.

"And this was an intelligence hit!" Aldington was incredulous. "My God! A fellow Peer......and you allowed them to put your father-in-law in the dock?"

"It's not like he was hanged, Toby," said Lovat, in all serousness. Eamon's hand went to his throat, so difficult was it to suppress an urge to laugh. Mother-in-law jokes no longer worked for him. In the course of his job he'd heard them all, but this one, about a father-in-law, it beat the lot .... framed for murder by his daughter's husband, but it's not like he was hanged. He closed his eyes. Were they to meet Jeremy's he would be rolling. GUSTAVE continued. "This again is about reputations. Jock and Diana, his wife......"

"......who briefly became Erroll's lover," interrupted Jeremy.

"......they were in on the plan," explained Lovat, "as was Phyllis Filmer....."

"......the woman who'd been his 'steady' prior to Diana's arrival in the country. She being married to the local boss of Shell Oil." Jeremy thought back to Moyne's letter, written to his niece Patsy, saved by Declan.

"So, in effect, he was snared by two contrived love triangles," explained Clark, "an old and a new, each sharing one corner."

"The trap being sprung by a telegram purporting to be from Phyllis," continued Jeremy, "who was in South Africa for a week or so. Her wire informed Joss that she was rushing back to Shell House to sort things out with her husband. Then came a phone call. He was told she'd arrived and they needed to meet, urgently. But with an evening already arranged at the Muthaiga with the Broughtons this, for Erroll, could only be at the dead of night."

"At a roadside rendezvous," said GUSTAVE, "where he was shot."

"By your imposter," added Jeremy, "the sharpshooter with the Smith&Wesson."

"An account radically different from that of James Fox," said GUSTAVE. "No doubt you have read *White Mischie*f."

"That and a lot more besides. His book concludes, of course, that Jock did it, and ….. "

"…..and you must therefore think the author was either frightened, or bought off."

"Let's just say that I await the film with interest. Perhaps it will stun me with its accuracy…..but somehow I doubt it."

"So when you say 'and a lot more besides' , this means what?"

"Declan," prompted Jeremy. McDaid obliged.

"When helping to tidy the garden at Ince, just after the Viscount died, I happened across an old letter that her Ladyship was throwing out. It had been addressed to her in '44 by an uncle, Lord Moyne. He was Colonial Secretary at the time of the trial in '41, and a close friend, Lord Lovat, to your mother-in-law."

"Yes, very close they were, he and Vera. I think, after her divorce from Jock, she would have preferred to have made it official……. but Walter was well used to his freedom, and then the Zionists got him."

"By the tone of his letter this was anticipated," continued Declan. "He writes of Jewish impatience with Westminster growing to an anger."

"By '44, with good reason perhaps," sighed Lovat, "but go on"

"Well going back to Shell House in '41, Moyne could ascribe the hit to a mysterious OPERATION HIGHLAND CLEARANCE overseen by a just as mysterious GUSTAVE. He only had the code names, the purpose of the first evading him and likewise the identity of the second……. but if he could arm his niece with these, the nomenclature as he put it, then he was sure that their mere mention could well earn some vital consideration for her husband, Alan Lennox Boyd, in his future Parliamentary career. Both Eamon and Jeremy read this as a starter. I also mention to them about the unexplained disappearance of Peg Willis. Then each sets off on a separate quest to pin that GUSTAVE down, and here we find you. Eamon, as we've heard, took the Belfast route, and Jeremy……."

well he'll tell you I'm sure."

"In a moment, yes." Lovat raised a frail palm. "But Declan, on that letter still, think...... was Moyne giving anything else away?"

"He was. In Cairo he'd come across two important items that had been kept well away from the trial...... a Smith & Wesson handgun, plus what he'd termed his Shell House Telegram."

"So what became of them?"

"It's something of a riddle. He informs Patsy Lennox Boyd that they are hidden in Shell House, concealed by the *African Tiger*."

"And you, GUSTAVE, you went through Ince," goaded Eamon, "and just a few weeks ago..... using me as pretext."

"Choose to consort with a terrorist organisation and you're fair game," countered Lovat, imperiously.

"Now boys," quipped Jeremy, "we're guests, remember. Sit and listen, and you'll hear of my route to this tea party." The lecturer singled the Minister. "Mr Clark, we've heard from GUSTAVE on the theme of reputations. If I now tell everyone that young Chas Cross was imbued, by his grandmother Jenny, with an active concern for his grandfather's reputation, you should be able to tell me who in your own family carries a similar concern for a wrongly impugned parent."

All watched the Minister's face..... the pale puzzlement, the deep thought, realisation, and then red anger. Now he was on his feet, and no longer so cool. "You've been talking to that dammed woman," he bellowed.

"Yes, to Nolwen, your step-mother, who has long resented the imputations that are repeatedly made against her mother, Alice de Janze, in this matter." Jeremy turned to GUSTAVE. "Lord Lovat, without wishing to play yourself off against your host, I find it ironic that these efforts of yours to manipulate authors and film makers have only worked to exagerate the notoriety of the by-standing Alice. All you've done, you see, is to stoke the distress of her daughter, and with this, her determination to identify the true assassins."

"Cow!" muttered Clark, roughly adjusting his chair so that he might resume sitting.

"I have found her gracious, intelligent, and honourable, and must express gratitude to you, Mr Clark, for facilitating our introduction."

"What!?"

"Through Chas Cross, who I've mentioned, and Sally, a young

lady friend of his. I sent them to you, initially, at your constituency clinic. You might remember their enquiry about film portrayals of the British in Africa. They were interested in your expectations of *White Mischief*."

"Yes," Clark's voice oozed self recrimination. "I remember now, and I referred them to Nolwen who was staying overnight at *The Duke of Cornwall*, prior to sailing from Millbay on the Brittany ferry. What an idiot I am, what a fool......"

"And never so often as when trying to please the young ladies," said Lovat.

Jeremy continued. "Curious about us, she challenged the youngsters with a coded riddle, as originally obtained by Cyril Connolly from Chester Kallman, just after the death of......."

".......Wystan Auden," nodded Lovat. "Go on."

"It was a test, our response to which won for us a related series of clues devised by Cyril himself. He'd got an answer, but one far too dangerous, then, to be released in plain terms. This was back in the '70s. Old, and soon to die, Cyril naturally wanted the best for his young wife and infant child. No doubt he'd had it pointed out to him that his conduct might have bearing on their prospects."

All looked to Lovat. GUSTAVE nodded again. Jeremy continued.

"With the further help of a friend of Mr Busbridge, a lady who proved a fund of knowledge on the collaborative work of Auden and Benjamin Britten, we managed to paint ourselves an overview of the political landscape that Menzies, with your help, was endeavouring to shape. Pivotal to his efforts, it appears was the cultivation of an ambiguity in the policy of the US Goverment towards defeated France."

"Because a visible Washington-Vichy accord was essential to the momentum of the more stealthily nurtured *Nordic Front*," explained Lovat. "But it couldn't be allowed to go too far, lest the sham became uncontrollable reality."

"And the awkward component in all this would have been de Gaulle," observed Aldington, thinking back to his time as an MP and Deputy Tory Chairman under Macmillan.

"Awkward, yes," agreed Lovat, "but a useful check. To the Joint Planners and the the bluffing Diplomats he was a pain, but the public and press loved him..... in the UK and in America. Many took Churchill's endorsement of the Free French as a test of his rhetoric."

"According to Auden," continued Jeremy, "this ambiguity was

realised in a balanced contest with Robert Murphy, Mark Clark, and Admiral Leahy, all beavering on the pro Vichy side, while Roosevelt, his wife, and Treasury Chief Morgenthau put their considerable, if less active, weight on the other."

"Yes," said Lovat admiringly, "and Menzies'remarkable coup was to keep this contest knife-edge poised for just long enough."

"And to keep himself fully informed on the situation he'd set up his own telegraph." Jeremy stood. He was gaining in confidence. "Your boss, Lord Lovat, was using the remarkable talent of Benjamin Britten, a genius, he, at putting words with music to give them special meaning. *Paul Bunyan*, his debut opera, was the work. The contestants became the pets on the one side, with Slim, Tiny, and Johnny on the other......and with each informant noted adjustment of political tune, so that of the corresponding character in the opera was revised. Thousands of revisions were made to the scores of scores sent from America to Ben's London publisher. There to be eagerly decoded under Menzies strict supervision. Connolly let on to Nolwen that he got a faint whiff of this when Auden independently sent him an early draft of the libretto. It was intercepted."

"Connolly was arrested and interrogated," confirmed Lovat. "Like you, Declan, he could have been shot......perhaps should have been. I can remember driving Menzies around to Cyril's house in London, after he'd been allowed home."

Could have been shot, thought Eamon again...... like I almost was. The gate clicked. GUSTAVE turned. "And I'd almost forgotten," he said. "Declan...... your answer, back at last from Church." An elderly figure limped towards the group.

"Peg!" called McDaid, almost tumbling from his chair in his eagerness to greet a re-found friend.

"Declan...... not a total surprise, nothing ever is these days, but......"

"Peg has been helping me at Beaufort," explained Lovat. "Peg, meet Jeremy, Alan, and Eamon, and my fellow Lords, Rothschild and Aldington. Declan, you've known longer than any of us......"

".......without being aware that he's no more an Irishman than I am," said Clark, leaving his chair to find yet another.

"But we can get on to that later," said Lovat. "We were hearing from Jeremy how we've been tracked down by way of a riddle. Yes, you've cracked Menzies' trans Atlantic musical telegraph. We did over react to

444

those words arriving at *Horizon*, because at that time Auden wasn't in on this. But he was an intelligent man, like Connolly, and he realised soon enough."

"So was this where the falling out between Auden and Britten began?" asked Jeremy.

"It was."

"And it had to be related to Auden's empathy for the persecuted Jew," joined Rothschild.

"Correct," confirmed Lovat. "Auden married a Jew, Erika Mann, to allow her to escape Germany on a British passport. The love of his life, Chester, he was an American Jew."

"So he would have been exposed and perhaps susceptible to the Stern-Yair logic," said Jeremy.

"Quite," agreed GUSTAVE, now grim voiced. "Where as Britten, with his pacifist leanings, would have been more inclined to earnestly embrace the concept of a *Nordic Accord*."

"This being the line that Berlin, Rome, and Vichy were trying to sell to Washington," added Clark.

"While Auden," continued GUSTAVE, "was persuaded that, now joined, this war against fascism had to be seen through to total victory. Moreover if the notion of a *Nordic Accord* was bad enough on face value, any suspicion that it was nothing more than a lure, a tactic to get the Nazis prematurely throwing themselves eastward had to raise the spectre of impending disaster for the European Jew."

"Moyne in his letter, is close to realising all this," said Declan. "He mentions the hunting down and killing of Avraham Stern Yair, sensing this to be linked to the Erroll shooting without fully grasping the nature of the connection."

"By the end of 1940 the state of Poland was no more, argued Stern." The game was up for GUSTAVE. He wasn't finding this easy. "The survival of his stranded relatives would therefore be best secured by raising a Jewish army to fight alongside Hitler's Afrika Corps and the Vichy divisions in Syria. That extra push, he argued, could, by finally bringing Britain to her knees, earn them their promised land. Deemed too dangerous to put on trial, we had him hunted down and shot, on Churchill's express instruction. And this is the dark side of Menzies' whole enterpise. If the *Nordic Front*, with HIGHLAND CLEARANCE, saved Britain, and Britain saved democracy, at the same time it surely hastened and exacerbated the disaster that both Auden and Avraham Stern so feared."

"The Holocaust," said Aldington, pensively. "I'm starting to get it now……. the arm twisting at Yalta. Stalin had by then worked all this out. As you've said, there's another side to the comforting legend of brave little Britain resisting the Nazi juggernaut alone. It wasn't the Home Guard that saved us, it was the Foreign Office, and specifically Menzies' department. And Stalin was well placed to measure the cost, the full sacrifice."

The Minister took over.

"When Declan saw that gold drop to the bottom of Whitsand Bay the '*Final Solution*' was still conceived in terms of rounding up the Jews of Europe and deporting them to territories on distant continents. If the Americans had put Indians into reservations, and we had penned Boers into concentration camps, was this any worse? Stalin's starving of millions of peasants was surely no better, and likewise our indifference to crop failure in India."

"All in the grand tradition of the potato famine," added Eamon.

"But forced deportation is still bad enough," answered Rothschild.

"Of course, Victor," agreed Clark, "But not as bad as systematic industrial scale extermination……. which was ordered only later, as what an enemy propagandist could maintain became a forced second choice option. What was in progress, during '40 and most of '41was the crowding of your people into transit camps and ghettos in preparation for a peace with the west, Menzies' phantom *Nordic Accord*. Hitler's people were fooled into believing that a part of this impending settlement would be a combined international assault on what would be seen as a European rather than German 'Jewish problem'. This would be the moment for the Colonial solution. Already land improvement schemes were underway in French North Africa, with Robert Murphy lending American money and encouragement. Vichy Madagascar was being assessed for similar….."

"….. and as a putative British contribution," continued Jeremy, "what better than a dusted off 'Uganda Scheme', the brain child of Joseph Chamberlain that had languished on a back shelf in the Foreign Office since the turn of the century. The proposal then had been to settle perhaps a million European Jews on a block of land close to Lake Victoria, an area then in Uganda but on subsequent border adjustment made over to Kenya. Already linked by rail to Nairobi and the coast, the potential was such that the idea won a majority approval when put by Herzl to his fellow Zionists at the Basle Conferencee of......." The lecturer hesitated.

"1903," finished Rothschild. "But the minority who opposed were stridently against. They were vociferous and active...... whereas the visionaries, Herzl and Chamberlain, they were in physical decline."

"The opposition being stiffened by another strand capable of punching well above its demographic weight," added Lovat. "The white settlers in Kenya, a patrician class who loved to lord it over the native with little regard for the kind of middle class mores that a Jewish influx would inevitably bring. For them, the threat posed by the scheme remained an anxiety right through to the '20s and '30s, poisoning any natural rapport they might have developed with those at the fore of the new European fascism. Erroll for instance...... he'd once been close to Tom Mosley, but by the late '30s they were hardly talking."

"Because while both anti-Semites, a solution for one amounted to a problem for the other," remarked Aldington.

"In a nutshell," said Lovat. "And by 1940 it was feared in Berlin that Erroll might have it in him to rally the whole of East Africa against a policy of mass Jewish deportation thereto. He could seriously threaten the success of the *Nordic Pact*, it was felt. He had to go....... so if we were in earnest then it was down to us to get rid of him."

"And you did," said Grigson, "and this show of earnestness, which is what HIGHLAND CLEARANCE was about, must have encouraged further the mass round-ups of Jews, with further mass confiscations of wealth and property. And what did Churchill and Menzies think that Hitler might do with his corralled hundreds of thousands when their promised homelands were suddenly revealed to be a mirage? They weren't all going to be sent home again, were they? Did the pair of them care?"

"The answer has to be that they cared more for this country and its precious democracy," replied Lovat.

"And for that enemy propagandist this means that Churchill and Menzies must take some responsibility for the Holocaust," added Clark. "This is why Stern's argument lived on after his death...... lives on to this today even."

"And this is what I currently fear," explained Lovat. "Plenty of clever anti-west propagandists still remain between Moscow and the east German border. Let them get their teeth into HIGHLAND CLEARANCE and they could reverse what we hope to be the tide of history"

"Holy Jesus," gasped Eamon. "Churchill responsible for the Holocaust, that's a new one."

"Not quite like he was for the Black and Tans, Eamon," said Busbridge. "Let's just say he suffered a failure of imagination."

"And who could ever have imagined industrialised killing on that scale," accepted Rothschild, "anything so evil, so mad?"

"Only Avraham Stern," answered Jeremy, "who our propagandists called mad. He saw the nightmare. He warned. Did anyone listen...... apart, perhaps, from Wystan Auden?"

Lovat seemed to shrink in stature. "And I had him killed," he sighed.

"Because those were you orders," said 'Peg' Willis, at last finding his moment to contribute. "Necessary orders, given by men big enough to realise what was needed, and rightly followed. Our concern must be for the present, and what's best for the future. This is what you said when you came for me, and bade me follow......and I did, there and then, for this was Lord Lovat, and if he wanted me for important work then I had to follow, and I will, to the end. For the Lord Lovat is a Shimi Fraser. He leads from the front and sees things through, as he did when we took and held that bridge."

"Thank you Peg," smiled Lovat, fondly. "It gets so much tougher with age, as the memory fades. How I've needed you these past few years. Why should we feel guilty? Trusting Menzies might have been Hitler's biggest mistake, but after that he still had choices. He didn't need to dig his country deeper into the hole."

"But that's what he did," said Jeremy. "Outmanouevred in the diplomatic stakes he allowed himself to be maddened to further reckless violence. He declares war on the US......"

"...... with all the temper of *Grimes* striking out at *Ellen*," said Busbridge. "A cooler head was required at this juncture, and he might have found one and stepped down in his favour."

"A man like that?" asked Rothschild, shaking his head.

"Never," confirmed Busbridge. "So even this can't entirely absolve Churchill from the terrible consequences of Menzies' game. Maybe this is what Britten tells us in *Grimes*."

"So *Grimes* might be Hitler, you say Jim." Jeremy liked this kind of thing. Busbridge hesitated, then;

"No, I don't. I say *Grimes* might be Germany, divided at the top between wanting to govern the world, and wanting its approval..... a personality split that Menzies was able to exploit, teasing the leadership to destruction. From Britten's standpoint, war can never be about good guys against bad guys. Instead it's a force of nature, like the storm. Once brewed it must blow itself out, the combatants as helpless in this cycle as are the innocent casualties. No one is to blame, not *Grimes*, not *Ellen*, not even the village bigots in all their vulgarity...... and yet, at the same time, all are."

"Valid point," acknowledged the lecturer. "This is the pacifists view, and Britten was one such....... but I'm putting it to you that his standpoint wasn't quite so detached. You've heard me say it just now...... that the composer, when he was in America, was *helping* Menzies...... Lord Lovat?"

"You're right," said GUSTAVE. "In fact he was ordered there for that specific purpose. And as you say, when, after *Barbarossa*, Auden realised how his words had been used, he was not a happy man....... but by then the job was done. The critical phase had been negotiated. Britten could come back."

"Nolwen has suggested that Wystan was ready to shop Ben to the American authorities," said Jeremy. "Chester Kallman said as much to Cyril, apparently. Was that just the lad's Jewish-American mischief?"

"Certainly the departure of Britten's ship was delayed," replied Lovat," and the composer did have a half completed manuscript confiscated, and yes, it was a setting of an Auden poem........"

"*The Hymn to St Cecilia*," said Busbridge. "Famously, he rewrote the lost part from memory during the crossing. He completed it even, and started the *Ceremony of Carols*, a piece that shortly afterwards I would be rehearsing at school...... but then my voice broke before the actual performance. I ended up turning the pages for the harpist!"

"But if Auden himself had a role in all this, I can't confirm," said Lovat. "I can confirm, though, that during the critical months, betwween the fall of France and *Barbarossa*, Benjamin Britten was working for Menzies, using the full extent of that considerable talent......but with the very best of intentions."

"Good intentions," sighed Rothschild. "With such was the road to Auschwitz paved."

"Easy to say in hindsight," said Clark.

"Except that Auden was offering foresight," countered Busbridge.

"But not as much as he may have subsequently tried to make out," said Jeremy. "This is something Kate and I discussed with your friend Enid. Consider the Auden worded song in the *Spring Symphony*, the one that begins '*Out on the lawn I lie in bed*.' The first three verses were chosen by Roger Burney, a young Naval Officer lost on the *Surcouf......* Declan will tell you that. The fourth, though, was added by Britten himself. Check it out. He would appear to be directing Auden back to his very own words. Speak it through for us, James, so we too might ask what qualifies this poet to accuse others of indifference to the fate of the millions of Poles and Russians imperilled by *Barbarossa*."

Busbridge began;

" ' *And gentle do not care to know,*
Where Poland draws her Eastern bow,
What violence is done;
Nor ask what doubtful act allows
Our freedom in this English house,
Our picnics in the sun. ' "

No one spoke. There they were, as a group, out on the lawn, looking across to Dartmoor, a forest of green; Rothschild the healer, Clark the brilliant talker, Busbridge the eccentric, Alan the silent walker, enjoying this garden where all could feel secure. GUSTAVE at last broke the silence.

"Point made, I think," he said."Now Jeremy, your path to this door, which must have been separate from Eamon's....... are you about to tell me that Auden identifies me from *Paul Bunyan*, that I rate a mention in these communications ?"

This is it, thought, the lecturer...... that famous conceit. If Lovat here saw himself as a rank equal to the likes of General Mark Clark or even Admiral Leahy, then he was ready armed. He had just the pin!

"Not in *Bunyan*, Lord Lovat," smiled Jeremy, beguilingly, "because what Auden and then Connolly point up in that work is a picture that Ben formed, and repeatedly up-dated, of part of the American political landscape. Yours was an operational role, on this side of the water."

"So might I figure in *Grimes* perhaps?" preened Lovat..... to

Jeremy's further delight.

"*Grimes* was written after the composer's return to this country," joined Busbridge. "The telegraph will have been long closed down. Best to read this work as an after-the-event allegory. Rather than specific individuals, look to identify group mentalities and sentiments, widely and not so widely felt."

"*Grimes* himself being a German national psyche, you said," prompted Grigson.

"Yes, and *Ellen* becomes all who yearned to bring out the best in this, offering love and understanding," continued James. "Britten would have counted himself amongst these, with his friend Peter..... who was a Quaker."

"As was Sam Hoare, Menzies' Prime Minister in waiting," added Clark, "a figure who could be used to make the deception all the more convincing."

"So my mentality?" posed Lovat.

"Is that also of Menzies and Churchill," continued James, "a stance which sees in *Grimes* a personality which for all its power and talent is divided against itself. The fisherman has dreams of settling with *Ellen* and becoming a respected member of the community, but running against these is the cruel ambition of a lone workaholic which causes him to be neglectful of his underlings. The stance that sees this split, and exploits it to madden the man to his watery grave, a stance that you were just a part of, Lord Lovat, is that personified by *Bulstrode*, the manipulative old sea captain. He uses *Ellen's* good nature as one of his tools to usher Grimes to self destruction....... for only then, he knows, will the village enjoy peace."

"So if we've no specific individuals in *Grimes*," said Lovat, with a hint of disappointment, "and I don't figure at all in *Bunyan*, then how is it, Mr Barnes, that Auden, with Connolly's help, and also Lady Clark's, can put you on a trail quite separate from Eamon's, one that you successfully follow, bringing you here?"

"For you, GUSTAVE, the poet finds a different kind of sketch, of the sort produced by a totally different kind of artist." The others were rapt. Jeremy was enjoying this, the playing on Lovat's vanity. "A sketch composed merely of words," he continued, preparing to puncture. "The words of a novelist whose wartime experiences coloured his output no less than Britten's did his."

"So this time it's straight storytelling," said Lovat, anticipating for himself a heroic persona. "And unlike the musicians, there were plenty of story tellers who went into battle."

"But few that knew you so well as this one," said Jeremy, almost cruelly. "Auden suggested that Connolly might ask *'Uncle Crouchback'*." Lovat's eyes momentarily widened, before narrowing viciously. "Yes," confirmed the lecturer, almost triumphantly, "and even though your old comrade in arms had been in his grave for a good eight years, Cyril dutifully trawled *Sword of Honour* to find an answer, one he chose to disguise beneath a third hint; ..... 'vaguest of clues'. Get it......vaguest? It had Nolwen stumped. Until Friday, that was, when, in a Bath tea shop, with the help of myself and a friend, she eventually arrived at Trimmer."

"Waugh," scowled Lovat. "That sneering little snob was always trouble. It goes back to *Vile Bodies*......"

"...... and *Lottie Crump*?" smiled Jeremy.

"Contemptible little brat......but as a family we rose to his taunts. That was our mistake. We should have known better."

"All the more odd then that he should have warranted that much ink in *March Past*," remarked Eamon.

"That was an attempt to smooth the crack. His kilted *Gustave* might have spelt trouble. We didn't want Waugh encouraging people to play detective........."

"........ so in your memoir you built the best part of a chapter around the hoax story," said Jeremy, "hoping to project him as a vengeful Malvolio. I see the rationale, but the repair was too late. While Evelyn and Wystan and Cyril have all now passed on, thanks to the last of the three and now Nolwen, and me, that riddle has enjoyed a life of its own."

"But this still doesn't explain how you got from Trimmer to me."

"We were in Bath," said Jeremy, "with an hour or three to spare. Why not ask 'Trim', we thought...... so off to Mells we went, to the wonderful old Church with the wonderful old Manor, and who should we find there but the Minister!" Lovat pinned Clark with an angry glare. "We know then that we're on the right track. I take Nolwen back for her train while leaving my friend, and she encounters Lord Oxford at *The Talbot*. The conversation is informative. I'm afraid Mr Clark that you are far from being the man's favourite politician. He was happy to swap his *March Past* just to see the back of you. This said, you did leave him nicely primed to dicuss the *Sword of Honour* books...... and the identity of Trimmer."

"Evelyn and Katherine Asquith," sighed Lovat. "It was like the woman needed a court jester. She was cruising the Med with my mother and my sister, and Father D'Arcy had suggested to Waugh that he should come along too."

"And she was finding it tiresome to be continually reminded by the Fraser womenfolk what a grand young fellow their brand new 'Shimi' was shaping into, the implication being that whatever her own son might achieve, young Trim could never compare."

"And Waugh was on to this in a flash," acknowledged Lovat.

"It became a private joke. For him and Katherine you would ever be Trimmer. And between them the caricature was spot on, even as, in *Sword of Honour*, it gets taken to the most absurd extreme. It didn't matter that the world at large wasn't going to see the joke, in fact it helped."

"It mattered to me, though," snarled Lovat. "Trimmer's heroism was a fraud. My battle scars are real."

"As, no doubt, were Evelyn's emotional scars," chided Jeremy. "Good looks, money, blue blood...... with all that and plenty to spare some might call it graceless to be slagging off one of the lower orders as a social climbing eunuch. Add to this the hoaxing, and the sacking, and I see a personality conflict stoked from *both* sides. You couldn't let it go, Lord Lovat, and in the end it betrays your identity."

"Thanks to that Cyril Connolly..... another poison-dwarf."

"Who, as *Everard Spruce*, knew too well Waugh's methods..... the relentless pushing of himself into informed circles. See how Evelyn found himself in Yugoslavia with Randolph Churchill and Freddie Birkenhead."

"So Jeremy," said Clark, "on Nolwen's prompting you and your friends......"

".....Kate and the kids......"

".... have managed to put all this together. That's very resourceful. Now your coming here today, does this mean you have a demand to make of us?"

"In the sense that the Lords Aldington and Rothschild, together with Mr Busbridge, have been brought here with a view to reaching some sort of 'understanding', then yes, I suppose I have...... though not strictly on behalf of myself. I've been enlightened, and that's fine, but this is more than just a watching brief you hold."

"Considerably more," agreed Clark

"When the alarm is tripped you move with strength. Peg here goes on the radio, and see how promptly he finds GUSTAVE on his doorstep. And had he not been willing to go ……. what then? And others too have suffered damage. Tony Cross flies his off- to-the-Caribbean kite, only for it to be down in flames before the end of the week. A minor matter, perhaps, relatively easily smoothed. But not so when someone like Eamon is dragged from his home, and then thrown from a train and shot at, with the likes of my friend Alan, here, being set up to take the rap for the contrived security breach. This stuff is of a different order. It's severe and it's sudden…….. so what can be the severe and sudden alarm?"

"Some things we'll let go," answered Lovat, "a lot of things in fact, at this stage of the game. On other things, though, we must move. Each threat must be considered on its own merits, in its own context. If we hear, for instance, of Mr James Busbridge and Mr Tony Cross both visiting the Vincennes Archive and sifting the same files on the *Surcouf* then we'll sit back…… but not when the latter expresses an intention to trawl the sea bed off the coast of Panama, for this is where the submarine still lies. The DNA testing we might have sabotaged," he nodded towards Declan, "but in the event we didn't have to…. To our surprise too!"

"So why invite me here?" asked Busbridge. "You must be wary of something."

"We actually anticipated your moving to obtain picures of the seaplane. We didn't think you would be so careless as to actually mention them in a phone call to Bovisand, but something in this direction was predicted," explained Lovat.

"Predicted and feared," said Busbridge defiantly.

"Because the lad was flown back in, almost to Kingsbridge. Then it was straight into Moorhaven. If the place hadn't been shutting down he would probably still be there. Proximity again……. we can't have any pictures of that plane near his brother."

"So you can agree with me that Norman is best left undisturbed," said McDaid.

"We can," confirmed GUSTAVE. "Likewise, proximity prompted my approach to Peg. It wasn't so much what had been said on the radio as the fact he lived so close to Ince. No harm done though." Peg was beaming. GUSTAVE's eyes creased to a rare smile. "And you'll be pleased to know that there's now very few who might qualify for summary execution."

"I'm honoured, I'm sure," said Eamon, sourly. "You can tell us now what the heat was at Ince..... something to do with that gun perhaps?"

"Which remains elusive," said Lovat. "It's also to do the circumstances of the Viscount's death, with Toby's determination to pursue his libel action against Tolstoy and Watts, and with the possible ending, or not, of the Cold War."

"The Cold War," repeated Eamon suddenly feeling out of his depth.

"I think you might begin with Viscount Boyd's death," suggested Jeremy. "Knocked over, wasn't he? London street......four years ago."

"Just after returning from West Berlin," said Clark, "having there checked out the conditions in Spandau Prison, on behalf of a Government nervous lest an action be lodged at the Strasbourg Human Rights Court on behalf of the sole in-mate, Prisoner Number Seven."

"Former Deputy Fuhrer Rudolf Hess," joined Busbridge unable to quite suppress his glee.

"So initially," continued Lovat, "Boyd's was merely an informal, precautionary mission......"

"......until," prompted Rothschild.

"......until Margaret's faithful fact finder was persuaded that he might be the man to save the House of Lords, and at the same time head off a movement that could shape as a serious obstruction to the cause of freedom for the Iron Curtain countries of eastern Europe."

"How so?" asked Aldington.

"Toby...... well might you be the one to ask. Let's say you win your libel action against Tolstoy. Would this be an end to it?"

"He might appeal."

"To the Court of Appeal, if given leave...... and ultimately the House of Lords."

"Losing all the way, and it will cost him," added Aldington, confidently.

"But he won't be bothered too much by that," said Lovat, "not with the kind of White Russian sponsorship he enjoys. If it goes all the way and earns full publicity then, for them, irrespective of the result, it's money well spent....... and this was what Alan Lennox Boyd was urged to reflect upon, in West Berlin, just a few days before he died. At that time, though, Tolstoy wasn't making *you* the target of his vilification."

"It was focussed on Macmillan."

"And it was put to Boyd that Tolstoy would hammer away with his wild allegations, forcing Harold to go to Court with a case which, like yours now, was sure to be frustrated by Foreign Office reluctance to come clean on the full story of the '44 Yalta discussions."

"Where Stalin, thanks to his knowledge now of Menzies' manipulation of Berlin, held a whip hand over Churchill."

"Moreover, it would have been suggested to Boyd that the tension between Law Lords, Foreign Office, and Stockton himself, a former Prime Minister, could bring the whole edifice that is the House of Lords into terminal disrepute....... especially if Tolstoy's side could find a way of throwing one particular piece of mischief into the fray, this being a document, a copy of which was actually given to Boyd to bring back to Westminster for inspection by the Lord Chancellor."

"And this document.....?" pursued Aldington.

"....... is an affidavit," explained Lovat. "One signed by Rudolf Hess, who, as we know, actually flew to Britain in the May of '41 in the expectation of concluding a truce that he was sure would herald the formation of the *Nordic Accord*, and with that an incisive joint-nation move against Russia. In this affidavit he attests that he'd flown with Hitler's knowledge and encouragement, neither of them doubting the authenticity of the *Nordic Front*, the sham joint nation initiative which seemed so convincingly to be promoting the *Nordic Accord* ..... a conviction cemented by, amongst other things, the business of the *Surcouf*, which miscarried, and the assasination of Lord Erroll, which didn't. This second episode is mentioned, I've been told, and, as was surmised just now, he points to it as being a particular spur for those dictating the pace and direction of the Reich's racial policies. The old Uganda scheme really was being dusted off, the Nazis thought........ what better indication than the proven readiness to burn poor Joss, that Hay in the manger."

"So Boyd agreed to take this to the Lord Chancellor," said Rothschild.

"In the expectation that he might consult with the Cabinet and the Foreign Office to produce a form of words that might defuse this time bomb. The idea was to draw Tolstoy away from specific lower ranking officials into a paper chase through a maze of now defunct, anonymously staffed committees...... the more vaguely constituted the better."

"So it would have been Hailsham then," said Aldington,

pensively. "Did he have a problem with such a precaution?"

"We were never to find out," answered Clark "Boyd got the affidavit back to London, only to be killed that same evening, before he could pass it over, and explain."

"With the thing being lost in the commotion of the accident," said Lovat. "We'd had him tailed, but a light fingered someone must have whipped it from beneath his companion's nose. He'd been eating with Bryan Guiness, no less……. Moyne's son."

"So it was gone forever," ventured Rothschild.

"No such luck," said Clark. "That affidavit would appear to be no less durable than its author…… and just as adept at turning up on the wrong side."

"The wrong side?" queried Jeremy.

"Useless to a thief, the case and contents were probably tossed aside, "explained Lovat, "only to be found by some well meaning soul who chose to pass it into the East German Embassy, thinking perhaps that Spandau was on their side of the wall."

"So the communists now have it, " reasoned Grigson.

"If only it were that simple," said Lovat shaking his head.

"Reports reaching us from inside the communist bloc give us every reason to believe that the seventy year old Marxist experiment has run its course. Common ownership within a centrally planned economy is failing to produce the necessary wealth. Industry is undertooled, the workers underfed, and the military under-equipped. In Russia, at the heart of the Soviet Empire, morale is sinking. The thousands of missiles and tanks guarding the periphery stand as a hard but brittle crust."

"So a wave of revolts such as the '56 in Hungary and the '68 by the Czechs might now succeed," suggested Jeremy, "hopefully restoring democracy."

"Hopefully……yes," said Clark. "but not inevitably. Such a breakup would threaten the very existence of a spread of military elites who, though originally trained and equipped to protect the revolution from the west, might now turn inward with reactionary fervour, moving to police their populations with even less regard for democratic convention. With survival the imperative, any squeamisheness about ideology would be forgotten. Look at Africa, at South America ……. a single party state doesn't need to be communist. Captains of commerce and inustry might be invited in to make common cause……"

"...... for since when had Adam Smith ever been regarded as a champion of one man one vote," agreed Jeremy, "or free speech. Find the right shopkeeper, put him on the right street, keep his queue in order and he'll pay handsomely for for a captive market."

"And at this point re-enter the *Ancien Regime*," continued Lovat. "Not all of White Russia went, as did the Tsar and his family, like lambs to the slaughter. The smart money was taken abroad in good time, to be switched and switched again, following cheap labour around the world, riding the depression, and being kept safely tucked away during the false dawn lit by Hitler's thrust at the Ukraine....."

"....... to cream a fat profit all the way," added Rothschild, "and now, if there's a fast rouble to be made out of the ancestral homelands, then naturally they'll be pushing for prime position. It could be the moment for the big shots and the big guns to stand together, you say."

"Particularly where there might be scope for discrediting modern western style democracy," said Lovat. "Remember, as enticing as our ways might appear to some, there remain many for whom the root might carry too bitter a taste."

"This root being Britain's survival in '41," said Aldington, "secured by the *Nordic Front* and HIGHLAND CLEARANCE with all its related cost, in land and in lives."

"*Barbarossa*," said Clark. "Think of the combat deaths, the devastated cities, the ruined harvests."

"And were that, and the Holocaust, not enough," continued Lovat, "we can add that cruel surcharge imposed by a resurgent and fully apprised Stalin in '44. The repatriation of the Victims of Yalta........ perhaps a million Russians to be added to Hitler's six million Jews."

"So with Stalin having known it all, Moscow wouldn't have learned anything from the Hess affidavit," said Alan.

"All they had to do was to start to believe what the likes of Kim Philby had been telling them for some time," confirmed Lovat, "and he, so trusted by Menzies, would have known more than Hess himself. In fact, on its own, the affidavit is of limited value. A Nazi, widely touted to be mad, can hardly be the most credible of witnesses."

"So what do you so much fear?" asked Eamon.

"Corroboration," replied Clark. "Which is why neither Toby here nor Tolstoy can be allowed too close to the Foreign Office records."

The cabbie nodded. "So from where else ....and from whom

else? Apart from GUSTAVE here, and Hess, I guess most of the main characters will now be dead….. not Philby though."

"With whom I have quite recently resumed contact," said Lovat, surprising all save the Minister, "and, for all his past misdemeanors it seems that now he's rooting for democratic reform. I suppose he always hated fascism, and consistent with this has been his recent warning to me that one chracter I'd always assumed to be dead is, in fact, still very much alive……. alive enough to be active on behalf this unholy tie up of White 'hot' money and former Red menace."

"Who's this ?" enquired Rothschild.

"I speak of my trained assasin, whose ruthlessness you witnessed, Declan, from your fishing boat on Whitsand Bay. After she'd dealt with Erroll we had her dropped into Yugoslavia, just after *Barbarossa* opened. The mission was deliberately betrayed."

"So for forty five years you've been thinking her feet wouldn't have touched the ground," said Eamon, "but they did."

"And, on this betrayal, with her at last coming to realise the full import of what she'd been involved in, and its possible consequences, she has an interesting and valuable story to trade in with her interrogators……"

"….. but not all at once," reasoned the Irishman. "For this is her ticket for survival."

"Survival of sorts," said GUSTAVE. "For she was marched off to some god forsaken Gulag, and there given protracted opportunity to reconsider her loyalties. And naturally, understandably, she would have played that story of hers for all its worth, and most recently it seems, in East Germany."

"Finding there some very eager listeners," continued Clark, "who would have said to her that with a little hard evidence to support the testimonies of herself and Hess then they might be on the verge of a substantial propaganda coup. With an *Aldington v Tolstoy* action attracting wide publicity throughout Europe, what better moment might there be for springing Hess from Spandau and putting him back in the dock. It needn't be a show trial…….."

"In fact all they need to set up for him is a fair hearing," said Busbridge, with naked relish. "Something he was denied at Nuremburg…… for then, it was the last thing we could afford."

"As it is still," confirmed GUSTAVE.

"So your concern, Lord Lovat, has been to tidy any evidence before it can be found," reasoned Jeremy, "either that, or tidy her."

"While tidying me in the process," scowled Eamon.

"And Philby," joined Alan, "has he offered any information on her movements?"

"I was only alerted this spring. She's visited Cornwall before, I was told, and might be back this summer with a view to making a further search of Ince. The word was that she wintered in Africa, in Mozambique, where East Germany currently makes a telling contribution to the communist side in the civil war."

"And from Mombassa," said Jeremy, "what's that? "Five hundred miles, and another hundred or so to Nairobi. I reckon she'll have scouted Shell House ...."

"....... and yet still not found what she'd hoped to," said Alan, "for why else come back to Ince? Tell me, is it swahili that's spoken in northern Mozambique?"

"I think it is," said Rothschild.

"And while we know the name 'Nyassaland' for the neighbouring former British colony changed to Malawi a good twenty years ago, might there be a province still called Nyassa, on the Mozambique shore of what we now call Lake Malawi?" asked Grigson. "If there is then it might well be that we've found the lady concerned."

"A quick phone call and I'll have that checked." Clark rose to his feet, and strode briskly inside.

"If it's who I think it is she's posing as a traveller down on Wacker Quay," continued Alan. "She does a line in herbal remedies. Her English is good, but not authentic."

"She was a Pole," said Lovat, "a Polish Jew, who'd managed to get into Palestine before the White Paper, in fact a cousin removed of the Avraham Stern who we later had shot....... he that sought the an alliance with Berlin."

"So at the time, even while related to the man she must have been strongly against Stern's line," reasoned Rothschild, "having enlisted, as she did, to be a special operative for us."

"She was," confirmed Lovat, "but while doing the business she was never told fully what HIGHLAND CLEARANCE was about. Like Ben in the US, and Sam in Madrid, she too thought herself to be working for a genuine *Nordic Accord*."

"So revised loyalies are a certainty," remarked Jeremy. "Indeed, Lord Lovat, were you and her to meet after all these years I can imagine her being ready with a few choice words...... and a re loaded gun."

"And all this time I've known her name," said Declan. "Those last words spoken by the guy in the water, the guy she shot.......Golda Stern."

"But known to us as Megan," said Grigson, as Clark reappeared to confirm there was indeed a Nyassa still. "Megan, Juma and Makesi.......and this weekend Chas Cross and Sally were planning to take a tent up there."

"Whose idea?" demanded Lovat.

"Megan's I think," answered Alan, "this after Chas had happened across the boys in Plymouth."

"When?" asked Busbridge.

"Might have been Wednesday," said Alan.

"Which was after you'd suggested to Chas that he might try them out on the African Tiger riddle," said Busbridge. "This could have prompted the invite. Do you think they're safe?"

"I think we should phone Tony Cross," said Jeremy, now on his feet. "And also the girl's parents....... I have their number here."

"Can you get Cross here?" Lovat wanted to know. "How much his mother passed on could be important."

"Let me do it." Busbridge produced an address book from his jacket. "I can persuade him." A pen was pulled from the breast pocket. "Minister .... the best way here from Plymouth please."

"Tavistock, then Launceston road before turning right through Chillaton for Lewdown. Right, then, along the old A30 to the village school. Left, there, to drop into the Thrushel valley, and we're on the other side. On a Sunday.....? Forty five minutes at the most." Clark led Busbridge and Jeremy to the phone. Lovat stayed.

"Declan, Toby," he said. "You both knew Boyd; Declan, from when he moved down to Ince........ Toby, since long before. You and he were MPs together in the '50s, Boyd making it to the Colonial desk, and you to the post of Deputy Party Chair. Think, the pair of you, think more laterally....... was there ever any mention from him of a Shell House, as distinct from what's come down to us from Lord Moyne, by way of his niece?"

And both did think ...... Declan, the gardener, favouring politics to mentally tick each of a sequence of visits made by Boyd to Kenya

461

during the '70, leaving Aldington, as a politician turning away from that field ....to find the spark to suddenly illuminate what had lain unconsidered beneath the other's nose.

"There was something, now you mention.........I recall being at his London home back when he was Colonial Secretary, and him there saying to me that he and Patsy had this dream of moving to a big place in the westcountry where they might properly concentrate on a garden. They would grow this plant and that, and also make something of a collection of shells that he'd gathered on his travels through tropical climes...... a small summer house for the garden, perhaps. These were stored away in sacks up at his constituency residence in Bedfordshire. At the time he was still adding to them. It might be that......"

"More than might," interrupted Declan. "This is precisely what Lord Boyd did. There is a Shell House in the garden, and he actually said to me that it had been started with some passed on from the uncle's estate......."

"....... this idea of building a house having been passed down with those shells," reasoned Lovat. "Right...... when the others are done on the phone we can make a call to the Viscountess. We don't know that she showed the letter to her husband, or even if she believed it to refer to anything other than Shell House Nairobi. If Moyne's shells were taken down to Ince and used for that structure then neither, including the Viscount nor Viscountess need have realised what could be amongst them."

"So what more might she then tell us?" asked Declan.

"She can say if there's been any recent damage done to this structure," said GUSTAVE. "And if so I want police surrounding that Wacker Quay without delay...... complete with armed support. I want helicopters at the ready, the lot."

Busbridge returned.

"Cross is on his way," he said. "He's heard nothing from his boy...... but to him, for now, no news is good news."

"Well let's hope so," said Lovat. "And Jeremy's speaking with the girl's people now?"

"Yes," said Busbridge, "and while he is, could you be so good as to tidy the mystery of how the *Surcouf* was lost."

"Once they were in the war, the Americans took charge of the thing, and this notion of the boat getting in and out of Martinique became more viable. The tide of war was turning and many of those French Generals and Admirals who'd fallen in behind Hitler were reconsidering. Position and prestige might be better preserved, it was thought, by coming to an understanding with the top brass in the States, by whom this view was encouraged….. "

"……. with talk of financial reward?"

"It'll often come down to that in the end," agreed Lovat, "and there on that island was a potential pension fund. If American lives could be saved with French gold then all the better. Who's going to argue with that?"

"De Gaulle for one," half-chuckled Busbridge.

"So this had to be kept secret still……but it was done, or at least partly so, this being the *Surcouf's* final mission. In February '42 she got in, and out again with one decent boat load. An American corvette was waiting for her in the Gulf of Panama. The swag was off-loaded at night, and then the submarine was destroyed……"

"……. just as the *Narval* had been, to silence all hands."

"But no limpet mine for the *Surcouf*," explained Lovat, "instead, a deliberate ramming beneath the strengthened bows of a carefully aimed a freighter. Dead in the water, unable to submerge, she was then polished off in the morning by air attack. This is why no one's keen on what's left of her being found."

"A difficult one to pin on the Luftwaffe," said Busbridge, grimly. "And Britten's friend, Roger Burney?"

"Remembering the *Narval*, he, like the rest of the crew must have been anticipating any kind of special mission with the utmost trepidation."

"Morale on the boat was reported to be low…… and understandably so."

"Because with America in the war that new arithmetic had to prevail," confirmed Lovat. "Landings in North Africa against a resolute Vichy defence would take thousands of GI lives. If this price could be lessened at the cost of a few dozen Free French sailors, plus the odd one or two from the RN, then this looked a good bargain. Cruel, yes, but such is war. Did Britten know of his friend's plight? He dared not say. By then Menzies had had him closed down ….. he could come back to England as soon as he liked. And he did, Auden's tale telling counting for nothing. By then the Grand Alliance was in place….."

"……and *Grimes*' fate sealed," added Busbridge. "Here's

Jeremy……. you got through to the girl's people? Any news?"

"They've already been over to Wacker," answered the lecturer. "They found no one there. The inflatable was tied still, and the tent up, with metal detector therein. All looked to be in order. Likewise the old woman's caravan…… but no sign of the big van that the Africans use."

"We need a description, then, of that van," said GUSTAVE. "It's to go to traffic police and coastguards. If the lad's been diving in Whitsand Bay then it could be that the woman's gathered all she might need, including the youngsters……."

"…….and be making her get away," said Jeremy, "but in that van……?"

"First she'll contact East Berlin. They'll want to waste no time in springing Hess from Spandau…… something we've got to stop."

Declan re apperared. "I spoke to the Viscountess. She went to check her shell house and was back to us almost immediately. Someone's been at it, she said, probably with a hammer, splitting open one of the larger shells. Foot prints there abouts, and a scattering of river mud suggests a number of intruders. They came through the fields along the edge of the Lynher River."

"So they might well have crossed from Wacker," said Clark.

"Time, I think, to cut the Gordian Knot," said GUSTAVE. "Mr Carroll, if I can prevail upon your services, I want Victor and Toby returned to *Jamaica Inn*. I then want you back here, where I'm going to leave Peg and Mr Busbridge to wait for Tony Cross. Peg can stay here as you then bring Mr Cross, with Mr Busbridge, over to the listening station at Morwenstow, less than thirty minutes from here. The Minister will take me there now, together with Jeremy, Alan, and Declan. I'll tell them at the gate to bring you through to where we'll be." Lovat was leading, in Lovat fashion. Peg glowed in admiration. "By the time you've caught up we should be installed in a fully functioning operations room." The Scot turned again to his fellow Peers. "Victor, Toby, thank you for coming today. I'd hoped to be entertaining you for longer…... but SANDMAN calls. So another time, maybe, perhaps soon…… I can come down to Westminster."

Rothschild and Aldington rose. "Well thank you, anyway, for this morning," acknowledged the latter. "We'll be intrigued, I'm sure, to hear how today's developments resolve."

"SANDMAN," repeated Rothschild. "Another contingency to be invoked?"

"Regretfully yes. Tuesday morning's newspapers, Victor.....and you'll know better than to believe all that you read."

*

(xiv) at sea (1)

"Treat this as you would a holiday. You'll be looked after well, with every comfort provided. See this, you've one of the best cabins on the boat."

Chas, queasy still, and far from steady on his feet, was unimpressed. "Tell me where Sally is, Megan."

"In a similar cabin on the deck above. She'll wake shortly...... to similar advice."

"You drugged us, kidnapped us....... and now you expect co-operation?"

"Once you've accepted this as the one sensible option, yes. We just need statements..... personal accounts, full and true, accounts that you might stand by in a Court of Law, if need be, under proper cross examination."

Chas stepped forward. Angry, dizzy, he was in no frame of mind to consider what might or might not be sensible. Behind the woman was a door, open. He could barge pass and through, he was sure...... but no, his legs were failing, folding. Hands groped for a wall, or a chair, or a locker, something to grip, but in vain. The floor loomed, until the two burly but hitherto un-noticed seamen moved as one from each flank, catching and easing him back to the bunk.

"You'll feel better for some food," said Megan, as if this might also deliver compliance. "I'll have some brought down. This door will be left open so that you might use the toilet opposite. Kurt, though, will be guarding the passage..... lest you be tempted to wander."

*

465

(xv) SANDMAN

Uncoded or encoded, little in the way of any form of radio communication will escape the tracking station at Morwenstow, one of the numerous trained ears which constantly feed the GCHQ nerve centre at Cheltenham. The broad, smooth, receiving dishes, angling attentively along the Sharpnose cliff-top, will also maintain a comprehensive log of all ship movement within the quadrant stretching from France to Ireland, the peacable and the potentially hostile.

'The Ghost' paused at the sternly patrolled barrier, the driver and front passenger commanding instant recognition. For the three in the back, this one entrance was clearly the only way out. Declan remembered similar. Until GUSTAVE said otherwise they would be as good as interned. In no time with no fuss they were through, parked and into the appropriate suite.

"I want a direct line up to the SAS," said Lovat firmly. "And this one should get me through to Faulds now." He picked up the receiver. In seconds the connection was made. "Faulds?....... Faulds, I'm at Morewnstow. Listen...... I'm having to invoke SANDMAN, and I need the task done and dusted within twenty four hours. I'll want an assent from number ten, but no one else at Cabinet level is to know, apart from Clark that is. He's with me now. Either we act, tell the PM, or all that Iron Lady stuff she's so fond of is out of the window. Also I want you to contact STANLEY. I want a hot line access to the General Secretary within the hour. Speak to you in thirty minutes." Lovat re-hooked the phone, turning now to scan a bank of six monitor screens. "While Cheltenham scrutinises recent phone traffic into the East German Embassy, we can play back through the last few days worth of shipping movements here abouts...... giving particular attention to vessels of eastern bloc origin."

"Would there be many?" wondered Jeremy.

"Trawlers, coastal freighters," said Lovat, "they hover off our coasts like flies might over a weary lion."

*

(xvi) at sea (2)

"So where's Chas?" demanded Sally. "He's OK I trust."

"He's downstairs," replied Megan, "and finding his feet. A spot of food and you'll both be fine."

"Can I see....."

"Later on, yes..... for the moment, though, you're best kept apart, until you realise that no one's meaning any harm."

For the girl there was just the one minder in attendance. She shot him a glance.

"No harm meant," she said, ruefully. "That's good to hear. So where are we going?"

"Nowhere, for the moment. Watch from that porthole and as we turn, every three hours or so, you'll see the same stretch of the Cornwall coast....... and quite a stretch it is, being as we're a good twenty miles out."

"Beyond the twelve mile limit."

"Purposely," confirmed Megan.

"So are we being held hostage? Has a ransom demand been isuued? Are we waiting while it's being considered? "

"Nothing so vulgar. This is about what you and Chas can give to us....... and it's nothing extortionate. All we ask is the truth."

"So why should we be out here," demanded Sally. "And why should we be waiting?"

*

(xvii) a skeleton case

"Mr Cross," said Lovat, to the second of the of the newly arrived three on their being ushered into the suite. "Welcome...... as one of your local MPs you'll be familiar with the Minister. Of the rest here, well, I know for certain that you're acquanted with Mr Busbridge. I shall ask him, therefore, to complete the introductions. Most, you'll find, have met either your son or his young lady companion, and all share a concern for their possible plight."

"Are they in danger?"

"No immediate danger," answered Lovat.

"But they might be in the hands of a dangerous person," added Declan.

"So our questions must be frank," said Clark, "and so must your answers."

"If I can help," assured Cross," then I will."

"For a start then," began Lovat. "Did you ever mention gold to your son, sunken gold in Whitsand Bay, and did you ever encourage him to go looking for it?"

"No, and no. What I knew of this I kept to myself...... but that wasn't going to stop the person who told me also telling Chas."

"That person being?"

"My mother, his grandmother......"

"Jenny Cross," said Declan. "I'm a Wakeham, Tony, a younger brother to Ben, who was once engaged to your mother. I was with her at Ince on the night she lost her job. She helped me, and, for her trouble, was left to endure the fiction that I was your father. This I most definitely am not."

"My mother preferred not to tell me that she'd let young Chas in on the tale, and to the boy she insisted that the he wasn't to mention her story when talking with me."

"So he started to search without your knowing," said Lovat.

"He did," confirmed Cross, proudly, "and he found what he was looking for."

"Are you sure?" asked the Minister.

"Actually it was the girl who brought it up, but she was diving under his direction."

"Recently?" asked Lovat.

"Very recently."

"So how come you've learned of this? What persuaded them to tell you?"

"The woman down at Wacker...... who would now appear to be more than she seems."

"But why shoud she have been told?" pressed Lovat.

"Her companions, the Africans..... they found the gold ingot after the kids had hidden it. It was Sally, she gave away the hiding place. You remember the skeleton....."

"...... I remember its owner," responded Declan.

"So it would have been you who buried him," Cross deduced. "And you'll remember where."

"In the cave along from Portwrinkle."

"The same where, by chance, all these years later, Chas and Sally chose to conceal their treasure trove. A few days later the girl wants to check that it's still there. Mr Grigson........ it was that evening you dropped her at the golf course. Her father had the metal detector in his car boot. She clambers around to the cave, and not content with a buzz, she has to have a peep. She digs down......"

"......and suddenly she's elbow deep in bones," added Jeremy.

"And this is too much," continued Cross. "She flees from the cave, but straight into the arms of our beachcombers. They gently see her on her way......."

"..... but are obviously curious as to what may have provoked such alarm," said Busbridge.

"And then, after an anxious night, Sally wastes little time in gettting down to Wacker. There she discovers that the boys have indeed found the gold, and brought it up to the caravan."

"So the woman has the gold," said Clark.

"She doesn't, actually," said Cross. "After listening to a distraught Sally, she proves remarkably helpful. Chas is summoned over to Wacker, the find returned, and the suggestion made that the trove and the bones be referred to separate coroners......."

"....... with her lads registering themselves as the finders of the bones," added Alan.

"Quite a favour," remarked the Minister. "So she let the gold go to the coroner."

"With the laudable suggestion that it might first be subjected to a proper independent assay."

"And what did this Megan take for her wise counsel?" said Jeremy.

"She wanted to meet me. And she did..... telling Chas that his gran's misgivings about me sharing their secret were no longer valid. What a sensible lady, I thought."

"And she took nothing else?" checked Lovat.

"Only a copy of the assay report."

"So not only sensible, but cunning," said the Scot. "This will confirm that it had been sourced from the British Treasury, as suspected by your father, Mr Cross, the Admiral Muselier." GUSTAVE turned again to McDaid. "What about the map, the 'original' piece that you, Declan, were left with after burying that body. You gave it to Jenny before crossing to Devonport and coming then to Scotland. She passed it down to her grandson. I trust he's put it somewhere safe, and it's not about to fall out of his back pocket."

"It's in a strong room now," said Cross, "again on the advice of this Megan, or Golda, or whatever you care to call her.......but......"

"Go on," urged Clark.

"She has seen it...... and begged to be allowed to snip a corner off the thing," Cross added.

".......and this, I suppose, was OK'd," sighed the Minister.

"So she treats herself to a tot of the real MacKay," said Lovat, "being that it was drawn on Admiralty paper. She's found that gun too. I know she has."

"And there could be something else," said Jeremy. "Though it might have been close by, it needn't have been the gold that activated Sally's metal detector when she went into that cave. She dug, and she found bones. Then she ran........ leaving them still more than three quarters buried, I would say. The fuller excavation would have been left to the Africans, and it's my bet that it was completed with the utmost care, from cranium to meta-tarsal, revealing amongst all that calcium a little lump of lead. With the help of the trial records from Africa, it could be that Golda Stern is now placed to account for every bullet loaded into that gun in pursuance of HIGHLAND CLEARANCE."

"Sounds like we might have an accomplished adversary," said Eamon Connors.

"She was well trained," said Lovat. "We must hope that her current colleagues in Berlin are less efficient."

"So have you alerted Spandau?" asked Busbridge. "Whose duty is it at the moment on the guard roster?"

"The Americans," replied Lovat. "Could be worse, could be better. For the moment, though, I'm preferring to keep them out of this....."

".......so that they might be better manipulated," said Busbridge, "much as in the spring of '41."

*

470

(xviii) at sea (3)

"Don't kick up, Chas, or they'll separate us again. We need to be taking the same line, so we need to be together." She sat on his bunk, reaching for his hand. He settled beside her. "It's Sunday...... right? She must have put something in that cocoa."

"And we had about thirty hours of sleep, missing Saturday...... and in that time who will have missed us? No one. People won't start asking questions until this evening...... and where will we be by then?"

"Not too far from home," said the girl. "There's a window to my cabin. We're still within sight of Cornwall....... down the coast a bit. I can see the clay tips."

"So no fast get-away. What then are they after?"

"It's got to be to do with that gun. There's a story to it, a big story that includes your grandfather, and the gold, those bones, and Ince too. It might even stretch to Kenya, to that *White Mischief* business that Jeremy's on to, and the Lady Clark."

"Things that happened a long time ago, Sally."

"But which might yet have a bearing on current issues. So it could be about getting that story straight, about the finding of evidence that might expose a cover up."

"Evidence that might be challenged, our role being to verify. Doesn't sound unreasonable."

"So tell me Chas, why this cloak and dagger all of a sudden?"

"Because that's what it's always been. The sweet reasonable Megan is a pretence. There's been murder done out in the bay, murder done in Africa, in Plymouth too, perhaps, and there might be more murder yet."

"Us?" shuddered Sally.

"Not while we're worth more alive than dead. Should there be hesitancy on the bridge then we have to hope it's not on this point."

*

(xix) an overview

"Take a look at this," said Clark, swivelling from the large monitor before him. A technician crouched at his side, staying with the picture, sharpening its images. The others gathered behind. "First, the wide picture; Prawle Point down to the Lizard, with each of these specks an Eastern Bloc vessel. Off Falmouth we have a cluster....... factory ships mainly, happily mincing up the fish that no one else wants. This was at 3pm yesterday. Now watch this one." He pointed with a pen.

"Starting to move up channel," observed the wrickleman, "but only slowly."

"So by 5 it's around the Dodman and crossing St Austell Bay, and by 7, a few miles out from Looe Island. Then it hangs around the Eddystone until dark, before creeping into Plymouth Sound, anchoring just inside the breakwater. In all that time it makes no radio transmissions, our fix having been obtained from satellite and radar. And it's to a radar picture of Plymouth Sound as obtained by locally sited and shipboard beacons sweeping into every corner of the port that we can go to now......," the technician touched the appropriate control, "....to the next part of the sequence." The screen flickered. A new picture formed.

"The Sound," recognised Cross. "The breakwater, with Drake's Island here....... and on this side, my diving centre, Fort Bovisand."

"And between," said Clark, also pointing, "dropping anchor just inside the breakwater, we have our mystery vessel. Above, twisting past Cremyll and then straightening northward we see the Tamar, with the Torpoint ferries here, the Dockyard of course, and the Saltash bridges at the very top. This, across from the Dockyard, is the mouth of the Lynher. Jupiter Quay is there, and also, at the very edge of proceedings, Ince Castle. Wacker Quay, unfortunately, is out of picture..... but watch what happens. It's almost midnight, and suddenly there's a faint blip in the Lynher."

"Something very small moving down river," said Busbridge, "quite quickly, and it's turning southward for the Sound......"

"......where it cuts to the 'wrong' side of Drake' Island," continued Clark. "And......." The larger image absorbed the smaller, to no one's surprise. "Then, if we fast forward through twenty minutes, look........"

"...... it starts back again," observed Busbridge, "retracing its outward route, all the way. So that's probably your inflatable, Tony."

"Where's my son, though, and Sally?"

"Keep your eye on the that ship," said Clark. "This is after a further twenty minutes."

"Yes, it's moving," said Eamon, "and this was in the very early hours."

"So what would you expect now?" asked Clark. "A run for home, perhaps......? Watch, we'll go back to the wider picture."

Grigson took up the commentary.

"Out towards the Eddystone again," he said. "Past the light, and then pointing herself to clear the Lizard by a good ten miles....... but in no great hurry."

"Cuba," suggested Eamon, lamely.

"Except after three hours she's turning back on herself," continued the Minister, "and then yet again, to and fro, but keeping outside the twelve mile limit." For the next four minutes they watched intently as the screen served them with a further six hours. Certainly the most anxious, probably the least hypnotised, Cross broke the silence.

"More than twelve miles, I know, but what's stopping us sending out a frigate?"

"Look here," said Lovat moving to a different screen. "What we've followed so far are radar and satellite images. These come from a different set of sensors, set in a network of sea bed cables. What they give us are submarine positions. We can identify ours well enough......"

"...... and by deleting each, then, from the remainder, identify the potentially hostile," muttered Jeremy, "and I see, you have one such tucked cosily below our humble factory ship. It would appear to have gathered itself a nuclear powered escort...... perhaps even nuclear armed."

"I shouldn't think so," said Lovat, "but we'll know in a moment. From the sounds these fish make our sea bed cables can even tell us the particular species. Here it comes now....... and, as I thought, we've got ourselves a diesel-electric, a Russian built Whiskey. Twenty to thirty years old, these are, several having been transferred to other communist countries, the GDR included."

"Can't we deal with that," pressed Cross.

"We can catch the thing and sink it any time we want," replied Lovat. "But if they've put the kids inside it then that's not something you would want us to do....... would you Mr Cross."

"Point taken," said the father.

"So Sally and Chas are out there as a pair of hostages," said Grigson, "as well as witnesses as to the dicovery of the the gold and the gun...... an extra something for Megan to take with all her evidence."

"All her evidence?" Jeremy wasn't so certain. "Why then are they hanging about still?"

"Because they won't yet have Hess in the bag," said Lovat, now with a gathered confidence. "And they don't know, yet, that we're on to them."

"What about the Africans?" said Grigson. "They're a double act. If one came back in with the inflatable then I would count it likely the two are together somewhere, probably in south Cornwall........"

"........but surely not waiting to be picked up," persisted Jeremy. "If this is a woman ruthless enough to shoot her own colleague, then she isn't going to be too concerned about getting the boys on board and then back home to Mozambique. They can make their own way."

"So what's the answer, Jeremy?" Alan demanded, pique sharpened by the lecturer's logic." Seeing as you're always so bloody clever."

Jeremy turned pensively to study the wall mounted chart. He didn't have to take this from Grigson, he knew, but he was thinking hard nonetheless. South Cornwall, and probably between Rame and the Lizard, in fact the Roseland might be far enough...... an area he'd once known well, and enjoyed too, until that night he'd lost Kate. His eyes drifted down to St Mawes, his mind slipping back. Two years, and he'd not returned there since. He pictured the harbour in summer. The river trippers, the cream tea punters, and the yachting set...... and yes, perhaps this was where they might be.

That Megan, she was a clever woman, just to have got this far. But it was all hanging on others, lesser lights probably, busting a nonagenarian out of jail. The whole thing was as fragile as that, so if there was time and there was chance, why not stretch for the something extra that might soften a still more than possible failure?

"The Trembaths, Alan...... do you have their number at Carwinion House?"

"It'll be in the book," said Grigson.

"The Trembaths," echoed the Minister. "Is that the Edward Trembath, he who was returned so regularly by the electors of Plymouth North?"

"The very one," confirmed Alan.

"His son Hugh, though, is the man I'm thinking to contact," said Jeremy. "He's an auxillary coastguard, and there's not much that gets past him down on the Fal estuary."

"So your enquiry......?" wondered Lovat.

"Would concern yet another of your fellow Peers. Tell me, how well do you know Lord Shawcross?"

"A lawyer politician, as was Lennox Boyd....... the one originally Labour, the other Tory, but after a few years in the Lords you wouldn't know one from the other. The place can do that."

"Save perhaps for Sir Hartley's specialist knowledge on the subject of Rudolf Hess," asserted Jeremy. "Attlee sent him over as our main man in the prosecuting team for the Nuremburg trials. Are you going to surprise me now by saying that he's not a member of your magic circle? If not you, then surely Menzies must have had a quiet word."

"Not to my knowledge," answered Lovat. "In fact I don't even know that Attlee was told. Four long years of war had passed since *Barbarossa*. The Churchill legend was established, with no room therein for HIGHLAND CLEARANCE. Stalin was no longer fooled, but with our keeping quiet about Katyn, together with the handing across of the *Victims of Yalta*, it was confidently hoped that we'd bought his silence. A legion of psychiatrists had dismissed Hess as mad, and it's my understanding that, at Nuremburg and since, Shawcross has never taken their reports at anything other than face value."

"But isn't there something about Hess having prepared a statement to make from the dock?" asked Jeremy. "It's said that he was blocked from reading it."

"Suggesting a testimony that might have approximated to the recently produced affidavit," added Busbridge, "mentioning a few of those HIGHLAND CLEARANCE sweeteners."

"But at that time he wouldn't have known that actual code name," said Clark. "And he would have had nothing solid to back his allegations. For Shawcross this was a madman who would make up anything to save his neck, a presumption we were happy to leave undisturbed. And all was deniable anyway."

"If any of it had been raised.......but it wasn't," said Busbridge. "All was suppressed, German war crimes being on trial, not Menzies chicanery, and certainly not GUSTAVE's summary execution of Avraham Stern."

"So what use can Shawcross be now?" asked Declan.

"The Hess affidavit will be attacked. A recently produced document implies a recently concocted story, the detractors will say. Shawcross might be the man to refute such a suggestion, and to that extent the case being made against the west is made harder to demolish."

"Useful," conceded Lovat, "so the connection with the younger Trembath is what?"

Jeremy turned again to the chart. "Lord Shawcross will probably be staying here, in St Mawes, now. His main home is up in Sussex, but he'll come down most Augusts for his sailing holiday. The family have a waterside mansion."

"Some socialist," muttered Eamon.

"He keeps a yacht on the Percuil, " continued the lecturer. "He'll take it out most days, usually with his son. The Africans will have watched, perhaps. If, during the night, they can get themselves onto that mooring, and into the cabin, then when the old boy comes out in the morning they have him there on a plate, ready to serve out to Megan in his own tub."

"So might Shawcross sometimes go out with a friend or friends?" checked GUSTAVE.

"He wouldn't go out alone," confirmed Jeremy. It's a big boat. The man's in his eighties.

"And would the Trembaths be counted amongst such friends?"

"Certainly Hugh, who knows the local waters so well."

"Then it sounds as if he might be the ideal man. Tell him there'll be four of us coming down this evening, that's me, you, Tony to dive, and Eamon to drive. Say that he has to be at St Mawes. We'll be going straight there, and that just after dark we'll be wanting to call on Lord Shawcross. The two Alans, and Declan, and you Mr Busbridge, are to stay and hold things at this end. We'll take one of the radio equipped cars they have here, keeping a channel open, constantly. You're to ensure that I'm available to the SAS, and to Faulds, ……. and that they're available to me.

*

476

(xx) a reckoning

Late morning
Monday 17th August

Ten metres of mahogany, every centimetre varnished to a glisten, slipped from its Percuil mooring...... the *Talisker of Lorne* was purring smoothly for the open sea. The younger man had taken the helm, the older having stepped down into the cabin on boarding and not yet reappeared. Normal enough, this was, under a breeze so light and so variable in direction. Better would be available out in the bay, but for perhaps an hour it had to be the motor. The canvas could be rolled out and hoisted at leisure.

Eamon had driven around to St Anthony. He and his two passengers, Jeremy and Tony, were now on the coast path, rounding Carrickneath Point as might a group of hikers, allowing the bare masted sloop to gently edge ahead. All seemed as in order as GUSTAVE could have been hoping it to appear...... for this was how it had to be to those watching from both land and sea. Yes, and particularly the latter, for make no mistake. From beyond the limit, every kind of scope or lens available to the kidnappers would be trained on the estuary mouth.

Climbing to St Anthony Head the followers temporarily lost sight the boat, impelling them to lengthen their strides until, on the drop to Zone Point they had her again in view, drawing for herself across the calm sea a bow-wave so regaular as to be seeming to direct them to their distant target vessel, faintly visible in the slowly clearing late morning haze. The watchers were as near now as land could take them. The die was cast.

But this couldn't have been known to Chas and Sally, even if, from its slight roll, it was clear to them now that the ship was at a halt. They were together and in Sally's cabin, with a portholed view of the distant Lizard.

"It must be Monday by now," said Chas. "Surely someone will have raised the alarm."

"But what kind of trail might bring a search here?" despaired the girl. Chas shook his head. He had no answer. He went to the glass, wiping it to gaze firstly across *The Manacles* to Goonhilly Down, and then, as his head dropped, to the depths below. And what was he to make of this?

"We have company, by the way."

"Company......?"

"Probably an escort. Unless I'm mistaken, within 50 metres of our port beam we have a submarine...... only the periscope up at the moment, but just as stationary as we."

"Waiting to whisk Megan and the two of us away to God knows where, I guess. Do we go quietly, Chas, or what?"

"If we don't, they can drug us again..... by needle if need be."

Early afternoon

Another two miles and the *Talisker* would be clear of British waters. For the steadily approaching yacht, binoculars were no longer needed......but there was the coast to watch still, and particularly the sky to the east where, if an alarm had been raised, she might expect helicopter activity. As yet, though, there was none. This was going well, thought Megan.

Her eyes returned to the sloop. That would be the young Shawcross at the tiller, helming to her boys' instructions while they guarded the old man.

Firmly but gently...... those were their instructions, and if he wasn't up to the lowered ladder then he could be lifted from yacht to ship by winch. With no pressure, it seemed that they could take this steadily, waiting until nightfall before transferring to the submarine...... just the four, herself, the two youngsters and Lord Shawcross. Juma and Makesi could hold the younger Shawcross here on the ship until they were well away.

As the *Talisker* drew alongside, though, it was apparent immediately, in his sprightly emergence from the cabin, that this man would have no need of any winch. Far from being cowed by this naked piracy, he was first to the ladder and climbing now without assistance. Cap, smock, cords, plimsoles, yes....... but looking very much the barrister. If a trespass wasn't careless, as this obviously was not, then there had to be a reason. The sooner it was heard the sooner it could be resolved.

Reaching the deck, and Megan, he straightened to give the woman a first opportunity to properly inspect her latest catch. Was there recognition in those eyes, she wondered. Ought she to know the man?

"Welcome aboard Lord Shawcross," she said. "I'm Megan to everyone else, so feel free to address me likewise. I trust the boys treated you with respect."

"There's very little that's respectful about being held at knifepoint. I suppose they were acting on your orders."

"Well if your son would also like to come aboard...... because I'm afraid we can't yet allow him to take your yacht back in."

"He's a friend, actually. Mr Hugh Trembath lives locally. He'll often crew, but he's not a Shawcross. What you might want from him, I can't imagine."

"Later, when we leave, he'll be the one to ensure your craft won't be left as a hazard to shipping."

"When we leave, eh? I would happily come were you to also let him take in the youngsters."

Megan took a pace back, to more deeply scrutinise this man's features. Youngsters......? Why should he be speaking of youngsters? The challenge shone from his eyes...... recognise me, dare to.

"And you're no Shawcross either," she stabbed.

"No more than you're a Megan...... Madam Stern, Madam Golda Stern."

"So......, " her hand felt into the more weighted of her two deep cardigan pockets, lightening it considerably with the smooth production of a gun, the gun. Lovat glanced down. There it was at last, still in working order, still lethal, back in her hands.....but now pointed at him. "Can it really be you?" she knew it was. "All these years, all those lives, the miles..... and I'm speaking again with GUSTAVE."

Lovat nodded, fixing her eyes with his. "I've come unarmed. Take me......but leave the kids. Let them go."

"I should shoot you now, with this same gun, given to me by yourself, to take with me onto the *Narval*, to use in Kenya. It was the next mission though, that I have best cause to remember.....the betrayal." Lovat closed his eyes, momentarily, bracing himself for the bullet..... but he wasn't to be despatched so cleanly. He had to be drilled, first, with invective. "I believed in HIGHLAND CLEARANCE, no less than Hess did, and the Haushofers. A *Nordic Accord*, with a colonial solution..... why not, I thought. This was the way to save my kinfolk, it had to be."

"If only they could have all agreed...... but no, still too many saboteurs, rejecting any suggestion of a greater Zion." Even at bay, the wily old stag had an eye for the split, that might just win delay.

"Yes, and some of them in my own family," obliged Megan.

"Trickery was afoot, they whispered, and were it to prevail then they could only see a bad prospect getting worse. I should have listened....... but didn't. I was taking the bait, preferring to believe that the likes of Erroll and his Muthaiga cronies were a genuine obstacle to constructive progress. I could smooth the way, you told me ...... and I was so convinced you were playing for real. I had misgivings when I heard in Cairo that Maisels had been eased out as Broughton's counsel, but foolishly, foolishly, even then I was still preferring to trust Great Britain, and you, and your Churchill, whose Zionism proved paper thin....... yes, White Paper thin, just as we'd been warned by Avraham. And, while I was still trusting, you thought you would put an end to me." Megan stepped forward. "Shall I tell you what those Slavs did to me?" She pushed the gun barrel against his lips. "Shall I show you? *That* was the ferocity of their hatred........and to follow, there was the fifteen years I slaved in that Siberian Gulag. Believe me, there were times when I envied those sent to Auschwitz." The spite seared from her eyes, she wanted more than to kill him, she wanted to flay him with her contempt.

"Orders, Golda, they were my orders."

"And such is the plea of every camp Kommandant called to account. We've a GDR sub to hand. Chas and his girl are coming back to testify. I'm taking you too, and when we've tried Hess as he should have been tried before, then you can answer for those who devised HIGHLAND CLEARANCE."

"You aim at a retrial for Hess, in East Germany? Is this serious?"

"By the time we reach Rostock he'll be out of Spandau and on our side of the wall. We have his affidavit.....a most interesting document. You might like to join in the cross examination."

Lovat glanced down at his watch. "And you think he can survive all this? He's over ninety.........fragile, physically and mentally. He's known to have been close to suicide."

Close to suicide ...... just three words, but uttered so coldly as if to say *'if you're not to late.'* Megan had to find out. Makesi was behind her, having followed Lovat aboard.

"Signal in to Berlin," she ordered him. "I want to know the latest on Hess. Hurry!" The African was smartly up to the bridge. Megan stayed, the Smith&Wesson trained still on the aged Scot. "I'm good with this gun, GUSTAVE, something you well know. The two bullets I have left can be enough. If Hess has been silenced then it'll be one for you, and one for me. The final sorting out between us we can do in hell."

Below, Chas and Sally were cheek to cheek...... noses pressed to the same porthole, eyes though, on separate things.
"Is that periscope still with us, Sally?"
"Constantly...... like us, hasn't moved."
"Look over there, then......... a hundred or so metres to the left."
Sally responded accordingly and, on pivoting, while pressing still, almost painfully, she caught sight of the suddenly raised wedge of black metal, almost twenty metres tall, just as it peaked. From within the wide splash of the subsequent forward flop she then saw revealed the fully levelled deck with its conning tower, replete almost at once with a busy complement of submariners. "Wow...... Chas! Is this the breeding season for these things. One of ours, I hope. You're the yardie. Are we saved, or is this just a further armed escort?"
"The latter I'm afraid. That's no NATO boat. There's only one machine that can break the surface under such thrust as that ..... and yes, see, it's marked with a Russian naval ensign. It's one of their *Liras*, known on our side as an *Alfa*. It'll do more than 40 knots submerged. "
They watched it swerve nearer, before surging from sight beyond their own screening hull, closing all the time, so obviously to them, with that one window on that side of the ship...... but to the total oblivion of all with a view of the deck, who remained rivetted to the drama unfolding theron. These eyes were instead locked on that pistol, and on the trigger finger of the hand that held it with such expert aim..... all save Lovat's. But did he so much as blink as the rifles were raised, knowing that he'd said that the sharpshooters were to take him too if need be? No more than he did at Pegasus when, leading from the front with brazen, upright, reckless, courage, he'd marched his men through girders pinging with snipers' lead.
More than forty years on now, and again he wouldn't be seen to flinch. He would take this in the manner of his ancestor the, the 11th Lord, last of the Jacobite Lovats, beheaded after the failure of the '45 and famous for his last words to the crowd as he mounted the Tower Hill scaffold;

' The more the mischief the better the sport! '

Chas and Sally heard gunfire, automatic gunfire...... a short burst from more than one weapon, but synchronised to the second. GUSTAVE heard it too, an instant after hearing the first bullet thud into the back of Megan's head. She was still standing as the second and third cut though her kneck, severing bone, muscle, artery and all, leaving her head to flail by the skin as a fourth and fifth below the shoulder blades lifted her to the rail and over....... the Smith&Wesson only then whirling from an unfeeling grip to splash and sink into the August warmth of a benign Falmouth Bay.

What had looked so menacing now lay inert, barely floating, a rag wrapped carcass. The submarine edged closer, those rifles still raised, confirming itself to be the promised *Lira*, declaring itself to be for reform..... and not a moment too soon. No one spoke, no one moved....... save for the two submariners armed only with the gaffs by which the body was crudely dragged from water to be lifted then below.

The intervention was achieved. The marksmen could retire into their shell, to resume duties as engineers, and weapons technicians, navigators and cooks. In they filed, without word or ceremony, in and down hatches thudding an emphatic closure. Away then powered the vessel, away and down, settling from sight to full performance depth.

*

(xxi) ashore

Surface appearances, though, can seldom give a complete story, such, of course, being the nature and indeed the very purpose of undersea warfare....... and hence installations such as that at Morwenstow, where on their screened overview Messers Clark, Grigson, Busbridge and McDaid have been well placed to note how, with the sudden arrival of that second boat, the *Lira*, or *Alfa*, as it was known to its trackers, the first, the *Whiskey*, had promptly scuttled away. And with having this vantage it is perhaps they who can best appreciate an irony in the episode.

Might it be that this brief but timely quadrille out in Falmouth

Bay, choreographed by GUSTAVE and STANLEY working together, had heralded an end to the Cold War? If so, then how fitting.......that it should have been just a little way along the Cornish Coast from where, 47 years before, another such submarine rendezvous had helped seed Stalin's epoch defining paranoia.

Now, though, of that transient present day foursome just the two surface vessels remained, and a signal was coming back from the *Talisker*, from GUSTAVE, to proclaim that his re asserted authority stood supreme.

Makesi and Juma, it had been decreed, were to be left with the factory ship, which was to immediately sail beyond sight of the British coast. Their van, which had been found in the main St Mawes carpark, was already on its way to the specialist dismantlers who waited at Culdrose. Nothing of this audacious attempt to reverse the tide of history was to escape scrutiny.

Both sets of parents, meanwhile, could be informed that Chas and Sally were on the yacht, safe and unharmed, and that they would soon be ready for immediate collection from St Mawes. Neither yougster would ever forget the 17th August 1987, and the breaking news story of that evening.......the suicide of Rudolf Hess. And whenever, later, generally to derision, it was suggested that prisoner number seven might have been murdered by an SAS hit squad, so as to further the development of a new East-West accord, then quietly they would think back to that last afternoon of a long, long weekend........ and find no difficulty at all in believing every word.

GUSTAVE returned with Peg Willis to Invernsess, from where his visits to Westminster became progressively fewer. He was to stay in touch with STANLEY throughout the final winter of his one time colleague's life, expressing gratitude for an intervention that had saved his own. In return he heard of the traitor's doubled delight at, firstly, having made a real contribution to his General Secretary's programme of reform and, secondly, having secured for him at least a partial return on the millions of roubles sunk into that absurdly expensive *Lira* project.

Having listened to the author of their misfortunes, Lords Aldington and Rothschild were placed now to better understand GUSTAVE's ruthlessness, and better fear its necessity. That other reputations might have suffered worse did little to console Toby, for how could private assurances deflect so wild and so public an assault? He battled on regardless, driving the writer into bankruptcy...... but more through a far from transparent collusion between the Legal establishment and the Foreign Office than by the disclosure of any vindicating records held closely in the archives of the latter. 'Foul!' cried young Nikolai on being refused an opportunity to appeal, this confirming a messy lose-lose outcome that left the stain merely smudged rather than truly lifted.

Victor....... beset by mere whispers, he was more able to choose circumspection, and reflect upon figures such as the Duke of Hamilton and Sam Hoare, names which had taken slanders to the grave, and beyond. Ingratitude.....? That could be accepted as one might a shabby envelope, which if taken carefully and opened slowly can reveal better within........ the due receipt, issued unknowingly by a posterity too well blessed to appreciate its good fortune.

At such sphinx-like repose did Rothschild remain. The soul, he was, of slighted discretion....... save for the one quiet mention made to Colin Daniels, which brought for an agent known to him as 'Alan Grigson' a prompt blemish free re-instatement to what the department could deem a further enhanced career.

Likewise, the cloud that had darkened Kate's professional prospects dispersed, in this case with McDaid's un wavering insistence that his and his brother's former identities were best re consigned to history. Declan would remain at Quarry Cottage, journeying no more than once a month down to St Lawrence where, on the suggestion of James Busbridge, he was to become a suppotive member of 'The Friends'. There was the occasional letter to and from 'Peg' in Scotland, but no visits. Their lives were too busy and too separate, the distance too great.

The closer friendship, now, came to be with Eamon Carroll, who returned summer after summer again for his stint at Whitsand Bay. 'Always a pleasant change,' he would say, of a working break made all the more enjoyable for his having shed the concerns of one doubly outlawed. Onside now, with both 'the Movement' and the security forces, he could take a(nother) leaf from Father Mulligan's book and likewise, alongside the Harrow Road, make an impartial stand for peace rather than armed conflict.

He would ever be grateful to the Declan McDaid, he who'd been in the right place at the right time to save his life, and had also guided him towards significantly strengthening the Republican position in a new peace initiative...... one which, ultimately, was to prove more successful than any hitherto.

Tony Cross, of course, had to be mindful of his tenure at Fort

Bovisand. It was unlikely, he'd been told, that anything useful might be divined from what was left of the *Surcouf*, particularly as the wreckage had long ago been secretly located and picked over by the Americans. It could be, though, that its small seaplane might have been scuttled somewhere in the waters around Plymouth, and that if a bar of gold could be raised then anything had to be possible. He could be assured, meanwhile, that between them the youngsters would receive appropriate bounty for both their find and the ordeal.

James Busbridge remained in contact, still researching the *Surcouf*, but a little less incisively now, so that the book which eventually emerged had something of the *White Mischief* about it...... in the sense that too little was made of such revelations as might overturn a somewhat rocky and afterwards patched-up-looking official version. Soon he was to be distracted, having noted more cracks in the foundations of the Churchill myth. Just how much forewarning had the war leader been given of the Japanese attack on Pearl Harbour? Enough to ensure that that the US Command could have been alerted far earlier? If so, then why wasn't it, he would ask...... entering a maze, then, in which his curiosity could find no bounds, and therefore no escape.

So it was left to Enid to get the best out of him as *Abraham*, to Kate's *Isaac*, their first public performance being given in October, at Bodmin's St Petroc's Church as part of an entertainment for an autumnal evening. Rapturously received, they were booked for the next festivals of music at St Endellion first, and after that at St Germans.

Understandably, justifiably, Kate was brimming with this when for the weekend following that October 'premiere' she travelled to Bath to stay with Jeremy. The Lady Nolwen Clark, who'd stayed overnight at Elspeth's, in Oaksey, joined them for protracted Sunday lunch at the same establishment they'd enjoyed back on that August afternoon which had taken them to Mells. While *White Mischief* (the film) still awaited general release, reports that increasingly confirmied the daughter's worst fears regarding the portrayal of Alice de Janze were, somehow, causing her progressively less dismay.

She'd been shown a wider picture, of a desperate last ditch bid for a better world. And now, following great cost, with so many others having had to sacrifice so much more, perhaps this was at last coming about....... not that this could in any way ease an increasingly fraught relationship between stepmother and stepson.

"So your friend Enid, Kate, she must have been delighted."

"Definitely, and not only with mine and Jim's singing. For her, that riddle of yours was a revelation. It indicated to her that the pacifist stand Britten had taken early in the war was sincere, that he'd allowed his talent to be used in earnest belief that it could shorten the conflict, and minimise casualties. And if Auden, being better informed politically and less naïve, guessed differently, and correctly, and saw Hitler being driven into a corner by this sham, and even saw ahead to all that barely imaginable evil that might be provoked......."

"...... and was provoked," joined Jeremy, "then even so, Britten still had his answer, as expressed in his *Spring Symphony.* "

"Yes, and if we're to believe Enid, it then came down to a matter between the composer and no-one else but his own tender conscience," continued Kate. "A conscience that he was always ready to search, time and time again. And with this fuller appreciation, she thinks she might at last be close to turning the key that will reveal the great mystery of what she holds to be the man's greatest opera."

"Remind us," urged Jeremy. "Nolwen lives just along from Glyndebourne. One day there might be an opportunity to see an actual performance. Which opera, Kate, and what insight would Enid have us take along?"

"*Billy Budd*........ in which, on realising he must sentence his loyal young foretopman to death, the virtuous Captain is so snared by guilt as to be brought to the very edge of mental disintegration, and this while his ship is at action stations in enemy waters, when one false move might imperil not only his company, and his fleet, but perhaps even his nation....

'*I am the messenger of death*'.....

Britten himself gives it to Captain Vere to sing those very words.........The composer's own confession, claims Enid. Her Ben, confronting the consequences of his role in Menzies' scheming...... an unknowing contribution to what he was subsequently to learn was a desperate trick."

"So no intent on his part," said Jeremy. "And freedom was preserved."

"But at massive, massive expense in terms of innocent life," said Kate. "Much as 'good order' on Vere's ship was only to be preserved at a price. Mens rea or not, can such a cost be forgotten? Can it be forgiven?

486

'Before what tribunal do I stand if I destroy goodness ?' Captain Vere asks, this man *'lost with all hands on the infinite sea.'* There he is, as Act Three closes, crippled by this agonising predicament in which his talents, his training, and his principles have all conspired to betray him...... and now he must attempt to explain himself to the boy."

"How does he find the words?" asked Nolwen.

"We don't know," replied Kate, "for even the composer is incapable. It's as if he too has succumbed to Billy's impediment. Does he need words anyway, when he has music, naked, profound music? No melody, just chords, their roots traceable, Enid says, in the shifting strains of *Bunyan,* ranging from the strong and confident to the distressed and indecisive. Searching chords, we hear, for where in all this is the remedy that might restore to Vere his 'starry' talent for leadership? Anywhere? Nowhere, for succour only comes with the blessing that Billy confers on his Captain as the noose is fitted..... a forgiveness as final and as public as is the execution. This, holds Enid, is what Britten himself must have yearned for..... and yearned in vain, for how, for him, could there ever be any equivalent......"

"........ so much having to remain secret," said Nolwen.

"And what can he do? He must work on as best he can," added Jeremy, glancing at Kate to remind himself how rewarding such a strategy had been in his own life.

"Exactly," continued Kate, knowingly smiling back to her refound partner. "For Ben there was some consolation in the incontestable fact of his own genius. If he owed the world something then it was from this that he could give........as he did, unstintingly. In *Grimes,* says Enid, the composer was pointing the finger...... but not so in *Budd* and the subsequent works. Instead, she hears self recrimination and a moving quest for atonement."

"So in your professional opinion, Kate," said Nolwen. "You knowing more than most about psychotherapy, and being also well acquainted with the woman herself, as you are too with the work of the artist she idolises...... would you say that this Enid's analysis was sound?"

Kate thought for a second, reaching for Jeremy's hand and smiling a smile which broke into a chuckle.

"Enid...... sound?" she shook her head. "We're all a little odd down in Bodmin. Living in that town, as she does, working in that hospital as do I, ... I'd say that it helps considerably if you are. She'll be the same as most of us in those parts, Nolwen....... a little strange, but totally harmless."

And that was it. Kate, Jeremy, Nolwen .... all three would be laughing, now, for the rest of the afternoon.

*

THE END

Whiskey (Class)

Introduced 1950s: Length 249ft: Displacing 1,371 tons: 50 crew:
Diesel powered: Surface range of 8,500 nautical miles.
Capable of 18 knots (14 knots submerged)

Alfa (Class)

Introduced 1970s: Length 265ft: Displacing 3,739 tons: 31 crew:
Nuclear powered: Unlimited range.
Capable of 20 knots (42 knots submerged)

ACKNOWLEDGEMENTS

Helpful books (enjoyed and recommended)
On the Erroll case include;
White Mischief by James Fox. (Vintage)
The Life and Death of Lord Erroll by Errol Trzbinski (4th Estate)

On the musicians and the writers include;
Benjamin Britten by Humphrey Carpenter (Faber&Faber)
Cambridge Companion toBenjamin Britten (a reader)
Edited by Mervyn Cooke (Cambridge)
Evelyn Waugh by Selina Hastings (Vintage)
Auden by Richard Davenport Hines (Vintage)
Cyril Connolly; a life by Jeremy Lewis (Pimlico)

On the Hess affair include;
Churchill's Deception by Loius Kilzer (Simon&Schuster)
Double Standards by Pickett, Prince, and Prior (Time Warner)

On Nazism
Nazism. The documentary readers compiled by Noakes and Pridham.
(Exeter University)

On the Surcouf
Who sank Surcouf by James Rusbridger (Century)
The author lived in Cornwall (near Tremorebridge) until his untimely death in 1994. He was said to have been a cousin of Peter Wright (of Spycatcher fame). He and my 'James Busbridge' share a number of interests.

On the Frasers
March Past. (Brave Shimi's memoir) (Weidenfeld)
Past Forgetting by Veronica Maclean (Review)

Other useful books include
Pegasus Bridge by Stephen Ambrose.
The Victims of Yalta by Nikolai Tolstoy.
The Blast of War by Harold Macmillan.
Alan Lennox Boyd by Philip Murphy.
Alan Clark Diaries.
Israel by Martin Gilbert.

also
The selected poems of W.H. Auden as edited by E. Mendelson
(Faber&Faber)

My thanks also to Mr Martin Lister for his help with spelling and Saltash area fact; and to the current owners of Ince castle for enabling me to take and use the cover photo of their home.

Illustrations: Acknowledgements are due to;

Imperial War Museum (Hess, Murphy, young Philby); Bedfordshire Times & Citizen (Alan & Patsy); G de Rougemont (Nolwen & Alice); Tatler (Jock & Vera); London & County Press (Bride & Groom); C Whiting (Menzies); P. Filmer (Phyllis); M. Biggs (Joss & Diana); ECPA (Emile); Curtis/Brown/Broadwater (Yalta); National Portrait Gallery (Ben); G. Auden (Wystan); Sunday Times (Cyril & son); Illustrated London News (Laura with daughters and son); Camera Press (od Philby); J Adams (Roger Burney); A McBean/ R. Wood (Peter); Francis Frith Collection (Mells Church and Manor); Grange Books (subs and plane).

Where the identity or location of a copyright holder has proved too difficult to ascertain the publisher will, on application, be ready to negotiate and settle appropriate terms.

The Author

Lliam West was born in Liskeard in 1949. He attended the Church School and the old Grammar School. After studying in Reading he moved to London, where he taught (in Brent South, close to the Harrow Road) before returning to his home town to continue the family business. This was sold up in 1985, enabling him to devote time to the care of his two sons and his elderly father while his wife returned to her career.

Delighted at the response to *Pandora Inn* (2001), the author hopes that *Frenchman's Gold* can continue to entertain and intrigue those who enjoyed that first story. Again he draws on his close native knowledge of Cornwall, and his fascination with mid-twentieth century British history...... times that coloured the remarkable output of talents so diverse as those of Waugh (*Brideshead Revisted*), Auden (*For the Time Being*), and Britten (*Billy Budd*).

Postscript
from Humphrey Carpenter's biography of Ben (p166)
(Faber and Faber)

"They found the company on the boat (bringing them back to England from America) uncongenial..... and their cabin was small, miserable, and airless. Britten had intended to work at the commission from Benny Goodman, and at a Hymn for St Cecilia for which Auden had written the words, but his drafts for both pieces were confiscated by customs officials on the look out for anything that might be coded information, before the boat sailed. Undaunted, he wrote out the beginning of the Hymn again, from memory, and finished it during the voyage......"

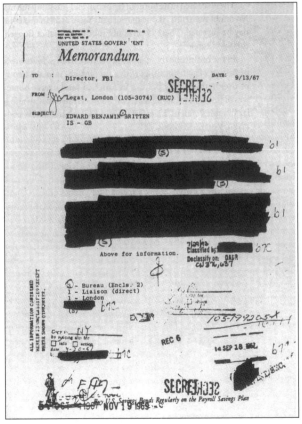

A heavily censored FBI document relating to Britten from 1967

Besson MB411

The spotter plane carried by the Surcouf
Weight: 1676lb   Span: 39 ft   Lenght: 27 ft
Top speed: 118mph   Range: 250 miles

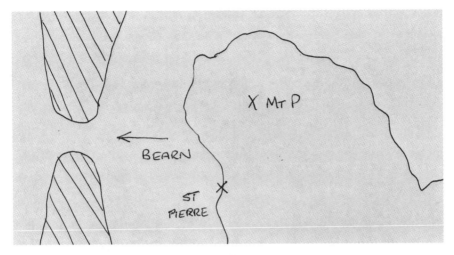

The full map.

**RAME
CHURCH**